"Surprisingly plausible, written with compelling narrative force and meticulous detail."

—*The Atlanta Journal-Constitution*

"Well-executed alternative history. The authors show thorough knowledge of the people, weapons, tactics, and ambience of the Civil War. A veritable feast."

—*Publishers Weekly*

"Gingrich and Forstchen write with authority and with sensitivity."

—*St. Louis Post-Dispatch*

"[*Gettysburg*] is believable and beautifully written . . . every bit as good as Michael Sharra's *The Killer Angels*. Not only do Gingrich and Forstchen bring the characters to life, and often horrible death, but they do so with memorable observations on the ways of war and vivid, technically accurate descriptions of frightful Civil War combat."

—*The Courier-Journal* (Kentucky)

"An eye-opener . . . filled with gore, smoke, heat of battle, and a surprise ending. The writing is vivid and clear. A ripping good read."

—*The Washington Times*

"As historical fiction this stands beside *The Killer Angels*. As an alternative history of Gettysburg, it stands alone. The mastery of operational history enables the authors to expand the story's scope. The narrative is so clear that the action can be followed without maps. And the characters are sometimes heartbreakingly true to their historical originals."

—Dennis Showalter,
former president of the Society of Military Historians

"*Gettysburg* is a creative, clever, and fascinating 'what-if' novel that promises to excite and entertain America's legions of Civil War buffs."

—James Carville

"The novel *Gettysburg* puts forth a highly plausible and exciting scenario of a Confederate victory in the Pennsylvania campaign of 1863. The authors exhibit an in-depth knowledge of not only technical details, but also the various personalities of the leaders and how they could have reacted had things gone quite differently from history as we know it."

—Don Troiani, noted Civil War artist

NEWT GINGRICH
WILLIAM R. FORSTCHEN
and
ALBERT S. HANSER, *contributing editor*

Thomas Dunne Books
St. Martin's Griffin ⚏ New York

Never Call Retreat

Lee and Grant: The Final Victory

THOMAS DUNNE BOOKS.
An imprint of St. Martin's Press.

NEVER CALL RETREAT. Copyright © 2005 by Newt Gingrich and William R. Forstchen. All rights reserved. Printed in the United States of America. No part of this book may be used or reproduced in any manner whatsoever without written permission except in the case of brief quotations embodied in critical articles or reviews. For information, address St. Martin's Press, 175 Fifth Avenue, New York, N.Y. 10010.

www.stmartins.com

Library of Congress Cataloging-in-Publication Data

Gingrich, Newt.
    Never call retreat : Lee and Grant, the final victory / Newt Gingrich and William R. Forstchen.
        p. cm.
    ISBN-13: 978-0-312-34299-9
    ISBN-10: 0-312-34298-2 (hc)
    ISBN-10: 0-312-34299-3 (pbk)
    1. United States—History—Civil War, 1861–1865—Fiction. 2. Grant, Ulysses S. (Ulysses Simpson), 1822–1885—Fiction. 3. Lee, Robert E. (Robert Edward), 1807–1870—Fiction. 4. Generals—Fiction. I. Forstchen, William R. II. Title.

PS3557.I495N48 2005
813'. 6—dc22

                                                        2005041366

First St. Martin's Griffin Edition: June 2006

10 9 8 7 6 5 4 3 2 1

For Our Fathers

WILLIAM R. FORSTCHEN

John J. Forstchen—a genuine cavalry trooper in our pre–World War II army who passed away while this volume was being written. "Gary Owen," Dad.

NEWT GINGRICH

Newt McPherson and Lt. Colonel Robert Gingrich—it was Robert, my stepfather, who took me on a tour of World War I battlefields when I was fourteen. The memory of that tour, the tragic waste I saw at Verdun, inspired me to try to make a difference in this world by entering politics and studying history.

STEVE HANSER

My father, Joseph A. Hanser, was a simple man of great wisdom and greater character. Our family has missed him every day since he passed away.

Acknowledgments

How to say thank you to so many as this trilogy is finished up is a daunting task. Seven years ago, the idea started with a few phone calls back and forth, e-mails and dinner together. It was just the three of us then, but in the years since, dozens have come into our lives to help.

To say the initial response to our idea was lukewarm is an understatement. Some publishers just "didn't get it," others said it would never work, and then Tom Dunne of Thomas Dunne Books came along and said he'd give it a try. So our first thanks must go to the incredible team at Thomas Dunne Books, and we're not just saying that because they're the publishers! Pete Wolverton, our editor, has been an incredible gentleman to work with. Patient, understanding, and from Bill's perspective especially, compassionate when his father fell ill and passed away while we were facing our deadline for delivery. Pete's ideas for inserts, changes, and editing have always been on the mark. The team working with Pete: his assistant, Kathleen Gilligan; Carolyn Chu, our patient map maker; and the copyeditor, Donald J. Davidson, have all been wonderful.

About a year into our project we met General Robert Scales, former commandant of the Army War College at Carlisle, and Dr. Len Fullenkamp, the senior historian at the War College. Both were enthralled with the idea for the series and volunteered their own time to advise, take us on staff rides, pick apart theories, and review our work.

One of the truly great discoveries was the wonderful team of folks at the Carroll County, Maryland, Historical Society and, through them, a truly gifted historian, Tom LeGore and his wonderful wife, Mary. Tom has an encyclopedic knowledge of the details of that region, historically and geographically, and his information was crucial in the framing of our story.

George Lomas, owner of the Regimental Quartermaster in Gettysburg, proved to be a great friend in the marketing of our first two books and offering advice as well along the way. As has Michael Greene, who has helped to educate us about the marketing side of this business. Our friends with the Civil War educational firm, Hardtack & Wool, gave advice especially related to marketing and the review of drafts.

Its been an honor for us to have the famous artist Don Troiani as our cover artist. Besides his incredible talent with the paintbrush he is a noted historian in his own right and offered detailed information we surely would have missed. Two advisers behind the scene have been the *New York Times* bestselling author W. E. B. Griffin and his son, William Butterworth. William has been an editor and friend of Bill Forstchen's for over twenty years with *Boys' Life* magazine, and provided great moral support and friendship throughout the creation of this series.

For Bill Forstchen, a special thanks as well to the administration at Montreat College: Academic Deans Beth Doriani and Abby Fapetu, and president Dan Struble for the offering of a year-long sabbatical, their enthusiasm for this project (which some colleges might not have embraced), and their understanding during difficult times.

There have been a number of people on Newt's Team who contributed time and wonderful advice: Randy Evans and Stefan Passantino for all the intricacies involved in coordinating the development of this series, Bill Sanders for a fine job of fact checking, and Amy Pearman and Rick Tyler for their tireless efforts with keeping our schedules together. Needless to say Kathy Lubbers, head of Gingrich Communications and our agent for *Never Call Retreat*, has been as tough as Grant in helping to keep this project on track and as understanding as Lee in helping to keep things coordinated.

And, of course, the "ever-suffering" companions in our lives, Callista, Sharon, and Krys. Some people seem to think that the life of an author has a certain romantic appeal to it. Just ask our wives and they will set you straight as to the reality!

There are so many fans, as well, who we wish we could acknowledge. People we've met while going through airports, doing book signings, those who have offered reviews and letters of encouragement. We especially appreciate those who "got" the idea behind the story and what we have tried to create with what we call "Active History," the examining of a crucial decision-making process in the past, and how if another path were followed, just how profoundly different our lives would be today. We see Active History as an exciting way to teach real history, to get students, "buffs," and anyone with an interest in our past to look back, to understand the courage, sacrifice, and strength of those who have shaped our nation. We can't resist mentioning with a smile, one critic who "dished" us with the comment, "These guys have PhDs? Don't they know Lee lost Gettysburg?" We hope that reader finally did "catch on," and we thank all of you who did "get it" and found pleasure in the reading of our story.

And in closing, a very serious acknowledgment as well . . . to those who lived the story for real. Approximately 660,000 young men lost their lives in our Civil War. Whether you are from the North or South, a citizen who just took his oath of citizenship today, or a descendant from the *Mayflower*, their story is our story. North or South, they gave the last full measure of devotion for what they believed in and have forever set for us an example of self-sacrifice and nobility.

Though of opposing sides, Robert E. Lee and Abraham Lincoln stand as two men of courage who shared as well a deep sense of Christian compassion, and at the end of the war set the example for a tragically divided nation that did indeed bind up its wounds and made us one again.

We are humbled by their example and we hope that in some small way our work pays tribute to them and pays tribute as well to all our veterans, right up to today and those who tonight stand the long watch for freedom on distant fronts. We believe firmly in that declaration by Abraham Lincoln that America is, indeed, "the last best hope of mankind."

Never Call Retreat

Chapter One

C.S.A. Capt. Phil Duvall of the Third Virginia Cavalry, Fitz Lee's Brigade, Army of Northern Virginia, raced up the steps of the Carlisle Barracks, taking them two at a time. Reaching the top floor, he scrambled up a ladder to the small cupola that domed the building.

One of his men was already there, Sergeant Lucas, half squatting, eye to the telescope. As Duvall reached the top step of the ladder, Lucas stepped back from the telescope and looked down at him.

"It ain't good, sir."

Lucas offered him a hand, pulling his captain up. Phil looked around. Morning mist carpeted the valley around them. At any other time he would have just stood there for a long moment to soak in the view. It was a stunningly beautiful morning. The heat of the previous days had broken during the night as a line of thunderstorms marched down from the northwest. The air was fresh, the valley bathed in the indigo glow and deep shadows of approaching dawn. The sounds of an early summer morning floated about him, birds singing, someone nearby chopping wood, but mingled in was another sound.

He squatted down, putting his eye to the telescope, squinting, adjusting the focus. He saw nothing but mist, then, after several seconds, a flash of light. It was hard to distinguish, but long seconds later a distant pop echoed, then another.

He stood back up, taking out his field glasses, focusing them on the same spot. With their broader sweep he could now see them, antlike, deployed in open line, mounted, crossing a pasture at a trot, their uniforms almost black in the early morning light . . . Yankee cavalry, a skirmish line . . . behind them, a half mile back, what looked to be a mounted regiment in column on the Cumberland Valley Pike.

He lowered his glasses and looked down at the parade ground in front of the barracks. His troopers were already falling in, saddling mounts, scrambling about.

"Lucas, get down there and tell the boys they got ten minutes to pack up."

"We gonna fight 'em?"

Phil looked at him.

"Are you insane? That's at least a regiment out there. Now tell 'em they got ten minutes to pack it up."

Lucas slid down the ladder, his boots echoing as he ran down the stairs.

Phil looked back to the east. He didn't need field glasses now. He could see them. The Yankee skirmishers were across the pasture, disappearing into a narrow stretch of woods bordering a winding stream. A few more pops, and from the west side of the creek, half a dozen troopers emerged . . . his boys. They were riding at full gallop, jumping a fence, coming out on the main pike.

Only six of them? There should be twenty or more. These were the boys at the forward picket just outside of Marysville. So the first rumor was true: They had been caught by surprise.

The Yankee skirmishers did not come out of the wood line in pursuit, reining in after emerging from the woods. There were a few flashes. One of his men slumped over in the saddle but managed to stay mounted. The mounted Yankee regiment on the road started to come forward, beginning to shake out from column into line, obviously preparing to rush the town.

He lowered his glasses and looked around one last time. It had been a lovely month here, duty easy, the locals not exactly friendly, but not hostile either. The land was rich, the food good, his mounts fattening on the rich grass, the bushels of oats, his men fattening as well.

Positioned here as an outpost they had missed the battles of the previous four weeks around Washington and Baltimore . . . and he was glad of it.

As a West Pointer, class of 1861, he knew he should be of higher rank by now, but that did not bother him. He had seen enough of slaughter.

Though others sought "recognition in dispatches" in order to gain promotions, that was a vainglorious game he felt to be childish. Staying alive and making sure his men stayed alive held a higher priority. Besides, Jeb Stuart trusted his judgment as a scout. That was recognition enough. Ever since Grant came east and started moving tens of thousands of troops into Harrisburg, it was his job to watch them from the other side of the river and report in with accurate assessments, and he had been doing that.

He had sent a report just yesterday that he suspected a move was about to begin on their part, and now it had indeed begun. What was surprising was the speed of it all. Carlisle was a dozen miles west of Harrisburg. Apparently, the Yankees had thrown a bridge across the river during the night and were now pushing forward with their cavalry to create a screen behind which their infantry would advance.

He ran his hand along the smooth polished brass tube of the telescope. There had been quiet evenings when he had used it to study the moon, the crescent of Venus, and now, on August mornings, before dawn, the belt of Orion.

Bring it along? It weighed a good thirty pounds.

Reluctantly he upended it, letting it tumble back down the stairwell, crashing on the floor below.

He took one last look, then slid down the ladder, boots echoing as he tromped down the stairs. Some men were running back into the building, darting into rooms, reemerging carrying some souvenir or keepsake picked up over the last month . . . a banjo, a wall clock, a quilt. At the sight of this, he regretted the destruction of the telescope. After the war it would have been nice to have it back home in the valley and take it up Massanutten to watch the stars at night or gaze out across a Shenandoah peaceful once more.

He heard heavy steps coming up the stairs. It was Lieutenant Syms, the man he had assigned to their forward station at Marysville. Syms was gray-faced, wincing with each step, his right calf bleeding, boot punctured by a ball.

"Damn it, Syms. Where the hell have you been?" Phil shouted.

"Sir, I'm sorry, sir. Didn't you get our report by wire?"

"Only part of it."

Phil stuck his head into the telegraphy station they had established on the second floor of the barracks.

Sergeant Billings was sitting by the key, looking at him calmly, awaiting orders.

"Read what Syms wired."

Billings picked up a scrap of paper.

"This came through at two-ten this morning. 'Pontoon bridge across river. Cavalry . . .'"

Billings looked back up.

"That was it, sir."

Syms shook his head.

"Damn all. I'm sorry, sir. They slipped some troopers across. Cut the line behind us before we could get more out."

"In other words, they caught you by surprise."

Syms was always straightforward, and after only a second's hesitation he reluctantly nodded his head in agreement.

"Something like that, sir."

"So what the hell is going on?"

"They jumped us at our headquarters. Ten of us got out. I sent a few boys down to the river, and in the confusion they were able to see that one bridge was already across and infantry on it. A civilian, reliable, he's been in our pay, told one of my boys that it was Ord's Corps leading the crossing."

"Do you believe that?"

"Yes, sir. I caught a glimpse of the bridge as we pulled out."

"How did you see it in the dark?"

"It was lined with torches, sir. I could see infantry on it. A long column clear back across the river into Harrisburg."

How did the Yankees get a bridge across the Susquehanna so quickly? They must have built sections of it upstream and floated them down once it got dark. He suspected that Syms and his boys were truly asleep, from too much drink, if they let that get past them.

Duvall sighed and looked at Sergeant Billings.

"Send the following to headquarters: 'Grant started crossing Susquehanna shortly after midnight. Ord's Corps in the lead.'"

Gunfire outside interrupted his thoughts. He looked up and saw what was left of Sym's detachment galloping onto the parade ground: one trooper leading the horse of a wounded comrade, who was slumped over in the saddle.

"'Believe Grant moving down this valley, heading south. Regiment or more of their cavalry about to storm Carlisle. Abandoning this post.' Now send it!"

Billings worked the key as Duvall went to the window and looked out. The Yankee cavalry were clearly visible on the main pike, deployed to either side of the road, forming a battlefront several hundred yards across. They were coming on cautiously, most likely not sure if this town was well garrisoned or not. Mounted skirmishers were now advancing less than a quarter mile away.

Billings finished sending the message, the confirm reply clicking back seconds later.

"Smash all this equipment, then get mounted," Duvall snapped, and he walked out of the room.

He reached the ground floor and saw three troopers upending cans of coal oil onto the floor, a sergeant holding a rolled-up newspaper, already striking a match.

"What the hell are you doing there, Sergeant?"

"Well, sir, this is Yankee government property, isn't it? Figured you'd want it torched."

The sergeant was grinning. There was something about arson that seemed to excite most young men, and the wanton destruction of this fine old barracks would be quite a blaze.

Duvall looked around, the corridor lined with old prints, lithographs of the war in Mexico, a portrait of Lincoln still hanging but the glass on it smashed, a rather scatological comment penciled across his brow. The barracks were a reminder that this was the oldest military post in the United States. It dated back to the French and Indian Wars.

The newspaper flared. The sergeant looked at him expectantly.

I grew up a little more than a hundred miles from here, Duvall thought. *We were neighbors once, a sister even marrying a fine young man from the theological seminary down at Gettysburg.* He had not heard from her in more than a year, not since her husband was killed at Second Manassas, fighting for the Yankees.

We were neighbors once.

"Sergeant," Duvall said quietly. "Don't."

"Sir?"

"You heard me. Let it be."

The sergeant looked disappointed.

"Go out and mount up."

The sergeant nodded, carrying his flaming torch, tossing it by the doorstep, where it flickered and smoked, his disappointed assistants following. Billings came running down the stairs and out the door behind them.

Duvall took one last look, walked over to the smoldering paper and crushed it out with his heel, then stepped onto the porch. His command of a hundred men was mounted, many with revolvers drawn, expecting to be ordered to turn out on to the pike and face the Yankees head-on.

Syms was kneeling over the wounded trooper, shot in the back, lying on his side, blood dripping out.

"We leave him here," Duvall said. "They'll take care of him."

"Sir, forgot to tell you," Syms said, looking up at Phil. "Your old friend is over there."

"Who?"

"George Armstrong Custer. That's his brigade dogging us. I saw him in the lead."

George, it would have to be him. No one spoke. All knew that he and George had been roommates at West Point.

An orderly led up his mount, and Duvall climbed into the saddle, turned to face his men, and pointed south.

"Let's go, boys."

"We ain't fighting 'em?" Sergeant Lucas asked, coming up to Phil's side as they trotted across the parade ground, angling toward the road out of the south side of town.

Phil shook his head.

"Hell no, Sergeant. That's not a regiment out there, that's Grant and the entire Yankee army. Now let's go."

Washington, D.C.

August 22
6:00 A.M.

M aj. Ely Parker, aide-de-camp to Gen. Ulysses S. Grant, turned off Pennsylvania Avenue and approached the east gate of the White House. A crowd milled about on the sidewalks, spilling into the streets. Guards lined the iron fence facing them. There was a low hum, as copies of newspapers, which had just hit the streets minutes before, were passed back and forth. He caught snatches of conversation. "Sickles is dead." "The rebs will be here by tomorrow I tell you . . ."

At his approach a detachment swung the gate open, a captain stepping forward to block Ely's approach. Ely leaned over, showing a slip of paper.

"Bearing dispatches from General Grant," he whispered. The captain examined the note, nodded, stepped back, and saluted.

"Hey, who's the Injun they're letting in?" a civilian shouted. "Injuns and niggers, Abe's got a helluva an army, don't he?"

Ely knew he shouldn't, but he was just so damn fed up and tired. Being a full-blooded Seneca in the army, he had often drawn comments, which he knew how to deal with, usually by a cold stare. But this morning he was tired, damn tired and fed up. He turned his mount and stared straight at the man who had shouted the insult.

The crowd parted back to the offender.

"Got a problem there, Major?" the man asked.

"Injuns and niggers are dying for you," Ely said quietly. "And you stand out here taunting. If you don't like us, at least have the courage to put on a gray uniform and fight us like a man. You're a coward, sir, and if you don't like that, wait out here for me after I meet the president and we can discuss it further.

"Pistols, swords"—he paused—"or tomahawks."

The man paled. A flicker of laughter greeted Ely's comments. "Bully for you," someone shouted. The loud-mouthed civilian turned and stalked off. Applause rippled through the crowd.

Angry that he had allowed himself to be baited, Ely turned back and rode the last few feet to the entry to the White House, dismounting wearily.

The captain at the gate came to his side.

"Can you tell me what's going on, Major?" he asked curiously.

Ely shook his head.

"Sorry to ask, sir," the captain pressed. "Just the city's been crazy with rumors for two days now. Word is the entire Army of the Potomac was wiped out and Lee will be here by tomorrow. That crowd has been out there all night. A lot of them are like that fool you dealt with. I have my men standing by with loaded rifles."

Ely said nothing, just nodded as he walked up the steps to the door, a sergeant opened it for him. An elderly black servant, waiting inside, offered to take Ely's hat.

"I'm bearing dispatches from General Grant," Ely said. "Is the president available? I'm ordered to deliver these to him personally."

"He's awake, sir. In fact, been up most of the night. Could you wait here, please?"

Ely nodded. The servant turned and went up the stairs, returning less than a minute later.

"This way, sir."

Ely followed him, looking around with curiosity. It was his first time in the White House, in fact, the first time he would stand before a president. If not for all that he had seen the last few days, the enormity of what he was bearing with him, he knew he should be nervous, but he wasn't. If anything, he was angry, damn angry.

The servant knocked on a door and seconds later it opened. Ely was surprised to see that it was the president himself opening the door.

The man towered above him, dark eyes looking straight at Ely.

"Thank you, Jim," the president said, then extended his hand to Ely.

"Come on in, Major. I was hoping you or someone would come down from our General Grant. Are you hungry?"

Caught a bit off guard, Ely lied and said no.

"Jim, could you bring our guest a cup of coffee?"

Ely stepped into the office. One other person was in the room, shirt half open, tie off, sitting on a sofa by an open window.

"Major Parker, is it?" Lincoln asked.

"Yes, sir. I'm on General Grant's staff, sir."

"Congressman Elihu Washburne," Lincoln said, nodding toward Elihu, who stood up and offered his hand.

"So do you think you'll fight that duel with that Copperhead down on the street?" Elihu asked.

Ely looked at him with surprise, dark features flushing even darker.

Elihu chuckled and pointed toward the open window.

"I heard you're a Seneca," Elihu said.

"Yes, sir."

"Noble tribe," Lincoln said with a smile. "I'm glad you're on our side."

Lincoln motioned for Ely to sit down on the sofa alongside of Elihu while he sank into an overstuffed leather chair facing them.

Even as he sat down Ely reached into the haversack at his side and drew out a sealed package and handed it to the president.

"These come directly from General Grant," Ely said. "I should add, sir, I was with General Sickles during the fight on Gunpowder River. After being separated from Sickles I recrossed the Susquehanna where a courier from General Grant met me, handed over the dispatches you now have, with orders to deliver them to you personally."

Jim came back into the room, bearing a small silver tray with several cups and a coffeepot, and placed it on a table, then filled the cups.

Lincoln placed the package on the table and motioned for Ely to take some coffee.

"So you were with Sickles during the fight?"

"Yes, sir, right up till he was wounded and taken from the field. After that, I felt it was my duty to retire and report on what I had seen."

"Tell me about it. Everything that's happened this last week. Why were you there with Sickles? What happened?"

Ely sighed and could not help but shake his head.

"Go on. I know you're tired, Major, but I want to hear it all."

"Of course, sir. No, I'm not really tired," he lied. "Well, sir, it's just the waste of it all, sir. It never should have happened.

"Sir, in brief. General Grant suspected that General Sickles was about to take the Army of the Potomac and cross the Susquehanna River to engage Lee on his own. That was specifically against Grant's orders.

"General Sickles, as you know, sir, crossed the river and fought Lee at Gunpowder River, and he was soundly defeated."

"Annihilated is more the word," Elihu interrupted.

"Sir, I was there throughout. That is why I felt I should come and report to you personally while carrying those dispatches at the same time."

He paused, taking a long sip of coffee. It was good, darn good, the best he had had in weeks. It hit his empty stomach, and for a second he felt slightly nauseous from it, suppressing a gag. He let it settle, Lincoln still staring at him.

"Take a minute, Major," Lincoln said, "then you can tell me the rest."

Lincoln had his shoes off, threadbare stocking feet stretched out, cup in his hand, sipping on it.

Where do I start? Ely wondered.

Lincoln put his coffee cup down, reached into his pocket and pulled out a folded paring knife, opened it, and cut the cords wrapped around the dispatch, peeling off the matches attached to the wax seal, and opening the cover.

He opened a dispatch of several pages and Ely immediately recognized Grant's handwriting. Lincoln scanned the sheet, features impassive, saying nothing, and then passed it to Elihu.

He picked up a second sheet, and scanned it. As he turned it over, Lincoln's features clouded. He stood up, turning away from Ely, and forcefully thrust the note toward Elihu, who took it.

"Damn it," Elihu muttered.

Lincoln paced over to the window and looked out for a moment, shoulders back, head lowered, lips moving as if speaking to himself.

Elihu tossed the second note on to the table. Ely looked at it, and Elihu nodded for him to pick it up.

The memo was authorization by Secretary Stanton for Sickles to move independently of Grant's command, and there, scrawled on the back in Grant's distinctive handwriting, was the question "Mr. President, did you authorize this?"

The silence in the room was interrupted only by the clock sounding the half hour.

Lincoln turned and walked over to his chair and sat down, with a long glance between him and Elihu.

"Go on, Major, tell me everything. Start with why you were sent down to General Sickles."

"Sir, on the afternoon of August 19 General Grant ordered me to proceed down to the Army of the Potomac," Ely began. "The general suspected that General Sickles was about to move, contrary to orders."

"Whose orders?"

"His, sir. There had been a staff meeting several days earlier that I attended as secretary. I did not bring a copy of that transcript, since it is highly sensitive, and if I were to be captured, it would have revealed in full detail General Grant's entire plan. It can be sent to you, sir, under escort if you wish, and it is proof that General Sickles acted against orders, for he was at that meeting as well."

"I think we'd like to see that at some point," Lincoln replied. "Now please go on."

"At that meeting General Grant outlined his plan for the forthcoming campaign. General Grant was waiting for the arrival of additional remounts, artillery, enough material for two more pontoon bridges, and at least another two divisions, planning that all would be in place by September 10. He would then have General Sickles cautiously move toward Baltimore to hold General Lee in place, while the Army of the Susquehanna moved to the west to outflank and envelop General Lee. As you can see, sir, those orders were not followed."

Ely hesitated. Lincoln nodded for him to continue.

"For whatever reasons, sir, General Sickles began to move independently, crossing the Susquehanna on August 19."

"And Grant did not authorize this?" Elihu asked sharply.

"Sir, he was not even aware of it."

"So why did he send you down to Sickles?" Elihu pressed.

"Because, sir, the telegraph connections between our command and Sickles went down. General Grant became suspicious, and there were rumors afloat that Sickles was indeed moving. I was sent down, carrying a direct written order from General Grant. Sickles was to reverse his march, fall back across the river, and then report directly to General Grant."

"So General Grant in no way whatsoever gave General Sickles any option to move independently?" Lincoln asked.

"No, sir."

Lincoln and Elihu again exchanged glances.

"Go on."

"Sir, I arrived at Havre de Grace on the morning of August 20 to discover that the Army of the Potomac was already across the river and pressing south toward Baltimore. I should add, sir, that I did a little checking at the telegraphy station there and, frankly, that was a wild goose chase."

"How so?"

"Well, sir, it was rather obvious the explanation that so-called rebel raiders had cut the lines north of Port Deposit was nothing more than a subterfuge. Those lines had been cut deliberately. I was met there by several of Sickles's staff. I told them I had to find the general at once. It was clear they had been waiting for someone from General Grant's headquarters to arrive."

Ely could not help but shake his head, the memory of that frustration apparent to Lincoln and Washburne.

"And they led you on another wild goose chase, is that it?" Elihu asked.

"Yes, sir," Ely said coldly. "I could have been up to General Sickles in two or three hours if guided correctly."

He shook his head angrily.

"I could have stopped that battle, sir," he said, voice heavy with despair. "I could have stopped it if I had gotten up to Sickles in time."

"I doubt that," Elihu replied.

"Sir?"

"Sickles was hell-bent on winning the war on his own. Major, you were outmaneuvered by one very slick general, and there was precious little you could have done to stop him, no matter what you tried."

"It took nearly the entire day of us riding back and forth," Ely continued. "I finally abandoned those damn . . . excuse me, sir . . . those staffers and headed off on my own. I could hear the sound of a battle developing and just rode straight to it. I found General Sickles at around four or so that afternoon.

"The battle was already on. I delivered General Grant's orders to disengage, but General Sickles argued that the battle had begun and he was driving them."

"Was he?" Lincoln asked.

"Yes, sir, and frankly, sir, once something like that starts, it's kind of hard to stop it. It looked as if Sickles did have the advantage over the rebels at that moment."

"Should he have disengaged anyhow?" Lincoln asked.

"Well, sir, at that moment, I guess not. He had two corps on our side tangling with but two divisions. But the point is, sir, if not led about so deliberately, I could have gotten up there before the battle even started. I had no doubt that General Sickles had the whole thing planned out."

Lincoln nodded thoughtfully.

"And the end of the first day?"

"Well, sir. They broke Pickett. Broke him badly. I saw that, but they pressed in too aggressively in pursuit, then ran smack into at least two more Confederate divisions and got mauled. I think, sir, at that moment it was obvious that all of General Lee's army was coming up and the battle had turned."

"Did Sickles see that?"

"Yes, sir, but he kept exclaiming that he now had Lee where he wanted him. I tried to press him yet again to follow the commander's orders. That, come morning, he would be facing superior numbers, while acting against the orders of the commanding general as well."

"But he pressed in anyhow."

"Yes, sir, he did." Ely sighed.

"He had to," Elihu interjected. "He was going for all or nothing."

"What happened then?"

"General Sickles misread Lee's intent, believing he was retreating. Sir, I would not care to second-guess a general on the field."

"Least of all General Grant," Elihu said with a bit of a smile.

"That's been my only experience up till then, sir," Ely replied. "But General Sickles had not yet fixed where Lee's new corps, under Beauregard, might be located. He pressed in anyhow and walked straight into a trap, Beauregard coming out on the right flank of the army and rolling it up.

"I was with General Sickles when he lost his leg. With that, sir, command broke down completely."

"There's a report that Sickles had his men carry him along the volley line, shouting for them to hold on," Lincoln said.

"Yes, sir. I'll give the man that. He had guts."

"Too much, I dare say," Elihu said coldly. "The ball should have taken his head off. He's already giving interviews in Philadelphia proclaiming the battle could have been a complete victory had not Grant failed to back him up as planned."

"That's a contemptible lie, sir," Ely snapped angrily. "General Grant up in Harrisburg had no idea that Sickles, a hundred miles away, was moving. It would have taken four days, at least, for Grant to come down and offer support. There was no plan. To say otherwise is a lie, a damned lie."

"I know that," Washburne said soothingly. "But there are a lot of people out there who won't."

"Sir, he directly disobeyed orders."

"Technically, no," Lincoln said quietly. Again he looked over at Elihu and then put his finger on the telegram resting on the table.

"He did have authorization from our secretary of war."

There was a long moment of silence.

Lincoln lowered his head, rubbing his brow with both hands.

"That does it," he finally whispered and stood up, going to the door. He stepped out of the office for a moment, Elihu watching him intently as he left.

"Your trip down here?" Elihu asked, finally looking back at Ely.

"I fell back to Havre de Grace sir. Once things broke down I thought it was my duty to report back to General Grant. Back across the river, sir, well, it was a madhouse there—wounded, broken troops, reporters shouting questions. By luck I saw one of General Grant's staff carrying the dispatches I have just given to the president. I took over that mission, sir. I thought it best to report directly on what I had seen as well, and I had the courier carry my report back to the general."

"Right decision, Major."

Ely leaned over and picked the coffee cup back up, draining the now tepid drink. Lincoln came back into the room and looked over at Ely, who stood up, sensing that his mission was complete and it was time to retire.

Lincoln extended his hands, gesturing for Ely to sit back down.

"I think you should stay a little longer, Major."

Elihu shifted, stood up, and started to button his shirt.

"Sir? Perhaps we should deal with this on our own," Elihu asked.

"I believe our major should see this," Lincoln replied, even as he sat down and struggled to put his boots on. "I want him to report it to General Grant exactly as he sees it."

Ely, a bit confused, looked at the two. Obviously, given the way Elihu was putting on his tie and then his jacket, something momentous was about to happen.

Lincoln said nothing, finishing with his boots and then running his fingers through his coarse hair. He walked to the window and looked out. Elihu settled silently back on the sofa and closed his eyes.

Ely felt uncomfortable, not sure why he was still there or what was about to happen. He filled another cup with coffee and drained it. He wished he could smoke, longing for the cigar in his pocket, but unsure of the proper protocol, he refrained.

The minutes dragged by, Lincoln silent by the window, Elihu drifting into sleep, the clock striking seven. Finally, Lincoln stirred.

"He's here."

The president turned away from the window, picked up the memo from the table, while nudging Washburne awake, and then stood in the center of the room.

Washburne stood up, and Ely did as well. Not sure of his place, he stepped back a few feet while Elihu walked over to stand behind Lincoln.

There was a knock on the door. When it opened, Ely immediately recognized Edwin Stanton, the secretary of war. The man came into the room, a bit of a smile on his face, which froze when his gaze rested on Lincoln, Elihu behind him. He shot a quick glance at Ely, who again felt self-conscious. He suddenly realized what a sight he must be, not having changed uniforms in over a week, mud splattered, face streaked with sweat, mud, smoke.

Stanton regained his composure and actually bowed slightly to Lincoln.

"Mr. President, you sent for me?"

"Yes, Edwin, may I introduce you to Maj. Ely Parker of General Grant's staff?"

Edwin spared another quick glance at Ely, who came to attention and saluted. Edwin did not reply and then turned back to Lincoln as if Ely was not even there.

"Sir, may I inquire as to the nature of this early morning call? I was over at the War Office reviewing dispatches when your summons came."

Lincoln extended his hand, offering the memo that Ely had delivered.

"Sir, let us not beat about the bush," Lincoln said coldly. "I just wish for you to explain this dispatch. Major Parker delivered it to me less than an hour ago. I should add that Major Parker was with Sickles at Gunpowder River, bearing a message from General Grant to General Sickles ordering him to withdraw. An order which General Sickles refused to comply with. Now, sir, please read what I've just handed you."

Edwin visibly paled, coughing, then held the memo up, adjusting his spectacles. He scanned the message.

"Sir, I am not sure of the meaning of this inquiry," Stanton said even as he read.

"When finished, please turn it over," Lincoln said.

Stanton did as requested, reading Grant's addendum, "Mr. President, did you authorize this?" and handed the message back to Lincoln.

"Sir, I think, yet again, there has been some miscommunication."

"Miscommunication?" Lincoln said softly, and shook his head. "Miscommunication? The Army of the Potomac all but annihilated and you call it a miscommunication?"

"Sir. I suspect here that General Grant failed to properly coordinate with General Sickles regarding the intent of the plans for the campaign. I warned you of that last month when Grant first came to Washington. If he had stayed here as I requested, this never would have happened."

Lincoln actually sighed and then chuckled softly.

Ely, outraged, struggled to contain a retort. Elihu looked over at him, and with a shake of his head communicated for him to stay out of it.

Stanton saw the gesture and cast a withering glance at Ely.

"Mr. President, I think we should discuss this in private." Now his gaze swept over to Elihu as well.

"No, sir, we will discuss this now. If you wish, you can sit down and listen to all that Major Parker has told me about what happened."

"I think, sir, there are better uses of our time than the report of a major obviously biased in favor of a general who has placed our cause in jeopardy."

Lincoln sighed again and raised his head.

There was a cold light in his eyes. All that Ely had heard of Lincoln never mentioned this. It was always "Old Abe," or just "Abe," but there was something different at this moment, a terrible anger that seemed ready to explode.

"Mr. Stanton, I expect your resignation before you leave this building," Lincoln said softly.

"What?" Stanton reddened.

"Just that, sir. Sickles moved on your authorization. I made it distinctly clear to all that when Grant took command in the field, all orders of troop movements were to be routed through him for his approval as well. You did not do so. Nor, for that matter, did you inform me of these orders you sent to Sickles."

He held the memo up, clenching it in a balled fist, shaking it at Stanton. Stanton started to speak but Lincoln cut him off.

"We lost maybe thirty thousand or more at Gunpowder River. A fine army destroyed. What in Heaven's name am I to say to the nation about that, sir? You, sir, have placed the plans of the last month in grave jeopardy; in fact, we might very well lose this war thanks to what you did."

"What I did?" Stanton fired back. "What I did? Mr. President, if you had but listened to me all along, we would not be in this fix. You have placed a drunkard in command of our armies."

"That is a lie, sir," Ely snapped, no longer able to contain himself and instantly regretting his words as all three turned to gaze at him.

"Damn you!" Stanton shouted. "You are relieved of your rank, Major. How dare you call me a liar."

Ely did not know what to say. Stanton turned to advance on him, but Lincoln stepped between the two.

"Mr. Stanton, you no longer have the authority to relieve anyone as of this moment. Now, sir, do I have your resignation, or do I fire you and release that information to the press waiting outside?"

Stanton looked back at Lincoln, breathing hard.

"I will not resign, sir."

"Then I shall relieve you of your posting, effective as of this moment."

Stanton now paled. For a second Ely thought he would collapse, as the man began to wheeze, doubling over to cough.

"Which shall it be?" Lincoln pressed, even as Stanton continued to cough.

Stanton looked up at him.

"Which shall it be?" Lincoln pressed.

"Go ahead and fire me," Stanton replied coldly. "I'll take this before Congress and the Committee on the Conduct of the War. Then we shall see."

"See what? Are you threatening me?" Lincoln snapped angrily. "Congress is not in session, nor shall I call it back into session until this crisis is finished. You can go to the newspapers and I shall counter with a copy of this memo, a direct violation of my own orders."

"It will ruin you, sir," Washburne interjected. "If you resign, you can claim reasons of health, your asthma. It's that or a fight you don't want and cannot win."

Lincoln sighed again.

"Or one the nation needs at this moment."

His tone softened and Lincoln drew closer.

"Edwin, you did fine to a point, but you overstepped yourself. Not just here but in the orders you sent to Meade during Union Mills. I am asking, as someone who once worked alongside you, please resign."

Edwin continued to cough, wheezing hard, then finally straightened back up.

"I'll resign," he whispered.

"Fine, then." Lincoln led him over to his desk, took out a sheet of White House stationery, and offered him a pen.

The stationery already was filled out with a statement of resignation. Stanton read it over once, then quickly signed it, straightening back up.

"And I assume my replacement is your friend there," Stanton asked, nodding toward Elihu.

"Yes."

"I figured as much."

Stanton looked over at Ely.

"Major Parker you said your name is?"

Ely felt a cold chill with the way Stanton looked at him.

"Yes, sir."

Stanton said nothing.

"Good day, Mr. President."

He turned and walked out.

Lincoln's shoulders hunched over, and wearily he walked over to his desk and sat down on the edge of it.

Again there was a long silence. Lincoln finally reached into a pigeon-hole of his desk and drew out a sealed envelope.

"Elihu, this is your authorization to assume control as acting secretary of war until such time as the Senate reconvenes to confirm your appointment. I expect you to go over to the War Office right now. Take an escort with you. Edwin's office is to be sealed. He is not allowed back in till such time as you review all records contained in there. Personal items will be returned to him once your review is complete."

"Yes, Mr. President."

Lincoln looked back over at Ely, who stood rooted in place.

"Don't let that little threat bother you," Lincoln said.

"Threat, sir?"

"His asking your name like that. Rather ungentlemanly of him."

Ely did not reply. After all he had seen the last few days, the threat of a former secretary of war seemed almost inconsequential.

Lincoln fell silent again for a few minutes, Elihu standing by the desk as if waiting.

"You know what to do," Lincoln said.

"What we talked about, sir," Elihu replied.

For the first time Ely realized the drama he had just witnessed had been planned out long before his arrival. His messages were simply the confirmation the president had been waiting for.

"Elihu, I'll drop by your new office a bit later this morning. I want all the arrangements made for my little adventure."

"Sir, I still caution against it. Stanton is on his way to the newspapers even now. It will cause an explosion in this town once the word hits. Plus the risk involved."

"Don't worry, Elihu, I'll have a good escort with me. I think Major Parker will serve as an excellent guide and traveling companion."

"Sir?" Parker asked, now thoroughly confused.

"I think it's time I paid a little visit to your general," Lincoln said.

Lincoln looked at the two, his features serious.

"Gentlemen, I think that the crisis is truly upon us now. Lee has out-maneuvered us again. Major, it is obvious that the word you bring to me is that General Grant has launched his attack prematurely, forced to do so because of Sickles's disastrous actions."

"Yes, sir, that is obviously the case."

"So the risks are far higher now. I must confer with Grant upon them before giving my own approval. The choice is ultimately mine."

He lowered his head as if speaking to himself.

"I am now convinced we shall either win or lose this war in the next two weeks."

Chapter Two

CSA It was the noonday lull, the cool breezes of morning giving way to a still midday heat. Gen. Robert E. Lee, commander, Army of Northern Virginia, rode in silence. The road before him was packed with troops, men marching at a vigorous pace. He trotted past the troops, edging along fencerows, cutting out into pastures and orchards to make speed.

The men were moving, maintaining a grueling pace of three miles an hour, hunched over, rifles balanced on shoulders or slung inverted, hats pulled down over brows to shield eyes from the noonday glare, faces sweat-streaked, dust kicking up in swirling, choking clouds. Some saw him and gave a salute or shout as he cantered along; others, sunk into the hypnotic rhythm of the march, were unaware of his presence.

These men had marched over a hundred miles in the past week and fought a brutal three-day running battle in killing heat, and it showed. The usual banter of a victorious army on the march was gone; the high spirits that should have echoed after their overwhelming victories over the Army of the Potomac were not showing this day. Exhaustion had overwhelmed exhilaration.

He rode in silence, lost in thought. Walter Taylor, his aide-de-camp, the staff, even the secretary of state, Judah Benjamin, sensing he wished to ride alone to think, trailed a respectful distance behind him.

After the smashing defeat of Sickles he expected Grant to wait, or perhaps even to start transferring his army by train and boat down to Washington, there to assume a defensive posture through the fall and winter.

But to take an aggressive path? To cross the river and move south, perhaps straight at him. No, he had not expected that. After every defeat dealt the Union Army over the last year, his opponents had always retreated, regrouped, and waited several months before venturing another blow.

It was like facing an opponent in chess. The traditional opening of a king or queen's pawn is expected, but then, instead, the man across the table puts his knight out first. That was usually the move of a fool . . . or could it be that of a *master* or someone who sensed or planned something Lee could not yet ascertain.

Who was Grant? In that tight-knit cadre of old comrades from West Point, the old professional army of the frontier, of Mexico, or garrison duty in East Coast fortifications, Grant was one man he could not remember. He knew the man had served in Mexico and gained distinction there for personal bravery and leadership, but as an army commander? He had beaten Beauregard at Shiloh, captured an entire army at Fort Donelson and Vicksburg. He was used to victory . . . perhaps that could be turned against him.

There were the rumors as well about the man's drinking, but then again, the army had always been a hard-drinking lot. In the case of Grant, the few who knew him said it had been brought on by a fit of melancholia when stationed out on the West Coast, separated from his wife and children.

Longstreet, who did know him, dismissed the drinking, saying that it was a demon his old friend would have overcome, especially when he had returned to the army and given the responsibility of command.

All the others he had faced so far, McClellan, the fool Pope, the slow-moving Burnside, the hard-driving but morally weak Hooker, even Meade and Sickles, he could read them, and he could read as well the thinking, the rhythm, the mentality of the Army of the Potomac . . . reft by internal dissent and political maneuverings, hampered by even more political maneuverings in Washington.

But he was no longer facing the Army of the Potomac, and even in Washington he sensed a change. Halleck was out, and just this morning Judah Benjamin had suggested that perhaps Stanton's days were numbered as well. A staff officer of Sickles's, a prisoner, had bitterly complained that his general had moved without coordination with Grant, and everyone at Sickles's headquarters knew that Stanton had sent out contradictory orders for which "someone would pay."

And Grant's corps commanders—Ord, McPherson, Banks, Burnside.

He knew the mettle of Burnside, knew the fumbling reputation of Banks, who survived due to political influence. Word on McPherson was his men worshipped him and declared him to be the best corps commander in any army.

And he knew him as well, as superintendent at West Point. The memory of McPherson caused him to smile. McPherson had risen to become the top-ranking officer of cadets. He was a moral man, honest, open-handed, respected by all. John Bell Hood had been his roommate and he loved him like a brother.

Of all the potential opponents this war had forced him to confront, James Birdseye McPherson was the one opponent he wished he did not have to face. There was a deep bond of affection, that of a mentor for a beloved student.

Now I will have to face him, and turn all that was good between us into a tool, a weapon to defeat him in battle.

Edward Ord, new to his rank of corps commander, was a man who supposedly loved a good head-on fight, a man like Hood.

And their troops. These Union soldiers from the West were used to victory; they were used to tough fighting in the scorching heat and bayous of Mississippi, the tangled forests of Tennessee, the swamps of Louisiana. They were fighters—and filled with a belief in themselves. In battle, such belief is often what tips the scale between victory and defeat. Though tough soldiers, the men of the Army of the Potomac seemed to carry an innate sense that defeat would always be their ultimate fate, and that had come true at Union Mills and Gunpowder River.

He wished he had another month, time to evaluate, to maneuver and observe Grant, to spar with him to get a taste of him, before moving in for the kill.

The pasture ahead dropped down into a glen and he welcomed the momentary pause as he loosened Traveler's reins and gave his companion a chance to drink in the shade of the willows lining the shallow creek. There the air was damp and rich, the brook rippling and sparkling with reflected light.

To his left a battery of guns was clattering over a rough-hewn wooden bridge, troops left the road to wade across the knee-deep stream. A few men playfully splashed each other. Sergeants called for canteens, handing them off to details to fill while the column pushed on, the water bearers enjoying their work for a few minutes, some tossing off packs, haversacks, and cartridge boxes and collapsing into the water to cool off, before picking up their gear and filled canteens to double-time back into the column.

More than a few men lay in the shadow of the trees, barefoot, soaking their feet, one of the men gingerly wrapping torn strips of cloth around his bleeding and blistered heels. At the sight of the general some came to attention. A provost guard watching the group nervously declared the men, exhausted troops from a Virginia regiment, had been given passes to fall out of the march for a few minutes but would catch up to their unit.

Lee said nothing. He nodded and then, gathering Traveler's reins, trotted across the stream and up the bank through the high river grass, birds kicking up around him.

Old Thomas Jackson would never have stood for the boys falling out like that. He'd have shouted for them to get back in the ranks and march till they dropped, but today was not the day for that. Reports from the previous week's march were that hundreds of men, listed as missing in action, had actually collapsed and died in the forced marching in hundred-degree heat. He therefore had sent word down that those unable to keep up today were to be treated leniently.

As he came up out of the streambed he saw a low church steeple, a small village of a few dozen homes, the windows of some showing limp Confederate flags, others shuttered and closed. Longstreet's headquarters flag fluttered out in a gentle breeze near the church, an awning set up in front of it, with staff gathering around.

Uniforms showed gold braid. He saw Stuart still astride his horse, leaning over, talking with Beauregard. Hood, sitting on a chair under the awning, head back, was obviously asleep. Seeing him coming up, men began to stir, staff moving about, setting chairs around a table.

A corporal offered to take Traveler's reins, and Lee with a sigh dismounted. On stiff legs he walked toward the gathering, returning the salutes of those waiting for him.

Someone nudged Hood, who looked around sleepily and then stood up. Stuart dismounted, taking off his plumed hat as he stepped under the awning.

These were his old warriors and Providence had been kind in this fight, sparing all of them yet again. Not a division commander had been lost in this last fight, thank God, though Pickett had lost three of his five brigade commanders and the others were wounded. He caught a glimpse of Pickett standing nervously to one side, the man breaking eye contact when Lee looked at him for a moment.

Under the awning Longstreet pointed to a chair at the head of the table. Lee settled down, a servant bringing to him what appeared to be a miracle, lemonade that was actually iced, and he gladly took it, draining half the glass. Benjamin sat down by his right side, Taylor moved in be-

hind Lee, while his cavalry escort dismounted, the men then walking
their mounts back down to the stream to water them.

The corps commanders gathered around the table and sat down, division commanders stood behind them.

"General Stuart," Lee began, "what is the latest news?"

"Well, sir, we lost our outpost and telegraphy connection at Carlisle."

"When?"

"Shortly after six this morning, sir. Yankee cavalry hit them hard. Our
men were forced to retreat and we lost all connection."

"And what other word is there?"

"Sir, all our telegraph connections that can report quickly on Harrisburg are down. The outposts we still have are at Shippensburg, Hanover
Junction, Frederick, and Gettysburg."

As he spoke he pointed out the positions on the map.

"We had a report at midmorning that the Yankees were also crossing
by ferry at Wrightsville, cavalry," he paused, "and infantry. It is also reported they are starting to build a pontoon bridge as well at that location.
We then lost our outpost at York about two hours ago."

"Grant's first move," Longstreet interjected, "is to cut our telegraph
outposts, blind us."

"We'd have done the same," Lee replied noncommittally. He had
hoped they could have held contact for most of the day. The use of
telegraphs for such reports was something new for the Army of Northern
Virginia, but given the vast front they now operated on, literally all of
eastern Maryland and south central Pennsylvania, he had hoped to keep
these precious lines up awhile longer.

"So any information we have now, sir," Stuart continued, "is nearly as
old as our first reports, couriers have to carry them back to our remaining
posts."

"And those reports?"

"The same, sir. Grant pushed the bridge across during the night at
Harrisburg, and they started moving before dawn. Railroad equipment
was sighted as well. Moved by train up to the bridge north of Harrisburg,
across the river, and down the right bank. Apparently they are already laying track and replacing bridges we'd torn up."

"Units?"

"Definitely corps strength or more. McPherson's Corps was in the
lead. The report I just mentioned from York indicated infantry in corps
strength preparing to cross at Wrightsville. That's it, so far."

"He'd lead with McPherson," Hood said softly. "We all know he is a
good man."

Lee nodded in agreement.

"And that is it?" Lee asked.

"I'm sorry, sir, but that is all I can report now."

"It is not your fault, General Stuart," Lee replied, holding his hand up.

He did not add that now, more than ever, he regretted the audacity of the raid attempted a week ago by Wade Hampton. He had felt some reluctance to adopt Stuart's bold plan, to launch Hampton on a raid up toward Reading to gather intelligence on Grant, sow panic, disrupt rail transportation, and perhaps even skirt the edge of Philadelphia.

Grant's cavalry, backed by infantry, had relentlessly hunted Wade down, killed him, and wiped out his entire brigade. Those men would have been invaluable now for shadowing Grant. The only forces deployed to shadow Grant were two regiments detached from his nephew Fitz Lee's Brigade. That was nowhere near enough to harass Grant, to slow him, and at this moment, far more importantly, to gain knowledge of his intentions.

Lee studied the map for a moment, finishing his iced lemonade.

What would I do? He wondered. *I will not put myself in Grant's shoes, not yet. I'll do so when I know the man better. Don't assume he will do what I would do.*

He leaned back from the table and motioned for another glass.

"Comments?"

"He'll come straight at us," "Pete" Longstreet said. "He's just securing his right flank at Carlisle. The main push will come from York to Hanover Junction, then to Baltimore using the Northern Central Railroad for supplies. He'll use the rail line for supplies and come straight down those tracks toward Baltimore."

Pete fell silent for a moment. Lee nodded for his old warhorse to continue.

"If he started this last night, I think he was hoping that we would still be tangled up along the Susquehanna, mopping up Sickles. Our men exhausted, worn down. He then pivots."

As Longstreet spoke he brushed his hand across the map to indicate the move.

"Pins us north of Baltimore."

"Precisely why I ordered this forced march back to Baltimore today," Lee replied.

He nodded toward the road down which the endless column flowed by, the men slowing in their passage at the sight of Lee and his lieutenants under the awning not fifty yards away. Guards along the road could be heard chanting over and over, "Keep moving, boys. Yes, it's General Lee. Don't disturb them. Keep moving, boys. . . ."

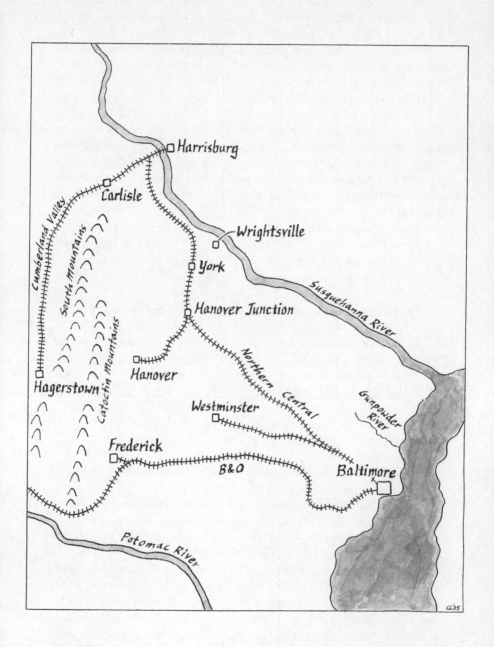

"If he does that," Lee said, "we've slipped the noose and Grant will just reoccupy the ground Sickles tried to take. Let him have it, then we are inside Baltimore, behind fortifications, and he can attack us till doomsday."

"I've learned to have a healthy respect for this man," Beauregard said softly, the lilt of his Louisiana accent soft and pleasant.

"Go on, sir," Lee replied.

"I'd be nervous about getting ourselves pinned inside of Baltimore. Look at the way he maneuvered between Forts Henry and Donelson, the way he encircled Vicksburg from the rear. If we stay in Baltimore, he might very well envelope us, circle around, and reconnect to his supplies through Washington. Do that, and he frees up the garrison of Washington to act as an offensive force, too. Sir, I'd be cautious about that move. We don't want Grant to gain control of the forty thousand men still pinned down there."

"Good advice, General Beauregard, but if that threat should arise, it will be five days, perhaps a week from now. But would you concur with General Longstreet that he will turn at Carlisle and come straight at us?"

Beauregard lowered his gaze, staring intently at the map for a moment.

"Honestly, sir, I don't know. I do not know this terrain, the land, the roads the way you men do."

Hood cleared his threat and Lee turned to face the commander of his Second Corps.

"Go on, General Hood. Your thoughts."

"I'd agree with General Longstreet," Hood replied, "except for one thing."

"And that is?"

"McPherson being in the lead and marching on Carlisle."

"And that is?"

"Sir. You and I know McPherson. I believe Grant brought him east to be his fast-moving corps, his Jackson."

Hood hesitated, realizing he had unintentionally offered an insult.

"Or the task you now do so ably, General Longstreet," Hood cried.

"No insult taken, sir," Pete said, just offering a smile and a nod.

"Please continue, General Hood," Lee interjected.

"If I was Grant, and wanted the strike to come due south, I'd have placed McPherson in Wrightsville and built the first bridge there, not at Harrisburg. I think we can read into this, sir, that perhaps Grant's intent is not to come due south, but rather to swing wide."

Hood gestured toward the map and motioned with his hand.

"A broad sweeping march down the Cumberland Valley. To turn our flank, perhaps even spring into Virginia."

Lee did not reply. Hood had raised a point. He next turned to Jeb.

"General Stuart? Your opinion."

"Most likely straight at us, sir. He can close in three to four days, using the intact railroad for support. Swinging down the valley will take more time, and the Yankees always are slower than us. Add in that repairing the railroad will tie them up further. We tore that railroad in the Cumberland Valley apart for just that reason, sir, but kept the Northern Central intact in case we had to eventually move back to Harrisburg. Grant will take advantage of that and come straight at us looking for a fight."

"May I interject something, sir?" Judah Benjamin, the Confederate secretary of state, asked quietly.

"Of course, sir. I always value your opinion."

"I am not a military man, sir, but I can look at this from the political side."

"Go on, sir."

"The Lincoln administration has suffered two devastating blows in less than two months. Your victories at Union Mills and these last few days on this ground. Your victories have brought Maryland officially to our side as well."

Longstreet shifted a bit but said nothing. Only the day before Pete had spoken derisively of Maryland's failure to raise even a single division to join the ranks. Only a few thousand Marylanders had so far volunteered; the rest were taking a wait-and-see attitude.

Judah looked up at Pete and smiled.

"I know, General, you are disappointed that there has been no levy en masse by our brothers in Maryland, but remember they have endured two years of oppression by Lincoln and his cronies."

"All the more reason for them to rally to the colors."

"That time will come."

"When the war is over and we have won," Pete replied coolly.

"Gentlemen, let us focus on the moment," Lee interjected smoothly. Longstreet lowered his head.

"The political pressure on Lincoln is, after what you achieved these last few days, all but overwhelming. His coalition is on the point of collapse."

"I wish to heaven he *would* collapse. When are they going to learn they can't beat us?" Beauregard interjected. If not for the presence of

Lee, he would have used more forceful words. All those around the table would have eagerly added to them, but none dared to voice their hatred of this effort to conquer them.

"Sickles was a War Democrat, the darling of that group, and now he is defeated and in disgrace," Benjamin said.

"Does anyone know how he is?" Lee asked.

"He's in Philadelphia," Stuart said. "He'll live, but I regret to say, sir, that we just got word that General Warren died this morning in one of our field hospitals."

There was a moment of silence, someone behind Lee sighing with a whispered comment, "Damn this war."

Warren had been one of them, or rather they had once been one with him. Another comrade of West Point gone, a devout man, well liked on both sides.

Benjamin had fallen silent out of respect. At a gesture from Lee he went on. "There is no real political motive for the War Democrats of the North to continue to support Lincoln, but there is precious little they can do at this moment to stop him. Congress is adjourned, the rats having fled when we first threatened the capital. For all practical purposes Lincoln has a dictatorship at this moment, but he must do something with that, and his lone remaining chance is Grant."

"So you think he will order Grant to come straight at us?"

"No, sir, I don't," Judah said quietly.

"Pray why not?"

"It's his last card. Lincoln is holding one last card, and he is now looking us straight in the eyes. Once he plays it, well, the drama will be decided as to whether that card is trump or not. I suspect he'll buy a little more time. The War Democrats can announce their withdrawal of support, riots can erupt again in New York and elsewhere, but I think our opponent will not lay that card down until something is in place to hedge his bet with."

"What about France?" Beauregard asked. "I heard that you said their intervention is all but certain."

Beauregard, proud of his French heritage, was always promoting the idea that France would eventually come to their side, as she did back during the First Revolution.

Judah smiled.

"Not a direct quote, sir," Judah replied with a cagey smile, "but close enough. Yes, Emperor Napoleon the Third will come in, but will that impact us here over the next month or two? I doubt it. If he sorties with his fleet to try to break the blockade at Wilmington, Charleston, or even at the mouth of the Chesapeake, I dare say the Yankee navy and heavy iron-clads will make short work of them.

"No, the French, as always, will play their own game to their own advantage. They will not help directly, only indirectly, and that will be along the coast of Texas, in support of their mad affair in Mexico. Even if they did break the blockade there, even if they broke the blockade at New Orleans, it would be long months before that impacted this front here.

"And frankly, gentleman, as secretary of state, though I wish for their help now, I certainly do not look forward to cleaning up the mess when we finally win and then have to kick them back out, because once involved on our side they will demand payment of some kind or another."

"So you don't see any change that will affect us here and now?" Beauregard asked. There was a trace of sadness in his voice.

"No, sir. And Lincoln knows that, too. Sorry, gentlemen, but don't look to France for any major changes in the situation you now face here in Maryland."

"Back to the original issue then," Lee said, "the here and now of this moment. For all these reasons, what do you think Grant will do, Mr. Secretary?"

"Wait you out."

"Sir?"

"Just that, General Lee. I heard the report you received but yesterday that a colored division had joined Grant's army. If he waits you out another two weeks, might he not gain another few divisions of colored troops, perhaps a few more battalions of artillery, more supplies, a few more brigades of remounts for cavalry? Might he not actually repair the rail line in the Cumberland Valley clear down to Hagerstown and thus give himself even more mobility? Might he not wait and force you to take the initative and in so doing choose the ground? Perhaps, sir, might he not just simply bypass you completely and march down the valley, cross into Virginia, and march on Richmond?"

"It is hard for me to see him doing that," Lee replied slowly, sipping again at his refilled glass of lemonade. "Moving on Richmond or waiting."

"Your views, sir?" Judah asked.

"If I were Grant, I would attack now, and with everything I have. My army has endured two months of hard campaigning; we took heavier-than-expected losses in our last action."

He could not help but raise his head for a few seconds and gaze again at Pickett, who stood silent, frozen in place.

"Five of the original nine divisions that started this campaign two and a half months ago have taken grievous losses. My sense of Grant is that he will come straight on, hoping to catch us exhausted, perhaps still strung out on a march back to Baltimore. Force us then to turn and fight.

"That is why I ordered this forced march today, no matter how painful it is for the men out there."

He gestured toward the road, where the weary columns continued to march by, and felt a wave of pity for his men. As they passed they undoubtedly knew that, yet again, he was deciding their fate. He had to do what was right for his country, and what was right for them, too. Dozens, perhaps a hundred or more, might die today during this march, but through their sacrifice all could rest in Baltimore, and by tomorrow the situation would be clearer. He pitied the thousands of wounded whom he had ordered to be loaded on ambulances and evacuated by any means possible back to the city. Their ordeal would be horrific this day.

Lee was silent and lowered his head. *Tomorrow we shall know. By then it will be clear whether Grant has turned south, coming straight on, or not. We can refit in Baltimore then and plan our next move.*

He hated this. He wished that right now telegraph keys were clicking, telling him which way Grant was moving, either coming straight on or, as Hood suggested, swinging wide on a flanking march to the southwest.

In almost every battle in the past, we knew their intentions. This time it was different, and that was indeed troubling. And yet, at Chancellorsville he had been caught off guard and turned near defeat into an overwhelming victory.

"Just one more victory, gentlemen," Lee said softly, surveying his lieutenants and the secretary of state. "Whether he comes due south or tries to flank us, all we seek is one more victory—and the war is over."

All around him nodded in agreement.

"Keep the troops moving, gentlemen. I want the entire army into Baltimore as quickly as possible, and then they can rest.

"General Stuart, starting tomorrow I want a strong screen moved forward toward General Grant. Give your men time to rest this afternoon and into tomorrow. Report to me tonight for orders."

"Sir, a problem."

"Go ahead."

"Many of our mounts are worn. I dare say half our horses need reshoeing."

"Then find new mounts in the city."

"Sir, city horses, well, they just aren't fit for cavalry. Draught horses, mostly. We're starting to sweep this area clean of remounts. I must have several days at least to refit after the hard ride of the last week."

Lee nodded.

"Rest your men today. Get them off the roads. Concentrate at a place of your choosing between here and Baltimore, then report to me as ordered. Send some of your staff back to the city to see what arrangements can be made for your refitting."

"Yes, sir."

"Gentlemen, I want this army to make twenty-five miles today. I know it will be a hard march. But I promise you at least a day of rest tomorrow. As I said before, be liberal with those who cannot keep up. We are not an army in retreat, and those who fall out will surely rejoin the ranks. They are good men, so treat the exhausted, the ill, with respect; make that clear to your provost guards."

All nodded in agreement.

"We meet tomorrow in Baltimore, and there will plan our next move."

The look in his eyes was clear indication of dismissal. The group began to break up, officers calling for their mounts, staff, and escorts.

Lee caught General Pickett's eye and motioned for him to come over, the crestfallen division commander yielding with a certain reluctance.

"General Longstreet, would you join us for a moment?"

Lee stepped out from under the awning into the warm afternoon sun.

"General Pickett, sir, I am disappointed in the report I received regarding your action at Gunpowder River."

"Sir, our blood was up," Pickett replied defensively. "We would not run before Yankees."

"And you destroyed your division, sir."

Pickett looked at him, eyes wide.

Lee looked over at Longstreet. Pickett was his old friend.

Pete gave no indication either way of his wishes. He knew Longstreet was in a quandary.

"I had hoped that in actions to come, General Pickett, it would be your division, which had been the heaviest division in my army, to see victory through. The honor might have been yours to lead a charge that could have won the war."

He paused for a moment.

"Sir, I shall not relieve you of command. But know, sir, that I shall be watching you closely henceforth."

"General Lee," Pickett replied icily, "if you do not have confidence in my ability, sir, then accept my resignation."

Lee flushed.

"I have no wish or time for such a result," Lee replied sharply, controlling his anger. "I need you and what is left of your division. I need every man, every experienced field commander I can find. Just do your duty, and follow orders, next time, to the letter. That is what I expect of you now."

Features pale, Pickett stood motionless. Slowly he saluted.

"Yes, sir."

He turned and walked off.

"I think you should have relieved him," Pete said quietly, waiting till Pickett was out of earshot.

"Perhaps. But controlled, under your direct observation, he can still lead. General Longstreet, I shall see you tonight in Baltimore. Perhaps by this time tomorrow the picture will be clearer and we will see our next move."

"I hope so, sir."

Lee looked at him closely. Now was not the time to show hesitation, even if it did whisper to him.

"I know so, General Longstreet."

He walked off, signaling for Traveler. An orderly brought his horse up; he mounted and fell in alongside the endless column, into the boiling clouds of dust, moving south toward Baltimore.

Chapter Three

Headquarters, Army of the Susquehanna
Carlisle

August 22, 1863
9:00 P.M.

The evening air was beginning to cool as he stepped out of the Carlisle army barracks, which had become his headquarters for the night. The corridor reeked of coal oil. A rolled-up newspaper, half burnt and then crushed, lay by the doorway, as if the rebs were going to burn the place then changed their minds. Whoever it was who had spared the building, he was grateful to him. The barracks was a fine old part of army history.

He lit a cigar and leaned against a pillar on the veranda, drawing the smoke in, sighing as he exhaled. He actually felt relaxed, all the weeks of tension, of waiting, what seemed to be interminable waiting, were over. They were on the move.

It had been a good day's march. McPherson's Corps had made over twenty five miles and camped ten miles southwest, at Centerville, and just behind him was Burnside's Ninth. Ord's men were still filing into Carlisle, and as he stood on the veranda, he watched them pass.

The town was rich, prosperous, not really touched by the war. Gaslight illuminated the main thoroughfare, this incredible valley pike, the type of road he'd have given a right arm for while struggling through the back lanes and swamps of Louisiana and Mississippi. Broad, well macadamized, the crushed limestone pavement glittering in the glow of the gaslight.

The troops marched by in good order, their spirits up. They were on the move and in the East. All day long the men he had brought with him from the Mississippi campaign had been in high spirits. Though over eighty degrees, the air was relatively dry. There were no foul humors in this Pennsylvania air carrying ague or yellow jack. For them twenty-five miles in such conditions was all in a day's work, though some had found the paved pike to be hard on the feet after the soft mud or powder of western roads.

What had captivated him and his army was the outright celebration of the citizenry. The pike was lined with thousands of civilians. They had been behind the rebel lines for over a month, and though Lee's men had treated them with the utmost respect, still it had been an occupying army, and now the liberators had come. It was a heady experience for all of them, civilians, soldiers, and even their general. For the first time on a campaign march they had been greeted as friends and not as alien invaders.

That thought, of being aliens in their own country, had often troubled him. Nearly twenty years earlier, during the buildup before the war with Mexico, he had spent a winter in Louisiana and had found it to be a pleasant memory, of cool winter nights and days usually filled with a nice touch of warmth when compared to Ohio or the freezing nights at the Point. Back then they had been treated as heroes about to go off to war. But those days were long gone. Not since the start of all this current misery had he seen such a march as they had experienced this day.

Pretty girls, many wearing patriotic ribbons of red, white, and blue, stood at farm gates, waving flags, cheering as each regiment passed. Mothers had looked on smilingly, passing out fresh-baked biscuits and bread; little boys had run up and down along the fencerows bordering the pike, laughing and playing friendly pranks. When the march broke for ten minutes' rest at the end of every hour, civilians had mingled freely among the men, bearing buckets of cool fresh well water and passing out yet more food.

So many soldiers in the ranks who were fathers found themselves, for a few minutes, transported back home, a child in their lap, tickling it, trying to get the infant or toddler to smile, and everyone laughing even when the child burst into tears and reached for its mother. Men began taking bullets out of a cartridge box, tearing them open and tossing a handful of loose powder into a quickly made fire to give the children a thrill as it burst with a puff of sulfurous smoke, then passing the minié ball to some wide-eyed boy as a souvenir. So many were doing this that word passed down the ranks that the practice had to be stopped before someone got hurt, and besides, multiplied a hundred thousand times, it was enough ammunition to keep an entire brigade on the firing line for a long day's fight.

When the bugles and drums sounded for the march to resume more than one man had tears in his eyes as he hugged and kissed a child who had been "his" for ten brief minutes. Younger men, boys of seventeen and eighteen, fell in love a dozen times that day, for at each stop there was a pretty lass, scores of pretty lasses. At such a moment all the restraints and decorum were set aside for a few minutes, though parents still kept a watchful eye, usually chatting with a captain or older sergeant as they watched. Boys who at home had stammered at the sight of a girl now boldly asked their names, how old they were, and if they had any brothers or sweethearts in the army. Girls looked into young soldiers' eyes and would not turn away, would smile, offer kind words, perhaps even the touch of a hand to a cheek or even a chaste kiss and a tearful, "Good luck soldier. I'll pray for you tonight." Addresses were hurriedly scribbled and exchanged, with the usually unfulfilled promise of writing after "all this is over."

And so the columns would form up and move on, passing through small villages of prosperous homes, past rich farms with neatly painted barns as big as churches. The fences bordering the pike were sturdy, well-built affairs of post and rail, enclosing orchards, wheat fields, and corn head high on the other side. The fences were often piled thick with honeysuckle in bloom and morning glories fading in the midday heat. The air was rich with the scents of an abundant land, of ripening apples, corn, flowers, and over all a sheen of softness, almost of a memory forming that could haunt those who outlived the weeks ahead, haunting them fifty years hence with dreams of at least one day when war did have a touch of glory to it as they marched ever west and south.

The column, stretching back twenty miles, all the way to Harrisburg, had thus moved throughout the day, thousands of rifles on shoulders swaying, sparkling as they caught and reflected the sunlight. Behind each brigade moved a couple of dozen wagons, the limit set by Grant before the march, one wagon with additional ammunition for each regiment, a second wagon for regimental supplies, and one ambulance per regiment for the surgeon, his equipment, and room enough for four men to ride who might be too sick to keep up with the day's march. It was a lean army marching fast.

Cresting low rises along the pike, a soldier could stop for a moment, looking back and then forward. As far as the eye could reach there were the long serpentine columns, dark blue, dull white canvas tops of wagons, the glint of bronze from batteries of Napoleon twelve-pounders, and always the flags. On this first day of march, a march carrying them down through loyal Pennsylvania, all the flags were uncased and held high, the light breeze out of the southwest gently lifting the banners.

National colors, the flag of the Union, state flags, many never seen before by the civilians, flags of Wisconsin, Iowa, Michigan, and Illinois mixed in with the more familiar banners of Ohio, New York, and, of course, Pennsylvania. Most of the flags were shot-torn, some little more than tattered rags, which had been lovingly patched, sewn, and resewn by those who bore them. Faded gold lettering was emblazoned upon them, names of distant battles from what seemed almost to be another war . . . Fort Henry, Fort Donelson, Shiloh, Corinth, Jackson, and in new, yet-to-fade letters, Vicksburg.

The colorful new flags of divisions and corps marked the head of each column, boys by the side of the road eagerly arguing with each other at the sight of them.

"Red means First Division, blue Second Division, and that is Thirteenth Corps!"

"No, Jimmie, you darn fool, white is Second and blue is Third, and I tell you that is Ninth Corps!"

At the passage of the colored division of Ninth Corps many at first stood silent, for such a sight had never been seen before, colored men, in uniform, carrying rifles on their shoulders and heading to war.

The men of that division, knowing they were being more closely watched than others, made it a point to march in proper style, rifles shouldered, not slung, hour after hour sergeants chanting the cadence, "Your left, your left, your left, right, left."

At the front of each regiment were brand-new national colors, beside them the unique yellow regimental flags of the United States Colored Troops. No battle honors were emblazoned on them yet, but all knew they soon would be.

As the first regiment in that division passed through hamlets and towns, past farms and workshops, most onlookers stood silent. But the sight of them, their new uniforms, the way they marched, keeping step, thousands of them, made their mark, and by the time the second brigade of the division passed, scattered applause would break out, and then cheers as the men, thousands of voices joined together, would sing "The Battle Hymn of the Republic." "He has sounded forth the trumpet that shall never sound retreat. . . ."

They must have sung it twenty times that day, each time as heartfelt as the last, and those lining the road joined in. And each time as they finished there was a strange, momentary silence. White citizens of a republic locked in the third year of a desperate war, looking now upon black men who perhaps indeed were the major cause of that war, armed and heading south. Such a sight would have been unimaginable passing through Pennsylvania only a few years before, but all things change, and war brings far more changes than anyone ever expects.

Their passage carried that message, that realization. More than one person watching them pass had lost a son, a brother, a husband to the inferno, and some felt tears come to their eyes. Perhaps, after all, there was worth in their loss; perhaps these men represented that.

For the men of Third Division, Ninth Corps, this was not just a war about the preserving of the Union, it was a war of liberation. When someone cried out, "Good luck, soldier," they felt a swelling pride within.

For those in that column that one word, "soldier," carried with it a weight undreamed of by those who cried it. It was no longer "boy," or even a kindly "uncle," or the dark, bitter insult of "hey, nigger."

Now it was "soldier."

And so this first day of the campaign had passed, hard marching to be certain, but lighthearted. For so many, somehow, war again seemed to have to it some distant glory, a thrill down the spine as song would sweep through the ranks. There was, there had to be, a meaning to what they were doing now; perhaps all the suffering might be leading toward something beyond them as individuals. They were swept up in this vast undertaking, joined together in a single spirit, the soul of the Union, and it gave to them meaning. It might bring them to death, to that terrifying moment when, a limb gone, life's blood flowed into the dust, but that was tomorrow. For the more philosophical, there was the thought as well that though death did indeed come to all men they would forever have this moment—and because of it, a hundred or, a hundred and fifty years hence, they would be remembered.

A captain with an Illinois regiment, a man of some schooling, would recite poetry to his men as they marched. Sometimes they'd listen, sometimes not; sometimes they'd laugh a bit derisively; on occasion the silence would mean deep thought. "We few, we happy few, we band of brothers," he said today. And Grant, standing at the bridge across the Susquehanna as they passed by just before dawn, had heard those words, coming louder as the regiment approached, then drifting off as they continued on. The words had stayed in his heart throughout the day.

The soldiers had marched from before dawn well into the twilight of evening before breaking at last and going into camp with word that they would roust out at four in the morning to start again.

The Cumberland Valley was broad, relatively flat, a dozen miles wide.

From Harrisburg to Carlisle it spread almost due west, then gradually began to arc to the southwest and then south, a broad open avenue that pointed eventually to the Potomac, to Maryland and Virginia beyond. As they moved down the valley the mountains that eventually would be the Catoctin Range stood to their left, a natural barrier that on the other side was still rebel territory.

The column marching past the Carlisle barracks thinned out as the wagons of the last brigade in line passed. At the end rode a unit of the provost guards, shepherding along those who had fallen out during the day because of illness and the heat. More than one of the guards had an exhausted man riding behind him on the rump of his horse. There had been almost no straggling this first day; that would come later as the relentless pace Grant had planned took its toll. Today had been easy for men well rested and eager. Two weeks from now it might be a different story.

"General Grant?"

An officer was approaching out of the twilight, the glow from the gaslights reflecting the glint of a single star on each shoulder.

Grant nodded and returned the man's salute.

"Sir, I'm Henry Hunt. You sent word for me to report."

"That was over a week ago, General Hunt. What kept you?"

"Sorry, sir. The doctor said it was a touch of typhoid. I thought you received my telegram about that."

Grant shook his head.

"Most likely lost in all the confusion, Hunt. Never mind that, though. Are you fit now?"

"Yes, sir, I am."

Grant looked at him closely, and for a second there was the memory of Herman Haupt, dead last week from dysentery. Anyone who served in the army sooner or later was stricken by the typhoid or dysentery, an occupational hazard that killed more than the bullets did.

"Walk with me, Hunt."

Grant stepped down from the veranda. The excitement in the town was beginning to die down, but curious civilians still lined the streets. He turned away and started toward the darkness of the parade field, Hunt by his side.

The last glow of twilight in the west was fading away, the sky overhead dark, clear with stars, the moon yet to rise.

"General, I know you are a good man. Your record at Malvern Hill, at Cemetery Hill the first day at Gettysburg, proved that."

"Thank you, sir."

"What happened at Union Mills?"

"Sir?"

"Tell me everything."

"Yes, sir," and for fifteen minutes he talked, Grant did not interrupt as Hunt described the debacle which had unfolded, the bombardment which had failed to dislodge Lee, and the horror of watching the futile charge go forward.

He finally fell silent. Grant, having finished his cigar, reached into his breast pocket, pulled out a silver case, opened it, gave Hunt a cigar, and took another for himself. Henry snapped a lucifer with his thumbnail, sparking it to light, illuminating the two of them as they puffed their cigars to life.

"A few questions," Grant said.

"Anything, sir."

"Could Meade have won? Or let me put it another way. When did it begin to go wrong?"

Henry shook his head.

"Sir, I really don't like speaking poorly of the dead."

"He was a brother officer. If the roles were reversed right now—if it was I who were dead, and Meade in command, he'd ask the same question."

Henry nodded in reluctant agreement.

"The entire army should have been on the move as soon as word arrived that we were being flanked at Gettysburg," Henry said. "If so, the following morning we could have cut Lee in half, his troops strung out on thirty miles of road from just outside Westminister clear back to Gettysburg. We'd have had him for certain then."

"I don't know about that," Grant said softly, gazing up at the stars.

"Sir?"

"You are talking about Meade not acting like Meade. I suspect our rival somewhere over there"—he looked at Hunt while pointing off to the east—"Lee, had the measure of the Army of the Potomac before even one man stepped out on that incredible march to Union Mills. You must admit, Lee was masterful in that campaign."

"Yes, sir, he was," Hunt said quietly.

"He knew Meade would be slow to react, perhaps even to the point of first seeking a council of war, not fully yet in command, his fellow corps commanders still his peers rather than his subordinates. He knew Sickles would be impetuous—that is clearly evident from how he played him at Gunpowder River—but that Meade would rein him in." He stopped and puffed on his cigar for a moment. "General Lee had the measure of all of you from the start and played it accordingly."

Grant sighed, and went on. "I remember once, down in Mexico, after the fighting stopped, some darn fool officers decided to go hunting. But it wasn't a hunt. They got their men to go up into the hills, form a line, and drive the game toward them. It was a slaughter."

The memory of it sickened him. How anyone could take pleasure in killing a dumb creature driven by fear was beyond him. War was little better.

"That was your Army of the Potomac," Grant said coldly. "You were boxed and driven."

"That has always bedeviled us," Hunt sighed. "It's as if Lee is always sitting in the corner at our meetings, wandering our camps at night. He seems to know even before we know."

Grant slapped the side of his leg with his hand.

"That stops now."

"Sir?"

"You speak of Lee as if he is a ghost or one of those mind readers at a county fair."

"Yes, sir, it was like that," Henry said.

"That bothers you, Hunt?"

"They were good men, sir. Damn good men. Warren, Reynolds, the boys with my command. They deserved better. A damn sight better."

"They will get it," Grant said calmly.

"Not those who are dead, sir."

"The dead are behind us, Hunt. What concerns you and me is now, and I tell you this, if you are to join my command, it stops now. I want you to understand that."

"So you want me then, sir?"

"Yes."

"For what, sir?"

"What would you suggest?"

"Artillery of course, sir."

"That was my intention."

Henry grinned. After his dismissal from the Army of the Potomac by Sickles he thought he would never get a chance for action again. Grant was now giving him that chance.

"I'll confess, Hunt, out west, in those forests, those bayous and swamps, artillery wasn't much use, too much of a tangle and too often slowed us down. I understand it's different here, and frankly I can already see that just with today's ride."

Henry grinned.

"Sir, this is the best damn artillery ground of the war, right here, clear down into northern Virginia. Almost all the land is cleared. You'll notice the lay of the land, sir. Ridgelines tend to run south to north, or southwest to northeast, spaced at good range, every four hundred to a thousand yards or so. It's damn good ground for guns."

"And Lee has your guns now, doesn't he?"

Henry, his spirit broken by that comment, said nothing.

"How would you organize yourself?"

"Sir?"

"What would be your preference in organization of artillery for this army?"

"What do you have with you, sir?" Henry replied, filled again with enthusiasm.

"I have twenty-three batteries, a hundred and thirty-eight guns—eighteen batteries of newly forged three-inch rifles, or Parrott guns, the rest smoothbore Napoleons. General Haupt tried to bring more up. If I had another couple of weeks I could have made it twenty-eight batteries, but things didn't play out that way."

"Yes, Haupt," Henry replied. "Another good man."

"You knew him?"

"Briefly, sir. Met him in Harrisburg after the retreat from Union Mills. He sent me on to Washington to report. I heard he died last week."

"Yes. I've sent for Grenville Dodge, who served with me out West, to replace him."

"I saw Haupt's handiwork coming up here today, sir. It looks like his men have repaired ten miles or more of rail line today alone."

"I know. Now back to the question, Hunt. If I give you command of artillery, how do you see it organized?"

"Under one unified command, sir."

"And that is you?"

"Answering directly to you, sir."

Grant nodded.

"Go on."

"A single unified command, sir. You are right in that Lee does have my guns, damn it. He must outnumber you"—he paused before correcting himself—"us, in artillery by two or more to one. But many of his gunners are amateurs. It takes months, years, to train good gunners. If you give me a unified command, I can pick the spot for you on any battlefield, concentrate the guns, and tear him apart."

"Offensively?"

Hunt hesitated and shook his head.

"Our guns just aren't effective for that. Don't get me wrong, sir," and as he spoke, Hunt warmed to his subject, "a three-inch ordnance rifle, with a good crew, can pick a lone rider off at a thousand yards, but once a battle starts, the smoke, the confusion . . ."

His voice trailed off for a moment, as if he were remembering something.

"You had over two hundred guns at Union Mills, didn't you?"

"Yes, sir, and we didn't budge them. We hurt them, at least I think we did, but not enough for Hancock, for Sedgwick, to break through. And in turn, their guns that survived our barrage just shredded our men down in that open field."

"What I figured," Grant said quietly.

"But if you need to anchor a position, or tear apart reb infantry out in the open coming at you—that I can give you."

"And Lee's superior numbers in guns?"

"Let him try and dislodge me. Just let him." There was a grim ferocity to Hunt's voice that Grant liked.

"The job is yours, General Hunt. You report directly to me. I'll cut the orders tomorrow morning to my corps commanders that all rifled guns are now assigned to your control. I know my corps commanders, and they'll squawk like crows over that order, so for now, let them keep their Napoleon smoothbores for close-in support, but the rest will go to you."

Hunt looked at him, more than a bit surprised. He had argued for this chance for two years, and now, with almost detached calm, this man from the West had finally given it to him.

"Thank you, sir, I won't let you down."

"See that you don't," Grant said. There was a note of dismissal in his voice.

"Set up your headquarters with mine for now. Pull together what staff you need. I'm promoting you to major general as well so you don't have to worry about any fights with others. Ord and McPherson know better, but Banks and Burnside . . ."

"I understand, sir, and thank you."

"Just do your job and we'll get along well."

Knowing that their conversation was finished, Hunt saluted and withdrew.

He watched Hunt leave. He sensed he had made the right choice with this man. He had a score to settle with Lee, and by giving Hunt his chance, not just to settle a score, but to prove his theory about a unified command of artillery, he would bind the man to him.

Alone, he walked the length of the parade ground to the flagpole. Someone had told him that for the last month rebel colors had flown from it, torn down just hours ago as their cavalry pulled out ahead of his advance.

He leaned against the pole, struck a match against it, and puffed yet another cigar to life.

It was good to be alone for a few minutes. He looked back at the barracks, aglow with light, staff inside, couriers riding up to the veranda, dismounting, and rushing inside, other couriers coming out, mounting, and galloping off.

He smiled. So many of them were boys, playing at this game, actually enjoying it. The day had been a good one, a fairly good march, though he would have preferred to make a few more miles.

He looked off to the southeast. Over there, just about a hundred miles away, was Lee.

Lee.

He wished for a moment that the old stories were true, the stories of Napoleon, Caesar, and Alexander, how they could slip into the mind of their opponents, sow doubt, and learn the deepest of secrets. It would be wonderful to turn the tables on this legendary soldier, to get into his mind as easily as he infiltrated the minds of so many of his opponents.

Foolishness, of course. This was an age of science, of machines, not of magic, and to waste another thought on such foolery was indeed a waste.

As he could not slip into the mind of Lee, he must ensure that Lee could never slip into his, never read his heart, never stir a note of discord or, worst of all, fear.

No, by simply doing that alone I can unnerve him. I've set my plans, made so hurriedly, thanks to that fool Sickles. I'd have preferred another three weeks, a month, to marshal more strength, but to have waited after the debacle by Sickles would have played against us, given Lee time to rest, to regather his strength and his nerve for the next encounter.

He sensed that just this move alone had most likely caught him off guard. Every other general whom Lee had faced, excepting Sickles, had always erred on the side of caution. Even Meade, in his blind panic to attack at Union Mills, was ultimately driven by caution, fear of how Washington would respond to his being outflanked and cut off.

Out west, in California, Grant had heard stories from mountain men who had seen wolves bring down their prey, elk, even old grizzlies. They did not charge in blindly, nor did they run away. Always they lurked, dashing in, pulling back, dashing in, in a hunt that might last for days, wearing their victim down to exhaustion. Always circling, always moving, never letting their victim rest, closing in, limiting their prey's movements, exhausting them—until at last the throat was bared and the kill made.

He continued to gaze southeastward, toward Baltimore. Chances were that Lee had forced marched back from the Susquehanna this day, concerned by word of the crossing at Harrisburg. *He will have to rest for a few days while I am fresh. He will have to refit, reorganize, rest his men after their mad dash and brilliant campaign of the last week; then they will venture out to meet me.*

He took another puff on his cigar, coughing slightly as he took it out of his mouth and looked at the glowing tip.

And yet I know this, he realized. *Even as I plot my moves, Lee will plot his. Neither of us will get fully what we want. In war one never does until the very last day, when the guns finally fall silent and one side submits.*

We both seek the submission of the other, and it won't come in one battle, one sharp moment of combat. It will be a grinding down, and tens of thousands will die in the weeks to come. I can move along several paths now, but then again so can he.

Was Lee sleeping now? He doubted it. *Most likely, even at this moment he is looking toward me, thinking the same thoughts I do.*

Grant let his cigar drop, and rubbed out the glowing embers with his foot. Turning, he went into his headquarters to get some sleep. Tomorrow would be a very long day.

Chapter Four

Ten Miles North of Hanover, Pennsylvania

August 23, 1863

6:00 A.M.

Captain, rider coming in."

Capt. Phil Duvall looked up from the simmering campfire where he and Sergeant Lucas had been frying some fresh-cut pork, requisitioned from the farmer whose yard they were camped in.

It was Syms. How the man was keeping to the saddle was beyond him. A local doctor in a town they had passed through had dug the rifle ball out of Syms's calf, bandaged it, and told him to stay out of things for a week. Syms had just laughed, asked the doctor to cut his boot down below the wound and bulky bandage, remounted, and fell back in. Besides, to "stay out of things" would have meant staying behind to be captured by the Yankee cavalry that had been pressing them back all day.

Duvall had pickets a few miles north of where they were camped, watching the road from Carlisle. The Yankee regiment went into camp at dusk. They had pressed, but not to the point of aggressively seeking a fight, rolling him back, trading shots at long range, probing forward, he retreating a mile or so, and thus it had been all day, with no casualties on either side—just a steady, constant pressure to mask what was behind them.

It was indeed his old friend Custer. He had spotted him just before sunset, riding in the lead, about a mile off. Strange that he was not coming on more aggressively, Phil thought more than once after confirming who his opponent was. That was an indicator right there that George was ordered not to seek engagement, but just keep pushing him back.

Syms halted and Lucas stood up to help him get out of the saddle, the man grimacing as he dismounted and hobbled over to squat by Phil's side.

"Some coffee?"

"Love it, sir."

Phil poured him a cup, and Syms took it, looking hungrily at the slices of pork in the frying pan. Phil handed him a fork; Syms stabbed a piece and took a bite, cursing and muttering as he gingerly chewed on the meat, then took a long drink of the hot brew.

He sat down with a sigh.

"What do you have for me?" Phil asked.

"Infantry, lots of infantry."

"Where?"

Syms reached into his haversack and pulled out a sketch pad. Drawn on it was a rough map.

"There's a road here, the one that runs south of the main pike out of Harrisburg. It passes through Dillsburg and on to Petersburg, which we rode through yesterday morning. I circled far out to the left as you told me to. Waited till dark, then cut north using farm lanes and back trails.

"Their cavalry screen is tight. You can tell someone new is running that show. Before, we used to punch through Stoneman or Pleasanton as a joke. Not now. Every crossroads was manned, every village had at least a troop of cavalry guarding the roads. So it was a lot of cutting through fields and keeping quiet.

"Near Dillsburg I finally saw the infantry. Campfires by the hundreds."

"That puts them fifteen miles due south of Carlisle," Phil said. "It means they're heading this way."

"Looks that way."

"You get any prisoners, identifications of units?"

Syms shook his head.

"I'm lucky just to get back with what I told you, sir. I lost two men coming back; we got jumped crossing a road. We wounded one man and talked to him. He's with Custer."

"But the infantry?"

"I can't tell you, sir, but from the campfires it looked to be division strength."

Their conversation was interrupted by the distant pop of rifle fire. The men camped around Phil looked up, some stood, a few going over their mounts, which had remained saddled through the night, and began to pack up, tying on blanket rolls, checking revolvers for loads.

"Our friends seem to want another day of it." Phil sighed. He looked over at Lucas, asked for Syms's notebook, and quickly wrote out a message.

Detachment, Third Virginia
Fifteen Miles Northwest of Hanover

Report has arrived that this night Union infantry in division strength camped at Dillsburg. Am facing at least a regiment of Custer's command. Will fall back toward Hanover.

Captain Duvall

He tore the sheet off and handed it to Lucas.

"Ride like hell to Hanover. Be careful, they might have tried to slip around us during the night. Get this message telegraphed to headquarters. Wait there for me. I suspect we'll not be far behind you."

Phil leaned over, forked a piece of pork, and wolfed it down.

"Mount up! We move in ten minutes," he shouted.

Three Miles Southeast of Port Deposit

August 23, 1863
6:30 A.M.

The train, pulling but two passenger cars, slid to a halt, steam venting around the president's legs. The engineer leaned out of the cab, looking at him wide-eyed.

"Are you Abe?" the engineer asked.

"Last time I looked in the mirror I was," Lincoln said with a smile. The startled engineer quickly doffed his hat and nodded.

A captain leaning out of the door of the first car jumped down, ran up to him, nervously came to attention, and saluted.

"Mr. President. I must admit, I can't believe it's really you, sir."

"It is."

"I thought the courier was mad when he grabbed me, told me to round up a company of men, and follow him to the rail yard and get aboard."

"Captain." Ely Parker stepped forward, the two exchanging salutes.

"That courier came straight from the War Department. You were, most likely, the first officer he spotted. Did you follow his orders and tell no one what you were about?"

"Yes, sir. I just rounded up my boys as ordered. I felt I should report to my colonel, but the courier showed me the dispatch with your signature on it, so I did as ordered."

"Good."

"May I ask what this is about, Major?"

"You and your men are to provide escort for the president up to Harrisburg. Absolutely no one is to know who is aboard this train. We'll stop only for water and wood. If but one man gets off the train and says a word to anyone, I'll have all of you up on court-martial before General Grant himself. Do we understand each other?"

"Yes, sir," said the captain, and he nervously saluted again.

"Son, I see you have a red Maltese cross on your cap," Lincoln interrupted. "Fifth Corps?"

"Yes, sir. Capt. Thomas Chamberlain, sir, Twentieth Maine."

"You were at Union Mills and Gunpowder River."

"Actually neither, sir. Our regiment was lost at Taneytown on July 2. We were paroled and just exchanged."

"We'll talk more about that later, Captain. I'm curious to hear your story."

"Yes, sir."

"Fine, now get aboard, and let's get moving."

The captain ran back to his car, shouting at the men leaning out the windows, "Get the hell back inside."

Ely looked up and down the track. They were several miles outside of Port Deposit, the length of track empty. The fast courier boat that had delivered them to this spot was resting in the reeds, the crew watching the show. Behind them was the broad open stretch of the Susquehanna, Havre de Grace just barely visible half a dozen miles downstream on the other shore.

Wisps of fog drifted on the river, several gunboats in midstream, anchored. On the far shore a huge Confederate flag, their "unstained banner," which could, when lying flat, be mistaken for a flag of truce, was displayed from the side of a barn.

He wondered if that just might be an outpost. Someone with a telescope could perhaps see what was going on here, yet another reason he had insisted that Lincoln, at least for once, not wear his distinctive top hat and black frock coat, covering himself with a cavalry poncho and a slouch cap.

The two walked to the back of the train. Without a platform it was a long step up, but Lincoln took it with ease, actually offering a hand back to the far shorter Ely, who was almost tempted to take it, but then pulled himself up. They got on board the car, which was empty except for the staff officer from the War Department who had come up several hours ahead to make the arrangements for the train.

"A good job, Major Wilkenson," Lincoln said. "All very cloak-and-dagger, something almost out of a play."

"It was the first good locomotive I could grab and get up here, sir. The engineer says she'll make sixty miles to the hour on the good track up toward Chester. The road ahead is being cleared, with the report there's several wounded generals on board."

"Very good."

"I'm sorry the arrangements are so spartan," Wilkenson said, gesturing around the car.

It was clear that the car had seen hard use in recent weeks. The chairs were simple wood; a stove stood at one end, a privy cabin at the other. As the major looked about, he noticed dark stains on the floor and many of the seats, and there was a faint odor of decay.

"Sorry, sir," Wilkenson said. "It just came back from taking wounded up to Wilmington, still hasn't been fully scrubbed out, but it was all I could find."

"That's no problem," Lincoln said softly.

The train lurched, whistle shrieking. After looking for a relatively clean seat, Lincoln sat down. He motioned for Ely to sit across from him.

Wilkenson stood silent for a few seconds, then said he was going forward to check with the engineer and come back with some rations.

For Ely it was a moment to finally sit back, one more hurdle jumped. Little had he dreamed this time yesterday that he would be escorting the president to meet Grant.

They had left Washington early in the afternoon, taking a gunboat down the Potomac and up the Chesapeake. Amazingly, they had slipped out of Washington without being noticed through a series of subterfuges and a report that the president had a mild dose of variola and had to be confined to bed and quarantine for several days.

Once aboard ship the president had retired to a cabin and within minutes was fast asleep, sleeping, in fact, for most of the journey. Ely, consumed with concern for the man he escorted, found he could not sleep.

The train was picking up speed, rails clicking, the car swaying as they went through a sweeping curve. To their right was the Susquehanna, at the moment still rebel territory on the far side.

Lincoln put his feet up on the seat and smiled.

"Now, Major, guess we have a long ride ahead. Please tell me everything about yourself, your tribe, how you came to wear the uniform."

"A long story, sir."

"We have plenty of time. You know, I sort of volunteered during the so-called Black Hawk War, nearly thirty years back. Glad as anything we didn't have to fight. Actually, my sympathies rested more with your side in that unfortunate affair."

"Well, sir, America is my country, too."

Lincoln leaned over and patted him lightly on the knee.

"I'm proud to hear that, Major. I wish we could all feel that way."

He leaned back, looking out the window. They were racing by an army encampment, survivors no doubt of Gunpowder River.

"So start your story, Major, and then, when you're done, I've got a few questions for you about General Grant."

The train thundered on, racing through the switching yard that put them on the main track heading north toward Pennsylvania.

Baltimore

August 23, 1863
7:00 A.M.

Wearily, Gen. Robert E. Lee swung his leg out of the stirrup. Trembling with exhaustion, he dismounted, grateful that Walter Taylor was holding his mount's bridle. He had left Traveler behind this morning to rest, borrowing an escort's mount to press the final miles into the city. The horse was feisty and skittish and had nearly thrown him when startled by a dog that had darted out of an alleyway to challenge possession of the road.

The city was quiet, provost guards out patrolling the streets, weary troops marching at route step down the main roads from the north, then turning to file west into their old encampment sites used prior to the start of the Gunpowder River campaign. The ranks were thin, thousands of men having fallen out during the last twenty-four hours from exhaustion, and again he had passed orders to deal lightly with such men.

Coming down the steps of the hotel flying the First Corps headquarters flag came Pete Longstreet. Pete had pushed on ahead at his request to ensure that the city was secure, and that no coordinated action might be coming from the Union garrison still occupying Fort McHenry down in the harbor.

"General, sir, good to see you," Pete said quietly, saluting. "Did you get some rest last night, sir?"

"Yes, actually I did."

He had stopped just south of Gunpowder River and was asleep within minutes. If he was to think this current situation through, he had to be sharper, and, besides, he felt secure with Pete heading back into the city while he slept.

"Things here in the town are secure, sir," Pete said. "Not a peep from the garrison down in the harbor."

"As I assumed. I doubt if General Grant could extend such control in a coordinated manner, but still it was a worry. Even a brief sally from the fort could have caused us problems."

"I talked with one of our citizens, a bit of an amateur spy, a minister who said he was in the fort last evening, under a pass to visit his brother, who is ill."

"He was under a pass?" Lee asked. "You know I don't like using such things for subterfuge."

"No one ordered him to do it, sir, from our army. He took it upon himself."

Lee hesitated, then nodded.

"Go on then."

"He said they were aware of Sickles being beaten, but had no word whatsoever of Grant moving."

"Good."

"He said they were all rather demoralized down there. Especially with word we were coming back into the city. That's about it regarding the fort. Garrison is still several thousand strong, with reports of more troops, mostly marines in the gunboats just outside the harbor. But nothing unusual to report from that side."

"And what else, General?"

"A rider came over the South Mountains into Gettysburg just before dusk, reporting in from Chambersburg. He carried a report that strong Yankee columns were seen coming down the valley past Carlisle.

"And then a report that just came in a few minutes back. Scouts report sighting Union infantry camped last night at Dillsburg."

Lee stood silent, trying to remember the location.

"At least ten miles south of Carlisle, a route that could take them toward Hanover. Also, Custer was screening that movement."

"Any indication which corps it was?"

"Nothing on any of that, sir. They are keeping up a solid screen."

Good move on Grant's part the first day out, Lee thought. *Blinds us and now moves in a shadow land to the north and west.*

As they spoke they slowly walked into the hotel lobby in which Longstreet had set up. Jed Hotchkiss, the army cartographer who had ridden ahead with Longstreet, was there to greet them. A table was set up covered with maps, and Lee walked over to it, with Longstreet by his side.

"Well, Major Hotchkiss," Lee said, "I see you've been busy again."

"Same maps as before, sir, but I thought you might want to get a look at them."

Longstreet leaned over the table, pointing toward York and then Carlisle.

"Sir," Hotchkiss began, "we know that they have a screen of cavalry, at least two divisions' worth, spread in an arc from York westward, over to here at Heidlersburg, about twenty miles north of Gettysburg. It was from Heidlersburg that our last report came in, and that outpost is now withdrawing to Hanover."

"I'll want General Stuart to start moving out a screen tomorrow, probing, across this entire front."

As he spoke he drew a line with his finger from Gettysburg eastward to the Susquehanna River.

"Tomorrow, sir?" Pete asked.

"Yes, I know," Lee replied slowly, and as he spoke he sat down, reached into his breast pocket to take out a pair of spectacles and put them on.

"Walter, my compliments to General Stuart, and please convey that order to him. Tell him I only want him to send out those regiments that he feels are relatively fresh. I fear our new rival has the jump on us on that issue. I suspect many of Grant's troopers have mounts well shod and rested, and the boys astride them as good in the saddle as our boys are. If there is to be a tangle in the next few days, I want our boys on good mounts, otherwise they'll be run down."

He was silent for a moment, staring again at the map.

By rights he should give Stuart at least a week to refit. The reshodding of one mount would only take a matter of minutes, but ten thousand? Every blacksmith and farrier in Baltimore would be busy for days with that task. Then there were the horses for the artillery, quartermaster corps, and medical corps to be tended to as well before this army could march on a campaign of maneuver that also might span a hundred miles or more in a matter of days.

I need a week, he thought, *but if I wait, that will give Grant a week to do as he pleases.* "For want of a nail a horseshoe was lost, for want of a horseshoe . . ."

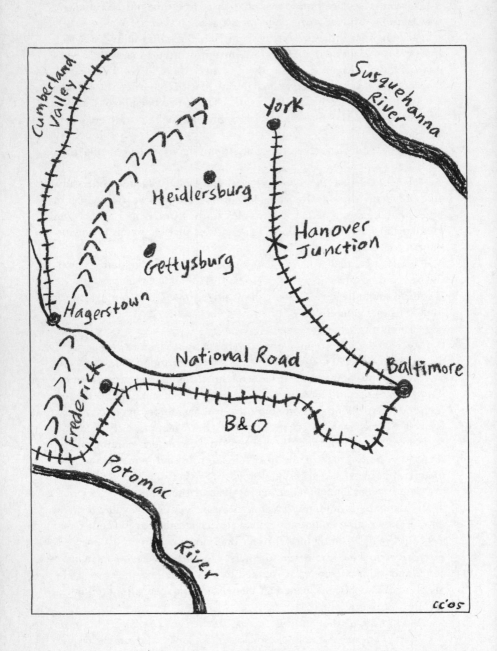

"Give the cavalry precedence in reshoeing the horses and drawing provisions. They have to move first or we will be blind.

"We need two things, General Longstreet," Lee said, adjusting his spectacles as he gazed at the maps, "time to rest and time to analyze what General Grant is about to do."

He forced a smile, accepting a cup of tea from Walter, who had fetched it from the kitchen in the hotel. He blew on the china rim before taking a sip.

"Don't worry, though, gentleman. We've faced others like this before. Remember Pope coming from the West with all his boasts?"

The staff chuckled.

"Headquarters in his saddle," Taylor laughed softly, and those gathered round Lee grinned with how that inane comment had been quickly turned into a meaning other than what Pope intended.

Lee looked over at Jed Hotchkiss and from him to Walter Taylor and the staff that was beginning to come in through the door.

"Gentlemen, two favors. First, Walter, would you be so kind as to ask the owner of this establishment if I might make my headquarters here? It is convenient and directly across the street from the telegraphy station. Also, Walter, I need you to see to the placement of the men as they file in. I want them to come in and find fresh rations. There's still plenty of beef and store goods in this town. Coffee, lots of coffee, tobacco, and fresh beef mean more now than three months of back pay. The men are to have tomorrow in camp, no drills, plenty of time to rest and for church services."

"I'll see to it at once, sir."

"The second thing, gentlemen. If General Longstreet and I might have some time alone."

Nothing more needed to be said. Within seconds the room was emptied except for Pete and himself. A minute later Walter came back in, offering him a key to a room on the second floor with the compliments of the owner, who said he was honored by Lee's presence. After whispering that a guard was being posted around the hotel, he withdrew.

Pete was sitting across from him, exhaustion graying his features. It had been a hard march for him, too, he could see that.

Longstreet stirred, took out a cigar, and looked over at Lee, who nodded his approval before Pete lit up.

"I think we need to have a talk, General Longstreet."

"I do, too, sir."

"Why so?"

"Things have changed, a lot of things."

Pete fell silent.

"Go on, General, I need you to speak freely. As I told you at Gettysburg, you are my right arm. I need to hear your opinions. Your insights gave us victory in the past; I am counting on you to help give us victory again."

Pete sighed, blew out a cloud of blue smoke, and leaned forward, looking Lee in the eyes.

"Sir, they just don't stop. I thought, after Union Mills, that would force Lincoln to give in. Certainly his abolitionist friends would stand by him, but the blow we gave them that day, I thought it was the beginning of the end."

"So did I, General," Lee said wistfully.

"We did it again at Gunpowder River. In some ways that victory was even more complete than Union Mills. It finished the Army of the Potomac, once and for all."

Longstreet sat back, shaking his head.

"I don't know anymore. I just don't know. I just thought that finally they would stop coming, but here they come again."

"You knew Grant. I mean before the war."

"Yes, sir."

"Tell me something about him."

"Well, sir, when I knew him, to be honest it was all rather tragic. He was a year behind me at the Point, graduating in forty-three. I knew him there as an honest sort. Didn't like to gamble, drink. A bit reserved. Curious, actually, since he didn't like the army all that much and would voice that in private. Even admitted he went to the Point simply because it was a free education. He planned to do his service afterward, then get out. The one thing he did enjoy was horsemanship. Underneath that gruff exterior there is actually a rather sensitive soul, though most would find that impossible to believe."

"This tragic side you mentioned."

"The word was he took to drink out of loneliness and despair when separated from his wife. He was, sir, a gentleman and many of the men stationed out in California after the war . . . well, sir, you know what I mean when it came to women out there and such. Grant wasn't one of them, and the loneliness drove him half crazy."

"That's why he left the army?"

"I think so. Also, killing just sickened him."

"As it should all of us, General Longstreet. Yet everyone says he is relentless, cold-blooded," Lee finally ventured, uncomfortable with his own thoughts.

"He is indeed that. At least I'm told that. I've never seen him in combat before. But from the word in the ranks he was absolutely fearless in Mexico. He doesn't lose his nerve under pressure the way many do, that is for certain."

"And yet, after leaving the army, he did not make much of himself." Longstreet chuckled softly.

"No, sir, he did not. Failed at most everything he did. But let me put the shoe on the other foot. How many officers do we know who were all great guns in peacetime and then failed miserably when the bullets really did begin to whine about them?"

Lee smiled sadly.

"More than any of us would like to admit, especially of old comrades."

"I think Grant is suited to this new kind of war that so many talk about."

"How so?"

"He doesn't stop. He just doesn't stop. Take Shiloh, for example, or his winter campaign around Vicksburg. Takes a reversal, what most anyone else would call a defeat, he wakes up the next morning as if yesterday didn't exist, and then pushes again."

"Like you, General Longstreet."

"Yes, sir, including me, but the difference is, he can draw on reserves we can only dream of. He understands that. Back in George Washington's time, an army fought a battle, it took weeks to resupply it, months to replace the men. Grant understands how different it all is now with trains, steamboats, factories. Fight a battle, he snaps a finger, brings up five million more rounds of ammunition, ten thousand more men, and pitches in again."

Both were silent for a moment.

"He is relentless once fixed on an objective. Though sensitive to the point of illness at the sight of blood, he can stand back and let it flow. Shiloh is an example we should look at carefully, sir. He turned it into a grinding match that finally broke Beauregard."

"Yet in many ways that battle was inconclusive."

"Inconclusive only because he did not have the authority to follow up. Halleck stepped in. I dare say, if Grant had been given full authority then, he would've pushed Beauregard clear to the Gulf of Mexico and not just to Corinth."

"Halleck. Sadly, those days are over," Lee said quietly, taking a sip of his tea.

"Precisely, sir."

"What do you think that portends?"

"That Lincoln has not yet lost his nerve, not by a long shot. In a way, he's sacked perhaps two of our best friends. Halleck, as you know, was always by the book. Stanton tended to work at cross-purposes to the administration in Washington."

Longstreet slapped the table with his fist and shook his head.

"Sorry, sir. I forgot to tell you. Lincoln did indeed sack Stanton yesterday."

Lee said nothing.

"Sorry. Word was out on the wires late yesterday. We have some boys who've tapped into the line from Washington that they've run across land to the Chesapeake. Stanton is out."

"Replaced by?"

"Elihu Washburne. Congressman from Illinois. The man who nominated Lincoln at the Republican convention. Perhaps more importantly he was Grant's congressman and apparently a close friend of his."

"That is news," Lee said quietly. "That means Grant has the full support of the administration. Carte blanche from now on."

"Sir, you just asked me to speak freely."

"Yes, I did."

"I think it's time for us to get back across the Potomac."

"Why so?" Lee asked.

"There is nothing more to accomplish here."

"I would disagree, General Longstreet. We hold Baltimore, we still threaten Washington, we have supplies to see us clean through the spring if need be."

"Sir, may I present my case?" Longstreet asked.

"Of course, General. I need to hear what you have to say, though it does surprise me, your thought of conceding this ground without a fight, when I believe we could finally settle the issue here once and for all."

"Sir, we've destroyed the Army of the Potomac, a stated goal of our mission back in June. We've brought Maryland into the Confederacy. I think, at this point, a strategic withdrawal into northern Virginia would be prudent.

"We do a methodical and orderly withdrawal out of Baltimore now, and Grant just swings on empty air when he comes in. We also take apart the Baltimore and Ohio Railroad as we pull back, take down every bridge, burn all the rolling stock left behind, tear apart the switching yards, burn the roundhouses, and take the heavy tools and machinery.

"If we pull out now, starting tomorrow, we can take with us every locomotive in this town, tear up track to take as well, even haul some of the machinery out of the factories as we go. Escort all that as we leave, and it would be a bonanza for our railroads in the South."

Lee did not respond.

Longstreet, warming to his position, pressed forward. "Sir, you might recall all the equipment that Jackson snatched from the Baltimore and Ohio back at the start of the war. It was brilliant and gave our side locomotives we desperately needed."

Lee smiled at the memory of how, in the early days of the struggle, Jackson had pulled off a wonderful hoodwinking of the Baltimore and Ohio, convincing them that they could only run trains in convoys at certain times, but he would not interfere with their operations in Maryland. Then, when the moment was right, he had raided across the river, blocked the track, and trapped an entire convoy of locomotives, supplies, and rolling stock. The equipment had been taken into Virginia and proved essential in keeping the Southern cause alive.

"Sir. If we take all their locomotives and rolling stock, then tear everything else apart, it would cripple their logistical support for months. It'd give us a lot of breathing room once out of Maryland with nothing but the wreckage of railroads behind us. Grant's offensive would grind to a halt."

"You know I don't like wanton destruction," Lee replied. "And remember, Maryland is now on our side. We cannot abandon it so lightly, or engage in such destruction in a state that is now part of our Confederacy.

"And what of our president's orders to hold Baltimore?" Lee asked. "To hold Maryland?"

Longstreet said nothing for a moment.

"Sir, you asked for my opinion, which means relating to the military situation, not a response to what the civilian government told us to do."

"Why the caution now, General Longstreet?"

"The cost, sir. Our total casualties have been well over sixty thousand since May. We've lost over a dozen generals, scores of regimental commanders. Some of our finest divisions have been fought to a mere shell. Pickett, Pender, Anderson, Johnson, Heth are all down to a fraction of their original strength.

"Withdraw across the Potomac, hold the fords—and in another eight weeks the campaign season will be over till spring. That will give time for the wounded to heal, to reorganize, bring regiments back up to strength. Our boys will understand it, sir. In fact, they'll welcome it."

"And yet that gives Grant time as well," Lee said. "We believe he has four corps with him at this very moment. Wait till spring and it might be six or seven corps."

"Sir, though it's not our realm, I think Secretary Benjamin would agree with me as well. It would give time for Europe to react to your victories, perhaps bring France into the picture, with luck maybe even En-

gland, too. This war is, ultimately, one in which we achieve a political victory. Either Lincoln is impeached or is voted out of office. All we need do
now is hold on till one or the other happens. Lincoln is undoubtedly
pushing Grant to fight. Let us not give him that opportunity, and then see
what happens."

Lee said nothing, letting his gaze drop to the maps on the table.

He had originally sought Pete's advice simply to examine the moment, what needed to be done the next few days, but instead his "right
arm" had opened a far broader examination: a fundamental decision of
what was to come not just tomorrow but in the weeks ahead.

"I cannot withdraw," Lee said, staring at the map.

"Because of President Davis?"

"Yes, in fair part. We have been ordered to hold Maryland and Baltimore, and I must not abandon such orders lightly. There is, as well, a logic
to his orders to us. If we do indeed win the peace this fall, it is essential
that Maryland be part of our new nation. It will force the Federals to
abandon Washington as their capital, will insure that the Chesapeake Bay
is controlled by us, and give us the one major industrial center in the
South. We abandon that, we abandon a major position of stability after the
war is over."

"Even if, in holding, we lose all, sir?"

"We will not lose," Lee said bluntly. "General Longstreet, we will not
lose."

"Sir, if I might be so bold, please enlighten me about your thinking,"
Longstreet replied.

"Just this, General. I see no reason to assume that an encounter with
Grant will go against us. Yes, he has caught us off guard for the moment,
but such is war.

"You were not with me in May, when Hooker made his move up the
Rappahannock. I will confess, in private, he did catch me completely off
guard with the audacity of that move. We were outnumbered, before your
arrival, nearly three to one. Whichever way I turned I would be flanked,
and yet we did fight our way out of that, turned the tables, and won a
stunning success, thanks be to God."

"The cost, though, sir—Jackson lost, nearly twenty thousand killed or
wounded."

"Yes, I know, but success we did have."

"We've paid that price twice more over these last two months. Sir, we
are running dry. Defeat Grant at a cost of twenty thousand and this army
will be a burned-out shell of its former self."

"I see no reason to anticipate that price," Lee said sharply. He leaned over the table and swept his hand across the map. "Grant will come at us from one of two directions and we will know what it will be within forty-eight hours.

"If he advances en masse, along the railroad, we either go for maneuver to flank or we dig in, perhaps near Relay Station, just west of here, and let him try us in the type of battle you always seek, good defensive ground for them to bleed out on."

"His other choice?" Longstreet asked softly.

"He takes the broader strategic move. Goes down the Cumberland Valley, takes Hagerstown and Harpers Ferry, then threatens to advance into Virginia or draw us westward into a fight along the South Mountain range."

"And your thoughts, sir?"

Lee sighed, rubbing his forehead.

"Too early to tell. This is, after all, only the second day of maneuver for both of us. The path down the Cumberland, to gain proper position, will take him a week or more, and he knows it will give us the time that we need. The direct advance would mean a crisis in three to five days.

"I suspect that even if Grant is operating on his own initiative, Lincoln will still put his finger into his plans. After the humiliation with the Army of the Potomac, I believe Lincoln desperately needs some kind of victory as quickly as possible. He'll push for the direct assault."

"But will Grant agree to that, sir?"

"If Lincoln orders it, he has to, the same as I would have to if directly ordered by the president," Lee replied.

"One more sharp battle, another day like Union Mills, where we lured him into a fight on our ground, and we have him, and this nightmare is finished."

"One more day, sir?"

"Yes, that should do it."

Longstreet nodded.

"Then you agree with my position, Pete?" Lee asked.

Longstreet forced a smile.

"Sir, you command this army, and I follow orders."

"But do you agree?"

"Sir, I've voiced my opinion," Longstreet replied. "But if you are confident of victory, then it is my job to help you in any way possible to achieve that."

"I will continue to weigh your suggestions, Pete," Lee replied, again using the more familiar first name. "Thank you. As I have said publicly many times these last seven weeks, your suggestion at Gettysburg that we abandon that field and go for a flanking march was the crucial element in creating our victory at Union Mills."

"Thank you, sir. May I offer one further suggestion?"

"Certainly."

"Either way, the B and O line will be important to us. May I suggest we contract with them now to get it fully operational as far as Frederick and position some supplies, perhaps some troops and artillery there."

"It will be the first time this army has relied upon such means for direct movement on a tactical level."

"Actually, sir, it was crucial at First Manassas, and Beauregard is familiar with its uses at Corinth and also the transfer of his troops up here. It is something I believe we should have paid attention to earlier."

Lee nodded in agreement.

"You're right. We should have looked into the use of the B and O earlier. I'll ask Secretary Benjamin if he would be willing to go over to their offices."

"And one other thing, sir."

"Go on."

"Get the pontoon bridges ready. We have enough captured bridging to run a span across the Potomac. I think they should be loaded on to flatcars and perhaps moved, prepositioned, over toward Frederick."

"Now? Move them now?"

"Yes, sir."

"General Longstreet, there is a chance that a sound-enough defeat of General Grant might afford us the opportunity to think aggressively, very aggressively, indeed. Perhaps even to span the Susquehanna in pursuit. We would need that bridging material shifted north instead of west."

"Sir, if we move the bridging material west to Frederick by rail, and Grant is indeed smashed, it will take but hours for us to return it to Baltimore."

"Why this insistence, General Longstreet?"

"Call it an ace up the sleeve, sir. If things should indeed go wrong, right now we are reliant on but several fords to disengage our army and pull back into Virginia. The pontoon bridges give us greater flexibility, and frankly, sir, I'd like us to have that extra ace."

Lee was silent for a moment.

"Sending them west, might that not give the wrong message to some, that we are preparing to evacuate?"

"If it does, so what, sir? Perhaps it might embolden Grant to move rashly and make a mistake. Either way, those pontoons are a nightmare to move. We all know that. It took Burnside weeks just to bring them up fifty miles last November and cost him the opportunity to get across the Rappahannock before we were into position. I urge you, sir, move them now."

Lee finally nodded in agreement.

"Who is in charge of them?"

"A Maj. Zachariah Cruickshank. He use to be in command of First Corps' supply train. After we captured the pontoons from the Yankees at Union Mills I transferred to him the responsibility for their movement."

"Transferred? Why?"

"Well, sir, he has a bit of a problem with the bottle. A profane man as well, but one of the best men for running wagons I ever saw. It's just he got a bit insubordinate with me a few times when drunk, and I felt it was best that we distanced ourselves for his good and mine."

"Insubordinate to you?"

Longstreet smiled.

"I'd rather not repeat what he said, sir. But regardless of that, like I said, he's a man who can be relied on when it comes to moving wagons."

"Tell this profane major to go down to the rail yards, find the right people there, and prepare to load for a move to Frederick."

"Yes, sir."

"But do not misinterpret this caution, General Longstreet. I want all my generals to realize and to know in their hearts that I plan to seek out General Grant, meet him in the field, and in one sharp action defeat him as we have defeated all others who have come against us."

"Of course, sir," Longstreet said quietly.

Chapter Five

CSA "You mick son of a bitch, come back here!"

The yard boss turned, glaring at Maj. Zachariah Cruickshank, commander of the pontoon bridge train, Army of Northern Virginia, with a dark eye. Several of his fellow workers gathered around behind their boss, one of them hoisting a sledgehammer and swinging it one-handed. Cruickshank's men, a hard-bitten lot themselves, stepped closer to their major, one of them unclipping the flap on his revolver, another beginning to uncoil a bullwhip.

"Go ahead and shoot me," the yard boss snarled, "but I'll be damned if I'll take your ordering me around like some damn slave. This is my rail yard, not yours."

Cruickshank was tempted to do just that, shoot the son of a bitch. Not kill him, just blow a hole in his foot or arm to make the point. General Longstreet had ordered him to get the pontoon train loaded up, and by damn he had to do it. Now this dumb Irish Yankee was giving him back talk.

He looked around as more of the yard crew came over. Tough-looking men every one of them. Some were grinning, expecting the start of a donnybrook, and were picking up sledges, pickaxes, pieces of ballast.

"Most of 'em are goddamn Yankees," a sergeant standing next to

Cruickshank whispered. "Let's go at 'em and take this damn place. I can get your trains for you, sir."

The men around Cruickshank muttered agreement.

Kill some of those sons of bitches, Cruickshank thought, *and it will be my ass hauled before Old Pete again, the threat of court-martial real this time.*

Cruckshank wearily shook his head, reached into his haversack, and pulled out a half-empty bottle of whiskey and held it up.

"Let's you and me talk," Cruickshank said, glaring at the yard boss. It galled him that he had to be reduced to making this offer, but damn all, he had orders from Longstreet himself and had to see them through.

The yard boss looked at the bottle, then nodded his head, turned to his men, and yelled at them to go back to work. Cruickshank ordered his men to back off, walked over to the yard boss, and together they climbed into an empty boxcar and sat down.

The two sides, like two street gangs waiting to see if it would be work or fight, stood apart, watching as their chiefs negotiated. A gesture from either would mean a bloodbath.

Cruickshank handed over the bottle; the yard boss uncorked it and took a long pull.

"Good stuff," he gasped. "This town's been dry as a bone ever since you rebs came in and confiscated all the liquor."

"There's plenty more where that came from"—Zachariah hated to say the words but had to—"if you help me out."

The yard boss looked over at him and grinned.

"So, got you by the short hairs, reb. One minute I'm a son of a bitch and the next you're trying to bribe me."

"I got a barrel of Tennessee's finest if you can help me work things out."

"This is my yard, not yours. You don't come in here ordering me around, especially in front of my men. Damn you, even the boss calls me Mr. McDougal, not 'Hey, you.'"

"I understand. Listen, McDougal—"

"Mr. McDougal."

Cruickshank sighed.

"All right then, Mr. McDougal. It's hot, I'm tired, and I got my orders."

"Listen, Major. I've had no word from the office about this. You just come wandering in here and demand four engines and forty flatcars. You have to be joking."

"I'm not."

"And I expect an apology for that son-of-a-bitch comment, you son of a bitch."

Cruickshank swallowed hard. Anyone else, at this moment, he'd have dropped him with one good punch.

"All right, one son of a bitch to another, does that satisfy you?"

"Barely," the boss said, taking another drink. He all but drained the bottle and tossed it out on the ground, where it shattered, then looked over expectantly at Cruickshank. Cruickshank motioned to one of his sergeants, who reluctantly came over, opened his haversack, and pulled out another.

For the first time, McDougal smiled, uncorked it, took another drink, then passed it back to Cruickshank, who took a long one as well.

Outside the boxcar this was read as a signal that things were simmering down. A few of his men, as Cruickshank had hoped, took out bottles and passed them to the work crew facing them.

"Let me guess," Cruickshank asked, "you're a Union man, aren't you?"

"And if I admit to that, do I get arrested?"

"No. We're not like Lincoln, who's arrested thousands."

"Well, before you and your men came and took over Baltimore, we had business here. Good pay. I've let go of nearly all my crews. Men of mine are starving, thanks to you."

"I don't see any colored around here," Cruickshank said.

The yard boss laughed.

"With you graybacks coming? Every last one took off, most likely working the yards up in Wilmington or Philadelphia now. I lost some good men, thanks to you."

"I could say the same thing," Cruickshank replied. "Look, you and I are stuck in the middle of all this. I drove wagons before the war; you put together trains. I've got orders, and I'm told you'll get orders, too. Our civilian boss, Mr. Benjamin, is supposed to be meeting with your boss right now to set up the contracts, but I was told to get over here right now and start things moving. So either we work together, or I'll shoot you here and now, say you attacked me, then get my men to take over."

"You do that, you'll have a riot on your hands," McDougal replied with a smile. "Besides, what kind of gentleman are you to give a man a drink, then shoot him?"

"I'm no gentleman."

"I thought all you Southern officers were gentlemen. And besides, you sound a bit like a damn Englishman."

"Listen, McDougal. Someday I'll tell you my hard-luck story. I'm not Irish, but the slums of Liverpool are just as tough for a working-class English boy. I'm an officer because I was a civilian teamster before the war running supplies to army posts out in Texas. You name the place and I'll run a hundred wagons to it, and be damned to whoever gets in my way. I've killed more than my share of Comanche and a few drunken Irish, too, when they tried their hand at thieving from my wagon train."

McDougal looked at him and burst out laughing, taking the bottle back, and after a long drink, handed it back.

Outside the boxcar the laughter was a signal for everyone to relax, and more bottles came out. Cruickshank watched them for a second. It was fine that they mingled, but get them too drunk and maybe a brawl would start just for the hell of it, unraveling all the concessions he had been forced to make so far.

"Four trains it is that you want?" McDougal asked.

"That's what I figure. Actually would prefer six, but figure I'd start with four."

"What the hell for?"

There was no sense in lying about it. Once they started loading up, the whole yard would see it.

"Ever seen a pontoon bridge?"

"You mean a bridge on boats?"

"Yes, damn them. Boats that you lay planking across. I hate the damn things."

"That's your job?"

"My curse. Each boat is nearly thirty feet long. It takes a dozen mules to move but one on a road, and if the road is too narrow or twisting . . . well, it makes you want to shoot yourself or get drunk. I got forty of 'em, plus the bridging lumber, and I need to get them to Frederick."

"Frederick?" McDougal laughed. "Between you and the Union boys, that line is a mess. Water tanks toppled, temporary bridges ready to fall apart, a helluva mess. The bridge over the Monocacy was blown last year during the fighting around Antietam, and she was a beauty. I helped put it up before the war, and then some dumb rebel blows it apart. The one we got up now is just temporary. You got a helluva job, Major. I wouldn't want it."

Cruickshank pushed the bottle back.

"I'll have a barrel for you tonight if you can at least get things moving."

McDougal picked up the bottle and looked at it.

"Your boys cleaned out every bottle of whiskey in town this last month."

"Like I said, I got barrels of 'em stashed in one of my boats."

"A deal then it is," McDougal announced loud enough that all could hear. "A barrel to get started, a barrel when you get loaded up."

Cruickshank nodded and stood up. Between one drinking man and another a deal could always be reached—when one had liquor and the other didn't.

The two shook hands. McDougal's grip was tight, rock-solid, and for a few seconds they played the game, the two looking straight at each other, neither relenting.

Finally, McDougal relaxed his grip and smiled.

"Guess you're not a gentleman after all," he said.

"You're damn right," Cruickshank replied without a smile.

He jumped down from the boxcar, McDougal by his side.

"I'll be back in an hour," Cruickshank announced and walked off. His second in command, Captain Sigel, fell in by his side.

"So you made the deal," Sigel asked.

"Two barrels. Supposedly the good stuff."

"Sir?"

"You know what to do. Empty the good stuff out and refill it with some of the white lightning you boys brewed up. Get some strong tea into it to color it right. That old Irishman will never know the difference. I'll be damned if he'll guzzle down my ten-year-old whiskey."

Cruickshank walked on, stepping around a pile of barrels leaking molasses, cursing as the sticky fluid clung to his boots.

"Damn job," he sighed. It was better than getting shot at, but moving those damn boats, what a rotten way to fight the war.

Baltimore

1:30 P.M.

 "Mr. Secretary, you realize the difficult position you are placing the Baltimore and Ohio in with this request?"

Judah Benjamin, secretary of state for the Confederate government, smiled at James Garrett, superintendent of the Baltimore and Ohio Railroad, but the smile hid an ever-growing frustration. "Sir, we are simply talking business," Judah replied warmly, putting on his best negotiating smile, "a business deal for which the B and O will be fully compensated."

"I could take a strictly business approach to this, Mr. Secretary, and ask how my company will be compensated. Are you prepared to pay up front for our services? Contracts with the federal government are paid for in cash, and on time. I am in no position to accept payment in Confederate money, which both you and I know has no real value."

"I understand your concern, sir. My salary is paid with that same money."

Garrett did not smile at the joke.

"Sir, I'll personally sign a promissory note, payable in gold upon the ending of hostilities."

"And suppose you lose?"

"Given our current position, the successes of the previous months, I think that unlikely," Judah replied.

Garrett was silent and Judah could almost read his thoughts. If Garrett agreed to contract with the Confederate army for troop and supply movements and the North then wins, he could very well find himself out of a job at the very least, perhaps even in jail if Lincoln was feeling vindictive. If the South should win, cooperation now would bring advantages after the war, but even then payment might take years, and the North could very well turn around and seize Baltimore and Ohio property outside of the Confederacy.

"I know you are in a difficult position, Mr. Garrett," Judah said smoothly. "I don't envy you at this moment."

"And if I don't cooperate?" Garrett asked coolly.

"Sir, I am afraid we will have to seize your line. There will be no payment, and after our victory the Confederate government might not be in a position to look favorably upon your property and the ownership by stockholders outside of the Confederacy."

"That does sound like a threat," Garrett replied sharply.

"It is not intended to be," Judah lied. "It is just a simple reality."

"If you do seize the line, realize that many of my workers will not cooperate. You'll have to man the lines with your own personnel."

"I know that, and we can do it."

Judah did not add that at this very moment one of Longstreet's officers was already down in the railyard negotiating with the workers there. He had suggested to Lee that the two meetings take place at the same time. Garrett was a known Union man, and it was best to be ready to move quickly if he refused to cooperate.

It was now Garrett's turn to smile.

"You don't have the logistical know-how," he replied, voice even and soft. "You don't have an organization like the United States Military Railroad, nor a man like Haupt or Dodge to run it for you. Is there a single man with your army now who can organize and run scores of trains, perhaps a hundred or more, as you've requested? I don't think so."

"That is why I am appealing to you," Judah said, still forcing his diplomatic smile.

"I think I will have to convene a meeting of the board of directors for this," Garrett announced.

Judah sighed. Garrett was taking the standard dodge. *He will not make a decision either way and therefore will come out clean. If the South wins, he can claim his hands were tied by his board, fire a few of them, and come out of it position intact. If the North wins, he can claim to have made a heroic stand.*

"And how long will convening this board meeting take?" Judah asked.

"To get a quorum? A week or two, and it will mean obtaining passes of transit through your lines for our members who are now in Northern territory."

"We don't have weeks," Judah said, an edge of anger to his voice now. "We need the line starting today."

"Then, sir, I am afraid I cannot help you at this moment," Garrett said, folding his hands across his waist.

"Then, sir, I must inform you that by the authority I hold in the government of the Confederate States of America, I am seizing control of your line for the duration, and compensation will not be offered."

"Be my guest," Garrett said calmly. "And I wish you luck with it."

Ten Miles South of Carlisle, Pennsylvania, on the Cumberland Pike

August 23, 1863
6:30 P.M.

 It was impossible to conceal who he was. The word had raced down the column hours ahead of his approach, and cheer upon cheer greeted him as he rode along the side of the road. His escort, a troop of cavalry, guided him around side paths, through cuts in the fence, and across fields to try to disrupt, as little as possible, the flow of the march moving at flood tide down the Cumberland Pike.

Passing an Illinois regiment, he got a resounding cheer. All semblance of marching discipline broke down as the men swarmed off the road to the fence flanking the pike, calling out his name.

He did not want to slow their advance, but at the sight of the Illinois state flag the emotion he felt was too much to ignore, especially when he recognized a captain in the ranks. He had once been a boy hanging around the law offices, running errands for a few pennies, then grown, gone off to school, and now to war.

Lincoln trotted over, reined in, leaned over the fence, and extended his hand.

"Robert Boers, isn't it?"

"Yes, sir!"

"How are your folks?"

"Just fine, sir."

"And you?"

"Delighted to see you, Mr. President," the captain cried excitedly, the men of his company pressing in close, extending hands as well.

Lincoln couldn't resist. He dismounted and climbed onto the top rail of the fence and sat down, grateful when one of the men offered up his canteen.

"Hot day, isn't it, boys?"

"Sure is sir," a sergeant cried, "but we'll make it a dang sight hotter for Bobbie Lee before long."

A resounding cheer went up with that, and Lincoln couldn't help but grin.

As he gazed out at their upturned faces, a smile creased his lined features. For the moment he would not think of all that was still to come, what these boys would have to face in the days ahead.

They were a tough-looking group. These were not the baby-faced recruits that he used to see on the drill fields back in the winter of 1861. These men had endured two hard years of campaigning in some of the worst climes in America. They reminded him of the line from Shakespeare in their appearance, having a "lean and hungry look," and in those hardened eyes and bronzed features he saw men of war and yet, down deep, neighbors, friends, still quintessentially American. They were professionals at what they did now, but given their druthers, all of them, to a man, would rather be back home tending their fields, working in their shops, perhaps getting some more schooling, perhaps trekking farther west to find new land to break to the plow and grow crops on, to raise a family on.

Several shouted out names of their kin he might know, one said he was born in New Salem and remembered him as postmaster, another proclaimed Lincoln had won a suit for his daddy and then, laughing, said his daddy had yet to pay the bill.

"Well, son, tell your dad the debt is canceled and you did the canceling for him."

More laughter.

He looked back toward the road. A brigade commander was watching, indulgent but also obviously impatient at the delay that had stopped the column.

"Boys, you gotta get back on the march now. That general back there, usually he's got to salute me, but on this day I think I better salute him and follow what he wants."

Lincoln offered a friendly salute and the general, grinning, returned it. Officers herded the men back onto the pike, shouting for double time, for them to pick up and fall back in with the next regiment in line, which was now several hundred yards down the road.

" 'Bye, Abe, God bless ya, Abe!"

The years had fallen away from them for a moment: They were boys off on an adventure, acting as if they had just met a favorite schoolmaster, who now had to shoo them along back to their work, the work of killing.

The brigade commander nodded his thanks, then, a bit shyly, rode up to Lincoln and formally saluted and extended his hand.

"Sir, it's a mighty big surprise to see you up here in Pennsylvania. Rumors have been coming down the line for hours that you were on the road behind us."

"Just thought I'd come up for a little look around," Lincoln said, again smiling.

"How did you get here, sir?"

"Well, General, let's just call that our military secret for now. But between us I rode over on one of Thaddeus Lowe's balloons."

The general looked at him for a few seconds, almost believing him, and then, shaking his head, broke into laughter.

"I'll remember that one, sir, you had me going for a second."

"Glad I can still do it at times."

"God bless you, sir. I better get moving. I think you'll find General Grant coming back shortly. Word came down the line from headquarters that if you were seen to have you escorted in. I think he's right in front of us."

"Then I think I'll wait right here," Lincoln said. "It's been a long day of travel. I'd like to sit for a spell."

The general saluted again and rode off.

Lincoln passed the word to the commander of his escort regiment for the boys to take a break and dismount. The colonel detailed men off to line the road to keep the men back and moving.

To Abe's delight, a sergeant came up grinning and shyly offered him an apple. It was still a bit green, but he didn't care. Taking out his paring knife he opened it up and studiously began to peel the fruit, doing it with skill, one continual loop of reddish-green skin coiling down from the apple as he turned it in his hand.

Another regiment came by, boys from Ohio whom he had passed at a near gallop minutes before. They broke into "Three cheers for Old

Abe!" as they marched by. He looked up and nodded, smiling, enjoying the moment.

Something inside him whispered that what he was doing now was exactly what he was supposed to be doing. He was president of the United States, and far too many took that office far too seriously. Not serious on the points that mattered, but rather in all the folderol, all the ceremonies, all the scraping and bowing, all the maneuvering and backslapping and backroom dealing.

These boys constituted the army created by his words, his dreams, his hopes. They were a part of him and he was a part of them. Being president for them at this moment meant he was to sit on a rail, peel an apple, cut it into slices, and munch them slowly to savor the tart flavor—and be seen as president doing it.

It was not so long ago I used to do just this. Sit atop a fence or lean on it, chatting with a constituent, or when riding the circuit, to stop at a farm for a drink of water, ask for directions, talk of weather and wind, summer heats and winter storms, find out who was dying and who was being born.

He ran his free hand along the fence rail and smiled inwardly. Just such a rail had helped him win the presidency, at the moment when loyalists carried it onto the convention floor in Chicago, claiming it was a rail Old Abe had split with his very own hands as a youth.

How I used to hate that work, he thought. *Backbreaking labor for a few bits a day.* A friend had once said if you were a failure at everything else, or too lazy for anything else, there was always schoolteaching or law. Schoolteaching was out, what with the few months of education he had ever received, so law it had been.

And yet, at times, he longed for moments like this, to sit on a fence, smell the honeysuckle and late summer flowers, the scent of ripening corn, and feel the warm, gentle breeze.

He was lost in such thoughts for a few moments until another regiment approached, more Ohio boys, who shouted with joy at the sight of him, taking off their caps and waving as they passed.

Someone had told him that, at Fredericksburg, Lee had said, "It is well that war is so terrible, or we should grow too fond of it."

At this moment he found he was fond of it, in fact, inwardly thrilled by the sight of it, if but for a moment he could suppress all that was implied behind this ceaseless parade marching by.

Where he had stopped was atop a low rise, just a gentle elevation of a few dozen feet that the pike came up and over, straight as an arrow. Looking either way he could see for miles, the road choked with men, artillery, wagons, all flowing ever southwestward. The steady tramp of the men echoed, almost timed to the beating of his heart.

They looked like tough campaigners. He always felt that the boys of the Army of the Potomac were too burdened down. Those darn foolish French caps, the kepis which did a man little good; a broad-brimmed felt hat was far better and to his mind looked far more American in spirit. These western troops carried blanket rolls slung over shoulders, rifles slung as well, though as the regiments passed him, officers called for the men to come to port arms in salute. The sound of marching, the rattle of canteens and tin cups, the shouts, the clatter of hooves on the macadam pavement, all blended together into what could almost be music for his soul.

"Sir, I think the general is coming," a lieutenant from his escort cried, pointing south.

Lincoln turned his gaze against the setting sun and shaded his eyes and sure enough, he could see a flag standing out in the evening breeze, moving along the side of the road.

The lieutenant drew out his field glasses and focused them. "That's him all right, sir. It's General Grant."

Someone was riding ahead—the inexhaustible Ely Parker, his mount lathered.

Lincoln nodded his thanks and then had a moment's quandary. *I can sit here, as informal as can be, or I can fall back into the role once more.* Given the gravity of the moment, he decided on the latter and stepped down from the fence, folding up his pocket knife.

Parker saluted. "The general is right behind me, sir."

"I can see that, Ely. Now why don't you just relax? You've done an admirable job getting me here and finding General Grant."

Ely sighed and leaned forward in the saddle, uncorking a canteen and took a long drink.

Grant leapt a low fence, rather than go around to an open gate, in a beautiful display of horsemanship. He came on at a near gallop, headquarters flag flying behind him. He reined in, snapping off a salute, Lincoln looked up, unable to hide a smile at what could only be taken as surprise on Grant's face.

"Mr. President, I hope this does not sound impertinent, but may I ask just what it is you are doing here?"

"Just thought I'd come up this way and see how you and the boys were doing."

Grant was silent for a moment, obviously caught completely off guard, and then dismounted. Lincoln extended his hand, and Grant, a bit shyly, took it.

"How are you, General?"

"Well, sir, to be honest, rather startled. Rumor came to me a couple of hours ago that you were in Harrisburg. Then that you were across the river riding aboard a supply train on the Cumberland line."

"Remarkable work those engineers are doing," Lincoln exclaimed. "I understand they've replaced bridging for fifteen miles just since yesterday."

"They're Herman Haupt's boys. They know their business."

"Yes, unfortunate loss. I heard of his passing," Lincoln said.

"Sir, if I had known you were coming, I could have arranged better accommodations for us to meet."

"General Grant, right here is just fine," Lincoln replied, and nodded toward the road.

The men of his escort, staff from Grant's headquarters, and provost guards were now having one devil of a time keeping the men moving, forming a cordon on the other side of the fence. The cheering was near to deafening.

"To be truthful, General, I think if we wish to sit and talk a spell, we better go someplace else. I don't want to inconvenience your march or you."

"No, sir, no inconvenience at all, though I do agree we should move. Perhaps up to a creek I just crossed."

"Lead the way then."

Lincoln climbed back into the saddle, Grant easily mounting and coming to his side. They rode south for a few hundred yards, between the fence bordering the pike and a farmer's orchard, gradually angling away from the road. The trees closest to the road had nearly been stripped bare of fruit but once back a dozen rows the trees hung heavy, and on impulse Lincoln plucked one. Grant saw him do it and smiled.

"That's foraging in friendly territory, sir."

Lincoln laughed softly.

"I'll tell the farmer he can call it a war tax if he should inquire about my indiscretion."

They reached the edge of the orchard, staff having opened a gate that led to a narrow path sloping down between elms to spreading willow trees.

Someone on Grant's staff had obviously been thinking, in spite of the surprise. A blanket was already spread under a willow, a small fire burning under a pot, two camp chairs set up.

The cavalcade reined in, eager hands reaching up to take the bridle of Lincoln's horse as he dismounted. Stretching, he looked around.

It was a charming spot. A narrow creek gurgled by not a dozen feet away, the bank grown high with rushes and cattails. The path was a shallow ford, perhaps tracing the original road, long since abandoned when the pike came through. All was shaded by willows, long branches hanging down in a canopy. It was all so peaceful, the air rich with the scent of moisture, cooling and relaxing. The shadows were already deepening, providing a diffused golden light to the setting.

Looking downstream, he could barely see the single-arch stone bridge which leapt the stream, men continuing to cross over it. But here under the shade of the trees the two of them were all but invisible.

"Some coffee, sirs?" the sergeant tending the fire asked.

"Yes, Sergeant McKinley, that would be fine," Grant replied.

Seconds later Lincoln had a battered tin cup in his hand, and he sat down on the camp chair, blowing on the rim before taking a sip.

"You keep fine accommodations, General," Lincoln said, pointing to the small fire, the blanket, and the two chairs.

He sighed and leaned back in the folding chair made of carpet and a few pieces of wood.

"This is actually a luxury, General," and he nodded to their surroundings. "I wish I had such a place on the grounds of the White House, a brook, some willows, and a bit of solitude."

"Well, sir, if you came to the army to seek solitude, I dare say you have come to the wrong place. We have over seventy thousand men on the march around us and a staff always in earshot."

Lincoln saw the dozens of staff that stood around expectantly. As he gazed at them, they stiffened, some saluting, some bowing, others just looking at him wide-eyed.

"Gentlemen, may I ask an indulgence," Lincoln said.

No one spoke.

"I'd like to talk with General Grant for a while. There'll be time enough later for us to chat a bit. So would you please excuse us?"

There were hurried excuses, and within seconds all had scrambled off, drawing back, moving away.

Lincoln leaned forward, staring down into his cup of coffee as if lost in thought.

"Your Parker is a good man," Lincoln said, breaking the silence. "I don't think he's had a wink of sleep in three days."

As he spoke he gestured across the stream, where Parker was sprawled out under a willow . . . fast asleep.

"One of the best. I'm glad he took it upon himself to report straight to you after being with Sickles."

"I assume he told you about Stanton."

"Yes, sir," Grant said noncommittally.

Again, there was a long silence, Lincoln sipping his coffee and then stretching his legs out.

Grant stirred, coughed a bit self-consciously, and Lincoln looked over at him.

"Well, sir, I guess I do have to ask you then, to what do I owe the pleasure of this visit?" Grant asked.

"I could be flippant and say that it is nothing more than a courtesy stop, General Grant, but you and I know that is not the case."

"No, sir, I assumed not."

"I need to see certain things clearly, General Grant. It has been nearly a month since we last met, much has changed, and the portents of what is to come are profound. I thought that was worth the journey to discuss these issues with you."

"Whatever you wish to know, sir, just ask."

Lincoln drew his legs in and then leaned toward Grant, so close they could almost touch, the president looking straight into the eyes of the general.

"General Grant, I will cut to the core. No foolery, no mincing of words. Win or lose, the fate of the Union now rests with you and those men marching across that bridge."

He motioned toward the pike, where the troops continued to pass, flowing endlessly, the men oblivious of the meeting taking place less than a hundred yards away.

Grant leaned back in his camp chair, the front legs lifting from the ground. After a long sip of the scalding coffee, he set the cup on the ground. "Sir, I understand that, and so do my men."

Lincoln fixed his gaze upon Grant's eyes. This is what he had traveled so far to gauge. It was one thing to meet Grant a few days after his appointment. It was another thing to see him now, a month later, a month after he had had time to contemplate the responsibility placed on him.

He had decided upon this long journey for precisely this moment. The original plan that Grant had devised to destroy Lee—an overwhelming advance using the Army of the Potomac and at least ten thousand additional troops—had gone out the window. And Grant, without any prior notice, had jumped across the Susquehanna. He had come all this way to see why. To see if Grant was going off half-cocked. And to see if this was indeed a man he could trust with this winner-take-all move.

"What do you wish of me, sir?" Grant asked.

"First of all, I need a straight answer. No speaking in vague terms, no concern for self. I want you to consider the future of our republic, the debt in blood owed to all those who have already died.

"I want a straightforward answer, sir, without puffery or the bombast so many others have given me.

"General Grant, are you and your men up to this task?"

"Yes, sir," Grant said quietly. He did not look at Lincoln. His shoulders were hunched, his gaze fixed on his cup of coffee. But his words were strong, filled with conviction.

"I cannot afford another mistake, another defeat, or even half a victory. Lee must be crushed," Lincoln said urgently. "Congress is on the point of rebellion. I've held them off as long as possible but they will soon reconvene, and when they do, there will be a call to end the fighting and negotiate a settlement. There's renewed rioting in half a dozen cities. Secretary of State Seward is constantly at my doorstep with warnings that Europe might soon intervene. This war cannot drag out any longer.

"General Grant, I need to know that you fully realize that and can rise to the occasion."

The years in courtrooms, the years of watching others, of leaning against fences and talking, had taught him much, taught him about when men lied and when they spoke the truth, when men had strength or did not, when men thought far too much of themselves and not of others. The last two years of war had sharpened those insights with bitter lessons of military failure and bombastic generals unable to match their deeds to their self-esteem when it came to fighting Robert E. Lee.

Grant stirred then. He looked into Lincoln's eyes. "I can bring it to an end, sir. I can win this war."

At that the tension Lincoln had suppressed uncoiled. He had come to this encounter with a terrible intent he had voiced to no one. If in this meeting he had doubts, he would not have hesitated. Lord knows, he would have had difficulty in that decision, but if need be, he'd have removed Grant and found someone else. Was this the voice of the naysayers, those who had planted the thought? Of Halleck, of Stanton, even Seward, saying, "Replace this man." If forced to, he would have.

Could I? He realized he would have. This decision, at this moment, he realized, was as momentous as the decision to relieve Stanton. One had been fired; the other was to be kept.

It wasn't just the statement, "I can win this war," that had laid to rest any lingering doubts; it was the look in the man's eyes, something he had never seen in any general before. There was a determination, a confidence that settled the issue once and for all. He trusted now that the plan Grant had would be one he would endorse.

Grant was, indeed, his man.

Both seemed to sense that a moment had passed that neither need worry about again.

There was a dropping off of tension. Grant stood up, going over to refill his tin cup and then to light up a cigar, which he had refrained from doing since they first met.

Lincoln was silent as he waited for Grant to settle into his chair.

"A few more questions, General."

"Anything, sir."

"Sickles, for starters. I know that derailed your plan. Why did you move so quickly after his defeat and why did you not inform me?"

"Sir, after such a blow I knew Lee would expect me to wait, to replenish our numbers. That would mean waiting well beyond September, more likely October. That would have risked winter weather stopping the campaign and forcing us into winter quarters with Lee still owning Maryland."

"We can't wait that long," Lincoln said forcefully.

"Sir, I know you cannot wait. The country cannot wait. We have to resolve this now and that is why I decided to make this move and do it with or without Sickles in support."

"Fair enough," Lincoln said.

"And besides, sir, though Sickles lost that battle, he bloodied Lee. I understand that Pickett's Division is a hollow wreck. To achieve his victory, Lee force-marched his army a hundred miles in killing heat and in the end was forty miles north of a line that he would choose to be on, right along the banks of the Susquehanna. With Washington as a barrier Lee is actually farther away from Virginia than we are, and we have better roads and railroads to support us. I knew that this first move had to be taken, and I took it, regardless of Sickles."

Lincoln nodded thoughtfully.

"Go on, sir," Lincoln said.

"By moving first I knew it would push Lee off balance. My reports are that he has force-marched once again, falling back into Baltimore. To march troops such distances, day after day, takes its toll. My men are moving fast, but doing so through friendly territory, and they are filled with confidence."

"Confidence in you?"

"Yes, sir. To be frank, yes," and he said so without any display of undue pride.

"Half this army marched with me across the Mississippi, abandoned our line of supplies, went to Jackson to block Joe Johnston and then doubled back on Vicksburg, bottling up Pemberton. They were there when Pemberton surrendered his garrison and reopened the Mississippi. They're good men. McPherson is superb, and Ord, though new to corps command, is a hard driver I trust. My boys are confident; they feel they have something to prove here, to go up against Bobbie Lee and thrash him the way they thrashed Johnston, Pemberton, Beauregard, and Buckner. Upon that confidence and desire to prove something much can be built."

Again Lincoln liked what he heard. It was not confidence in him personally, it was confidence in his men, which Lincoln sensed was mutual from what he had observed while riding down here.

"Coordination, General. I've always felt we never truly coordinated all of our strength. Before coming here Elihu showed me a roster of total strength. Good heavens, General, we have nearly three quarters of a million men under arms. Can you bring additional strength to bear?"

"I agree, sir. But realize this. Half of those numbers are nonexistent. Take off ten percent or more just as deserters. Then add in governors holding back pet units filled with their political appointees. Many of those hundreds of thousands are ninety-day militia, of no value in a stand-up fight against Lee's veterans. There is an old saying I learned at West Point—it dates back to the Romans—'To send untrained men into battle is to send them to their deaths.' "

Lincoln nodded in agreement, remembering the tragedy of First Bull Run.

"I have nearly twenty thousand militia under Couch. To send them straight into a fight would be cruel and wasteful. If I had six months with those men, they'd prove to be as good as any, but we don't have that time, sir. But they are serving a valuable purpose right now, which I'll explain when we go over my plans in detail, but don't expect them to stand on the volley line at seventy-five yards and trade it out with an elite, well-trained unit like the Stonewall Brigade.

"Others are sitting out garrison duty as far north as Portland, Maine, and as far west as Council Bluffs, Iowa. Sir, what I am marching with is all that I will have for this campaign. But I should add, sir, that General Lee faces the same crisis. Governor Vance in North Carolina is notorious for keeping men back as home-guard units in the western mountains. Every other governor does the same down there. That is the paradox and the curse of their system even more than ours, states' rights. Each Southern state is doing right for its own purposes, but making it impossible for Davis and Lee to organize Southern resources for the common purpose. With your leadership and the strength of our Constitution we can do a far better job of mobilizing all our assets over time than they can."

He was warming to his subject, and Lincoln nodded for him to continue.

"For every man on the front line we need at least one more to guard our lines of supply, to shepherd along ammunition, food, fodder for horses, medical supplies. That eats up our numbers rather quickly. That's a second service Couch's men will give us once their first mission is completed. They'll provide security to our rear and the relaying of supplies. That means that every man that marches with me now will be in the fight."

"And your other fronts?"

"On other fronts I can tell you this, sir. Sherman has driven Bragg out of Chattanooga. That is a major victory for us. I have ordered him to not stop, to relentlessly press southward now and invest Atlanta before the end of autumn. I have confidence in Sherman. He's grown and is ready for independent command, and I think he'll make the most of it. He has seventy thousand men with him, I wish it was a hundred thousand. He'll need fifty thousand more just to secure his supply lines back to Memphis and Louisville.

"We've abandoned our operations before Charleston, as you know. The navy can handle that. Bottling it up is all we needed, nothing more, along with Wilmington. Additional troops still need to hold Vicksburg, Port Hudson, and New Orleans. When you get right down to it, sir, that comes to less than two hundred thousand on the front lines, though heaven knows I'd give my right arm for fifty thousand more right now."

"The colored troops?" Lincoln asked.

"Yet to be proven in battle, sir, but I think they'll fight. I understand their training has been intensive, unlike most white regiments, and all their officers are handpicked volunteers with extensive experience in the field prior to promotion to command those regiments.

"I just worry that their spirit will continue when they get hit by their first volley."

"They'll hold," Lincoln said forcefully. "I saw that when our line was broken at Fort Stevens and the colored men from Massachusetts charged forward. They'll do their duty when the time comes."

"And that regiment is still in Washington?"

"Yes, along with over forty thousand other men," Lincoln said. "Why do you ask?"

"Sir, I'd like to replace General Heintzelman as commander of the Washington garrison."

"Why?"

"Because that is part of my plan, sir."

"This is something we did not discuss before, General Grant."

"Sir, if you have come this far to talk, now is the time to talk about it. I did not want to trust the core of my plan to dispatches. That is also the answer to why I did not promptly inform you of my change of plans. I simply could not at that moment. Too many dispatches have been lost in the past, or leaked to the newspapers before the ink on them was barely dry."

"Nor did you want Stanton to interfere," Lincoln said, a cagey smile lighting his features.

Grant said nothing.

"That's over with. You will answer to Elihu Washburne. The two of you know and trust each other. General Grant, you still must answer to the civilian government, but I agree with your keeping your cards close in this opening stage. It was a sound move, and I would have done the same if in your shoes."

"Thank you, sir. I did not want to hold information back from you, but at the moment I felt the risk was too great. It was utter chaos at the Port Deposit transfer, and things could have gone awry there. General Sickles was doing everything possible to intercept any information I would pass along. Also, I cannot trust a civilian telegraph network with such sensitive information. That is why I am glad you are here. In the future, sir, knowing our lines of communication are secured, I will keep you posted on all issues and follow your orders. I have some plans I'd like to share with you to insure a speedy transfer of information in the days to come."

Lincoln nodded, liking what he heard. In contrast, he remembered his visit to McClellan after Antietam. The general was obviously disturbed by his presence, giving him the runaround, in subtle ways actually moving to insult him to the point of giving him a horse far too small for his stature during a review of the troops. In contrast he and Grant were now sitting alone, talking. Grant, though a bit nervous at first, was now obviously relaxing and being open. He was impressed as well by Ely Parker, who had held nothing back during their long journey together.

"General, I do not want you to wait for orders from Washington or worry about any day-to-day interference. Lord knows we had too many generals in the East looking over their shoulder for political manipulation and strict instructions. Stanton is gone, and Washburne will support your every effort. You will issue orders both here and to the armies throughout the country. I want you to keep your eye on Lee, and Sherman to keep his eye on Bragg. I will keep my eye on Washington and the politicians.

"As commander in chief I have to know what you intend to do. That is my duty. However, as long as I give you the command, you must give the orders. All I ask is that you keep me informed so I know what your plans are both here and throughout the country, then I can support them and get reinforcements where needed. That also enables me to answer the newspapers and the politicians."

He paused.

"That is why I came here to see you. And, General Grant, I think we see eye to eye on these issues."

"Thank you, sir," Grant replied.

"Now, how do you propose we end this terrible conflict?"

Grant stood up, and taking several puffs on his cigar, he began to explain his plan, Lincoln sitting quiet, hands folded in his lap as he leaned back in his camp chair.

"You are asking a lot, sir," Lincoln finally said, when, after fifteen minutes, and a tracing of a map with the toe of his boot on the ground, Grant at last fell silent.

"I know that, sir."

"It means a trust in your decisions, sir, that I've given to no other before. Washington would be stripped bare, something I've never allowed in the past."

"Sir, if I might be so bold. To quote you, you once said, 'The dogmas of the quiet past are inadequate to the stormy present.'"

Lincoln could not help but smile.

"Did you ever consider politics, General Grant."

"Heaven spare me that," Grant said with a weary chuckle.

"You are asking for a winner-take-all shake of the dice. You are talking about some very hard fighting within a week, perhaps the hardest of the war. The losses might very well be appalling, and Washington itself could fall if things turn against you."

"Something like that, sir. The loss of Sickles means having to draw on every reserve in this theater of operations. I no longer have a reserve as was originally planned. But I will tell you my greatest fear."

"Go on."

"That General Lee does indeed flee south. That he abandons Maryland, crosses the Potomac, fortifies the river crossings, and then drags this war into another year. Sir, I do not want to imagine another year of this contemptible war. We'll have to fight him to gain that river. From there into northern Virginia, cross the Rappahannock, and most likely into where Hooker fought at Chancellorsville. From there across the North Anna, and then crawling and fighting every inch of the way to Richmond. No, sir, I want him to stay here, in Maryland, or better yet even in Pennsylvania. His victories here, sir, I want them to be a trap that will enable us to destroy him in the end."

"But suppose, General Grant—dare I say it—suppose it is Lee who wishes the same thing, who seeks that same battle with you and in the end we lose both you and Washington."

"Then, sir, we have lost the war," Grant said quietly.

"And do you believe that can happen?"

Grant smiled.

"No, sir, we are going to win this one."

Chapter Six

Near Hanover, Pennsylvania

August 24, 1863
4:00 A.M.

"General, sir, I hate to wake you, but this could be important."

Gen. George Armstrong Custer groaned and sat up, confused for a second as to where he was. A staffer stood in the doorway holding a lantern.

Custer sat up, holding his head. He realized now he had indeed taken a little too much Madeira with dinner.

"What the hell is it?"

"Sir, a civilian just came in. I think you should talk to him."

"Couldn't it bloody well wait? What time is it?"

"Four in the morning, sir, and frankly, no, sir, I think you need to hear this man's story."

"Go on then, bring him in, but it had better be good."

The staff lieutenant disappeared for a moment. There was muffled conversation out in the corridor of the house he had requisitioned as headquarters, and then the lantern reappeared.

A strongly built man, with massive shoulders, stood behind the lieutenant.

"Who the hell are you?" Custer asked.

"James Donlevy, I work in the B and O rail yards down in Baltimore."

"So?"

"Well, if you don't want to hear it, General, the hell with it."

Custer sat back down on the edge of his bed.

"Lieutenant, get me some damn coffee. Now, Donlevy, tell me why you're here."

"I was sent up by my boss."

"Who's that?"

"Mr. McDougal."

"Never heard of him."

"Frankly, sir, he's most likely never heard of you."

Custer took a deep breath and exhaled. This wasn't getting off to a good start at all. Wasting time being irritated with civilians was not going to get the job done. *Patience, George,* he told himself.

"All right, James. Just tell me why it was so important this Mr. Mc-Dougal thought I should be woken up at four in the morning."

"Well, General, he had a little information about the rebs and their movements he thought you should be aware of. Or at least General Grant should be."

"And that is."

"Something about pontoon bridges being moved about on the railroad."

This finally caught Custer's attention, and he looked up. The lieutenant came back in, bearing a cup of coffee.

"You want some, Donlevy?"

"Wouldn't mind if I do."

Custer motioned for him to take the cup and sent the lieutenant out for another.

"Go on, then."

"Yesterday afternoon a damn surly rebel officer came to the rail yard for the B and O, looking for engines and flatcars to pull what he called pontoon boats to Frederick."

The lieutenant came back with a second cup and Custer sent him back out.

"How many cars did he want?"

"At least forty, he said."

Custer did a quick calculation. That was enough bridging to span more than a quarter mile. Not enough for the Suesquehanna but definitely enough for the Potomac. This was interesting, damn interesting.

"I heard something about the boats being captured from General Meade."

Custer knew that was true. The pontoon train had been overrun in the retreat, some of the equipment destroyed, but word was the rebs had captured enough for at least one good bridge.

"Where did they want to move these pontoon bridges to?"

"Mr. McDougal said they want to use the B and O to move them at least to Frederick."

Custer took that in.

Frederick. Once there the rebels could move the bridging down to Point of Rocks, to half a dozen different locations along the Potomac. It'd give them a bolt hole back across the Potomac without having to rely on a ford.

Now he was fully awake. Does this mean Lee was retreating?

"How and why did you get here?"

"My boss is a Union man, same as me."

"So why aren't you in the army?" he asked, just to see how this civilian would respond, and he watched him carefully.

"My brother was," Donlevy said quietly. "I'm all my mother has left now. My brother died at Fredericksburg with the Seventy-second Pennsylvania, the Philadelphia Brigade. After that I promised my mother I'd stay home and take care of her."

The man seemed slightly embarrassed by the admission, and Custer nodded.

"How did you get up here?"

"The rebels took over the railroads yesterday. Mr. McDougal said something about them seizing all the lines. A train was coming up to Westminster to check the track and perhaps to establish a depot for supplies. Mr. McDougal got me on the train, told me to steal a horse once into Westminster, and ride north till I ran into your patrols."

"What about the rebs? How did you get around them?"

"Wasn't too hard. There aren't many out there. I had a good horse and outran one of their patrols.

"I avoid the rebels, then almost get killed by your men, General," Donlevy said indignantly. "Your damn men are trigger-happy. They fired a couple of shots at me before finally letting me come in."

"Sorry about that, but a healthy-looking man like you, on horseback at night. It would rattle a patrol."

"Still, what would have happened to my mother then, damn it? Precious poor gratitude I call it."

"If your information is correct, I'm certain our government will show proper gratitude, Donlevy."

He didn't add that Donlevy would be a guest of his headquarters until the report was confirmed. If it turned out he was a rebel agent, sent to sow false information, he'd soon be dangling from a tree.

"Make yourself comfortable, Donlevy. We'll be moving out in a few hours and you can ride with me."

"I didn't plan to join the army."

"You are now my guest."

"I see," Donlevy said quietly. "But if I get docked pay for not going back, well, I expect someone to take care of that."

"We will. Consider yourself on my staff for the moment at a pay equal to your railroad pay."

Custer left him and stepped out into the corridor, where his lieutenant had obviously been eavesdropping.

"What do you think?" Custer asked.

"He seems real enough. He's right, our boys almost shot him. His horse is outside, blown and lathered. He's dressed like a rail worker, greasy as hell, no look of a cavalryman to him. I think he's telling the truth."

"If true, that means Lee is pulling out," Custer said. "By damn, he's pulling out of Baltimore. He means to skedaddle back to Virginia and hold us off from there."

"It does look that way."

"Damn all. We got to get that bridging material. Burn that and we can block him."

Custer slapped his hands together with sudden glee.

"I want the entire brigade mounted and ready to move within the hour. Get the fastest rider you can find and send him back up the line to General Kilpatrick with this report."

Custer grabbed a sheet of paper and a pencil from the lieutenant, who then held a candle while Custer leaned against the wall and jotted out a note:

Headquarters, Second Brigade, Third Division
Hanover, Pennsylvania

Aug. 24
4:00 A.M.

    Have received word from civilian who took train to Westminster, stole a horse, and rode into our lines, claiming to work in Baltimore and Ohio yards in Baltimore. States that Army of Northern Virginia pontoon train, loaded on forty rail cars, to be moved by rail to Frederick and perhaps beyond. States as well, same railroad now taken over by rebels. Will set out this morning, moving west and then south to Frederick to intercept.

Signed,
Custer

.   .   .

Sir, what about our orders to hold here and screen Couch?"

"The hell with that now. We can sit back and do nothing, waiting a day for orders, or show some dash and, with that, win glory. Now what's it to be?"

The lieutenant knew better than to respond to that question. He saluted, dashed out the door, and in less than a minute "boots and saddles" broke the early morning silence. Within seconds the camp began to stir.

Custer stepped out the door and in the twilight of dawn took in the scene, the sight of the men of the First Michigan standing up, cursing and muttering, but answering the call.

It was going to be a great day for a ride, Custer thought with a grin.

Headquarters, Army of the Susquehanna
Near Shippensburg, Pennsylvania

August 24
11:30 A.M.

The early lunch under the canvas awning had been simple army fare: hardtack, salt pork, some roasting ears purchased from the farmer whose yard they were camped in, and, of course, coffee, plenty of hot coffee, Lincoln taking his with some cool sweet cream.

A hundred yards away, down on the Valley Pike, the troops continued to move, a seemingly endless, procession, regiment after regiment passing by, these men the tail end of Ord's Corps, General Ord having ridden over to join them for lunch.

The talk around the table had been on anything but the war, perhaps a mess tradition, Lincoln thought, and, if so, a wise one. A young lieutenant proudly showed off a daguerreotype of his wife and newborn son. Grant shared a story about California and its beauty, his hope of perhaps settling out there after the war. Ord told of how some eastern men had challenged his men yesterday, asking what their corps badge was. One of his men had proudly slapped his cartridge box, proclaiming, "Here's our corps badge, a cartridge box with forty rounds."

Ord had already decided that this would be the insignia for his command, a black cartridge box with the gold U.S. oval in the middle.

From there they had talked about military standards of old, Napoleon's famous eagles, the eagles of Rome, the horsetail standards of the Mongols. A captain shared the story of Varus and the lost eagles of the legions, taken by the Germans during the reign of Augustus, and how Augustus wandered the palace crying out, "Varus, give me back my eagles?"

The group fell silent at that story, some looking sidelong at Lincoln, wondering if he might have done the same after Union Mills. And yes, he knew that story, and it did indeed haunt him when he thought of those bloody slopes, the thousands of dead and dying. He thought, as well, of the story already circulating across the country—how, several weeks after Union Mills, a rebel soldier had slipped through the picket line at Washington, calling for a truce, taking from under his jacket a green banner stained with the blood of the Irish Brigade. He said he had retrieved it on the battlefield, taking it from a dying Union officer's hands and pledging he'd return it. The reb, a son of Ireland as well, refused any offer of money, or even food, and was escorted with honor back to his own lines, where his comrades gave him three cheers.

As he was sipping his second cup of coffee, realizing that his mission here was completed and it was time to leave the pleasant comradeship of the army and return to the turmoil of Washington, an officer came galloping along the roadside, leapt a fence, and rode straight toward the group. His stallion was sleek, jet black, the officer astride it cutting a sharp figure in a neatly fitting uniform. He reined in hard and dismounted with a flourish.

Lincoln's first instinct was a dislike of this man. He had the look of George McClellan about him, his uniform a little too neat when contrasted to Grant's simple four-button private's jacket, or Ord, covered with dust and sweat, and other officers begrimed. The man was short, about the same height as McClellan, and perhaps that was a trigger for Lincoln, who like many who were tall, saw military men of diminutive stature and too much braid as being "little Napoleons."

The officer came up to Grant, grinning, and saluted.

"General Sheridan, may I present you to our president?"

Sheridan turned and actually looked startled. He had not seen Lincoln sitting in the shade, slouched in a canvas-back chair, sipping coffee.

The man instantly snapped to rigid attention and saluted.

"Excuse me, sir, I mean, Mr. President, I didn't see you, sir."

He looked a bit flustered, and Lincoln's first sense of dislike dissipated. He stood up, nodded, and extended his hand, which Sheridan took warmly.

"Sir, an honor to meet you," Sheridan said enthusiastically.

"Thank you, sir."

"I heard you were with the army. I was hoping to be able to see you."

"You came here in what seemed to be a hurry, General Sheridan. Do you bear important news?"

"Yes, sir."

"Report then."

Lincoln was caught by the fact that Sheridan pulled a dispatch out of his breast pocket and handed it straight to him. With McClellan's army there would have been all sorts of secrecy, officers huddled outside, McClellan with a touch of pomposity excusing himself to go confer in whispers before coming back to tell Lincoln what was occurring—and often distorting the news. This openness was refreshing. The note, he saw immediately, was addressed to Grant, yet Sheridan had handed it directly to him. A small issue to be certain, but one that was telling.

"I think this is for our general," Lincoln said, handing the note over to Grant, who opened it up.

Grant scanned the memo and stood silent for a moment, as if lost in thought.

"Interesting news?" Lincoln asked.

"Yes, sir, it is."

Grant looked around at the gathering.

"A report from General Custer." He paused for a second.

"Good man, Custer," one of the staff said, "promoted to brigade command just before Gettysburg. Aggressive as all hell."

Lincoln realized that Grant had taken the pause in order to be prompted, to get a little background on Custer before proceeding in front of the president.

"It was sent this morning at four A.M. from near Hanover. The report says that a civilian informant, whom Custer believes is truthful, came through the lines from Baltimore. General Lee is preparing to move his pontoon train via the B and O to Frederick, perhaps beyond."

"That's news," Ord said softly. "Is he running?"

Grant handed the memo to Lincoln.

"If I'm not mistaken, General," Lincoln said softly after scanning it, "Hanover is not that far from here. Why has it taken nearly eight hours for this message to arrive?"

Grant nodded in agreement, looking over at Sheridan.

"Sir, I was at the telegraph and railhead five miles north of here when it was carried in by courier. Seems some pro-Southern civilians, or perhaps rebel raiders, are cutting our telegraph links as Grierson advances on the east side of the mountain. Apparently the courier from Custer wasted several hours looking for Kilpatrick and then Grierson before moving it back up the line to Carlisle, where it was telegraphed to our railhead. See-ing the importance of it, I rode it down here myself."

Lincoln handed the dispatch back to Grant, saying nothing.

Grant motioned for the table to be cleared, and within seconds plates and cups were pushed back, a map quickly spread out, men gathering round.

"Is this reliable?" Grant asked, looking around. "I don't know this Custer. His dispatch states that he is moving on his own toward Frederick to intercept. Did Kilpatrick or Grierson authorize this?"

"Apparently not," Sheridan replied. "There're no endorsements or comments from either of them yet."

Grant looked around at the gathering.

"Again my question," Grant said sharply. "Custer. Is he reliable?"

"A glory hound some call him," Ely said quietly, "but from what I've been able to pick up, he's at the front of a fight."

"Last in his class at West Point. Damn young to command a brigade. Class of 'sixty-one," a captain added. "A staff officer with McClellan."

There was a momentary pause in the conversation, Lincoln standing quiet, watching.

"Captain, you are a staff officer under Grant. Should that disqualify you for field command if the need arises?" Sheridan asked.

The captain stood silent, then shook his head.

"How did he rise so quickly?" Grant asked.

"He can fight," Ely replied. "After Union Mills, he was one of the few who brought his command out relatively intact. Even defeated a couple of rebel infantry regiments trying to cut him off from Harrisburg. That's how he wound up under our command rather than back with the Army of the Potomac. He was in Harrisburg when we came in and did good ser-vice patrolling the western bank of the river."

Again there was a moment of silence as Grant examined the map.

Lincoln studied him carefully. This was strictly a military decision, and he was curious to see how Grant would handle it, what advice he'd solicit. Would he make his decisions on his own, and do so boldly, or con-vey timidity and lack of confidence?

Grant lit a cigar, and that seemed to be a signal for the others gathered round to fall silent. He puffed intently, staring at the map, picking up the dispatch for a moment, setting it back down.

"One thing to note here," Grant said at last. "Custer, by moving, has left a gap ten miles wide in our cavalry pickets shielding Couch's slow but steady advance. That was always a decoy, but one I hoped would hold for another day or two. If but one patrol of rebel cavalry attacks that opening, gets through, and takes a few prisoners, they'll realize that move is nothing but a feint. It's twenty thousand militia playacting at being our main force to direct Lee's gaze to the north rather than the west."

There were nods of agreement.

"We must assume Lee will know by the end of the day we are not coming straight on, but attempting to flank to the west of the mountains, so that game is up."

He was silent again for a moment, puffing on his cigar.

"Lee is playing the safe move. Get the pontoon train west and to the rear of his operational area."

"Do you think he's pulling out?" Ord asked.

Grant shook his head.

"Not like Lee. No, but he will play the safe move first. He needs to secure a line of retreat if we should outmaneuver him or defeat him outright. We'd do the same."

Grant looked over at Ely.

"What pontooning material do we know they have?"

"Their bridging material at the start of Maryland campaign was laid at Williamsport, and then washed away in the floods right after Union Mills. We know he captured some of ours after Union Mills."

"How much?"

"Enough at least to get across the Potomac."

Grant nodded.

"That gives him a secure line of retreat if he can get it in place, say here, or here," and as he spoke he pointed toward several potential crossing spots south of Frederick.

Grant leaned back from the table, hands clasped behind his back.

"Two potential choices here, gentlemen. The first, that Lee is preparing for a general pullout, the first action to be the moving up of his pontoon bridge and getting it in place, followed within hours by the evacuation of Baltimore."

"Do you think he is pulling out?" Lincoln could not help but ask.

Grant emphatically shook his head.

"No, Mr. President. Everything we know of Lee is that he is extraordinarily aggressive. He has won three great battles in a row, starting with Chancellorsville, and he has destroyed the Army of the Potomac. I am confident he will want to face us and seek a single battle of decision. But Lee is not a wild gambler. He is a very smart, calculating risk taker. I believe he is simply taking a safe move at the start. Chances are he has no idea we are even aware of it. In fact, it is fair to assume he has no idea at all. He is just doing what any general does before an action, no matter how aggressive he is, to secure a line of retreat before moving forward to action. Lee will stay and fight. There will be another battle soon, and it will be in Maryland."

Grant paused, hands on the table, looking down at the map again.

"I do not want him to have that line of retreat. We allow him to do that, things go against him, he can then get out and retreat to Virginia to lick his wounds and prepare for yet another campaign. We've got to stop that train from getting any farther than the east side of Monocacy Creek, just outside of Frederick."

Lincoln took all this in with great interest. He sensed that Grant was already thinking beyond a single battle, the events of tomorrow or the day after; he was thinking out an entire campaign, perhaps two battles, half a dozen, but all with the ultimate intent of keeping Lee north of the Potomac and destroying him.

He continued to watch, saying nothing, but feeling an ever deepening reassurance.

Grant stood up and looked around at his staff.

"Ely, send a dispatch to General McPherson. The easy marching is over. His current location?"

"Sir, according to our schedule, by noon the head of his column should be down near Greencastle."

"Fine. I want a fast courier down to him now. Write out the orders for me and I'll sign them. General McPherson is to force-march through Hagerstown, then cross over the South Mountains and Catoctin ranges. I expect him in Frederick by late tomorrow, to secure that town and block the west bank of the Monocacy. That will be thirty-five miles of tough marching, and his men had better be ready to fight at the end of it."

"Second order," and as he spoke, Ely had a notebook out, scribbling away furiously. "Get a courier over to Custer, tell him he is authorized to gain the west bank of the Monocacy, secure the rail crossing at Frederick, and burn all the bridges. That will bottle Lee upon the other side."

"Sir, there are three bridges at Monocacy."

Henry Hunt, who had been standing quietly with the staff officers, stepped forward.

Lincoln caught Hunt's eye and nodded an acknowledgment. This was the officer who had brought in the first report to him of the debacle at Union Mills.

"I was there, sir, June 28, reporting to General Meade after he took command of the Army of the Potomac. I remember the railroad bridge as a temporary wooden structure. The iron bridge was blown last year during the Antietam campaign. There's also a solid covered bridge, double wide, two spans, within rifle range of the railroad bridge. Then there's a heavy stone bridge where the National Road crosses the river, a half mile or so north of the rail bridge. I don't think Custer will have the munitions to destroy that one."

"Thank you, Hunt. But at least Custer can make a fight for that."

"If they can push him back, regain the west bank, and have some engineering troops, that railroad span could be brought back up in fairly short order," Hunt continued.

"That's why I want McPherson in there," Grant said, and Hunt nodded in agreement.

"Third order, I want the pace of the corps following McPherson to be picked up. We are not going to leave him out there dangling. Now get to work, gentlemen."

The group scattered, calling for their mounts; Ely remained seated. He tore off a sheet of paper and began to draft orders.

Lincoln watched, taking it all in. There was no panic, no confusion, no debate. Orders had been given decisively and were now being acted on, all done in a matter of minutes.

Grant looked over at Lincoln and nodded. Sheridan stood to one side, saying nothing.

"Phil, stand by me, for I might need you shortly."

"Yes, sir."

A subtle gesture on Lincoln's part indicated that he wished to talk. He and Grant stepped out from under the awning and slowly walked halfway down to the road, where troops were continuing to pass, not yet aware of what was transpiring.

"Did this catch you off guard, General?" Lincoln asked.

Grant shook his head.

"Not seriously. A standard opening move."

"So Lee is not escaping?"

"I can't promise that, sir, but if the shoes were reversed, I know I would not give up all the gains I had achieved without a fight. As I said yesterday, we want his victories to be a trap, to hold him in place. He is just displaying a bit of caution here with the movement of the pontoon train."

"So why block him?"

Grant smiled.

"Two reasons. First off, he'll wonder how we knew. If Custer sweeps down ahead of the trains, burns the bridge, or better yet captures the bridging material, Lee will be caught off balance and it will set him to wondering, something I want him to do. Second, it sets the stage for our meeting. McPherson coming down on Frederick, that's an open challenge for a fight he cannot resist."

"And yet this seems to disrupt your plans?"

"Not seriously. I planned all along to maneuver west of the mountains as far as Frederick, then come down and face him. If time had permitted, perhaps even push far enough eastward to block him entirely from the Potomac and link up with the Washington garrison. I don't think that will happen now. He'll figure out Couch by the end of this day and the diversion I set for him with the militia. Then it is fair to assume he will ascertain the rest, but we will be on the move to block that."

"This Custer left a wide-open hole in that screen," Lincoln asked. "Suppose he is off on a fool's errand, planted by some rebel agent."

"Then General Custer will be Captain Custer doing garrison duty in Kansas or the Dakotas," Grant said coolly.

"But I was not there when this civilian came in, so for the moment I'll have to trust Custer's judgment. He made the decision of a general, and I will back him until proven wrong. If I don't do that, no general under me will have the audacity to take a chance. I only get angry when they've done so on what is obviously information they should have seen through or do not act when the evidence before them is as plain as day but they lack the courage to act.

"Besides, our little farce with Couch could not have lasted much longer. We wanted the rebels to see him at long distance but not get close enough to figure out the truth. That was bound to unravel at some point."

"The Baltimore and Ohio, though."

"Yes, it gives Lee an interesting advantage. Plenty of rolling stock and locomotives in Baltimore. He might use that to move swiftly, while my men will be on foot."

Grant smiled again.

"My men will just have to move hard and fast."

"A curious point, General, from earlier," Lincoln said casually. "You mentioned how a general always keeps a line of retreat open. Yet you risked all back in May when you crossed the Mississippi, then cut a hundred miles into that state with no line of supply or retreat. Isn't that a violation of the rule you just said Lee would follow?"

"That was different, sir. Frankly, I knew the mettle of my opponents, and knew I could do it and win."

"I see." Lincoln looked at him intently.

His cigar almost finished, Grant let it drop, crushing the embers out with his heel.

"Mr. President, I hope this does not seem rude, but I must move south. You are welcome to join me."

Lincoln laughed softly.

"But tending to a president might be a hindrance at this moment."

"I didn't say that, sir."

"But you might be thinking it."

Grant looked up at him, not sure how to react, and Lincoln smiled.

"I've seen all I need to see here, General. I know the armies of the Republic are in good hands. Do your duty."

"Yes, sir. Of course, sir."

"And do not let Lee escape. Finish him and finish this war," Lincoln said forcefully.

"I will do all in my power to achieve that, sir."

Lincoln extended his hand.

"I know you will."

The two turned and walked back toward the awning, where Ely was still busy writing out orders and Sheridan stood silent, waiting.

"This Sheridan. He's from the West, isn't he?" Lincoln asked.

"Yes, sir. Fought under Rosecrans, gained a reputation as a hard driver at Stone's River and Perryville."

"You ever see him in action?"

"No, sir, not personally."

"Why did you bring him east?"

"I heard this man just doesn't know when to quit. He's tough, aggressive. Yes, a bit of a showman, but it's always good to have one like that in your army. I didn't want to strip any more officers out of Sherman's command, but word was Sheridan is good, so I ordered him east a couple of weeks back."

"His job?"

"At the moment, a general in my back pocket. I've been watching him carefully. He's acting right now as an assistant, being my eyes where I can't be, and doing a fine job of it."

"I don't get your meaning. About him being in your back pocket."

"In case I need to fire someone, sir, or someone is wounded and can't continue in command," Grant said quietly.

Lincoln nodded. Good planning. Long before he had crossed the line with his decision to replace Stanton, he had Washburne marked for the job.

The two paused, Lincoln putting out a friendly hand, resting it on Grant's shoulder.

"I'll be back in Washington by this time tomorrow. I've thought it over and agree to your replacing Heintzelman with Winfield Hancock if the man is physically up to the job. I'll see that your request regarding the garrison in Washington is carried through and will inform Secretary Washburne of your other plans. I will confess I hesitated as I contemplated it last night. Perhaps it was this latest news, this thought that Lee just might escape south of the Potomac because of the pontoon bridge."

He looked Grant straight in the eyes.

"Perhaps instead it's the trust I now have in your judgment. You did not hesitate a few minutes back when Sheridan came in with that dispatch. There was no panicking, no running about, no calling for yet another staff meeting and hours wasted as a result. You run things as I've wanted to see them run for over two years, Grant. I trust you."

"Thank you for that confidence, sir. I will see that I continue to hold it."

"God be with you, General Grant."

"And with you and the Union, sir," Grant replied.

Lincoln said nothing more, turning and walking off to where an orderly already had his horse ready to go. Grant looked over to Sheridan and gestured for him to join Lincoln. Phil mounted and trotted over to the president's side to escort him back to the railhead.

The two rode off.

Grant watched them leave, troops along the road cheering as they saw Lincoln riding toward them, then turning north, heading up the valley for the long trip back to Washington. Soon they were gone from view, while before him the endless column continued to march by.

"Ely," Grant said, without looking back, "I want those dispatches now."

Chapter Seven

After riding hard, Capt. Phil Duvall reined in before the mansion on the outskirts of Taneytown. In the previous few minutes he and his command had crossed through the battlefield of the previous month, an experience that had cut into his heart.

Everywhere there were shallow sunken depressions of upturned earth, the graves of the thousands who had died here on July 2.

Phil remembered a quote from Wellington he had learned at West Point, that the only thing as depressing as a battlefield lost was a battle-field won.

No one could tell the difference between won or lost now. The air was thick with that sickly sweet smell of death, more than one of his troopers, hardened as they might be, vomited even as they rode.

Ever since leaving Hanover they had crossed over the ground the armies had campaigned across and fought on in the Gettysburg–Union Mills campaign. Sunken graves, decaying horses still unburied, overturned caissons, burnt wagons. He was stunned to discover in Gettysburg a hospital tended by Union volunteers of the Sanitary Commission filled with hundreds of patients, Union and Confederate. The men had been there ever since the battles of early July, too sick or injured to be moved.

One of the volunteers, a woman, had burst into tears at the sight of him. "Not another battle here," she cried. "Not another battle."

The memory of her was sobering. He could see in her his own mother and sisters. Such women were always there after the fight, to clean up the wreckage after the armies moved on, to hold hands late at night as boys continued to die, long after the gods of war had gone elsewhere in quest of victims.

Taneytown itself was a scene of utter wreckage—homes burned, crops trampled down and rotting, civilians silent and sullen as he rode in.

They had passed a regimental graveyard, a rough-hewn plank marking it as men of the Twentieth Maine. He had heard of their stand and annihilation by Pickett. Over three score were buried there, shallow graves that had washed out in the rains, and then been scavenged by wild pigs and dogs. The sight sickened him. Rotting blue fragments of uniforms, a skeletal hand half raised out of a grave, an overturned wagon, burned out, broken remnants of ammunition boxes littering the field.

Waste, nothing but damn waste. *Is this where I shall be a month from now?* he wondered. He wondered as well what his men thought as they trotted across the battlefield, silent, grim faced.

As he dismounted before the mansion, he looked about. Supposedly, both Meade and Lee had used this mansion during the earlier campaign. He walked up the steps of the mansion, knocked on the door, and waited. No one answered at first until finally, after a long minute, a black servant opened the door.

"May I use your home?" Phil asked.

"The owners aren't home."

"I just need to use your top floor for a few minutes," Phil said politely.

The servant opened the door and let him in.

"Sir, is there gonna be fighting around here again?"

"No. We're just riding through."

"General Lee used this is as his headquarters during the last fight. It was terrible, sir, the fighting around here."

The servant pointed to broken windows, covered over with pieces of paper, bullet holes pocking the side of the house facing the town, a shattered eave struck by a shell.

"Don't worry. We're just riding through."

As he walked down the corridor to the main staircase Phil saw that whoever owned this place had simply left. Bits of paper still littered the floor. A table in the room to the left rested in the center of the room, chairs drawn up around it, a map marked with penciled lines still there, as if Lee and his staff had departed only minutes before.

"I'm the only one here to look after the place," the servant said apologetically. "Been meaning to get around to cleaning all this up."

The opposite parlor across the hallway had obviously been used as a hospital. Carpets and walls were stained with dried blood, furniture was upended and piled in a corner, the room still having a lingering, sickening smell to it.

He bounded up the stairs, going to the third floor, then scaled the ladder up to the cupola, Sergeant Lucas behind him.

Breathing hard, Phil uncased his field glasses and looked back down the road he had just traversed with his small company. Behind him, not three miles away, was a column of Yankee troopers. Not a company or regiment, it had to be a brigade or more the way the dust swirled up behind them, clear back to the horizon.

"Custer?" Lucas asked.

"Yup. It's gotta be him."

"Driving damn hard," Lucas said.

"That's George," Phil said drily.

He remembered many an afternoon, George and he, out for a ride after seeing to their duties as cadets, trotting along the heights overlooking the Hudson, talking about all their hopes and dreams of glory. The war was still ahead, the arguing and shouting of politicians of no concern to them during those wonderful days but four years ago. Their talk instead was of what it might be like out on the great prairies of the West, with endless horizons ahead of them, or perhaps a posting to California or Charleston and the lovely belles that might await them there.

He smiled with the memory, how on so many nights, after lights out, they'd lighted a candle concealed behind a blanket and he'd sat up with George, reviewing yet again plane geometry or French, trying to coax his roommate along, to keep him, last in his class, from flunking out.

On those rides together George would inevitably challenge him to race, and off they would gallop together, George usually winning and teasing him about the legend that southern boys could always beat a Yankee on horseback.

So now we are in race again, old friend, Phil thought as he raised his field glasses and scanned the horizon, *but this time, I have to beat you at it.*

He scanned the horizon. The day was clear, no haze. Taking out a map, he propped it against the windowsill, orienting himself. The hills to the north must be Gettysburg, the South Mountain range beyond. He scanned that way. Nothing. No troop movements, at least on this side of the range, but what was happening beyond it? Well, that was a mystery.

Looking toward Gettysburg he thought he caught a gleam of reflected light, perhaps some dust. Infantry? It was impossible to tell.

George, though, was obviously driving southwest, coming straight at him. If so, what was his goal?

Shadow the east side of the mountains? Why moving so fast? If he was to provide a screen for the advancing infantry, they'd still be a dozen miles back. Was he heading for some objective this way? Phil traced a finger down the map.

Frederick?

Why there, if the bulk of the Union army, as seen by the patrol by Syms, was now north of Hanover? He had sent Syms and a dozen men back north even as they had pulled out of Hanover to try to identify a unit, but so far nothing had been heard from them. He feared Syms was most likely lost.

Frederick. Push hard and he could be in there by tomorrow morning. Block the pass or perhaps take the railroad.

A distant line of skirmishers emerged along the road back to Littlestown, advancing at a trot. Now less than two miles away. In another fifteen minutes they'd be into the town.

Give them a punch here? he wondered. Leaning out of the cupola he looked down at his ragged command. They had been retreating for nearly two days. Horses were blown, half a dozen men left behind because of a thrown shoe, a mount collapsing.

No, he had to keep pulling back until Stuart sent up reinforcements.

"We keep moving, Sergeant Lucas," Phil said bitterly.

The two raced down the stairs, ignoring the servant, who, amazingly, had actually made up some tea and had it waiting for them.

Coming back out on the porch Lucas shouted for the men to remount and get ready to move.

Duvall leaned against a porch pillar, casing his field glasses, dreading the thought of getting back into the saddle. He had been riding since dawn, was exhausted, and just wished for an hour of uninterrupted sleep.

A clatter of hooves echoed, some of his men turning, raising carbines or pistols, looking toward the road from the mansion back into the village. They relaxed at the sight of Lieutenant Syms. His mount was lathered, foaming, Syms's features pale as he reined in, grimacing with pain.

"Can't believe I found you here," Syms gasped, leaning forward in his saddle, breathing hard.

"You look like hell," Duvall said.

Syms smiled weakly and fainted. Lucas went to his side to help him out of the saddle. Half a dozen willing hands came to his side, carrying him up to the porch of the mansion.

Syms opened his eyes and looked around in confusion. The servant from the mansion knelt by his side and gently held a cup of tea to his lips. Syms took a drink and nodded his thanks.

"Where are the rest of your men?" Phil asked.

"Dead, captured, or played out."

"What did you find out?"

"I must have ridden fifty miles since dawn. Circled around Custer's men. By God, are they moving fast!"

"I know."

"We hit a Yankee infantry column about twenty miles north of here. Phil, it's a sham, all a sham."

"What do you mean?"

"We came over a rise and there they were, a column marching on the road, not even any skirmishers forward. Scared the hell out of me. I mean we were less than fifty yards away when we ran smack into them."

He grinned weakly.

"One sight of us, though, the mighty cavalry of the Confederate army"—Syms chuckled at the memory—"and the entire column bolted and ran like sheep. Not a shot fired, they weren't even loaded up.

"We ran them down, took a dozen prisoners, the rest of them just disappearing, jumping fences, throwing their rifles and packs away, running off into the woods and across the fields. Hell, if I had fifty men, I could have bagged five hundred."

"Militia?"

"You're damn right. Nothing but militia. If it wasn't so funny, I'd of been disgusted with 'em. One of them, a lieutenant, cried like a baby and spilled everything when we threatened to shoot him."

"My God, you didn't!" Phil said.

"Hell, no." Syms grinned weakly. "He said all the boys in his division were in the army for ninety days to avoid the draft. The entire army was just like him. They'd been lying about Harrisburg for weeks. Just hating Grant's men who lorded it over them. Grant's boys are moving to the west, behind the mountains. These boys, under Couch, crossed the river by ferry down at Wrightsville. Supposedly close on to twenty thousand of them. They were even told they wouldn't have to face a battle, just march about for a week or so."

Phil sat back on his heels.

"Damn all."

The realization hit. McPherson's men, tough veterans, had crossed at Harrisburg. If they weren't in front of him, that meant they had to be on the road over the other side of the South Mountains.

It was fitting together. Custer makes a dash to seize the pass at Frederick; McPherson comes through with the rest of the army behind him.

"The rest of your men?" Phil asked.

"We got jumped riding through Gettysburg on the way down here looking for you. Some troopers from your friend's brigade."

He seemed to drift away for a moment, then sighed. "I had to leave my men behind, Phil. I had the best mount. The boys even told me to ride for it and carry the news back to you. My boys, they're dead now or prisoners. They turned back to fight while I rode off."

Phil knelt by his side, holding his hand, and shook him slightly.

"Look at me," Phil said softly, and the lieutenant gazed up at him.

"Are you certain of this report? The entire army north of us is militia?"

"That's what the prisoners we took told us. They were scared. Hell, I hated to do it, but I had a cocked gun to the lieutenant's head and said I'd blow the man's brains out if the others lied. We kept them separated, then brought them up before the lieutenant one at a time, and they all said the same thing. One of 'em even identified the four corps marching with Grant—McPherson, then Burnside, then Ord, and finally Banks. That poor lieutenant soiled his britches, he was so frightened."

"Wish you'd brought him back."

"Couldn't. So we just told them to strip naked—they thought we were going to shoot them—and then we sent them running with a few shots over their heads."

Syms chuckled at the memory.

He laid back, breathing hard.

Phil put a hand to his forehead. Syms was burning with fever. He looked down at Syms's right leg, hit the day before. The man had been riding with his boot off. Leaning over, Phil sniffed the bandage and suppressed a gag reflex.

Lucas was up by their side with a blanket, and the black servant was on the porch, bringing a pillow and blankets as well.

"Lieutenant, why don't you rest here awhile," Phil said softly. He looked up at the servant.

"I'll take care of him, sir," the servant said quietly.

Syms didn't argue.

"I'm played out, Phil. Just played out."

"Custer's boys will take care of you."

"Hate to lose the leg. Damn me. Sally sure did like to dance. I can't picture her marrying a cripple."

"You'll be dancing soon enough," Phil lied. "And besides, she loves you and will be honored to marry you." This time he spoke the truth, his voice choking.

Syms forced a smile.

Phil stood back up, looking at his men.

Their mounts were blown, and in this region finding new horses would be impossible. It had been picked over clean the month before.

They'd have to ride with what they had.

"Let's go," he said quietly. He'd have to find someone to push ahead, to get down to the nearest telegraph outpost and send the word of what was happening here. That might take hours.

Sadly, he looked back at his old comrade that he was leaving behind.

He pulled out his notebook, opened it, and scribbled out a quick message.

To General George Armstrong Custer,

> *As a favor to your old roommate. Please take care of my friend, Lieutenant Syms. He is an honorable soldier of the South. After the war he plans to marry my sister Sally. When all this is over, I look forward to a chance to see you again under less difficult circumstances.*

> *Yours truly,*
> *Phil Duvall*
> *Class of 1861*

He handed the note to the servant, then tore off another sheet, jotting down his report.

"Sergeant Lucas, find someone with the best horse. Have him ride to Westminster."

"Sir?"

"The telegraph station there might still be open. If Custer is driving southwest toward Frederick, they might be bypassing that place. Tell the courier to ride like hell."

Lucas took the note, walked down the line of mounted troopers, picked one out, handed up the note, and the man was off at a gallop.

There was a rattle of carbine fire at the north edge of town. He caught a glimpse of some Yankee troopers. A few rounds hummed overhead.

"Let's go," Phil shouted, mounting up and turning to look back one last time at his old friend, who weakly raised a hand in salute.

The small column turned and rode off, heading toward Frederick.

Baltimore, Maryland

August 24
6:30 P.M.

General Lee rode alone through the early evening, long shadows descending on the camps that ringed the west side of the city. The days were getting shorter, a touch of a cooling breeze was a welcome relief after a day of heat.

Campfires were flaring to life, men standing about them. There were snatches of laughter, a banjo and hornpipe playing, a few of the more energetic men dancing to the tune. The air was rich with the scent of fresh roasting meat. Each regiment had been given a bullock or a couple of pigs for dinner, and the meat had been roasting throughout the afternoon.

Several of the regiments were planning evenings of entertainment, amateur skits, song and dance presentations, a minstrel show, and a theater group from Baltimore was appearing before the boys of Scales's Division with a presentation of Shakespeare's *Julius Caesar,* starring one of the Booth family, John Wilkes, as Brutus. He wished he could attend but was pressed by other matters.

As he wove his way through the camps, men who saw him approaching lined the road, cheering, taking off caps and holding them high, officers with a flourish drawing swords to salute. A young lady, visiting one of the camps, actually stepped in front of him, blocking his path, and offered up a bouquet of flowers, which, a bit embarrassed, he took and then, once out of her sight, handed to Walter Taylor, who trailed along behind him.

He was taking his ride for several reasons. One, of course, was to be seen by the men. The second was to see them, to evaluate their spirits after the grueling efforts of the previous weeks, and the third was just to have time to think.

He could see that though the men were tired the morale of his army was as good as ever. They had known nothing but victory since Fredericksburg. After but a single day of rest their spirits were returning, though in one sense that was deceiving. He had spent most of the day reviewing with his three corps commanders the muster returns. Dozens of regimental and brigade commanders again needed to be replaced. Promotions by

the dozens would have to be written up. Many regiments were now commanded by captains, companies by sergeants. If given time, he would
most likely break down Pickett's Division and reassign the remnants to
beef up Scales, whose division he was now passing.

Scales had been out of the fight, shadowing Washington, but he had
been ordered north to Baltimore. Lee sensed that every rifle would be
needed and that division, the remnants of Pender and Pettigrew, having
sat out the last fight, would now be his vanguard when the time came to
move. Besides, the sham of threatening Washington was past.

It was Grant whom he wanted now. It all rested on that, one sharp action with Grant. Lure him into an action as decisive as Union Mills or
Gunpowder River—break him, and in breaking him, break Lincoln as
well. Finally, leave the stubborn Illinois lawyer with no choice but to accept that he could not coerce the South.

He stopped under a spread of elms canopying the road, loosening his
reins, Traveler moving to the side of the road to nibble at some tall grass
growing along the fencerow. A steady stream of traffic moved by in both
directions, a company of troops marching by, a couple of supply wagons
heading back into the city, a drover leading half a dozen cattle. Lee's staff
kept a respectful distance, whispering for those passing to let the general
have a few minutes alone, and all obeyed the request, the passing column
of infantry silently coming to present arms as they marched by.

He dismounted, going over to lean on the fence, looking out over the
encampment that spread out across the open fields outside of Baltimore.
More fires were flaring up, cheers erupting from where Scales was camped.
Most likely the acting troupe had arrived, a circle of torches being ignited
to illuminate the stage where the story of Caesar would be enacted.

He felt that the clock was now ticking. He wished for nothing more
than to give these men a few more days like this. Plenty to eat, time to
sleep as much as they wanted, to write letters home, to horseplay, to forget for a brief moment what they had been through, and to ignore what
faced them again.

An inner sense told him, though, that such would not be the case.
This was a last night of peace, a single night of peace before it would all
start again.

He bowed his head.

"Dear Lord, please guide me in the days to come," he whispered.
"Give me strength to do what is right. Guide me always to seek the honorable path and in so doing bring this terrible struggle to an end.

"For those whom I lead, dear God, and for those whom I face. I know
many will fall in the days to come. Forgive them their sins and bring them

into your loving embrace. Let friend and foe come together before your holy throne as brothers once more. Amen."

"General Lee? Forgive me, sir, for interrupting."

He looked over his shoulder. It was Walter, his hat off.

Walter was pointing toward the road that wove past the defensive earthworks of Baltimore. Coming toward them was a carriage, and he could see Judah Benjamin, Jeb Stuart, and Pete Longstreet.

"Thank you, Walter."

Lee saluted Judah as he stepped down, followed by Pete and Jeb.

The three came over to the side of the road to join him.

"I suspect, gentlemen, you bring news," Lee said.

Judah nodded and Lee could see the look in Longstreet's eyes.

"A telegram just came in from Westminster. It's troubling, sir."

"Go on."

"Sir, a report from a captain with the Third Virginia. The same boys who were covering Carlisle. He states that the Yankee infantry moving on the east side of the mountains are nothing but militia. It looks like Grant's main striking force is west of the mountains."

Lee listened in silence. He nodded, saying nothing, taking the information in.

"How reliable?" Lee asked.

"I know the captain of that troop," Jeb said. "A good man, West Point. I was slating him for promotion to a regimental command. He's done excellent scout work in the past."

"How did he get this information?"

"The first telegram just gave the general details, a second one came in a few minutes later. It stated that a patrol had encountered a column of infantry north of Gettysburg and taken prisoners. The sender declared the information to be reliable."

Lee looked over at Jeb.

"I wish we had more to go on," Lee said.

"I know, sir. I do, too. It's taking a devilish long time to get our mounts rested, reshod, and refitted. I've already detailed two regiments up to Westminster with orders to force a probe. Jones and Jenkins, minus about half their men, are moving down the B and O right now, covering that line."

"The B and O," Judah sighed, shaking his head.

"One other thing," Pete said, interrupting Judah before that conversation over the railroad started. "The report from Westminster also stated that an entire brigade, under Custer, is driving hard, is already into Taneytown, heading southwest, apparently pushing toward Frederick."

Lee turned away, going back to lean against the fence.

So it was beginning, the mask starting to slip away. It was all becoming clear now. Grant hoped to hold his attention northward until into position to sprint toward Frederick. Once in Frederick he'd close off the railroad to Harpers Ferry, to a possible crossing at Point of Rocks.

Lee looked back at Longstreet, who stood silent.

"So now we know," Lee said.

Pete merely nodded.

Lee turned his gaze on Stuart.

"I want every one of your men mounted and ready to move before dawn tomorrow."

"Sir, that will be tough to accomplish. I have thousands of men still waiting for shoes for their horses."

Lee shook his head.

"We need your cavalry moving, General Stuart."

"Yes, sir," Jeb replied.

"And then there's the railroad," Judah said.

"It didn't work out, did it?" Lee asked.

"No, sir. Garrett refused."

Lee, in an uncharacteristic gesture, slammed a balled fist against the fence rail.

"General Longstreet, any suggestions?"

"First and foremost, we must secure that bridge over the Monocacy."

"What do we have there now?"

"Just an outpost and telegraphy station."

"I want Jenkins and Jones up there by tomorrow morning to secure the crossing. General Stuart, I want you up there as well. Take a train if you can, otherwise, sir, I think you'll just have to ride."

Stuart nodded, offering no protest.

"Sir, I've been doing some checking," Judah interjected. "We face some real problems using the B and O."

"I'm not certain we really have to use the B and O," Lee said. "We've moved quickly in the past without use of rail."

"I think, sir, it's different this time," Pete said.

"How so?"

"If a fight is brewing at Frederick, and if we can get the bulk of our forces there ahead of Grant, we can bottleneck him. He'll have only one road, the National Road, to bring everything up. It'll be a race, and the railroad can help us tremendously. Fifty trains can bring up an entire division with supplies in just two hours, compared to two days of marching. Plus the men will be fresh.

"There's our artillery reserves as well. We have nearly two hundred and forty guns total. That's over forty batteries. Sixty trains can move those guns, with horses and men. Three days if we move them overland."

"The B and O has some fine locomotives," Judah announced, "capable of pulling twenty cars. It can give us a tremendous advantage."

"But it won't cooperate," Lee replied sharply.

"I've already informed Garrett we are seizing control for the duration of the campaign. I suggest, sir, tonight, that word be put out to every regiment in this army. Any man with railroading experience, especially engineers, mechanics, brakemen, report to the main depot in Baltimore."

Lee said nothing for a moment. If only he had an organized division of military railroad troops, this would not even be a bother.

He looked over at Walter and nodded in agreement. "Get the word out at once. Men to report by dawn.

"Pete, find someone to put in charge."

"Major Cruickshank."

"I thought he was in command of the pontoon bridges."

"He's a hard driver. I think he's our man."

"Promote him to brigadier general, and get him working on it. Now what about the pontoon bridges? Weren't they supposed to already be up at Frederick?"

Pete sighed and shook his head.

"They're still at the depot."

"What?"

"Sir, nearly every yard worker just sat down or took off once word came that Garrett was not cooperating. Cruickshank has apparently struck a deal with the yard boss, though, and we should be moving around midnight. But it's going to cost."

Lee looked at Judah.

"I do have some cash reserves," Judah said. "Silver coinage."

"Fine, then," Lee replied. "Have Cruickshank offer five dollars a day to any man who will come back to work. Jeb, I want you up there when the pontoon train goes forward. Take the bridge at Monocacy and hold it at all cost."

"We definitely need that bridge," Longstreet interjected. "It's not just the bridge, it's the junction just on the other side. There's a water tank there, and also a turntable."

"Aren't there other turntables along the line?"

Judah shook his head.

"I looked at the maps in Garrett's office. There's a turntable at Relay Station, just outside of here, the next one on the line is at Frederick Junction, on the west side of the Monocacy. We don't have that, and every train will have to be backed up. Also, there's a bottleneck. It's double track most of the way, but there's a thirteen-mile stretch between two tunnels, east of the Monocacy, that's single track. Everything will have to route back and forth through that."

Lee sighed. During the winter at Fredericksburg he had sweated out the movement of but half a dozen supply trains a day coming up from Richmond. But one engine breaking down meant short rations for that day. Now they were talking about moving hundreds of trains.

"Gentlemen, we are racing through too many issues at once here. Let us focus on the overall issue, and then all will derive from that."

The group around him fell silent.

"I think it is clear that General Grant will move on Frederick rather than toward Harpers Ferry and crossing into Virginia. It is clear as well that our concern to the north was nothing more than a masterful feint on his part.

"I had hoped for a few more days' rest for our army, that is now finished. Grant's intention in taking Frederick was perhaps to threaten our potential line of retreat if we had planned to withdraw, but we all know that was never our intent. We are here to stay in Maryland."

"Could we not let him come to us?" Judah asked. "He'll wear his men out; we can continue to rest and refit."

"Impossible," Longstreet replied. "Do that, let him envelope us here and reunite with the Washington garrison, and we'd be pinned in this city with no line of retreat. He could then wait us out, forcing us to attack on his terms."

Lee nodded in agreement.

"No, Mr. Secretary, it has never been the policy of this army to let our opponents choose their ground. From Harrisburg to Hagerstown and then over the National Road to Frederick is more than a hundred miles of marching. All of it in the end funneling down to one road over the Catoctin Mountains. We marched that same road last year during the Sharpsburg campaign. It's a good road but a steep climb over the South Mountains and then the Catoctins.

"No, sir, that will be a hard march. He's been on the road for three days now. I'd place the head of his column at Greencastle, perhaps lead elements as far as Hagerstown, but he is more than a day away, more likely two, from Frederick. And even then, all will have to funnel over that one road.

"If we can take advantage of the railroad, and get our army up and marching before dawn, we can have all our strength there in two days, the bulk of our army there ahead of Grant.

"Then we choose the ground and let him come at us. Lincoln is un-doubtedly pressuring him to attack, and attack us he will. We will have the better ground, and by heaven's help we will smash him."

He looked around, and even Pete nodded in agreement.

"Another battle like the ones you talk about, General Longstreet," Lee said enthusiastically, looking over at Pete. "A good defensive line, like the one we had at Union Mills, and we bleed him out."

"I hope so, sir."

"I know so," Lee said emphatically.

"Now, gentlemen, you know your orders. Walter, find Generals Hood and Beauregard and have them report to me back at my headquarters in Baltimore immediately. I want those trains moving, infantry to be on the march at dawn with five days' rations and full cartridge boxes. General Longstreet, please accompany me back to headquarters and we shall lay out the routes of march for our corps. If we can get the trains running cor-rectly, General Scales's Division will lead off by train, sparing them the march and placing them ahead of the Union cavalry.

"Gentlemen, this is the battle we have been waiting for, and with God's help this will finally end the war."

B & O Rail Yards, Baltimore

August 24
11:30 P.M.

McDougal, damn it, are we finally ready to move?"

"Yes, Major, I think so."

"It's general now, McDougal. Remember that."

"Yes, your worship," McDougal said with a grin while shifting a wad of tobacco and spitting.

Former major, now general, Cruickshank muttered a curse under his breath. A job that should have taken only three or four hours had con-sumed a day and a half. The pontoons and bridging material had been la-boriously hauled through the streets of Baltimore to the rail yard. Then there had been the nightmare of maneuvering each wagon carrying a thirty-foot-long boat up onto a flatcar. Easy enough when talking about it, but bloody chaos when turned into a reality. Each flatcar had to be backed up individually to a loading ramp, mules unhooked, then the cumber-some wagon pushed by several dozen men from the ramp onto the car. Several of them had slipped, the clearance of wagon wheel width and rail car width being only a few inches to either side, and one of the boats had been staved in when it tumbled off the car.

Once loaded, the wheels had to be chocked, cables hooked to secure the wagon in place, the single car then pulled away from the ramp and sidetracked, another flatcar hooked to a locomotive and backed into place.

Meanwhile cantankerous mules had to be forced aboard boxcars or open-sided cattle cars, kicking and braying. After hours of waiting in the heat, men then had to go into those same cars, lead the mules out to feed and water them, then lead them back in again.

If the full Baltimore and Ohio crew had been around, he knew the job would have gone off without a hitch; instead, he was primarily reliant on his own men and a hundred or so workers who had shown up just after dark, when word circulated around that each man would be given five dollars, in silver, at the end of each day's work.

That alone burned him. His boys were getting a few dollars a month in worthless Confederate scrip and that issue alone had triggered more than a few fistfights with the civilians.

McDougal, who had agreed to stay on as yard boss for twenty dollars a day, silver, watched as the first of the locomotives began to inch forward.

Jeb Stuart was aboard that train. An extra car hooked on to the end, an open cattle car now carrying half a dozen horses and the "cavalier" himself, sitting astride the siding of the car, hat off and waving a salute to Cruickshank as they passed.

"Damn show-off," Cruickshank muttered.

"He's off to war and you ain't," McDougal said. "Count yourself lucky."

"I'm stuck here now, McDougal," Cruickshank said. "I'd rather be going with my pontoons. Get the hell out of this place."

"Oh, you'll have grand fun these next few days," McDougal said cheerfully. "I figure you'll have to help organize two hundred trains or more. A snap if you know what you are doing."

"I don't, and you do," Cruickshank said coldly, looking over at McDougal. "And by God, you better do it right."

McDougal smiled.

"But, of course, Major . . . I mean, General. Of course."

Chapter Eight

C.S.A. "Stop the train, stop the damn train!"
Jeb Stuart leaned over the side of the car. Mules in the boxcar up ahead were kicking, screaming in panic. Flames shot out from under the wheels of the boxcar, streaming back.

The train whistle was shrieking, a couple of brakemen running aft, leaping from car to car, clamping down the brakes as the train skidded to a halt. As the train slowed, flames that had been trailing in the wind started to lick upward.

Jeb jumped off the car he was riding on, nearly tripping, regaining his footing and running alongside the train. The mules inside the burning car were terrified. A brakeman was by his side, helping to fling the door open, and the animals leapt out, disappearing into the darkness.

The front left journal box of the car was glowing red hot, flames licking out. The engineer of the train and the fireman came back, lugging canvas buckets which they threw on the box, steam hissing. More buckets were hauled by several soldiers, dousing the side of the railcar.

"What in hell is going on here?" Jeb roared.

"Happens all the time, General," a brakeman announced. "That's a journal box. Filled with grease to lubricate the axle of the wheel. Sometimes it just catches fire."

Another bucket was upended on the box, the water hissing.

"Open the damn thing up."

"Once it cools, we'll repack it," the engineer said.

"How long?"

"Once it cools."

"Just open the damn thing."

A brakeman with a crowbar flipped the lid of the journal box open, the engineer holding a lantern and peering in at the steaming mess.

"I'll be damned," he whispered.

"What is it?" Jeb asked.

"Packed with wood shavings and scrap metal."

"What?"

"Sorry, sir. Someone sabotaged this car. It should have caught fire twenty miles back. Was most likely smoldering and we didn't even notice it in the dark."

"You mean someone deliberately wrecked it?"

The engineer said nothing, finally nodding his head when Jeb gave him a sharp look.

"Where?"

"Don't know, sir. Most likely back in Baltimore. Should have burned miles back down the track. Lucky we got this far. We're going to have to check every single box on this train now."

"Damn all," Jeb hissed, turned away, slapping his thigh angrily.

Looking down the track he saw the headlight of the following train, hauling ten more cars loaded with the pontoon bridging. One of the brakemen was already running down the track, waving a lantern.

"How long?"

"In the dark like this?" the engineer said. "An hour or two to check all the boxes. Better check the ones on the following trains as well. Sorry, sir, but we're stopped for now."

Exasperated, Stuart looked around at his staff, who had climbed off the cattle car to witness the show.

"Mount our horses up. How far to Frederick?" he asked.

"Follow the track, another twenty miles or so to Frederick, sir."

"You wait to dawn, sir, we'll have things ready."

"I have no time, Custer isn't waiting for some train to get fixed," Stuart snapped. "Mount up. We ride to Frederick."

Two Miles North of Frederick, Maryland

August 25
5:30 A.M.

Morning mist clung to the fields flanking the road. To his right George Armstrong Custer could catch occasional glimpses of the Catoctin range, rising up nearly a thousand feet, the ridge-line golden with the glow of dawn.

It was a beautiful morning after an exhausting night. Turning in his saddle, he looked back, the column of his troopers, led by the First Michigan, were quiet, many slumped over in their saddles, nodding. Ever since they gained the pike at Emmitsburg the ride had been an easy one, a broad, open, well-paved road, and not a rebel in sight as they swept southward through the night, taking four hours for men and horses to rest before remounting two hours ago.

He could see the church spires of Frederick just ahead, rising up out of the mist, which was starting to burn off the fields, but still clung thick to the winding course of the Monocacy on his left.

A scout, a young lieutenant, came out of the mist, riding fast, reining up and grinning.

"Was just in the center of the town, sir. Not a reb in sight. Talked with some civilians. They said a reb patrol rode through about an hour or so ahead of us and turned east to head down to the Monocacy."

"How many, Schultz?"

"About a hundred or so. There was some commotion at the telegraph station there. The rebs had that occupied, and then all of them pulled out heading east."

Most likely Phil, he thought with a grin. The wounded prisoner taken at Carlisle had told him who he was facing: his old roommate from the Point. *Usually I could beat Phil in a race and that's what it is now.* He had hoped to spring on him during the night but Phil had always stayed a jump ahead.

Well, my friend, now I got you against the river. Will you turn and fight?

And part of him hoped he would not. That he would just get the hell out of the way.

"You know the way to the bridge?" Custer asked Schultz.

"Easy enough, sir. Get to the center of town and turn east. Few blocks, you'll be at the depot for the town. We can follow the track for the spur line that runs up to the center of town. If you just keep heading south through town it turns into a toll road that heads straight down to the river, a covered bridge crossing the Monocacy just south of the railroad bridge. I think that'd be the quicker path. Civilians said that's the route the rebs took."

Custer nodded, trying to picture it. He had come through here the year before with McClellan.

"I'll take the lead with the First. You go back up the line, tell Colonel Alger to take his Fifth. Once he's in the center of town, he's to pick up the tracks and come down that way to the river. Tell Colonel Gray. I remember the National Road crosses the Monocacy via a stone bridge. Have Gray send a company down to take that bridge, rest of his command to stay in reserve. Mann with the Seventh to stay in town as reserve also. I can be found at the railroad bridge."

Lieutenant Schultz set off at a gallop.

"Let's move it!" Custer shouted.

He set the pace at a quick trot, buglers passing the signal back up the column.

Out front, as always, he thrilled to the thunder behind him as his troopers picked up the pace. Guidons were fluttering as he looked back. Colonel Town, commander of the First, spurred his mount to come up by Custer's side.

"George, bit impetuous just riding straight in like this, ain't it?" Town shouted.

"No time to feel things out, Charles. Schultz is a good scout. His boys have the center of town already. But it's the bridge we want."

Cresting a low rise, they passed the last farm flanking the pike. The town was directly ahead. It was so typical of this region, the houses built close together, facing right onto the street. A scattering of civilians were out, a few were unfurling Union flags from their windows.

He thought of the story of Barbara Frietchie. Most said it was all made up, others said it was the truth, how she had hung a Union flag out the year before, when the rebels marched through on their way to Antietam. Some troops threatened to fire on the old lady and her flag until Stonewall himself came up and supposedly exclaimed, "Who touches a hair of your gray head, dies like a dog, march or . . ." He'd have to look her up afterward and find out if the old lady really did confront Stonewall.

As they approached the center of town the thunder of their arrival echoed in the canyonlike street, more and more civilians leaning out of windows, some cheering and waving, others staring in silence.

He saw Schultz's boys at the main crossroads, still mounted, carbines drawn. He slowed and shouted for the toll road. The men pointed south.

"The Fifth will follow the railroad track! I'm taking the First in on this road!"

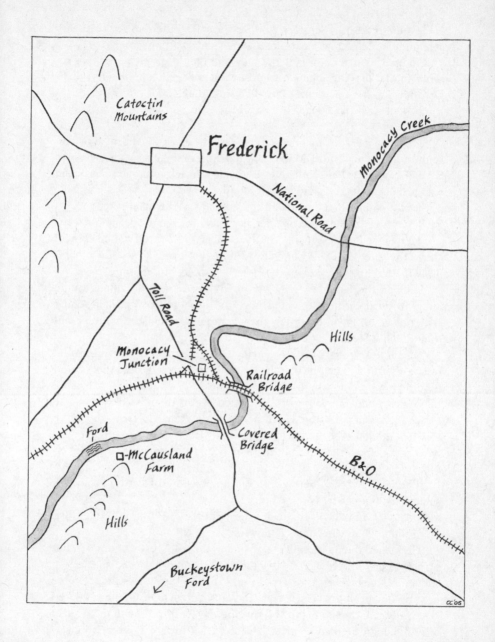

"The rebs are down at the main junction," a sergeant shouted. "Saw them not ten minutes ago."

"Guide the Fifth, Sergeant, and Seventh. Tell them to set up at that columned building that looks like a school and await my orders."

He knew that, according to the book, he should stop here with his reserve and let his lead regiments go forward and, as his professors would say, "develop the situation." Only then should he go forward.

To hell with the book! He was in the lead and would always be in the lead.

The men of the First, coming on fast, were almost up to him. He spurred his mount hard and took off, heading straight through the town. Several blocks farther south and he was again back into open fields, the road just ahead forking, and for a second he slowed.

Schultz hadn't told him about this. Which was the main pike?

The road to the left was broader, partially macadamized, and not waiting, he followed it. Less than a minute later he saw the toll station, a small shack, the gate up. The ground ahead started to slope down. It was obviously the way to the river, which was still cloaked with morning mist.

Hills on the far side were clear of fog. They were less than a mile away. Broad open fields greeted him, the usual patchwork of ripening corn, rich green shoots of winter wheat coming up, orchards, pastures, and squared-off woodlots.

No cattle or cows were out grazing. This area had been well picked over last fall and again two months ago as the armies recrossed this ground heading toward Gettysburg. Here and there fences were missing, passing troops from the previous two campaigns using them as firewood. He reined in, coming to a stop. He turned, pointing toward a farm lane to the west, shouting for the men to form into line. Troopers turned, urging their mounts on, chickens scattering and squawking as the boys galloped to either side of a farmhouse and barn.

The owner of the farm was out on the porch, red-faced and shouting something, but Custer ignored him.

"Colonel Town, you command the right flank. I'll be in the middle. Have four of your companies follow me."

He judged the fence on the east side of the road, ready to jump it, but several troopers were already dismounted, tearing down the stacked-up split rails. The owner was down by the road, shouting curses about having just rebuilt the fence. Custer just looked over at him, grinned, saluted cheerfully, and then rode through the opening, cutting around the edge of a cornfield and into an orchard. Looking back toward Frederick he saw where the men of the Fifth were coming out, riding to either side of the railroad track, going a bit slower. It'd take another ten minutes before they'd be up and deployed into line.

Turning, he gauged the distance to the river. He could see his goal now, a wooden trestle. The road he had just been on headed down to a covered bridge a few hundred yards south of the railroad crossing.

Dismount and go in carefully or rush it? He pulled out his field glasses and scanned the river bottom and could see nothing. All was cloaked in mist.

If it's only Phil down there, he most likely has only a hundred or so. But give them a little time and they could work some mischief and prepare a defense, or worse, perhaps some reinforcements are coming up.

Rush him on horseback before he has time to get ready. He cased his field glasses and drew his saber.

The men of the First were lined up, covering a front of a couple of hundred yards, pistols or carbines out of holsters, officers with sabers drawn.

He could feel that their blood was up. There was nothing like the anticipation of a mounted charge to do that to a man. The tension was building, horses sensing it as well, snorting, a few rearing up, men grasping reins tighter. Men were looking over at him wide-eyed, some grinning.

He hesitated for a second. *Go straight in, or wait for the Fifth to come in on my flank? I've got nearly three hundred men with the First. Five to ten minutes is often the difference between victory and defeat. No, this is the moment!*

"First Michigan! Forward at the trot!" He pointed toward the railroad bridge.

Monocacy Junction

August 25
6:10 A.M.

 "Typical George Custer," Captain Duvall announced, shaking his head.

With field glasses focused on George, he watched as his old friend drew his saber, pointed, and then set off, moving to the front of the advancing line.

A thousand yards, three or four minutes, and they'll be on us. He scanned the ground, so far only one regiment. What looked to be a second was just becoming visible, along the bed of the spur line leading into Frederick. Why didn't George wait for them?

Phil lowered his glasses. Perched on the roof of the depot, he had a clear view, except for the mist still gently rolling up from the river directly behind him.

He had deployed half his men to the left, about a hundred yards over, where the toll road came down to the covered bridge. There was a nice little cut there made by the railroad, about fifteen feet deep, with steep, sloping sides, a perfect entrenchment and place of concealment for his mounts. The rest of his men were in the depot, toolsheds, and outbuildings.

The depot was inside a triangle of rail track formed by the main line of the Baltimore and Ohio right after it crossed the river, the main track running west. The other two sides of the triangle were formed by the spur line that came down from the town of Frederick, branching to either side of the depot so that trains from the city could head west or east.

There were two blockhouses as well. Rude affairs, abandoned. If only he'd had a few field guns he could have held this place against anything George threw at him. One blockhouse, on the far side of the river, looked straight down on the bridge. A single Napoleon twelve-pounder in there could have swept the bridge. The other blockhouse, inside the western edge of the triangle, commanded the railroad cut and the spur line. He had placed a half dozen of his best shooters in there.

George's advancing line was down to less than a quarter mile. He could hear their bugle calls floating across the morning stillness, a beautiful sound. They were picking up speed, George a good twenty yards in front. Phil focused for a few seconds on the distant figure, hat off, golden shoulder-length hair waving in the breeze, a match for the crazy-quilt patchwork of braid on his uniform.

Phil smiled. George always did like those things, a true seeker of glory. And in his heart he prayed that none of his men now singled him out. His own boys knew they'd been friends at the Point, but still, George was a target that just begged to be shot.

Phil slid down from the roof, knocking off a few shingles, jumped to the solid awning that protected passengers waiting for a train, then climbed through an open window to the second floor. His men were hunkered down by the windows, carbines raised, waiting. Many had the new Sharps breechloading carbines, captured during the Gettysburg–Union Mills campaign, cartridges laid out on the windowsills. More than a few were grinning. George was coming straight on, mounted, in the open.

Three hundred yards, now two hundred.

The Yankee bugle call echoed the charge!

The men over in the railroad embankment to his left waited, maintaining good discipline. *Let them get close.*

A hundred yards. Damn, they were coming on fast, yelling like demons.

A solid volley rang out from his forty men. Good shots all of them, a dozen saddles emptied. The men around him in the depot opened up, enfilading fire pouring into the flank of Custer's charge.

Monocacy Junction

6:20 A.M.

"Charge!"

The bugles picked up the command, echoing across the valley, the sound all but overwhelmed by the pounding of hoofs, the high-pitched cries of men loosed from all restraint, caught up in the mad, magnificent splendor of a full-out cavalry charge. He looked back for a second at these good troopers, up off their saddles, knees braced in tight, leaning forward, holding reins with one hand, weapon in the other, crouched low over the necks of their mounts.

The first volley caught him by surprise. He felt a bullet wing past, puffs of smoke ahead.

He looked back. Several troopers had dropped, tumbling from saddles; four or five horses were down, men pitching off their mounts, tumbling end over end. And yet the momentum of the charge was now unstoppable, men and horses weaving around the fallen, riding full out, the first blow not slowing them, instead now driving them forward, weapons raised high.

"Come on, Wolverines! Come on!"

The charge swept down through open pasture and fields.

What appeared to be a ravine, perhaps a railroad cut, was straight ahead, marked by puffs of smoke.

"Come on, boys!"

He urged his mount onward, the horse moving uncomfortably, favoring its right side. He spared a quick glance down and saw where a shot had sliced its right leg, blood streaming out.

Fifty yards, now twenty-five.

Rebs stood up from the edge of the ravine, carbines lowered. He hunched down low in the saddle. Another volley. His horse just collapsed, throwing him, knocking his wind out. Troopers of the First Michigan were reining in around him, as he struggled to stand up, their pistols drawn, firing blindly at the puffs of smoke, cursing, yelling.

He judged the moment. Not too many over there, maybe not more than fifty or sixty. He stood up, feeling dizzy, looking for his saber. A trooper leaned far over from his saddle, picked it up from the ground, and tossed it to him.

"Come on! Keep pushing!'

Men, yelling wildly, rode up to the edge of the ravine, pistols out, firing left and right. Men pitched out of saddles. Some rebs were up out of the ravine, pistols drawn, emptying cylinders, tossing revolvers away and drawing sabers, swinging wildly. A mad melee erupted.

A volley erupted from his left. The railroad depot. Puffs of smoke swirling from windows, mingling with the early morning fog. A blockhouse caught his attention. Aperture for a field piece.

My God, did they have artillery here?

Saddles were emptying around him from the enfilading fire. A trooper came up to his side, leading a riderless mount.

"General, sir, might I suggest we get the hell outta here?" the sergeant shouted.

Custer remounted.

He scanned the action. The ravine was full of horses; it was hard to count them in all the confusion. A reb came up out of the ravine, raised a carbine, pointing straight at him. The sergeant next to him dropped the man with three shots from his revolver.

"General, sir!"

Custer nodded.

"Sound recall. We'll wait for the Fifth."

The bugle call sounded, the well-disciplined men of his command turned about, many glad to do so, and broke into a ragged gallop back across the field they had traversed minutes before with such confidence.

A few hundred yards out Custer looked back. More than a few rebs were up out of the ravine, shouting defiance.

He looked off to the north. The men of the Fifth were deploying from column into line.

"Let the bastards cheer," Custer announced. "We'll bag them before the hour is out, boys."

Three Miles East of Monocacy Junction

6:30 A.M.

G eneral, is that gunfire?"

Jeb Stuart reined in, stopping, the aide by his side, head cocked, listening.

Yes, it was. Distant, a soft, muffled popping, almost drowned out by the clatter of hooves behind him, men of Jenkins's Brigade riding to either side of the track in a sinuous column that stretched back for over a mile.

Damn all. What the hell was going on? If not for the damn train he'd have been in Monocacy a couple of hours ago. Looking back down the track, which after the tunnel they had ridden through was again a double line, he saw nothing but his men on horseback.

"Pick up the pace!" Stuart shouted.

Leaving the column behind he broke into a gallop, heading toward the sound of distant battle.

Monocacy Junction

6:40 A.M.

D ismount!"
George Custer, himself, remained mounted, ignoring the snapping whine of .52 Sharps carbine rounds whistling over his head. The troopers of the First, their blood up after the initial repulse, gladly followed orders, drawing carbines from saddle holsters, levering breechings open, inserting rounds, deploying out into heavy skirmish line, every fifth man detailed off to hold the reins of the four who dismounted.

He wished now for just a few guns, even a section of three-inch ordnance rifles to sweep the edge of the ravine with canister before going in. But he had traveled fast, leaving his one battery of light guns behind.

"Boys, forward at the double!" Custer shouted, "Take that damn depot!"

The men started forward on foot, running flat out. A few tumbled over before reaching a shallow ravine, pausing, hunching down, a ragged volley ringing out as they began to return fire. The more venturesome then stood up, racing forward, closing the range to a hundred yards.

The rebs, though, were in an excellent position. Phil had picked his ground well. The railroad cut was a trench offering protection, the depot, especially the log blockhouse, an impregnable position. To his left the troopers of the Fifth were doing the same, advancing dismounted, shooting, pushing up a few dozen yards, sprawling out on the ground, firing again. Scanning the depot building with field glasses he saw shards of wood explode from the side, windows shattering, a reb out in the open for a second, sprinting from a shed back to the depot, collapsing on the track from a well-aimed shot.

George pushed up, ignoring the danger, furious that his charge had been repulsed.

"Here comes Gray!" someone shouted.

George looked back. He had sent word for Gray to come up in support, and the column was coming out of the town, riding hard.

"Keep pushing them, keep pushing!"

CSA Phil Duvall raised his field glasses and saw the distant column coming out of Frederick. This time, damn it, George was doing it right. A regiment, dismounted, was coming down on his right. Custer's lead regiment, dismounted as well, was pressing on the left. The third regiment meant that well over a thousand men would be pushing in on him in a matter of minutes. At better than ten-to-one-odds he would simply be pushed back from the bridge. It was just a matter of time.

Several of the men by the windows were already down, one dead, another cursing, holding his shoulder, a third man crying, a spray of shattered glass having torn into his face.

He walked to the far side of the room and looked over at the ravine. His men were up at the lip, firing away, but he knew it was useless now to try to hold longer.

Damn all, where was Stuart? He gazed back at the railroad bridge, hoping against hope that he'd see a column crossing it even now, reinforcements coming up to hold this crucial junction.

"They're starting to deploy out, sir."

He looked back to the north. The column coming out of the town was swinging out into line, preparing to charge. They'd ride through the dismounted skirmishers and this time overrun him.

"Time to get out, boys," Phil shouted. "No bugle calls, just mount up. I'll see you on the far side of the bridge. Sergeant Lucas, get up to the ravine, tell them to bring down our horses!"

Lucas raced down the stairs.

He lingered a few seconds longer, again shifting his field glasses to George. He could tell his old friend was loving the moment. Mounted again, riding along the skirmish line, urging his men to get up, to press forward.

He certainly led a charmed life. He had seen George go down, and for a second feared he was dead, but then the man had stood up, brushed himself off, remounted, and was back in the fight.

"Your day, George," he said.

Phil ran down the stairs and out under the awning of the depot.

The men over at the ravine were disengaging, sliding down the slope, running to their horses, mounting up. It was going to be a tight race. As soon as his boys stopped shooting, George would press in.

The first of them came galloping down the track, more following, troopers leading the empty mounts of the men who had been holding the depot. The telegraphy crew from Frederick were already riding for the bridge.

Lucas brought up Phil's horse, and he climbed into the saddle. He didn't need to give any orders now, the boys knew where to go and just wanted to skedaddle before the Yankees closed in. They raced for the bridge. Fortunately, the wooden structure, wide enough for two tracks, had planking laid to either side between the crossties, otherwise they'd have had to cross dismounted, leading nervous mounts.

His men galloped across, Phil slowing as he reached the bridge. Bullets whined about him. Yankees were up to the ravine, tumbling down its side; others were running toward the depot. He caught a glimpse of George, raised a hand in salute, and, turning, urged his mount across the bridge at a gallop.

Was that Phil? George wondered, quickly uncasing his field glasses and focusing them on the bridge. It was hard to tell with the smoke and the mist still rising off the river.

The way he kept his saddle, the wave—it did indeed look like his old friend.

He edged his mount around the ravine, leaning back in his saddle as he finally went down the slope and out onto the track. His men, breathing hard, grinning, faces besmirched with powder, sweating, were down into the ravine, running toward the depot.

Half a dozen rebs lay along the lip of the railroad cut, dead. A dozen more, wounded, were down by the track, several of his men already there helping them.

"What regiment are you?" Custer asked.

"Third Virginia," one of them announced, looking up at him defiantly.

"Captain Duvall?"

"That's our man. What of it?" the reb said.

George nodded and then saluted.

"My compliments, boys. You put up a good fight."

So it was Phil.

"Any trains come through here since yesterday?"

"How the hell would I know. We just got here ahead of you Yankees."

George rode up to the depot, looking around. If the rebs had moved trains up here, there would have been more men defending this place than an outpost patrol he'd been dogging since yesterday. *By damn, we got here ahead of 'em.*

The depot itself was pockmarked with bullet holes. He studied the bridge that Phil had just ridden across, the far end obscured by smoke and fog. The bridge, a rough affair, looked like something military railroad crews would have thrown up after an earlier bridge was destroyed. He drew closer, and saw down in the river twisted lengths of cable, iron girders. Obviously the wreckage of what had been here, most likely before the Antietam campaign.

Already his mind was working. Hold it or destroy it?

His gaze swept back over the depot. Blockhouse, a turntable, the triangle of track. *If the rebs get hold of this they can easily turn trains around. With a double-track system, in a matter of hours they can bring up a hundred trains or more out of Baltimore, move an entire army.*

He had no idea where Grant was at this moment. Maybe ten miles off, maybe fifty. *Destroy the bridge, perhaps it will get Grant's dander up, but then again, we can replace it in a day or two. No, I came here to block the rebs from moving their pontoon bridge and by God that's what I'll do.*

"General, sir."

He looked over his shoulder. Lieutenant Schultz was riding up.

"Sir, Colonel Gray's compliments. His boys are deployed, but he is shifting two companies over to the stone bridge, the one for the National Road. Says that reb skirmishers are on the other side. Colonel Mann is in place as reserves."

George nodded, saying nothing.

Skirmishers on the main road heading back to Baltimore.

"Infantry or cavalry?"

"Sir, he didn't say."

Most likely cavalry, George thought. *I've got a thousand men with me. It has to be cavalry coming up. It is surprising they're not already here.*

That decided it.

"Lieutenant Schultz, do we have any ammunition reserves, raw powder?"

"Sir?"

"Just that, barrels of powder?"

He already knew the answer, but felt he had to think out loud at this moment.

"Sir, just what our men our carrying with us. We left the supply wagons behind."

"Get back up to Frederick, see if any shops have blasting powder. Check the depot here as well."

"Sir, I doubt that we'll find any. Both armies have been through here twice in the last year."

George nodded in agreement. Four or five barrels under a main trestle would do the trick, but to find that many now might take hours.

"We've got to destroy that bridge, Lieutenant."

Trying to burn it might sound easy but he knew it wouldn't be. He'd have to get at least a couple of cords of kindling wood. There was enough of that in a wood rick next to the depot, but hauling it out there, placing it under a trestle, with Phil's boys popping away from the other side at less than a hundred yards would be damn difficult.

Schultz looked over at the bridge and seemed lost in thought.

The lieutenant suddenly grinned.

"Sir, there are two locomotives in the depot up in Frederick, both with passenger cars and boxcars. Maybe we could use those."

Custer grinned, too.

"I always enjoyed the sight of a good train wreck. Get on it, Lieutenant."

East Bank, Monocacy Creek

7:00 A.M.

Jeb Stuart reined in, an exhausted, begrimed captain coming up to him on foot and saluting.

"Capt. Phil Duvall, sir, Third Virginia."

"What is going on here?" Stuart asked.

"Sir, didn't you get the telegraph message we sent out an hour ago?"

"I've been riding up here, Captain," Jeb said, exasperated. "No, I did not get the telegraph message."

"Sir, we've been withdrawing in front of Custer's Brigade since yesterday, from Hanover down to here. We tried to hold the depot on the other side of the river, but he pushed us back about twenty minutes ago. He has at least three regiments over there."

Jeb looked toward the bridge, the far side obscured by fog.

"How many men over there?"

"Like I said, sir, a brigade. I'd guess at a thousand or so."

"You couldn't hold?"

Phil pointed to the exhausted men, still mounted, who were gathered behind him.

"Sir, we put up a fight, kept them back for a half hour or so, but if we'd stayed five minutes longer, sir," he sighed, "well, we'd either be dead or prisoners now."

Jeb contained his exasperation. It was obvious that Duvall's men had put up a fight: At least a quarter of them were nursing wounds, while a score of horses without riders was testimony to those left behind.

"Where can I maneuver here?" Jeb asked.

"Sir, down there to the south, about two hundred yards downstream you got a covered bridge, double wide. To the north about two miles or so, I'm told there's a stone bridge. I suspect there's a number of fords here as well."

Stuart nodded.

"Jenkins will be up within the half hour. Jones is right behind him. Duvall, you keep your men posted here."

Phil wearily nodded and saluted.

"Yes, sir."

Stuart, realizing this man had done all that was possible, drew a deep breath then leaned over, offering his hand.

"You did good, Captain, real good. You did all you could. Now it's our turn. Give me an hour and we'll have that bridge back!"

Chapter Nine

Headquarters, Army of the Susquehanna
Near Greencastle, Pennsylvania

August 25
7:10 A.M.

"Excuse me, sir, I thought you should know. It's started."

Grant looked up at an excited Phil Sheridan standing at the entryway of his tent.

"Frederick?"

"Yes, sir. It was actually a reb dispatch, sent to Baltimore, but the line was open, and it was also transmitted up the B and O telegraph line to Harpers Ferry and also to Hagerstown. We had a Union man at the station there. He just dispatched it up to us here."

"What did it say?"

"It was a rebel outpost reporting from Frederick. Said they were abandoning their post and would attempt to hold the railroad bridge at Monocacy. Brigade-strength Union cavalry, believed to be Custer, in pursuit."

Grant sat back in his chair, rubbing his brow. The beginnings of a migraine were upon him, the tingling in the fingertips, a slight ringing in his ears. Why now?

He looked down at the map spread upon his desk.

"McPherson?"

"This morning's report, he's into Hagerstown, head of his column about five miles beyond."

"Burnside?"

"Lagging a bit. McPherson pushed his men until midnight, Burnside had them fall out after dark. He's between here and Greencastle."

"I'm going up."

"Sir?"

"You have a problem with that, Sheridan?"

"Well, sir. I'm sort of a fifth wheel here. I could go forward for you."

Grant studied him and yet again was glad of the decision to bring this man east. Sheridan wanted to go forward because he smelled a fight coming and wanted to be in the thick of it.

"No, Phil, you stay here for now. Dispatches and such are being routed to this position. Send a message back up the line for Ord and Banks and Hunt with the artillery to pick up the pace. I'm going forward. By the end of the day I should be into Frederick. I'm taking Ely Parker and my staff with me."

He sat back for a moment, studying the map. It was beginning to look like a meeting engagement. He had hoped to be able to secure the Catoctin Pass, perhaps even move all four of his corps down into the plains in front of Frederick, before Lee caught wind of his maneuver. If now, after the triggering of this fight by Custer, Lee came up quickly, he could block the pass and in so doing secure a defensive barrier that would allow him to maneuver as he pleased, either to retreat across the Potomac or shift the bulk of his force back on Washington. That thought was chilling, especially given the agreement he and Lincoln had arrived at only yesterday.

Send a countermand to Lincoln, suggesting a change? It'd take at least a day for that to catch up. It would show, as well, a loss of nerve.

No, we have to take the pass first and hold it.

"Keep them moving, Phil, and then report to me in Frederick by the end of the day."

Headquarters, Army of Northern Virginia
Baltimore, Maryland

7:10 A.M.

C.S.A **G**eneral Lee, there's action at Frederick."

Walter had allowed him to sleep hours past his usual time of rising. For that Lee was grateful, having been up half the night with Longstreet and Judah Benjamin analyzing the reports that increasingly confirmed that the so-called army coming down from the north was a sham, and that Grant was pulling a wide flanking march, either to cross the Potomac into Virginia or come out of the mountains at Frederick or Point of Rocks down on the Potomac.

Lee was already half-dressed, a servant helping him with his boots, when Taylor knocked on the door. He reached up, taking the dispatch Taylor was holding.

He scanned the message from the outpost at Frederick and put it down on his bed.

"Has General Stuart arrived there yet? What about the pontoon train?"

"Sir, a report came in about four this morning that the trains carrying the pontoon bridge were sabotaged. Wheels on the cars were not greased prior to leaving the depot and several caught on fire twenty miles east of Frederick. General Stuart got off the train and went on by horseback."

"This is disturbing," Lee said softly. "I thought we would have that position secured by now."

"Stuart's last report, sent by telegraph from about ten miles east of Frederick, a place called New Market, said he was riding up fast, the brigades of Jenkins and Jones were moving to secure the junction and hoped to secure the railroad bridge and the National Road bridge upon his arrival. He has two brigades of cavalry, compared to Custer's one light brigade."

"What trains are readily available down at the depot?"

"We have a convoy of fifteen trains forming up now, sir. Scales's Division is loading up even now. General Longstreet rousted his corps out three hours ago, and they are already marching west."

"But that will take two days for them to arrive."

"Yes, sir. But we are forming a second convoy of twenty trains to move by midmorning with Johnson's boys loading up."

"Good, Stonewall Division, excellent," Lee whispered.

He stood up, leaning over the map. It was becoming clear now. Grant meant to move over the mountains into the central Maryland plains at Frederick.

Lee smiled slightly as he contemplated that. *Grant will only have one road to do his maneuver, while I'll have the railroad, the main pike of the National Road, and numerous secondary roads.*

We get into position ahead of him, it will be the classic position for destroying an opponent, with him feeding troops in piecemeal while we are already in place . . . if we can get there first.

"Walter, get down to the rail yard. I want a train ready to take me up as soon as possible. Pass word to Generals Longstreet and Beauregard to keep their men moving west. The railroad will move up Hood's Corps and our artillery, then once that is done will start shuttling back to pick up the infantry."

"Sir, I'm concerned about this sabotage problem. It stopped our pontoon trains cold this morning. A few more acts like that could paralyze our movements."

"Tell that man Longstreet appointed . . ."

"Cruickshank," Walter prompted.

"Tell him to make sure every car, every engine, is inspected before departure. If there is a Yankee spy or agents working in that rail yard, men not in uniform, they are to be dealt with swiftly and harshly as spies and saboteurs."

He hated to say that, it went against his nature, but at this moment half a dozen provocateurs could wreck the entire movement of his army.

Walter saluted and left the room.

Putting on his jacket, Lee gazed once more at the map. So it was beginning. He'd have liked to have had two or three more days to rest and refit his men, but the Lord had willed differently. So perhaps this was now the moment after all. One more swift victory, to drive Grant back, and surely Lincoln would be forced to negotiate or collapse.

Monocacy Junction

7:30 A.M.

George Armstrong Custer crawled up on to the roof of the depot, standing up, using one of the two chimneys as a brace. Balanced precariously, he took out his field glasses and scanned the opposite bank.

A column of rebel troopers were coming up along the track that clung to the side of a hill on the other side. Men were dismounting, pulling out carbines, horses then being led back. He saw guidons of at least two regiments, hard to tell which.

He braced himself, leaning field glasses on top of the chimney. A bullet zipped by, another smacked the chimney in front of him.

There! He caught a glimpse of him and smiled. It was Jeb, Jeb Stuart over there, plumed hat, gold braid, a group of men standing about his horse as he pointed, the men saluting and running off.

So I've got Jeb on me. How many men? A brigade? No, not Jeb. He'd come on with everything he had, two brigades, maybe three, but it will take time for that column to come up the rail track. He turned to look north. He couldn't see the stone bridge of the National Road, but the morning was still, the last wisps of fog burning off the stream, and it was impossible to miss the plumes of dust to the north. *More rebels coming that way?*

Infantry? No, he doubted that. They had obviously caught the rebs by surprise here. It would be cavalry first.

Another bullet slapped a shingle by his foot, bits of wood flying up.

He looked back to the rail bridge. Reb skirmishers were on the other side, puffs of smoke. His study of the bridge confirmed his first impression. It was a temporary affair, made of wood that had been soaked with pitch and tar, smeared with grease and oil from passing trains. If not for the rebs on the other side, he'd have it aflame within an hour, but old Jeb, of course, made that all but impossible.

Another puff of smoke, another bullet zipping dangerously close.

The rebs on the far side of the bridge were hunkered down behind support beams, a few sprawled on their stomachs on the tracks, others down in brush along the stream embankment. The volume of fire was beginning to pick up as the first of their reinforcements sprinted along the track, spreading out, finding cover. For an instant he thought he could catch a glimpse of Phil, waving his arm, standing up, pointing out a position, then quickly ducking down as a volley rang out from his own side.

He looked to his left, at the covered bridge for the toll road. On the far side reb skirmishers were already deploying. The bridge was double-wide. A column would take casualties but could indeed storm it if he didn't act quickly.

Taking a deep breath, he slid down the roof, leapt to the awning, and ducked through a window, bullets pocking the wall around him.

"Sir, I think that was rather bold of you," a sergeant quipped, looking up at Custer as he landed in the room, "and frankly, sir, damn stupid."

Custer gazed at him for a second then broke into a grin.

A bullet slammed through the room, passing clean through the plank siding and plaster interior.

Cursing, the sergeant knelt, aimed through the window where Custer had just entered, and fired back.

Custer looked around the room. A dead reb lay in the corner, two more of them, wounded, sitting by the body. The face of one of the rebs was a smear of blood, eyes swollen shut.

He ran down the stairs and out behind the depot. Men of the Fifth Michigan were swarming across the spur line, dropping behind stacks of railroad ties, woodpiles, anything that could offer protection.

Colonel Town was already waiting for him, as was Alger of the Fifth and Colonel Gray of the Sixth. He had already sent orders back to Colonel Mann to take his entire command to block the National Road bridge.

"It's going to get hot," Custer announced. "I saw Jeb Stuart over there. A brigade is coming up. I suspect he'll have another one or two up shortly."

"Let 'em come," Town growled. "We got this side now and we'll hold it."

Custer grinned, then shook his head.

"If I knew we had infantry coming up, I wouldn't worry, but we don't know. Colonel Town, get a couple of your troopers, ones with the best mounts. Send them west on the National Road toward Hagerstown. Have them report to whoever is at the head of the infantry column they should find. Tell them we're holding the west bank of the Monocacy and will attempt to burn the bridge, but we need support."

"That thing? We can burn that in no time," Town said, leaning around the side of the depot for a few seconds to point at the bridge. A bullet whacked into the clapboard siding beside his face.

Custer laughed softly when he pulled back.

"See what I mean? We have to do it under fire, and it's going to get worse. We just can't send men out there with kindling and coal oil, they'll get mowed down."

The three colonels around him nodded in agreement.

"Mann is to hold the north flank. Alger, you hold the center here with your Fifth. I doubt if they'll try and rush the bridge, but they might get desperate and try it. Gray, for the moment you'll be in reserve. Move your boys back to that woodlot behind us, keep them mounted, though, and ready to move quick to where I need them. Town, your boys get the right flank. And I want that covered bridge burned as well before they try and get a column across. It should be easier than burning the rail bridge.

"I sent some men up to Frederick. There's a couple of locomotives there. Check with your own men, anybody who has railroading experience, detail them off to go back to town and help out. We're going to take those two trains, get them on the bridge, and blow them. That should take things down."

"Should be fun," Town said.

"Unless you're on the train," Gray replied.

Monocacy Creek

7:45 A.M.

CSA "Jenkins, Jones, we cannot let the Yankees burn that bridge!"

Jeb Stuart, with his two brigade commanders, stood pointing out the window of the top floor of the mill just south of the railroad track and north of the toll road on the east bank of the Monocacy.

The volume of carbine fire was rapidly increasing as the first of Jenkins's men, of the Fourteenth Virginia, dismounted and pushed down to the river's edge. Behind them the men of the Sixteenth and Seventeenth were dismounting as well, forming up to go in.

"We keep it under fire," Jenkins offered, "and there is no way in hell they can get out on to it and set it ablaze."

"From what I've heard so far about this Custer, he's impetuous," Jeb said. "Remember, he did fight his way out after Union Mills. He might try anything."

Jeb walked to the other side of the top floor of the mill and looked over at the covered bridge just south of the railroad. With his field glasses he could see Yankees deployed across the front of that bridge and along the riverbank. He studied them intently and saw that some of them were bringing up armloads of wood, kindling. So they were going to burn that first. Good move, he'd have done the same.

"Jenkins, think you can storm that bridge?" Jeb asked.

Jenkins looked out the window, studying the double-spanned bridge for a long moment.

"It's over a hundred yards long, sir. We try to charge that, we'll have four men across inside the bridge, but one volley and our boys will get tangled up."

"I want that bridge," Jeb said. "We take it, we flank Custer, then drive him back from the depot."

"Sir, do it on horseback, I don't know. Two or three wounded horses inside a covered bridge . . ." His voice trailed off. They were all experienced enough to know that inside a covered bridge a few downed horses could stop an entire charge.

"Your boys of the Thirty-fourth, are they still mounted?"

"Coming up now, sir."

Jeb hesitated, then looked over reassuringly at Jenkins.

"We've got to try. Send them in. The Yankees will have that bridge afire in a few more minutes. Send in the Thirty-fourth. First company mounted, the rest on foot behind them. With luck your first company can rush it, then the dismounted men secure it."

Jenkins nodded, but his features were grim, as if Jeb had just given a death order.

"There must be fords along this river. It's not that deep."

"Send out patrols to look for them, but I want that bridge now. We fail in that, well, then try to find the fords. Get the boys of the Thirty-fourth ready. Have the rest of your men sweep the rail bridge with carbine fire. How long before some artillery comes up?"

"Jackson with the Charlottesville Battery is still an hour or more off, sir," Jenkins said.

"Send a courier back and tell them to move it, to move it! The next hour could be the decisive hour."

He turned on Jones.

"You have the north flank. If you think you can rush the National Road bridge, do it now! Probe for fords. Secure your left flank to Jenkins's right."

"What kind of reinforcements can we expect?" Jones asked.

"Fitz Lee's boys are back at Sykesville. I've pulled them off shadowing the north and I'm bringing them here, but it will be midday or later before they come up. Scales's infantry division was supposedly loading up in Baltimore after midnight. They should be up any time now."

"Artillery with them?" Jenkins asked. "A battalion of artillery could smother those damn Yankees and push them back."

"A couple more batteries. Combined with the Charlottesville boys and your light battery, we can pound the hell out of them, but that is still hours away. I want that covered bridge before then, and once we take it, we flank Custer and secure the rail bridge."

He pointed toward the distant crest of the Catoctin Range, four miles away, standing out dark blue in the morning light.

"I'm not sure when, but today most likely, Grant and his infantry will come pouring out of that pass up there. He's only got one road to traverse those mountains. We take the ridge and block the road, we got the bastard bottled, no mistake. General Lee wants us to secure that pass and then the Yankees will bleed themselves white trying to get over it. I want that ridge today, and not just the railroad. Now move it!"

Baltimore and Ohio Rail Yard

8:00 A.M.

"God damn it, McDougal, now what!" Cruickshank roared.

A billowing vent of steam was blowing out from the lead locomotive of the convoy. The engineer was out of his cab, stamping his feet, cursing, looking around, bewildered.

McDougal, cursing, left Cruickshank's side and ran up to the engine, stopping at the edge of the plume of scalding steam.

"Stephens, you stupid son of a bitch!" McDougal roared. "What happened?"

The engineer looked back at him and then simply shrugged his shoulders, but his eyes were focused nervously on Cruickshank, who was up by McDougal's side.

"I don't know, sir. I started to feed in steam to get moving and a line just blew wide open."

"Well, shut the damn thing down," McDougal screamed, trying to be heard above the high-pitched whistling roar of the venting steam.

Stephens climbed back into the cabin, worked a valve, and the roar drifted down to a whisper. McDougal cautiously approached the locomotive, shaking his head, and then pointed toward the steam line that fed into the left-side cylinder of the locomotive.

"Busted, sir," McDougal sighed. "Just blown wide open. It'll have to be replaced."

"How long?"

"Four hours at least."

"Too many things have broken, McDougal."

"You accusing me of somethin', sir?"

Cruickshank raised his arms, then slapped his sides in exasperation. He looked back down the line. Fifteen trains were fully loaded with an entire division of infantry, men piled so thick on the cars that many were riding on the cowcatchers of the locomotives, the wood tenders, and atop the boxcars.

The locomotive that had just broken down was the lead one in line.

"Get this wreck pushed out of the way," Cruickshank said.

"How?"

"You idiot, the locomotive behind it."

"Too much weight sir."

"Then damn you, disconnect it from its own train, push this wreck to a side track, and clear the line. I need this convoy moving now. General Lee will be here any minute; I need an express for him as well.

"Just move 'em," Cruickshank shouted.

"What about the broken-down train with the pontoon bridge on the single-track section?" McDougal asked.

Cruickshank stepped closer to McDougal. They were of the same height and build and anyone watching would have expected a brawl to break out.

"I'm raising your pay to fifty dollars a day in silver," Cruickshank said coldly. "Telegraph up the line, make sure those pontoon trains are clear of the single track. This division needs to move up now. But so help me, McDougal, I'll string you up myself if I think you're playing double with me."

"Me, sir, at fifty dollars a day?" McDougal laughed. "Like hell, sir. I'll take care of you."

The Toll Road on Monocacy Creek

8:15 A.M.

Colonel Witcher of the Thirty-fourth Virginia nervously turned and looked back at his men. First company was mounted, guidon at the front. Behind them, the rest of his command was dismounted, carbines and pistols out, the men in a column stretching up the road for fifty yards.

He lowered his head, whispering a silent prayer, then drew his saber and pointed toward the bridge, its roof just visible through the trees.

"Bugler, sound the charge!"

Custer was just riding down to the covered bridge when he heard the high clarion notes of the charge. The west end of the bridge was beginning to smoke. Someone had found a can of coal oil in a nearby farmhouse, cut it open with a knife, and was hurling the contents on to the shingled siding. Troopers were sprinting up, tossing loads of kindling against the side of the bridge, then dodging for cover. Three men were already down, one of them dead by the side of the bridge.

George urged his mount to a gallop, riding down the length of track, reining in where the toll road crossed the track and looked straight down the tunnel-like length of the bridge, the interior already coiling with smoke, the sides licked by flames.

He saw the head of the charging column appear at the far end.

"Someone get back to Gray," he shouted. "He's in reserve back in the woodlot a few hundred yards north of here. I need him here now!"

 The entry to the bridge was directly ahead, and Witcher caught a glimpse of a sign WALK YOUR HORSES WHEN CROSS-ING.

He leaned into the neck of his mount. Once into the dark tunnel of the bridge the noise was stunning, pounding hooves, echoes doubling and redoubling off the roof, the walls, the floor of the bridge, men shouting. A Yankee trooper, hunched down by a support beam at midpoint, was out from concealment, running, the far end obscured by smoke, licks of flame. No gunfire yet.

Thirty seconds, dear God, thirty seconds and we're across and back into the open.

The charge thundered forward, men shouting, a few shots, men caught in the madness of the charge, firing pistols blindly.

Saber out, he pointed the way, leaning forward, caught in the madness of a charge across a bridge, yelling insanely.

Halfway across, fifty yards, ten seconds, five seconds, and we're out.

The smoke was blinding, he couldn't see, his mount nervous, slowing at the sight of the flames licking the walls on the far side. He spurred her viciously; the horse lunged forward.

Almost out of the smoke.

And then he saw it. A double file of Yankee troopers, standing, carbines lowered. A suddenly flash, and then just a quiet stillness and a slipping away.

The lead horses of the charge collapsed not ten yards away, riders thrown, men and horses screaming, tangling up. The third and fourth ranks of the column colliding with the horses that were already down, more men falling, a lone horse jumping the tangle, the rider superbly keeping his saddle, crashing into the double file of the volley line, slashing left and right with saber, two men staggering back, screaming, one just collapsing, a headless corpse.

"Reload! Reload and fire!" Custer roared.

Men were levering open their carbines, slamming in rounds, cocking pieces, firing blindly into the smoke. Another horse came out, riderless, then two more, men still holding their saddles, one with pistol out, firing, emptying his cylinder, then pitching backward off his horse.

The bridge echoed with a roaring shout. Through an eddy in the smoke George saw a packed column of dismounted troopers racing forward.

More of his men from the First were up on their feet, running up, forming a volley line three ranks deep, a lieutenant shouting for volley fire.

The men reloaded, waiting the extra few seconds. Several pitched over even as they waited.

"Present! Fire!"

The interior of the covered bridge was now all smoke and confusion. Men screaming, cursing, a horse with a broken leg staggering out in blind panic, knocking its way through the volley line, a trooper coming up to its side and putting a bullet in its head, the animal collapsing and the same trooper then dropping down behind it, reloading his carbine.

George had his revolver out, drawn, cocked, waiting... and then the charge hit with full fury, two hundred dismounted cavalry of Virginians swarming forward, pistols, carbines, sabers out. His thin volley line began to step back, men dropping carbines, drawing revolvers, blazing away.

George felt something slap his left arm, numbing it. He pivoted on his mount, saw a rebel trooper with pistol raised, cocking his revolver, and George dropped him with two shots. The rebels were out of the bridge, beginning to swarm outward, pushing the men of the First back, but as they emerged from the bridge they stepped into a firestorm. Troopers hunkered down in the ravine that Duvall's men had held but two hours ago now turned and poured in a withering fire. Few rebs made it more than a dozen feet before collapsing.

George caught a glimpse of men still inside the bridge, tearing off their jackets, using them to beat out the flames that were licking up the sides of the bridge. The one side, soaked with the can of coal oil, was now burning hotly, but it could still be stopped.

"Come on, boys!" Custer shouted. "Take it back!"

Men from the ravine flanking the bridge stormed forward, and a mad bloody melee ensued at close range. Troopers firing into each other's faces from not five feet away, men down on the ground grabbing, kicking, punching.

He heard a bugle call from behind him, looked back, and saw Gray riding down hard, a ragged line of mounted troopers behind him. George stood in his stirrups and waved, cheering them on.

The mounted column slammed into the melee. His boys on horseback firing left and right, pushing their way through the confused struggle . . . and the rebs began to fall back, one or two at first, and then within seconds the entire command, turning and running.

Gray, caught in the madness of the moment, pushed into the flaming bridge, saber drawn, slashing to either side, his mount jumping the tangle of dead and dying horses. The column thundered down the bridge, pursuing the retreating rebs across its entire length.

Custer fell in with the column, his mount screaming with fear as they pushed through the flames licking up the side of the bridge and over the blood-soaked bodies. Dozens of Union troopers were inside the bridge, yelling, cursing, firing blindly. Far ahead he could see that Gray had reached the far side in pursuit, and then was blocked seconds later by a volley that dropped half a dozen men around him.

"Sound recall!" Custer roared.

But he did not need to give the order. Already Gray had turned about, the turn difficult in the tight confusion of the bridge, more men dropping.

The survivors of Gray's countercharge emerged, Gray leading the way, hat gone, blood streaming down the side of his face. The men were panting, some cursing, others filled with the wide-eyed look of troopers who had known the moment, the thrill of a charge, the driving of their enemies.

"Good work, Gray. Now get your boys back in reserve!"

Gray gasping for air, nodded, saluted, and shouted for the men of the regiment to follow him back.

All around Custer was chaos. Half a hundred or more men were down, dead, wounded, screaming, their screams mingled with the pitiful screams of the horses and those of the wounded trapped on the burning bridge.

The bridge was now ablaze. Flames licking along the eaves, gradually spreading toward the center of the span. In short order it would spread to the underpinnings, the support beams, the dry wooden floor. For the moment his right flank was secure.

He caught the eye of a sergeant and motioned him over.

"Sergeant, get a flag of truce. Tell Jeb Stuart my compliments, but I'm asking for a fifteen-minute truce on this bridge to get the wounded and dead off before they burn."

The screams of the horses and men caught in the flames were horrific.

"And for God's sake, shoot those poor animals. They deserve better than to die like that."

J eb Stuart lowered his field glasses, shaking his head.

He had spotted the Yankee trooper waving a white flag on the far side of the bridge and sent word down to honor it. The bridge was rapidly disappearing in flames, smoke billowing hundreds of feet into the air, and it was obvious they were trying to rescue as many of the wounded as possible.

Damn all. For a brief instant he thought Witcher had actually carried the bridge. Now it was going to take time, scouting, finding a ford that could be taken without too much loss.

Nothing yet at the railroad bridge, just heavy skirmishing fire back and forth. Word had just come that the light battery of the Charlottesville Artillery was even now arriving, and he had sent a courier back to guide it into place next to the blockhouse that looked down on the bridge. The Yankees had no artillery yet to counter with, a carbine was next to useless much beyond three hundred yards, and with the guns he could dominate the position. For starters, they could flatten the depot.

Frederick

9:10 A.M.

Lieutenant Schultz, what the hell is holding you up?"

Schultz looked up in surprise. It was Custer, left arm hanging limp, blood dripping from his fingertips.

"General, you're hurt."

"Don't bother me with that now. I want to know what the hell is going on with these locomotives!"

"Sir. The boilers were dead cold. We had to get them fired up. It's taking time to build up a good head of steam."

"How long?"

"Another hour at least."

Even as they spoke Custer turned in his saddle to look back toward the river where a different sound had just mingled in with the cacophony of battle—artillery fire.

A couple of dozen men were gathered around the locomotives, cavalry troopers, one of them a corporal, obviously having taken charge, shouting orders. Custer rode up to him, and the corporal saluted.

"Who are you?"

"Tyler, sir. Rick Tyler, First Michigan."

"Why are you here?"

"Was an engineer for three years before the war. Heard the word you needed railroad men up here, sir, so came up to help out."

"You're in charge then, Tyler, and I'm promoting you to sergeant. Will make you a lieutenant if you pull this off. Now why is it taking so damn long?"

"It's a cold start, sir. Got to get into the firebox, build a fire from scratch, start shoveling wood in. Then heat the water to a boil, build up steam pressure. It ain't healthy, but I'm throwing some coal oil in to get it going faster."

"Coal oil?"

"We're in luck, sir. Found five hundred gallons or more of it, sir, in that warehouse over there. We're going to put it all in the passenger cars pulled by the trains. Also found some turpentine, barrels of grease as well. That will really let go."

"Any blasting powder?"

"None to be found, sir. We've been asking around, but folks here say it was all cleaned out by the armies passing through. Also, sir, found a third locomotive in that engine shed over there. It's an old teakettle, twenty years old at least, but we're firing that one up as well."

"At least an hour, then?" Custer asked, and even as he spoke he fought down the light-headedness overtaking him.

"Sir, to be honest, two hours, but I'll push it. We need a damn good head of steam if you want to do it right."

"Why's that?"

"Well, sir. Figure once we get the train on the bridge I can smash down the safety valves. The fire in the passenger cars, they'll burn, but it will burn up, sir, not down. It might damage the bridge but they can still fix it. I seen that happen once with a string of boxcars just outside of Detroit that caught fire on a bridge. The bridge was back in service the next day. We get the boiler to explode, though, and, well, sir, that'll be a helluva show."

"Good work," Custer said softly.

"General?"

He looked over to Schultz, a regimental surgeon from the Fifth who was by his side.

"Let me look at that arm."

"Not now."

"Sir, looks like you are about to keel over," the surgeon replied. "Just give me five minutes, sir."

Custer nodded reluctantly, and with a grimace dismounted, sitting down on a bench under the awning of the station. Schultz helped Custer take his uniform jacket off, Custer cursing softly. The doctor bent over, examining the entry wound a couple of inches below his left elbow, an assistant by his side handing him scissors, which he used to cut the shirt back.

"This is gonna hurt, General," the doctor whispered, and then there was a flood of pain as the doctor slipped his finger into the wound.

He thought he was about to faint. The doctor drew his finger out.

"Got some bad news for you, sir. The bone's broken. Sir, I think you're going to lose that arm."

"Like hell I am," Custer hissed.

"Sir, I can have you under in five minutes; it'll be over in ten. From the way you're bleeding I think an artery is severed in there. You'll bleed out if I don't take it off now."

"I've got a battle to run, damn you."

"Not today, sir. You'll be back in action in a month, sir, but today is finished for you," the doctor said gently.

"Tie it off."

"What do you mean, sir?"

"Just that," Custer snapped. "Get a tourniquet on it. That will stop the bleeding, won't it?"

"For a while, but why?"

"Because I've got to get back to my command."

"Sir, I put a tourniquet on that arm, it'll be above the elbow, and you'll lose that, too, if it stays on too long."

"Just do it, goddamn you. Get a tourniquet on it. You can hack at me once this is over."

The doctor stared at him intently for a moment, then reluctantly nodded, actually patting him lightly on the shoulder. He motioned to his assistant, who set to work, taking a tourniquet out of the doctor's medical bag, wrapping it around the general's arm just above the elbow, then clamping it down so tight that Custer struggled not to cry out.

The flow of blood slowed and then nearly stopped.

The assistant rigged up an arm sling, helped put it on the general, who sat back, pallid.

"Promise, once this is over, you'll come straight back to me," the doctor said.

"Sure," Custer said, forcing a weak smile, looking up at him.

"I can give you a little morphine for the pain."

"Addle my mind. Just a good shot of whiskey will do."

Several of the troopers who had gathered round to watch reached into pockets and haversacks, pulling out bottles. Custer grinned, took one of the bottles, knocked down a good long drink, and then rose shakily to his feet.

He had not commanded these men long, and he knew some resented him and his meteoric rise to command. But by God this was his day now.

It was almost worth losing an arm for. A week from now the illustrated papers would be plastered with images of him, arm in sling, leading a charge, bridge blowing up in the background. It could very well mean a second star.

"Help me up."

Again more eager hands reached out, helping him slip his jacket on, then up into the saddle.

"Get a report down to me, Tyler, once you're ready to roll. Until then I am going to keep Stuart and his rebs off the bridges."

"Yes, sir."

He turned and galloped off.

"You know I used to hate that son of a bitch," one of the troopers said, "too much glory seeking, but, damn me, he sure has the stomach for a good fight."

One Mile North of Boonsborough, Maryland

9:45 A.M.

Riding as he always did at the head of his column Gen. James McPherson, commander of Seventeenth Corps, Army of the Susquehanna, saw the swirl of dust ahead, two troopers riding hard as they came out of the village. They had slowed for an instant as they approached his advance line of mounted skirmishers, several of the skirmishers then falling in by their side to lead them in.

McPherson urged his own mount to a quick trot and forged ahead to meet them at the edge of town. The troopers, their mounts snorting, lathered with sweat, reined in, saluting, the men gasping for breath.

"General McPherson?"

"You have him."

"Thank God, sir," one of the troopers gasped. "Afraid we'd kill our mounts if we pushed them much farther."

"What's your report?"

"Sir, we're with General Custer's Brigade. He's in one hell of a fight just east of Frederick, facing two or more brigades of rebel cavalry."

"What is Custer doing there?" McPherson asked. Though he had no details of what was supposed to be happening east of the Catoctins, his information was that the cavalry was to slowly push south, acting as a deceptive screen to keep Lee's attention focused north until his corps gained the pass and were into Frederick.

"Sir, yesterday," a trooper gasped, "the general got word the rebs were moving a pontoon train through Frederick. He decided to get there first and block the bridge over Monocacy Creek. We got there just minutes ahead of a whole swarm of rebs. Sir, he's asking for infantry support."

"The railroad bridge there—what is it made of?"

"Wood, sir. But the creek's only a hundred yards wide or so. Doubt if we can get a fire burning on it; anybody steps out on it is bound to get shot."

"Artillery?"

"None, sir, we left it behind in the dash down to Frederick."

"Which rebel brigades?"

"Don't know, sir, but I can tell you, as I was riding up over the pass through the Catoctins, I looked back. That whole riverbank a mile wide was just swarming with them. You could see a lot of dust in the distance, maybe infantry, maybe more cavalry. I couldn't tell."

McPherson nodded, still studying the map. Twelve miles at least to Frederick. He looked east. The high expanse of the South Mountain range was only a couple of miles ahead, a tough climb.

"The road ahead?"

"It's the National Road, sir, well macadamized. Tough on the horses, though. Mine was going lame. About six miles across the next valley and then up over the Catoctin Pass."

Custer had certainly triggered something. *If Lee takes the bridges, then blocks the pass, Grant's plan unravels.*

He didn't hesitate any longer with his decision. He turned and looked back. His massive column, fifteen thousand men, was visible for miles back across the valley, dust swirling up, morning light glinting off shouldered rifles, white canvas tops of ammunition wagons and ambulances standing out.

They'd been marching since before dawn, having already covered nearly ten miles. He was planning for them to break in another hour to cook up their midday meals.

He looked back at the troopers. "If I get you fresh mounts, can you guide me?"

The two hesitated, then nodded.

McPherson turned to his staff.

"Pass the word to every regimental commander. I want the men pressed. Three miles to the hour, ten-minute break to the hour and not a minute more. No straggling, provost guards to keep them moving until they drop on their faces. I want this column moving and moving hard. Round up my headquarters guard detail and find fresh mounts for these two boys. I'm going up to Frederick. I expect to see this column crossing the Catoctin Pass no later than midafternoon. Do you understand me?"

"Sir, it looks like hard pushing getting over those mountains," one of his men said, pointing toward the looming South Mountain range directly ahead.

"Get all wagons off the road, just infantry. The wagons can fall in behind them after the corps has passed. Ambulances, tell the surgeons to pack what they can on a horse and then fall in riding with the column. Pull ammunition out of the wagons, get the extra rounds passed out to the men as they march by, eighty, a hundred rounds to each man if possible. Send word back to General Grant describing everything you've just heard here. I don't have time to write it out. Tell him I'm going ahead to Frederick."

He pointed at one of his young, eager lieutenants.

"You, get back up the road to Burnside. Inform him of what you've heard here and my decision to force-march on Frederick. Tell him I hope he will press forward with all possible speed to my assistance."

The two couriers from Custer were off their mounts, one of them patting the animal's neck with affection, pouring water into his hat, emptying his canteen, the horse eagerly gulping down the few drops.

Troopers from the headquarters company came up, a lieutenant detailing two men off to trade horses. The cavalryman from Custer's Brigade was reluctant to leave his mount, handing over the reins.

"Her name is Ginger. She's a good horse, carried me through three charges. I'll come back for her after this is over."

The trooper receiving the horse nodded, the two understanding each other and their love for their mounts. There was a pause and they shook hands.

"William Bradley, I'll take good care of her. Mine is Sarah, she's got a tender mouth and hates spurs, so go easy on her."

Bradley gently led the horse over to the side of the road where it could crop some grass while he took its saddle off.

McPherson saw the exchange and could not help but smile. The two men trading horses were actually not much more than boys, their mounts beloved pets, companions.

He looked to the mountains ahead. *So close and yet so far,* he thought, but it was not of the fight ahead he was thinking. Who he thought of now was beyond the imposing range, little more than fifty miles away, in Baltimore.

If not for this rebel invasion of Maryland I'd be married now. Grant had promised him, once Vicksburg fell, he could have a furlough to go to Baltimore to marry Miss Emily Hoffman. And then the rebels took Baltimore, and not a word from her since.

Ironically, he knew her parents were delighted. They were devout se-
cessionists and at the start of the war had forbidden their marriage.

So close, he thought. *Perhaps we can end this war as Grant said we would,
and then I'll ride into Baltimore and, parents or not, Emily and I will marry.*

Custer's troopers finished their exchange of mounts and saddled up,
coming over to his side, disrupting his thoughts.

McPherson motioned to one of his staff, who pulled out a flask, handing it to the two troopers.

The one gladly took it, draining it half off, the second shook his head.
"I'm a temperance man," he said.

"Good for you, son," McPherson replied. "Now let's go see what your
General Custer has started."

Monocacy Junction

11:00 A.M.

The depot was burning, the pounding of the last hour from
the four guns arrayed on the opposite bank having torn it
to shreds and then finally ignited it. The last of the troopers within
poured out of the building, running and dodging as another shell
screamed in, detonating on the track of the main line, ballast and shrapnel
spraying.

George Custer sat behind the blockhouse just west of the depot, feeling light-headed, his anxious staff gathered round.

Mann was still holding the National Road bridge but had just reported that a second rebel battery was deploying on the far side, and
could expect to engage at any moment. Also, it appeared that more rebs
were coming up and already across the ford between him and the railroad
bridge. Word had just come back from Town that several companies of
rebs were across the river to the south as well, at a place called McCausland's Ford. Town already had a picket line out and, for the moment, was
holding them, but more troopers, a regiment or more, could be seen on
the opposite bank, heading in that direction.

"Gray, you detach half your men, send them to back up to Town,"
George said.

Gray nodded to one of his staff, who galloped off. Seconds later a shell
nicked the side of the blockhouse, bounded off, then exploded on the far
side of the track, the group hunkering down.

"Sir, maybe it's time we get out of here," Gray offered. "We're being flanked on both sides. They got two batteries. I just had a rider come down from Frederick. He was up in a church steeple and said he saw plumes of smoke, from trains approaching. My God, if they have infantry on those trains, they'll force the bridge regardless of loss. By then we'll be cut off from retreat as well."

"We hold," Custer said coolly.

"Sir, we did our best," Gray countered. We can still get out, pull back to the top of the Catoctins behind us."

He pointed to the mountain range now standing out boldly under a late morning sun. "There's only one road. We can block it all day. We get cut off and wiped out here, the rebs will have the bridge and the pass, too."

"What good is holding the pass if Lee keeps this bridge, gets his pontoons across, and then escapes?"

"Escape, sir? It's time we thought about escaping. Besides, the men are damn near out of ammunition. If infantry are coming up, what are we supposed to do, throw rocks at them?"

Custer shook his head, feeling so weak he couldn't respond. He looked up at Gray.

"May I suggest, sir, you're seriously injured, perhaps you should get back to the surgeon."

"And have you take command and order a withdrawal?" Custer snapped angrily.

Another shell slammed into the blockhouse, the building shaking from the impact, the men still inside cursing.

Their argument was cut short by the distant cry of a steam whistle and Custer looked up expectantly. For a few seconds he wasn't sure of the direction the sound came from. Could the rebel reinforcements already be coming up? A second whistle sounded and he struggled to his feet.

"We are going to blow this bridge, then we'll get out," Custer announced. "Get my horse!"

CSA Jeb Stuart shifted his field glasses. It was hard to see with the smoke that billowed up in the still summer air, but then he saw it, two trains, coming out of Frederick.

What is going on?

He watched them intently, and then the realization hit.

"Tell Captain Jackson with the battery, I want his guns to hit those trains before they reach the bridge. Order the Fourteenth onto the bridge now."

His staff looked at him, confused by the suicidal order. Only minutes before, Jeb had been exuberant, the river had been forded at two locations, he was funneling men across even now, and in another hour they'd have the depot.

"Those trains!" Jeb shouted. "They'll blow them on the bridge. Move it!"

Every step of his horse was agony to him, but George kept his saddle, galloping up the length of track toward Frederick. There was a sharp curve ahead, a small white clapboard schoolhouse to one side. He saw the smoke of the lead locomotive; it wasn't moving fast but it was coming on, rounding the curve, the locomotive not pulling anything other than its tender.

George slowed. He saw Lieutenant Schultz on the cowcatcher, the excited lieutenant leaping off as the train skidded to a stop.

The smoke of the second locomotive was several hundred yards back.

"We got a plan, sir!" Schultz cried.

"Where's the cars loaded with coal oil?"

"That's the second train, sir."

"Where's Tyler?"

"He's piloting the second train. He sent me ahead, but we got to talk quick, sir."

"The third train?"

"Another ten minutes or so before its steam is up."

"I don't understand," Custer said, again feeling light-headed.

Schultz quickly outlined the details, the idea registering with George, who in spite of his pain grinned.

"Do it!"

Schultz ran up to the cab of the locomotive waving his arms.

The venting of steam stopped, pressure built up, smoke billowed from the smokestack, and, finally, the engine began to inch forward. As it slipped past Custer the engineer and two firemen on board leapt out.

The locomotive continued, unpiloted, down the track, and for a second George was hit with a deep fear. He had never thought to pass the order to make sure the switches had been set properly. He could only pray that someone down at the burning depot knew what to do.

He turned about and started to ride back down the track. To his left he saw puffs of smoke. Men, his men, on horseback, pulling back along a road, reb skirmishers pressing them.

The next engine came around the bend, pulling a passenger car and boxcar. It was picking up speed as it thundered past him. Sergeant—hopefully soon-to-be lieutenant—Tyler leaned out and waved.

George loosened his reins, spurring his mount. The pain forgotten for the moment, he galloped down the track toward the depot, riding just behind the train.

C.S.A. Phil Duvall looked around anxiously at his men. Over half his command was down after five long hours of fighting. Men were tearing open the cartridge boxes of the dead and wounded, trying to load back up. Wide-eyed, he gazed over at the colonel of the Fourteenth, who was breathing hard, gulping.

The man was scared. *Hell, who wouldn't be?*

"Alright boys," the colonel cried. "Let's go!"

The colonel stood up and then stepped out right to the middle of the bridge, standing between the two tracks, saber out, pointing.

There was a hesitation and he looked back.

"Come on, you bastards!" he shouted. "Don't let it be said that the Fourteenth is filled with cowards!"

Men stood up and began to run forward, hunched low, hugging the sides of the bridge, dashing from one support beam to the next.

Phil looked around at his own small command that the colonel of the Fourteenth had "volunteered" into this mad charge. He caught Sergeant Lucas's eyes, the man looking at him as if to say, "Do we really have to do this?"

"Come on, boys," Phil said, swallowing hard. "Let's go."

He stood up and ran forward. There was no rebel yell this time. The situation was too grim for that. It would be a mad dash into a blaze of fire erupting from the other side.

They reached the middle of the bridge, several men already down, one tumbling off the side of the bridge into the stream. Others were dropping, crumpling; some were slowing, returning fire.

There was the discordant hum of an artillery shell, followed by three more soaring overhead, but he could not see where they landed.

And then he heard it coming. Looking up, he saw a locomotive, near to derailing it seemed, coming through the switch from the spur line to Frederick and on to the main track. It was thundering straight toward him on the eastbound side.

He jumped back, flattening himself against a trestle beam, the engine roaring by. He caught a quick glimpse of the cab. No one was on board.

What the hell is going on?

The engine raced across the bridge, the temporary structure shaking and rattling with its passage. All the men in the charge stopped for a second, looking back as the train cleared the bridge and then disappeared around the bend.

"Here comes another!" someone shouted.

Phil looked back to the west, the smoke of the passing train making it difficult to see.

Another locomotive was coming off the spur line on to the main track, this one beginning to slow down. Sparks were shooting out from the wheels as it began to brake.

"Get it!" someone screamed.

And instantly dozens of shots rang out, sparks flying off the brass and iron siding of the locomotive. To his absolute amazement he saw three Yankees aboard the locomotive, one of them now swinging a heavy sledgehammer, as if smashing something. Phil raised his revolver and fired it, emptying all six rounds. The man staggered but swung again. From out of the passenger car several Yankees emerged, jumping down. One of them made a dash for the side of the bridge as if to jump off, but he was shot before reaching the railing.

From inside the passenger car he could see flames erupting, blowing out the windows, a popping sound, like muffled explosions within, each pop setting off more flames.

Phil stepped up to the side of the locomotive and pointed his empty revolver at the man with the sledgehammer.

"Make a move and I'll blow your damn head off," he threatened.

The man looked at him, grinned, and dropped the sledgehammer, putting one hand up in the air, his other arm hanging limp.

"Get down!"

"You're damn right I'm getting down," the Yankee said, reaching for the railing by the steps and then leaping off. He hit the bridge flooring and cursed, going over on his side.

"Reb, give me a hand up."

"Why?"

Already carbine fire from the far side of the bridge had resumed. Torn, Phil felt he should go forward and still try to capture the other side.

"I'll tell you a secret, reb."

"And that is?"

"This son of a bitch is going to blow up in a few minutes, and there isn't a damn thing you can do now to stop it. I've smashed up the works good and proper, and that boiler is getting set to let go."

Phil looked around at his men. The way ahead was already almost impossible to traverse; the passenger car was burning fiercely, flames like blowtorches blasting out of the windows, which were shattering from the heat.

The Yankee was half up to his feet, looking at him wide-eyed, his features pale.

"You want to live, reb, get off this bridge *now!*"

Phil reached down and pulled the man roughly to his feet.

"Pull back!" he roared. "Get off the bridge!"

His men needed no urging. They had had enough of this fight.

Shoving his prisoner along, Phil broke into a run, the two crossing the final feet back off the bridge and tumbling down into a culvert.

The Yankee grunted as he hit the ground next to Phil and then, to Phil's amazement, the Yankee reached into his pocket, pulled out a bottle, and uncorked it.

"You first, reb."

Phil nodded and took the drink. A minute ago he figured he was a dead man, and for the moment was damn grateful to still be alive. He realized that if this damn fool had not come along with his train, he'd have been forced to continue in that bloody charge. Many of the men of the Fourteenth were now cut off by the burning passenger car, some daring the flames, crouched down low, running back, others just giving up and jumping off the bridge.

"What's going to happen?" Phil asked.

"You just watch," the Yankee said, taking the bottle back and gulping down at least half a pint in three or four hard swallows. "But stay down low."

Peeking up over the side of the culvert Phil now saw a third locomotive appear, a small switch engine. It looked like an antique from twenty years ago, but it was moving fast, men jumping off as it rounded through the switch on the spur line. It thundered on to the bridge, artillery shells detonating to either side of it.

The switch engine came onto the bridge, still building speed, and plowed into the train ahead of it. The boxcar at the rear of the second train collapsed, and an instant later exploded into a fireball of flame as hundreds of gallons of coal oil sprayed out. The boxcar then telescoped into the passenger car, the burning car bursting asunder, spilling out rivers of flaming oil on to the bridge. The switching engine upended, tipping over, crashing through a trestle railing, careening off the bridge with a roar. It plunged into the river below, tearing out the side of the bridge, ripping up track, an explosion of steam and smoke erupting as it hit the river.

"I'll be damned," Phil whispered, standing up.

"Get down, reb!" the Yankee shouted, reaching out with his good arm to pull him down.

The second locomotive had lurched forward half a dozen feet from the impact, breaking the rail, tipping over slightly.

"About ready," the Yankee said. "Now stay down!"

There was a thunderclap and Phil could not resist peeking over the edge of the culvert. He felt a wash of heat and steam, the boiler of the locomotive erupting. Debris soared heavenward: part of a drive wheel, the smokestack, nearly intact, hunks of metal, flaming coals that looked like meteors or mortar shells fired at night.

He could feel the ground shudder. The bridge itself seemed to lurch, almost as if it had jumped from its foundation, and then settled back down. Wooden beams collapsed, spraying fire across most of the structure.

On both sides, everyone stopped shooting. Like schoolboys they stood up to watch the destruction, some even shouting excitedly.

"Down, reb!"

The Yankee pulled him back into the culvert, curling up as he did so. A hunk of red-hot metal, part of the boiler, hit the side of the culvert and then bounced over them, spraying Phil with a shower of boiling hot water so that he cursed and slapped at his face.

The echo of the explosion rumbled across the valley.

George Armstrong Custer, still mounted, watched, mesmerized by the spreading cloud of debris. He could barely keep his saddle now, and perhaps, if not already injured, he would have been more alert and seen it coming, the expanding explosion, shards of iron, wood, part of a train axle spinning end over end, the axle killing his mount and tearing him out of the saddle.

A Mile East of Monocacy

11:10 A.M.

The train lurched even as a fireman leapt atop the tender and down to the door of the passenger car.

"Out, get out!" he screamed.

Lee, half dozing, opened his eyes, men looking up at the wide-eyed fireman.

"We're gonna wreck. Jump for it!"

Their train was slowing, skidding, the locomotive brakes shrieking as if they were about to be torn apart.

Walter leaned out the window to look and then turned on Lee, grabbing him by the shoulder, hauling him physically out of his seat and pushing him back to the rear door, the rest of the staff now following him. The train was still moving at ten miles an hour or more. Lee reached the last step and hesitated.

"Jump, sir! Jump!"

Lee leapt off, hitting the ground hard, rolling, Walter coming down by his side. Seconds later Hotchkiss was on the ground twenty feet away. More men piled out.

Lee sat up, confused, actually feeling a bit humiliated, and undignified by this sudden action. Then he saw it. Coming down the track, straight at them, was a locomotive, moving frightfully fast.

Walter grabbed Lee by the shoulder, pulling him up and away from the track.

The firemen and engineer were the last to leap, hitting the ground on their feet, and began to run up the sloping embankment away from the train.

The locomotive coming toward them appeared to be slowing down but still it was coming on at a good thirty miles an hour or more . . . when it collided head-on with their train, both boilers exploding, debris soaring heavenward. The passenger car they were on disintegrated, and then actually slid backward, its shattered remnants rolling into the ditch Lee had landed in.

Stunned, he looked about, oblivious to the debris showering down even as Walter protectively stood at his side, looking up, watching for danger.

Fire and steam boiled across the track, the two locomotives seemingly mated in a single tangled pile of scrap metal, both tracks torn up and mangled by the collision.

Lee looked back. Fortunately, the head of the convoy bearing Scales's Division was skidding to a stop, a good hundred yards back from the wreck.

"What in heaven's name was that?" Hotchkiss whispered, coming up to Lee's side, brushing himself off.

"Did all the men get out?" Lee asked.

Walter looked around.

"I think so, sir."

There was a voice inside him that whispered that he never should have thought of using the railroads to move his men. It was a strength of the Yankees, but sometimes also a weakness, since a single derailment could tie up movement for days. He looked back at the trains bearing Scales and his men.

"Get them dismounted," he said. "Traveler is back on the second or third train. Bring him up to me. I'm riding forward."

He walked up the line to look at the wreckage, shielding his face from the heat of the fire. One of the men had indeed not gotten out, the fireman who had leapt to their car to give the warning, thereby saving Lee's life. The man had apparently been caught between the passenger car and the tender, his body nearly torn in two.

He knelt by his side. Fortunately, the poor man was already dead. He whispered a prayer and then stood up. Someone with Scales had already thought to bring Traveler forward, and Lee mounted up.

"I'm going forward, gentlemen. Get Scales up as quick as possible," he said quietly, and, edging around the wreckage, he pushed on toward Monocacy.

Monocacy Junction

11:50 A.M.

Custer knew he was dying. It wasn't the arm that got him. It was the hunk of red-hot metal, bursting from the explosion, that had shattered his legs, killing his horse as well. Several of his men had tenderly carried him back behind the depot and into the blockhouse.

He chuckled. *Hell of a way to die. Hope the artists make it look good.*

The rebs were now closing in from all sides. He had ordered Gray and Mann to try to get out, to get up to the Catoctin Pass and hold it till Grant arrived.

The bridge was still standing, but barely. The north side was collapsed between the second and fourth piers, the south side a twisted jumble of torn-up track, smoldering wood. A scattering of shots still echoed, now a circle of fire as the rebs who had forded the river to the north and south closed in.

Alger had not made it out. Shot in the stomach, bent double but still game, he raised his revolver to fire at the rebs coming down the main track from the west.

The ring closed in tighter. The rebs flanking him now circled the higher ground around the blockhouse, firing volley after volley into the gun ports. The inside of the blockhouse was a shambles, a shell having pierced a gun port, striking down a dozen men within.

Numbed, George looked around. *Damn rotten place to die,* he thought. *Out in the open, after a damn good charge. That's how I wanted it, Custer's Last Charge. Not inside this shambles.*

"Cease fire," he whispered.

Alger looked over at him.

"Cease fire," George said again.

Alger nodded, looked around for something white, finally tearing off the bloody shirt of a dead trooper, putting it on the point of his sword, and sticking it out a port.

The gunfire outside slacked and then stilled.

"Put your guns down, boys," George said softly.

The begrimed men around him said nothing.

"You done good. You just might have given Grant the time he needs. No shame in surrender after what we did."

"You Yanks, come on outta there."

Four men picked up the makeshift litter, made out of a blanket, and carried George, blinking, into the sunlight. They set him down against the blockhouse after he asked to be able to sit up.

Directly ahead the railroad bridge was still burning. To his right the remnants of the covered bridge had already collapsed, hissing and steaming into the creek. He had certainly made a fine job of destruction here this morning.

Dozens of his men were being rounded up, hands over their heads, being herded to the far side of the depot, which had just collapsed in on itself.

A thin line of rebel troopers were now coming across the railroad bridge on foot, edging their way across over broken beams, twisted track, barely able to negotiate the collapsed section except for a single stringer that had somehow survived.

"George, how are you?"

He felt a hand slip into his.

"Phil?"

"It's me, George."

"Think I'm dying, Phil."

Phil hesitated.

"You are, George."

A blanket had been placed across George's legs. He looked down and saw part of a leg sticking out at an impossible angle, other leg gone nearly at the hip. *So damn stupid, killed by an exploding train.*

"How are you, sir?"

It was hard to see.

"Who is it?"

"Corporal Tyler, sir. You said I'd make lieutenant if I blew up the bridge."

"I did, didn't I. What are you doing here, Tyler?"

"He's my prisoner, George," Phil said. "A brave man. Figure he saved my life. I'll see he gets taken care of, and will sign a statement of your promoting him if you wish."

George smiled, no longer able to speak.

"Hell of a fight, George. You certainly put a twist into us. You always wanted glory," Phil said, his voice suddenly choking. "Well, you got it, my friend."

But he was already slipping away, to visions of other places, and, of course, of glory.

Chapter Ten

CSA **F**rustrated, President Jefferson Davis tossed the latest dispatches on his desk. It was turning into another hot day, and slipping off his coat he walked about the room, hands behind his back.

Something was brewing, that was clearly evident, but what he could not tell. The latest word from General Lee was dated from yesterday morning, indicating that Grant had indeed crossed the Susquehanna, that he appeared to be coming straight south toward Baltimore, and that Lee was preparing to engage.

He could sense the difficulty Lee was facing. The *Richmond Examiner* was still hailing the great triumph at Gunpowder Falls, predicting now that Washington would fall within the week and the war would be won.

His own experience, though, whispered to him that it would not be that easy. Lee's dispatch indicated they had sustained over eight thousand casualties, many of regimental and brigade rank. His leadership ranks were sorely depleted and the Army of Northern Virginia had always relied on its midlevel officers to give it a speed and flexibility the Union army did not seem capable of matching. The battle had been fought in hundred-degree heat. Of course, he'd prefer to rest and refit before seeking action yet again. Grant had disrupted that.

The disturbing part was all the other news. In the pile of dispatches was a report, taken from the telegraph line at Harpers Ferry, sent over to Winchester and from there to Richmond, with the information from an outpost that a Union cavalry brigade had occupied Frederick. Another report had come in from a scout, who rode down from Greencastle during the night to Winchester, claiming that all of Grant's army was in the Cumberland Valley, heading straight to the Shenandoah Valley.

Did Lee know this?

The news from the west was of equal concern. Bragg had lost Chattanooga without a fight, pulled back, and yesterday turned at a place called Chickamauga, where Sherman had fought him to a standstill, Bragg complaining that had he been properly reinforced with but one more corps he could have destroyed Sherman. Bragg now claimed he might have to retreat as far as Atlanta if he did not receive sufficient reinforcements. He had already dispatched Joe Johnston's small force to Bragg, but sensed that would not help much. If anything, those two would quickly turn on each other.

Unless Bragg could somehow turn the tables on Sherman, Atlanta might be threatened in another month.

But if Lee could indeed destroy Grant, then take Washington as ordered, what Sherman did in the West would be moot. Lincoln's coalition would fall apart, and whether it was Lincoln or there was a coup and a new president was in place, the North would agree to peace terms. Word had yet to come back from France as well, but after the recent great victories in Maryland, he fully expected the French now to be in the fight within a month, putting yet more pressure on Lincoln.

The problem still remained, though: There were no more reserves. Governor Vance of North Carolina was supposedly holding back ten thousand militia, claiming they were state-controlled and needed for coastal defense. Other governors were doing the same. There were simply no more reinforcements to send to Lee.

He sat back down, picked up the copy of the *Examiner,* and again read the supposed details of the victory at Gunpowder River. For the moment, that was all that he could do.

The White House

Noon

G eneral Hancock, sir."
      Lincoln stood up from behind his desk and came to
      the door to greet the general, who leaned shakily on a cane
while trying to offer a salute.

Lincoln reached out, took him by the arm, and led him over to the
sofa in his office. Hancock smiled, moving slowly, and sat down.

His features were pale. He was obviously in pain and had lost weight,
a bit of a grayish hue to his complexion. At first look, Lincoln regretted
the decision to order him down here. It was clearly evident the man had
come straight from his bed in Philadelphia to be here.

"Your wound, sir?" Lincoln asked. "How is it?"

"Mr. President, if you are asking if it prevents me from doing my duty,
then the answer is, I am doing fine."

Lincoln smiled at that reply, his first doubt receding a bit.

"Personally though, sir, and forgive the language, it hurts like hell."

"I can imagine," the president responded sympathetically. Curiosity
got the better of him. "Is it true they pulled a tenpenny nail out of you?"

Winfield smiled weakly.

"Have it as a keepsake back home. That and a few other things pulled
out of me, but the wound is healing, sir."

Lincoln looked down at the man's lap and noticed a bulge where a pad
and bandage were wrapped around Hancock's upper thigh underneath his
trousers. The wound was most likely still open and not yet properly healed.

"Either the rebs are getting short of standard canister ammunition or
the nail came from the saddle," Hancock said.

"General, forgive me, but I must be blunt with you, sir," Lincoln
replied, leaning over and gently patting Hancock on the knee. "Do you
feel fit to take field command?"

"Yes, sir. Of course, sir."

Lincoln looked straight into his eyes.

"How will you ride a horse, sir?"

Hancock hesitated.

"Well, sir, old Dick Ewell used a carriage. Both Grant and Lee did,
too, after taking bad spills from their mounts. If that is the only con-
straint regarding your concerns, please dismiss them, sir. I want a command, and if given it, I will command." Hancock's voice deepened as he
said "will."

He paused for a few seconds, looking off, past Lincoln.

"Especially after what they did to my boys of the Second Corps. I owe it to them to do everything possible to make sure our cause succeeds."

There was a cold edge to his voice. This man carried an anger, a bitterness, for what had happened to a command that all knew he loved.

Hancock looked back at Lincoln.

"Sir, at Union Mills, my corps was destroyed in a futile charge. I could have accepted that, even those who died, God rest them"—his voice came near to breaking—"could have accepted that if we had won. Sir, we could have won. I could see it just before I got hit. If all of Sixth Corps and Third Corps had gone in after my boys, we'd have taken that ridge and shattered Lee."

Hancock lowered his head, saying no more, as if lost in a nightmare.

Lincoln still wasn't sure, though, as he watched Hancock. The man could barely walk, even though he sensed his soul was afire to get back.

"Sir, it's been nearly eight weeks since I was wounded," Hancock whispered. "I survived it, I'm healing. I have to get back into this fight."

"The pain, though?"

"Yes, sir, there's some."

"Are you taking anything for that?" Lincoln asked, again being blunt.

"I did, sir. Morphine. I remember hearing how Jackson once said he didn't drink because he found he liked it too much."

Hancock chuckled softly.

"Well, sir, it was the same for me. I stopped it a month ago, right after the doctor finally probed and found the nail, draining the wound. No, sir, no concern there. My mind is clear, and I want back into this fight."

There was a knock at the door and Lincoln turned, a bit surprised. He had just come back to the White House, arriving in a shuttered carriage from the Naval Yard. The carriage had to force its way through a huge crowd gathered at the gate, and when he got out, the reaction was mixed: some cheered, others openly booed.

When he heard that Hancock was already at the White House, waiting to see him, he had left word they were not to be interrupted. After spending a few brief minutes with Mary and Tad, he had come to his office and asked for Hancock to be escorted in.

The door opened, it was Elihu Washburne, and Lincoln relaxed.

"Mr. President, thank God you are back."

"Just returned an hour ago," Lincoln said, standing up. "I was going to come over to your office immediately, but our good General Hancock was waiting to see me."

Hancock, as if to show his strength, stood up smoothly, a slight grimace wrinkling his face as he came to attention and saluted Elihu, who came over and shook the general's hand.

"You are well, sir?" Elihu asked.

Hancock chuckled softly. "The president and I were just discussing that, sir. Well enough to command is the right answer, I think."

"How were things with Grant?" Elihu asked, looking over at Lincoln.

"Splendid," and he briefly described his journey there, what he had observed, and his return.

"Not so good here," Elihu said after listening patiently.

"How so?"

"Stanton for one. It will come out in the papers this evening that he is calling for Congress to reconvene and begin impeachment proceedings. Says that his removal was illegal. He's already filed charges about my orders not to let him into his old office, claims we've illegally seized personal property of his."

Elihu shook his head.

"I fired Halleck from his staff position, a couple of dozen others. All of them are howling for blood, and the papers are picking it up. They're arguing I have no authority to do so since I've yet to be officially confirmed by Congress as secretary of war."

"To be expected," Lincoln said. "I can stand the heat if you can, Elihu. You did what I hoped you would do."

"There's worse, sir."

"Go on."

"There are rumors floating that one or two others in the cabinet might side with Stanton, saying that you have lost the war and repeatedly exceeded your constitutional authority. Your authorizing me to act with the authority of the secretary of war without proper confirmation by Congress being an example."

"Who?"

Elihu looked over at Hancock.

"Gentlemen, if you wish me to withdraw." Hancock said.

Lincoln shook his head.

"What Secretary Washburne is now talking about, General, will take weeks before anything happens," Lincoln said coldly. "Long before the Congress can do anything, the war will have been decided. That is why your being here is so important. We need your help to ensure the war is decided in our favor."

He walked away from the two for a moment, then turned back.

"Weeks before they can crawl out and do anything. Let them howl. Let them try and fiddle while Rome burns. I don't care, I tell you." His voice was filled with a cold anger. "My concern is of the moment, here, now, what we can do within the next two weeks before those howlers have any chance to act."

"Still, sir, eventually it will happen, and they'll come for your blood," Elihu said.

"I don't care now," Lincoln snapped angrily. "Let them impeach me. If we win, I don't care what comes next. I'll have done my job as I believe the Founding Fathers would have wanted it done.

"And if we lose"—he sighed deeply—"it won't matter."

He lowered his head, and his two companions were silent.

Lincoln walked over to a map pegged to the wall, motioning for the two to follow him.

He studied it intently for a moment, then turned to Hancock and smiled.

"General Hancock. You are my man. You are to take command of the garrison of Washington. I am relieving Heintzelman today. He's a good officer but not up to what General Grant and I want done. We both agreed that you, sir, were the man to see it through."

"Sir?" There was obviously a tone of disappointment in Hancock's voice.

"Is anything wrong?"

"A garrison command, sir. I hoped I'd be returning to the field."

Lincoln smiled.

Near Boonesborough, Maryland

August 25
Noon

General Burnside, why are these men resting?" Grant snapped, riding up to where Burnside and his staff were gathered against the side of a church in the center of town. Several were sipping tin cups of coffee, others standing about as enlisted men worked a cooking fire, frying up some fresh cuts of pork, the slaughtered animal hanging from a nearby tree.

Burnside, obviously flustered by this sudden appearance of the commanding general, came to attention.

Grant glared down at him, breathing hard, his mount snorting and blowing. More of his staff were coming up behind him.

"Sir, it is noonday. I thought I could get better marching out of them this afternoon if they were fed a good meal."

"Did you not receive the dispatch from General McPherson?" Grant asked sharply. "I most certainly did, and it requested that you press forward with all possible speed."

"Sir, I am indeed doing that," Burnside said quietly, "but you can only ask so much of men's legs when their stomachs are empty."

"How far ahead is McPherson?"

"Sir, I'm not sure."

Grant lowered his head, an obscenity about to break out of him. He held back, drawing his mount closer to Burnside.

"The front man in your column should have been ten feet behind the last man with McPherson. Now you tell me you don't know how far ahead he is?"

"Sir, an hour or so ago I could see them cresting over those mountains," and Burnside pointed toward the South Mountain range.

"Then by heaven's, man, I expect to see your men cresting those same mountains and catching up! I'm going ahead to join McPherson. I expect you up to Frederick with all possible speed. Do I make myself clear?"

"Yes, sir," Burnside said icily.

Grant jerked the reins of his mount, turned back on to the National Road, and was quickly up to a gallop, heading east.

Burnside and his staff watched him ride off.

"Westerners," one of his men sighed. "Wait until he comes face-to-face with Bobbie Lee and the men are exhausted."

As Grant reached the east side of the village, he saw thousands of the colored troops, in the fields on either side, building fires, rifles stacked, backpacks off, the men milling about. It'd take a half hour or more, Grant knew, to get these men formed up, out on the road, and marching again.

Uttering a whispered curse and a frustrated "What does Burnside think he is doing?" he pressed on.

Monocacy Junction

12:50 P.M.

General Lee, thank heavens, we were worried sick about you!"

Jeb Stuart rode up to Lee's side, saluted, and then reached over in an uncharacteristic gesture and took his hand.

"I'm just fine, General Stuart."

"We heard about the wreck of your train. First reports were that you were trapped in it."

"Foolishness," Lee said, even as he thought of the fireman's scalded and mangled body. "I'm just fine."

Lee looked away from Jeb for a moment to take in the scene of destruction. The depot was burning, the water tower, punctured by a shell, was trickling water. Behind him the bridge was burning, teams of troopers were working around the edge of the fires, trying to beat them out with blankets, a few buckets of water hauled up from the river, shovelfuls of dirt.

One entire side of the bridge was completely destroyed. The smoldering remnants of two locomotives and what appeared to be a passenger car now lay in the river. The north side of the bridge was still tenuously holding together, a few stringers connecting the piers, but all planking and track gone.

Lee turned to Jed Hotchkiss.

"That's the bridge we needed?"

"Yes, sir?"

"No other crossings for rail?"

"No, sir."

Lee sighed.

"How long do you think it will take to get a track laid back across it?"

Jed shook his head.

"Not my department, sir. We don't have the railroad men the way the Yankees do. But it looks like the stringers are still intact on one side. Put three, four hundred men on it, and maybe in a day or two we can have it back for at least one side with lightly loaded trains."

Lee looked back at Jeb.

"Situation here?"

"We took out most of Custer's Brigade. Sir, he put up a darn good fight. That's him over there."

Lee looked to where a small knot of captured Union soldiers sat around a blanket-covered body, a lone Confederate officer sitting among them. As he looked at them, the Confederate officer stood up and saluted, most of the Yankees standing and doing the same.

"That's Captain Duvall, sir," Stuart whispered. "He and Custer were close friends back at the Point. Duvall was the one who sent the warnings from Taneytown and first tried to hold this side of the river. I think he should get a regiment, sir. He's ready for it, and he's earned it."

Lee edged Traveler over to the group, the last of the Yankees still sitting coming to their feet as he approached.

"My compliments, gentlemen, on your stand here," Lee said, returning the salute of a begrimed Union captain whose arm was in a sling. "I understand you fought with honor and bravery. My thanks to you for that flag of truce so our wounded could be taken off the burning bridge."

"You'd have done the same, General," the captain replied.

"I'll see that you and your men are paroled as quickly as possible," Lee said. "Men such as you should be allowed to return safely to your families."

The captain looked up at him.

"Thank you, sir."

"Captain Duvall, my sympathies on the loss of your friend. Sadly, such is the nature of this war. I shall pray for you and for his family this evening."

"Thank you, sir," and there was a catch in Duvall's voice.

Lee motioned for Jeb to join him. Together they rode around the blockhouse, which was now serving as a field hospital, and up a gentle slope to the edge of the railroad cut, which was littered with bodies from both sides. Behind him, remnants of the covered bridge, sticking out of the water, still burned.

Uncasing his field glasses, Lee quickly scanned the town. He remembered it well, having ridden through it the year before during the Sharpsburg campaign. Well-ordered, neat homes, the citizens not necessarily pro-Confederate but at least respectful of him and his men.

Beyond, he could see where the National Road rose up, curving back and forth to the crest of the Catoctin Mountains. He could see puffs of smoke, hear a distant echo of gunfire.

"Do we have the heights yet?" Lee asked.

"No, sir. My first concern was to try and envelop Custer and at the same time seize the railroad bridge intact. I've detailed off Jenkins to push the heights, Jones to secure the town. Fitz Lee is bringing his brigade across the National Road bridge even now, and I've ordered them up to the heights."

"I know, I just passed my nephew while coming here."

"Sir, we could use infantry and artillery."

"Scales is bringing his division across the ford just north of here and is halfway up to the town, but it will still take time to deploy and get them into action."

If only we had held this bridge, Lee thought. *We could have brought the trains in, run them right up the siding to Frederick, and Scales would already be in action.*

"What's up there?"

"What's left of Custer. I'd say two of his regiments got out."

"Surely we can gain the heights from them with what we have?"

"Sir, my boys rode all night."

"So did Custer's."

"Sir. That's a steep slope fighting dismounted. It'll take some doing to get up it."

Lee reluctantly found he had to agree.

"Any word of their infantry?"

"Nothing, sir. With luck we just might've stolen the march on them. We gain those heights with Scales and my boys, and Grant is bottled up in the next valley over. He'll bang his head against us all day along. That ridge makes our ground at Fredericksburg look like a billiard table in comparison."

Lee looked about at the ground, hay and winter wheat trampled down by the passing of both armies, smoke cloaking the river valley. Even as he watched, a thirty-foot section of the bridge gave way with a creaking groan and dropped into the river.

His engineering training allowed him to work a quick calculation. He'd have to find good timber, shore up at least one side of the bridge for a single track, get men to find rail, best bet being to tear some up from the spur line. It'd take a day, at least, maybe two. Bottle Grant up at the same time and force him to attack, filling him with the anxiety that he could very well escape back into Virginia once his pontoon train moved down to Point of Rocks. That would force Grant to come on.

"I want those heights, at least for the moment. I want to see what is going on over on the other side," Lee said. "Either we'll see all of Grant's army coming on, or nothing. If it's nothing, then we'll know that Grant is heading toward Virginia, or just perhaps moving behind the screen of militia to the north. We need to confirm that right now.

"Round up every extra man you have and send them up there. I'll set up headquarters back at the National Road bridge."

Stuart saluted and galloped off.

Though caught off balance for the moment, Lee found himself sensing that he was recapturing that balance, that with luck Grant was indeed coming in from the west. If so, he could now choose the ground and force Grant to come at him, the same as at Union Mills.

Braddock Heights—Catoctin Ridge

1:45 P.M.

Here it comes," McPherson announced, but no one needed to be told.

The few hundred cavalry troopers with him, joined by his headquarters staff, were played out; barely a man had half a dozen cartridges left.

On the road below, a column of infantry was advancing with impunity. At such range, artillery would have torn them apart, but there was no artillery up here.

McPherson turned and rode but a few dozen yards to the west. Below him he could see his own column, dark blue, like a long coiling serpent moving across the valley between the Catoctin Range and South Mountains, the head of his column still a half hour away.

He had sent back several couriers, urging the column to press forward, but the race would apparently be lost by not more than a few minutes.

"They're deploying, sir!" someone shouted. Colonel Mann, one of Custer's men, who was dismounted, his horse dead, was pointing.

He didn't need to go back to look. They were most likely down to two hundred yards, lead regiments shaking out from column to line for the final sweep up to the ridge.

A scattering of shots echoed, and a dozen troopers, still mounted, came over the crest of the road, slowing at the sight of McPherson.

"Sorry, sir, we ain't got a round left, and don't ask us to draw sabers and charge."

McPherson smiled and shook his head.

"You did good, boys, the best I've ever seen cavalry fight. Get yourselves out of here."

The sergeant leading the group saluted and led his men down the road to the west.

One of McPherson's staff came up, leading his horse.

"They'll be on the crest in a minute, sir."

McPherson sighed, mounting, watching as Mann rallied what was left of Custer's men, pointing to the rear.

"Sir." One of McPherson's staff was pointing down the road. A knot of officers, riding hard, was coming up the slope. Behind the officers he could see that the head of the column was double-timing, men running, sunlight glinting off of rifles. With field glasses raised he could see as well that with every yard gained a man was staggering out of the column and collapsing from exhaustion. Men were shedding blanket rolls, haversacks, but still pressing on.

The officer in front . . . it was Grant, of course.

As a volley rang out behind him, he turned and looked back and saw the first of the rebel infantry, mingled in with dismounted reb cavalry, reaching the crest.

Suicide was not a gesture he cared for today. He spurred his mount, starting down the slope, staff about him, Custer's men, most on foot, some mounted, staggering along.

Grant spotted him, leaned into his mount and, with his usual display of brilliant horsemanship, came up the slope at a gallop. McPherson rode down to meet him.

"What is happening here?" Grant shouted, reining in hard by McPherson's side.

"Infantry just on the other side."

"How many?"

"Full division. It stretches all the way back to Frederick. Lead regiments deploying into line."

Grant looked up to the crest of the road and then back to their own troops, still coming on at the double, several hundred yards away.

A few shots whistled past them but Grant ignored the threat.

"Can we take 'em with your men?"

Grant pointed back to the great blue serpent weaving across the valley.

"Hell, yes," McPherson replied.

"Lead them in. I'll head back down and urge them on."

He leaned over and shook McPherson's hand.

"Stay healthy, James. And you did a good job, moving your men forward. Half an hour later and Lee would have had this ridge for good."

Grant turned and rode off, McPherson grinning. That man already assumed they were going to sweep the rebs off the crest.

By heavens, if he believes it, then I'm the man to do it, McPherson thought, even as he rode down to the head of his column, shouting for the boys to keep moving but to shake out into line of battle.

Braddock Heights

2:00 P.M.

CSA "Come on, South Carolina, form up here!"
Sergeant Major Hazner, following the lead of Colonel Brown, urged his men on at the double. Men were doubled over, panting, some peeling off blanket rolls and dropping them even as they ran up the steep grade of the road. Then they broke to the right, climbing over a post and rail fence, and then into a tangle of second-growth trees, low branches whipping back into men's faces, the column turning into a pushing, shoving, cursing crowd.

To their left a volley rang out and Hazner could see the smoke swirling up from the road. Cavalry troopers were mingled in with the infantry, firing with carbines; some had pistols out, waiting for the range to close. Shouts ahead; a staff officer, hat off and sword drawn, was waving to Brown.

"Fall in here. Fall in here!"

The ground began to slope away, dropping down. They were over the crest and Hazner felt as if his legs were about to buckle and give way.

"What the hell is going on?" Brown shouted to the staff officer.

"We got the crest, but by God, they've got infantry, thousands of 'em, coming up the road. Get ready, they'll hit any minute. Scales says we got to hold this ridge!"

The staff officer saluted and, turning, ran northward, shouting for the next regiment behind the Fourteenth South Carolina to fall into line.

The men were already loaded, Brown shouting for all ten companies to fall in by line, Hazner pushing the men along.

Another volley from the left, then a switching over to independent fire. *Must mean they are close*, Hazner thought.

Directly ahead, the second-growth timber gave way to an orchard, and as he looked that way, he stood goggle-eyed. He could see them, see them clear back to the next mountain range, which had to be five or six miles off. A long column of blue that seemed endless, surging forward, weaving its way clear up to the crest beyond.

"There's thousands of 'em," someone gasped.

"Just worry about the ones in front of you," Hazner shouted. Even as he spoke he saw Yankee skirmishers on the far side of the orchard. They were moving slow, either cautious or exhausted. A few stepped out into the orchard and dropped within seconds from the fire going downslope delivered by the regiment astride the road.

More skirmishers appeared, dropping down behind the fence bordering the other side of the orchard. Puffs of smoke, but so far none in the direction of the Fourteenth.

"Get down, men, get down," Brown shouted.

No one needed to be told what he was thinking, and all were grateful to collapse to the forest floor. After the heat of the climb up the road, the cool leaves, ferns, and undergrowth were a blessing. Some of the men pulled their canteens around, lifting them to drink. Hazner said nothing, but if they came begging for water an hour from now, the hell with them.

But the sight of them drinking got to him. He took a few sips himself, the water a bit muddy, having been scooped up while they crossed the Monocacy. They waited, fire from behind the fence building in intensity, still directed toward the regiment astride the road and open yards of the small homes and tavern atop the crest.

"Check your caps, boys," Hazner said, even as he drew up his own rifle, half-cocked it, and saw that the percussion cap was still in place. He waited, glad for even a few minutes to catch his breath, the trembling in his legs stopping, but hunger hitting him so, that he reached into his haversack and pulled out a piece of hardtack.

As he reached in, his hand brushed against the journal of his comrade, Maj. John Williamson, dead at Union Mills. Why he still carried it was beyond him. It was an extra pound, its details, its questionings too disturbing, but somehow it was still a link to a childhood friend he could not quite let go of.

Two months ago John was still alive, the two of them marching side by side up the Cumberland Valley, filled with hope that soon the war would be over. John had died at Union Mills, shot through the head.

Brown leaned up on one elbow to survey their line. The regiment was little more than a third of those who had marched that day back in June. Gone were the men lost at Gettysburg, Union Mills, and in the disastrous charge in front of Washington.

Always they were told the "next one" would be the "last one." Though he found it hard to believe in a God who cared, who intervened for those who prayed, still he could not help but utter a silent wish, *Let this be the end of it.*

He looked down the slope while biting off a piece of hardtack and saw a flicker of red, white . . . a Union flag. A regiment was coming up. Shadowy glimpses of men in dark blue, shaking out from column into line, moving up to the edge of the fence row.

"Get ready," Colonel Brown hissed, crouching low, moving down the length of the line.

The flag emerged from the other side of the orchard, held high, a state flag beside it, Hazner could not tell which one.

The men approaching gave out three "Huzzahs!" as they knocked over the split rail fence, stepped into the orchard, and with poised bayonets started through the orchard.

"Up, boys, up!" Brown shouted.

The regiment stood.

"Volley fire on my command! Take aim!"

The two hundred rifles of the Fourteenth South Carolina were lowered, aiming downslope. The Yankee regiment, angling toward the men holding the road, had not expected this. Their colonel, out front, still mounted, shouted something, pointing his sword toward the Fourteenth.

"Fire!"

Dozens of Yanks dropped. Miraculously, their colonel still kept his mount.

"Reload! Independent fire at will!"

The Yankees, as if guided by a single hand, raised their rifles to their shoulders and took aim.

"For that which we are about to receive..." a wag in the line shouted, even as the Union volley hit. They had the advantage of being up slope, protected by the trees, but still a dozen men dropped or staggered back from the volley line. Hazner was showered with bits of bark and tree sap from a spruce he was standing next to.

The fastest had already reloaded, and now the fight was truly on. Fire rippled up and down the line, men shouting, cursing, laughing, tearing cartridges, capping nipples, taking aim. The calmer ones braced their rifles against a tree before firing.

Hazner stepped back from the volley line, walking its length. He spotted young Lieutenant Hurt, so green at Fort Stevens, now calmly directing his men to pour it into the men around the colors. Smoke cloaked the orchard. Then the return fire slackened.

A cheer went up from the Fourteenth, the Yankees were falling back. But they did not retreat far. Once out of the orchard they stopped, some of the men taking a few dangerous seconds to grab fence rails and pile them up as a barricade before dropping behind them.

Well-aimed fire began to slam into the ranks of the Fourteenth. Some of the shots were high, but some were hitting, men grunting, cursing, or silently collapsing.

"Down, boys!" Hazner shouted.

His men needed no urging. They hunkered down behind trees, rocks, some crawling up the dozen or so yards to the edge of the orchard, tearing down the fence that flanked it on their side, piling the rails up the way the Yankees did on the other side, a hundred yards away.

Within a few minutes a deadly game was on. Both sides seasoned, both knowing how to fight, trading fire across a narrow orchard, neither willing to give any ground.

Braddock Heights

2:30 P.M.

G.S.A Geneeral Lee, I must urge you, sir, please come up on foot," General Scales begged, standing between him and the incoming fire sweeping the crest.

Lee could not help but nod in agreement. To take Traveler the few dozen yards to the crest would be madness, for him, his staff, and his beloved mount.

He swung down out of the saddle.

On the road beside him men from Scales's Division were continuing to push up the road. He had passed them on the ride up here, too restless to remain any longer at the bridge.

As he rode by, the men struggled to cheer, but they were moving fast, doubled over, pounding up the steep slope to the roar of battle, which now swept the crest.

"Sir, please come no further. It's too dangerous up there."

Lee smiled and simply stepped around Scales, who came back to his side and deliberately placed himself in front of Lee.

"Sir, if you insist, please follow me then," Scales said, and crouching down slightly, he led the way.

They angled off the road to the left and slipped behind a small tavern.

"From the top floor you can see what is happening, but please do not stand close to the window, sir."

Lee walked into the building, which was already transformed into a hospital, dozens of men on the floor, and followed Scales up the narrow steps to the second floor. When Scales opened a door, several cavalry troopers near the window looked back at their guests in surprise, the sergeant leading the three coming to attention.

"Good log walls, General, is stopping the bullets," the sergeant said, "but this window is mighty dangerous."

Even as he spoke splinters of glass from a windowpane sprayed back onto the bed in the middle of the room.

Lee nodded his thanks and approached to within a half dozen feet, and raising his field glasses, he looked out.

Smoke obscured the road directly below, but what he saw beyond was what he had come to find out. A corps at the very least, the column visible clear across the valley and back up to the mountain beyond.

"It's their Seventeenth Corps," Scales said. "We've taken a few prisoners. James McPherson is their commander."

Lee sighed inwardly.

It was far too bitter, and he looked away for a moment.

James was brilliant, tough, a good leader. He'd push straight in, sensing that if he let his opponent consolidate his hold on this ridge, the campaign was already over, the initiative now on the Southern side.

He remembered conversations with the young cadet about military history, about Napoleon's use of mass at the crucial point of battle. McPherson would not wait; he'd come slamming in; he was already doing that. Studying the road again, Lee saw the regiments were shaking out of column and coming up the slope in battle line, moving fast.

"Sir, when can we expect reinforcements?" Scales asked, interrupting Lee's thoughts.

"Sir?"

"Reinforcements?"

"Hood's old division is coming up. They took trains from Baltimore and should be getting off now."

"Back where we dismounted?" Scales asked. "That's several hours of marching."

Lee nodded, saying nothing.

"Artillery, sir, a few batteries would be mighty helpful."

"Back with the trains as well."

Scales fell silent as Lee raised his glasses again.

He scanned the advancing columns of blue. They were moving hard; he could see scatterings of men by the roadside, collapsed. McPherson would be calling for double time to bring up his men; his corps would be exhausted by the time they reached this crest. Back at the opposite crest, the South Mountain range, Lee saw that the road was empty except for some wagons. A break in their column of march? Maybe there was an opportunity presenting itself. Catch McPherson by himself and defeat him in isolation.

He watched, ignoring another shower of glass that sent Walter Taylor nervously to his side, almost blocking his view.

"Let them come," Lee said quietly, his voice almost tinged with sadness. "Let them come."

"Sir?" Scales asked.

"Hold as long as you can," Lee said, "but don't overextend. I want your division intact, sir, not a wreck. Hold as long as you can then pull back."

"I don't understand sir."

"If we hold here, McPherson will finally halt, build up, and then come on in full strength against your one division. But there is a chance we can actually lure McPherson in. He is impetutous when he feels he is winning. We lure him over this ridge and then hit him with our reserves coming up."

Lee stepped away from the window and began to outline his plan.

Below Braddock Heights

3:00 P.M.

James McPherson, hat off, shouted for the next regiment in line to break to the right, cross the field, and deploy into line. The men were pale with exhaustion.

The Second Brigade of his Second Division was now up and deploying out.

The fire coming from the crest was murderous, but through eddies in the smoke he could see his own volley lines, extending out farther and farther to either flank as each new regiment fell into line.

They were stretching them out up there. *The rebs must be damn near as tired as my boys going up that slope.* Just one good push and he'd be through them; he could sense that.

The Third Brigade was now approaching, men moving fast.

"Straight up the slope, my boys!" McPherson shouted. "Straight up till you're engaged, then give them hell!"

Braddock Heights

3:35 P.M.

The men of the Fourteenth South Carolina were starting to run short of ammunition. They had been trading fire across the orchard for over an hour. Nearly a quarter of the men were down.

Hazner, crouched behind a tree, struggled with his ramrod to pound another round down the fouled barrel of his gun. Reloading he rolled over on to his stomach, leveled the barrel against a log, and waited. The smoke parted for a moment; he caught a flash of black, a cap, aimed carefully, and fired. The hat disappeared and he grinned. He might not have hit the man, but he sure had given him something to think about.

The orchard between the opposing sides was shredded. Two regiments fighting it out on either side had most likely fired more than twenty thousand rounds back and forth during the last hour. Trees were nearly stripped bare, apples exploding so that there was the interesting scent of cider, more than one man commenting that they wished they could crawl down there and gather up some of the shattered fruit. The trees inside the woodlot they were deployed in were torn and splintered, a few smaller ones actually toppling over.

The fire from the other side began to slacken and then stopped.

"Everyone load, hold fire," Brown shouted.

It was obvious something was building. They were going to try another charge.

A distant hoarse cheer, the Yankee "huzzahs" given three times, rolled up the hill.

A staff officer, this one mounted, came through the woods toward the Fourteenth, Brown standing up to meet him, but making it a point to keep a tree between him and the Yankees.

"Column coming up the road. Enfilade it, but then you are to pull back."

"Fall back?" Brown asked, obviously confused. "Hell, sir, just get me some more ammunition and some water. We'll hold."

"Orders from General Lee himself. He doesn't want this division torn apart. We're pulling back into Frederick. Rally your men in the center of town."

The officer turned without waiting for a reply and rode to the north, toward the next regiment in line.

Brown turned. "You heard him boys. We're pulling back. Wounded who can walk, start moving now."

A couple of dozen men who had been resting just behind the volley line struggled to their feet and began staggering back. Those who could not move looked toward Brown beseechingly.

"Sorry, boys," Brown said sadly. "We got to leave you. Don't worry. The Yankees will take good care of you."

"Yeah, right," one of them hissed. "Point Lookout for us if we live."

"Here it comes!" someone shouted.

Hazner turned and saw the head of a column coming up the road. At the same moment the regiment they'd been facing across the orchard stood up and came out into the open, advancing at the double.

"Take aim straight ahead, boys," Brown shouted.

Hazner agreed. To hell with the column. It was the men they were facing they had to worry about.

"Fire!"

A ragged volley swept the orchard, dropping another dozen, but this time the Yankees did not slow; they just kept on coming.

"Fall back, men, stay with me!"

The Fourteenth moved woodenly at first. After the long march, the bitter fight, they were exhausted. Behind them the Yankees, sensing the breaking of their opponents, let out a cheer, and seconds later a volley ripped through the woods, the Fourteenth losing a half dozen more.

Hazner reached the crest of the ridge. Along the road to his right he could see where troops were falling back, cavalry mounting up, infantry pushing around them. A thunderous fire erupted from the road, a sharp volley sent into the advancing column, and then those men turned and started to run.

Over the crest, Hazner, falling in by Brown's side, started down the slope. It was steep and he ran like a drunken man, nearly tumbling over, men around him cursing, panting, some tangling up in the brush and falling, getting up again.

Behind them he could hear taunting yells. Looking back, he saw where the Yankees had gained the ridge. Some were pushing on, others stopping to reload.

Ahead and below the town of Frederick was two miles off. Beyond, he could see smoke cloaking the river valley and a distant column of troops moving along the National Road.

Brown staggered and tripped, cursing as he hit the ground. Hazner pulled him up, the colonel's hands badly skinned from the tumble.

"Come on, sir," Hazner cried, "but by damn, there better be a good reason for this."

Braddock Heights

3:50 P.M.

"McPherson!"

James was atop the crest, glasses raised, studying the ground ahead. A half mile downslope he could see where the rebels were swarming along the road and fields, heading back toward Frederick. Beyond the river he could already spot another column coming up.

Grant came to his side, grinning.

"Good work, McPherson."

"Cost us," James said quietly. "We fought entire battles out west and lost fewer men than I just did taking this ridge."

"It's only started," Grant replied coolly. "Are you pressing them?"

"My boys are exhausted, sir. I've double-timed them for miles, threw them into this fight. They need a few minutes at least. We got the good ground now. Isn't that what we wanted?"

Grant was silent for a moment, field glasses raised, studying the terrain ahead.

"That bridge is out of artillery range from up here. We give Lee time, he just might get it back up again. Besides, if we sit up here, he will not come at us."

McPherson looked over at him.

"We just had a meeting engagement up here, both sides equally tired. If we dig in here tonight, what will Lee do tomorrow? Attack?"

McPherson found he had to agree.

"No, sir, of course not."

"I want him to fight us. We've got to grab hold of him and stay in contact. I don't want him to have time to think, to maneuver, to repair that bridge, to think about the Potomac River at all. We give him good bait, though, and he'll bite it and then hang on to us the way I want."

"And that means my corps, sir, doesn't it?"

Grant grabbed him by the forearm.

"You know what to do. But you, personally, don't go doing anything foolish. Push down there and grab hold of Lee. I'm setting up here for the moment. Give your boys twenty minutes to catch their breath, try and find some water, then send them in. I want that town and the river beyond."

McPherson knew without even having to ask what Grant was ordering him to do. To stick his corps out forward and let Lee bite into them. He thought of all the quiet afternoons he had spent with Lee at West Point, the admiration he had always held for him. He wondered if Lee knew whose corps this was that was about to come down to meet him. It was going to be one hell of a bloody mess this day.

McPherson saluted and rode off.

Chapter Eleven

Good heavens, sir, they're coming down."

Lee said nothing, sitting astride Traveler at the edge of the city, looking up at the Catoctin Heights. Yes, indeed, McPherson was coming down, battle lines deployed out a quarter mile to either side of the National Road. Flags flying, regiments came down the steep slope, skirmishers to the fore. It was a grand sight. All about him stopped to look. The battle line was studded with national flags and state flags, and he found a swelling of admiration within himself. His star student from the West Point days was doing a remarkable job. Despite himself, he was proud of him as a mentor might be of a cherished younger person.

A half-mile front, late afternoon sun behind them, bayonets flashing, disciplined in their advance even on such difficult ground.

"Half a league, half a league, half a league onward," Walter whispered.

Lee nodded in agreement. These were brave men indeed. Brave and foolish. They had taken the bait. *McPherson has courage but he is going to give us an opportunity to defeat him in isolation before Grant can arrive.*

"Walter, tell Robertson he must come up. Scales is to hold the town as we talked about. We'll fight them street by street if need be. I want their entire corps pulled into this fight."

"Yes, sir!" Walter galloped off.

Lee turned about and rode into the center of town, General Scales by his side. Regiments were still forming up after their retreat off of the ridge; men gathered around wells, filling canteens; wounded being carried into churches and homes; citizens standing silent, watching, looking up at the heights, worrying that their homes would be destroyed if Frederick became a battlefield.

"General Scales, get your provost guards out and order these civilians into their basements. There's going to be a fight here, and I wish to avoid injury to them."

"Yes, sir. So we hold the town, sir?"

"I want to pull McPherson in here. Yes, you will hold the town. Grant has done what I hoped. If he had sat up on those heights, he could have waited for days, concentrated, or perhaps even shielded us from a maneuver down into the northern Shenandoah. Now he will be forced to come on in support of McPherson. We have an opportunity to defeat his army in detail, one corps at a time."

Lee looked to the east.

"Robertson should be up in a few hours by train and will roll in from the north and smash McPherson. If Grant is so impetuous, he'll then funnel more men in and we will smash them in turn. By this time tomorrow the rest of our army will be concentrated here, but we will have taken out a quarter, perhaps a half of his army. Then he shall dance to our tune. He will learn that the East is a more dangerous place than his Western campaigns prepared him for."

Two Miles East of Monocacy Junction

4:25 P.M.

Cursing soundly at the engineer of his train General Robertson rode past the hissing engine. It had taken them six hours to come up from Baltimore, rather than the two promised to them back in the rail yard. Two locomotives had broken down, one of them obviously sabotaged with a hole punched into a cylinder and then plugged with tallow and hemp that had finally blown out. It had forced his entire convoy to shift tracks, then shift back again, to get around the stalled engine, leaving two regiments behind. The scene just east of the river was chaos. Dozens of trains were backed up, the ones that had brought up Scales waiting to begin a backward shuttle all the way to Relay Junction before being able to turn around. The pontoon bridges were parked to one side, blocking the westbound track, and straight ahead was the wreck that he had heard almost killed General Lee.

On the way up they had passed Longstreet's Corps, marching on the National Road, fifteen miles out of Baltimore but still a good day and a half away from the spreading battle at Frederick.

He turned and looked back. His men were piling off the boxcars, passenger cars, flatcars, and even coal hoppers pressed into service for this troop movement. The men were forming up into columns of march, beginning to surge forward on either side of the tracks.

"Keep 'em moving!" Robertson shouted. "Boys, General Lee needs us. Now keep moving!"

Braddock Heights

4:30 P.M.

General McPherson spared a final glance back at the South Mountain range, five miles away. The valley between him and the distant ridge was empty. No troops were coming up.

Where in heavens name was Ninth Corps? They should already be over the crest, flooding in to support him.

But orders were orders and he knew what Grant wanted—to hold Lee in place here while he cast his net wide. If only the rebs had come on again. Holding this ridge he could have pounded away at them all day. His reserve ammunition trains were coming up the slope, along with a battery of three-inch rifles, the only battery Grant had allotted to him. But he understood his orders, the mission Grant wanted, and that he was now a pawn, or perhaps a knight, ventured out into the middle of the board.

Downslope, a mile away, skirmish fire was erupting, reb infantry and cavalry falling back into the town.

He looked around at his staff.

"A moment of prayer, gentlemen," he said softly, and removed his hat.

Lowering his head he silently commended his soul to God, asking for a blessing upon his men who this day might fall. All were silent.

"Let's go," he said, his voice matter-of-fact, as if they were out for an afternoon's ride down into a friendly village to visit old friends.

He raised his field glasses one last time, looking to the far horizon. It should be possible on a clear day to see the church spires of Baltimore. So close to Emily, and yet so far. Battle smoke obscured the view. He lowered his glasses and cased them.

General McPherson and his staff set off down the road to Frederick.

Frederick

4:45 P.M.

CSA Sergeant Hazner raced up the steps to the top floor of the building and flung a door open. He stopped for a few seconds in amazement. It was a photographer's studio, the owner, a dyspeptic-looking frail gentleman gazing at him with surprise, the air thick with the odor of ether and other chemicals.

"Sir, might I suggest you go to the basement," Hazner said, stepping back from the doorway and then directing the half dozen men with him to take positions by the windows.

One of the men started to smash the window panes with the butt of his rifle and the photographer shouted a protest.

"Please just open them," Hazner said. "Let's not get carried away."

He had to laugh inside at this little point of etiquette. If what was about to happen, did happen, this place would be a shambles in fairly short order.

The men did as ordered and Hazner walked over to the table the photographer had set up in one side of the room. A number of wet collodion plates were lying on black felt, others were hanging up, drying. Hazner studied them for a few seconds. Some were just blurs, but a few were really quite remarkable, a blurred column of men moving up the road just below, but there, in a different picture, remaining stock-still at the main intersection of the town, was General Lee on Traveler, General Scales by his side. Another photograph showed the Catoctin Heights wreathed in smoke, blurred columns moving up the National Road, and in the foreground General Lee with field glasses raised, looking up at the battle.

"So you've been busy today?" Hazner asked.

"Quite so! A dozen images, many of the battle itself. Quite extraordinary. I hope to get more," and he pointed to the camera on the far side of the room.

"Could I convince you gentlemen to pose for me right now?"

Several of Hazner's men looked at him, grinning. He was almost tempted, but then shook his head.

"Sir, I don't think you realize how dangerous it will be here in a few minutes. Please go to your basement."

"You can't force me," the photographer said loudly. "Good heavens, man, no one has ever photographed a battle before, and I plan to do so today."

Hazner shook his head.

"Just be careful, sir," he said, nodded to his men, and then ran down the stairs and out into the main street.

The last of the Confederate infantry were disappearing into buildings, men running. A block to the west a two-gun section was set up, both pieces firing at the same instant, recoiling, filing the street with roiling clouds of smoke. The guns were hooked to their caissons by trail ropes, the guns being dragged down the street even as their crews worked to reload. They stopped at the main intersection.

"Fire!"

Both guns kicked back, several windowpanes shattering from the blast, the solid shot of the twin Napoleons screaming down the street.

Still hooked to the caissons by twenty feet of rope, the team started to move again.

"Better get off the street there, Sergeant," the section commander shouted. "They're coming on fast!"

Hazner looked up the road, and sure enough, he could see them a half dozen blocks away, Yankee infantry, running hard, dodging into buildings, rifle fire already erupting from upper-floor windows. A minié ball hummed past him, and then another; a gunner collapsed, holding his arm and cursing, his comrades quickly picking him up and helping him to get up on the caisson.

The crew moved another block. Hazner pressed himself inside the doorway as they fired again, the scream of the shot tearing down the street and slapping him with a shock wave. He peeked out and saw it slash through a file of troops on the street, knocking them over. More shots came down the street. From the window overhead his men were opening up, leaning out, shooting, ducking back in.

It was time to get inside.

He dashed back into the building and up the stairs. The photographer was in the corner of the room, head under a black hood behind the camera, asking if the men would stand still for a moment, but they ignored him. Two of the best shooters were at the windows, the others passing up loaded rifles. Glass was shattering, the room filling with smoke.

Strange, all their other fights had been out in the open. Usually towns were bypassed in a fight. Why Scales had decided to stand here, men broken up into small units, was beyond him. This was going to be one ugly fight.

Hazner settled down by a window, back pressed against the wall, and then leaned over to look out. Swarms of Yankees were coming down the street, men dropping with every step forward, the column breaking up,

an officer out front shouting, waving his sword, the formation disinte-
grating as they broke and ran toward buildings, ducking into doorways.
Within seconds the return fire became intense, bullets smacking into
windowsills, tearing across brick fronting. Across the street a man tumbled
out of a third-floor window, smacking into the pavement with a sickening
crunch.

"Gentlemen, just please remain still for fifteen seconds, that's all I
ask!"

Hazner ignored the man, raised his rifle, and joined the fight.

Braddock Heights

5:10 P.M.

Grant stood silent, field glasses trained on the town below.
It was turning into one hell of a fight. McPherson had
waded straight in. Buildings were ablaze, a church steeple wreathed now
in smoke, fire licking up its sides. Beyond, he could see where a large column of infantry was coming over the National Road bridge across the
Monocacy, the distant smoke of locomotives barely visible through the
haze.

Lee's Second Division was starting to deploy, preparing to sweep into
the town from the north side. McPherson had placed his men well. One
division was forming to the north to meet the counterthreat, at least another division into the town, and what looked to be a brigade pushing to
the south side of the town, fighting what appeared be dismounted cavalry,
and steadily moving toward the river.

Now, if only I had more men up, Grant thought. A Confederate division
with Lee's army carried almost as much strength as a Union light corps.
Though McPherson had fifteen thousand at the start of the day, several
thousand at least had fallen out in the forced march. Even now those stragglers were walking past him, small groups, a few men, a couple of dozen
being shepherded along by a corporal or a sergeant, more than one stopping to ask one of his staff where the fighting was or where they should go.
And always they were directed down the road into Frederick and told to
get into the fight.

McPherson had, even by conservative estimates, lost two thousand
men taking these heights. Hospitals were already set up on the western
slope, the wounded, Union and Confederate alike, being carried in. Grant

dared not even to watch that too closely. Unlike many another general, hospitals terrified him, turned his stomach.

So McPherson, at best, had carried nine or ten thousand into the fight and Lee had twenty perhaps twenty five thousand down there closing in. Yes, McPherson was the bait, but now he needed a solid line to hang on to him.

He turned and looked to the west. Only now did Grant see the head of Burnside's column coming over the South Mountains, and the sight filled him with rage. *Those men should be up here now, forming up just behind the slope, and ready to sweep forward in mass to catch Lee off guard.* He wondered if Lee had realized that. He had conceded the heights too easily. *Even as I set the bait, was Lee urging me to cast it in?*

No. Never think that. Do that and I start to become like all the others who faced Lee, worrying more about him than what my own plans are.

"I think that's General Sheridan coming up," Ely announced, pointing to the west.

Indeed he was—coming on hard, lashing his mount, Rienzi, up the final steep slope.

"Damn that man," Sheridan shouted, even as he reined in.

"Burnside?"

"Exactly. Says he can't possibly push his men any faster."

Grant looked back to the boiling cauldron of battle down below, Sheridan falling silent by his side.

"My God," Sheridan said, "what a fight."

"It is. I sent McPherson down there to hold Lee in place. If we had dug in here, Lee never would have sought battle and perhaps slipped off."

Grant turned to Sheridan. "I will not leave McPherson down there to be slaughtered. I need Ninth Corps and I need Hunt's guns. We've sucked Lee in and a good counterblow right now would hurt him."

Sheridan did not reply.

"He's got his colored division in the lead, sir. What about that?"

"I don't care which division he's got in the lead. I want them into this fight before nightfall!"

Grant looked around at his silent staff. Ely gazed at him and simply nodded, as if reading his mind.

"General Sheridan. You are to take command of Ninth Corps." Even as he spoke he motioned for Ely to write out the authorization. "Relieve Burnside of command on the spot. Tell him he can report to me tomorrow for reassignment. You will take command of the corps and push them forward with all possible speed. Any division or brigade commander who fails in doing that, relieve them on the spot and find someone who can do the job. Send word back to Hunt to push forward even if it takes all night. If we can save McPherson, Lee will surely hang on for a rematch tomorrow, and we need guns in position to meet him. Do you understand your orders?"

"Yes, sir!" Sheridan said with a grin.

Ely finished writing the dispatch, tore the sheet off, and handed it to Grant who scanned it, then signed the document relieving Burnside.

Sheridan snatched it, turned, and, with staff trailing, set off at a gallop.

Frederick

6:00 P.M.

"General, they're hitting us from the north!"

James McPherson turned to look as a courier came riding in from the north side of town.

"Full division. Robertson's I'm told. Hood's old command."

"Good," McPherson said with a grin. "The more the merrier."

"Our boys are falling back. They can't hold."

"Then go back there and tell them to get into the houses, hunker down, and, damn them, hold. We've got to hold!"

All around him was blazing wreckage. The pleasant town of Frederick had become a battlefield much like Fredericksburg the year before. The entire western end of the town was afire, flames leaping from building to building on the westerly breeze that had sprung up. There was a touch of coolness in the air and he looked up at the dark clouds gathering on the other side of the mountain, filled with the promise of an evening thunderstorm.

It was always said that a battle brought rain, and it was hard to tell at this moment whether the thunder rolled from the heavens, the incessant rifle fire in the center of town, or the burst of artillery streaking through the streets.

Monocacy Junction

6:20 P.M.

L ee stirred anxiously, sipping a cup of coffee, leaning against a fence rail, looking toward the town wreathed in smoke. It sickened his heart to see a church spire collapse in flames, and he whispered a silent prayer that if it was being used as a hospital that those within had been evacuated.

He looked back at the bridge. All the fires were out hours ago, and hundreds of men were now at work. Men were tearing up track from the spur line, bringing it down, along with the ties. A crew of men were tearing at the timbers of a barn, dismantling it piece by piece to get at the precious beams, which would then be dragged down and slung into place to provide bridge supports. A captain with Stuart, who had worked on this same line before the war, said he could get a bridge in place for at least one track by late tomorrow and was now running the job.

Robertson's boys were going in. The volume of fire on the north side of town was clear evidence of that. Now if only Johnson's division was up, he could make a clean sweep of it, envelop McPherson from the left, and close the trap. But the latest dispatches from Baltimore indicated Johnson's men were still on the rail line, twenty miles back.

Longstreet and Beauregard were reporting good marching on the roads, but were still a day away, and his artillery reserve, so dependent on the railroad, had not yet left Baltimore.

This was unlike any battle he had ever fought. He had hoped, when first he grasped Grant's maneuver, that he could catch him by surprise here, at the base of the Catoctins, tear apart one, perhaps two, of his corps, and then chase him down and finish him. He had placed too much reliance on the railroads, and now it was telling.

He finished his coffee, set the cup down, and walked over to his staff, who were hurriedly eating while standing about the smoking ruins of the depot, watching the work crews scrambling about the wreckage of the bridge.

"Gentlemen, I think we should go into the fight," Lee said.

Several looked at him with surprise. It was obvious they had assumed that after the long day he would establish his headquarters here for the night.

"General, let me go forward," Stuart said. "My boys are blocking that Yankee brigade on the south side of town. I can manage things."

"No, I want to see how Robertson is doing," Lee announced.

Everyone knew better than to argue with him. An orderly brought up Traveler. He mounted and headed into the cauldron, staff following anxiously.

The White House

6:00 P.M.

Lincoln ate alone, his servant Jim Bartlett had delivered a tray with a few slices of fried ham, some potatoes, and coffee to his office.

Finishing his meal he stood up to stretch, the sound of his chair scraping on the floor amounting to a signal. Jim politely tapped on the door.

"Come on in."

"Sir, should I clear your tray?" Jim asked.

"Thank you," Lincoln replied.

Lincoln had gone to the window. Crowds had gathered in Lafayette Park, with troops ringing the White House.

Lincoln suddenly turned.

"Jim, a question."

"Anything, sir."

"The colored of Washington. I know this might sound like a strange question. But with all the news of the last few days, what do you hear?"

"Well, sir, I've spent most of my time here in the White House, but I do hear talk with the staff."

"And that is?"

"Frustration, sir."

"Frustration? Over what?"

Jim stood holding the tray and Lincoln motioned for him to put it down.

"Jim, let's talk frankly. I need to hear what you have to say. This war is your war, too."

"Precisely why so many are frustrated. They want to be in on it."

"What about volunteering for the Colored Troops."

"Sir, both my son and grandson are already with them."

Lincoln sensed the slightest of defensive notes in Jim's voice, as if the president had implied that those who were frustrated should join the army.

"I meant no insult, Jim, and yes, I am proud of the service of your son and grandson."

"Sir, so many men here are working folk with large families to support. Day laborers, men who work the rail yards, the canal docks. They can't afford to go off for twelve dollars a month the way some can like my son. But still they feel it's their war."

Lincoln took this in and nodded.

"Perhaps a way can be found for them to volunteer for short-term service," Lincoln said offhandedly.

Jim suddenly smiled.

"Can I take that as a request, sir?" Jim asked. "To talk with folks and see if there'd be some interest in that."

"By all means," Lincoln said absently, and then, lost in thought, he returned to looking out the window.

Frederick

6:45 P.M.

Sergeant Hazner ducked down as a spray of shot slammed through the window. It had been fired from across the street. He leaned back up, drew a quick bead on the half dozen Yankees leaning out of the windows on the opposite side of the street, fired, and saw one drop.

He ducked down, motioning for one of his men to hand over a loaded musket. The photographer, long since giving up his quest for a photograph, was on the floor moaning with fear.

The stench in the room was dizzying, the air thick with ether. Bottles of chemicals had been shattered, and to the photographer's horror, several of the glass plates, including the precious one of Lee astride Traveler, watching the fight, had been blown apart, bits of glass sprayed across the room.

"Want a picture now?" Hazner shouted.

The photographer simply shook his head.

Hazner peeked up, caught a glimpse of several Yankees running across the street toward his building, fired, but wasn't sure if he'd hit one.

Below, he heard the door slam open, shouts.

"Come on, boys," Hazner shouted, standing up and running for the doorway. Of the six he had led in, only three were still standing. They followed him out. He hit the staircase, ducking as the two men below aimed and fired, plaster flying.

Hazner leapt down the stairs, bayonet poised. One man parried the strike, another edging around to swing a clubbed musket at him.

He countered the parry, bayoneting the man before him, ducking under the blow. One of his own men behind him shot the man with the clubbed musket, shattering his skull. The two others fell back, running out the doorway.

Panting, Hazner looked down at the man he had just killed. Damn, just a boy. Rawboned, uniform of dark blue, weather-stained, threadbare, patches on his knees, shoes in tatters.

Damn near look like us, he thought sadly.

He grabbed one of his men.

"Sit at the top of the stairs, shoot anyone who comes through that door."

The man nodded and Hazner went upstairs, ducking low, crawling to the window.

Frederick

7:00 P.M.

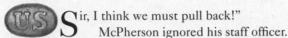Sir, I think we must pull back!"

McPherson ignored his staff officer.

The entire west end of the town was ablaze. In places Union and Confederate wounded were helping each other to get out of buildings. Hundreds of his men were streaming to the rear, limping, cradling broken arms, slowly carrying makeshift litters with wounded comrades curled up on them. A hysterical officer staggered past him, crying about losing his flag.

From the north side of town a steady shower of shot was raining down. Looking up a side street he saw men of his Second Division giving back, running down the street, shouting that the rebs were right behind them.

He had never fought a battle like this. Always it had been in open fields or a tangle of woods and bayous. Here it was impossible to tell anymore who was winning or losing. If he had been sent down here by Grant to be the bait, he had most certainly succeeded in his task. He was being hammered from three directions by two full Confederate divisions and at least a brigade or more of cavalry.

Down the street, several hundred yards away, a fireball went up, brilliant in the early evening sky. Across the street a pillared building was burning, dozens of men coming out of it, carrying wounded, and he shouted for his staff officers to find some additional men to help evacuate the wounded.

For a moment he was tempted to somehow try to arrange a cease-fire, to ask Lee to stop fighting for one hour. The town was burning; thousands of wounded were trapped in buildings, and they needed to be taken out.

But how? A fight in a town like this was utter confusion. Rebs might hold a block, a building, while across the street his boys were holding on. In several places, columns of troops advancing had turned a corner, only to collide with their foes, with the fight degenerating into a vicious street brawl until one side or the other pulled back.

"Sir, for God's sake, let's pull back."

He turned on the man, shouting the advance.

"No, sir. We go forward. Grant will bring up Burnside and we are going to hold this town!"

Frederick

7:15 P.M.

 eneral Robertson!"

Lee rode to Robertson's side, his division commander saluting.

"How goes it, sir?"

Robertson shook his head and looked up at the darkening sky, now streaked with lightning.

"Sir, it's chaos in that town. Can't keep any control or command of troops. Its street by street, and those Yankees just won't give up. Frankly, sir, I can't tell you what is going on."

"Are we driving them?"

"Yes, sir," Robertson said, "but it isn't like any fight we've been in before. Hard to tell in a town like that. The men we're facing aren't like the Army of the Potomac. Never seen anyone try to hold a town like this before."

He pointed toward Frederick, the city ablaze, driving back the approaching darkness. It looked to Lee like something out of the Bible, apocalyptic, the air reverberating with thunder, explosions, the crackle of rifle fire.

"Drive them! Keep driving them," Lee shouted. "I want those Federals in there taken. Tonight."

"We'll try, sir."

Lee spurred his mount, going forward into the fight.

Frederick
7:20 *P.M.*

C.S.A. Sgt. Maj. Lee Robinson, First Texas, Hood's old Texan brigade, was at the head of the column, not carrying the colors for the moment, instead directing his men to keep moving, to drive to the center of the town regardless of loss.

Yankee snipers were at a score of windows, shooting down. He urged his own on as ordered. If they got tangled up in a building by building fight all semblance of order would vanish. The orders were to seize the center of town and that was only one block ahead.

"Keep moving, keep moving!"

Frederick

7:21 *P.M.*

U.S. This way!" McPherson shouted.

Leading part of an Illinois regiment, McPherson pointed the way straight into the center of town.

Two of his staff had dropped in the last block and a dozen men of the Illinois regiment. *The center of the town*, he thought. *Hold that intersection and we can hang on awhile longer.*

"Come on boys, come on!" He spurred his mount ahead.

C.S.A. Sergeant Hazner leaned up on the windowsill. If not for the spreading fires it would have been impossible to see a target. He saw the column, an officer on horseback, rose up to shoot, and a volley from across the street drove him back down.

C.S.A. Sergeant Robinson stopped dead in his tracks, stunned as a Yankee officer, alone, came around the corner on horseback. His own men staggered to a halt, the column around him confused for a brief instant, then raising their weapons up.

Robinson, rifle poised, aimed straight at the officer. He was less than ten feet away.

"For God's sake," Robinson shouted, "surrender!"

The officer looked straight at him, grinned, offered a salute, and then started to turn as if to ride away.

Robinson shot him, feeling as if it was murder. The man jerked upright, swayed, and then tumbled from his mount.

A few seconds later Yankee infantry appeared, and at the sight of the downed officer a wild shout of rage rose up from them and they lunged forward.

Robinson's Texans deployed, delivered a volley at point-blank range, and charged in with bayonet. A frightful melee ensued.

"McPherson! McPherson!" the cry went up among the Yankees, even as the Texans waded in, clubbing and lunging.

Within seconds the Union troops broke and fell back, driven around the corner by the advancing Texans.

Robinson, however, stopped, and knelt down by the Union officer, who was still alive.

"Sir, why didn't you just surrender?" he asked.

"Not in my nature," McPherson gasped. "Could you do me a favor, soldier. Can't breathe. Help me sit up."

Robinson set his rifle down and propped McPherson up against the side of the building. McPherson coughed, clearing his lungs, blood foaming from his lips. "Thank you."

"Sergeant?"

Robinson looked up and was stunned to see General Lee approaching, oblivious to the battle raging around him, staff nervously drawn in close in a protective ring.

More troops of Hood's old Texas brigade were running past, going into the fight.

"Who is that, Sergeant?" Lee asked.

Robinson looked at the man's shoulders.

"A major general, sir."

Walter took the reins of Traveler as Lee dismounted and stepped up to the two. Robinson, not sure whether he should come to attention, decided to continue to help the wounded officer and kept him braced against the wall.

"Oh, God," Lee sighed, "James."

McPherson opened his eyes.

"General, sir. Sorry we had to meet again like this."

Lee knelt by his side and took his hand.

"James. Dear God, James, I'm so sorry."

"Fortunes of war, General. Remember old Alfred T. Mahan always talked about that, the chances of war."

Robinson did not know what to do. Should he draw back, stay to help the Union general, or rejoin his command?

The sergeant looked over at Lee.

"I'm sorry, sir," he said, voice near to breaking. "I asked him to surrender, but he wouldn't. I'm sorry, sir." His voice trailed off.

"Not your fault, Sergeant," McPherson whispered. "Did your duty. Foolish of me, actually. Don't blame yourself."

Robinson found himself looking up into Lee's eyes, and was filled with anguish.

"I'm sorry, sir."

Lee shook his head.

"No, Sergeant. War, contemptible war, did it."

Lee looked back at McPherson.

"Are you sorely hurt, James?"

McPherson nodded. "Can't seem to breathe."

Blood was spilling out from just under his armpit, trickling down from his lips and nostrils.

"General?"

Lee looked up. It was Walter.

"Sir, it isn't safe for you here. Word is more Yankees are coming into the town. Sir, you must move!"

Lee nodded, then looked from his old student to Robinson.

"Sergeant, get a detail together. Carry General McPherson back to the depot down by the river. Stay with him, I'm ordering you to stay with him. Find my surgeon down there, and see that the general is tended to immediately."

"Of course, sir," Robinson replied.

He wondered for a second whether Lee remembered the incident at Taneytown, where he had defied Lee, grabbing hold of Traveler's reins and blocking his advance. But the general seemed lost in misery.

"I'll see he is taken care of, sir," Robinson whispered.

"General Lee, a favor," McPherson whispered.

"Anything, James."

"My fiancée is in Baltimore. We were planning to marry but then this campaign started. Interfered with our plans."

He paused, struggling for breath, coughing up more blood.

"Could you send for her?"

"Of course, James. Anything."

"Her name is Emily Hoffman." He paused again as if already drifting away, Lee leaning closer.

McPherson chuckled and then grimaced with pain.

"Can't remember her address, it seems. But it's on her letters in my breast pocket."

"She'll be on a train and up to you by tomorrow, James."

"Would like to see her again."

"You will, my friend. God forgive me. I am so sorry."

"Duty divided us," McPherson whispered, "but you are still my friend, sir."

Lee, head lowered, could not suppress a sob, squeezing McPherson's hand.

"General, sir!"

It was Walter, dismounted, placing a hand on Lee's shoulder.

"Sir, it is too dangerous here. They have reinforcements coming in from the pass. We must move!"

Lee stood up woodenly, his gaze turning again to Robinson.

"Sergeant, this man is your duty now. Please see to him, and I shall be grateful."

"Yes, sir."

Lee mounted and rode off.

A number of soldiers who had gathered round to watch had already made up a litter out of blankets and muskets strapped together. Robinson gently helped to pick up the general and place him in the litter.

"Help me sit up, Sergeant," McPherson gasped. "Can't breathe lying down."

"Certainly, sir," Robinson said softly, as if to a sick child. "I'll keep you up. You'll be all right, sir."

McPherson looked at him and smiled weakly.

"Don't think so. You're a damn good shooter, Sergeant."

Sgt. Lee Robinson found he could not reply.

As the group set off he caught a glimpse of Hazner standing outside a building, remembering him from the charge at Fort Stevens. As they passed, Hazner saluted.

Braddock Heights

7:30 P.M.

"Come on boys, that's it, that's it!" Grant shouted.

The lead division of Ninth Corps was storming over the heights, running at the double, Sheridan in the lead.

Whatever had been said before about colored troops, he now laid to rest as he watched them pass. These men were tough, unbelievably tough, rifles at the shoulder, moving at the double, still keeping columns. A few collapsed as they passed, but then struggled to get to their feet and press forward.

Sheridan barely paused to salute, obviously in his glory. He had driven these men forward without pity, and they had answered to his call.

"How did Burnside take it?" Grant asked, as Sheridan rode up to his side.

"Like a soldier actually," Phil replied. "I think he expected it. I don't like the man leading these colored men, Ferroro, but for the moment he'll do. He, at least, is at the front. Tough men, double-timed them the last two miles."

"Hunt?"

"Courier came back, saying if Burnside's boys will get the hell off the road he'll have the first guns up by midnight."

"Good, very good," Grant replied enthusiastically.

"Sir, I've got a battle to fight," Phil announced excitedly, and turning, he fell in with the column, heading down the ridge into Frederick, and as he rode the heavens opened and the rain began.

Frederick

8:00 P.M.

General Lee stood at the edge of the town watching it burn even as the storm swept down from the hills. By the flashes of lightning he could see a column of Union troops coming down off the ridge.

It had to be another corps. Reports were they were colored, men of Ninth Corps.

The battle for today had served its purpose. The Union Seventeenth Corps had been shredded in the town. There was no sense any longer in trying to hold it. It was afire, all semblance of control lost. Throughout the night Grant would keep pouring more men in while Johnston would not arrive much before midnight, and it'd still take several hours to bring him up.

No. The day had started off poorly with the bridge, but he felt confident now. They had smashed a corps, and Grant would not let that pass lightly. *He'll bring in the rest of his men. Now is the time for us to take the good ground.*

He turned to Walter.

"Order Scales and Robertson to evacuate the town, to pull back to the other side of the river."

"The other side, sir? What about the bridge?"

"The other side has higher ground, Walter. You saw the survey Jed Hotchkiss did for us today. It's a good defensive position, and I will not venture a fight on this side. Grant's blood is up, and he'll hit us, come tomorrow. Let him think we're retreating and that will bring him on. I want everyone back across the river and then let us see what Grant will do. Once we defeat him, we can repair the bridge and move our pontoons."

"Yes, sir."

Walter rode off.

Lee sat silent, watching the town burn, the wounded coming out, and he lowered his head.

"Merciful God," he whispered, "forgive us what we did to each other this day. Please let this be the last fight. Let it end here so that no longer friend is turned against friend."

Braddock Heights

1:00 A.M.

In spite of the rain, Frederick continued to burn. The moon was out, its light reflecting off the thick haze of smoke that cloaked the valley below.

Word had just come back to Grant that McPherson was wounded, perhaps already dead, and now a prisoner. His corps was a shambles, according to Sheridan, at best six thousand troops still effective.

A bloody first day, upward of nine thousand men killed, wounded, or captured between McPherson and Custer. The damage to Lee, Grant wasn't sure about, though hundreds of rebel wounded were now in the hospitals behind the heights or being tended to in the town, what was left of it.

Ely came up to him with a dispatch to sign, a request to be carried through the Confederate lines to Lee, asking for information on McPherson. Lee's nephew, Fitz Lee, had been taken prisoner, his horse shot out from under him. His leg was badly broken in the fall and might need to be amputated and he wished to inform his uncle, as well, that his kin was being well taken care of and would receive the best treatment possible.

Grant signed the note, and Ely went off to find a courier willing to brave approaching the Confederate side, under flag of truce, at night.

The clattering echo in the valley behind him was building. Coming up the road he saw a band of officers, one of them carrying a sputtering torch. It was Henry Hunt.

Hunt spotted Grant and came over.

"Damn, sir, wish I could have gotten here sooner," Hunt gasped. "Just the road was clogged with infantry, that damn Ninth Corps."

"That damn Ninth Corps, as you put it," Grant replied, "has come through now, under Sheridan. They're down in the town."

Grant pointed to the smoldering nightmare below, and Hunt nodded, whistling softly.

"Looks like it was one helluva fight."

"It was, and it will be. Where are your guns, sir?"

Hunt proudly pointed down the road. Already visible by the light of the torches and lanterns around the hospital area, the first team was pulling hard, coming up the slope. As they rounded the final curve the dismounted gunners were leaning into the wheels of the lead piece, horses panting and slipping on the macadamized road, which had turned soft and greasy after the heavy thunderstorms. The driver was shouting, cursing, trace riders spurring their mounts, and the piece lunged forward, gaining the crest. Behind it was a double caisson pulled by six more horses, behind that another gun, and then another double caisson, all of them struggling and lunging forward to gain the final slope.

"We've been on the road eighteen hours, sir. Getting down the road over South Mountains was tough going since the rain had just passed. I lost several pieces upended, teams killed, and several men when the guns went out of control. I'll send horses back in the morning to get them. My men are beat, but where do you want us?"

"That's the spirit, Hunt," Grant said approvingly. "That's the drive I want. Take them down the slope. You'll find General Sheridan has set up headquarters, I'm told, in what's left of the railroad depot in the center of town. Report to him."

"Sheridan, sir?"

"McPherson's down," Grant said quietly.

"Sorry, sir. I didn't know."

"Sheridan's in command down on the field at the moment. I'm waiting up here. Don't worry, Hunt, you'll get your chance at your grand battery; I'm not splitting you up. Phil has the lay of the land down there and will tell you where you should set up for the moment. Report to me down in the town at dawn."

"Yes, sir."

"Where's Ord? Have you heard from him?"

"He's right behind my column, sir. Cursing at me all the way, says I'm slowing his march."

"That's Ord," Grant said with a smile.

"He should be along once the last of my guns has passed. I'd say he's about three miles back."

"You've done good today, Hunt. Now get to work."

Henry looked at him and then grinned, saluted, and rode off, yelling at his men to move faster regardless of the downslope ahead.

"Sir?"

It was Ely.

"The dispatch is going off now. May I suggest you grab a little sleep. It's been a long day."

At the mere mention of sleep, tiredness overcome him. He'd ridden nearly thirty miles, been in the thick of it, and for the first time directly matched wits with Lee. He had also sent a good friend to his death or captivity.

Ely pointed to a house, a small clapboard affair on the other side of the road.

Grant walked over, dodging around a gun team pushing by him, the trace-horse driver swearing at him to "get the hell out of our way," the driver not realizing whom he was yelling at.

Lights glowed within the house.

"Hospital inside, sir," Ely said, "but a couple of the boys arranged a spot for you on the porch."

A bed was made up, an actual mattress under a couple of blankets.

Wearily he sat down, not turning aside the offer when Ely knelt to help pull off his boots. The migraine which had bedeviled him all day still held on, and he suddenly felt nauseous, as if the awareness of his affliction intensified it.

He lay back with a sigh. Migraine or not, within a few minutes he was fast asleep. Guards quietly circled the porch with orders from Ely to maintain a silent vigil. Ely sat down on the porch, leaning against the railing, struggling to stay awake to intercept any dispatches that might come in, but even he succumbed, falling asleep with his head resting on his drawn-up knees.

Out on the road the guns continued to pass, Napoleons, Parrotts, three-inch ordnance rifles, caissons, forge wagons, teams panting and struggling, crews cursing, moving woodenly in their exhaustion. They responded to Grant's orders for speed as he slipped into a dream wracked by nightmares of McPherson, of so many dead, all looking at him as if to ask whether it was indeed worth it, whether he was worthy of them.

Baltimore

2:15 A.M.

US "E mily. Wake up, dear. Wake up."
      Startled, Emily Hoffman sat up in her bed, her mother
by her side, holding a lit candle.

"What is it?" she asked.

"Dear, there's a soldier downstairs. A captain, he insists on seeing you."

"A Confederate?" she asked, still half asleep and confused.

"Yes, dear," Her mother stifled a sob.

"James!"

She was out of her bed, snatching up her dressing gown, slipping into it, and half-lacing the top as she raced barefoot down the stairs. A light was glowing in the parlor, and as she stepped into the room, the soldier, who had been talking with her father, turned and stiffened.

"What is it?" she gasped.

"Miss Emily Hoffman?" the captain asked nervously.

"Yes."

"Ma'am. I bear a telegram from General Lee, addressed to you, ma'am."

He held out the envelope, and she stood frozen, fearing to accept it.

The captain just stood there, red-faced, unable to speak, hand still extended with the envelope.

Her mother stepped forward, and the captain bowed slightly as she took the envelope and tore it open, her father holding a lantern up so she could read it.

Her mother began to shake, lowering her head.

"It's James," her mother gasped.

"Papa?" Emily looked at her father imploringly.

Her father took the telegram.

"It's addressed to you, sweetheart, from General Lee." He began to read:

"It is with a heavy heart I must inform you that your fiancé has been severely wounded. I regret to tell you he is not expected to live. He was a beloved student of mine, and this tragedy touches me deeply. If you wish, you may take the next train out of Baltimore to come to his side at Frederick, where even now my physician attends him. The officer bearing this letter will escort you and your family."

Her father stepped forward, as if to hand her the letter, but she backed up, collapsing on to the sofa, sobbing.

"It's not safe," her mother said. "I think she should stay here. There's fighting up there."

"I'm going," she gasped.

"Madam," the officer said, "General Lee will provide for your safety and protection."

He paused.

"If it was me," he whispered, "I'd want my Eleanor to be at my side."

Emily looked up at the officer. She felt at this moment that she should hate him with all her soul. It was someone in that uniform who had shot her James. But the look in his eyes, which were brimming with tears, stilled her anger.

"Thank you, Captain . . ."

"Cain. Bill Cain, ma'am. Headquarters staff for General Lee, stationed here in Baltimore. It's where I grew up."

He forced a smile through his tears.

"You might not remember me, Miss Hoffman, but I once danced with you at a social before the war. I met your fiancé that night, an honorable gentleman."

"Mama, pack my things," Emily whispered.

Washington

August 26
6:00 A.M.

He almost wished that he was back on the train racing across Pennsylvania. At least for those wonderful twelve hours he was able to stretch out and sleep. No one disturbed him, the passenger car sealed and guarded. No news, no decisions, just peaceful rest.

He and his escort rode down the narrow streets of Georgetown, which in spite of the early hour was awake, filled with traffic. Troops by the thousands lined the roads, fully laden with backpacks, haversacks stuffed to overflowing, the men in long lines shuffling forward a few dozen feet, stopping, then moving again.

As he rode past them, the soldiers looked up, saluting. A few called his name, but they were tired, having been up nearly the entire night, filing down from the fortress lines. Thet kept the city awake with the constant tramp of their marching, the rumble of field pieces, the cracking whips of drivers urging on supply wagons. Men leaned wearily against muskets, swaying, some actually falling asleep standing up, then comrades nudging them awake when the column moved forward again a few dozen feet.

He caught sight of Winfield down by the docks. Amazingly, the man was actually on horseback, his features pale in the morning light, Elihu by his side. At his approach Winfield smiled and saluted.

"How goes it?" Lincoln asked.

"Oh, sir, the usual chaos." Winfield pointed to the docks and wharfs of the old Chesapeake and Ohio canal. Dozens of barges were lined up, troops filing aboard. A hoist was swinging the barrel of a thirty-pounder Parrott gun out over a barge and slowly lowering it down. The men were nervously standing back as the barrel came to rest in the hull, the boat sinking deeper into the water as it took on the burden.

It did indeed look like chaos, hundreds of workers hauling boxes of rations, ammunition, barrels of salt pork, and stacking them up inside the bulk-hauling boats, many of them coated with layers of coal dust from their years of service bringing coal down from the mountains of western Virginia. Troops were filing aboard passenger boats, a hundred men or more to each, and he could see a procession of barges was already heading up the canal. Once aboard and settled in, the men relaxed, lying down to sleep, some sitting up, digging into their haversacks. One man had a small concertina out and was playing a lively jig.

"Ready to go!" The barge carrying three of the Parrott guns cast off, the four mules hauling it braying, digging in, their driver cursing at them, snapping a whip. The barge inched away from the wharf.

Resting in a sling by the side of a wharf was the massive barrel of a hundred-pound Parrott gun, twenty tons of metal, its iron carriage in another sling, dozens of men swarming around the monster, hooking cables to the thick woven mat the barrel was resting on. A work crew was busy carrying individual shells aboard, a hundred pounds each, and massive bags of grape and canister shot. Farther down the wharf, another boat, surrounded by sentries with bayoneted rifles, was loading barrels of powder, with hand-lettered EXPLOSIVES signs marking the entrance to the wharf.

"I should be leaving soon," Winfield said. "I think they've got the system down. I'll leave staff here to keep moving it along. I want to get up to the front. We have a brigade of mounted troops moving up the canal ahead of all this. Word will get out, and Mosby and his boys might try some mischief. I want to be up there if he does."

Lincoln nodded and extended his hand.

"Be careful, Winfield. You're a good man. Take care of yourself."

"Oh, I will, sir."

He started to dismount and a couple of young staff officers moved quickly by his side. It was not so much a dismounting as it was a lifting-down. He grimaced with the pain, but then, remembering Lincoln, he smiled.

"See, sir, no problem at all." He accepted his cane and leaned heavily on it. Then he limped off.

"Think he can handle it?" Lincoln asked, looking over at Elihu.

"If anyone can, it's him. He spent an hour with me yesterday morning, went over the details, and then was down here at the docks all day and clean through the night. He knows his job."

"Fine, then. We made the right choice."

"Something curious going on you should know about," Elihu said, and motioned to a sidestreet, leading Lincoln as they wove through the columns of troops queuing up to get aboard the canal boats.

As they turned the corner Lincoln was startled to see hundreds of black men standing about in a crowd, many with shovels, picks, and axes on their shoulders. Others had wheelbarrows loaded down with baggage. Two men had between them a large two-man whipsaw. A scattering of them were armed with old muskets or pistols.

At their approach the milling crowd fell silent, many of the men taking their hats off, stepping back at Lincoln's approach. To his amazement Lincoln saw Jim Bartlett standing in the crowd—rather, standing out, since he was dressed in a fine suit while most of the men wore the ordinary clothes of laborers.

"Jim?" Lincoln asked. "May I ask what is going on here?"

Jim braced his shoulders back, staring Lincoln straight in the eye.

"Mr. President, remember last night when you asked me to see if men would be interested in volunteering short-term for some work?

"Well, we know where them boats are going." He nodded toward the canal barges loading up.

"How do you know that, Jim?"

With that a number of the men started to chuckle.

"Ain't no secrets from us colored folk, Mr. Lincoln," a burly worker replied, and that brought on more laughter.

"Too many of you white folks think we're invisible. We're cleaning the dishes and the missus starts gossiping with other ladies about what her husband just told her, we're sweeping the floor at Willard's and the officers are boasting, or we're emptying trash in the War Office and pieces of paper just come falling into our laps. Oh, we know."

That brought renewed laughter, and Lincoln could not suppress a grin. He instantly saw the wisdom of it, thinking himself of so many conversations in the White House with servants walking in and out of the room. By heavens, of course they'd know.

"What are you and your friends proposing, Jim?" Lincoln asked.

"Our hands, our backs. There are tens of thousands of colored in this city who want to do something, anything. Let us go with the soldiers. We can dig for them, and, sir, we know that's a worry of yours."

The burly man nudged the man next to him, a thin, frail gentleman with graying hair who stepped forward nervously.

"Begging your pardon, Mr. Washburne, I hope you ain't mad, but I brought coffee into the room while you and a general were talking. I heard you say something about moving the men, but maybe not having time to dig in proper, building forts and such."

Washburne looked at the speaker in amazement.

"You know I oughta fire you," he blustered. "What you overheard is a military secret."

"Oh, I heard Mr. Stanton talking all the time, a lot of things, sir, maybe you should know about, considering all the fuss he's kicking up in the newspapers."

Lincoln threw back his head and laughed, a laugh unlike any he had experienced in weeks.

"He's got you, Elihu. We need this man."

Elihu shook his head, then leaned out of his saddle and extended his hand.

"All right then. We'll talk after this is over, but by heavens I'll never speak a word again when you are around."

The man grinned and took Elihu's hand.

"We're on the same side, sir. Maybe for different reasons, but the same side."

"For the same reasons now," Lincoln said quietly, and he looked back at Jim. "Troops have to have priority on the boats, but wherever there's additional room, you men get aboard."

A cheer went up.

Lincoln extended his hand.

"I should warn you, though. It will be dangerous. I cannot guarantee that you will be treated well if things turn against us and you are captured."

"Then we fight," Jim said quietly. "A pick or an ax is as good as a bayonet."

"Not against disciplined troops," Elihu said softly.

"It'll be hours, most likely, before there will be room on any of the boats," Lincoln said.

"We already figured that," the burly man said. "We'll just start walking if you don't mind. Follow the canal path."

Lincoln suddenly was overcome by emotion, his face limp with sadness.

One of the men held up a banner made out of a bedsheet. Emblazoned in red letters: WASHINGTON COLORED VOLUNTEERS.

The crowd cheered again and then spontaneously poured down the street, turning on to the canal path to head toward the front. As they surged by him, Lincoln remained motionless.

Looking back toward the boats, he saw Colonel Shaw leading the men of the Fifty-fourth Massachusetts aboard several barges. Shaw caught his eye and snapped to attention, saluting, his men cheering as they saw their brothers pouring down the street and then turning to follow the canal path.

"How the world is changing," Lincoln whispered. He reached over and took Jim's hand.

"God be with you, my friend."

"And with you too, Mr. President," he paused, "and thank you."

Chapter Twelve

Gen. Pete Longstreet rode up the steep slope past a wooden blockhouse, pausing for a moment to watch as a gun crew struggled to maneuver a twelve-pound Napoleon through the back doorway, then rolled it into place inside, positioning it at a gun port looking down on the river below.

The blockhouse was perfectly positioned to cover the ruins of the railroad bridge and the still-smoking wreckage of a rail depot on the other bank, less than four hundred yards away. To either flank of the blockhouse men were digging in, cutting trenches, a work crew dragging cut lumber from the mill just south of the track to pile atop the barricades.

A scattering of Yankee skirmishers were around the depot on the other side of the creek, but for the moment there seemed to be one of those informal cease-fires between them and the Confederate skirmishers. Many were up, walking about, examining the wreckage, both sides adopting the live-and-let-live attitude of soldiers who were more than willing to fight when called upon, but considered sniping to be little better than murder if there was no immediate purpose to it. Like schoolboys they prowled around the wreckage, coming to the river to examine the bridge and gape down at the two shattered locomotives in the creek. A few had started fires to fix one last pot of coffee before battle was rejoined.

Even Pete stopped for a minute to look at the ruins. It was obvious there had been one hell of a fight here yesterday. Bark had been peeled off trees by bullets, hunks of metal from the exploding train littered the riverbank, and burial details were at work on both sides of the river, as if clearing the ground for the next harvest, which would begin soon enough.

"Hey, reb, who's the general?" a Yank with a booming voice shouted from across the river.

Several of the Confederates down by the bridge looked back and saw Pete.

"Why, that's old Longstreet!" one of them shouted back. "Now that he's here, there'll be hell to pay for you boys."

Pete shook his head. A compliment in a way, but the men would be in Yankee headquarters within the hour. Curious, this war: no matter how often the men were lectured on it, skirmishers on both sides tended to gossip and give away secrets, just like old women at a quilting party.

Pete pressed up the hill to a flat plateau where Lee, Jeb Stuart, Walter Taylor, and John Hood stood, all with field glasses raised, looking toward the distant ridgeline.

Pete offered a salute as he approached, and Lee, lowering his glasses, smiled.

"General, good to see you. You must be exhausted after such a long ride."

"I'm fine, sir," he lied. He was numb after the twenty-four-hour ride, the anxiety of what was happening ahead, and the frustration he felt as he paralleled the railroad track and saw the colossal traffic jam that stretched for miles. The hope had been that during the night, once Hood was finished moving his divisions up, the trains could start shuttling troops from his own corps forward, sparing them the rest of the march. That was clearly impossible. Only a few engines were moving, while dozens waited to back up through the single-line track between the two tunnels.

"Tell me, General, when can we begin to expect your troops?" Lee asked, as Pete dismounted. One of the staff handed him a cup of coffee, which he gladly accepted.

"I left them during the night, sir. The lead division, McLaw's, should be up by noon."

"Good. And General Beauregard's Corps?"

"Behind the rest of my column, sir, but he is also moving on parallel roads, not the National Road. He should start filing in late this afternoon."

Lee nodded approvingly.

"How are things here, sir?" Pete asked.

"Grant is living up to his reputation," Lee said and motioned to the Catoctin Ridge.

Pete uncased his field glasses and focused on the distant ridge. Though it was wreathed in early morning mist and smoke from the burning town, he was able to catch glimpses of troops moving down the road.

"Ord we think," Walter interjected.

"McPherson and Burnside are already accounted for," Lee said. "That only leaves Banks. Scouts with General Stuart reported a number of batteries coming into the town during the night."

"I heard you really chewed into McPherson yesterday," Pete said.

"Yes," Lee replied, his voice now barely a whisper.

"Sir, I'm sorry. I meant no disrespect to James. He was a good man."

"He's still alive," Walter said.

"Will he pull through?"

Lee shook his head.

"Again, sir, I'm sorry."

"It is God's will," Lee said softly.

"Most of McPherson's Corps was destroyed yesterday," Walter said. "We briefly tangled with some of Burnside's men last night. Colored troops."

"Damn all," Hood said coldly.

Lee turned and looked over at Hood, who lowered his gaze.

"They are to be treated like any other troops we face," Lee announced. "If taken prisoner, they and their officers are to be shown all due respect, as has been our tradition. I want everyone to understand that."

"Yes, sir," Hood said.

"So that leaves one of Grant's corps unaccounted for," Longstreet said, feeling it best to change the topic. "Banks, supposedly his strongest unit."

"I suspect he is on the far side of that ridge even now," Lee announced.

"There's nothing to the north," Stuart said. "My screen is still holding, though there has been some heavy skirmishing with Grierson. The only cavalry unit to break through so far was Custer, and we saw what happened to him yesterday."

"But he did burn the rail bridge and covered bridge and mauled several regiments in the process," Hotchkiss interjected. "I'd consider that a fair trade."

"Yes, indeed, a fair trade. And it also fixed this place as the one where this war will be decided, once and for all," Lee announced.

Pete, sipping his coffee, looked over at Lee.

"It has to be here," Lee said. "We could have held those heights up there." He pointed to the Catoctin Ridge. "But if we had, Grant would not have taken the bait. The position is simply impregnable, and even Grant would not have attacked us if we had stayed there. He'd have stopped his advance and dug in along South Mountains."

Lee turned to face his officers.

"Remember last year. But one of our divisions held that ridge for an entire day while we regrouped at Sharpsburg. The Catoctin Ridge was an even better tactical position, with only one road crossing it versus three at South Mountains."

"Then, sir, why did you concede it?" Longstreet asked.

Lee smiled.

"Because it was too good. If Scales had stayed there, and then been reinforced by Robertson's Division, no force on the face of this earth could have pushed us off. Grant would have remained concealed behind South Mountains, and that would give him time. He could have sat us out for weeks or perhaps pushed down to Harpers Ferry, crossed into Virginia, and thus forced us to follow him. No, when I saw this ground, I wanted him here."

Lee turned and pointed to the flat open plain between the river and Frederick.

"They will deploy out there, gentlemen. Our elevation here, according to Jed Hotchkiss, is a good hundred to two hundred feet higher, with excellent fields of fire for our preponderance in artillery. We have the range of hills to our south bordering the river; they can act as a tactical shield if we should wish to maneuver that way. But I think Grant will come straight on."

"Just like Burnside at Fredericksburg," Hood interjected.

Lee nodded in agreement.

"I believe I am getting the measure of Grant. He is tenacious. He pushed McPherson's Corps forward yesterday afternoon to seize the town and perhaps the bridge regardless of the losses. We bloodied him. It is obvious by what we see over there that blood has not deterred him. He has pushed two more corps in, and they will begin to deploy down to the river and then come straight at us. And I say, let them come!"

He slapped a balled fist against the palm of his hand.

Longstreet turned to look at the ground. Lee was right. It was indeed ideal ground for a fight. The Monocacy Creek formed a natural barrier to slow any assault. There were numerous fords, and the still-intact stone bridge of the National Road, but each of those fords and the bridge faced, on the east side, excellent ground for artillery, infantry, and observation. Union attacks would have to funnel into those points, and it would be a killing ground. There were also fairly good roads on the east side, running north to south, which could provide for rapid redeployment of troops.

"Then why will he attack?" Pete asked. "We do hold the better ground here. Not suicidal, as would be the case if we were atop Catoctin Heights, just slightly better ground than those on the west side. But why attack us? Why not wait? I think, sir, if it was us over there, we would definitely not attack."

"Because he is under pressure, General Longstreet, from Washington. And because everything we know about Grant tells us that he is aggressive and persistent. I think Grant is not a fool like Burnside. When he hits, as he did at the second day of Shiloh, he will come on with everything at once. But he will come on."

"Only if he thinks he can win, or has a broader plan," Pete said. "I wish Beauregard was here to see this and offer his opinion."

At this Lee turned to look at Pete with fire in his eyes, a flash of anger even. Pete had seen that look before. So many spoke of the gentleman Lee, the courtly Lee, but when battle loomed, a cold side could come out, even one of anger. That had truly flared to the surface at Union Mills when he fired Dick Ewell from command and sent him home in disgrace.

When word had first come that Grant was on the move he had seen Lee surprisingly off balance for over a day, pondering, unsure. That was now washed away. He was confident, eager for battle, perhaps too much so.

"We both want this to end," Lee snapped. "We received a report yesterday that not three days past Lincoln was with Grant up by Carlisle. Lincoln is facing a firestorm back in Washington over his removal of Stanton and the defeats. If Grant cannot win it for them in the next week or two, their government might collapse."

"Therefore, might not the seizing of Catoctin Heights have been a wise move?" Longstreet ventured. "It would have forced Grant to either make a suicidal attack or maneuver, which would have taken too much time."

Lee looked at him sharply, and Pete realized he had overstepped his bounds. It was something he could have said to Lee in private, but to second-guess a decision which could no longer be reversed, in front of others, was a major mistake.

"I apologize, sir," Longstreet said softly.

"No offense taken," Lee replied, and his features softened.

"No, General Longstreet, I want this settled now. We have lured Grant down out of the pass. Once our guns are up and in place, we can turn that field across the stream into a slaughterhouse. We break him in his attacks, then counterstrike. He'll have only one road out as we converge in. We break him, then unleash Jeb here to finish the job. I dare say that in three days we can annihilate Grant here, push him up over the Catoctin Pass, and what is left we can annihilate in the valley beyond."

Longstreet said nothing. He could see that the Old Man's fire was up, the same as the first day at Gettysburg, and there was no arguing with him now. It was just that there was one question unanswered. If this was indeed a killing ground, why was Grant marching into it?

Braddock Heights

8:00 A.M.

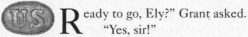

R eady to go, Ely?" Grant asked.
          "Yes, sir!"

Grant looked around at his staff. Lohman would stay behind at the crest to keep an eye on the approach of Banks's Corps, which, though slow, was now cresting the South Mountain range. All of Hunt's guns had long since passed. Behind Banks would come the tangle of supply wagons, twenty-five miles of them, with orders to go into reserve behind the Catoctin Mountains, with priority given to ammunition, rations, and medical supplies.

A report had just arrived that the railroad crews had completed the repair of the Cumberland Valley Railroad down to Hagerstown, and the first trains were coming in even now, carrying extra supplies. A dozen trains a day from Harrisburg would free up a thousand or more wagons that could be used to improve his supply line from Hagerstown to here. With the double mountain barrier, other than the problem it presented with the steep slopes, he now enjoyed a very secure line of supply. With the extra wagons, the load per wagon could be lightened to speed up the passage over the mountains. By midday his telegraphy crews promised they'd have a direct line completed from Hagerstown to Frederick. With that in place he'd be linked to Harrisburg and the North.

Another crew a hundred miles away was hard at work stringing a connection due east out of Washington to the Chesapeake and another line on the east shore connecting into the line that ran up to Dover. By late in the day, messages from Washington and back, which only yesterday took days, would be cut to not more than an hour or two.

There were times in his past when he had wanted to be as far away from contact with Washington as possible. But not now, not with the confidence among himself, Lincoln, and Washburne. If his plan was to work, they had to have this intricate web of wire to hook it all together, encircling Lee with tapping signals made of electricity that Napoleon and Caesar could never have dreamed of.

He was grateful to Ely for the five hours of uninterrupted sleep. All of Hunt's Artillery had passed, and now the second division of Ord's Corps was slipping and sliding to the top of the crest and then sliding down the opposite side. Ely had told him that Ord had passed by without even wakening him, saying he and Phil would figure out where to deploy.

Both these men were new to corps command. Ord only in May, Phil just since yesterday, but he felt a sense of confidence in them. They understood every detail of the intricate plan he had worked out even before Sickles went off half-cocked. Though he had yet to actually see Phil under fire, he knew Ord had a good eye for ground and would act correctly. If he had encountered any real questions, he would have sent a message back.

The men of Ord's command were indeed exhausted. Typical of Ord he had pushed them remorselessly. As Grant rode out into the road, he took one last look to the west and saw Ord's Third Division struggling forward. The side of the road for miles back across the valley was dotted with blue specks, men who had collapsed after a day and a night of marching, with only a two-hour break at midnight. Perhaps twenty percent of his strength was thus scattered, but he had learned long ago that each regiment had its core, the hard-bitten lot of two or three hundred who did ninety percent of the fighting. Some of the stragglers, he knew, were good spirits in a fight but physically unable to keep up on a forced march, some were the shirkers, worse than useless in a fight, and many were just ill with the usual complaints of the "two steps," ague, or lung sickness, and to slow an army for them to keep pace was senseless.

A collecting point had already been established for them in the village of Middletown, appropriately named, for it was midway between the two mountain ranges. Hospitals were set up there for the sick, and once the road was cleared, those capable again of marching would be pushed forward.

He started down the slope, taking in the details. At least half a dozen of Hunt's guns and even more of the double limber caissons had wrecked on the way down. Crews had lost control and jumped off, with horses, guns, and caissons going over the side of the road in a horrifying tangle. And yet Hunt had pushed on.

A scattering of dead from both sides lined the sides of the road. Boys in tattered gray and butternut mingled with the tattered blue of McPherson's boys. No one had bothered to move them, other than to drag off the road those who blocked the way.

He tried not to look; the sights were far too distressing: sixteen-year-olds clutching a Bible or daguerreotype, older men twisted up in agony, others so peaceful, as if asleep. Two boys, identical twins, lay arm in arm, their blood commingled in the mud. The bodies were all so still, but strangely, if you stared at them too long, they appeared to be breathing still. A reb sergeant and a union private lay side by side, an open canteen between them, and yet ten feet away were two more, transfixed in death, one with a knife buried in the stomach of the other, the faces of both frozen in a terrible rage.

One man, a Confederate captain, was sitting against a tree, letters scattered about him, one still clutched in his hand. Letters from a mother, a sweetheart perhaps? He looked for a second, then turned his gaze away, forcing himself to again look straight ahead. None would ever go home; they'd be buried here. Perhaps weeks or months later a letter might arrive from a company officer or comrade, "Dear Madam, I regret to inform you . . ."

Wellington was right, the only thing as terrible as a battlefield lost was a battlefield won. Win or lose was still not decided, but for those now carpeting the sides of the road, victory or defeat no longer mattered.

I can never dwell on that too long, he thought. *Will Lee and I one day answer for this,* he wondered. It was a thought he knew was not healthy for him at this moment, and he forced it aside.

The migraine still bedeviled him, and he rubbed his brow. Ely was watching him with concern. He had tried to eat breakfast, a fine feast of fresh eggs, some salt pork, and even a few links of smoked sausage, and then slipped into the woods to vomit it all up. He smiled away Ely's concerns with the simple, "I'm fine."

A cigar helped a bit, and he puffed on it continually as he rode down the slope. The random thought came to him that a drink right now would taste awfully good, would settle his stomach, perhaps push the headache back, but that was something he knew he could never do now.

Maybe years from now, when I think of this moment, he thought, *perhaps then I'll get a good bottle of whiskey down and drink it dry, but not now, definitely not now.* But if there was anything that could turn a man back into an alcoholic it was this nightmare road and the wreckage of battle strewn along it.

The headache intensified. He tossed aside the cigar he was smoking, half finished, and then in a couple of minutes lit another.

They rode into the western end of Frederick, dozens of buildings smoking ruins. Ord's lead division was by his side, men moving slowly in their exhaustion but looking around, exclaiming over the wreckage, the obvious signs of a hard-fought battle.

Collapsed buildings still smoldered, civilians picking through the wreckage, a dazed woman standing by the side of the road clutching a flame-scorched portrait. A detail of soldiers, several of them Confederate prisoners, was hauling buckets of water, flinging them against the side of a home which was partially burned and still flickering with flames. A brick house, windows shot out, had a hospital flag flying in front of it; dozens of homes now displayed that flag, or just white bedsheets hanging out of windows. Wounded Union and Confederates lay on the sidewalk, while from within came ghastly cries of anguish.

An upended limber wagon blocked a sidestreet, several of the horses still alive, whimpering in pain, and Grant turned to one of his men, asking him to put the poor beasts out of their misery. He loathed the sight of an animal in pain.

In another section of town, nearly an entire block had been leveled by fire, smoke billowing up from the ruins. A church, its steeple tilting at a drunken angle after being hit by an exploding shell, had its doors flung open. On its doorstep he saw Union and Confederate doctors, working together, doing the grisly task of admitting some within and quietly telling many stretcher bearers to carry their burden "around the back," which meant they were too far gone for help.

The windows of nearly every shop were smashed in, and from a tree two bodies dangled on ropes, one a rebel, another a Union soldier, signs hanging from their stiffening bodies: LOOTERS & COWIRDS.

He edged his way toward the center of town. Here the battle had been at its fiercest. Dead carpeted the sidewalks, dangled from windows, were sprawled into shop windows, and laid curled up in alleyways. A cavalry detachment, a few weary men from Custer's command, were mounted and at the center of town, directing Ord's column to keep moving eastward, to not stop till the far side of town.

"General Sheridan's headquarters?" Ely asked, and a trooper pointed down the road.

"At the Frederick railroad depot, about four blocks ahead, sir," and the men saluted as Grant rode by.

"General Grant!"

He looked over at his inquirer, a civilian carrying a cumbersome box with tripod over his shoulder.

"Sir, a favor!"

"What is it?" Grant asked.

"Sir, General McPherson was shot right over there." The photographer pointed toward a corner building at the center of town, several bodies lying in the gutter, bloodstains still in the street.

Grant stared at him.

"May I have your portrait there, sir? Surely the *Illustrated Weekly* will want this one. General Grant mourns at the place McPherson fell."

Though obscenities were rare for him, one spilled forth now, and turning, he rode on, staff glaring coldly at the photographer who stood there, mystified by the response. Then, shrugging his shoulders, he moved on, setting up his camera for another shot of the troops when they paused for a break.

He pushed on, past a house where a tattered Confederate regimental flag dangled from a third-floor window. He saw a column of exhausted rebel prisoners, fifty or more, being escorted by several equally exhausted guards, a minister saying a prayer over a dozen blanketed bodies, a Catholic priest giving communion to several men who had stopped for his blessing, and then to his amazement, an embalmer who was selling policies.

Men like him always trailed the armies. They'd sell an "embalming policy" for fifty dollars to any soldier and issue him a receipt. If a comrade brought the body in with the receipt, the deliverer received five dollars, the body was supposedly embalmed, usually poorly done, and then shipped to the family.

Some of McPherson's men were negotiating with him, dead bodies lying around his wagon.

"Drive that scoundrel off," Grant snapped, and several of the men of Grant's headquarters detail were more than happy to comply, one of them deliberately smashing the embalmer's bottles of fluids with his sword, then drawing a pistol on him and telling him, "Get the hell out of this town, you son of a bitch."

Grant did not look back, but rode on. At last he saw it, the rail depot. It was a wreck, a small roundhouse burned to the ground, several cars still flickering with flames, a warehouse all but flattened by fire except for the skeletonlike eyes of its windows.

He spotted Sheridan out front, Ord by his side, and Hunt leaning against a tree, smoking a cigar. At his approach the three came to attention.

"Quite a mess here in town," Sheridan announced, as Grant rode up.

"I can see that."

"No fighting to report, sir. The rebels gave back during the night and retreated across the Monocacy."

Grant nodded. No news there. At dawn he had seen it clearly enough. Frankly, he did not expect Lee to try to fight him on this side of the creek. There was no good tactical ground for him to hold, other than to try to maintain his grip on the town and block the one road.

Grant dismounted, tossed his cigar aside, and walked over to a table where Phil had a map spread out, pencil marks indicating troop movements. The other officers fell in around him.

Grant puffed on his cigar as he leaned over the map and studied it intently, examining where Sheridan had sketched in the rebel positions.

"We fight him here," Grant said.

"But he has chosen this ground," Hunt replied. "Sir, I know you said we should stop trying to worry about what Lee wants, but still, from experience, sir, when that man chooses ground, it means a tough fight."

"And that is precisely why I will fight him here," Grant replied sharply. "He wants this fight, and so do I. Let him choose this ground, this particular place. It will fix him in place the way I want it."

He leaned back, rubbing his brow again.

Ord grinned and said nothing.

Grant leaned over the map again.

"We just had a report come up from the depot," Sheridan said, "that General Longstreet was spotted."

"Is Beauregard up yet?"

"No indication of that, sir," Sheridan replied. "We've accounted for two divisions of Hood's. About a hundred guns are deploying along the heights above the depot and also over on our right flank here."

He pointed to where the creek took a turn to the southwest for a mile or so before bending back to the south.

"It's called the McCausland Farm. A good open hill. Guns there can enfilade the depot area."

"Sir," Ord interjected, "we have two intact corps up. Hunt has his batteries up. Why don't we go for them here?"

He pointed toward the McCausland Farm.

"There's a ford below the farm. My boys could force it."

Grant nodded, looking at the map, remembering the lay of the terrain he had spent hours studying yesterday.

"Your boys have marched for nearly twenty-four hours," Grant said.

"My command, then," Sheridan offered. "They've had several hours' rest."

"I want you to hold the center of the line and the left flank," Grant said. "You're already in position for that."

He contemplated the move and then finally nodded.

"I want to keep the pressure on Lee, but Banks is not yet up. General Ord, a limited attack, later in the day. Do not bring on a general engagement, though."

"Sir?"

"The last thing I want now is to push Lee out of this position, but I do

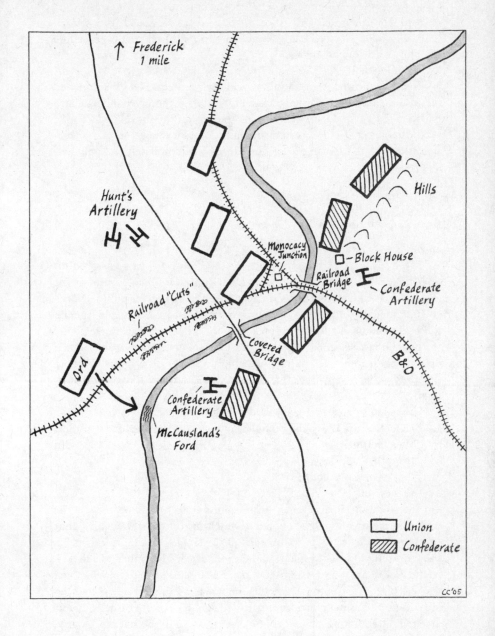

↑ Frederick
1 mile

Hunt's
Artillery

Monocacy
Junction

Railroad "Cuts"

Ord

Covered
Bridge

Confederate
Artillery

McCausland's
Ford

Hills

Block House

Railroad
Bridge

Confederate
Artillery

B & O

Union
Confederate

CC'05

not want him to think we are suffering from temerity. Commit as if we are about to try a serious lunge, but conserve your boys."

"If I gain the ford?" Ord asked.

"Hold it, of course. That will force him to want to take it back, but do not bring on a general engagement."

"I understand, sir."

Grant sat down on, of all things, a church pew that had been carried out of the church across the street and his staff gathered round as Sheridan held a map up, Grant behind him, tracing out the move.

He hated giving orders like this for a limited attack. A "demonstration" they use to call it at the Point. Still, such a demonstration might cost a thousand lives before it was done.

One Mile Southeast of Monocacy Junction

2:00 P.M.

The train drifted to a halt. Emily Hoffman gazed out the window, the spectacle around her not registering, for at such a moment the world collapses into itself, and the struggle, the anguish, the drama of a hundred thousand others become meaningless.

For the last six miles they had passed train after train stalled on the other track, locomotives puffing, backing up slowly, foot by foot. Troops lined the tracks, marching westward, battle flags at the fore of each regiment.

"Miss Hoffman?"

She looked up. It was the kindly Captain Cain, and she forced a smile.

"Miss Hoffman?"

"Yes, Bill?"

"We're here, ma'am."

"Thank you."

She stood up. Her parents, sitting across from her, stood as well, her mother reaching out to take her hand, which she refused. She took a deep breath and followed Cain to the back of the single car, empty except for the four of them. Troops piled off the other cars in the train and she realized this was one more part of the war she hated. As she stepped out onto the rear platform, she found a detachment was waiting for her, Confederate cavalry and a small carriage, a battered country type of carriage, barely able to hold four, its top gone, a single aging horse in the traces.

"Sorry about the carriage, ma'am," a major said as she stepped down, taking Cain's hand. "It's all General Lee could find for you."

She forced a smile as she stepped into the carriage, Cain taking the reins, her mother and father squeezing in on the seat behind her.

The major rode out front, escorts flanking the carriage, and they set off. The road they were on, heading south, was packed with troops, the major riding ahead, shouting for them to clear the way.

The men, grumbling, stepped aside but, at the sight of her, many removed their hats. "That's her," she heard one of them announce as they passed.

The road turned off to the west, and after another turn to the south, they pulled into the drive of a modest two-story frame house.

She recoiled at the sight confronting her. Several hundred men lay in the yard, under the trees of a small orchard, some out in the glaring sun, others under quickly erected awnings of shelter halves and tarps. A tent was set up outside the building, and to her horror a pile of bloody limbs rested outside the tent.

The major barked a sharp command, and one of his troopers dismounted, grabbed a blanket from behind his saddle, ran up, and threw the blanket over the grisly sight, but it was too late; she had already seen it.

She felt as if she would faint but then whispered a silent prayer for strength. *James must not see me weak, not now.* Behind her, her mother began to cry.

Cain got down from the carriage and offered his hand.

"This way, Miss Hoffman."

She stepped down from the carriage. All in the yard fell strangely quiet at the sight of her, men whispering to each other. Some of the wounded were boys in blue, and one of them, leg missing below the knee, propped himself on his elbow.

"Let's hear it for old McPherson!" he cried, and a ragged three cheers echoed weakly.

She looked at her escort of Confederate troopers and officers. They were silent, but she could see in their eyes there was no rancor, instead she saw looks of compassion, and she nodded to them, one of the men offering a handkerchief so she could wipe her eyes.

She mounted the steps. A minister was standing there, and for a horrified second she feared she was too late.

"I'm Reverend Lacy," he said. "I used to serve with General Jackson. Now I'm on General Lee's staff. He asked that I attend you, miss. Your fiancé is still with us."

"Thank you, Reverend," she whispered.

He extended his hand and she took it.

"He's upstairs, resting at the moment."

"His condition?" her father asked.

The reverend looked straight at her.

"You must be strong, my dear, and place your faith in Our Lord."

"He won't live, will he?" she asked.

He shook his head.

"How long?"

"A few hours perhaps."

"Is he in pain?"

"No. The doctor gave him morphine, though he tried to refuse it. Miss, he is shot through both lungs. It is only a matter of time now."

She said nothing but felt a frightful urgency to see him and stepped into the house. Again she wanted to recoil. It appeared to be the home of a country physician, his office to her right, but the sight within that room filled her with horror, for the doctor was operating on a man, blood dripping to the floor, the doctor bent over, cutting into the man's open thigh. In the parlor to the left, a dozen men were on the floor, a woman, most likely the doctor's wife, bandaging a boy's face, slashed wide open from scalp to jaw. She looked up at Emily, but said nothing.

"This way," Reverend Beverly Lacy said and led her upstairs to the second floor. In what was obviously the doctor's bedroom she saw him as she reached the last step, doorway open.

She took a deep breath, prayed yet again for strength, and slowly walked in. He was under the covers, which were pulled down to his waist. Chest bandaged, the left side soaked red. A trickle of blood frothed his lips. He was breathing raggedly, gasping, each breath another froth of blood.

She knelt down by his side and took his hand. It was cool to the touch, graying, so unlike the warm strong grasp she once knew, the way he held her when they danced, when they walked together beneath the moonlight, the way his hands had so lovingly cupped her face when they kissed for the first time.

"James."

She leaned forward and whispered. He moaned softly, eyes fluttering.

"The morphine," Lacy whispered behind her.

"He knows I'm here now," she replied.

"James, it's Emily."

His eyes opened. He turned his head slightly, looked at her, and smiled.

She took the handkerchief given to her by the Confederate officer and wiped his lips.

"Emily." It was barely a whisper.

She leaned forward and kissed him.

She had to be strong, she knew that, and though she wanted to collapse, to cry, to just curl up and die with him, she knew she could not.

She stood up and looked at Lacy.

"A favor, Reverend."

"Anything."

"James and I were to be married. In fact, if not for what is happening now, General Grant had promised him a furlough once Vicksburg was taken for him to come to Baltimore so we could be joined."

She looked back down at James.

"We want to be married," she whispered.

"My dear?" It was her mother standing in the doorway.

A look from Emily silenced her mother. She looked at her father, who nodded in agreement.

Lacy hesitated.

"My dear, at this moment? He is drugged and his time approaches."

"You attended General Jackson at his deathbed, did you not?" she asked.

"Yes, miss," Lacy whispered.

"And his wife was present?"

"Yes."

"Then let General McPherson's wife attend to him."

Lacy did not respond.

"Marry us."

It was McPherson, eyes open, a smile on his lips.

Lacy nodded in response.

"No years together," McPherson whispered, "no wedding night, but still we have a little time, and then we will be together for all eternity."

Forcing back her tears she took James's hand and turned to face the minister.

Chapter Thirteen

Go, boys, go!"

Ord was standing in his stirrups, saber drawn, urging his men on as they ran down the slope on the double, in column by regiments. Shells rained down into the packed ranks, men screaming; at the ford, smoke swirled up from volley after volley blazing from the other side of the Monocacy.

"A splendid fight!" Ord shouted. "A splendid fight. Now drive 'em to hell!"

He turned and galloped down to the edge of the creek, violating strict orders from Grant to stay to the rear. He knew the general standing at the edge of town might see him, but he no longer cared. The fury of battle was upon him and he loved every second of it.

An Indiana regiment was in the lead, terrifyingly shredded by a volley delivered from the other bank, but they piled into the river anyhow, regardless of loss, plunging into the thigh-deep waters, pushing forward, men collapsing at every step, to be carried off by the waters.

Overhead was an inferno as Hunt's batteries, firing at long distance, plowed up the field on the other side of the creek and tried to suppress the dozen rebel batteries up next to a brick farmhouse that overlooked the ford less than a quarter mile away.

The Indiana regiment buckled as it reached midstream and started to give back, boys from Ohio pushing up behind them, gaining another twenty to thirty feet before they, too, started to collapse. Another Ohio regiment pushed in after them, plunging across, and barely gained the muddy bank on the other side. The Union was paying in blood for each foot gained for what was, as their commanding general declared, "a demonstration to fix Lee in place."

On those banks it turned to hand-to-hand fighting, men screaming, cursing, lunging with bayonets. Ohio just barely gained the opposite bank and then the artillery thundered in. The reb infantry gave back, coming out of the willows and ferns that lined the stream, running across the open field, dodging around the exploding shells of Hunt's batteries. As they fell back a terrible inferno erupted, battery after battery lining the hilltop around the McCausland farm opening up, sending down volleys of case shot that exploded over the Monocacy. Any shot that went high detonated or plowed into the ranks of the supporting brigade coming up to join in the assault. Treetops exploded in flames, solid shot slamming into the water threw up geysers thirty feet high pockmarked by the iron and lead balls of case shot slamming into the stream.

Ord, hat off, screamed with fury, urging his men to press in. A courier rode up, the side of his mount dripping blood, the horse limping badly.

"From General Grant, sir!" the courier shouted. "Call it off. Pull back!"

"We have the other bank!" Ord cried.

"You are ordered to call it off, sir!"

Ord reluctantly nodded, shouted for one of his staff to get across the stream, another to order the Second Brigade to turn about and retreat. Buglers began sounding recall throughout the attack.

The first courier into the stream went down, a shell detonating directly over him. Another dashed off, young lieutenants looking for glory were always thus, hoping a general would notice them. He barely made it to the other side, shouting to a regimental commander, and then he, too, pitched out of his saddle.

Within seconds the Ohio regiments on the other side broke and fell back across the stream. The supporting brigade, the men obviously not at all upset about the order to pull back, reversed and started to double-time back up the open slope.

As the last of the Ohio and Indiana regiments came up out of the river bottom, picking up wounded as they retreated, the rebel artillery ceased fire, a taunting cheer rising up from the other side.

"Some demonstration," Ord hissed, as he looked at the hundreds of dead and wounded piled along the riverbank or floating downstream. "I certainly hope Grant is right and this brings about an effect worthy of the lives of these young men.

"Tomorrow, you bastards," he shouted defiantly, and, turning, he retreated with his men.

Baltimore

5:30 P.M.

The last train of the artillery reserve rolled out of the Baltimore depot twenty-four hours behind schedule. Cruickshank wiped the sweat from his brow and looked over at McDougal, who had pulled out a bottle and was taking a "wee nip," something he tended to do at least twice an hour.

"Useless now to try and move Beauregard," Cruickshank said, "but there're the supplies, hundreds of tons of it. Rations, additional ammunition, evacuation back of the wounded, replacement horses and mules."

"And not a locomotive to be seen," McDougal said with a shrug.

"They'll be back tonight." There was almost a pleading note in Cruickshank's weary voice.

"A few perhaps, but you seem to have forgotten something, General."

"And that is?"

"Wood and coal."

"What do you mean?"

"You have over a hundred locomotives up the line and all snarled together. Their boilers have most likely been cooking away all day. They're short of wood and coal."

"I thought the order was given to send the necessary supplies for them up the line."

"Never got out, what with you rushing about, countermanding orders, then countermandering them again."

"Damn it, you should have kept me informed."

"I did, twice today, don't you remember? But you kept saying, 'Get the guns, up, McDougal, get the guns up.'"

He glared at the man, honestly not sure whether he was telling the truth or not. After two days with barely any sleep it was hard to tell anymore what was said just ten minutes ago.

"I'd say two thousand tons should do the trick," McDougal announced, fingers out as if calculating on them. "That'll be ten of our heavier trains, but we seem short of hopper cars."

"Where the hell are they?"

"A fair number of Robertson's boys rode up on them, General, sir. Don't you remember?"

"No, I don't, damn you," Cruickshank hissed, turning his back on McDougal.

What a simple, stupid, and yet all-too-obvious concern. When he drove supply wagons in Texas before the war, hauling along extra water and grain was a given. If the trains had simply gone up and off-loaded, then come straight back, he would not have a problem now, but many had been stranded up there for over a day, and their crews had undoubtedly kept the boilers lit and steam up.

Of course they'd be running short of fuel by now.

"What is stored along the line?" Cruickshank asked, not looking back.

"What do you mean 'stored'?" McDougal replied.

"Fuel, damn it."

"Wood ricks at the stations usually have a couple of cords that local farmers bring in. Coal for some of our newer engines, a few tons at each station. But you got more than a hundred locomotives up there, General, and they're all hungry and thirsty."

McDougal's tone was flat, showing he had enough sense not to rub the general's face in the problem. He knew he could take him on in a good knockdown, and if there had been the slightest hint in his voice, there would have been a fistfight, or better yet knives or pistols, one that had been building for days.

"How many locomotives still in the yard?"

"Three, and all of them are old wheezers."

"Load one of them up with wood and get it up at least to the tunnel and the changeover to a single track."

"Won't haul more than a hundred cord or so."

"I don't care. Just get something up there."

Cruickshank turned to one of his dwindling staff. He had been sending them out on assignments all day and none had yet returned.

"Get a message up to General Lee. Write something down and I'll sign it. Tell him about our fuel problem, and also what you see along the line."

The captain, one of his old drivers, sat down on a barrel and laboriously began to write out the dispatch.

The yard was strangely quiet after the mad bustle of moving out two divisions of infantry and over two hundred artillery pieces. Men who worked for the Baltimore and Ohio were sitting about in the shade, eating their evening meals, laughing and smoking, and somehow he felt that many were looking at him and secretly grinning.

If only Garrett had been cornered into a contract or, better yet, this army had had a trained railroad detachment the way the Yankees did. There were just too many details—and then he inwardly cursed himself, knowing he was trying to justify his own failings.

McDougal was off, shouting for some of his men to warm up one of the three remaining engines, several of them laughing when McDougal called out the number.

"I could pull more with me own hands," a derisive reply came back.

"Just do it, damn ya," McDougal shouted.

The staffer finished writing out the dispatch, Cruickshank cringing a bit as he read it, with all its misspellings, but the content was correct and he signed it.

Cruickshank walked over to McDougal's side.

"Not much to do here, General, until the engines start coming back. If they come back. Why don't you go sleep."

"I think I should stay," Cruickshank replied.

"Don't trust me?"

"No, I don't."

"General, darlin', would any of my lads be so stupid as to get themselves shot now? You have guards all over this place watching their every move. Go back to the company office and get some sleep."

Cruickshank reluctantly nodded in agreement.

"One question first," Cruickshank said.

"And what might that be, General, and if you are asking me if I am sabotaging your plans, of course, the answer is no."

"No, it's about one particular train."

"Which one?"

"This morning, the one for Miss Hoffman. Even though it was pulling troops, you had an extra car on it within minutes, had a good crew on board. It left here without a hitch except for the traffic farther up the line."

McDougal fell silent. After another sip from his bottle he handed it to Cruickshank.

"Wouldn't you have done the same?"

Cruickshank finished the bottle and threw the empty on the tracks, the glass shattering.

He looked at McDougal, nodded, and then went off to find a place to sleep.

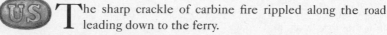

The sharp crackle of carbine fire rippled along the road leading down to the ferry.

Winfield Scott Hancock had worried deeply about this moment, for two reasons. First, would they arrive here ahead of any strong Confederate detachments or would they have to fight for possession of the crossing?

It looked to be no more than a company of Confederate cavalry which were already drawing back as his cavalry regiment, escorting the lead boats, had pushed ahead. They had been ordered to try to drive all the rebels off before the first barge arrived, to keep concealed what was going on, but Winfield knew that was an impossible hope.

By midday, on the other side of the Potomac, they had been steadily trailed by Confederate scouts, most likely Mosby's men, who had laid down an occasional harassing fire. For a while they had simply taken to firing on the barges, the men aboard them delighted with the challenge and giving back entire volleys, dropping several of the raiders.

Then Mosby's men had switched tactics, firing on the draft horses pulling the barges, killing or wounding several, which had really set tempers aflare among his men, who thought this was unfair and downright cruel.

Strange how war is, he thought. *Killing men is part of the game, but to deliberately shoot horses, except in the heat of battle, is thought unfair and draws howls of protest.*

Mosby's men had pushed ahead, crossed the river at Edwards Ferry, and just above it tried to destroy one of the locks, which would have tangled the entire operation. Fortunately, the cavalry escort on his side had second-guessed them and raced ahead, stopping them just in time.

So to think that word had not gone ahead and up to Lee regarding their move was now senseless.

What had worried him more, though, was his own reaction to fire. He had seen it with more than one officer or soldier. A man of courage, or the sublime few, were as calm under fire as they were at a church service, until finally they were hit. They lost a limb, took a bad wound, and something within died, never to return. When again under fire the calm was gone, some broken completely, to be relieved of command or sent back to the rear, old comrades watching their departure with pity and, yes, also a touch of disdain.

His own experience, he knew, would haunt him the rest of his life. It was not the pain at the moment of being wounded. Surprisingly, there had only been numbed shock and deep rage that fate had pulled him out of the fight at Union Mills just when he was needed the most. No, it was what had happened afterward.

The doctor had withdrawn the bullet from his inner thigh just below his crotch and stanched the bleeding that, at first, he thought might kill him. It was later, in Philadelphia, when the wound festered, his leg swelled to twice its normal size, and the heat, the terrible heat.

At that moment he knew he was dying, in fact, inwardly he begged for it to end the agony. The mere touch of a sheet on his leg sending shock waves through him, the morphine dulling the pain, but still it was there. Doctor after doctor would come in and stick probes into the wound to keep searching for something, anything, and the room would spin in circles, and he would break, whimpering for more morphine. He lived for the next injection and prayed for death in between.

Then one doctor struck upon a plan, and when he was told of it, he begged to just be left alone to die, not to be moved, not to endure what was proposed but then relented when his wife asked him to try for life, to stay with her and the children.

They then brought a saddle into the room, set it up on sawhorses, lifted him naked from his bed and had him sit on the saddle, feet in the stirrups. The doctor then marked where the entry wound touched against the saddle, crawled under the sawhorse, and carefully drilled a hole through the saddle. He was matching up the trajectory of the bullet with how it struck him while he was upright, astride a horse. All the other doctors had probed his wound with him flat on his back, legs spread wide. This one doctor had figured they should put him back into the position he was in at the moment he was struck and perhaps in so doing a probe could find whatever it was that was now killing him. He reasoned that the bullet which had struck him had not creased up the side of the horse, but instead had gone straight through his mount's neck, then into the saddle and finally lodged in his upper thigh.

Several assistants now braced him as he sat in the saddle, feet forced into the stirrups, the mere act of bending his swollen leg a living, burning hell. The doctor was on the floor under him and took a long hooked probe out of his medical bag.

"Be brave, General," the doctor said, and then he slipped the probe through the hole in the saddle and into Hancock's body. Groaning, sweat pouring from his face in the ninety-degree heat, he hung on, gripping the hands of an orderly, struggling not to scream.

"Got it!" the doctor cried, and he pulled the probe out, its hooked blade snagged onto a tenpenny nail, bits of uniform, saddle, and rotting horsehair and flesh.

The wound exploded, decaying flesh and pus cascading out onto the floor, now that the plug within had been removed.

He fainted.

When he awoke the fever was abating, the wound still draining... and he was alive.

And since that moment the fear had eaten at his heart. *Can I stand battle again? Will terror of facing such an ordeal again unman me? Can I still command?*

And there was the other aspect of it. He had ordered the morphine to be stopped the day after the ordeal, but the wound was not healed, perhaps never would be, leaving a suppurating hole in his leg. His doctor had raged with protest when Winfield had told him he had orders to report to Washington.

"Three months from now, maybe," was the reply, "but for God's sake, General, you did your duty. I didn't put you through that agony and save your life just to see you throw it away. Let someone else carry the burden now. You have a loving wife and family to think of."

"Doctor, thank you for my life, but you are talking about what is now my duty, my country's call." With a smile he limped out of the doctor's office.

What he had not told the doctor was the wish that he could somehow take a supply of morphine with him. Its memory haunted him, its soothing call, the strange dreams, the easing of pain.

All that was set aside at this moment. A minié ball snicked past him. He did not flinch, though several of his staff did. It was a test, and he had passed it.

He looked around at his staff and grinned with delight.

"I don't think they've made another ball to hit me just yet."

"Maybe not you, sir," one of his men replied, "but maybe there's one out there for us."

The group chuckled at the gallows humor.

Infantrymen converted from soldiers of a Maine heavy artillery regiment were jumping off the lead barges, deploying into skirmish line, double-timing up the road to fall in with the cavalry skirmishers driving back the few rebs contesting the position.

Hancock waited for a landing plank to be laid to his barge before he stepped off, leaning heavily on his cane for support.

He looked around. A typical river crossing for the Potomac. He remembered it from an earlier campaign when he had crossed here on a pontoon bridge. The ferry was a standard affair, cable strung across the river as towropes, but the boat was gone, the position abandoned after the war swept through back in June.

With even a modest pontoon bridge it'd be an excellent crossing point, a clear but narrow road straight up to Frederick to the north and Leesburg, Virginia, a dozen miles to the south.

The low river-bottom ground quickly gave way to a rising slope which even now his skirmishers were taking.

He set off at a slow walk, heading up the slope. Pausing for a breath, he looked back. A bridge on the road from the ferry crossing rose up over the canal, and the barge crews were now using it to run their horses across, and with practiced skill the first barge was already being pulled back toward Washington, narrowly passing those barges still coming up.

Just ahead was what was considered to be one of the engineering marvels of the Chesapeake and Ohio Canal, the viaduct over Monocacy Creek.

It was a stone arched bridge, carrying not a railroad track but the water of the canal, flat and level from one side of the Monocacy to the other, well over thirty feet above the river's flood plain. The towpaths on either side were excellent crossing points for infantry and it was essential to hold this position.

He was surprised that neither side, at some point during this war, had not decided to blow this viaduct; it would have shut the canal down for months.

Looking back down the canal, toward Washington, he could see a long procession, boats riding low in the water, the men in high spirits. They'd been garrison troops for far too long, enduring the endless gibes and often scuffles with the men of his beloved and now gone Army of the Potomac.

He had felt a bit of the same disdain for them once. While his boys were up at the front, battling it out with the Army of Northern Virginia, the Washington garrison had sat out two years of the war, in heated barracks, with cookhouses, fresh rations, and even beds to sleep in. They had, however, won their honor with the holding of the city in July. Reinforced now by tough veterans from the South Carolina campaign, they were out of the city that many themselves had come to hate, were in the field on a new adventure, and had not seen so much action that they dreaded the next shock. In a way they reminded him of how he and his men had once looked, long ago, in the early spring of 1862, when McClellan had led them forth to the Peninsula, fresh, eager, neat, and ready for a fight.

He worried some about how they would react when they were hit by the hardened combat veterans Bobbie Lee would throw at them. He

knew that in an open running fight he would bet on the veterans of field combat over heavy artillerymen converted into infantry. However, dug in, with a defensive role of stopping the rebs and not maneuvering against them, he thought his Washington garrison troops might just do the job. He was certainly going to do everything he could to stiffen their resolve and get them ready before Lee got to them.

He gained the top of the slope. The view was magnificent, the Potomac River coiling behind him, the canal with its boats, the sun low over the Catoctin Mountains to the west.

The last of the skirmishing ahead was dying down. No casualties to either side, the rebel patrol far back now on the road, a mile or more away.

His staff was coming up around him, several of them survivors of the Second Corps who had escaped the debacles at Union Mills and Gunpowder River and who he had requested to join him now.

"Right here, gentlemen," Hancock announced. "I want a good survey done right now along this rise. We dig in close to the river."

"This close?" a major asked.

It was Jeremiah Siemens, his old topographical engineer when he commanded a division at Chancellorsville. Jeremiah had missed Union Mills, having been wounded at Chancellorsville, his empty left sleeve rolled up.

"Yes, here."

"No room for withdrawal, sir, if things go against us."

He knew Jeremiah well enough to know that the question was not so much for himself, but as an answer to those gathering round.

"There will be no withdrawal, gentlemen," Hancock announced. "Our orders are to secure every potential crossing spot between here and Point of Rocks." He pointed toward the Catoctins, ten miles to the northwest.

"That's here, Nolands Ferry just on the other side of the viaduct, then Point of Rocks. We leave five thousand men back at Edwards Ferry across from Leesburg, but the rest come up here."

The group, now including several officers from his First Division, were silent.

"If Lee should come on us with everything he has," one of them finally ventured, "we have to defend four crossings, and picket in between. He can focus on one point and outnumber us there five, maybe even six or seven, to one."

"That's why we dig in," Hancock replied sharply. "Jeremiah, I want surveys completed here and at Nolands before dark. Then up to Point of Rocks by dawn, but defending that position will be easy, it's a narrow squeeze down to the crossing and three thousand men there would be like the three hundred Spartans at Thermopylae. Remember, we don't

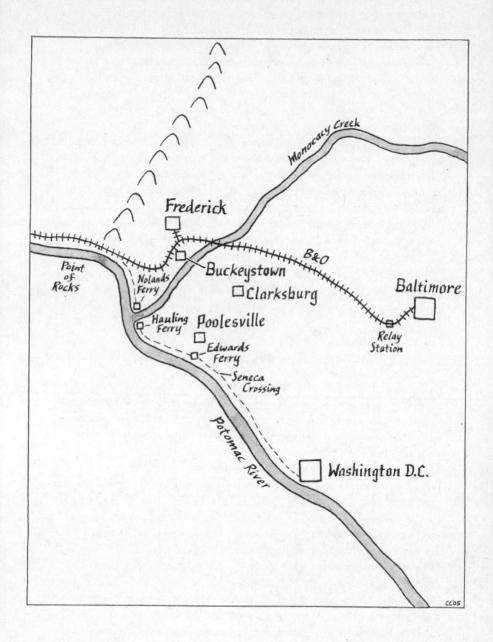

Monocacy Creek

Frederick

B&O

Point of Rocks

Nolands Ferry

Buckeystown

Clarksburg

Baltimore

Hauling Ferry

Poolesville

Edwards Ferry

Seneca Crossing

Relay Station

Potomac River

Washington D.C.

CC'05

have to defeat Lee by ourselves. We simply have to stop him long enough for Grant to catch up and hit him from the rear. If we do our job, Grant will do his. Somewhere along here Lee is going to try to get home to Virginia. We are the cork in the bottle to stop him."

Hancock looked upriver and then downriver. He made a summary judgment of what he saw and what he remembered from the maps of the region.

"No, I doubt that it will be Point of Rocks or Edwards Ferry. If Lee should turn, it will be here."

"That's a lot of work," someone said. "Our boys are good diggers, Lord knows. They did their share around Washington, but to make it secure, while also putting out pickets, keeping back Mosby . . ."

No one spoke for a moment. All had fallen silent, for in the distance, like a summer storm, came a dull, rolling thunder.

"Then let's start now," Hancock replied sharply. "The sooner we are dug in, the safer we will be. Make sure the men understand that. They are digging for their lives."

Headquarters, Army of the Susquehanna
Frederick, Maryland

7:00 P.M.

A cool evening breeze wafted down from the heights behind the town and Grant sighed with relief as the temperature dropped several degrees within minutes. Not like Mississippi at all, where the muggy heat would linger through the night. No mosquitoes either, and that was a blessing.

He had moved his headquarters from the town depot out to a low rise just east of the toll gate south of town. At the edge of the rise, a quarter mile away, Hunt was busy with his guns, crews digging in, throwing up lunettes around each piece, constructing rough bombproofs to store limber chests in. Occasional harassing fire came from the rebel guns on the far side of the river, but nothing serious, just a growling back and forth like two old neighboring dogs reminding each other of their existence. It dropped off as dusk settled over the countryside.

All orders had been given; Sheridan and Ord knew their tasks. Of Banks he was not sure yet, but his men had come up in good order during the day, filing down out of the mountain pass and falling in on the north flank. Banks's men, at least, he knew were good troops that had fought through the swamps of the lower Mississippi, though ironically many of the regiments were recruited from New York and New England. It had been easier in the first year of the war to ship men from there to New Orleans while the Confederates still held Vicksburg and Port Hudson.

They had seen action before, though not on the scale of battles here in the East, but he had a sense of them, that they were grateful to be out of the Deep South and eager to prove themselves . . . and tomorrow would definitely be a day of proving. He hoped they would rise to the occasion.

The orders were straightforward and simple. At dawn, all three corps were to engage: Sheridan in the center, Ord on the right, Banks on the left, with what was left of McPherson's Corps to be in reserve in the town. The three attacking corps were to go for the fords, but also force a general action up and down the length of the river for five miles or more, to fight like hell and hold Lee in place, to not give him a breather or the room to maneuver, but to lock hold of him and hang on. And they were not to throw men away senselessly. Ord, his blood up after barely taking the ford, was ready to do so, to storm straight in against a hundred or more guns. *No, first we have to wear the other side down, exhaust them, and then let the plan unfold.*

Campfires by the thousands were springing to light along the river, on both sides, the scent of wood smoke, coffee, and frying salt pork filling the evening air. To him it was a comforting smell, part of his life, a better part of the army life he had always loved. The day's march done, the men settling down, songs drifting on the air, rations being cooked, the first stars of evening coming out.

If only war were like this forever, I would love it so, he thought, *but only if this moment could be frozen, not what had been or what was to come.* Behind him his staff was having their supper, spread out on a rough plank table, the men laughing at a joke. They were used to his going off like this, especially before a fight, to be alone, to smoke, to think, to recalculate, to think again, in silence. Besides, the migraine still tormented him and the thought of trying to eat anything beyond some hardtack made his stomach rebel.

Was everything in place? *Is there anything I forgot?*

He knew it was senseless to try to reason those questions out now, and yet always he did it on the eve of a confrontation. It was not a question of resolve, however.

He had resolved on this moment on the day the telegram arrived from Lincoln bearing news of Union Mills and of his own promotion to command. He knew the focus of his task, to track Lee down, bring him to battle, and then destroy him.

So many would die tomorrow. He knew that; they all did, on both sides of the river. Even as the men around the campfires joked and sang, many others had drawn off. Some sat alone, looking up at the heavens, in wonder, in prayer, or, for a tragic few, in terror. Others knelt or stood in prayer. Some stood in circles around a trusted minister or simply a man of the regiment who everyone acknowledged "had the ear of the Lord." Some sang hymns, others recited psalms, a group of Catholics knelt before a makeshift altar while a priest offered up mass and then absolution.

Others wrote letters home, or if they could not write, dictated a few lines that a comrade would jot down. The darkness deepened, the sky a deep indigo, and he sat in silence, smoking, and watching the far bank of the river.

Home of Dr. O'Neill
Near Monocacy Junction

7:30 P.M.

Emily looked out the window, watching as the hills to the west darkened, the last glow of twilight fading, a cooling breeze fluttering the curtains.

"Emily?"

"Yes, James."

She reached out and took his hand. Her father, on the other side of the bed, wiped James's brow with a damp towel.

"Is it dark out?"

"Yes, dearest."

He smiled.

"Thought I couldn't see anymore."

Reverend Lacy sat by her side, hand on James's chest. He looked over at her and she could see in his eyes that he sensed something.

He suddenly arched his back, struggling to take a breath, the struggle continuing for long seconds.

"Dearest, dearest," she gasped, standing up and leaning over him.

"You'll always love me, Emi?"

"You are my husband now."

"I'll wait for you. Please wait . . ."

He took another breath and then seemed to fall back, his body beginning to relax.

"The Lord is my shepherd," McPherson whispered as he gently exhaled.

"I shall not want. He maketh me to lie down in green pastures," Lacy replied.

She could feel his hand relax. Leaning over, she felt his last breath drift out of his body and, instinctively, she breathed in, as if by so doing she could take his soul into hers.

"He leadeth me beside the still waters," Lacy continued.

She whispered the psalm with him, and when finished stood up and let James's hand slip from hers.

Strange, she felt as if his presence were still there and then was, ever so gently, drifting away.

Lacy stood up. He closed James's eyes and pulled the sheet over his face.

He was silent as Emily walked to the window, the evening breeze drifting in. In the west the evening star was shining. She knew then that if she should live another fifty years, every time she saw it, she would think of him, of this moment.

There would never be another in her life. There would be no children, no years of growing old together, of watching a family grow even as they faded away. This war had taken all that away.

In the fields below her, hundreds of campfires glowed. It was a beautiful sight, and at that moment she could see why her husband had loved it so. This world of men—of such violence—was a world also of comradeship. Behind her she heard muffled sobs, of her father, her mother, and of young Captain Cain, weeping for a fallen enemy who had become a comrade.

The campfires flickered and glowed. *How many of those gathered about them tonight will be with my husband tomorrow?* she wondered. *How many wives at home prayed tonight, mothers and fathers, children and friends, and tomorrow their worlds will end as mine just has.*

Would anyone realize that? she wondered. *Yes, those who suffered what we have. But later, long afterward, would anyone care? Would anyone remember?*

And long years from now, when others spoke of this time and dwelt upon its supposed glories, who would think then of those left behind? Who would think of a childless, aging widow, dying alone, hoping that her young love did indeed wait for her in heaven?

Headquarters, Army of Northern Virginia

8:00 P.M.

General Lee smiled and nodded as Pete Longstreet came to his side carrying a folding camp chair.

"Mind if I join you, General?"

"Glad for the company."

Pete unfolded the chair and sat down by Lee.

"Beautiful evening," Lee said.

Pete nodded in agreement, lighting a cigar and puffing it to life.

The valley below them was aglow with campfires, the evening air cooling, darkness cloaking the mountains, the woods, and fields. From both sides of Monocacy Creek came singing, some boys shouting out "Bonnie Blue Flag" and seconds later the other side of the creek echoing to "The Battle Hymn of the Republic."

"A regular song fest by the bridge tonight," Pete said quietly. "I dare say, those must be Irish boys over there; they have some good tenors."

"Strange isn't it? Serenading each other on the eve of battle."

"Happened before, week before Chancellorsville," Lee said. "They finished with both sides singing 'Home Sweet Home.'"

Lee fell silent for a moment, voice near to choking at the memory of it, the way it had started out with patriotic airs, then to songs from before the war, and then finished with the haunting refrain, "Be it ever so humble, there's no place like home."

"Tomorrow should decide it," Lee said, regaining his composure.

"I hope so, sir."

"You don't sound the way you did that night before Union Mills," Lee said, looking over at his old comrade.

"That seems a long time ago," Pete replied meditatively.

"Why?"

"It's just that they don't stop. They just keep coming at us. Before Union Mills, I saw it clearly. Lure them into that one great fight, which we did, and they would see our resolve and bring an end to it. And now, two months later, here we are again, another army before us."

He gestured to the campfires on the far side of the creek.

"Just about a year ago we crossed through this same ground. Just on the other side of those mountains we fought Sharpsburg, and I remember those campfires and the evening rain. Then the cold night before Fredericksburg and the thousands of fires."

The chorus from the other side echoed. "I have seen him in the watch fires of a hundred circling camps."

Pete fell silent.

"It will end here," Lee whispered.

"I hope so."

"I know so."

Lee reached out and patted Pete on the knee.

"It will end here. That army across from us is the last they have. They will venture it tomorrow. We saw their first lunge late this afternoon, and they drew back and spent hundreds to our few score. That was just a probe, a test. Tomorrow Grant will come at us with everything he has. They will come again tomorrow, and it will be like Fredericksburg, like Union Mills."

Lee smiled.

"And you, my old warhorse, will hold the center."

"Yes, sir."

"Generals."

Walter Taylor approached and Lee could tell by his demeanor that the news was not good.

"Go on, Walter."

"Sir, a message just came up from Doctor O'Neill's house. General McPherson is dead. Sir, my condolences, I know how close you were to him."

It was inevitable. Reverend Lacy had told him earlier in the day that it was only a matter of hours.

"And Miss Hamilton?" Lee asked. "Did she arrive safely?"

"She is now Mrs. McPherson. The reverend married them when she arrived."

"I see," Lee said softly and lowered his head.

Though Pete was present, he did not hesitate to go down on his knees. With bowed head he recited the Twenty-third Psalm, Pete and Walter joining in.

He was silent for a moment, reflecting on James, just how young he was at the Point, how enthusiastic and cheerful, always eager to help underclassmen, even protective of plebes, admonishing others one day in chapel that the usual hazing endured by first-year cadets was unchristian and unprofessional. It was an unpopular view with the cadets and even many of the instructors, who saw hazing as a way of toughening boys into men, but Lee had wholeheartedly agreed with him and admired his courage for standing up and speaking out.

"Miss, I mean, Mrs. McPherson. Walter, please convey my deepest sympathies to her. Inform her that when this crisis is over and time permits I wish to personally convey those sympathies but cannot do so at this moment."

"Yes, sir. I've already written out a brief note for you to sign."

"Thank you, Walter, but I'll do that myself later."

"Yes, sir."

"Please be certain that Reverend Lacy stays with her. If she wishes to join a train back to Baltimore and to take her husband with her, we are at her disposal."

"Yes, sir."

He stood up and saw that there was something else.

"What is it, Walter?"

"We've just had a scout come in. Says he is with Mosby and he carries a dispatch from him."

"Concerning?"

"Sir, a large convoy of canal barges carrying Union troops moved this day up the Chesapeake and Ohio Canal. They have traveled as far as Hauling Ferry, where they started to unload."

"How many barges? How many men?"

"The note doesn't say, other than 'dozens of barges.'"

"What about the courier?"

"He says it looked like thousands of Yankees. He got across the river just ahead of their patrols and rode straight here."

"Looks like they are trying to close the back door," Pete said, slapping his hands together.

Lee nodded in agreement.

He was silent, looking again at the flickering campfires on the far bank. The Union boys had long ago finished their "Battle Hymn" and both sides were now singing "Tenting Tonight."

"It won't affect us tomorrow," Lee said.

"I don't like it, though," Pete replied. "We've always had a way out of Maryland if need be. They're trying to block it now."

"It won't affect us tomorrow." Lee repeated himself, this time more forcefully. "So what if they block the fords and ferry crossings at this point? Once we destroy Grant, we can destroy each of those positions piecemeal. Scattering troops like that just makes it more certain that we can mass and destroy them. It will just take a little time. First we must win here."

"I'd feel better, though, sir, if we had managed to get our pontoon bridge across that creek and down to the Potomac. We've always operated in the past with a secure line of retreat if need be."

"Those days are finished." Lee replied. "And Grant—did he have a secure line of retreat in May when he crossed the Mississippi and hit Johnston's army and then moved north to invest Vicksburg?"

Pete shook his head.

"No, sir, he didn't. He took the gamble."

"And won. We are all gamblers in this game, General Longstreet. Grant wants to make us nervous. Let him. But if I was one who actually gambled with money, I'd bet a hundred to one that, come dawn tomorrow, Grant will attack. If he attacks, we defeat him, then it is moot whether the crossings are blocked or not. It will be Grant who will have to try to escape us as we push him back on to that one road over the mountains."

"Grant will attack," Pete agreed.

Lee sat back down in his camp chair.

"The troops blocking the fords. They must be the garrison from Washington. If so, then so much the better. I will order Mosby to let them pass, then once up here he can do a night raid, get across the Potomac, and smash a few of the canal locks. Canals are even more vulnerable than railroads. Destroy a single lock and the entire section above floods out, leaving the boats stranded, while down below the canal gets washed to overflowing. They will be stranded, and we can either turn on Washington or finish them at our leisure."

Pete found he had to nod in agreement.

"I think you should get some rest, General," Lee said. "It will be a hard day's work tomorrow and we must be up early."

"Yes, sir."

Pete stood up and then, strangely, came to attention and formally saluted.

"Good night, sir. And please get some rest as well."

"Thank you, General."

Pete walked off, trailing a cloud of cigar smoke, and Lee watched him leave.

Sighing, he turned around and gazed out over the valley, the thousands of fires flickering low, the song from the valley below becoming softer. This time it was "Lorena."

"The years creep slowly by, Lorena . . ."

James is dead, and so many out in those fields will be dead this time tomorrow . . . Please God, let it end here. Bring us victory if it is Your wish . . . and let it end here.

Chapter Fourteen

General Hunt, sir."

Henry Hunt opened his eyes. A sergeant was leaning over him, holding a lantern. He didn't recognize the man and for a moment was disoriented.

"Sir, you told me to wake you an hour and a half before dawn."

Henry grunted and sat up. A low campfire glowed in front of him, several enlisted men squatting around the fire, one feeding in small sticks while another reached out with a gloved hand and pulled out a battered tin pot.

Henry stood up, stretched, mouth feeling gummy, stomach a bit weak. He had misled Grant about the typhoid; it still troubled him a bit. He stepped away to discreetly relieve himself, then came back to the campfire.

The men were part of his new staff. He was never really good with names and had yet to learn theirs, but they were about the business of morning chores, one looking up with a smile and offering him a cup of coffee, another handing over a plate that actually had fried eggs on it and a slab of ham.

He nodded his thanks, the men talking quietly among themselves as he ate his breakfast, glad that it stayed down and settled his stomach. Finished, he set the plate down, took his cup of coffee, and stood back up and lit a cigar.

It was still dark, a mist rising off the river, filling the valley, pale moonlight reflecting off it. In the fields about him there was a thin layer of mist and wood smoke. Many were still asleep, or pretending to sleep, lying in their blanket wrapped in thought. Around low fires small groups were gathered, some silent, some talking.

He walked the few yards down the slope to where the right flank of his grand battery was deployed. A handful of men were still digging; most, however, were asleep, some lying curled up on the ground, others resting under a caisson or field piece.

He started to walk the line. Guns were well placed, intervaled at ten yards, lunettes thrown up around each piece, some well built to shoulder height on the flanks, a bit lower in front to offer an open field of fire. The horse teams for the ammunition caissons had been unhooked and sent to the rear, a quarter mile back. Lunettes had been thrown up around the dangerous cargo, and bombproofs for the ammunition had been dug by some of the crews and even roofed over with logs.

As he passed, an occasional officer would come to attention, salute. A few offered comments. "We'll give 'em hell today." "How you doing, General?" "Wait till you see the shootin' my boys can do."

He acknowledged each one and walked on.

Every piece was a rifle, either a three-inch ordnance gun or a ten-pound Parrott. He had always liked the look of the Parrott, with its extra band of iron wrapped around the breech, and though it was more cumbersome to move than the three-inch ordnance gun, he always felt that it was a better piece for true long-distance work.

Ammunition was well organized. Each of the forward caissons carried but two rounds of canister—for use if by some chance the rebs did get up close; every other slot was filled with case shot or solid bolts. Each battery had one limber to the rear loaded just with canister if an emergency should arise. During the night twenty additional limber wagons, each loaded with two chests of ammunition, had come up; an additional two thousand rounds and more was on the way.

Even now trains were hauling ammunition down from Harrisburg to Hagerstown, off-loading it to be sent the final miles along the National Road. Grant had assured him he would be kept well supplied.

He turned and slowly walked back to his headquarters. More men were up. He could feel the tension in the air.

There was a faint brightening to the eastern horizon.

"Gentlemen, time we went to our posts," Henry announced quietly.

East Bank, Monocacy Creek

4:55 A.M.

C.S.A. Phil Duvall, now a major, sat up and tossed his blanket aside. Sergeant Lucas was by the fire, poking at the flames with a stick. Their horses were calm, lined up on their tether line; a couple of his men were already up, tending to them, one brushing his mount down and talking quietly to her, rubbing her ear, the horse nuzzling in to him.

"What time is it?" Phil asked.

"About five I'd reckon, sir," Lucas replied.

Phil went over to the fire, extending his hands. There was a slight chill in the air, rather a comfort after yesterday's heat.

It had been a wonderfully still night. They were no longer down by the bridge. Jeb had assigned a couple of additional companies to him and told him to probe south at dawn, down to the Potomac, that there were reports of Yankees there. An easy day, he hoped.

Lucas handed him a cup of coffee.

"Better get the boys up," Phil said. "It's time to move."

C.S.A. Sgt. Lee Robinson of the First Texas stood at attention as steam vented from the train and it slowly began to inch its way down the track, a locomotive pushing a single passenger car.

The men around him were silent, saluting as the car drifted by, engine bathing them in steam, bell tolling slowly.

It disappeared into the dark.

He relaxed, looking around at his men.

"A brave lady she was," one of his comrades whispered.

Robinson said nothing. He had followed the orders General Lee had given to him, helping to carry McPherson to the rear. No other orders had come after that, and he assumed that he and his boys should stand by as guards, which they had done throughout McPherson's ordeal of dying, helping to fetch small things, some of the men volunteering to help with other wounded when there was nothing to do for the general. Their final task was to carry the body, draped with a Union flag, back to the rail line, since no carriage or wagon could be found. The widow had walked with them, never saying a word, and he had been overwhelmed with guilt, at times wanting to blurt out that he was the one who had shot McPherson. That would bring her no comfort, he knew; in fact, it would forever put a name and a face to the man who had killed her husband.

He looked to the west, to the dark sky, still filled with stars. To the east Orion was up, a faint glow of indigo and scarlet spreading beneath it.

"Let's go find our unit," Robinson said. "That's where we belong now."

C.S.A. Sergeant Hazner stood up cautiously. The truce had lasted through the night, men gossiping back and forth across the river, but all had become silent as the eastern sky began to brighten, a Yankee shouting across, "You boys better hunker down now. The ball is about to commence."

The fog lifting from the river floated just below him, rising up so close it seemed almost solid, as if he could leap out of the trench and walk upon it to the other side.

He hated their position, the one that fate had cast for his regiment, right smack in the middle of the line.

After their fight on the heights, and in Frederick, all had figured that Lee would put them into reserve. Instead they had filed in, just after dusk, directly in front of where Lee had established his headquarters, the Fourteenth South Carolina on the left flank of the log blockhouse overlooking the shattered bridge. No one needed to be told that one hell of a lot of fire was going to be coming their way, and the work of the unit they replaced, though they had dug in, had left something to be desired. He and his men had labored until midnight deepening their trench, dragging up lumber to pile atop it, cutting back brush and small trees to the front to improve fields of fire.

When they paused in their work, they could hear the Yankees engaged in the same work on the other side, not a very comforting sound.

Finally, Colonel Brown ordered them to stand down at midnight and get some rest.

"How are you doing, Hazner?"

"Fine, sir," and he saluted as Brown came up.

"Still quiet," Brown said.

"Not for long, sir."

West Bank of the Monocacy

5:10 A.M.

U.S. Sgt. Washington Madison Bartlett of the United States Colored Troops was already up. It had been impossible to sleep. His men had been restless during the night, many sitting around the campfires, already using the old soldier slang for what it would be like to "see the elephant," meaning their first day in battle.

Some boasted, others were silent, many prayed. More than a few who could write spent the night penning letters, first for themselves and then for their comrades. A preacher who claimed to have been a recruiter for the Fifty-fourth Massachusetts had joined them just before leaving Philadelphia, Reverend Garland White, walked from campfire to campfire, kneeling with the men, offering a prayer, a few words of encouragement, then stood up and went to the next group and knelt again.

He reached into his breast pocket and pulled out two letters: one from his father and the other, now almost in tatters from having been passed around so much, the letter from Lincoln. It was too dark to read them, but simply holding them was like a prayer in itself.

His father, at least, was safely back in the White House, personal butler now to the president. He wondered what his father would say if he could see him now, on this morning of battle.

"Father?"

He turned. It was his son William smiling up at him nervously.

He had been forced to play the role of the sergeant with his son since they joined the army together, ignoring him, yelling at him when need be, even picking him up a few times by his collar and pushing him to his task. But they were in the dark, alone.

"Afraid, Father?"

"Yes, of course, Son."

"I'm terrified."

He put a hand on his son's shoulder.

"When the shooting starts, just remember to stay at your post with the other drummer boys and help the stretcher bearers."

He wanted to say, for God's sake, stay directly behind me, let me be your shield this day, but of course he could not say that.

"Your granddaddy is proud of you, William."

The thought of his own father gave him pause. At least his father was safe, a servant in the White House, who, until last week, when they moved out, had sent along daily and often eloquent letters about Lincoln and the reasons for this war of liberation.

He could feel the boy trembling, and he pulled him in close to his side.

"Granddaddy is proud of you, I'm proud."

"I'm proud of you, too," William said, and then with a loving gesture reached up and buttoned the top button of his father's uniform.

"You gotta look right for the men today."

The sergeant major laughed. The darn collar was too tight, but the boy was right.

"I will and so will you."

"Sergeant?"

He looked up. It was Sergeant Miller, company sergeant of A Company, approaching. The man was tall, massive expanse of shoulders, at first look a tough roustabout, but he was always soft-spoken, almost to the point of gentleness, in a tough sort of way. He sensed that Miller had been watching the two and Washington suddenly felt embarrassed.

"Go along now, Son, make sure the drummer boys are up and ready for business."

"Yes, Father . . . I mean, Sergeant."

He turned and ran off.

"I just wanted to report, Sergeant, that Company A is formed and ready to go."

"Thank you, Miller."

Miller hesitated, then nodded in the direction of young William.

"How old is your boy?"

"Fourteen."

"Doesn't it make you nervous, him being here like this?"

"Do you mean, could I leave him behind?" Washington said and then shook his head. "No, Sergeant. When he said he had to come, too, the way he looked in my eyes, I couldn't say no. It's his future even more than mine that we're fighting for now."

Bartlett chuckled and shook his head.

"Now his mama, now there was the fight, but I told her, 'Woman, if he's old enough to say he wants to fight for freedom, I will not stop him, nor will you.'"

"Still, a son," Miller whispered.

"You have any boys?" Bartlett asked.

Miller stiffened and looked away.

"I did."

There was a moment of silence, and then Miller, voice almost breaking, told about the mob fighting in Baltimore, how his son was gunned down before him as they tried to escape the city.

"I'm so sorry. I didn't mean to go into your personal business," Bartlett offered.

"No, Sergeant. No, it's why I'm here today."

"The name is Washington."

"John here," and the two shook hands.

"I guess if my boy had been given the chance to reach fourteen he'd want to be here, too," Miller finally said.

"That's why mine is."

He paused.

"He'll be safe back with the drummer boys. At least I hope so."

"Think today will make a difference?" Miller asked.

"If we get into this fight, it will," he said sharply.

The two said no more, standing side by side, the regiment finishing its breakfast and lining up, the eastern light brightening.

The White House

5:15 A.M.

He arose early. Dressing, he slipped out of the bedroom, walked down the hall, and quietly opened the door to Taddie's bedroom. The boy was asleep, sheet kicked off, a toy stuffed dog on the floor. Lincoln tiptoed in, pulled the sheet up over his boy, picked up the stuffed dog, and set it beside him. It used to be Taddie's favorite, in fact, still was, though he would no longer admit it, saying such things were for little boys, but when it came time for bed he still had to have "Scruffie" by his side.

He kissed Tad lightly on the forehead, slipped out of the room and down the corridor to his office. His secretary, John Hay, as was so often the case, was within, asleep on the sofa, a scattering of newspapers and dispatches on the floor by his side.

Lincoln walked over to the window and opened it slowly so as not to disturb John. Down on the White House lawn below, troops were still camped, some of the very few still left in this city. A couple of sentries walked their beat on Pennsylvania Avenue, the two stopping for a moment, leaning on their rifles to chat. Then an officer approached, and they quickly resumed their monotonous pacing, the officer turning away. The man paused, looked up, saw Lincoln in the window, and saluted. Lincoln nodded, gave a friendly wave, and the officer disappeared into the morning mist rising off of the Potomac and the marshland behind the White House.

Lincoln went over to his desk, sat down, and, striking a match, lit the lamp, adjusted the wick, and replaced the glass chimney. It was an ugly, elaborate thing, with three insipid brass angels holding up the base, that Mary had picked out at Tiffany's on one of her "decorating sprees" that cost so much it was still causing him headaches with Congress.

He looked at his desk. Nothing new had come in since he had retired at midnight. But it would start coming in, and quite soon. He put his feet up on the desk, tilted his chair back, and closed his eyes, but could not fall asleep.

Frederick

5:20 A.M.

Gen. Ulysses S. Grant, rubbing his brow, walked out of his tent and his staff came to attention. Ely came up, offering him a cup of coffee. Ord, Sheridan, and Banks were waiting.

"Anything new?" Grant asked.

"Quiet on the other side except for digging," Phil reported.

Grant nodded. That had been a lingering concern, that Lee just might try to pull the first move, but he was not noted for night attacks. If roles were reversed, he would have ordered his men to stand down, to rest, just as Lee had done, other than for the front line of troops, who had commenced digging once darkness fell.

Campfires were flickering up, men cooking their morning rations, something he had ordered the afternoon before. He wanted these men well fed, with full canteens, before the day started.

A few drums rattled, a distant bugle called. On the slope below him Phil's reserve division, the colored troops, were already up, beginning to form ranks. Backpacks, any unnecessary baggage was left behind; each man was to carry just rifle, haversack, canteen, and eighty rounds of ammunition. A surgeon was already preparing for the day under an awning, his staff unloading boxes of bandages from a wagon, a stack of crutches piled up behind the awning, and two men were digging a pit to receive the severed limbs.

Out in the fields beyond, regiments were forming up, the reserve units, just beyond gunnery range. The forward edge of this fight was already down on the line, hidden within the bank of fog filling the Monocacy Valley. There was a slight temptation to order them in right now, under cover of the fog, but it would take a half hour or more for the orders to be sent, and in that half hour the fog would undoubtedly burn off. *No, the plan has been set, don't change it now.*

"You better get back to your commands," Grant said. "I'll come along later to check. Just remember your orders, our mission this day."

The three corps commanders saluted, mounted up, and rode off, Phil with a bit of a wild dash, saber drawn while standing in his stirrups. Yes, he was something of a showman, but every army needed at least one like that, just as long as he didn't go off and do something reckless.

Grant took the cup of coffee offered by Ely and walked back to where he had sat the night before, camp chair set up, the open plateau, the sloping plain down to the creek, all wide-open ground, except for the squared-off farmers' woodlots. It was getting brighter by the minute, the stars of Orion's shoulder fading, washed out, the horizon now a brilliant gold.

He sipped his coffee and waited, Ely standing by his side, silent. The sun broke the horizon, a brilliant shaft of light marking the start of the day, of August 27.

6:00 A.M.

Remember!" Henry Hunt shouted. "I want measured fire. I want every shot to count. You Western boys claim you're so damn good, now prove it to me!"

His booming voice carried up and down the line. Gunners looked up from their pieces, officers standing behind them, gazing in Hunt's direction, his last comment producing some grins, but also a few catcalls about the kind of "damn" shooting he was about to see.

He waited a few more minutes, the red-golden orb of the sun now clear of the horizon, the top of the fog bank catching the light, wisps of it curling up like glowing streamers.

A bit of fog and wood smoke clung to the opposite bank, but the higher hills were clearly visible. Behind him the Catoctin Range stood out boldly; looking back he saw the white tops of wagons coming down out of the pass, supply trains, an endless column of them, most likely clear back to Hagerstown.

He continued to wait, feeling the tension, for all of it now rested on him, his one command.

Again it was like Union Mills, when he was ordered to open the action, Meade by his side, waiting expectantly for the rain to ease, the fog and smoke to clear enough, so that he and his gunners could see their targets. The tension was the same, but this morning the air was clear, and what he wanted was directly in front of him. It was a bit similar to Union Mills, too, rebel batteries were dug in, but due to the twisting Monocacy and the lay of the land, he would have them in a partial enfilade. At least eighty guns lined the crest of the McCausland Farm, fourteen hundred yards away. Their only advantage was they were a good hundred feet higher, but still they stood out clearly.

One other thing was different. Grant was not by his side. They had discussed the plan of action yesterday afternoon, a brief conversation again just before sunset when Grant rode down to survey the position, and now he stood alone. He liked that. Meade had clung to his side throughout the bombardment at Union Mills and had even subtly tried to force him into actually taking responsibility for the ordering of that disastrous charge.

No, Grant was leaving him to do the job, and he liked that trust.

A few more minutes passed.

Scattered rifle fire began to crackle down in the fog, which was beginning to burn off, skirmishers opening up.

It was time.

"Battalions, make your shots count!" Henry roared and then raised his fist.

"On my command!"

He slammed his fist down.

"Fire!"

The battle of Monocacy Creek had begun.

Headquarters, Army of Northern Virginia

6:10 A.M.

here it goes!" Walter exclaimed, unable to contain his excitement.

Puffs of smoke, scores of them, erupted from the Union grand battery a mile away, guns fired almost in unison. Lee stood silent, watching.

Approximately seven seconds later the first shell landed, impacting in front of the batteries rimming the edge of McCausland Farm. Then dozens of geysers of earth erupted, explosions in the air from well-cut fuses, smothering his own batteries in smoke and fire. A caisson went up with a flash; a gun upended, flipping over; another collapsed, pieces of its wheel flying through air.

The concussion of the guns rumbled over them, a continual roar, followed seconds later by the softer popping of exploding shells, and the thunderclap of the exploding caisson.

"So it will be our left," Longstreet announced, coming up to join Lee.

They waited, banks of smoke covering the Yankee gun position. No fire for several minutes, the smoke slowly clearing, and then a few guns fired, followed seconds later by dozens more.

His own batteries started to reply, and Lee raised his field glasses to study the result. Shots went wide, plowing up earth several hundred yards ahead of the enemy batteries, others struck behind it, one lucky, or well-aimed, shot dismounted one of their pieces.

Several minutes passed, another gradual rumbling, several more of his own guns were destroyed.

Lee watched, saying nothing. The Yankees were firing very slowly, deliberately, waiting for the smoke to clear. Well-trained crews rolled their pieces back up. Then section commanders took the time to carefully aim their piece, removing the delicate rear sight, stepping back, then giving the command to fire.

The guns at McCausland Farm were his reserve batteries, and crews were primarily infantrymen "volunteered" into the artillery after the huge haul of equipment at Union Mills. They had trained for the last seven weeks, but seven weeks did not equal two years of battle experience. It was going to be hell for them down there.

His own trained batteries were deployed on the slope just below him, the range to the enemy guns almost a mile—very long shooting indeed.

He had noticed it yesterday, the way Grant was deploying, and it demonstrated a good judgment of ground, and of target. He was tempted to order the batteries to pull back, but decided against it for the moment. It was a grim calculation. Pull back now and it might actually trigger an effect not desired, for Grant might hesitate, wondering what he was up to. Also, regardless of the measured pace of the Yankee fire, long experience had taught him that, over time, accuracy would decrease due to smoke, fatigue, due even to such factors as the heating of gun barrels, which generated subtle changes in trajectory.

He knew, as well, that even if he wound up trading guns at four to one down at McCausland Farm, it would seriously cut into Grant's small artillery corps, and still leave Grant with well over a hundred and twenty pieces to face whatever came next.

"Walter, tell our batteries below to open up, but with very limited and controlled counterbattery fire."

"Range is rather long, sir," Walter said.

"Precisely why I want it limited. We have a lot of ammunition but should not be profligates with it at the start. Tell Alexander to pick out his best crews and have them start to reply. I want the Yankees to know we will not just sit back and do nothing."

Minutes later the first of Alexander's guns opened up. It was already getting hard to see the opposing battery. In the still morning air smoke was piling up, like a vast fog bank drifting slowly, mingling with the natu-

ral fog down in the river valley, which was slowly burning off as the sun cleared the ridgeline behind him.

All up and down the length of the river rifle fire was erupting. The Yankees had dug well during the night, establishing a forward line that at places bordered on the creek. Already a particularly bothersome spot was becoming evident, the railroad cut on the other side, the curve of track behind the destroyed depot. The cut could almost be enfiladed by the guns of Alexander's main battery and the blockhouse. He sent another courier down, ordering him to turn his Napoleons in that direction.

The first of the wounded started to come back, the men who could walk, cradling a bloody arm, or moving woodenly, face and scalp bright red. And mingled in with them were the inevitable shirkers, men shamming wounds or acting as if they were helping an injured comrade, the provost guards shouting out the age-old litany "Show blood!" and, if the man could not, turning them about with the flat of their swords, driving them back into the fight.

A half hour passed, the bombardment pounding McCausland Farm dropping off slightly, but still hitting in with a couple of dozen rounds a minute, the fire still well aimed, a dozen pieces on his side destroyed. He watched the men through his field glasses, ghostly in the smoke, standing to their work, firing back.

All along the front now, from north of the National Road bridge, to south of McCausland Farm, there was a continual blaze of fire, occasional spent rounds humming overhead, cracking into the trees behind him.

He pulled out his watch. It was not yet past six-thirty in the morning. Still no assault, but he knew it would come.

In the Railroad Cut

7:00 A.M.

Phil Sheridan ignored the scream of a solid shot plowing in, striking the edge of the cut, then bounding up with a howl, passing over head. Still mounted on Rienzi he slowly trotted down the length of track.

"How you doing, boys?" he shouted.

Men, faces begrimed with powder, up on the lip of the cut, looked down, grinning, surprised to see a major general right in the thick of it.

Phil knew they had a special attachment to their old Burnside. He had to dispel that here and now, and there was only one way to do it, regardless of Grant's orders to not "recklessly expose yourself."

Hell, that's what a good general had to do at times.

There are moments when if you do not lead by example you can't lead at all.

Another shot screamed in, this one striking the heavy barricade that had been erected six feet high across the east side of the cut to offer some protection from enfilade. It was made of piled-up railroad ties and rails, wrenched up during the night, the solid shot sending a fifteen-foot section of rail whirligiging through the air like a deadly scythe, cutting two men in half.

The blockhouse, just on the other side of the barricade was getting absolutely pounded to shreds. He had ventured a Napoleon for that position, but word was it was already dismounted by a direct hit through the gun port, but half a dozen volunteers, all of them sharpshooters had stayed on, peppering the rebs across the creek.

The best men of the three regiments holding the cut were up on the lip, taking careful aim as ordered, firing, then passing empty muskets down to men within the cut who were busy reloading and passing the guns back. Sheridan dismounted and crawled to the edge of the cut, stuck his head up, and looked to the other side.

It was hard to see anything. All was veiled in smoke, flashes of light rippling up and down the riverbank. The air was alive with the hum of miniés zipping past, a splatter of dirt kicking up nearly directly in front of his face. He deliberately remained motionless for several seconds and then slid back down.

"Hot enough up there for ya, General?" someone shouted, and the men began to laugh.

"Not as hot as you're making it for those damn rebs!" Phil replied and a cheer went up.

He mounted and rode on.

Hauling Ferry

7:30 A.M.

The growl of gunfire was a continual wave from the north. Men as they labored on the entrenchments would pause, look up, talk to each other until a sergeant came along and shouted for them to get back to work.

Winfield walked the line. It was easier than riding. He noted with interest how the Catoctin Ridge seemed to act as an acoustical reflector, like a cliff returning an echo, the sound of the artillery up at Frederick bouncing off of it, reverberating the length of the valley.

It sounded like one hell of a fight, and, for a moment, he regretted being here. *But then again, at least I'm here, near it, rather than back in Philadelphia reading about it.*

"General, sir." He smiled as Jeremiah rode up, his horse lathered, saluted, and dismounted.

He reached into his oversize haversack and pulled out a folded sheet of paper, opening it up.

"Sir, I'm sorry this took so long, but what with the darkness, I finally figured it was best to wait till dawn to finish my work, rather than make a mistake."

"You decide what's best when it comes to mapmaking, Jeremiah," Hancock replied warmly. "I trust you."

"Sir, I'm afraid you aren't going to like some of what I got to tell you."

"Go on." Jeremiah looked around for something to put his map against and finally opted to press it against the flank of his horse, who, completely exhausted, was now cropping on the rich pasture grass.

"I think we have to link the defensive line from here all the way up to Nolands Ferry. That means a front of over three miles. If we try to hold these points individually, particularly Nolands, Lee could easily flank it, moving between us here and there, roll the Nolands position up, and then have a means of getting back across the river, while blocking us at this position."

"That's a long front for this command," Winfield said.

"That's why I said you might not like it, but that's the lay of the land, sir."

Winfield studied the map sketched out by Major Siemens. He saw the point of it, that the Potomac behind them curved slightly to the north, cutting off Nolands Ferry from observation here, and also a shallow ravine cut down between them. Lee could force his way between these two strongpoints, isolate one, then annihilate the other. He had to keep the two positions linked if they were to hold.

"It's one tall order for digging," Jeremiah said. "I've sketched out what I would like, though. Strong bastions here, then one every six hundred yards, right up to Nolands, thus providing interlocking fields of fire. One of those hundred-pounders in each of the bastions, backed up by several thirty-pounders, would make it a grand killing ground. We also have to drop a lot of timber to open up the fields of fire, however."

Winfield nodded in agreement.

"I've calculated the amount of digging it will take," Siemens announced. "Three to four days at least with the men available."

Winfield said nothing, continuing to smile, which caught Jeremiah off guard.

"Sir, I figured you'd be kind of upset about this news, but that's the way I see it. I've also drawn up some fallback plans, bastioning each of the ferries, but I'm not comfortable with it."

Winfield held up his hand for Jeremiah to stop talking, and then, with his usual dramatic flair, he pointed down to the canal to a line of barges unloading and to the towpath beyond.

Thousands of black men were moving along the banks of the canal, getting off the boats, slowly walking up the towpath, pushing wheelbarrows, nearly every man armed with a tool—an axe, a shovel, a saw, a pick.

Winfield motioned for Jeremiah to follow him. Together they slowly walked down to the canal, the men from Washington, under a bedsheet banner, gathering around them.

"Mr. Bartlett, is it?" Winfield asked, approaching an elderly black man dressed in, of all things, formal attire of black jacket, vest, clean white shirt, and cravat.

"Yes, sir," Jim replied.

"May I introduce Maj. Jeremiah Siemens, my topographical engineer."

"You mean a mapmaker, sir?" Jim asked.

Almost involuntarily, Jeremiah masked a smile behind his fist. "Something like that, Uncle, but I'm also an engineer who lays out fortifications."

"Yes, I am an uncle, and a grandfather as well," Jim said, bracing his shoulders slightly. "I have a son and a grandson with Burnside's Corps; they're fighting even now up there. And I worked in the White House as the head butler before volunteering."

As he spoke, he motioned to the north and the distant gunfire.

Slightly humbled, Jeremiah dropped his condescending tone and extended his hand.

"Maj. Jeremiah Siemens." He paused. "Mr. Bartlett."

Jim took his hand formally. "How may we be of service to you this morning, Major."

Jim looked over at Winfield.

"Mr. Bartlett," Winfield said, "we need miles of trenches and fortifications in place no later than tomorrow. Major Siemens here has laid out the plan, but we are short of men, short by tens of thousands of the men needed to build them."

"That is why we volunteered," Jim replied.

Even as they spoke, another barge came up, several dozen black men getting off, then turning around to lend a hand with off-loading the barrels of salt pork and heavy small crates marked MUSKET ROUNDS, .58 CALIBER, ONE THOUSAND.

Behind them, farther up the towpath, more men came forward slowly, having walked the entire distance from Washington.

"Well, Jeremiah?" Winfield asked.

"Ah, let's see."

Confused, he looked down at his map and then at Winfield.

"I'm waiting, Jeremiah," Winfield said calmly.

"Mr. Bartlett, I am hereby appointing you as my assistant and commander of the Washington Colored Volunteers," he blurted out.

There was a chorus of chuckles from those gathered round, a few cheers, and offers of congratulations to Jim.

"I want you to start organizing your men into groups of a hundred. Appoint a . . ." he hesitated, "a captain to command each group of a hundred, and that captain to appoint sergeants who will command ten men. I'll have my men down here within thirty minutes. One of my men will then lead each group of a hundred and will be assigned a section that we'll start to stake out, and your men are to, well, start digging in and cutting out trees to create fields of fire."

"What we came here for, boss," someone in the crowd shouted, and there was another chorus of cheers.

Jeremiah, still a bit flustered, looked over at Winfield, who simply nodded.

"I'll be back in thirty minutes, so I think you better get busy, Mr. Bartlett."

"Some of the boys are mighty hungry," Jim said. "They've walked all night."

Winfield stepped up and motioned to the men off-loading the barrels of salt pork.

"Our infantry came up with five days of rations. I think we can use the reserves for your men," Winfield said. "Mr. Bartlett, have someone who was a cook pick out fifty men to stay behind from the digging. They can set up kitchen areas down here."

He pointed to the ground between the canal and the river.

"Also, appoint another hundred men to work on setting up encampments, digging latrines, and making shelters for your volunteers."

"A lot of orders," Jim said.

"Welcome to command, Mr. Bartlett," Winfield said with a smile. "I'll countermand only one of the major's orders. You don't answer to him. From now on you will report directly to me."

"Yes, sir," Jim said.

Winfield nodded and limped off, Jeremiah following him.

"What a blessing," Winfield said. "A message caught up to me from Elihu Washburne during the night, said that the colored men of Washington are pouring out by the thousands, maybe ten thousand or more, to volunteer their help up here."

"Lord knows, we can use them," Jeremiah replied, "but, sir, getting them organized, setting them to organized work. Building entrenchments, bastions, and clearing fields of fire isn't just simply digging a ditch."

"Who do you think built most of the fortifications around Washington? No one ever gives them the credit. I'm willing to bet, sir, you will find some damn good engineers, not formally educated but practical and experienced, back in that crowd."

"And what if the rebs come?"

"They will come."

"I mean, sir, what if they come and break through? Those men—" and he motioned to the volunteers who were now milling around Jim, shouting, asking for orders, asking for command positions, arguing with him that they didn't hike fifty miles just to be cooks.

"What about them?" Jeremiah asked.

"If it comes to a breakthrough, I'll tell them to fight, and they will fight. They walked here to help win their own freedom and their relatives' freedom. They are prepared to risk their lives as well as their sweat."

Two Miles North of Hauling Ferry

9:30 A.M.

Phil Duvall slipped up cautiously to the edge of the tree line. Yankee troopers and infantry occupied the ground just ahead, spread out in a thick skirmish line, hunkered down behind a low split-rail fence bordering an open pasture. It had cost him seven men to get up this far, and he knew he'd only have a few minutes before the Yankees began to push back.

He scanned the sloping ground ahead, this low crest dropping down into an open pasture, then undulating back up to a low rise a half mile away. An open ravine with a creek weaving through it dropped down to his right, leaving an open vista to the Potomac. He could barely see the canal. If he had had the nerve, he might have tried to climb a tree for a better view, but the Yankees on the other side of the pasture were proving to be damn good shots. He wouldn't last long in a tree.

One of his troopers, providing covering fire for him, knelt, took aim, and fired, and a split second later crumpled over, shot in the head.

Phil raised his field glasses and scanned the opposite slope and his heart dropped. All along the opposite low-lying ridge men were at work. He could see dirt flying into the air, the diggers invisible below their thighs in places. Curiously, many wore blue trousers, their uniform jackets discarded, white shirts standing out clear, but mingled in, in far greater numbers, were colored men. An entire woodlot of several acres was rapidly being cut down, trees crashing, teams of a dozen men harnessed to ropes, laboriously dragging trimmed logs up the slope. Others were taking the branches and weaving them into large oversize baskets, as thick around as a barrel and nearly as tall as a man, setting them in place atop the earthworks while others then shoveled dirt into them.

One crew, of well over a hundred men, working with a team of a half dozen mules, was slowly dragging what appeared to be a long black tube along the crest. He tried to focus in on it. It looked to be the biggest gun he had ever seen, one of the legendary hundred-pound Parrotts.

It was. Behind them, coming into view, was another crew of a hundred colored men, dragging a heavy iron gun carriage, the mount for the piece.

A spray of bark and splinters and tree sap smacked against the side of his face. He ducked back behind the tree. Two more minié balls whizzed in, kicking up dirt to either side of him.

"Major, sir, I didn't ride with you for two years just to see you killed now," Sergeant Lucas hissed, lying flat on his stomach behind the tree next to him.

Phil looked up.

Damn, mounted troops, a hundred or more, were coming down from the crest, riding hard.

"Major, sir, really I think it's time we got the hell out of here."

Phil forced a tight smile and nodded. He had seen what he had been sent to see, and now it was time, as Lucas said, to get "the hell out of here."

"Come on!"

He stood up and sprinted to the rear.

Headquarters of the Army of Northern Virginia
Monocacy Creek

10:00 A.M.

"hy don't they come on?" Lee asked impatiently, pacing back and forth, looking over at Pete, who paced alongside of him.

The firing had been going on since dawn. Of the hundred guns down at McCausland Farm, barely half were still firing. Ten thousand shells or more had turned the ground around the farm into a plowed-up wasteland, the brick farmhouse pounded into wreckage.

All along the riverfront the firing was continuing, both sides taking losses, but nothing that would even begin to indicate a clear decision.

A thunderclap rolled up from the south, another caisson going up, and that decided it for him.

"Walter, my compliments to General Alexander. Tell him to pass the word down to the battery commanders at McCausland to mount up and withdraw out of range."

Walter almost seemed to breathe a sigh of relief with that order. The men all along the ridge had been watching the duel since dawn, cheering when an enemy gun was wiped out, groaning when two, three, and four of those at McCausland fell victim.

Walter mounted and rode off.

It was impossible to see anything now. The entire riverfront for miles was enveloped in a dank, yellow-gray smoke.

"Perhaps that will draw him in," Lee said.

Longstreet did not reply.

This fight was proving to be different. Grant was showing a cagey side, the hours of bombardment, as if to indicate he had ammunition to burn. *And I do, too, and more will be on its way from Baltimore once the tangle of trains is unsnarled.*

Burnside would have just come in blindly, Hooker would have at least made a lunge, then perhaps frozen, and McClellan . . . well, if it was McClellan over there I would have already crossed the river myself and gone after him.

For a moment he was tempted to order just that. To send Beauregard's men, who made up most of his reserve, into an attack, but the Yankees had dug in well on the opposite bank, and though they would not advance, he knew they would not give back easily.

So far we've most likely lost a thousand, perhaps two thousand, to an equal number. Something has to break soon, Lee thought. *He has to come on.*

Hunt's Battery

10:45 A.M.

amn good work, boys!" Hunt shouted. "Damn good work!"

Now mounted, he trotted down the line, shouting his congratulations, the men cheering as he passed.

"What do you think of Western gunners now, sir?" one of them yelled out.

The question actually gave him painful pause for a second, remembering the bloody defense at Gettysburg, the sacrifice of Stevens's Battery, the final stand in the cemetery. And all of them gone now.

He slowed, then remembered to stay in this moment, not to dwell on the bitter past.

"You're damn good lads and I'm proud of you!"

His response drew a cheer and he rode on.

The men were exhausted; many had stripped off their jackets, sweat streaming down their bodies. The August sun beat down on them; gun barrels were so hot that to touch them would fry a man's flesh.

As his batteries ceased fire, men were already swabbing and reswabbing the bores, the sponges hissing and steaming as they were slammed in.

Limber wagons were coming up, circling around, ignoring the incoming fire that still rained down from the center of the rebel line, crews rushing up to off load ammunition and carry it into the bombproofs.

He passed an entire team of gunners who had been wiped out, all of them killed when a well-placed case shot detonated directly above them. Stretcher bearers ignored them, going down the line to pick up the wounded. Even in victory there would be the casualties.

Eleven of his guns had been disabled in the fight, wheels taken off, barrels hit and dismounted, or bursting case shot killing everyone gathered around a piece.

As always, the wounds to artillerymen were the most horrific. A solid shot had torn off the wheel of a Parrott gun, then slashed clean through the solid oak of the trail piece, killing or wounding the entire crew; one man was impaled against the side of the lunette, a spoke from the wheel driven through his stomach, pinning him to the wall. To Henry's absolute horror, the man was still alive, groaning softly, several comrades gathered round him, debating whether to try to move him or not. A surgeon came up and Henry prayed that the man had the courage to inject him with so much morphine that he would slip away.

He turned his head away and rode on.

Another shot winged in from the distant rebel position, this one either damn well aimed or pure luck. It hit a caisson moving up. The caisson, loaded with fifty shells and over a hundred pounds of powder, exploded with a roar, the entire team of six horses blown down, debris soaring heavenward. Seconds later a distant roar went up. It was a defiant rebel yell.

His own gunners turned, facing the rebs, waving clenched fists, vowing revenge.

Henry continued to ride on, inspecting his pieces. He knew the next stage was about to begin. The question now was simply when.

Headquarters, Army of the Susquehanna

11:00 A.M.

Grant lit what was now the tenth cigar of the day, coughing slightly as he puffed it to life, remaining motionless in his camp chair, just sitting silently, watching the fight. Actually, it was now impossible to see much of anything. No wind had stirred, the day was getting hot, typical of late August, with only a few puffy clouds overhead to indicate a storm later in the day.

The entire river valley was hidden in smoke, the rattle of musketry and the booming of the artillery incessant. And yet it had settled into a dull steady pattern, punctuated only by loud huzzahs from Hunt's batteries about twenty minutes ago when it became evident that the rebels they had been pounding all morning were pulling back.

A telegraph line had been run out from the town during the night. The men within the signals tent were bent over their strange machines and cases of batteries that emitted a strange acid smell.

The key started to clatter again, and he stood up, unable to contain himself. This had to be it. It had to be.

He realized he was making a display of anxiety and forced himself to turn back, acting as if he was continuing to survey the smoke-filled valley and the battle that thundered there, which, so far, had not changed ownership of even one inch of ground.

Ely was over at the tent. From the corner of his eye Grant saw his adjutant running toward him, grinning.

"Sir, it's from Port Deposit."

"Go on."

"Fleet left at dawn. Should be coming into position by now. Second report from observation post opposite Baltimore confirms the report."

Grant smiled.

In one sense, it was a miracle. Here he was on this battlefield, and yet news from a hundred miles away had just been handed to him.

He took a deep breath.

He had held Lee's attention since dawn. Now would have to come the bloody part to keep that attention fixed.

He looked over at Ely.

"Tell General Ord to go in," he said calmly.

Baltimore

11:00 A.M.

M r. Secretary, I think you'd better come out and see this."
Judah looked up at the Confederate officer, one of Pickett's men standing in the doorway of his hotel suite.

"What is it?"

"Sir, General Pickett requests you come out and have a look. Something is up with the Yankees."

Judah headed for the door, leaving his jacket behind. It was another typical Baltimore summer day. The day had turned hot and sultry. Leaving the hotel, he followed the officer up the street to Battery Park. Scores of civilians were heading in the same direction, talking excitedly, and already he had a good guess as to what to expect as he crossed through the picket line at the entry to the fort and then up to where George Pickett stood, looking out over the harbor.

Directly below, within easy gunnery range, was Fort McHenry, its large garrison flag coiling and drifting above the fort. But that was not what was drawing interest. In the outer harbor a flotilla of several dozen ships was just visible in the late-morning haze on the water, dark coils of smoke rising from ships a half dozen miles away.

Pickett turned and bowed formally as Judah approached.

"Mr. Secretary, I think the Yankees are up to something."

"How long have they been out there?"

"Lookouts first reported the smoke an hour ago coming down from the north." Pickett motioned for Judah to take a look through a telescope.

He bent over, the telescope focused on a side-wheel steamship with three masts. It was a heavy oceangoing vessel. Its side wheels were churning the water, bow almost straight on. He studied it carefully. It was hard to tell, but it looked as if the deck was packed with blue . . . Union infantry.

At the head of the flotilla came a half dozen gunboats and four heavy monitor ironclads, guns pointing menacingly toward the city.

He stood back and looked over at Pickett.

"What do you think, General?"

"Don't rightly know, sir. But if they do move into the inner harbor, should I fire on them?"

"What did General Lee order you to do."

"Hold this city until he finished off Grant."

Judah could detect a bitterness in Pickett's voice. He made no comment about it. It had been reported to him that Pickett was heard complaining that Lee was blaming him for the devastation of his division at Gunpowder River, and that he had only been "following the old man's orders."

He wanted in on the fight now taking place out at Frederick and chaffed at being left behind.

Shortly after dawn everyone in Baltimore knew that something was happening in Frederick. In the early-morning silence all could hear the distant thunder. Windowpanes were rattling and excited boys, climbing to the tops of church steeples, shouted down that they could see smoke on the horizon.

But there was no news, other than the fact that a bombardment had started at dawn . . . and nothing else.

An officer came riding up, arm in a sling, and dismounted, coming up to join the two. It was Lo Armistead.

"So what is it?" Lo asked.

"We're not sure," Pickett replied.

Lo looked through the telescope for a moment.

"It's an assault force," he announced.

Judah had to nod in agreement, even as Pickett returned to the telescope, bent down, and scanned the approaching ships.

"Who is it?" Judah asked. "Where did they come from?"

"First observations were that they were coming down from farther up the Chesapeake," Pickett said, eye still glued to the telescope.

"Then it's got to be that damned Army of the Potomac," Lo replied. "They just won't die, they just won't die."

"I thought we destroyed them last week," Judah said.

Lo looked over at him and shook his head.

"Yes and no, sir. Maybe ten thousand or more eventually got out. A few, a tough few. Last report was that old Sykes was in charge of them. A slow and deliberate man, but tough in a fight. We faced him at Taneytown.

"The Yankees also have marines that were stationed in Washington, some naval troops, even a few infantry and heavy artillery units stationed down at Fortress Monroe. Combine those with the garrison down there and we have a major problem on our hands."

As he spoke he pointed toward Fort McHenry.

"If we had that fort, they wouldn't dare to come into this inner harbor. Now they can land with impunity by early this afternoon. I wish now we'd taken that fort."

Judah looked over at Lo, suddenly filled with curiosity.

"Is it true, sir, that your uncle commanded the defense of this city against the British?" Judah asked.

"Yes, sir. He commanded the garrison in that fort right down there." Lo pointed to McHenry. "In fact the original flag from that night, the Star-Spangled Banner, is still in my family's possession."

"A curious war we have here," Judah said quietly.

Neither of the officers replied.

He could see that the fleet was drawing closer by the minute, and then, to his utter amazement, a flash ignited from the fort, and seconds later a shell burst directly over where they stood.

Judah ducked down, Lo by his side.

"I guess the truce between us here is over," Judah said, trying to act game, even though the explosion had terrified him.

Pickett slid down beside the two, the men within the battery scattering. Though they still had a half dozen guns in the position, none were currently manned, the other pieces having been pulled out during the feint on Washington at the start of the Gunpowder River campaign.

A half dozen more shells screamed in, exploding, kicking up showers of dirt, scattering panic-stricken civilians out in the street.

"Mr. Secretary," Lo said, "I think you better get back to your quarters, pack up, and, frankly, sir, get out of this town."

"What?"

"Just that, sir."

"Damn them," Pickett gasped. "We've been hoodwinked. At least they could have shown the common courtesy to send up a flag of truce and announce they were about to fire."

Another shell screamed in, missed the fort, and blew up against a house across the square.

"I don't think it's time for courtesies," Judah replied. "General Pickett, sir, can you hold against that?"

Judah half-leaned up and pointed out to the ships steaming into the harbor.

Pickett looked at him coldly and shook his head.

"Against that, sir?"

Pickett was angry.

"My boys did their duty at Gunpowder River. I get blamed for it, I'm left with little more than two brigades, and given the number of ships out there, there could be fifteen thousand or more Yankees."

"Your orders were to hold," Judah said coldly.

Pickett hesitated, then reluctantly nodded his head.

"I'll try, sir, but I can tell you, before evening we'll be on the run. I suggest you, sir, get out of Baltimore now. Go up and join General Lee."

"There are some home-guard units," Judah argued, trying to remain calm.

"Maryland, my Maryland?" Pickett replied sarcastically. "A rabble. A few thousand. If that's Sykes out there, they'll mow them down. We're finished here."

"I shall tell General Lee your exact words," Judah snapped.

Judah stood up, tried to act dignified by brushing himself off, then ran out of the fort and down the street to his hotel. The crowd of curious civilians of but minutes ago was now a terrified mob, running in every direction. He saw one man leaning out of a window, tearing down the Confederate flag that hung from it, letting it flutter to the street, and then slamming the window shut.

A crowd came pouring out of a tavern down the street, some cheering, and with their cheering a fight broke out.

Madness, all of it madness, Judah thought.

He ran up to his room, grabbed a carpetbag, and quickly stuffed into it every document he thought might be of value and two small heavy bags of gold coins, the official funds for his venture here. His black servant, showing good common sense, had just finished packing his suitcases.

Judah looked around the room that had been his unofficial office for the last five weeks. He had come into it with so many hopes and dreams, that from here he could engineer an alliance with France, perhaps England, perhaps end this carnage. Maybe Lee could still retrieve that, but his job here was finished.

He picked up his carpetbag and headed down the stairs. To his amazement the owner of the hotel confronted him.

"Sir, regarding your bill," the man said with an unctuous tone. "You
have run up quite a few charges."

"You said you were honored for me to be here when I first checked
in," Judah snapped.

"Sir, we are talking about nearly five thousand dollars. The bill for the
champagne and oysters alone is rather significant." The man held up a
long charge sheet. "And should I add, this is calculated in standard cur-
rency, not Union greenbacks," he paused, "or Confederate paper."

"Send the bill to me in Richmond when the war is over," Judah
snapped.

He shouldered past the man and out on to the street.

To his amazement he saw a single-horse carriage come up, top down.
It was his old friend Rabbi Gunther Rothenberg.

"Figured you'd need a ride," the rabbi said.

"In the name of the Eternal," Judah gasped. "You are indeed a friend.
The rail yard of the B and O, my friend."

"What I assumed, Mr. Secretary."

Half a dozen trains had finally returned from the front and
Cruickshank was back at work, ordering the loading of the
stockpiles of ammunition, when he heard the first shell detonate, the explosion echoing against the brick buildings. All had stopped work, looking toward the center of town. Less than a minute later a civilian had
ridden through, whipping his horse, crying that a Yankee invasion fleet
was coming.

All work had stopped, the single explosion now followed by a continual thumping roar, half a dozen explosions a minute. The report of the
panicky civilian was confirmed minutes later when a staff officer from
Pickett rode in and took Cruickshank aside.

"We're abandoning the town," the officer said. "General Pickett orders you to load up what you can of the supplies, then set the rest afire."

The man had then ridden off without waiting for a reply.

Cruickshank watched him leave, McDougal coming to his side.

"Well, General, looks like that's it for you."

Cruickshank stared at him.

"Quite a few tons of explosives in those warehouses," McDougal said
quietly. "Light them off and you'll burn down half the city. Now, frankly,
I don't care about them rich folks, but it'll ruin us being able to work here
for a long time to come."

"Orders are orders," Cruickshank said coldly.

McDougal did not reply. He simply stuck his hands in his pockets.

Two more trains backed into the station, one carrying wounded, the second, a single passenger car. The second came to a halt at the main depot, and after several minutes an escort of Confederate soldiers came out, struggling to maneuver a stretcher out the door, the body on it draped with a Union flag.

"That must be him," McDougal said.

Cruickshank did not reply. He watched as the small entourage stepped down from the train and then walked off, a Confederate officer helping to hold up a young woman, all of them oblivious to the spreading confusion, the rumble of explosions.

"Cruickshank!"

He looked up and saw a small carriage coming across the yard, jostling and shaking as it crossed the tracks. He recognized the man as Judah Benjamin.

The driver of the carriage, wearing what to Cruickshank appeared to be a strange small round cap, reined in, and Judah stepped down.

"You've heard?"

"Ah, yes, sir. At least that there's fighting."

"There's a flotilla of Yankee ships coming up the harbor loaded with troops. Fort McHenry is bombarding our positions, and General Pickett will undoubtedly pull back without putting up much of a fight."

Cruickshank did not reply.

"Where's the telegraph station?"

"This way, your honor," McDougal said with a smile and led Judah off.

Cruickshank, unsure what to do next, finally turned to one of his lieutenants and told him to round up all the men of their command at once. They were to leave their packs, just grab their rifles, and come on the double.

He looked at the man with the strange hat in the carriage. The man smiled, extended his hand, and introduced himself.

"Do me a favor, General," Gunther asked.

"Yes, sir?"

"Keep an eye on my friend. He has a hard road ahead, as do you. I shall keep you both in my prayers."

McDougal came out of the telegraph office, motioning to the train that had brought in McPherson, and began to shout orders.

With amazing speed the yard crew set to work, the locomotive and the lone passenger car shifted over to a sidetrack with a water tank, crew swinging over the pipe to refill the tender, other men scrambling to toss up wood, others with large oilcans checking the drive wheels, while yet others opened the journal boxes of the passenger car and, from buckets, slathered in hunks of grease.

"All but five of the men are reported in, sir."

Cruickshank turned to see his rough-looking detachment lining up, nearly a hundred men in all.

"Who is missing?"

"Oh, Vern Watson and several of his friends." The others chuckled.

"Where the hell are they?"

The lieutenant looked up at Gunther.

"Are you a man of the cloth, sir?" the lieutenant asked, features a bit red.

"A rabbi."

"What?"

"He's Jewish," one of the men shouted.

"Go on," Cruickshank snapped.

"Well, Vern and his friends went down to a house of ill repute, said they'd be back by noon, and you wouldn't notice them missing."

Cruickshank sighed.

"Well, let the Yankees roust them out of bed. Now get aboard that train."

The men broke ranks and ran to the passenger car, piling in to overflowing, some scrambling up onto the roof, others atop the wood tender, a few even perching on the cowcatcher.

Judah came out of the telegraphy office, followed by several Confederate soldiers who had been manning the post. He walked up to Cruickshank.

"We're leaving now. That Mr. McDougal said he'd have a train ready for us."

"Over there, sir."

Judah nodded, walked over to the carriage, and extended his hand to Gunther.

"God be with you, my friend," Gunther said.

"Someday, when this is all over, come to Richmond as my guest," Judah said.

"We'll see," Gunther said sadly.

Judah looked straight into his eyes, smiled, then, taking his carpetbag, he headed for the train. Gunther turned his carriage about and rode off.

Cruickshank found himself alone looking over at the row of warehouses stockpiled with munitions, boots, tents, heavy machinery that was to be transported back to Richmond to aid in artillery production, crates of tools, armored plating for ironclads, rail for track, machinery to make breechloading carbines, tens of thousands of horseshoes.

It'll take ten minutes to set it ablaze, he thought, *and what a fire that will be.*

He noticed as well that McDougal's workmen stood about, gazing at him. A few had picked up shovels, heavy wrenches, pry bars, axes, and picks.

He could order his men out of the car, one volley would scatter the workmen, and they could then level this damn place. In the distance he could hear more explosions and the distant crying of a mob, rioting yet again.

McDougal came up to his side.

"Your train is ready, General. You have a clear road up to Relay Station, then a thirty-minute delay until a convoy of a dozen trains passes on both tracks, though I dare say that plan will change now, what with you having all them locomotives up there and not wanting them back here."

A dozen locomotives, all they could have carried, Cruickshank thought. *Enough to equal two thousand wagons of supplies.*

"Just one question, McDougal, and be honest for once, damn it," Cruickshank asked, gaze still fixed on the warehouse.

"Anything at all, General, sir."

"You were playing me double the whole time, weren't you?"

McDougal laughed softly.

"Honestly? An Irishman to an Englishman turned rebel?"

Cruickshank looked him the eyes.

"Honestly."

"Of course I was, sir."

"Why?"

"Wouldn't you if we was reversed? You know, Cruickshank, though you're a bloody Englishman by birth, why you ever sided with them is beyond me. Slavery, all that. It's no different than the way we was treated in Ireland or you in the slums of Liverpool.

"So if you be wishing to shoot me, go ahead. But my boys over there, they might not have guns, but you should see the way they can swing a pick or pry bar into a man's head when they got to. And if you try to burn the warehouses, that's what you'll face."

Cruickshank was silent.

"Don't do it," McDougal said quietly. "I wouldn't want our friendship here to end in a bloody brawl. Besides, you'll burn half the city down and things here are hard enough as it is. My men have families, as do I."

Their gazes held for several seconds.

"A deal then," Cruickshank said, "the last of our deals."

"Go on."

"Help me to load two or three trains with ammunition, and I'll spare everything else."

"How do I know you won't burn it anyhow, once loaded up?"

"You have my word on it."

McDougal hesitated then nodded.

"Deal."

McDougal turned to his men and started to shout orders, Cruickshank doing the same to his own command, having them stack arms.

Within minutes hundreds were at work at a pitch Cruickshank had not seen once across the last several days. Cases of small-round ammunition were lugged out and hauled into boxcars or carted over to the train where Judah still waited and piled into the passenger compartment. Boxes of artillery shells, two men to a box, were trotted out and put on flatcars.

Locomotives were uncoupled while the crews worked, moved up to the engine houses, where fuel and water were taken on, grease and oil checked, then returned to the cars and hooked up.

It took little more than an hour to have three entire trains loaded up.

All the time the sound of gunfire was increasing, now counterpointed by the shriek of heavy shells, most likely from the monitors.

Finally, McDougal approached Cruickshank.

"I've given you three trains, as promised. They'll run fine."

The three engines were already maneuvering out of their sidings, pulling the precious supplies that could sustain the army through an entire long day of battle.

Again a moment's hesitation. Cruickshank looked back to the warehouses crammed with enough for a dozen more trains but already, across the far side of the railyard he could see a column of infantry pulling back, heading northwest, out of town.

"A deal is a deal," Cruickshank replied and stepped past McDougal, walked to the passenger car, and mounted the back steps. Leaning out, he waved to one of his men who was in the locomotive cab. The engine lurched, beginning to inch forward with a blast of steam.

"General, darlin'."

He looked down, McDougal walking alongside him.

"What now?"

"You know you forgot my day's wages for today. Since I only worked half the day, that'll be thirty dollars in silver."

"Go to hell!"

"Where I expect to meet you, too, sir."

McDougal reached into his back pocket, pulled out a bottle, and tossed it up to Cruickshank.

"We'll drink another when we meet in the lower regions," McDougal shouted.

Cruickshank almost allowed himself to smile. Uncorking the bottle, he took a long drink and climbed to the back platform of the train.

McDougal stood in the middle of the track, waving, growing smaller and smaller as the train picked up speed . . . the last train out of Baltimore, smoke boiling up from the city beyond.

Headquarters, Army of Northern Virginia

12:45 P.M.

They're going in!" one of his staff cried.

He did not need to be told. Though the smoke all but masked the movement, he could see the dark columns coming down the slope toward his left flank, heading toward the same ford they had attempted to breach the day before. This would be the obvious point of attack now that his guns had drawn back.

Alexander was already redirecting his fire, shifting from long-distance counterbattery to direct support, pounding the heavy columns, which looked to be of corps strength, perhaps fifteen thousand men. At last Grant was committing himself.

He felt it was time to move, to go down behind the McCausland Farm, to see directly to the repositioning of the guns and to ensure the movement of one of Beauregard's divisions into a support position if the pressure on Hood's men down at the ford became too heavy.

"Sir?"

It was one of his staff, holding a note, his hand shaking.

Lee took it and scanned its contents and felt as if he had just taken a visceral blow. It was from Judah Benjamin.

He looked back to the west.

Was this coincidence or part of your plan? he wondered, looking toward what had been identified as Grant's headquarters area.

If planned, it was masterful. Seek battle here, block the river, for that report had just come in a half hour ago, and now strike my base of supply.

He looked down at the assaulting column, his own troops having opened up on it with a thunderous volley, Union troops by the scores dropping, and still it pushed forward.

He crushed the telegram in his fist.

Fine, then, he thought. *Let it be here. It will take two, perhaps three days for whatever is hitting us in Baltimore to take effect. So come on and attack, and let us see how we match each other. In that time I will crush you, and then all your maneuverings will be meaningless.*

He went over to Traveler, mounted, and rode down to face the approaching charge.

Chapter Fifteen

It had been a bloody nightmare; in fact, it still was. Ord slowly walked up the long slope from the ford to the burned-out ruins of the farm.

Never had he seen such carnage, and all joy of battle, all enthusiasm, was purged out of him. Barely a step could be taken without tripping over a body.

It started two hundred yards back from the ford, clusters of men dropped by rebel artillery, then lines of them down by the crossing itself. He had finally waded the stream on horseback and just below the crossing the slow-moving water was tinted pink from the dozens of bodies that had drifted down from the crossing and then snagged on rocks or broken tree limbs, cut down by the incessant fire.

At the first Confederate entrenchment the ground was churned up, muddy, from the deadly hand-to-hand fighting, bodies and wounded intermingled.

Slowly he moved up the long, deadly four-hundred-yard slope to the farmhouse. Over half the men of his First Division carpeted the ground. In places it looked as if they were a line of battle down on the ground, just resting, having been cut down by terrifying volleys that had dropped up to a hundred at a time.

He rode on, the air overhead a constant hum of miniés, spent canister, and shrieking shells fired high.

He stopped by the farmhouse, stunned by what was before him. He had missed Shiloh, but had often heard stories of the absolute destruction around the Hornets Nest. This, he realized, must far transcend it.

The ground for several dozen acres was nothing but churned up dirt and mud, the result of Hunt's morning barrage. Nearly thirty destroyed guns littered the slope, some collapsed down on one wheel, others overturned, others with entire crews and horses from the limber team dead.

But it was the infantry fight here that had been truly horrific. On the one side it had been men of Early's command, tough veterans; on his side were three divisions, and they had fought it out toe to toe. He actually had to dismount to weave his way through the carnage. Dozens of stretcher-bearer teams, some of them Confederates with white strips of cloth tied around their sleeves or hatbands, were gingerly picking their way through the chaos, pulling men out, rolling them over, making a quick judgment, picking some up, leaving others behind.

He had ordered up the corps ambulances, the few that had pressed ahead after the forced march of the infantry two days before. These were parked at the bottom of the slope, loading up, and then splashing across the ford to the hospital area.

The roar of battle ahead was a continual thunder. He pushed forward through a constant stream of men staggering to the rear. Most were walking wounded, men hobbling along, two comrades, one with a shattered left leg, another with a broken right leg, with arms wrapped around each other, moving slowly. A man, stripped to the waist, dirty, lank hair hanging to his shoulders, a bullet hole in his stomach, came back, waving a leafy branch, eyes glazed, hysterically chanting the refrain from the "Battle Hymn." "Glory, glory, hallelujah . . . glory, glory hallelujah . . ."

"Edward!"

He saw Grant riding up, cigar clenched firmly in his mouth, gingerly maneuvering Cincinnatus through the piled-up bodies and then coming forward.

Exhausted, Ord did not bother to salute.

"How goes it?"

"How goes it, sir?" Edward asked. His normally high-pitched voice was near to warbling. Unable to contain himself, he pointed across the slopes to McCausland Farm.

"That's my corps there," he said.

"What's ahead?"

"Not sure. I know we shattered a division, Jubal Early. Tore them apart once we gained the farm. Reports say that a reserve division ahead, not yet identified, but supposedly Beauregard's, is blocking our advance. Also, the guns not destroyed by Hunt are still over there."

Grant did not need to be told. He could hear their thunder, shot that missed the ranks ahead skimming overhead.

"General, there's no further purpose to this advance," Ord announced. "My corps is fought out."

"Tell your men to stop, to pull back to here, form a salient around the ford."

"Thank you, sir."

Ord saluted, bowed his head, and rode forward.

Near McCausland Farm

5:30 P.M.

The gunfire beyond McCausland Farm was rippling down, slowing in volume and pace. Lee rode along the line, watching as Beauregard's men slowly pushed forward, the Yankees giving ground. What had once been a cornfield was now as flat as the one at Sharpsburg. Every stalk cut down, the ripening corn replaced by a grim harvest of blue and gray.

In a significant way, this fight had indeed been like Sharpsburg and the cornfield. Charge and countercharge had swept the field repeatedly until all semblance of order, of meaning too, perhaps even why they were fighting for this ground, was forgotten. It had simply devolved into a murder match by both sides.

Jubal Early was limping across the field toward him, and for once even this tough old fighter seemed shaken.

"My boys," Jubal said, coming to Lee's side and looking up. "Sir, my boys. That's my entire division out there." He gestured across the cornfield toward the farm.

Lee could not reply, leaned down, patted him on the shoulder, and turned back to ride to his headquarters.

If this was the way Grant intended to fight it out, it was time to turn the tables.

Sergeant Hazner slipped back down in his trench. In the last few minutes it just seemed that a terrible exhaustion had set in on both sides. Almost all firing had ceased. Colonel Brown crept past, patting men on the shoulder, telling them to stand down, to clean their weapons, and watering parties would be formed. Hazner was not at all surprised when Brown called on him to form that detail.

He looked around at his men. The regiment had not taken too many casualties this day, twenty dead and wounded, more dead than wounded actually, mostly head shots, and one section of men knocked down when a shell detonated directly above their trench.

The blockhouse, just to their right, had been a favorite target of sharp-shooters all day, its front and flank absolutely shredded by hundreds of bullets.

"Man could take that thing down and open a blacksmith shop with what he found in that wood," someone quipped, but no one laughed; they were all too damn tired and thirsty.

Hazner pointed to a dozen men.

"Get canteens," he said, voice so hoarse he could barely speak.

The men spread out, bent double, moving down the entrenchment, picking up canteens as they moved. Hazner ventured to stand up, taking off his cap, peeking over the lip of the trench.

What a damned nightmare, he thought. What little vegetation there had been in front of his position, clear down to the river, was beaten to pulp. The tops of trees along the riverbank were shredded. The Yankee en-trenchments on the far side were again becoming visible, the smoke from the long day's fusillade starting to lift on a building westerly breeze. At the edge of the railroad cut, held by the Yankees, he saw stretcher teams, bent low, climbing out the back of the position and sprinting up the slope to the rear. The understanding that both sides had always held fire for stretcher details continued to hold; no shots were deliberately aimed at them, but random shots could still take them out, and more than one man carrying a stretcher suddenly collapsed.

The more aggressive on both sides began to resume fire now that the smoke was clearing enough to see the other side, and Hazner ducked down after one round zipped by a bit too closely.

The water detail gathered around him, men with ten, fifteen canteens slung around their necks.

"Let's go," Hazner said. He led the way down the trench. They passed through the next regiment to the left, the entrenchment curving back to the southwest, following the bend of the hill. Their dead were piled out on the far side of their stronghold, the bottom of the trench car-peted with tens of thousands of pieces of paper, torn cartridges. The men looked as if they had come from a minstrel show, faces blackened by smoke and powder, rivulets of sweat streaking their faces.

"Fired a hundred fifty rounds, I did," he heard one of them boasting wearily. "Know for sure I got three of 'em. Boy, what a shooting gallery we had today."

Even as he spoke the man rubbed his shoulder.

He passed through another regiment and then another and then finally the trench just ended. Directly below was the railroad track leading to the bridge but they were now a good four hundred yards back from the front.

"Be careful there," said a sergeant posted at the end of the entrenchment. "They got a few real good shooters over there."

Hazner nodded his thanks, took a deep breath, and climbed out of the trench and slid down the slope to the railroad track. Men were scurrying back and forth, bent on the same duty, carrying canteens for Scales's Division posted up on the slope looking down on the center of the line.

Long-distance harassing fire was indeed coming from the railroad cut on the other side of the Monocacy, nothing accurate, but an unaimed ball at six hundred yards could kill just as quickly as an aimed one.

"Come on, boys," Hazner said, and he slid down off the track and into an open field. A mill was directly before him, at least what was left of it, the building having caught fire during the day. Behind the mill was a small pond, all but concealed in the drifted banks of smoke. In spite of his exhaustion he ran down to it. Scores of men were lying along the bank around the pond, and he slipped down between two of them, the man to his left a Yankee, but he didn't care.

Brushing the water back with his hand he stuck his head in, delighting in the tepid water, and drank deeply.

"Ah, thank God," he whispered. Splashing water up over his neck, he was half-tempted to just take off his cartridge box and jump in.

"Ah, Sergeant, maybe we better go someplace else," one of his men said softly, tugging him on the shoulder.

"Why?"

"Most of these boys is dead."

Hazner half-sat up, looked at the Yankee lying next to him, head buried in the water, and shook him.

The man's head turned slightly and Hazner recoiled with horror. He had no face, the jawbone and nose completely blown off. He had been drinking right next to him, only inches away.

Before he quite realized what he was doing, Hazner got to his knees, bent double, and vomited.

Gasping, he leaned over, ashamed of the fact that he had vomited on the dead soldier.

"It's all right there, Sergeant," one of his men said. He looked up. It was young Lieutenant Hurt, the boy he had braced up before the assault on Fort Stephens. Hurt put his hand out and pulled Hazner up to his feet.

"We thought you seen it," Hurt said, and he pointed to bodies around the small pond, not just on the banks but floating in the middle of it, one of the bodies having jammed in the millwheel. The water was actually tinted pink. Some of the men were still alive, but so weak that after having collapsed into the water they were now drowning.

Hurt ordered the detail to drop canteens and pull the poor wretches out. The men set to work, some of the wounded so badly injured that as they were pulled out they screamed with pain, one of them a man scorched black from the waist up.

Hazner, still in shock, said nothing.

The men, having finished their task of pulling the drowning back, were not sure what to do next. Hurt looked at Hazner, as if expecting the experienced sergeant major to resume control.

"Nothing we can do for these boys now," Hurt said. "I'll tell Colonel Brown when we get back and he can get Scales to send ambulances down."

He said it loud, as if offering an excuse to the injured and the dying around them.

"Come on, boys. Let's get above the pond."

Hazner picked up a dozen of the canteens and said nothing, following along woodenly. They reached the ground above the pond, and all along the banks of the stream hundreds of men were at work at the same task, so that by the time Hurt found a spot for the men to start filling, there was barely a trickle of water.

After twenty minutes the last of the canteens was filled, and Hurt motioned for them to start heading back. Hazner brought up the rear, the detachment crossing over the railroad tracks up the slope and tumbling into the trench. Moving down the line Hazner just walked along tall, while his comrades moved bent double until they reached their regiment.

Hazner leaned against the side of the trench, still standing, saying nothing as the men around him greedily took canteens, tilted their heads back, and drank deeply.

"Sergeant?"

He focused his gaze. It was Colonel Brown.

"Yes, sir."

"Maybe you should get down, Sergeant."

"Sir." Hazner looked around, suddenly aware that he was still standing erect, his men gazing up at him. He slid down to the bottom of the trench.

"Lieutenant Hurt told me what happened back there, Sergeant. How are you?"

"Me, sir?" Hazner said, forcing a smile. "Just fine, sir. Just fine."

Brown patted him on the shoulder and crept off, calling for the men to save a little water to pour down their barrels so they could swab their guns clean.

Someone offered Hazner a canteen. He tried to drink the water, but to his utter shame, seconds later, he vomited it up.

No one spoke.

Can I ever drink a drop of water again without seeing him? he wondered.

Hauling Ferry

6:30 P.M.

Jim thought he knew what labor was, but the long years of life in the White House, the formal protocol, the softly spoken and ever-so-polite conversations, even between the servants, had never quite braced him for this.

For hours he had stood out in the sun, until someone, surprisingly, a young white officer, had brought over a chair and pointed out that an awning had been set up for him, complete with desk.

He had gladly taken this position, along with the offer of a half dozen colored men who were fairly well dressed, most of them clerks who said they could write with a good hand, and were now his staff.

The makeshift bedsheet banner WASHINGTON COLORED VOLUNTEERS hung limp from one side of the awning, now fluttering slightly with the evening breeze that carried with it the scent of rain.

Thus he had worked through the day, struggling to keep things organized. As ordered by the general, he had first assigned fifty men, largely chosen at random, to be captains, told them to pick ten sergeants each, and then for the sergeants to pick ten men as workers.

Within an hour that had all but threatened to fall apart as some men started coming in complaining, declaring their captain was drunk, or they would be damned if they would take orders from a dockyard roustabout while they had actually taught school or owned a barbershop.

At first he tried to reason with them, but within minutes was overwhelmed, until finally one of Winfield's staff officers settled the bombardment of complaints with a drawn pistol fired into the air. That had silenced the gathering crowd.

"Either take orders or get the hell out," the officer had said, pointing back to the towpath.

Several dozen, to Jim's shame, actually threw down their tools and walked off.

"Best to be rid of them anyhow," the officer had said. "Every unit has its whiners and malingerers."

Before leaving, the officer had hesitated, handed the revolver over to Jim, and told him to feel free to use it if need be, and no questions asked.

He actually had threatened to use it twice. Once on a "sergeant" who was dragged in after beating the hell out of his captain, the second time, on of all things, a white corporal, drunk, who came up and started taunting Jim and the men in the cookhouse, saying he'd be damned if he'd ever fight alongside of "goddamn niggers."

After so many years' experience in the White House, dealing with all kinds of guests, some of them downright hateful of the colored race, Jim at first tried to speak quietly and politely in reply, until the drunken corporal, with the foulest of oaths, raised a foot, slapped it into Jim's lap, and ordered him to polish his shoe.

The startled corporal was greeted with the revolver, cocked and aimed straight into his face.

"You son of a bitch," Jim snapped, amazed at the words coming out of him, but no longer caring. "Now kindly remove your foot from my lap. President Lincoln would never have done anything like this, and I sure as hell will not take it from trash like you."

Jim shouted for a white officer, and then started to shake, not sure of the reaction that was about to unfold over a black man waving a pistol at a white man, as the officer came running up.

When Jim told the officer what happened, there were a nervous few seconds, the corporal swearing that "no nigger is gonna talk to me like that," even though the cocked revolver was still aimed at his face.

The officer, grinning, then drew his own revolver and suggested that the corporal "comply with Mr. Bartlett's orders," placing an emphasis on the word "mister."

The world was indeed changing this day, Jim realized.

The corporal and the black "sergeant" were "bucked and gagged," the object of ridicule by all who passed. That support from the white officer seemed to have settled things down significantly, and there was little backtalk to Jim as he checked off work schedules, reassigned some men who obviously were not working out as leaders, and detailed off new crews to work as men continued to swarm in throughout the day.

So many were now at work that Jim had assigned his six assistants to be "colonels," each responsible for fifteen work crews, and yet still more were coming in.

Surprisingly, in the last several hours, the chaos had given way to a fair semblance of order. Crews worked four hours on, then were given an hour off to go down to the makeshift cookhouse, where salt pork, hardtack, and coffee were being served out. There were few plates or cups available, the men passing around a bucket with the hot coffee, taking the hot slabs of salt pork, slapping them onto pieces of hardtack, and wolfing them down, then lying down in the shade until called back to work.

At midafternoon he was offered a horse. A Yankee cavalry trooper came leading an old swaybacked nag.

"She ain't much, sir," the trooper said, "but me and the boys figure that with you in command it was only proper you should have a horse. We took her from a nearby farm."

Jim smiled with delight, especially over two facts. One that the young trooper had called him sir. The other was the fact that this was not some sad foolish prank to humiliate him; it was a dead-serious gesture of thanks and respect.

He gladly took the horse, though he would never admit it had been years since he had been astride one.

Now mounted, he rode along the line with his six colonels following along, several of them mounted now as well. It gave him the chance to see the progress, and with his makeshift staff he inspected the line. Major Siemens rode over to join him.

"Your men are a wonder, Mr. Barlett," Siemens said as they traveled the line. The preliminary trench had already been dug to shoulder depth and now the rectangular bastions, spaced at regular intervals so as to provide interlocking fields of fire, were going up, too. Men worked on the moats that would surround each, tossing up the dirt to form the fortress walls, which were reinforced with the woven baskets filled with dirt. Clear fields of fire were being opened up, entire woodlots disappearing to saws and axes, the lumber being dragged up to pile into the bastions. Smaller logs were being hammered into the ground at a forty-five-degree angle and then the exposed end sharpened. Brush was being stripped of leaves, tied into bundles, and then staked to the ground to provide barriers that would slow and even break up an advancing charge.

Other men were setting to work digging potholes, just eighteen inches deep and eighteen inches wide, a hundred yards or so out from the trench line. A few branches and then brush would be laid over each hole. A man stepping into one at the run, at best, would have a sprained ankle and perhaps even a broken leg. It only took fifteen minutes or so for a good man to dig one and then conceal it, but thousands of such holes could help to shatter a charge, and the men at such work chuckled about how many Johnny Rebs they were going to trip up. A few took the extra effort to drive a sharpened stake into the bottom of the hole, but others said that was unfair, a broken leg was injury enough.

The really hard labor was moving the giant hundred-pounder guns. Each tube weighed over twenty tons, the iron carriage another five tons. No wagons were capable of handling the weight, and the crews had resorted to something that looked like it was out of stories from the Bible. A hundred to two hundred men would be roped to each gun, a few mules added in, if available, greased logs were laid underneath the rough-cut lumber frame the gun rested on, the entire crew then straining to pull the dead weight up the slope and into the half-built bastions. Other crews labored at lugging up the heavy hundred-pound shells, one giant of a man making a display of his attempt to carry two at a time. At most places black laborers and white troops were mingled together, digging side by side.

That, too, thrilled Jim. There had been some hesitation at first by the soldiers to do menial labor next to black men, but Winfield had laid that to rest, hobbling up and down the line, shouting, "Boys, it's either dig or eat bullets, so I'm telling you, start digging! I tried eating one of those bullets, and by God they don't digest very well."

A day of labor, the way their black comrades worked on without complaint while many a white soldier was near to collapse, was making them one. Black laborers too tired to walk down to the kitchen areas suddenly found themselves handed a piece of hardtack and salt pork out of the haversack of a soldier who sat down beside him during a break and then offered a canteen to wash it down.

Jim had also organized watering crews, mostly young boys carrying a couple of buckets, moving up and down the line; when the buckets were empty, they'd run down to the river and refill them.

The dangerous job of moving up the bagged gunpowder Jim was more than happy to leave to the white gun crews. Too many of his men were fond of cigars and pipes.

The first of the thirty-pounder Parrotts had come up just after midday, but these arrived with full limbers and one horse-team for every three guns, so they could easily be moved into place.

They rode as far as Nolands Ferry, where the line finally curved back down to the river. A dozen barges were moving up the canal, heading toward the farthermost work site at the upper Point of Rocks.

"Once it gets dark," Siemens said, "have your men stand down, get some food and rest. They've put in one hell of a day."

"Thank you, sir."

"No, it is I thanking you," Jeremiah said with a smile, leaning over to offer his hand.

Headquarters, Army of Northern Virginia

7:00 P.M.

 Lee slowly walked under the awning and sat down, taking off his hat and wiping his brow.

Longstreet, Beauregard, Stuart, and Hood were all present, as were Jed Hotchkiss and Walter. Judah Benjamin, who had just arrived from Baltimore, sat slumped over in his chair, nursing a glass of wine.

"A hard day, gentlemen," Lee said, looking about at the gathering illuminated by the glow of coal oil lamps.

No one spoke for a moment.

He knew he had to brace them up. They had anticipated a full-out frontal assault, as at Fredericksburg, and instead there had only been the one limited, but very bloody, attack on the left, while all across the day the rest of the line had been engaged in a long-distance firefight of an intensity they had never seen before.

"If only they had come on," Beauregard said, "we would've mowed them down and be in Frederick tonight."

"But they didn't," Lee retorted. "Grant, it seems, is no Burnside."

"They most certainly did on my front," Hood replied sharply. "Jubal Early's Division is a wreck and out of this fight."

"We lost well over eight thousand today," Lee said, "six thousand with Jubal, two thousand at least from the firing along the line, and, frankly, I do not see any permanent results from that loss."

"We tore Ord apart," Beauregard interjected. "That's two of his four corps wrecked so far. Grant has most likely lost upward of eighteen, perhaps twenty thousand men since this started."

"Twelve thousand, though, of ours across three days," Longstreet said. "We can't afford that rate of exchange much longer."

"I concur," Lee announced. "The question before us now is our response."

He nodded toward Judah.

"You gentlemen all know we lost Baltimore this afternoon."

"Damn Pickett," Hood snapped. "If I was there, I'd have fought them street by street."

Lee looked over sharply at Hood and his breach of the rule against profanity at headquarters but said nothing.

Hood was right. Even though Pickett had only the equivalent of two brigades with him, surely he could have put up some kind of a fight, slowed them down for a day or two. His command, at last report, was at Relay Station, where George now claimed he'd put up a fight.

That was too little far too late. The precious reserve supplies, enough to have sustained him in a slugging match with Grant for weeks if need be, were now gone, sitting in Baltimore warehouses.

"Fire him," Longstreet said sadly, for he was speaking of an old friend.

"I already have," Lee replied. "I sent a telegram back informing General Pickett to report to me here, and for Lo Armistead to take command of the division."

He looked around at the gathering.

"And nothing more is to be said about him," he announced. "If Armistead can at least delay their advance, that should give us three days, perhaps as many as five before we face any real threat to our immediate rear."

He looked around at the gathering of commanders, who nodded in agreement.

"Then that means if Grant will not come to us, we must go to him," Lee replied.

No one spoke.

"Gentlemen, our situation is by no means lost. Do not give way to pessimism, for I most certainly have not. General Beauregard is right. We have bloodied him. Two of his four corps are fought out. Granted, though Early's Division is out, Scales's, though heavily fought, is still relatively intact, as are Robertson's men, who sat out the day's fight in reserve, as did two of Beauregard's divisions and McLaw's."

No one replied, waiting for what he would say next.

That gave Lee a reserve of four divisions, calculating in their losses across the last two weeks, about twenty-five thousand men, just about the same number Jackson had used at Chancellorsville.

"If we wait again tomorrow, gentlemen," Lee said, "I assume we shall see a repeat of today. A massive fusillade along the entire front, but one that will not decide anything. Perhaps he will send Banks on his north wing to try our right flank, but I doubt that. I think he proposes to wait, to hold us in position until this secondary force comes up from the rear to reinforce him."

There was no disagreement to what he had just said.

"Then we must attack before Grant can be reinforced."

"Where, sir?" Longstreet asked, shifting uncomfortably.

"General Stuart, I asked you to do some scouting. What can you report?"

Stuart stood up and leaned over Hotchkiss's maps spread out on the table.

"I still have Chambliss's Brigade to our north and west," Jeb said. The mere mention of that troubled Lee. It was the old brigade of his son, Rooney.

"They are reporting increasing pressure from Grierson. His men have pushed down across a line from the Catoctins eastward to fifteen miles below Westminster. Nothing very aggressive, other than George Custer's dash. A few raiding forces did reach the railroad tracks but quickly fell back. But by tomorrow they might be astride the Baltimore and Ohio line."

"That is no longer a concern," Lee said sharply.

"Yes, sir, but I thought you should know."

"I have Jenkins moving down now to develop out the situation at the fords on the Potomac," Stuart continued.

"Sir, that does trouble me," Pete said. "The report that came back this afternoon, about their digging in at four points along the river. If, and I must emphasize if, we need one of those crossings, it will be a tough fight now."

"We will not need them," Lee said sharply. "If anything, that move might be to our advantage. As I said last night, we defeat Grant here, then have Mosby cut several of the locks on the canal. That will strand the bulk of their Washington garrison far outside the city. I was thinking at first of turning on them and defeating each in detail, but that is senseless and an additional waste of our few remaining men."

"What then, sir?"

"We defeat Grant, then march straight at Washington."

No one spoke, though Hood and Stuart did nod and smile.

"If Lincoln has emptied out the garrison of Washington, that is the first time he has done so since this war started. He has gambled, but we shall pick up the cards. We take Washington, and regardless of the price here in destroying Grant, we will truly win this war, once and for all."

He looked over at Judah.

"Would you not agree, Mr. Secretary?"

Judah stirred from his exhaustion and looked at Lee.

"Yes, sir," he replied softly. "It would end the war."

Lee nodded his thanks. He realized that now, at this moment, he had to imbue his men with renewed hope. They were all exhausted; so was he. They had fought a pitched battle just a week and a half ago and were now in another, this one against what was proving to be a far more wily foe. Defeat Grant, though, and then within days deliver the double blow of taking Washington, even if he had but twenty thousand men left, the war would be finished, once and for all. It would be a blow Lincoln could never recover from.

"The lower ford I was asking about on the Monocacy," Lee said, looking back at Stuart.

Stuart leaned over the map and looked to where Lee was pointing.

"Yes, sir, Buckeystown. Yes, sir, we scouted it out, have pickets now on the other side."

"What's holding it?"

"Not much, sir. A light outpost, a company or two of infantry. Did not see any cavalry."

"And the road down to it?"

"Starts back behind our headquarters, sir. One road does skirt fairly close to where Ord pushed in today, but a second road farther back is far enough behind the lines. The hills to the south of here, sir, are a good shield. High. We have pickets all along the crest. The only problem, though, is that at several points the road rises up high enough that it can be seen from the Catoctin ridge."

Lee nodded, studying the map intently, Hotchkiss up by his side.

"I surveyed some of this last year," Hotchkiss said, "when we passed through here before Sharpsburg. I rode it again today with General Stuart. He's right. It might be a potential flanking route, but at several points the road crosses up over hills, the tops of which are not concealed by the ridge running along the river."

"Distance."

"Just under three miles, sir, from the rail tracks down to the Buckeystown ford. A tough climb then of about two miles, I'd estimate, up to the plateau on the other side. From there I'd calculate six miles into Frederick. We've all seen the ground on the other side. It's a flat, wide-open plain, no real defensive positions on it. Fight on that, and it will be who is quicker and has more courage that will decide it."

Lee took in what Hotchkiss was saying. And again that magical moment began to form, of lines of march, distances to be covered, who would move when, how they would deploy out, the same as he had felt after the first night at Gettysburg and again in laying the trap at Gunpowder River.

"That will be it, gentlemen," Lee announced quietly, standing back from the table.

He looked over at Beauregard.

"Do you wish the honor of leading this, General?"

Beauregard smiled and nodded his head.

"Two of your divisions, along with Robertson and McLaw. Generals Longstreet and Hood, I hope you have no objections to these detachments of your divisions."

"It means no reserves," Longstreet said quietly.

"We had none at Chancellorsville and, gentlemen, this is beginning to feel a bit like Chancellorsville, though, in fact, our odds are better. Their secondary force is not literally at our back as it was at Chancellorsville; it is over forty miles away in Baltimore."

"It's not Hooker this time," Longstreet said. "Remember this is Grant."

Lee looked over at Beauregard.

"He does have tenacity," Beauregard said. "Any other general would have caved in after what we did the first day at Shiloh."

"Then let him stand, and thus, unlike Shiloh, we will indeed finish him."

Beauregard's features shifted ever so subtly.

"I meant no disrespect, General," Lee said, bowing slightly to Beauregard.

"None taken, sir," he replied softly.

"What about their observing it from the Catoctin Heights?" Stuart asked.

"We do it now, tonight," Lee said.

"Sir, that's a tall order," Hood said. "My old division, though not in the fight, stood to arms all day. They fought a pitched battle the day before."

"It has to be tonight," Lee said. "I want the attack to start just before dawn. Jeb, you will lead with a brigade of cavalry and post guides at regular intervals along the road. Take the ford a few hours before dawn. General Beauregard, your two divisions to follow, and you must gain the plateau by first light, followed by McLaw, then Robertson.

"Artillery?" Beauregard asked.

"Whatever is left of our old experienced crews will be in this as well. I'll have Alexander detail off a battalion to each of your two divisions, General, two batteries to each of the other divisions."

He pointed at the crossing point and then up to the plateau on which Buckeystown sat.

"Deploy out, then start sweeping north. Nothing piecemeal. I want a solid two-division front, with McLaw and Robertson behind you in support. Do not stop until you have rolled up his line. As you advance across our front, Scales, Johnson, the brigades of Rhodes and Anderson's old commands will come in on your right. A grand assault across the river at a right angle to your attack. Your primary goal then will be for your left flank to capture the National Road, but not too quickly."

"Sir?"

"I want panic to set in. If we bolt the escape hole shut, Grant just might be able to rally in his desperation and turn on us. I want them in a panic, running for that road. The ones first on it will, as always, be the ones we don't care about, the teamsters, the staffers, supply wagons, those who have already run. Finally, bolt it shut when their main forces are on the road and partway up it."

Beauregard took the orders in, taking a sheet of paper from Walter and jotting down notes, sketching a copy of the map as well.

"General, you have a lot to do," Lee said. "I will come down to see you off. Can you be ready to move by midnight?"

"Sir?" he hesitated. "Yes, sir, I can."

"Fine then," Lee said with a smile.

"Jeb, get your lead brigade ready to move as well. Go with him on this and once across, provide cover to his left flank."

Jeb grinned, saluted, and left, Beauregard by his side.

"I better go see to my old command," Hood said. "Sir, if any boys will take down Grant, it will be my old Texans."

Walter left, calling for Jed Hotchkiss to follow and start working on additional maps for the various commands.

Longstreet, however, remained, Judah sitting by his side.

"Anything else, General?" Lee asked.

"No, sir, not really, but one suggestion."

"And that is?"

"Start moving the pontoon train south by road. You have a good screen with Jenkins. Moving those pontoons is a nightmare once off a main pike."

"Why the caution?" Lee asked.

"Why not, sir?"

Lee nodded and Longstreet stood up and left.

Lee finally sat back down and looked over at Judah, who was gazing down into his glass of wine.

"Hard day for you, sir?" Lee asked.

"Not as hard as yours," Judah said quietly.

"You look exhausted."

Judah smiled.

"Just sad, that's all."

"Why so?"

"Three days ago I was sitting in Baltimore, just waiting for that dispatch ship flying a French flag to come in with word that the emperor, that mad emperor, had thrown in with us. Baltimore would have, after the war, quickly rivaled New York as a place of industry and commerce, which we desperately need. Chances are Washington would have wound up as our new capital."

"It will still happen," Lee said with a smile. "As my boys say, 'We ain't licked yet, not by a long shot.'"

"I wish I carried your confidence," Judah replied.

"You have to think back on our history, sir. Perhaps because you were not born here, and no offense intended, you don't fully sense that."

"How so?"

"My father fought with Washington. Many in our ranks had sat at the knee of a grandfather and heard tales of Valley Forge, that terrible retreat across New Jersey the year before, the bitter fighting in the Carolinas. Half a dozen times our cause seemed all but lost, and yet each time a kindly Providence saw fit to save us. Our situation at this moment is no different. We endured then, we shall endure now. Of that I am still confident."

Judah held up his hand.

"I'm sorry to have disturbed you."

Lee sighed and nodded.

"Not your fault. I am tired, just so very tired as well."

"General, I think you need to get some rest."

"Yes, sir, I do," Lee replied. "Again, no offense taken by your comments."

Judah stood up, bowed slightly, and left.

Lee looked over to his tent, the flap open. He went in, his servant having set a candle and his Bible on a table by the cot. Lee sat down, struggled to take his boots off, and then picked up his Bible and thumbed through it, turning to the One Hundred Forty-fourth Psalm.

"Blessed be the Lord, my strength, which teacheth my hands to war. . . ."

Headquarters, Army of the Susquehanna

9:00 P.M.

A hard day for Edward," Phil Sheridan said, pouring another cup of coffee and offering it to Grant.

Grant watched Ord walk over to his horse, mount, and ride off.

"Yes, a hard day," Grant replied, sipping at the coffee, then setting it down to pick up a stick and resume the whittling that had taken it from a couple of feet in length to a last few inches. Shavings piled up around his feet.

"How's the headache, sir?"

Grant raised his gaze and stared at Phil without responding, at that moment teaching Sheridan one of the taboos of this headquarters: when the general had a migraine, no one, except for Ely, should ever dare ask about it.

Grant resumed whittling and Phil was silent, staring into the campfire. A mild breeze stirred. To the south, there were lightning flashes but it looked as if the storm would skirt by them, perhaps soaking the boys down along the Potomac.

"Tomorrow, I want you to shift one of your divisions down in support of Ord. He has no reserve left."

"Which one."

"The colored one. That's your reserve, isn't it?"

"Yes, sir."

"And they sat the day out, so they're fresh."

"Yes, sir, but they've never seen battle."

"Time they did."

He finished whittling, tossing the fragment of stick into the fire, hesitated, then drew out another cigar and lit it, offering the case over to Phil, who gladly took one of the fine Havanas.

Grant offered him his half-burned match, and Phil leaned over, puffing his cigar to life.

Grant studied him intently as Phil lit his cigar, sat back, and exhaled.

He missed Sherman. There was a man he did indeed confide in. Many was the night the two sat up and talked. Talk of plans, talk of what had been and what they still intended to do.

McPherson had filled a bit of that role since coming east, but poor James was dead. An hour ago, under flag of truce so that wounded from both sides could be pulled back from the riverbank, a message had come through the lines informing him of that fate, and also that before he died James had married his beloved Emily.

"Wish I'd given him that furlough back in the spring," Grant sighed. "Perhaps now there might at least be a child on the way."

"What, sir?"

"Nothing. Nothing, Phil."

He was silent again and grateful that Phil understood the need. When he was silent, he was in no mood to talk, and idle chatter to fill the dead air was an annoyance.

The stars were not out as brightly tonight, a thin high haze moving in. Rain in a day or so, he sensed, perhaps a lot. *Can't change that, though, so don't worry about it.*

The day had been a hard one. Phil was right, especially for Ord.

His entire corps was a hollowed-out wreck. He had lost more men in this one assault than during the entire siege of Vicksburg. Where an entire corps had been this morning, barely a division could be mustered now, and those men were beat to hell, disorganized, brigades down to regiments, and regiments to companies. It had been the bloodiest assault he had ever launched.

And he did not regret it, though Ord was all but shattered by the experience.

He had seen it himself when he rode across the river late in the afternoon to watch the fight up close. Yes, he had lost ten thousand or more, but Lee had been forced to match him, and from all accounts the dreaded Jubal Early Division was smashed beyond any hope of repair, along with a couple of brigades from one of one of Beauregard's divisions.

He had presented to Lee a different kind of fight today, one of sustained firepower on the rest of the front. No mad charges, no standing out in the open in volley lines while Lee's own men were dug in, as at Fredericksburg. Instead, just a continual grinding down of fire.

Lee's men had most likely fired off nearly as much ammunition as they had at Union Mills, but with only one-tenth the impact along the rest of the line. His own supply officers were already sending in reports that two million more rounds of small-arms ammunition would have to be sent up during the night, and the wagons crossing over the pass were indeed hauling that and more.

How many millions did Lee have?

Hunt reported firing nearly eleven thousand rounds of bolt and case shot. One of his staff, earlier in the day, had laughed while reporting to Grant that he had overheard Hunt shouting, "Make every shot count, boys; it's costing the taxpayers two dollars and sixty-seven cents a round."

He stirred, looking back at the fire.

"Yes, the colored division," Grant said, and Phil did not respond, still puffing on his cigar.

"Move them down to support on this side of the Monocacy before dawn. I think our General Lee over there will counterstrike us, and it will come straight in at Ord, to try and push him back across the river and then break our right flank."

"Yes, sir."

"I want your blackbirds to be ready to go in. They claim they have something to prove. Now's their chance."

"I'll see to it personally."

"Phil."

"Yes, sir?"

"I spotted you today down in the railroad cut, right in the middle of it. I thought I told you to avoid recklessly exposing yourself."

Phil smiled, but then shook his head.

"Sir, I'm sorry. Three days ago those boys were under Burnside, and' they still are fiercely loyal to him. I needed them to see I was different somehow, and that meant getting up into the thick of it. I figured the risk was worth it."

"I know, we all do it at times. But I lost James. Ord, well, I think poor Edward is a bit shattered at the moment. Banks, he's an amateur, the same as Sickles, a political appointee I find myself saddled with, and come a crisis I'll personally see to the running of his corps. So I need to count on one of my corps commanders, and it seems that's falling on your shoulders. Don't do the same tomorrow. Keep back a bit."

Phil smiled.

"Of course not, sir."

Three Miles East of Monocacy Junction

11:45 P.M.

 God damn it, I can't believe these damn things are still here," Cruickshank groaned.

He walked the length of three trains still loaded with the pontoon bridges, cursing and swearing every inch of the way, his staff and old teamster crews following behind.

Their train from Baltimore had indeed made good time, as McDougal had promised, until it stalled ten miles from the front line. A locomotive had run out of fuel on the single-track line and ground to a halt ahead of them, and then three more had stalled. Judah Benjamin had left him there, finding a horse to go forward to report to Lee.

A scattering of men, most of them skulkers from the rear, plus a few squadrons of cavalry troopers who had rounded the skulkers up, were busy scavenging the countryside for enough wood to get the boilers going again, the troopers driven to distraction because every time they turned their backs the skulkers dropped their loads and attempted to disappear into the surrounding woods.

"Find some teams. God damn it, where are the teams of mules we sent up with these trains?"

The men stood around silent. The boxcars which had been carrying the mules were open, all the mules gone, most likely commandeered by some other unit.

"Find some damn teams!" Cruickshank roared.

"Major Cruickshank?"

A courier approached out of the dark, riding, of all things, a mule.

Cruickshank glared up at him, the courier lit up by a railroad lantern he was carrying.

"It's General Cruickshank now!" he roared.

The courier stood his ground.

"General Longstreet sent me out here hours ago to look for you." He paused. "Sir. May I inquire where you have been? I was told you would be with these pontoon bridges."

"No, damn you, you may not inquire. Now what the hell do you want?"

"Sir, I carry orders from General Longstreet to you, informing you of his wish that you begin to move these bridges south toward either Nolands or Hauling Ferry."

"Where the hell is that?"

"Sir, I don't know. I assume, sir, you being a general, you would know."

That was too much. Cruickshank walked up to the man, grabbed him by the leg, and lifting, tipped him right off his mount.

The lantern went flying, shattering on the adjoining track, spreading flame, which gradually winked out.

"Damn you, sir. I demand satisfaction," the courier cried.

"Look me up after the war is over," Cruickshank snapped.

"I shall inform General Longstreet of this affront."

"And he'll laugh in your face, sonny. Now go tell good old Pete that when he can find me two hundred and fifty mules, I'll start moving these bridges."

"I'll tell him that and more."

"You do that."

The humiliated officer went to grab the reins of his mule.

"Don't touch him! That mule belongs to me now."

"The hell you say."

Cruickshank reached for his revolver, half drawing it.

"He's mine, so start walking."

The officer glared at him angrily, the men around Cruickshank laughing. He turned on his heels and strode off.

Cruickshank handed the mule off to one of his men.

"Now go find two hundred and forty-nine more," he said.

He leaned back against one of the flatcars bearing a pontoon bridge, reached into his pocket, and pulled out the bottle given to him by McDougal. He had not dared to drink it in front of a secretary of state, and, for that matter, he was in no mood to share it with any of his men, so he waited till they wandered off, most of them chuckling about the fight.

Once alone, he uncorked it and drained it down neat, crawled up under a pontoon, and was soon asleep, oblivious to the column of troops that began to pass by, swarming over the railroad tracks, falling in along a road on the opposite side, and heading south.

Chapter Sixteen

That's it, sir."

Jeb Stuart reined in, the forward scout by his side gesturing straight ahead. He dismounted, and followed the scout. The two of them walked slowly, almost as if they were actors tiptoeing across the stage.

The gesture struck Jeb as a bit absurd, but he followed the scout's lead, not sure how far off they were from the river. Sound was drowned out by cascading water. An overcast was beginning to set in, stars dimming, and it was hard to see much, but he could see glimpses of what he assumed was a dam, the white sparkle of water flowing over it.

"Mill on the other side," the scout whispered.

They walked thus for another hundred yards, and then Jeb saw some of his men, lying to either side of the road, as if resting, but they were spread out into a skirmish line.

The scout crouched down, Jeb joining him.

"Can you make out the ford?"

Yes, he could, low flowing water, again sparkles of white, they were almost at the edge of the creek. Enough starlight still shone through, and he thought he caught a glimpse of someone on the other side.

"Hey, who's over there?"

It was a Yank on the other side, and Jeb froze.

"I'll shoot. Now who is over there?"

The scout stood up.

"Don't get riled up, Yank, we're just sitting over here, same as you on your side."

There was a pause.

"What you doing, reb?"

"Sent down to picket this place, make sure you don't try and sneak across here. And you?"

"The same."

"Got any coffee, Yank?"

Again a pause.

"Yup. Trade you a pound of coffee mixed with real sugar for a pound of tobacco."

"Sounds good to me, Yank. Let me ask my boys for their tobacco. I'll be right over."

Jeb grinned. This scout knew his business. Now standing in the open he walked down the skirmish line.

"Come on, boys, give it up," the scout whispered.

Some of the men cursed softly, one of them complaining they already had plenty of coffee, but the scout took their pouches.

"Take that hat off, sir," the scout whispered as he strolled past Jeb. "You stick out like a sore thumb with it on. And crawl down a bit closer so you can listen."

The scout went down to the water's edge and held his hands up.

"Meet you halfway, Yank, and no foolery now."

"Promise, reb."

The scout splashed into the creek and Jeb watched him carefully. It wasn't more than knee-deep. The scout slowed, luring the Yank closer to their side.

"How are you, Yank?" the scout asked.

"Fine, and you?"

"Damn glad to be down here rather than up in the thick of all that fightin' today."

"Damn right," the Yank said.

"Where you from, Yank?"

"Name's Michael Greene. I'm from Illinois. And you?"

"Luke Snyder. I'm from Virginia."

The two shook hands.

"Got that tobacco? Ain't had a smoke in days."

"Sure enough. Same for me with coffee. Would you boys mind if we lit a little fire to boil some up?"

"Naw, we won't shoot, but keep it back a ways from the creek."

There was an exchange of packages, and then the flare of a match, which startled Jeb, causing him to crouch down lower. The two were lighting their pipes while standing right in the middle of the creek.

"Glad when this is over," Snyder said. "Just want to go home. My wife just had another baby."

"How's that?" the Yank chuckled.

"Oh, a furlough about nine months ago, right after we whipped you at Fredericksburg."

The two laughed softly.

"We weren't at Fredericksburg. You sure wouldn't have whipped us. We was busy taking Vicksburg. I'm with Ord."

Jeb smiled. This scout was damn good.

"I heard you boys are tough."

"Damn right we are. Sorry to tell you this, reb, but we're gonna whip you for sure this time, and then we can go home. Our boys ain't never lost a battle."

"We'll see about that, Yank."

"Grant is gonna just grab your Bobbie Lee by the nose. You'll see."

"Again, we'll see. Don't count your chickens before they hatch, Yank."

"Seemed like a hell of a lot of fightin' further up the creek today," Greene said. "Bunch of bodies came floating down right around dark."

"Yeah, there was."

"You in it?"

"A bit," Snyder replied.

"We win?"

"You got across the creek. Kind of figure that's where the fighting will be again, come morning."

"I sure as hell hope so. And I'll just sit tight right here. Been in five battles, reb, wounded once. I've seen the elephant enough."

"Same here," Snyder said. "You sit on one side, and I'll sit on the other. I got about fifty men with me, and we were told just to sit tight but spread the word if something was up."

"About the same for us here. Reb, tell your boys we won't shoot if they won't, and let's outlive this one."

"Agreed. Come dawn we'll do some more tradin'."

Again there was the shaking of hands.

"Yeah, guess you're right, reb. Just wish the hell it was over with. Not married yet. My girl Lucy said she'd wait. Sure would love to have a baby with her the way you did with yours."

"Better yet helping her to make one," Snyder said, and they both chuckled.

"Well, I better get back," the Yank said. "My captain can be a stickler. Take care, reb."

"You, too, Yank."

"Go ahead and make your fire now, but keep it back a couple of hundred yards. Like I said, the captain is a stickler, he'd tell us to shoot at you, and frankly, that's murder to me, especially when I know a fella's name."

They shook hands, parted, and the scout waded back to shore and walked past Jeb as if he didn't exist. Jeb waited a few minutes, crawled back, and then joined Snyder.

Snyder was silent, looking over at him.

"You hear it?" Snyder asked.

"Every word. Good work."

"Damn, sir, I hated it."

"Why?"

"Lying to him like that. He was for fair play, same as me. I hated to do it."

"Duty, son," Jeb said softly, patting him on the shoulder. "We pull this day off and you can say you led the patrol that led to the march that won the war."

Jeb walked back to his horse, mounted up, and started back up the road. Just around the bend and out of sight of the creek lanterns were set every couple of hundred feet by the side of the road. The head of Beauregard's column was coming down.

Beauregard was at the fore.

Jeb rode up, and the two saluted each other.

"The way ahead is clear, General. Not more than a company garrisoning the ford. You have clear ground just around this bend, then two hundred yards to the ford. I would not suggest forming a battle line. When ready, just have your men come on at the double, hit the water, and get across. I really couldn't see the road on the far side, but am assured it leads straight up to Buckeystown and the plateau."

"Thank you, General Stuart."

Beauregard took out his pocket watch and Jeb struck a match. It was three in the morning.

"An hour and fifteen minutes to first twilight," Beauregard said. "My Second Division is two miles behind this one. That should give them time to come up. We'll start the assault at four."

"I'll take the lead if you don't mind," Jeb said. "My boys can be up to Buckeystown in fifteen minutes and then hold it if there's any additional Yankees up there."

"Sounds fine with me, General."

The two shook hands.

Beauregard passed the word back for his column to halt marching, the men to ground arms and sit down in place. No fires, no talking. The men were more than happy to comply, most, at least those with strong nerves, asleep in minutes.

Near McCausland's Ford

3:45 A.M.

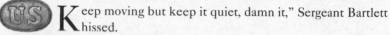 "Keep moving but keep it quiet, damn it," Sergeant Bartlett hissed.

The column of his regiment moved silently across the open fields, the lead in a formation that stretched back nearly a mile. Shortly after midnight Phil Sheridan himself had come into their camp. There was a hurried officers' meeting and minutes later word was passed, without drumrolls or bugles, for the men to fall in, leaving packs behind. As each regiment formed, men were handed an additional forty rounds of ammunition and then told to form in column by company front.

Company A was in the lead, in fact, in the lead of the entire division as they set off across the fields.

Bartlett, moving at the side of the column, looked back and thrilled at the sight, limited as it was by the darkness. An endless column, moving across fields, through torn-down fencerows, skirting the edge of the artillery batteries whose crews were awake, silently watching them pass. For a half mile or so they tramped along a road, then turned off, heading downslope, and as soon as they were off the road, the going became difficult.

The ground ahead was strewn with dark forms. At first just one or two bodies here or there, and then dozens, and, finally, in one horrid place, scores of corpses in a line. The men started to whisper, some recoiling as their booted foot stepped on the back or the severed limb of a man, and the white officers repeatedly hissed to the men, "Keep quiet, damn you!"

They reached the stream and it was a nightmare. Wounded by the hundreds were still on the ground. Sheridan had ordered the ambulance crews to douse their lights while the division passed, but even in the darkness Sergeant Bartlett could see the work, men being loaded up, crying softly, some screaming.

He braced himself and kept going forward, beginning to chant soothing words to his men. "It's alright, boys, it's alright. Keep your courage boys, keep your courage."

They hit the creek and began to wade across. On the opposite bank there were a few lanterns lit, and by their light he could see dozens of men staggering back, or just collapse along the riverbank.

An officer raced ahead, splashing through the water, and kicked over the lanterns.

"Come on lads, almost there. Come on," the officer hissed.

The column of Third Division, Ninth Corps, crossed over the Monocacy, heading east into the salient, even while, but four miles to the south, four divisions of Confederate troops prepared to strike in the other direction.

Buckeystown Ford

4:50 A.M.

Stuart looked around. Minutes ago he could barely discern the clump of trees behind which many of his men waited. Now it was barely beginning to stand out. He remembered at the Point how one of the professors had talked about the old Mohammedan tradition that first light was the moment when one could distinguish a black thread from a white one. That always struck him as foolish. Many a night, if the stars were out, he could tell the difference.

But here, now, at this moment, he knew first light was breaking, in spite of the increasing overcast.

"Let's go," Stuart said, drawing out his heavy LaMat revolver.

Men came out from the trees behind him, already mounted, forming up on the road, most with pistols drawn, a few with sabers. They started to walk down to the Monocacy.

"General, sir?"

It was his scout, Snyder.

"Yes?"

"A favor, sir?"

"Be quick about it," Stuart said as he continued to ride forward.

"Sir, that Yank was a fair fellow, and it's stuck in my craw that I lied to him. Please let me give him a warning. Just one minute to get the hell out of the way."

Jeb hesitated but his old sense of chivalry took hold.

"You got a minute."

The scout, still on foot, ran ahead, straight down the road to the creek.

"Hey, Greene. Private Greene!" he shouted.

"Snyder, that you? What are you yelling for? My captain will be god-awful mad!"

"Get out now! We're coming across, a whole bunch of us. Skedaddle! Greene, listen here, get home, marry that girl, and have a dozen babies! Name one after me!"

A pause.

"Thanks, Snyder!"

There was shouting now on the other side, Private Greene running off, and unfortunately spreading the alarm.

"Let's go, boys!" Jeb shouted.

He spurred up to a near gallop, pistol raised. Just before hitting the edge of the creek he saw Snyder, who was preparing to mount, the scout offering a salute.

His mount jumped into the creek, spray of water going up, and in seconds he was across.

A few shots whizzed by. No one was hit. Up out of the creek he turned to the right, following the road. It rose up a steep slope and he took it at the gallop. At the mill some men were tumbling out, most half-naked, and as he galloped past he fired a few shots in their direction, the startled Yanks ducking back inside.

Laughing, he rode on. In the early light the road ahead was barely visible. To his right he could see the mill dam, some shadowy figures down by it running about. And then just a climbing road, no one on it, him in the lead.

He burst out laughing, filled with joy. Riding at a full gallop, he pressed on, the road twisting and weaving, his staff and the mounted first regiment of Virginia boys behind him, struggling to keep up, all the boys hooting and hollering.

After a mile his mount began to slow and he eased back slightly, staff catching up.

"Damn it all, sir. You're gonna get killed someday doing that," one of them shouted as he pushed past Jeb to lead the charge.

"Damned if you'll lead it, Captain!" Jeb shouted, and now it was a race between the two.

They pressed up the road, neck to neck, both horses stretched out, pounding hard. The exuberance of the moment was overwhelming. Behind him were four divisions of infantry, two full battalions of guns, and his own brigade. Near on to thirty thousand men. They had the Yankee flank wide open; it was going to be one hell of a day.

Headquarters, Army of the Susquehanna

5:30 A.M.

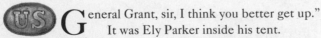 G eneral Grant, sir, I think you better get up."
        It was Ely Parker inside his tent.

"What is it?" Grant asked, opening his eyes.

"Sir, it looks like Lee is flanking us."

Grant sat up with a start while Ely adjusted the mantle on the coal oil lamp on the desk, the inside of the tent brightening, Grant squinting for a moment, inwardly groaning, for the light was like a bolt shot into his brain. The damn headache was still with him.

"Sir, a rather frightened lieutenant is outside. He's part of an Illinois regiment, Ord's Corps. They were assigned to picket our right flank."

"Coffee," Grant whispered.

Ely already had a cup, not too hot, so he was able to gulp it down. He stood up, still in his stocking feet, pulling up his suspenders over his shoulders, not bothering to put on his jacket, and stepped out.

His staff was up, milling about, some gathered round the lieutenant who was on a lathered horse. Several of the enlisted men, old vets, were simply sitting by a campfire, frying up salt pork as if this were just the start of another day. One of them tried to catch Grant's eyes, as if to inquire whether he would care for some.

Dawn was approaching. The sky overhead was gray, the east glowing brighter, but the approaching sun would be concealed. The air was still, but smoke from fires rose up a couple of hundred feet then flattened out to form a haze over the entire area. On the opposite bank, nothing stirred, the smoke of campfires concealing the hills.

Grant walked up to the lieutenant, who was breathing hard.

"What's your report?" Grant asked sharply.

"Sir. My company was detailed down south, to Buckeystown ford to guard it. About an hour ago, reb cavalry stormed it."

"Did you see anything else? Infantry, artillery? What was their strength?"

"No, sir. Figured I should report in."

"Who's in command down there?"

"Sir, we were just a company, a few more companies stationed back at

Buckeystown above the ford. The rebs, they just came out of nowhere, shooting, hollering, killing everyone. I thought I should get back here to report. I seen Jeb Stuart myself leading the charge."

"How did you know it was him? An hour ago it was near total darkness."

"I knew it was him. He had on that funny hat and was out front, sir. I know it was him."

"Did anyone send you?"

"No, sir, came on my own."

Grant looked at him. The boy was obviously frightened and had experienced a hard ride, his mount blown.

Grant said nothing and turned away, Ely following him.

"Boy's in a panic," Grant said.

"Could just be a raid?" Ely offered.

"Or more," Grant replied.

He had long ago memorized the maps and knew every detail.

"About six miles down to there. One of several things. It just might be a raid, perhaps to secure the road south, make us nervous. Second, it might really be Jeb, though I won't take that boy's word for it. Third . . ."

He paused and looked back to the east, where all was still.

"Lee is flanking us."

He whispered the last words, but with so many at headquarters, several overheard, and within seconds the entire headquarters area was buzzing.

Angrily, Grant turned.

"Silence!"

All the men turned toward him, some coming to rigid attention.

He gazed at his staff, ice glittering from his eyes.

"No panic, no running about like chickens with your heads cut off. We know Lee is a good foe, better than Pemberton or old Joe Johnston. If he's flanked us, he's flanked us. But that also means he is where I want him, out in the open. Now go about your business. And not a word to anyone outside of this headquarters. If but one of you starts spreading a panic, by heavens I'll have you court-martialed."

He was a bit embarrassed by the outburst but knew it had to be done. In spite of their confidence, the boasting of so many of his men about what would happen, how they would show Easterners how men from the West could tame Lee, he knew that down deep for many that was a lot of bluster. Lee was indeed a legend. Lee was famous for the surprise flank march, and now he was testing Grant with one.

Inwardly, he cursed himself for a moment. He should have detached a brigade to the ford, but he wanted every man available into this fight.

Too late now to change that. I have to find out more.

Directly to his front a scattering of distant rifle fire began to open up and within minutes started to build. This time it was Lee who had opened the day's match. Up and down the length of the creek his men began to blaze away. His own boys, many of whom but minutes before were out behind their trenches, cooking breakfast or relieving themselves, dashed back into the trenches and began to return fire, the volume building.

Henry Hunt began to open up, this time engaging in a measured and very long distance duel with Confederate guns in the center of their position.

Was this a mask in itself? Grant wondered. *Of course Lee would open up, threaten perhaps a local attack to keep me focused as long as possible on this place.*

"Ely, get a couple of men, our best mounts. Men with good eyes and brains who won't get carried away or exaggerate. Send them down toward Buckeystown to scout things out, then have them report back here."

Ely nodded.

"Sir, any other orders."

Grant looked back to the east.

I will not dance to his tune, he thought. *Not based on the report of one frightened lieutenant. Besides, if he is flanking me, it'll be several hours before he really hits.*

"No," Grant said. "Everyone is to stay in place until I say different."

He turned and walked over to the fire where the enlisted cook looked up and grinned, offering up a plate of fried salt pork, mixed in with crumbs of smashed-up hardtack.

Stoically, Grant tried to eat the meal, if only to set an example, but knew that within minutes he would be down by the latrine, bringing it up again, his head still throbbing.

Buckeystown

6:00 A.M.

Come on boys, move it, keep it moving!"

General Beauregard was at the crossroads leading up from the ford that intersected the road that headed up to Frederick.

Regiment after regiment marched by at the quick step. Some were beginning to flag after the sharp two-mile climb up from the river bottom. They'd been up all night but there was definitely a fire in their eyes, more than one shouting good-natured gibes to their general as they flowed past.

These were tough men and he was proud of them. Men who had defended Charleston for over a year in boiling heat, clouds of mosquitoes day and night, many ridden with ague and living on bad rations.

Up here in the North they had lived off the fat of a rich land, had seen victory against the vaunted Army of the Potomac at Union Mills, having delivered the crucial flanking blow, and it looked like they were about to do it again.

Staff officers at the intersection were directing each regiment as it approached. First Division was to file off to the left of the road and form line of battle. Second Division, which was a half mile down the ford road but coming on fast, would break out and form to the right. Behind them was the battalion of artillery, twenty-two guns, and they would form up in the center, still mounted and ready to move forward.

Beauregard pulled out his watch. Six in the morning. At this rate, on this road, it'd be at least three more hours before every last man was up. Too long.

Anxiously, he looked to the north. Jeb's mounted skirmishers were already forward by a half mile, occasional pops indicating that the Yankees were out there and by now had to know what was up.

"Keep moving, boys! Keep moving! In one hour we go in!"

Buckeystown Ford

6:20 A.M.

Sgt. Lee Robinson waded across the stream, marching with his Texans at the head of Robertson's Division, the general just ahead of him on horseback.

The going had been frustratingly slow throughout the night. Move a few hundred yards, halt for ten minutes, double-time for a minute, back to marching pace, then halt again.

It was typical of a night march and had left him and his men exhausted. The road they had been on was open, and some of the regiments had actually departed the road and simply moved across the fields, paralleling it until stopped to wait until first light.

First, though, Beauregard's two divisions had to cross, followed by the battalion of artillery, which clogged the road ahead.

On the far side of the creek he could see the narrow lane that all of them were trying to funnel into. Artillery clogging the road.

Robertson looked at them in frustration.

"It'll take hours," he hissed.

He turned to his staff.

"Go straight up this slope. To hell with the road," Robertson exclaimed. "Find farm lanes, anything. If need be, just cut across open fields. I want my boys into this fight!"

Minutes later Lee Robinson was given the word.

"First Texans! Right up the hill, now move it!"

They'd done this before. It meant hard marching and climbing, but if it got them in quicker, then that was part of war.

Without complaint, he led his men forward, through the yard of the mill, and then straight up a narrow farm lane and into the woods above.

Headquarters, Army of Northern Virginia

6:50 A.M.

Lee paced back and forth, unable to contain his nervousness. Pete sat silent by the morning campfire, sipping a cup of coffee. Down below the entire valley was again cloaked in the fog of battle. The day was very still, the air heavy, damp, which held the smoke in place, so that it was impossible to see more than three or four hundred yards.

Lee went over to the campfire and sat down.

"It should be starting by now," Longstreet offered, breaking the silence.

"Yes, it should be," Lee replied, trying not to sound cross.

If Jackson was in charge, as he was at Chancellorsville, he would not be worried, as he was not worried then.

He knew the crossing had started before dawn. A courier had come in an hour and a half ago confirming that.

It was now just a matter of waiting, and waiting was hard this morning.

Grant had outfoxed him on several points. Baltimore was gone, the river was blocked, but in doing these things Grant had left Washington open.

Beat him now, today. Beat him fully, and send him and his men running, and then the promise of that first night at Gettysburg will be fulfilled. All things will still be possible . . . and the war won.

One Half Mile North of Buckeystown

7:00 A.M.

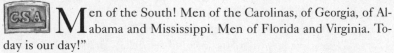 en of the South! Men of the Carolinas, of Georgia, of Alabama and Mississippi. Men of Florida and Virginia. Today is our day!"

Beauregard, standing in his stirrups, trotted down the long double-ranked battle line, sword held high. The moment was transcendent, his eyes clouding with tears. Never had he seen such as this, an open field, two divisions deployed across a front nearly a mile long, battle flags held high.

"Let history one day record that it was we, we here, who on this day won our independence!"

A wild cheer went up, the rebel yell. Though only those within a few hundred yards could hear his words, that did not matter. All could see him, the cheer racing up and down the battle line, resounding, swelling, deafening!

"Forward to victory!"

Drummers massed behind the center of the line started the beat, a steady roll. Buglers picked up the call, echoing the advance. Beauregard turned to face forward, sword resting on his right shoulder, horse rearing up, and then stepping forward with a noble prance.

Behind the line were arrayed twenty-two field pieces, elevated to maximum. As soon as he turned and started off, they fired in unison, the signal to the assaulting force, and to Lee, that the attack had begun.

The mile-wide battle line began to sweep forward.

Behind them, the exhausted troops of Robertson were just beginning to emerge on the main road, McLaw's men not yet up in place. But he could wait no longer. They had to go in now while surprise was still on their side . . . and victory was ahead.

Headquarters, Army of the Susquehanna

7:10 A.M.

All were turned, facing south.

They had heard the distant report of the massed volley of artillery in the south. Distant, but distinct above the general fusillade roaring along the river bottom.

One of the scouts Ely had sent out was coming up the hill to headquarters, urging his mount on. He reined in before Grant and saluted.

"At least two divisions, sir," he announced. "Sorry I took so long, but I wanted a good look at them, try to count their flags and such."

"Where's Lieutenant Moore?" Ely asked.

"He got hit. Killed, sir, some of them reb skirmishers are damn good shots."

His horse was bleeding from two wounds, testament to the accuracy of fire he had faced while scouting.

"Continue with your report," Grant said quietly.

"Sir. I counted enough flags for at least two divisions. It's Beauregard. I remember seeing him at Shiloh, sir. It's definitely him."

"Just two divisions?"

"No, sir. They were deployed out into a front of two divisions, behind them about twenty, maybe twenty-five guns. But I could see more men coming up from the road, also moving through fields. I'd reckon at least one more division, maybe two. I caught sight of a Texas flag with those men."

"Robertson perhaps," Grant said softly.

"Could not say, sir. Did you hear those guns fire off?"

"Yes, we did," Ely interjected.

"That was a signal. They're advancing. Like I said, two divisions wide, right flank on the river, coming straight up the road from Buckeystown."

The man fell silent and Ely offered him a canteen, which he gladly took and drained half.

"Good report, soldier," Grant said. "Take care of your horse and get something to eat."

Grant walked away from the scout, Ely following.

"Ely," he said quietly, "send for Ord and Sheridan *now*. No hurrying about, no panic, but I want them up here quickly."

Grant turned about and walked to the campfire, knowing all eyes were upon him. Everyone at headquarters had heard the report.

He sat down by the cookfire. He was hungry again, and after losing his first attempt at breakfast he was tempted to try again. This time he'd have to keep it down. Everyone was watching, and if he threw up, all would think it was nervousness and not just the headache. Besides, he'd need food; it was going to be a long day. He sat down, took a piece of hardtack offered by the cook, and chewed on it in silence.

Chapter Seventeen

McCausland's Ford

8:15 A.M.

U p, men, up!"
Sgt. Maj. Washington Bartlett knew something was happening long before the order was given. The division had deployed just behind the crest of a ridge, a ruined brick farmhouse above, obviously the site of yesterday's terrible battle. Just beyond the ridge a steady fusillade was resounding, the men of Ord's surviving troops engaged just on the other side of the rise. Since deploying, the men had been busy scratching at the ground with bayonets, tin cups, anything to dig out a little protection from the long-distance artillery bombardment coming down out of the hill to the left.

A few dozen had been hit, the first blooding of the division, but the men had held steady.

Minutes earlier he had seen Sheridan galloping up from the ford, and the way he rode, flat out, told Bartlett that something big was about to take place.

He quietly worked up his nerve, at one point looking over at John Miller, who returned his gaze, tight-lipped.

"Think we're going in?" Miller asked.

"Well, that general didn't ride over just to ask us how we were doing." And now the command. "Up, men, up!"

Within seconds, like a giant dark wave, the ten regiments of the United States Colored Troops were up, preparing to dress into line of battle.

"By column of regiments, starting from the left!"

"That's us," Bartlett shouted, and he started to move to the left of the line, the position the colonel said he should assume when they went into a fight.

"By column of companies, to the left wheel, march!"

Surprised, the men looked at each other, not responding at first. They were being ordered to turn about and head back to the ford, away from the fight.

B artlett looked back. The other regiments were repeating their maneuver, stepping away from what they thought would be their assault position, shifting from battlefront into columns by company front.

Sheridan came back from the front line, still riding hard, one of the white officers of Bartlett's regiment trotting over to meet him.

"Sir, I thought we were going to fight?" the officer cried. "My boys are ready."

"You will fight, damn it!" Sheridan cried. "We're being flanked to the right and rear on the other side of the creek. You are going to have to meet Lee's flank attack head-on. Now get your boys moving!"

Sheridan galloped off toward the ford several hundred yards away.

That stopped the grumbling and a few even offered a cheer as Sheridan rode off.

The officer turned, grim-faced.

"Move it! Back to the ford! Move it!"

From the lip of the crest Bartlett could see small formations of white troops coming as well, running fast.

8:30 A.M.

B eauregard was still out front, now riding with Jeb's troopers, who were deployed in a forward battle line, a quarter mile ahead of the infantry. He turned to look back, the divisions moving steadily, but slowly. It was the old problem of any advance in line versus column. Units were weaving their way through farmyards, woodlots, fields high with corn, open pastures, knocking down fencerows before pressing into the next field.

He regretted now not keeping them in column formation, to shake out into line when the Yankees were in sight, but that could be a problem as well. It could take up to a half hour to shift a divisional column into line of battle, and if they were caught by surprise, especially while trying to change formations, a debacle could ensue.

Also, he did want impact. The sight of a mile-wide battlefront advancing could be overwhelming to an enemy force if they were still in column and marching rapidly up to meet them.

Besides, he could not help but marvel at the sight. It was grand beyond anything he had ever witnessed before, a fulfillment of all old dreams of glory to be found in war. He knew it was inspiring to the men as well, occasional cheers still rippled up and down the lines, battle flags to the fore, drummers keeping the beat.

The ground ahead was opening up, broadening out into a vast open plateau. The Catoctin Range was clearly visible, straight ahead, the church spires still standing in Frederick and the town itself becoming visible as well.

A gentle rise in ground was almost directly ahead and to the right of that the creek was bending to the left, the ground leading down to the Monocacy, a long open slope.

"That's the ford over to the McCausland Farm," Jeb announced, "just behind that low rise. We take that and if Ord is on the other side, he'll be bottled up. But it don't look that way now."

As he spoke Jeb pointed ahead, straight up the road. They were still a mile off, but he could see a dark column, concealed in dust, moving at a right angle to his own advance, heading to the west. . . . No, they were stopping, shaking out from column into line.

Beauregard grinned. It was about to begin.

Jeb shouted an order, a regiment of troops, spurring their mounts, pushing forward.

"Maybe we can still catch them while they're moving," Jeb announced.

US "Form here, form here!"
Sergeant Bartlett ran down the front of the regiment, following his white officers, as the regiment, soaking wet after having double-timed across the ford, began to swing back out into line of battle. Men were breathing hard, some pointing south, exclaiming.

"Here they come. God, look at 'em!"

"Silence!" Bartlett screamed. "Damn all of you. Come to attention and remain silent!"

The men looked at him, braced themselves. Bartlett caught the eye of the colonel, who nodded his approval.

They had been the first across the creek and were immediately pivoting. Their left was nearly at the stream, the right just about up to the railroad tracks; the next regiment was falling in beside them, and then another and another.

Bartlett stepped a dozen feet forward, first glaring at his men, then curiosity got the better of him and he looked up the line.

It was a grand sight, three regiments already in place, a fourth falling in, extending their front now to a quarter mile. The last of the black regiments from the Second Brigade ran by behind them, and right behind them, the first of Ord's men were crossing the stream.

They were a grim-looking lot. Their uniforms were filthy, some not much better than tattered rags. Their faces were blackened, some with uniform jackets off, others with hats missing. They moved slower, obviously numbed and exhausted, some helping along wounded comrades.

And from the direction they had come, distant gunfire erupted.

An occasional round whizzing by overhead, Bartlett's men involuntarily looking up as if they could see the passage of the ball.

"To the front!"

Bartlett turned.

A cornfield was directly in front of them but the ground sloped up enough that he could see mounted men, about six hundred yards away, coming toward them.

The colonel was studying them intently with his field glasses. He lowered them and looked over at Bartlett.

"Those are rebel cavalry. Forward screen. They'll start opening with a harassing fire, Sergeant. The men are to kneel down, not return fire, until their infantry comes up. I want the first volley to hit them like a sledgehammer."

"Yes, sir."

"Scared, Bartlett?" the colonel asked.

"No, sir."

The colonel winked at him.

"I am. Any sane man would be at a moment like this. Remember, Sergeant, courage is being afraid but then doing your duty anyhow. Just remember that and you will do fine."

"Yes, sir."

The colonel slapped him on the shoulder.

"When it starts, I want you close to me. We'll be behind the volley line, directly in the center, same way we drilled it a hundred times back in Philadelphia."

"Yes, sir."

"If I should fall," the colonel said, "Major Wallace will take command. If he falls, then it's up to the company officers and especially you sergeants to keep the men fighting."

"You won't get hurt," Bartlett said.

The colonel smiled.

"I was in every fight with the Army of the Potomac from Gaines Mill to Fredericksburg, where I got wounded. Believe me, Sergeant, officers fall."

He gave a tight-lipped smile.

"Prove something today, Bartlett."

"Sir?"

A minié ball hummed overhead, a puff of smoke erupting from the middle of the cornfield, the shooter invisible. Dozens of more shots ignited, a man in the ranks cursing, dropping his rifle, staggering back, clutching his arm. Men to either side looked at him nervously.

"Kneel down, boys, kneel down," the colonel shouted. The men quickly did as ordered, down on one knee, rifles still poised to the front.

The colonel looked back at Bartlett, who realized at that instant the colonel was playacting. He remained standing, talking with the regimental sergeant major as if the two were just standing about, having a friendly conversation, with not a care in the world.

From the opposite bank, a quarter mile up the slope, puffs of smoke were visible, more rounds coming their way, minié balls whining overhead, another man going down, this one silently, the man next to him beginning to scream, frantically wiping blood and brains from his face.

"We're going to be enfiladed from that crest," the colonel said, nodding back to the opposite bank. "Hope Ord at least left a good skirmish line out there to keep them back."

Behind the USCT battle line, the rest of Ord's men were still trudging across the creek, some running, some limping, some barely able to move. Farther down the line at the end of the right flank of the Colored Division, the first of Ord's men were falling into place to extend the line.

"I was saying, Sergeant Major, today is a day to prove something."

"And that is, sir?"

"You and your men stand this fight, and for the rest of your lives you will be able to look any other man in the face and say you are his equal."

"Some might not see it that way, sir," Bartlett replied quietly.

The colonel laughed, then shook his head. He slowly began to pace, a dozen yards in front of their line, and Bartlett knew this was the continuation of the act. And he was now part of that act, to play at being totally unconcerned, and by their example, brace up the men about to face their first action. A quick look to the flank showed him other officers doing the same. A few were extolling their men, others were just quiet, pacing back and forth. One had a Bible out and was reading aloud from it.

"You know, I'm from Ireland," the colonel continued. As he spoke, he reached into his pocket and pulled out a cigar, lit it, and then looked at Bartlett. He pulled out a second cigar. Though Washington Bartlett had never smoked, he took it now, the colonel holding the match while he puffed it to light. He made the mistake of inhaling and started to cough.

Several of the men in the ranks chuckled, as did the colonel.

"I was born in Ireland," the colonel continued, while slowly walking in front of the men, Bartlett by his side. "Came over in 'forty-seven, fleeing the potato famine, a starving lad, nothing but skin and bones and rags when I got off the boat."

Another scattered volley from the cornfield, another man went down, hit in the knee. One of the officers in the next regiment on the line collapsed, and an angry shout went up, the line actually beginning to surge forward, their officers shouting for the men to stand back in place.

For a second Bartlett looked back behind his own men and saw his son, with the other drummer boys. They were down on their stomachs, clustered near the regimental surgeon.

"I first worked as a navvy," the colonel continued, "digging for the railroads at four bits a day plus keep. Became a section boss finally. War comes and I'm a sergeant. My Alice was my salvation; she kept telling me to get some book learning while I was in the army. Had a good company officer, used to teach us reading, history, literature, and such in the evenings to pass the time in winter quarters. Found I liked the learning and began studying. Lot of things, history of our country, biographies of the Founding Fathers, and, of course, Hardee's drill manual.

"While I was in the hospital after Fredericksburg, word came around they were forming up colored regiments and looking for good men with combat experience to volunteer as officers."

He smiled.

"And now here I am a colonel."

Bartlett noticed a change in tone as the colonel talked on. He had fallen into a bit of a brogue when talking of his life, different from the studied attempt at sounding like he was educated, a professional man.

"I heard about that letter the president sent to you. Can I see it?"

Washington proudly unbuttoned his jacket, reached into his breast pocket, and pulled out a pocket Bible, the letter folded inside. He opened it up and handed it to the colonel.

Men in the ranks nodded. "The letter, he's reading the letter," some of them said.

The colonel held it reverently, read the contents, then handed it back.

"God bless old Abe," the colonel said, this time loud enough for the men of the regiment to hear.

Several repeated his words.

"I understand your father works in the White House."

"Yes, sir," Washington replied proudly. "Been there near on to fifty years. My middle name is Quincy, named after the president who gave me a silver cup when I was baptized. I'm mighty proud of my father."

"And that's your son back there?" the colonel motioned toward the surgeon, where the drummer boys were mingled in with the stretcher bearers.

"Yes, sir."

"Make sure you keep him back today," the colonel said quietly.

"Thank you, sir. I will."

"Sergeant Major, you know there was no love lost between us Irish and you colored."

"I know that, sir."

"Both fighting for the same jobs, both treated as trash. This war is changing that forever."

"I hope so, sir."

"I know so. Today is your day to win what we Irish won at Fredericksburg."

Bartlett's back was to the south as the two talked. The colonel paused, looking past him.

"They're coming," the colonel whispered.

Bartlett turned and for several seconds he was frozen in place.

Bayonet tips showed just beyond the opposite slope six hundred yards away. Rising above the bayonets, at regular hundred-yard intervals, were the banners of the Confederacy. Within seconds the bayonet tips were rifle muzzles, then a wall, a wall of gray and butternut, cresting up over the apex of the low rise. Onward they came, not slowing, reaching the edge of the cornfield and then disappearing again, except for the rifle muzzles and bayonets projecting above the stalks.

In the silence he could actually hear them coming, the tramping of feet, cornstalks snapping, wavering, and collapsing. It was wave, a tidal wave, an ocean of armed men, relentless, coming forward, the silence broken by cheers from their side now that their enemy was in sight.

"To our duty, Sergeant Major," the colonel said. He turned and casually walked back to the middle of the regimental line. He paused, looked up at the flags, the distinctive yellow regimental flag of the USCTs, beside it the national colors. He formally came to attention and saluted both.

"Fight like hell, boys!" the colonel shouted. "Keep an eye on your glorious flags! If they go forward, you go forward!"

He stepped back through the ranks, the men still kneeling except for the color guard, and took position directly behind them, Bartlett by his side.

Three hundred yards out and the rebels were still advancing. Bartlett looked at them in astonishment. Their advance was a solid wall, some officers mounted and out front. Drummers beat out a continual roll. Another cheer that sent chills down his spine, the legendary rebel yell. He had heard it often enough yesterday, from a distance, now it was truly real, coming straight toward him.

More than one in the ranks was looking back at him, eyes wide with fear.

Suddenly John Miller stood up.

"Damn rebels!" he roared, shaking his fist. "Come on, you sons of bitches."

With that a loud shout erupted from the regiment, some of the men began to stand up, officers shouting for them to remain kneeling.

"Check your caps, boys!" The cry went up and down the line, and men half-cocked their muskets, looking down to make sure their percussion caps were in place. A few fumbled in cap boxes to replace a lost or forgotten cap.

Two hundred yards.

Again another defiant rebel yell. An increase in the drumroll beat. It was hard to see the men through the corn but their rifle tips and bayonets stood out clearly, the tidal wave coming forward, not slowing.

"Up, boys, up!"

The regiment stood up, the regiments down the line doing the same. The colonel drew his sword and tilted his head back.

"Set your sights for one hundred yards!" he roared.

Men looked down at their Enfield rifles, some adjusting the rear sight.

"Volley fire on my command!"

They waited, rifles at the shoulder. The rebs kept on coming; they were not going to stop; they were coming straight in. Some of the rifle points disappeared, the men carrying them leveling their weapons for a straight-in bayonet charge.

"Take aim!"

The cry was picked up, each man shouting out the words, "Take aim!"

Across the regimental front six hundred rifles were lowered.

"Pick your targets, boys!" the colonel shouted.

Barrels shifted slightly, men searching for targets, hard to find in the cornfield, many therefore aiming straight in to where the enemy colors floated above the advancing line.

Bartlett felt as if he wanted to scream out the order himself. They were close. A hundred yards, yes, but it seemed as if within seconds those glistening bayonets would be right in his face.

The seconds dragged out, as slow as eternity itself.

"Fire!"

The volley let loose as if delivered on the drill field. Six hundred rifles firing as one. Jim stood silent, awed. Before, they had always fired across an empty field. The corn directly in front of them just flattened, or flew up into the air. For a few seconds he wondered if any round had even been able to reach the rebs, but then through the smoke he saw rifles tips pitching backward, a regimental flag going down.

"Reload!" Bartlett roared, no longer able to hold himself back. "Hurry, boys! Reload!"

And then he heard it . . . a Southern voice yelling, "Charge, boys, charge 'em!"

It came from the cornfield.

A yell resounded, a high-pitched yipping like that of a pack of mad dogs on the scent of blood.

"Load, load, load!" A white officer was pacing in front of their volley line, gesturing wildly, urging the men on. Bits of cartridge paper flew into the air as men tore them open with their teeth, poured powder down barrels, squeezed bullet into barrel, and threw the paper aside. Ramrods were out, hundreds of arms rising up, pushing charges down the barrels.

All of it was combining together . . . "Charge! . . . Load, boys, load." . . . the maddening rebel yell almost on top of them . . . "Load, boys, load!"

"Volley fire, present!"

The colonel had remained absolutely still throughout, not budging an inch, not saying a single word, and Bartlett, looking at him, drew inspiration. Yelling would change nothing; it was calmness now that counted, calmness and nerves of steel.

"Take aim!"

He looked straight ahead. Cornstalks collapsing, flashes of bayonets, faces of men, distorted with battle fever and rage, rushing toward them.

Some of the men were not yet loaded, but most were, rifles leveled.

"Fire!"

A shattering roar. Then nothing but clouds of smoke. Men started to reload. Those who had not loaded quickly enough for the volley lowered their guns, aimed into the smoke, and fired.

And then a few men came out of the smoke, still at the run, bayonets lowered . . . and smashed into the line.

Wild oaths, screams, men slashing out, rebs lowering rifles in the last few seconds and firing at waist level into the solid ranks. More men going down, the line bowing back just to the flank of the colors, the national flag bobbing down for a moment.

Bartlett looked left and right. The battle line almost broke open where a couple of dozen rebs had waded in, slashing, jabbing, a rebel officer with revolver drawn dropping several men before being clubbed down.

At the center the national flag was half down, its holder bayoneted in the stomach, a reb reaching out grabbing the flagpole, wrestling to pull it out of the grip of the dying man.

Bartlett leapt forward, bayonet poised, and dived into the melee, bayoneting the reb who had hold of the flag, and was hoisting it up, shouting with glee. The man collapsed, flag going back down.

"Volley fire, present!"

It was the colonel, still motionless, oblivious, it seemed, to the near breakthrough.

"Take aim!"

Less than half the men complied; the rest were fighting hand to hand or were so rattled by the onset that they moved as if trapped in mud. More than one had thrown his rifle down and was already running.

Bartlett pulled the colors back from the dying reb, using the staff as a club, waving it back and forth, several rebs trying to close in on him.

"Fire!"

Another volley and the few rebs directly in front dropped, some riddled by half a dozen or more rounds.

Washington stepped back into the line, panting for breath, his rifle gone, the flagstaff clutched with both hands.

Someone slapped him on the back and he half turned, ready to fight. It was John Miller.

"Sergeant Major, I'll take that, sir. You got other jobs to do."

He was reluctant to give it up, looking up at the banner, red stripes, part of the flag torn by a bayonet, blood on the white stars.

"Sergeant Major, if you don't mind, please."

It was the colonel.

He nodded, handed the flagstaff to Miller, picked up a rifle lying on the ground, and stepped back through the line.

"Volley fire on my command!"

The line had held, half a hundred were down, but it still held. A glimpse through the smoke showed him a second rebel line was up, in the cornfield, about a hundred yards back, the corn in between already shredded down to the ground. Beyond them, up on the low rise, artillery pieces were wheeling into place.

He stepped back beside his colonel.

"Take aim!" the colonel roared.

Rifles were aimed downrange.

"Fire!"

"Reload!"

Bartlett, panting for breath, looked over at his colonel, who smiled. And to his horror he saw that the man was clutching his midsection, blood trickling out. Washington reached out to grab him, but the colonel waved him off.

"Just a scratch," the colonel said with a smile.

"Surgeon!" Bartlett shouted, but his voice was drowned out by men yelling, explosions, the steady tearing zip of miniés coming into their lines.

"Leave off of it," the colonel snapped. "I'm still fine."

He looked at Bartlett and grinned.

"No one will ever take that flag away from you ever again, Sergeant Major."

The colonel turned back to face the rebel line.

"Take aim!"

"Fire!"

9:15 A.M.

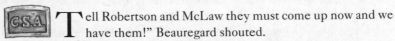 ell Robertson and McLaw they must come up now and we have them!" Beauregard shouted.

A staff officer saluted, turned, and galloped back down the road.

Across his mile-wide front the battle had opened, volleys rattling, the air above and around him alive with bullets. He rode behind his regiments, the reserve brigades, one to each division advancing, already going in to strengthen the assault. Directly to the front of his First Division more than one man had gone into a near frenzy with the realization they were fighting colored troops.

He thought those would break with the first charge. The lead regiments had leapt forward without even firing, figuring to panic and bowl them over with the sight of the bayonet.

Those regiments had been shredded, and now a vicious firefight raged across the cornfield.

The first of his guns, a battery of Napoleons, were already in play but the shooting was tight for them. There was no good prominence to deploy on that would enable the gunners to fire safely over the heads of the infantry in front. The range was short at six hundred yards, and missing in elevation by even a few feet would send case shot plowing into the backs of comrades, so most of the shells were going high, bursting far behind the enemy line.

He sent another courier over to the gunners, telling them to shift target, to bombard the crossing where Yankee infantry were drawn up defending the far side of the ford from increasing pressure by Jubal Early's battered survivors.

He looked back down the road—dust. It had to be Robertson; it had to be.

Headquarters, Army of Northern Virginia

9:20 A.M.

He had not gone in as one solid blow, Lee thought, high enough above the smoke that he could clearly see the spreading battle on the other side of the creek.

Two divisions were in, trading blow for blow with what looked to be two divisions of Yankees. One division was far stronger than the other, and close examination had revealed them to be the colored troops. Most likely fresh from training fields, numbers not yet depleted, perhaps five thousand or more.

They had just sustained a mad frontal charge and held, his own men forced to give back, and now it was a stand-up firefight. Beauregard was right to try that tactic; if the blacks had broken in panic, that panic could easily have infected the rest of the army and sent them running, the way the German Eleventh Corps had at Chancellorsville.

The Yankees had taken a bad position to try to hold. Their left flank, on the far side of the creek, was at a right angle to the ford. They should have conceded that point, pulled back several hundred yards to the north, but if they had done so, the Yankees still on the east side of the creek would have been completely surrounded.

There was a great opportunity now.

"Tell General Alexander to return his guns on our left back to their position of yesterday, to open a general bombardment on the Yankees below them. Also, tell Jubal he must push forward and retake that ford. That could begin to roll up their entire right flank."

An orderly saluted and galloped off.

Hood and Longstreet were by his side, both silent, glasses raised, watching the spreading fight.

"I should go down, help Jubal," Hood said. "I can bring up what's left of Rhodes's old division as well."

Lee nodded in agreement, not saying a word.

"We're losing a lot of men down there," Pete said.

"So are they," Lee replied.

Headquarters, Army of the Susquehanna

9:40 A.M.

He could sense the growing anxiety of his staff. Men were moving about hurriedly, couriers setting off a bit too quickly, spurring their mounts hard.

There was so much smoke now it was hard to see, the air absolutely still, filled with dampness, the kind of conditions that could cause battle smoke to become a thick, impenetrable fog.

Banks came in. Dapper-looking, fifteen years older than Grant, he saluted in a perfunctory manner.

"You sent for me, sir?"

"I want you to prepare to shift your reserve division back into the center of Frederick, then move south of town to cover the Catoctin Road."

"Is this the beginning of a pullout?" Banks asked quietly.

"No, it is not!" Grant snapped, loud enough for everyone to hear. "We stand here, we fight here, we win here. We are not pulling out."

"Sir, may I be so bold," Banks said with almost a lecturing tone. "You have been flanked, sir, and that is Lee down there. He is already preparing to come in from across the river. I suggest we consider evacuation of this plain and pull back to the high ground."

"You are being bold and completely out of line, General Banks," Grant said icily. "I have given you an order. Now see that it is carried out. Keep your division in town. When I pass the order, they are to come out on to the plains south of town."

He paused, stepping closer to Banks.

"Those are my orders."

"Yes, sir," Banks said calmly. He saluted crisply, and without a look back, rode off.

The roar of battle continued to intensify. Hunt's batteries were fully engaged, half the pieces sending shot into Beauregard's guns, the other pieces pounding the ground on the other side of the ford, where increasing numbers of rebel infantry were pushing down toward the river.

"More rebs going in!" someone exclaimed.

Grant shifted his field glasses back to Beauregard's advance, but could see nothing, the smoke too thick. He lowered the glasses. It was hard to discern, but watching closely he could see a dark tide moving through the smoke, coming up to merge with the enemy's forward battle line.

"Bet that's the Texans," Ely Parker said softly.

First Texas

9:50 A.M.

Men panting, bent double, the battle line of Hood's old Texas brigade surged forward. Behind them the rest of Robertson's Division was filing in behind Beauregard's right-flank division, having broken column from the road to swing into line.

They crossed over a railroad track, gray-clad bodies scattered along the right-of-way. A shell screamed in, bursting directly on the track, showering them with case shot and fragments of ballast, five men going down.

"Keep moving, boys!" Lee Robinson shouted. "Keep moving."

Men were cursing, a few falling out from exhaustion. Directly ahead he could see Monocacy Creek, and at the sight of it some men cried out that there was water.

At the head of the column was a staffer from Robertson's headquarters, mounted on a bloody horse, sword drawn, now pointing to their left.

"Turn and form line!" he screamed.

The men around Robinson cursed, one of the corporals snatching canteens from half a dozen of his comrades and ignoring the orders, dashing the last few yards down to the creek.

Lee let him go. Those who were still with this column were the solid hard core of the old First. No skulkers. They had been driven out long ago. Every man was a veteran, a veteran of the cornfield at Antietam,

Fredericksburg, Union Mills, the debacle before Washington, the slaughter last week at Gunpowder River. An officer shouted for the corporal to come back, but the man ignored him, jumping into the creek, forcing the canteens down, then but a few seconds later coming back up the slope, muddy, water dripping, passing the canteens back to his comrades, who drank greedily and then passed the precious liquid to friends forming line around them.

"Forward at the double!"

The First Texas set off, a ragged line, but then again they were never noted for parade-ground performance, but when it came to a fight, they were the ones called upon.

"I heard it's niggers up there," someone cried.

"They can kill the same as a white man," someone shouted back, and from more than one there were dark oaths about what would happen to prisoners.

"None of that," Robinson shouted. "General Lee said prisoners will be taken and treated properly. I'll shoot the first man that disobeys."

No one spoke in reply; all were now too exhausted, too focused on what was ahead.

They swept past a battery of Napoleons, gun crews busy at work, pieces kicking back, gunners rolling their pieces forward while swabbers ran sponges down the bores to kill sparks and keep the barrels cool.

As the men passed in front of the guns the crews stopped work for a moment, a few cheering "old Texas!" on.

They hit the edge of the cornfield, or what had been the cornfield. It was mowed flat, barely a stalk standing, bringing to Lee's mind dark memories of Antietam, where the brigade had lost nearly eighty percent of its men in twenty minutes.

Hundreds of bodies littered the ground, the wounded who were unable to walk trying to crawl to the rear. Walking wounded staggered about, seeing Texas coming on, a few of them cheering, others just standing silent.

The roar of battle ahead swelled. Nothing could yet be seen, only smoke, a shell bursting overhead, more men going down, a riderless horse dragging a body, the foot of a dead man caught in the stirrups, the litter of battle, drums, cartridge papers, smashed and twisted rifles, and bodies and more bodies.

Finally he saw it, a shadowy line, men no longer standing, most down on their knees or lying flat as they fought.

"Forward, Texas!"

US Sergeant Major Bartlett remained by the side of his colonel, whose features were pale, graying, lifeblood seeping out between the fingers of his right hand clasped to his stomach. But the man was still on his feet.

They had long ago gone to independent fire at will. Most of the men had fired off the forty rounds in their cartridge boxes and were now reaching into haversacks and pants pockets or scavenging in the cartridge boxes of the dead and wounded.

Bartlett had left his colonel a few times to pace down the line, detailing off parts of companies to stand back from the fight for a few minutes, to upend canteens into barrels to loosen the gummy powder and swab their barrels clean. Those without water he ordered to pee down the barrels, a few of the men, in spite of the horror around them, laughing about getting shot in the wrong place while they did as ordered.

Guns were so hot that to touch them with bare skin would blister the flesh off, and men actually laughed as one soldier, following Bartlett's orders, suddenly dropped his gun and began to hop about in agony.

As he reached the right flank of the line he looked for Major Wallace, to report that the colonel was badly wounded and would not last much longer, but Wallace was dead, shot through the forehead.

The line was still holding, but over half the men were down. In sections they were stretched out in nearly a straight row, a gap of a dozen feet in the front, and Bartlett ordered men in to fill the gap, calmly telling them to close the line, center on the flag, and keep firing.

Fifty yards back, down in a shallow depression he saw the surgeon at work, and in spite of the call of duty he ran back, looking around frantically. The surgeon looked up at him, pausing while he bandaged off the arm of a corporal and caught Bartlett's eye, nodding over to his right. His son was helping to drag in a man shot in the face. He nodded and ran over to his son.

"Daddy." The boy looked up at him wide-eyed and then smiled.

"Not afraid now," his son gasped. "Too much to do, but wish I could play the drum."

He patted his son on the shoulder then bent low and sprinted back to the colonel's side.

Just as he reached the colonel the intensity of fire from the enemy side redoubled, swelled, a shattering volley taking down half the men of the color guard. Miller was still standing, though, keeping the national flag aloft.

Washington looked over at the colonel.

"Reinforcements on their side, another wave. Make sure the boys stay low and keep pouring it back."

"For God's sake, sir," Bartlett shouted, "then you get down, too."

"Can't," the colonel gasped. "Once I lie down, won't get up."

He was using his sword now as a cane to keep himself up.

The enemy fire sweeping in was deadly. After the first volley from the reinforcements, it was now aimed independent fire, bullets whistling in low.

Cursing, Miller went down, clutching his arm, another man snatching the colors from him, that man then getting hit, and then another took his place.

'They'll come in hard, all at once," the colonel said. "If the flank breaks, we have to pull back. Keep the men together, rally them round the colors and keep them together. Try to get them up on the road to town, if not, then back along the railroad track."

Bartlett nodded, unable to speak.

10:15 A.M.

M ove your battery out to the right," Hunt shouted.

The captain in charge of a battery of Illinois gunners saluted, shouted for his men to hook up their pieces and pull them out of the lunettes. He was changing front now with nearly all his guns, shifting from fire across the river to the pounding of the rebel flanking attack. There was little they could actually shoot at, the smoke was too thick, but the sound of battle to their right was swelling, punctuated now by more rebel yells. Anyone with experience knew a breakthrough was coming, and would roll straight toward them.

He looked back toward town. The reserve limbers, loaded with canister, had yet to appear. He needed that canister, and he sent the last of his couriers off to urge the limbers on.

"They're starting to break," someone shouted, pointing.

On the road below, hundreds of men were emerging out of the smoke, Union troops, white and black mixed together, some running, some giving ground defiantly, clustered around a flag, falling back thirty or forty yards, turning to fire, then falling back again.

In ten minutes the rebs would be on him.

T exas!"

The men of the Texas Brigade were up on their feet, pushing through Beauregard's men and starting forward. It was not a mad, impetuous charge. They came on low, crouching, standing up to fire, going down low to reload, weaving forward a few dozen feet, standing to fire again. The range was so close that now, at last, Lee Robinson could see his enemies, maybe thirty yards off, shadowy dark figures, down low, firing back. No solid volley line, they were shredded, but the survivors were hanging on, refusing to budge.

It was going to take the bayonet.

10:20 A.M.

A courier came up on foot, crouched over, clutching a hand that had taken a bullet.

"Colonel!"

"Over here!" Bartlett cried.

The courier came up and at the sight of the colonel, still standing erect, he forced himself to rise up and then salute.

"General's compliments, sir. Our right has collapsed. You are ordered to pull back."

The colonel nodded, oblivious to the rebel infantry, shadowy and yet clearly visible not a hundred feet off, flashes of light winking up and down their line.

"Sir, try and get over the railroad and back toward town. But frankly, sir, I think that way is cut off by rebel troops."

"To where then?"

"Along the river and the railroad track. There's a railroad cut 'bout half a mile back—"

He collapsed, shot through the head.

The colonel looked around.

"Hardest maneuver," he said trying not to bend over from the pain.

"I'll take care of it, sir."

The colonel nodded.

Bartlett went up to the colors, stood up, and looked around.

"Men, listen to me! We're pulling back. No panic. No panic. I'll shoot the first man that turns and runs."

Men looked over at him.

"Load for volley but don't fire!"

Men began to stand up and the sight of it was pitiful. He did not realize until that moment just how many men were down for good. Of the six hundred who had opened fire, barely two hundred and fifty now stood, clustering in close to their flag.

He could hear the rebel yell resounding to his right and now heading toward the rear.

John Miller was down on his knees, and Washington reached down, pulling him up, John wincing.

"Don't stay behind," Bartlett shouted.

John nodded.

"Fall back! Keep your formation, men. Don't run, fall back at the walk!"

He grabbed the colonel, who gasped and went double.

"Leave me, Sergeant."

"Like hell."

"I'm dying. Now leave me. If you don't, they'll get you, too!"

Washington tried to pull him along.

"Damn it, soldier. An order. Leave me!"

The colonel straightened up, looked at him, and then actually smiled.

"Good work, soldier," he gasped. "Just take me over to the surgeon. I'll see you later when you come back."

Tears in his eyes, Bartlett realized he could not lead these men out while burdened with a wounded man who could not walk on his own.

He picked the colonel up and carried him over to the makeshift hospital area down in a gently sloping ravine. A hundred or more were on the ground, the surgeon frantically at work. At the sight of his approach the surgeon came to his feet and ran over.

"I'll take him."

Together they helped the colonel to lie down.

"Where's my son?" Bartlett asked.

"I don't know."

Frightened, Washington stood and looked about. He saw several drummer boys dragging a man with a leg shot off, two more struggling with a stretcher, but his son . . . he could not see him.

"William!"

His voice was drowned out by the roar of battle, the rebel yell as the enemy before them, sensing the pullback, began to surge forward.

"William!"

Someone shoved him. It was Miller, his left arm dangling but his right still strong.

"They're on us!" Miller cried.

Washington looked up. The rebs were already over the position they had held but a few minutes before.

"Sergeant Major Bartlett, act your role," the colonel gasped. "I'm proud of you. Now take command like a soldier."

Washington, fighting back tears, saluted, looked once more for his son and then as the colors passed him, he fell in by their side, then got behind the men, racing back and forth, up and down the line, ordering the men to fire, reload, pull back, fire, reload, pull back.

The rebs swarmed over the hospital area.

10:40 A.M.

Sheridan came up the slope to army headquarters, hat gone, his uniform torn where a ball had plucked his shoulder, barely breaking the skin but now marked by a trickle of blood.

Grant stood silent, cigar clenched firmly in his mouth.

"The line is breaking," Sheridan announced.

"I know, I can see that."

"They've split the front. Ord's boys to the north of the road, my division of blacks to the south."

He paused.

"General, they fought like tigers. Held them back for an hour and a half."

Grant said nothing, just nodding.

"Sir, my entire corps is about to be flanked, pinned down by the river. Some of Ord's men mixed in. The rest were up on the right of my black division but have given way. Robertson is swinging on to my flank now. Early is crossing the ford and I think Scales is preparing to come down from the heights."

"Hold exactly where you are."

"Sir? They'll have three divisions coming up this road. They're coming up even now. Shouldn't I pull back to block?"

He pointed down the road toward Buckeystown and he was indeed right. What was left of Ord's command had broken, was coming back across the plateau. In a matter of minutes Hunt's batteries, unsupported yet by infantry, would be in the thick of that attack.

"Shouldn't I pull back, support Hunt?"

Grant shook his head.

"That railroad track, the ground around it, turn it into the Hornets Nest like at Shiloh. It will stop Lee cold for hours and he'll bleed out if he turns on it. You take command down there. Let me worry about here."

"It means I'll be cut off."

"Yes, it does," Grant said quietly. "At least for a while. You start moving back, though, and those boys will just keep moving and then start running. That's happened too many times in the past. They are to stand and hold their ground. That is your job. Let me deal with the rest."

"Yes, sir," Sheridan replied.

"You will hold throughout the day. Let him bleed out on you. Do you have extra ammunition?"

"Yes, sir. Twenty wagonloads during the night, about three hundred boxes of a thousand rounds each."

"You got a battery down there as well. Use them to fire down the tracks in both directions. Now go!"

Sheridan forced a grin, turned, and rode off.

Directly ahead, on the road toward Buckeystown he saw a division deploying out, coming forward, a staff officer shouting that it was McLaw.

"Let him come," Grant replied sharply, sat back down, tossed aside his cigar, and lit another one.

10:45 A.M.

 Robert E. Lee turned to his old warhorse, Pete Longstreet. "Attack all along the line, General Longstreet."

"Sir? Beauregard is nowhere near Frederick yet. In fact sir, I think he bungled it. He should have waited for Robertson and McLaw to fully deploy out, hit them with four divisions at once."

Yes, Pete was right on that point. Beauregard went in too soon, he should have waited the extra hour. But then again, that had always been a curse to them, to any army in the past attempting to flank a foe by a back road. It could take hours to deploy out into battle formation, and in the interval an opponent could either draw back or prepare. What did surprise him was that Beauregard going into battle formation four miles back, before engaging. He should have gone forward in columns and covered the ground in half the time.

Chancellorsville, in one sense, had played out that way. The first of Jackson's divisions had completed the march shortly after noon, but it was another four hours before he went in. Though the victory was overwhelming at the start, darkness had intervened, and thereby saved the Army of the Potomac.

Nothing of that could be changed now. But Grant's right flank was indeed crumbling. He could see a clear breakthrough opening a breach between the two divisions first sent out to stop him. Up by the National Road, a division of Union troops that had been in reserve position yesterday was now filing back toward the town.

That left but two of Banks's divisions to cover several miles of front. What was left of Sheridan in the center, and Ord on the right, was collapsing.

His original plan, for Beauregard to sweep up the west bank of the Monocacy, literally to have the sleeve of the man at the right of the line brushing the water, apparently was not happening. The position from just back of McCausland's Ford, up to the depot was acting as a breakwater, while Beauregard seemed to be pivoting more to the west with his assault, following the road up to Frederick.

"General Longstreet, push your men down to the ford just south of the National Bridge. Drive across, open a wedge there. Put every man in. We are not to hold back now. I want every man in."

"Sir," he said and hesitated.

He had rarely seen Lee this agitated, this focused on the moment at hand.

"General Longstreet, did you hear me, sir?"

"Yes, General Lee. It is just that I suspect General Beauregard's assault will stall when he reaches Frederick. The Yankees right down by the stream below us are hanging on. Our original plan was for the divisions on this side to link up with Beauregard as he swept past, thus reinforcing his attack, and our assault would go in on the enfilade against them. What you are ordering now instead is a frontal assault."

Lee turned away from the fight, eyes fixed on Pete.

"We must venture that. I think they are ready to break."

"Sir, that is not the Army of the Potomac over there. That is something different, men used to victory. We must factor that in."

"Then we shall teach them that they can indeed lose."

"Sir," again he hesitated, "I beg you to reconsider. We have lost our base of supply, an enemy force is advancing on our rear even if it is still a few days off. We fight a full-scale battle here, even if we win, we just might lose. We have no reserves; we'll have ten, maybe fifteen thousand additional wounded, and Grant most likely will slip back over that pass and still be a threat."

Lee was silent, gazing at him, and for a few seconds he hoped that indeed he was reaching through, penetrating the fury of battle that was now upon him.

"Order Beauregard to halt. He did not do a good job, but at least he finished what was left of Ord and part of Sheridan. Grant is down to but one corps capable of an offensive. We hold, let him then try to hit back."

"No, sir," Lee snapped angrily. "I want this finished, now, today. This is our chance to defeat them once and for all. Now see to your duty, General Longstreet."

We hold here!"
    Sergeant Major Bartlett looked up as Phil Sheridan rode among their ranks. Most of the men of the Third Division had given ground in fairly good order, but to his shame several of the regiments had broken entirely and run.

Of white officers he saw precious few. Three captains from his own regiment, one of them clutching a head wound, one whom he knew to be a drunkard and obviously drunk now, the third of decent caliber who had kept his company together and in good order but seemed lost in shock.

The rebs had not pursued hotly; their fire had slackened as the Third pulled back. Sheridan was pointing up toward the railroad track, to where it edged along the side of a low ridge for several hundred yards, with several cuts through the low ridge for the grade. There was a thick cloying scent in the air; the ground about the cut had a scattering of bodies that had been out in the heat for two days. They all looked as if they had on uniforms two sizes too small, bodies swollen, knees drawn up, one with both hands clenched and raised.

To his right he saw the piers of a bridge about a hundred yards upstream, smoke curling from collapsed timbers still protruding above the water.

"Rally along the railroad track, boys," Sheridan cried. "You hold the west end, the rest of the corps the east end. And you've got to hold!"

Bartlett led his men as they scrambled up onto the track and looked around. There was a shallow railroad cut. Good protection if hit from the river or from the north, but if the rebs came straight in from the west, it was bad ground.

"Track and ties, boys!" someone shouted. He wasn't sure who said it, but within seconds a couple of hundred men were at work. There were no tools, though, men prying at the spikes with bayonets.

Some of the black soldiers waded in, shouting they knew what to do. The Baltimore and Ohio's rails were bolted together, and on the outside of the track, at the joint, a wooden block was wedged in to keep the joint tight. A heavy sergeant took the butt of a musket and started to hammer on the side of the wooden wedge. It began to move. Several more joined in, working in unison. The wedge popped out. Up and down the line men were popping the wedges. The sergeant ran along the track, grabbing men, shouting for Bartlett to get his boys, three or four to each tie on one side.

Seconds later, with more than two hundred men lifting and pushing, the track with ties still attached rose slowly, the rail bending. Bolts popped and the long section of track rose up and crashed over. Men swarmed over the torn-up section, prying loose the six-foot-long ties, tearing them free, running them up, and stacking them across the open end of the cut; others came up with twisted pieces of rail, tossing them on.

A company of white soldiers from farther up the line came to them, carrying pry bars and wrenches, a shout of joy going up among the men around the sergeant directing the operation.

"You boys need help?" one of the white soldiers shouted, holding up a wrench.

"I was a Reading Railroad man," the black sergeant shouted, and the white soldier slapped him on the shoulder.

"Could see you knew your work. Erie Railroad here."

The few precious tools were passed around, easing the job, the sergeant directing men to unbolt sections of track. The barricade, though low, had to span over thirty feet. Gradually, it was beginning to build up. Men scooped up ballast with their bare hands and threw it over the barricade. Others started to drag ties to the top of the cut, to give a little more protection and to make them the perfect height for a rifle rest when lying down.

"They're coming!"

The few men who had the stomach to remain behind as skirmishers came running down the track. Their approach was announced as well by a rebel volley that tore straight down the ravine, dropping half a dozen men.

"My men over here!" Bartlett screamed. "Rally to the colors, men.

A white officer came up. He didn't recognize the man, a colonel.

"Sergeant, where're your officers?"

He looked around and recognized no one in the confusion, the bustle of men working to tear up the track.

"I don't know, sir."

"Take your colors. Plant them on that barricade and hold it!"

Even as he spoke there was a loud clattering, a shouting to clear the way. A field piece, a bronze twelve-pound Napoleon, was being moved up the track, crew shouting for the men to clear back.

The ravine was so narrow that the crew stopped at the eastern entryway, unhooked their piece, and swung it around, beginning to drag it forward by hand. Bartlett could see where it was going to be positioned, and he shouted for his men to pitch in, even as he approached the barricade with the color guard. Sergeant Miller, arm in a rough sling, was still with them, features gray, but he was hanging on.

With men pushing from all sides the Napoleon was run up to the barricade. The team that had pulled it up were backing up to open ground where they turned their horses around. Men unhooked the limber box, nearly half a ton of weight, and manhandled it down, dragging it the length of the ravine and depositing it ten yards back from the gun. The team took off.

Bartlett's men fell in on either side of the gun crew.

"What are we facing?" a gunner asked.

"Texans I heard," Bartlett replied.

"Oh, lordy," the gunner sighed. "You boys, stick to us like ticks on a dog."

"We will."

"They're coming!"

He could hear them now, the high-pitched yelping. The smoke had cleared just enough that they were visible, a couple of hundred yards off, a line astride the railroad track, spread a couple of hundred yards to either flank, red banners to the fore.

He looked back. Up and down the railroad cut for as far as he could see men were up against the embankments; a roar was thundering back from the east end, down by the river. From what little he had learned so far in the army, he knew their position was a bad one. They were like a long thin line, men almost literally back-to-back along the railroad line. The rebs coming at them had them at a right angle. Other rebs were swarming around to either side; from the far riverbank long-range shot and shells were beginning to rain in.

They were cut off, surrounded.

Someone slapped him on the shoulder, and he turned. A young white soldier pushed two packs of cartridges, ten rounds in each, into his hand. Behind him half a dozen other white soldiers had laid down two wooden cases of ammunition. One had already pried it open with a bayonet, torn off the tin waterproof cover, and was piling out ten packs of cartridges, men coming over to scoop them.

We're going to need every round, Sergeant Major Bartlett realized.

"Case shot, one-second fuse!"

The gunners were well practiced, a young boy running up bearing the shell, which was rammed home.

"You colored boys, stand back!" a gunnery sergeant yelled, even as he stepped back from the piece, his lanyard taut.

He jerked the lanyard—an explosive roar, the Napoleon kicking back several feet. The shell detonated directly ahead of the advancing line, dropping several. A man was screaming on the other side of the gun, clutching a crushed foot, the gun having gone over it.

"I told you to stand back!" the sergeant screamed.

"Case shot, one-second fuse!"

The rebel advance stopped. He could see them raising their pieces up, then bringing them level.

"Down! Get down!"

A second later the volley swept the front of the barricade, minié balls striking iron railing, railroad ties, snapping through the flag, and striking men as well.

"Aimed fire, boys!" Bartlett shouted. "Careful aiming. Now give it to them."

The fight was on again. Seconds later the Napoleon fired, the shell disappearing into the smoke. To his horror, Washington Bartlett realized at that moment that his son, if still alive, was somewhere over there, in the direction they were shooting. Any round going high was most likely plowing into the hospital area.

He raised his own rifle, aimed very low, and fired.

10:55 A.M.

Oh, this is beautiful, just beautiful," Henry Hunt exclaimed as he paced behind the new line he had just set up, facing south. He ignored the enfilading artillery fire coming from across the river, which had already dismounted or struck down two of his guns.

It was the target before him that counted.

The last of Ord's broken men had streamed past his position, and now, four hundred yards out, an entire division of rebel infantry was coming straight at him. He had over sixty guns lined up. Not as many as Malvern Hill, but more than Gettysburg.

He had full faith in his gunners. They had proven themselves yesterday in the bombardment of the McCausland Farm. And now they had infantry before them, a beautiful wide target spread out over a half mile. Three brigades in the lead, two more a hundred yards behind. And behind them another division four hundred yards farther back, struggling to re-form after their initial clash earlier in the morning.

"Fire!"

This was not a single salvo. He had ordered his battery commanders to carefully check aim and elevation and make every shot count.

The guns directly in front of him went off. Seconds later more opened up, the last firing maybe thirty seconds later. Commands were being shouted, "Case shot, two-second fuse!" "Roll 'em up, boys." "Sergeant, check that elevation screw. Raise it half a turn!"

Field glasses were useless in the smoke. He squatted down, trying to see under the billowing clouds created by the guns just fired, and was delighted. Shells were bursting right in front of the advancing line, puffs of dirt geysering from the shells with percussion fuses, some of the shots going high, but some of the high ones hitting the second line.

Excellent shooting.

He knew when to fall silent, to step back, which he now did. And his men went to work.

11:00 A.M.

I want my divisions back in!" Beauregard shouted.

Robertson's and McLaw's divisions had taken the lead in the assault, passing through and beyond his own two divisions, which had delivered a savage beating to the Yankees but in turn had been torn apart.

He regretted now, more than ever, not waiting for them to come up, to have sent all four in at once. They could have gone through like a battering ram, but then again, the delay might have allowed the Yankees to do what they were now doing, shifting guns about, bringing up more men.

Johnston had not listened to him at Shiloh about his deployment before the attack, packing the men in too close so that all command and control had been lost, and he had been saddled with the blame.

Now Lee would blame him for the loss of momentum. *Damn it, well, let Lee try to maneuver twenty-five thousand men on one narrow road, then go into a fight.*

To his right the Yankees were digging in along the railroad track. Already the position reminded him of the infamous Hornets Nest of Shiloh.

Turn on it, wipe it out completely, or push toward Frederick and leave Robertson behind, or order Robertson to echelon to the left and avoid it as well?

But battle was already joined. Robertson was sending his men straight in. He would have to leave him behind.

Beauregard pointed up the road toward Frederick, shouting for his own men to form and get back into the attack.

"Come on, boys, come on! We can still take them! Come on, move it!"

His two divisions started forward, not with the beautiful formation and élan of dawn. They had marched over six miles since they began and fought one pitched battle already, but nevertheless they went forward, heading toward the sound of the guns.

Relay Station
Ten Miles West of Baltimore

11:15 A.M.

Gen. George Sykes leaned out of the railroad car that served as his headquarters. On the parallel track an engine inched forward, railroad workers jumping off the flatcars they had been riding on, a team handing down several rails, eight men shouldering the rail and running forward.

"Two more breaks in the line, General, sir."

The yard boss, some Irishman by his brogue, gave a bit of an impertinent salute and ran forward with his men.

George stepped down from the car and walked forward. Behind him another train was easing to a stop, in front of the engine was a massive flatcar converted into a rolling fortress, an armored car they called it, the barrel of a thirty-pounder protruding from the iron-plated front.

A similar car was at the front of his own train and the one on the parallel track.

Ahead there was the rattle of skirmishing, some rebs visible on the track perhaps six hundred yards away, a marine detachment pushing them back.

Strange, all this, George thought as he leaned against the armored car to watch the laborers at work.

After surviving the debacle at Gunpowder River, he had assumed the few battered survivors of the Army of the Potomac would be disbanded and sent to other units, the name of that famed command stricken from the records forever.

Then had come the hand-delivered dispatch from the War Office, countersigned by Grant, specifically laying out a detailed plan that had stunned him.

He was to reorganize the survivors into a single corps, out of deference to him, the Fifth Corps. Units were to be banded together by the states they came from. The men would be resupplied, which they were, then told to rest and wait, which they did for five days.

And then word had come to prepare to move. The men had marched up to the Northeast River, ten miles back from the Susquehanna, to Charlestown. That night a flotilla of transport ships arrived, and the next morning they had steamed out, racing south.

Off the mouth of the Patapsco River at the entrance to Baltimore they had joined a second flotilla, this one actually commanded by Farragut himself, many of the ships having come up from the siege of Charleston. There were deepwater ships: transports crammed with marines and sailors converted to infantry, ironclads, and long flat barges carrying the trains he and some of his command now rode in.

Baltimore, contrary to expectations, had fallen with barely a shot being fired, except by the garrison at McHenry.

There had been some rioting, which the sailors were assigned to put down while he and his valiant few, his Army of the Potomac, reinforced by the marines, set off.

His first concern was that the rebs might blow up the huge stone viaduct at Relay Station. Thus once the armored cars and their locomotives were rolled off the trains at the dockyard and switched onto the Baltimore and Ohio's main line, he had set off. The charge by rail worked. Their arrival at dark sent the rebs scurrying back across the bridge, and dawn revealed that their commander, who he now learned was Lo Armistead, had indeed been trying to find enough powder to stuff up under one of the arches of the bridge to bring it down. Armistead had failed, and so they had been able to continue pushing west.

Today, though, had been frustratingly slow work. The rebs kept tearing up the track ahead, smashing switches. An armored car would be raced forward, firing its massive gun, and they'd scatter, pull back, and then resume their desperate work.

And yet they were moving forward, mile by mile. He knew his nickname, whispered behind his back, "Tardy George."

The hell with them. His tardiness, as some called it, was being methodical and, by God, he certainly was not tardy at Taneytown. If only Sickles had listened to him at Gunpowder River and gone a bit more slowly, this whole operation would be different now.

The yard boss stood up, waved his hand, indicating the rail was fixed. The engine vented steam and George walked back to the command car behind the locomotive, climbing aboard. During their stop a telegrapher had hooked into the line and handed George the latest news.

"Heavy fighting all along the line at Frederick. Grant."

There was no need to be told that. Whenever the train stopped all could hear the rumble in the distance.

The yard boss ran back aboard his own train on the parallel track, saw George, saluted again, then turned to one of his men, who reluctantly offered up a bottle out of his pocket.

"How much we paying that man?" George asked of one of his staff.

"Sixty a day."

"Damn, I don't even make that much. I don't even think the president himself makes that much."

"Well, sir, he said that's what the rebels paid him, and he did his utmost to play hell with them. He was the only one around, and he does good work. Almost everybody with the Military Railroad command are still up in Harrisburg or repairing the Cumberland line."

"More than the president," George mumbled.

The train moved forward, gaining a little speed. Through the window he could see where the rebels had torn off several rails, heated them, and then bent them around a telegraph pole. The train shifted slightly as it crossed over the patched section, rolled forward another half mile, then slowed again.

Another break, damn it.

It was slow, he knew, but it was relentless. On the road parallel to the track, infantry was marching forward, the shot-torn standard of the old Fifth Corps at the fore.

The Army of the Potomac was marching toward the battle. Slow as ever, perhaps, but it was in the field again—and looking for a fight.

Hunt's batteries were lost in clouds of smoke. It was impossible to see them other than by the flash of their guns. Grant looked back toward Frederick. McPherson's boys were up, forming at the edge of town, four thousand of them, but ready to refight a battle the way they had done two days ago, street by street.

Around Grant his staff was hurrying about, packing up map cases and field desks and piling equipment into the single wagon that served as his headquarters, now harnessed to a team, back end open. Several enlisted men started to drop his tent.

"Leave that be," Grant shouted. "It's not important now. Get mounted and ready to move."

The rebel charge was still coming forward, picking up momentum. Hunt was already flanked but still holding on. He was tempted to ride down to him, but decided against it.

I am not a corps commander. He had to force himself to remember it. *Nor even in command of a mere army.* The telegraph connection that was being taken down even now was his link to an elaborate operation on three fronts in Maryland as well as to Sherman down in Georgia; the battle directly before him was not his only concern.

And besides, if I go dashing about, that will infect everyone. It always does. Stay calm, stay calm.

The last of the headquarters gear was packed up. The telegraphy wagon was already on the move toward town.

He motioned for the headquarters wagon to set off, the driver looking back anxiously toward the rebs swarming up the road less than a quarter mile away now.

Ely led over Grant's horse and he mounted, making it a point to do nothing for a moment, taking the time to light a cigar.

He could see Ely was agitated. Miniés were zipping by.

He puffed on the cigar for a moment, watching them. Nodded and turned Cincinnatus.

Without a word he rode toward the town.

Chapter Eighteen

G en. Robert E. Lee reached the edge of the ford, several companies of cavalry deployed around him in a protective circle, carbines and pistols drawn.

The Union position here had just collapsed, nearly a thousand men taken prisoner, nearly all of them Ord's men, including General Ord himself, with a scattering of colored troops mixed in.

The ground was carpeted with bodies, ambulances from both sides now picking men up, six and seven to an ambulance, to be taken into the Confederate lines. Several surgeons were at work in the field, awnings set up, a vast sea of agony around them.

He spotted Jubal Early, standing by one of the tents, leaning on one of his staff, pants leg torn off just above the thigh, blood streaming down from his knee.

Lee rode up and dismounted, going to Jubal's side.

"I'm sorry to see you are hurt, sir," Lee said.

"Think I'll lose the leg," Jubal said weakly.

"Perhaps it will not prove to be that bad," Lee lied, a quick look down revealed that a bullet had shattered the poor man's kneecap. That he was even coherent at this point with such an agonizing wound was a mark of the man's strength.

"I've turned what's left of my division over to John Gordon," Jubal said, motioning toward the creek, "but sir, frankly, I no longer have a division. It is completely fought out."

"You did well this day, sir," Lee said, touching him lightly on the shoulder and then returned to Traveler and mounted.

The Union prisoners were slowly shuffling to the rear, many of them detailed to help carry wounded from both sides. It was a procession of agony, men crying, many in shock, some looking up at Lee in wonder, more than a few in defiance.

He saw a small number of black prisoners, with one white officer, being herded off to one side, the men surrounding them shoving with rifle butts and bayonet points. Lee went over to them.

"What is going on here?" he snapped.

A surprised sergeant looked up.

"Sergeant, what is your name?"

"Len Gardner, sir, Third Louisiana."

Lee turned to Walter.

"Note that name, Walter. Sergeant Gardner, if I hear of any accounts of abuse of prisoners I shall personally hold you responsible."

The group ducked down as an errant shell screamed overhead.

The white Union officer stood up first and stepped to Lee's side and saluted.

"Capt. Averall Heyward. Thank you, sir. I think they were getting set to execute us."

"That's a damn lie," Gardner cried.

Lee looked at Gardner and fixed him with a cold gaze.

"I tend to believe this officer's word over yours," Lee snapped.

"Captain, take your men, fall in with the other prisoners. You will be well treated. Walter, write down the following:

"I have spoken personally with the Union officer bearing this note. He shall report to me after the action of this day to inform me of any abuse dealt to him or any other man or officer serving with the United States Colored Troops."

Walter jotted down the note and handed the pad over. Lee signed it, tore the sheet of paper off, and handed it to the officer.

"As more colored prisoners come in, use this note to round them up and keep them with you. One of my staff will stay behind with you to insure all of you are treated properly. That note will serve as a pass to my headquarters after this battle is over as long as you give me your parole now not to try to escape."

"God bless you, sir," the captain replied and saluted. "And I give you my parole on my word of honor as an officer."

"And God be with you, Captain."

Lee turned and rode to the edge of the ford and then spotted Ord. The man was surrounded by several staff officers and a lone Confederate guard. He was wounded, hit in the arm, which was already in a sling. Lee approached him and dismounted.

"General, are you sorely hurt?" Lee asked.

Ord looked at Lee and actually grinned.

"Not as badly as your men are, sir. Pardon me, sir, but we gave you a hell of a fight here."

"That you did, General."

"We bled you out here. My boys put up a hell of a fight to the bitter end."

"You can be proud of them, General."

"Thank you, sir."

"A question, General. Are any of the colored troops with you?"

"No, they are with Sheridan."

"Sheridan?"

Ord grinned. "He took over Burnside's command two days ago. Maybe that explains why they are fighting so ferociously over there." Ord pointed toward the smoke-shrouded railroad cuts."

Lee remounted and rode off. He shook his head with anger.

"We must not lose our heads, our moral compass as an army. If our men start executing prisoners now, then we have indeed lost God's blessing at a time that we need it the most. It will bring shame to our entire cause."

Lee edged Traveler into the water. His mount wanted to drink but he would not let him, the water was so tainted with blood. He pushed across, staff following.

To his right, a quarter mile away, Robertson's Division was engaged in what was already being called the Hornets Nest. The railroad cuts for the Baltimore and Ohio had been turned into bastions. He could not see the fight from here. There was too much smoke, but the air was alive with bullets zipping and screaming overhead.

He paused and watched it with frustration. Taking that position now did not serve the plan. It was Frederick and the pass over the mountains that Beauregard should have focused on.

"Walter, send someone in there. Find Robertson. Order him to report to me now. I will be up on the road."

Several staff, escorted by a half dozen troopers, rode off.

He turned and continued up the field. Several of his escorts dropped from their saddles as they rode up the hill, weaving past a hospital area for the black troops. He detailed off another staff officer to stay with the hospital, bearing the same orders he had given on the other side of the stream.

They crossed over the killing ground of the corner field, raced over the railroad tracks and up to the Buckeystown Road. Again chaos, wounded by the hundreds staggering back, fence rails down, crops trampled, a farmhouse on fire, wounded being pulled from inside even as it burned.

Turning onto the road he now saw the rear of Beauregard's divisions, pushing up, ranks thinned, a terrible bombardment striking into them.

Lee clenched his fist in frustration. Not against the guns. Not another Malvern Hill.

He wanted to go forward, but Walter rebelled, pushing in front of him.

"Sir, I am sorry, sir, but I cannot let you ride into that inferno."

Lee hesitated. Walter was right. The battle now hung by a thread, the orders he had so often given to his beloved generals, to stand back, to manage the fight, to not go into the middle of it, had to apply now to him, too.

"Send some men up there," Lee snapped. "Find Beauregard. Bring him back to me now!"

12:10 P.M.

 "Feed it to them! There they are! Feed it to them!" Hunt cried.

Gun after gun recoiled, sending deadly sprays of canister downrange to the rebel lines in the corn and grass, and they were returning fire. The ground ahead was a killing ground, casualties piled up by the hundreds, his gunners hard at work in the last fifteen minutes, following his order to retreat by recoil. After firing, the pieces were not rolled forward, but were loaded in place, the elevation checked, and another canister round was blasted down the field. But canister was running short, many of the crews changing over to case shot cut with a half-inch fuse, blowing as they barely cleared the barrel. Those out of canister were converting back to solid bolts, the shock of one of those bolts passing through the ranks causing the enemy to scatter even if it struck down only one or two.

They were bleeding McLaw out, and his men were shouting with rage, sweeping the position with rifle fire, a good third of Hunt's gunners now down.

He took a deep breath.

"Hook up trail lines, retire by fire!"

Caissons were backed up, cables run out to the trail pieces of the guns. A piece would fire, and the caisson crew would urge their horse forward a dozen paces while the crew reloaded, then the gun would fire again.

It was only a matter of time before they were overrun. Rebel infantry was swarming about both flanks, horses were going down, stalling pieces in place, desperate crews trying to push their pieces back by hand, but they were still firing, holding them back.

"Feed it to 'em. God damn 'em. Feed it to 'em."

With Lee

12:30 P.M.

P. G. T. Beauregard came riding up, sweat streaming down his face in the humid heat, hat off, and Lee braced himself inwardly for the confrontation.

"General," Lee said, "my orders to you last night I thought were clearly understood. Cross at the ford, establish contact, deploy, then sweep due north into the town and take it."

"Sir, it is not that easy," Beauregard replied. "If I had waited for McLaw and Robertson, we'd have wasted another hour, maybe two. I felt it was important to strike hard and fast."

"You hit without waiting. All four divisions at once, backed by a battalion and a half of artillery and a brigade from Jeb, should have overrun them in the first strike. Besides, you have let your command split. One division is wasted now containing that pocket down by the river."

"There is an entire corps trapped down there," Beauregard replied. "Destroy them and Grant's final offensive power is gone."

"It is costing far too much. You should have advanced, echelon to the north, aiming at Frederick. That and the road are the prize."

"It is too late to call back Robertson now; he is too hotly engaged, and his action protects my right flank."

"And the guns," Lee replied sharply. "Why are you sending McLaw straight at their guns?"

"That's all of Hunt's batteries up there, sir. Without infantry support. We take them and we cripple Grant."

"Sir," Lee said stonily, "you have lost focus. You are caught in the mo-

ment. Four of your divisions, angling toward Frederick, would have caused Grant to abandon the entire line, and I could have brought in Longstreet and Hood efficiently. Now we are split apart."

"So should I withdraw?" Beauregard asked sarcastically. "We have them on the run."

"No, you will not withdraw, but, sir, I am taking command here."

"Am I relieved, sir?"

Lee hesitated. If it had been nearly anyone else, he would have done so. But these were Beauregard's men, new to the Army of Northern Virginia.

"No, sir, you are not relieved, but I shall now ride with you. I want your men to echelon to the left and drive for the pass. I expect that within the hour. Now go see to your duty and we shall win this fight, regardless of loss."

Railroad Cut

12:30 P.M.

This was beyond anything he had ever imagined war to be. There was no place for the wounded; they lay where they fell. All were deafened by the slapping roar of the Napoleon whose crew had expended all their canister and case shot and was now reduced to firing solid shot, aiming low so that the ball would strike in front of the rebel infantry, kicking up a spray of ballast and splintered railroad tie, which hit with deadly impact.

If not for the barrier, all within the cut would have been swept away. The worst casualties were up on the slopes of the ravine, the men exposed to fire from the flanks even as they fought to keep back the rebels circling in from both sides. Men of several regiments were mingled together at the barricade, some of them whites from the next division who had brought up more ammunition and decided to stay.

"Granddaddy was at Oriskany," one of them kept saying with a grin. "It was like this. Injuns just circling all around, whoopin' and hollerin'."

Several times the rebs surged to within yards of the cut, threatening to push the men on the lip back down. If that happened, it was over, but the men had held them back, the rebs going to ground.

"Raining, thank God," someone announced.

Washington looked up, felt a few soft splashes on his face, a light drizzle—cooling, a true relief.

12:35 P.M.

CSA Grim, near to shaking with fear, Sergeant Hazner kept low, back in the same gully he had been in the day before when the train exploded. They had been ordered down from their dug-in position an hour ago, to try to force the ruined bridge or, at the very least, to enfilade the railroad cut just west of the depot. A few had made a valiant rush onto the ruined bridge, jostling across broken ties, then trying to catwalk across the stringers in the midsection. Not one had made it.

So they had settled down to a steady, raging fire, adding to the smoke and confusion. The artillery above them pounded the opposite position. The blockhouse, which had guarded the entry into the cut, had finally collapsed in on itself after repeated hits, but even in the ruins the Yankees hung on, firing back.

Men were dropping, but no ground was being gained, no advantage to be found, just a steady wearing down by both sides until finally exhaustion, lack of ammunition, or the fact that there was no one left to fight would decide it.

Headquarters, Army of the Susquehanna

12:40 P.M.

US Grant stood at the edge of town, field glasses raised. The town was directly behind him. McPherson's boys were hard at work, piling up barricades across the streets at the south edge of town.

Looking up toward the pass, he saw only a few wagons coming down. He had ordered all wagons to stay on the far side of the mountain except those bearing small-arms ammunition or artillery rounds.

A few shells were winging over toward the road, fired from a rebel battery deployed out on the left of their line. It was very long-distance fire, but nevertheless an indicator of what would be coming.

Banks's support division was up, filing in with McPherson's men.

Every regiment was now engaged, or soon would be. He had no reserves left. Banks's men up by the National Road were now reporting an assault supposedly led by Longstreet and backed by a dozen or more batteries.

Lee was indeed pushing all out.

Down below he could see the first of Hunt's guns coming back, drivers lashing their exhausted horses, emerging out of the smoke. The artillery fire within the smoke was slackening.

More guns came out, bouncing across the fields, and then he spotted Hunt. He sent a staffer down to lead him in.

Hunt looked like he had come out of a blast furnace, uniform scorched, face bleeding from a blistered burn, an eye nearly swollen shut.

"Sir, beg to report, I had to pull the guns back. We were getting flanked on both sides and nearly out of ammunition. By God, we emptied everything we had into them."

"You did fine, Hunt, held them up an hour or more."

"What a slaughter, sir, never seen anything like it. Worse than Malvern Hill, Gettysburg even. But they just kept coming. No ammunition left. We've been firing continually since just after dawn. I'm sorry, just couldn't get ammunition up fast enough . . ."

He bent double, breathing hard, and Grant remembered this man was still recovering from the typhoid.

"Get your guns to the far side of town. Post them up to guard the road to the pass."

"Yes, sir."

Grant walked back and forth along the street that led down to Buckeystown, men to either side of him dragging out tables, fence rails, a busted-up sofa with its owner, behind the two men, howling in protest, anything that could stop a bullet.

A light drizzle was coming down, pleasant at first, cooling, actually cutting the smoke down a bit.

He could see them. They had stopped for the moment, positioned just north of where his headquarters had been. He took out his field glasses and in the diminishing smoke could make out some details.

Three divisions. The one that had overrun Hunt, on the right, reforming ranks. The second, to the left, the third moving behind the second to reinforce their left. It was taking time, valuable time. Their guns were moving up the road, going ahead of the infantry and swinging out into an open field. In a few minutes they would start shelling him.

He turned to look out across the rest of the field. The Hornets Nest was an inferno. Rebs had it completely surrounded but so far had not closed in for the kill. If anyone would hold it to the end it would be Sheridan. It was tying up a lot of the Confederates. *Those men should be focusing here,* he realized.

To his left gunfire raged along the northern flank. Rebs were across the river just below the National Road, trading long-distance volleys with Banks's men. The rebs had moved a lot of artillery support up on that flank and were heavily pounding the infantry guarding the bridge, perhaps in preparation for a frontal assault directly across.

Grant took it all in. Lee's attack had degenerated into three separate uncoordinated fights.

He could afford to lose the center completely, even if not one man came back from Ninth Corps; they had more than traded their numbers. Banks's fight was almost a different battle, without coordination on their own left. The guns trapped on the far side, if moved over in support of the main attack, might make a difference, for his own artillery had been worn down to exhaustion.

No, it was going to be here, right here, today, that it would be decided. The three Confederate divisions deploying out, forming up. *They just might knock me back and secure the Catoctin Road.*

He had already decided that if the road was threatened, he would not try to pull back over it. That would turn retreat to utter rout. He'd order the supply wagons on the far side to turn about and evacuate back to Hagerstown, while he extracted the army to the north, following the pike up toward Middleburg and Taneytown.

That would draw Lee after him, even while Sykes came up and Hancock, in his turn, threatened Lee's rear. At some point the combined weight of his three converging forces would outweigh Lee, no matter what happened here in the next few hours.

He felt calm, and he tried to convey that calmness even as the legions below him continued their intricate maneuvers, shifting an entire division to the left of the assault. The first of their guns opened up, solid shot winging in, smashing into buildings at the edge of the town, brick flying, windows shattering.

All he could do now was wait.

With Lee

1:00 P.M.

 Patience, he thought. *Patience, just a few more minutes to get it right.*

Lee remained silent, watching as Beauregard's Division that had been down on the right flank filed behind their comrades drawn up a couple of hundred yards ahead. The maneuver was relatively easy. They had already been formed into battle line, so it was simply a matter of having them face left and start marching. But over a mile of ground had to be

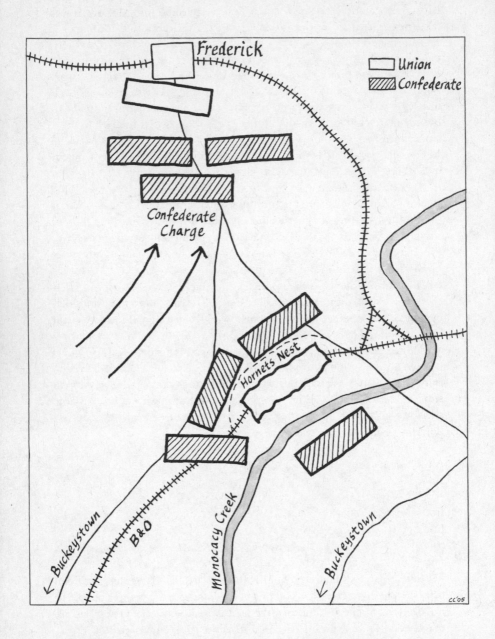

covered, over hillocks, through half-trampled corn, pushing over ground devastated by the Yankee artillery that had smashed into McLaw. It was taking time, and the men were tired.

The other divisions had advanced slightly, in echelon to the left, meaning that as they moved they did not advance straight ahead, but rather at a forty-five-degree angle to the left.

Lee was still on the road, Beauregard by his side. The man was fuming, embarrassed that the general commanding had seen fit to come down here to take direct control of his men.

"I still wish we had more," Lee announced and he looked back to where Robertson's men were attempting to storm the railroad cuts. Scales had yet to get across on the other side.

"I ordered Robertson to break off an hour ago," Lee snapped. "He should be coming up."

He turned and looked at Walter.

"Perhaps the message didn't get through," Walter offered.

"Then send another."

"Sir, might it not be too late now?" Beauregard offered. "That will take another hour."

Lee looked over at Beauregard and reluctantly had to agree. It was indeed too late now to bring Robertson up, and even if he did, after so many hours of protracted fighting, Robertson would need several hours to rest and refit his men before going into another assault.

"Walter, get another courier down there. Tell Robertson, if he feels he is on the edge of a decisive breakthrough, to go ahead. Otherwise he is to stop the attack. Those people down there are pinned and it is useless to shed more blood trying to dig them out. We can take care of them after we defeat Grant and seize the town."

The long, sinuous column of troops marching behind Lee stopped. All up and down the line they turned and faced right, poised for a straight-in assault on the town about a mile ahead.

The formation was at last as he wanted it. Two divisions wide in the front. Two brigades of each division forward, a third brigade deployed two hundred yards to the rear.

The secondary line, three brigades wide, deployed two hundred yards farther back, behind the reserves of the first line. The guns ahead were keeping up a steady fire into the town with hardly a Yankee gun firing in return.

He wished he could see Longstreet having broken through on the other side, the bridge there taken, his men closing in on Grant from the other side, but there was precious little movement, other than those troops who had forded the stream below the bridge but were being held back.

He could not wait any longer. The tattoo of rain was beginning to pick up. It did not look as if a downpour was approaching, but if it came down any harder, in a few hours movement might be difficult.

He turned in his saddle and his heart swelled.

So it had come down finally to this: a grand assault, in the old tradition of the great charge, to finish the battle. He had broken their right, pinned their center. There were no more reserves for Grant.

Grant's men must be exhausted, all the more so after the pounding and pullback.

Flags were held up all up and down the line. Three divisions, perhaps upward of eighteen thousand men, shoulder to shoulder.

It had all come to this, Gettysburg, Union Mills, Washington, Gunpowder River. *One more charge, one more glorious charge and we break them forever and the war is won.*

· *Win this charge and the enemy behind me will be but an annoyance to sweep away. The men down by the river are trapped. We destroy Grant this day and three days hence we will be in Washington, the war won.*

He thought of Arlington. *I could be home in two weeks.*

He thought of Shakespeare, *Henry V. Yes, indeed, this might be our Saint Crispin's Day.*

Like Napoleon at Borodino the moment had come to break the enemy by frontal assault.

Jeb Stuart was by his side, hat off, grinning.

"General Stuart, you will command the left of this assault. Remember it is echelon to the left, keep obliquing to the left to flank the edge of the town and secure the road. General Beauregard, the right division will go into the town."

"Sir, I object," Beauregard replied haughtily. "Stuart is commanding my division, and I am commanding men I do not even know."

"Sir, it is either that way," Lee said testily, "or I shall command it myself."

"Yes, sir," Beauregard replied carefully.

"I will be with the Third Division and commit them to one of you or the other. Do we understand each other?"

"Yes, sir," Jeb said with a flourish, removing his hat. Beauregard simply nodded.

"I am not one for theatrics before the troops, gentlemen," Lee said quietly. "Now go forward!"

Jeb let loose with a wild rebel yell and galloped across the field, his actions a signal that the attack, the attack that would win them this war, was going forward. Beauregard trotted straight up the road.

Drummer boys were up, and began to tap out the long roll. Regimental officers, those still surviving from the earlier fight, stepped forward, extolling their men.

Several minutes later the left division stepped off, Stuart actually out front, waving his hat.

Lee took off his hat and lowered his head.

"Into thy hands, O Lord, I commend my spirit and the future of our cause. Thy will be done."

Headquarters, Army of the Susquehanna

Here they come! My God, look at 'em, like on parade!"

Men gathered about Grant were up, pointing. The light rain had washed the air of some of the smoke and all could now see a division advancing toward their right. A few minutes later a second division emerged, and then, as if guided by a single hand, the entire advancing line turned and obliqued to their own left, shifting the center of the advance more to the west side of town.

Grant watched silently, nodding with approval at the precision of the movement. They were working to flank him, pull him back farther from the embattled men down at the Hornets Nest, working to envelop the road up to the Catoctin Pass.

"Tell Banks's Division to leave the center of town and shift northwest," Grant announced, not looking back as someone galloped off with the news.

He had fifteen minutes, maybe twenty, before the storm hit. The men barricading the streets, the entrances into the town, had stopped in their labors for a few minutes to watch the approaching wave, but now returned to work with determination, ignoring the shot that still screamed into the town, detonating against buildings, setting a house afire, smashing through eaves, brick walls, and passing clean through clapboarded homes.

The few civilians who had come down to watch did not need to be told what to do. They were fleeing in panic. One hysterical mother was screaming for her son. A couple of soldiers, laughing, pulled the boy down from his perch in the branches of a tree and handed him, kicking and screaming, to his mother, who ran off, dragging the boy with one hand and slapping him with the other.

"As terrible as an army with banners . . ." Ely whispered, coming up to Grant's side.

Grant bit the end off another cigar, cupped his hands to light it, and said nothing.

The Hornets Nest

U.S. "Here they come, boys!"

Phil Sheridan was up among them, having come over on foot from the next cut.

Bartlett did not need to be told. This time they were charging straight in at the run. Men leaned in against the barricade. The gunners, out of all ammunition, pulled out pistols, drew short sabers, or hefted ramrods.

C.S.A. Robinson pushed his men forward, scarcely believing what they were about to do. A few minutes before, a lone courier had come up to Robertson, the division commander, shouting that General Lee wanted him to disengage or finish the position. The courier had then questioned him about the previous couriers.

None had arrived, Robertson shouted. He turned, looked at the Hornets Nest, and then pointed straight at it.

"Let's finish this now!" Robertson shouted. "Are we gonna let it be said that a bunch of darkies beat us?"

A terrible roar went up in response.

Robinson shook his head. They had been fought to a standstill. A rumor was coming down the line that Lee himself was about to lead the assault on the center of town to finish Grant. *Shouldn't we be there?* he wondered. *Is there any purpose to this slaughter here other than us killing each other like animals in a frenzy?*

But the charge went forward, and, dutifully, he went forward with it. The charge rushed the barricade that was heaped with the fallen from the two previous attacks. Flashes of gunfire rippled on the other side. Robertson was actually in the lead, on foot, pointing forward, and one of the first to gain the top of the barricade.

"Come on!" he screamed and jumped over to the other side.

Robinson slammed in against the side of the barricade, looked up over it, caught sight of a man not ten feet away, and dropped him. Sliding back down, he reloaded. He came back up, men pushing up around him, and was up and over the barricade. In the narrow confines of the railroad cut, it was no longer combat, it was a primal act of murder on both sides. All the hatreds of the war, the causes, the fears, played out. He saw Robertson lunging for a regimental flag, a black sergeant major clubbing him down. Robinson started for the sergeant major, almost was in reach, the black sergeant major turning to face him, screaming with rage, then was shoved back as the man in front of him was bayoneted.

Men were trampled underfoot, screaming, the fighting surging back and forth.

On the Catoctin Road

US **H**enry Hunt stood with raised field glasses, watching the advance. He felt he would sell his soul now for a dozen limber wagons. His batteries were wearily coming up the long slope, nearly all with empty ammunition chests, and then, as if in answer to his unholy prayer, a couple of canvas-topped wagons came over the ridge and started to slide down pavement that was increasingly slippery from the rain.

In the back of each wagon were two limber chests, a total of two hundred rounds of three-inch ammunition, solid bolts, case shot, and a few rounds of canister.

He ordered two of his batteries to stop, unlimber, and runners to begin fetching the ammunition. It wasn't much, but he could certainly put down one hell of an enfilade into the left of the advancing rebel line. After several minutes, his first gun kicked back with a sharp recoil. He was still in the fight.

C.S.A **R**obert E. Lee nodded to the commander of the third division in the assault. The man turned, stood in his stirrups, and pointed forward.

The wave of men set forward and as ordered did their first oblique to the left. Lee rode by their flank as they advanced, staff and cavalry escort around him.

No rifle fire yet from the other side; the head of the advance was not more than six hundred yards from the town. His heart swelled. This could be his Austerlitz, the one battle spoken of so often at the Point. The climactic battle of decision. He could sense it now. All the fighting of the previous two months had at last led to this moment.

"Sir, we'd better get back," Ely announced.

The advancing wall of rebs was now just four hundred yards off.

Grant reluctantly nodded, deliberately pacing parallel to his line for a hundred feet so that the men would see him, then climbed up over a barricade blocking a street. These were McPherson's boys. Tough-looking, more than one with a bandaged head or arm, and they looked angry, damn angry.

"McPherson!" Someone screamed. "Remember McPherson!"

The cry was picked up, racing across the front, and it sent a shiver down Grant's spine. Even in death that young hero still led.

It was hard to gain a vantage here to watch the fight or direct it. One of the problems of defending a town was that units were impossible to control once they were into the streets. He was anxious, though, about going to the west side of town. If by chance Lee did seize the town, he'd be cut off from what was left of his command if he was to the west of it.

Ely had already found a place, leading him back one block to the burned-out depot on the east side of town. The telegraphy link there had been reestablished, and to his amazement several reporters were gathered round clamoring for some time on it, one of them from the *New York Tribune*. At his approach they turned and started to shout questions.

He ignored them and followed Ely up a flight of stairs in a burned-out warehouse. Part of the second floor was intact and from there he had an excellent view of the entire assault coming in and the sweep of battle to the east as well.

The Hornets Nest was completely hidden by smoke; to the northeast Banks, to his disgust, had conceded the National Road bridge, but at least was holding the ground above it a couple of hundred yards back. The rebs seemed reluctant to cross, however, for a battery of Napoleons was pounding any who tried to cross.

The rebel advance was down to a couple of hundred yards. Some of the rebels were no longer visible, the buildings before him blocking the view.

A spattering of fire erupted from the edge of the town and then a torrent as regiments stood up from concealment and opened up. The impact staggered the rebel advance, which slowed across a division-wide front, and then thousands of rifles were raised up, then lowered, and a tearing explosion ripped across the plain. A couple of seconds later bits of charred wood and shattered brick exploded around Grant, the reporters and hangers-on down in the street below ducking at the sound.

The fight was now truly on as the rebel's second division, on their left,

advanced another fifty yards, slowed, stopped, and fired into Banks's reserve division, catching some in the flank as they continued to file out of
the town.

Within a minute, all ahead was cloaked in smoke, explosions flashing,
huzzahs and rebel yells echoing. Never had he witnessed anything like
this. Never. Smoking his cigar, hands in his pockets, he waited for the
fight to play itself out.

1:30 P.M.

Lee continued to ride with the advancing division, ignoring
the protests of Walter and others. The charge ahead was
stalled; the men had opened fire too soon. Regardless of their losses they
should have pressed in to fifty yards or less before firing. Through the
smoke he could dimly see where hundreds were falling.

"Straight in, boys!" Lee shouted, and he stood in his stirrups, pointing
now to the western edge of the town and the open field beyond.

"Straight in at the double, and remember—home, boys, home is just
on the other side of that town!"

He spurred Traveler forward, and with this movement the rebel yell
tore down the line, men held rifles up, flags tilted forward, and the charge
to cover the last three hundred yards was on.

Traveler suddenly jerked around as if hit, and Lee felt an instant of
terror. Their bond was close, going back years, and in so many fights his
comrade had never been scratched.

It was Walter, leaning over, jerking Traveler's reins, pulling his head to
one side, causing him to slow and stop.

Lee glared at Walter.

"Let go of me!"

"No, sir."

"That is an order!"

"No, sir! Court-martial me after this is over, sir, but no. Your place now
is here, sir!"

The cavalry escort had pushed in around Walter, many staring straight
at Lee, a few too frightened to do so.

"Listen to him, please, sir," one of them shouted, and that brought on
a chorus of agreements for Walter.

Lee found himself suddenly in tears, tears of pride for the gallant men
streaming past him, shouting his name as they charged, for the sight of
the flag, his flag, held high, disappearing into the smoke, the sight of Jeb

Stuart, hat off, waving it high, urging the men forward, even for Walter and the love he showed at this moment.

He lowered his head, nodded.

"You are right, Walter,"

Walter sighed, tears welling up.

"Sir, forgive me. But if we lose you, we lose the cause."

"No, Walter," Lee replied, "the cause is being decided now, by them."

He pointed toward the wall of men surging forward.

In his heart he knew this was the highwater mark. If they could wash over it, all would be won. If not . . . he dared not think of it at this moment.

Behind him, guns were already hitched up, beginning to roll forward, ready to support the breakthrough, the lead piece coming up, slowing, waiting for the infantry ahead to surge into the town and beyond.

1:35 P.M.

C.S.A. All across that front, men of Florida and Alabama, men of Virginia and Arkansas, sensed the moment. They could see it in Lee as they charged forward; they could see it in that gallant cavalier, Jeb Stuart, shouting wildly, waving them on. They could see victory.

Some had been marching since First Manassas or the Peninsula, fought a dozen battles, waded the Potomac many times, and then in June, with such high hopes, had those hopes fulfilled at Union Mills, when final victory was within their grasp. So many, far, far too many comrades who had marched with them, were gone . . . and now the moment of final reckoning.

Others had marched in the West and had known one bitter defeat after another; others had come from Charleston, where the war had dragged on through days of scorching heat and sweltering nights, all to join this legendary and victorious army.

Lee was right, his cry echoing down the line, home, home was just on the other side of this town.

The charge rolled forward, pushing into the reserve ranks of the lines before them, men exhorting each other on, screaming to go, to go, to keep going forward. The reserves joined them, swarming into the main volley line, tripping and leaping over the bodies of hundreds who had fallen in the initial exchange.

"Come on! Charge!"

The wild enthusiasm spread, sweeping the entire front. Once twenty-five thousand before dawn, then eighteen thousand, now barely sixteen thousand, they began to race forward, a tidal wave, officers caught up in the maelstrom, flags of regiments mingling together, an ocean of armed men bent on victory.

At the barricades, in the ruined houses facing the charge, in the field west of town, Banks's men, tough fighters all, regardless of their dandy leader, saw it coming. They were nearly all from the West and had never known defeat. Or when defeated, they had believed in their hearts it was but a setback of the moment, and tomorrow would set it right.

This was tomorrow. Stand here and it is over. Run and you might live, but run here and there will be another tomorrow in which you will have to face it again or, worse, live out your life wishing you had stood but a few minutes longer.

Officers, some behind, but many now stepping out in front of the men, shouted and pleaded, "Hold, boys! You got to hold! Reload, let 'em get close. Reload!"

Several flag bearers stepped out of the ranks, holding tattered standards aloft, shouting for the men to stay with them, to not leave the colors, and the ranks surged forward a few feet to rally round those colors.

Ramrods were worked down fouled barrels, rifles then raised, some fixing bayonets.

"Hold fire, boys. You'll have one good shot. Hold fire!"

The wall was a hundred yards off, now breaking into a run, the ground thundering at their approach, men standing wide-eyed, officers shouting, a few throwing down rifles and turning to run, the rest ignoring them.

"Hold now, boys. Hold!"

"McPherson!"

"Hold!"

A few more seconds.

"Take aim!"

Nearly five thousand rifles were leveled, men crowding round each other, those few still in ranks presenting, the second rank leaning in between those in front, in most places just crowds of men behind barricades or individuals leaning out of shattered windows and doorways, the metallic sound of thousands of hammers being cocked back.

Those in the front rank could see it, that strange illusion when a volley line presented directly in front of you and it looked as if every single rifle was aimed at you, so close you could see the open muzzle, the eye squinting down the sight. Some slowed, hesitated, others crouched low, as if bending into a storm, those who tried to slow, now pushed on by the mob surging forward behind them.

F ire!"

N early five thousand one-ounce minié balls snapped across the intervening ground in little more than a tenth of a second. Many went high, but many, so many, came in low, hitting legs, stomachs, chests, arms, heads. For a blessed few there was nothingness, that final split second of sight, of looking at the man about to kill you, or gazing down, seeing grass, a clump of weeds, a flower, or a dreamlike vision of home, of someone waiting, a child running toward you . . . and then whatever it was that waited beyond the nothingness.

For many there were a few seconds, a tumbling backward, a collapsing forward, a few more pumps of the heart, a chance perhaps to realize that this world was finished, it was goodbye, goodbye to summer evenings, to the touch of a girl's lips, the embrace of a mother, the laughter of friends, the pleasure of a Southern evening under the stars.

For many more it was numbness, a falling down, if blessed, no pain in those first seconds, just a numbness, then a mad tearing at a jacket, knowing you were hit, but not sure where. *God, don't let it be the stomach. Take a leg,* they would bargain now, *I can lose a leg, not the stomach.* And they would feebly tear at their clothes to see where the hole was.

Yet for others there was pain, the terrible grinding agony of a thighbone shattering, collapsing, splinters of bone tearing through flesh and uniform, an arm flying back as if pulled by a giant behind them, the elbow shattered, hand nearly torn off, jawbone shot away.

It wasn't just bullets that did this. A musket stock of the man in front would be blown off and spin into another man's face, breaking his jaw, parts of other men's bodies would punch into the those following, canteens, tin cups, cartridge boxes, twisted rifles, broken swords, pieces of shoes, belt buckles, all these became deadly projectiles as well, showering back into the third, fourth, and fifth ranks.

The entire charge staggered. For so many cheering wildly but seconds before, all thought of cause, of glory, of victory, was gone. The world had focused down to them, to them alone. To the hole in the body they were staring at numbly, to a frantic tearing at a breast pocket to pull out a Bible, the letter of a sweetheart, the daguerreotype of a child, for at such a moment, that was truly all that mattered anymore, all thoughts of rights and wrongs, of what had taken them a thousand miles to this place . . . forgotten.

And yet, though fifteen hundred or more had fallen, there were over fourteen thousand still surging in.

Regardless of the thrust of those pushing in from behind, it took terrible long seconds for the charge to continue forward. Men had to push around the fallen, the dying, the blinded men screaming, dropping weapons and turning to stagger back, and for nearly every man down there was another in shock, reaching down to support a falling brother, a beloved friend, a favorite officer, or just coming to a numbed stop, their face covered in blood from the man in front of them.

"Come on! Keep moving! Come on!"

The charge surged up over the dead, wounded, shocked, and dying and pushed forward, but those few precious seconds gave the defenders the chance to start to reload. Most of them veterans, they glared defiantly at the rebs pushing in, even as they poured powder, slammed ball down barrel, some now just thrusting ramrods into the ground or against a barricade, cocking the piece, pulling out the percussion cap.

There was no time for orders now, no measured volley. Madness on both sides was taking hold, but several thousand completed the mad race, some now firing so close that the discharges burned the men in front of them. Hardly a shot could miss at this range, some of the rebels absorbing five and six bullets. Those up in the second floor of buildings merely had to aim down into the seething mass.

Thousands more collapsed literally at the edge of town, and then the charge was upon them.

Rebels swarmed over the barricades, screaming insanely, aiming and firing down at their tormentors. Men behind the barricades lashed out with musket butts, some swinging them like clubs, catching their foes across legs and knees, breaking bones, the injured collapsing back.

There were bayonet thrusts, pistol shots, shouts, oaths, curses, hurrahs, men fired into faces not five feet away. None now really knew what he was fighting for, other than the raw primal instinct of survival. All speeches, all talk of causes, of rights, of freedom, of land, of honor, of who had wronged who were forgotten by these nineteen- and twenty-year-old boys swept into a nightmare not of their making, a nightmare that they would enact.

If there was any sense beyond the immediate, it was a vague consciousness that somehow, for some reason, at this moment, what they did would finish it forever, one way or the other, and those not yet into the melee were driven forward by that thought, that and the hysteria that sweeps all men being sucked inexorably into the hurricane of battle.

CSA Jeb Stuart was down, horse riddled by a half dozen bullets, sending him flying forward, a fall that saved his life, for at least a dozen more rounds were aimed straight at him. As he pitched forward one round tore open his left sleeve, another creased his brow, a third struck a uniform button over his stomach at an angle, and painfully drove it in, but barely breaking the flesh.

He laid there semiconscious, troopers dismounting around their beloved "cavalier."

Beauregard had stepped back in the last hundred yards, letting the charge sweep past him. Dismounted, he stood silent, watching the slaughter. The fight was now beyond anything he could ever control. If victorious now, he would go in; if defeated, he would fall back to confront Lee.

Farther back, Lee stood silent, head bowed in prayer.

"Please give them strength, Lord, please give them strength," he kept repeating over and over.

US Another wagon had come up over the pass, this one loaded down with, hope beyond hope, cases of canister rounds. They were prepackaged straight from the factory in Troy, New York, having only been cast and made the day before yesterday, the railroad bringing them through Harrisburg straight from the factory—tin can, serge powder bag attached to the can containing fifty iron balls, each one inside a wooden tube ready to be transferred into a standard limber box. Hunt shouted for one of his batteries still mounted to turn around, and leading the way, he raced back toward Frederick, six three-inch ordnance rifles behind him and the wagon driver, terrified to be heading into the storm. A gunner had climbed up alongside the mule driver, grinning, telling him that he had just joined the artillery and would be shot if he slowed down.

Grant, hands still in pockets, continued to stand silent. It was impossible now to see with all the smoke, the steady drizzle of rain.

His lips suddenly felt warm, and he reached up to his cigar and burned his fingers. In his agitation he had smoked it clean down to the stub. He spat it out, fished for another in his pocket, and swore. The silver case was gone, most likely dropped on the retreat into the town.

Ely came up, offered a cigar, a reserve he always carried for the general, and lit it. No one spoke. Even the reporters down in the street were silent, all looking south.

CSA The wall of men had broken across the front of the town into six funnels, swarms of men, all formation lost, pushing against the barricades across the six streets facing south, barricades giving way under the sheer pressure, while up in the buildings Union troopers were firing away frantically, five and six men loading for one man at a window, until he dropped and another stepped up to take his place.

To the left, at the edge of the town, Banks's Division was buckling back. The charge was already across the pike that led to Harpers Ferry and now beginning to approach their goal: the pike over the Catoctin Mountains. Victory was in sight.

Jeb was back up on his feet, staggering like a drunk, not yet aware that he was suffering from a concussion and a broken wrist, but turning about, shouting for a horse, screaming for the infantry to go forward, for the cavalry to turn oblique and to start swarming up the National Road to take out the Yankee artillery that was enfilading them with such deadly effect.

One barricade in the center fell, the next one to the left collapsed, Union troops giving back, a swarming wall of rebs pouring over, battle flags to the front, and beginning to push into the town.

US They're breaking through," someone announced.

Grant ignored the comment. Wounded were trickling back, a few cowards running, but the provost guards did not bother with them; they had been ordered into the fight as well.

I have no more reserves, Grant realized, *and yet . . . my God, what a price Lee is paying for this.*

There was a clatter of hooves in the street below, and he walked to the edge of his precarious ledge and looked down. It was a battery of guns, three-inch ordnance rifles, Hunt in the lead. At each street corner one gun was being detailed off, unlimbered, men swarming around a canvas-topped wagon at the rear of the formation, unloading boxes.

Hunt rode to the warehouse, looked up at Grant, and saluted.

"Hundred rounds of canister!" Hunt shouted.

Grant nodded and actually grinned.

"Good work, Henry! Good work!"

Hunt positioned a gun directly below Grant, pointing due south, then shouted for the last gun to cut down an alleyway to the next street and position.

Looking down the street, Grant could see where the rebel charge was over the barrier, only a block away, beginning to fight its way up the street.

"Sir, we had better get ready to pull back again," Ely announced.

Grant said nothing, heading for the shattered stairs and back out onto the street.

The reporters who had been shouting questions were long gone, except for one, the *Tribune*'s man, who was silent, wide-eyed, looking down the street. The telegraphy crew had left their station, drawing pistols as they ran out of the building. Grant's staff, standing about in the ruins of the depot, waited for the order to mount up and evacuate the town.

He said nothing, going to Hunt's side.

"I can hold them," Hunt gasped.

"You'd better," was all Grant could say in reply.

The terrified wagon driver reined in behind the gun, the crew reaching into the back, pulling out boxes of canister rounds, one of the gunners tearing the wooden shipping lid off, slipping out the tin can and cartridge.

"Double canister!" Hunt shouted.

A second wooden cylinder was opened, the serge bag torn off. The first charge went down the barrel, the second can then rammed down on top.

The sergeant in command of the piece plunged a pick through the touchhole tearing open the powder bag within, fished into the primer bag at his side, pulled out a friction primer, set it in the touchhole, hooked the lanyard on, and stepped back.

"Stand clear!"

He drew the lanyard taut and waited. The road ahead was still packed with Union men, fighting hand-to-hand with the rebels surging forward.

C.S.A. The charge was up all six streets leading into Frederick, and Lee could see that on the left, his primary goal had all but been reached. Part of Beauregard's Second Division had indeed swarmed over the Catoctin Road. Jeb's troopers were on to the road. Their mounts were blown, but they appeared ghostlike to be rising out of the mist, pushing upwards. If not for the Yankee artillery blocking the way, they'd be to the top within minutes.

What I wouldn't give right now for one more fresh division, he thought. *One division to support Jeb and to flank the town.*

Ahead he could, at times, make out men pushing in toward the town. His heart thrilled at the sight of it, the flags of the Confederacy held high!

Unable to contain himself, he rode forward, a stern glance at Walter silencing protest.

"We have them now!" Lee shouted. "We have them now! Go, my boys, go!"

The charge up Fourth Street toward the depot was gaining some small momentum. The men who had held the barricade but minutes before were nearly all dead, wounded, or captured. The surviving Yankees were beginning to break, to scatter into homes, shops, rebel officers at the front screaming for their men to ignore them for now, to press on through the town and to the open plains beyond.

"Out of the town and we've won!" more than one screamed.

Another rebel yell now, wild and defiant, filled with hopes of victory as they swarmed up the street.

Get ready!" Hunt screamed.

A few Union men were still out in the street, running, and then they saw the gun aimed directly at them. They knew what would happen in a few seconds. Men dodged, threw themselves into doorways and alleyways.

The rebel charge, swarming forward, was gaining momentum until the men up front saw, through the smoke, the muzzle of a three-inch ordnance rifle, not a hundred feet away, aimed straight at them.

Fire!"

The ordnance rifle recoiled with a thunderclap roar, the charge of canister bursting from the barrel. As the first tin cleared the muzzle the tin sheathing peeled back, the fifty iron balls beginning to spread out, deviating to one side or the other, up or down an inch or so for every foot forward; the second can emerged, peeling back, its shot spreading as well. At a hundred feet the spread would be a deadly cone a dozen feet wide.

The impact was devastating, twenty pounds of iron balls, each weighing a little more than two ounces, each traveling at over seven hundred feet a second. A single ball could decapitate a man, tear off an arm, a leg, go clean through a man, tear apart a second, and drop a third behind him.

The entire front of the charge collapsed in a bloody heap.

"Double canister!" Hunt roared.

The swabber leapt forward and ran the sponge down the barrel to kill any lingering sparks. Another prepackaged charge went in, a second tin on top, and was rammed down, crew to either side working the wheels to reaim the gun straight down the street.

"Stand clear!"

The battery sergeant drew the lanyard taut and jerked it.

A hundred more balls tore down the street, plowing like a giant's hand into those not swept away by the first blast. Windowpanes shattered from the blast, glass tinkling down, sometimes entire sheets slashing into a man; canister that had gone wide ricocheted down the narrow valley of the street, bouncing off walls, then tearing into men fifty, a hundred feet, farther back.

"Again, double canister!" Hunt roared.

To the west, from Fourth and Fifth Streets, the guns were firing as well, recoiling. At Third Street the charge was far enough forward that it spilled out onto Main Street, almost overrunning the gun, the crew keeping their nerve. The rammer went down, staff still in the gun, the battery sergeant firing it off anyhow, one hundred iron balls and the ramrod blowing down the street, shattering the charge.

Out of the smoke enveloping Fourth Street a charge began to surge forward again, the men in the fore disbelieving. Victory had been so close, so goddamn close, just past that gun.

An officer leapt out front.

"Home, boys, home!"

He ran straight for the piece, the men at the fore raising rifles, firing, the gun sergeant going down, and half the crew. Grant, startled, realized that a ball had plucked the rim of his hat. He remained motionless.

Hunt shouldered his way in, picked up the lanyard, waited a few seconds, a few maddenly long seconds, the rebel charge getting closer, ready to spill into Main Street, where, if once gained, the rebs would swarm around the gun.

"Look at 'em!" Hunt was screaming. "Can't miss, look at 'em!"

Even as he stepped back, shouting for the crew to jump clear, he jerked the lanyard again.

The rebel major leading the charge disappeared, as did scores of men behind him.

Sickened, Grant turned his back for a moment. He had actually caught a glimpse of a man decapitated, the rebel major, head spinning up into the air, bringing back the nightmare memory of Mexico, a comrade standing next to him, head blown off by a round ball fired by a Mexican battery.

"Double canister!" Hunt roared, wild-eyed. While waiting for the gun crew to reload, he pulled out his revolver and emptied it into the smoke.

Another man picked up the ramrod, shoved the round in, crew forgetting to sponge the piece in the heat of battle. Hunt plucked a friction primer out of the haversack of the dead sergeant, fixed it in place, attached the lanyard, stepped back, and jerked it, another roar, the gun recoiling up over the curb.

"Double canister!"

"Hold, Henry," Grant shouted.

Henry looked back at him.

"For God's sake, Henry, hold fire."

2:00 P.M.

If ever there was a moment when the vision of all that could finally be had materialized, it had been but ten minutes ago. The flags going forward into the town, Stuart's men were going up the slope, the rebel yell was resounding.

Now the dream was dying.

He was silent, back astride Traveler, oblivious to the shot whistling by, spent canister rounds whirling overhead. No one was advancing now. Before the front of the town clusters of men were still fighting, aiming up at second- and third-story windows, riddling anyone who leaned out, but in the sidestreets he could catch glimpses of Union troopers leaning out of windows, firing down.

It was from the streets themselves that the horrible message was now clear. Hundreds of broken men were running back, flags missing or held low, a few officers, hysterical, trying to get in front of the broken formations, urging men to rally, to go back in again.

More artillery fire from within the town, counterpointed by horrific screams.

What had been a surging forward but fifteen minutes ago was collapsing into a rout.

"My God," Lee whispered.

The first of the uninjured to fall back were streaming past him, men silent, walking as if already dead, pulling along wounded comrades, a half dozen men, sobbing, carrying a blanket with an officer in it, McLaw, face already gray in death.

Lee slowly urged Traveler across the front of the retreat.

"My men, my men," he cried. "What has happened?"

"It was too much."

He looked over. It was Beauregard, riding toward him.

"What do you mean too much?"

"You asked too much, General Lee. They had artillery waiting in the town, each street covered with guns, double canister. It was too much."

Lee stared at him, unable to reply. Beauregard rode on.

Lee looked at the beaten, retreating men.

"Can we not still rally?" he cried.

Some of the men stopped, boys of McLaw's old command.

"We'll go back if you want," one of them gasped, and a feeble cry went up. "Order us back in," another shouted.

But even as the small knot gathered around Lee, thousands of men to either side of him were streaming back in defeat.

From the town he could hear a deep-throated cheering, a Union regimental flag defiantly waving from a rooftop, a tattered Confederate flag being held up beside it and then pitched off the roof.

"Can we not still rally?" Lee asked, but this time in barely a whisper.

He looked up toward the slope of the Catoctins. Jeb's boys were giving back as well, artillery farther up the road pounding them hard. They were beginning to draw back.

"General Lee, sir?"

It was Walter, reaching over to take Traveler's reins.

"Sir, I think we should withdraw. We are coming under fire here."

Lee wanted to tear the reins out of Walter's hands to turn and madly ride into the town, to somehow retrieve the victory that should have been theirs this day.

"No, sir," Walter said quietly. "No, sir, not today."

Lee nodded and turned away.

"Hurray for the Union! We whipped you damn good!"

Lee stopped. It was a Union soldier down on the ground, his legs shattered, but up on his elbows, glaring defiantly at Lee. His escort circled in closer. One of the cavalry troopers, cursing, half-drew his revolver.

"No!" Lee snapped.

He looked down at the soldier and then dismounted and walked up to him. The boy looked up at him wide-eyed.

"Who are you?" Lee asked.

The boy gulped nervously.

"Private Jenrich, Forty-third Ohio."

Lee knelt down by his side and took his hand.

"Private, I shall pray tonight that you get safely home to your loved ones and that someday we can meet in peace."

Lee stood back up and looked at his men, all of whom were stunned, silent.

He said nothing more, riding on, leaving Private Jenrich who bent his head and sobbed.

The Hornets Nest

C.S.A. **L**ee Robinson and what was left of the First Texas gave back, retreating toward McCausland's Ford. Precious few of his one once gallant regiment remained. To the north, through the drifting smoke, he noticed that the sound of battle was falling away into silence, and through the smoke he could see ghostlike figures heading to the rear.

It was a defeat. He had never known such a sensation before, defeat. They had nearly taken the first of the railroad cuts but the damned Yankees just would not give back, not run, not surrender. Was it because they were colored, or because they were Yankees?

Or was it because they were both?

He reached the ford, waded in, splashed the tainted water over his face, and knelt down in it for a few seconds as if it were a cooling baptism to wash away the sins of war.

Standing up, he led his men over the river.

US **S**ergeant Major Bartlett led the skirmish line that cautiously advanced toward the ford. The regiment was, in fact, nothing more now than a skirmish line, maybe a hundred men still standing. Sheridan rode behind them, a regiment of white troops spreading out.

Bartlett scanned the ground ahead and finally saw what he was looking for, the hospital area, and sprinted toward it. It was indeed a charnel house, several thousand men on the ground, many Confederates now mixed in, men left behind by their retreating foe.

He ignored his duty for the moment, his friend John Miller by his side, walking back and forth until he spotted the regimental surgeon, down on the ground, a Confederate soldier lying on his side, groaning, as the surgeon probed into his shoulder and then pulled out a rifle ball.

"Doctor!"

The surgeon looked up and recognized Washington, his features grim. "My son?"

"Over there."

His son was lying by the colonel's side as if asleep.

Both of them were dead.

Washington stopped, unable to move. Washington felt as if struck. He could not move or speak, then he slowly sank to his knees, gathering the limp body, still warm, into his arms.

Washington started to rock back and forth, cradling his son.

"Sergeant Major!"

He looked up. Phil Sheridan was gazing down at him.

"What's wrong?"

"My son," he whispered.

Phil stiffened and said nothing for a moment.

"What's your name, Sergeant Major?"

Washington could not reply.

"Washington Quincy Bartlett," John Miller said.

"I saw you today, Bartlett, the way you held the barricade, rallied the men. Do you know what the Medal of Honor is?"

Washington could not reply.

"I'm putting you in for one," Phil said, and he paused, as if adding an afterthought, "and my condolences, Sergeant."

Phil rode on.

Washington did not even really hear what he said. All that he had fought for now rested limp in his arms.

It was far too much for Washington, and he dissolved into tears, still rocking back and forth, Miller kneeling by his side.

Headquarters, Army of Northern Virginia

7:00 P.M.

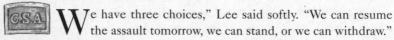

"We have three choices," Lee said softly. "We can resume the assault tomorrow, we can stand, or we can withdraw."

None dared to reply. Longstreet was absolutely silent, staring off. Hood had been wounded in the arm down by the Hornets Nest, and the surgeon had just reported he would most likely lose it. Beauregard, claiming fatigue, had withdrawn to his tent. Jeb, head and arm bandaged, sat across from Lee.

"I say fight," Jeb said softly. "I was within a couple of hundred feet of the heights before the attack collapsed. I still could have taken it."

Lee did not reply directly. He knew Jeb had barely gotten halfway up, losing scores of troopers trying to charge the guns while still mounted.

Lee looked over at Walter and then to Judah.

"Withdraw," Judah Benjamin said calmly.

"Why so?"

"Sir, I am no general or tactician. But the campaign here in Maryland is over."

"We came so close today," Lee whispered, as if in shock. "So close. I could see victory like a golden light above our colors. So close."

He fell silent.

"Grant's army is as badly mauled as ours," Jeb said. "We can finish him tomorrow."

"And how many more armies will be here this time tomorrow?" Judah said. "Another Confederate army perhaps?"

Lee looked over at him stonily.

"No, there will be no more armies," Lee replied, "no more reinforcements. We are it."

"And how many men are still capable of fighting?"

Lee looked over to Walter.

"Sir, there are no clear reports yet. It will take days. Every division was engaged. Robertson is dead, so is McLaw, both their divisions fought out. Beauregard's two divisions in the assault, I'd guess, fifty percent or more lost."

"General Longstreet, your command?" Lee asked.

"Fought out, sir."

Lee looked at him carefully. He had not yet asked why Longstreet had not pushed the attack more boldly from the northern flank and in the center. But he suspected he knew the answer. Longstreet was trying to hold some strength back.

Longstreet finally stirred.

"This army has lost nearly half its fighting strength in the last three days. I suspect casualties will be in excess of twenty-five thousand, perhaps close to thirty. Added to our losses of last week at Gunpowder River and the earlier losses in front of Washington and at Union Mills and Gettysburg— the Army of Northern Virginia is finished as an offensive force."

He had said it straight out. Bluntly and without tact.

Lee nodded, dipping his head.

"Sir, it is time to get this army south of the Potomac," Judah said, forcing his way back into the conversation.

"And the president's orders?" Lee asked.

"He is not here. I am, sir, and I think that gives me some authority as the civilian representative to order you to do so."

Lee forced a smile.

"To take the responsibility from my shoulders?" he asked.

"If you would let me."

"No, sir, I will not let you take that responsibility before our president. I am commander in the field. I must act at this moment in best accordance with the needs of this army, the main surviving hope of our cause."

"Washington faced worse after Brandywine and Germantown," Judah said.

Lee smiled but shook his head.

"He was not facing what I now face."

He sighed and lowered his head.

"Those wounded capable of being moved, with what transport we have left, to be loaded up tonight. Take only those men with good prospects of healing, of returning to the fight. All others to be left behind."

The men around the table stirred.

"Walter, we will leave a note for General Grant asking for his charity to our men. I am sure he will comply."

"Yes, sir."

"General Longstreet. Can you hold this position through tomorrow?"

"Sir?"

"I want Grant to think we are still in position, considering a resumption of the fight. Meanwhile I will take what is left of Hood's and Beauregard's commands and head south, down toward Hauling Ferry, along with our pontoon train."

"Sir, my scouts reported yesterday, and again today, that the Yankees have heavily fortified that crossing."

"We will move with speed. If God is willing, we will launch a surprise attack at dusk and overrun that position. They are, after all, garrison troops. Once the ferry is taken, the pontoon will be laid during the night, I will secure the position, and then, General Longstreet, you will withdraw down to it."

"Yes, sir, I think that is possible."

"Gentlemen," Lee sighed, "if we are finished as an offensive force, so is Grant. We return to Virginia and the war will continue. Perhaps what we've achieved here will be sufficient to overturn the Lincoln administration and victory can yet be ours."

He stood up, the gesture an indication of dismissal, and walked out from under the awning.

The rain was coming down steadily, not hard, just a constant drizzle. Through the gloom and smoke that still clung to the fields, he could see on the far side of the river hundreds of lanterns, bouncing about like fireflies, details of men looking for lost comrades, bringing in the wounded. All was silent except for distant cries of pain, prayers, pleas for help.

He lowered his head.

"My fault, it's all my fault now," he said.

Chapter Nineteen

The War Office
Washington, D.C.

August 29, 1863
4:00 A.M.

"The line is still down," Elihu Washburne announced, standing in the doorway of his office where Lincoln had spent the night, anxiously pacing back and forth.

There was no need during the late morning and early afternoon of yesterday to be told there was a battle on. The rumble had been steady from the northwest until the rain finally came, buffering the sound.

And then the telegraph line had gone dead.

Rumor of that had spread through the city within minutes, anxious crowds gathering again around the White House, the War Department, and the Treasury Office, which was the hub for all the telegraph lines.

Lincoln had stayed in the War Office, not wishing to confront the crowds out in the street.

His pessimism had taken hold during the night. The line had gone down shortly before two in the afternoon. If it was only a temporary break, it should have been up again within minutes. The long hours of silence now told him but one thing. Grant had lost Frederick and was in retreat. The silence could only mean that.

What do I tell the nation now? He wondered. *Be disciplined and wait for the facts*, he counseled himself.

Dawn

en. Ulysses S. Grant stood silently, then stretched and looked out over the plains surrounding Frederick, Maryland.

He had not slept at all. The migraine, the sounds coming from every house in the town and from the surrounding fields, the horrid memory of the Confederate major, head blown off, connecting to the nightmares that still haunted him of a comrade dead in Mexico.

Phil Sheridan wearily came to his side, emerging from the gloom, the smoke, the fog wrapping the field, rising up from the Monocacy and the rain that had fallen throughout the night.

The battle fury was out of Phil; exhaustion was etched in his face and in the way he walked, shock overtaking him as well.

"It's a nightmare down there," Phil said softly, nodding a thanks as Ely handed him a cup of coffee, which he took in both hands. They trembled as he raised it to his lips.

"How could he do it?" Phil asked.

"Who?"

"Lee. My God, sir, he drove his men in relentlessly. It was madness, absolute madness."

"He had this one final chance," Grant said, "and felt he could grab it. If the shoe was on the other foot, we might have done the same."

"I've never seen anything like it before."

"We don't end this now, we might see it again," Grant replied. "It's finished this week or they could regroup across the Potomac and hang on for years."

Phil, still holding his coffee with trembling hands, looked over at Grant.

"I want pressure put on him."

"With what, sir? My corps is gone, McPherson's, Ord's. Sir, I never thought I'd admit something like this, but the army is fought out."

"I'm not talking a full-scale attack," Grant replied. "Even if I wanted to, the men are finished, at least for today. But we still must find a way to keep pressure on Lee, no matter what."

He looked away from Phil.

In one sense Phil was right. The Army of the Susquehanna was indeed fought out. Three out of the four corps that had marched with him only days ago were hollow, burned-out wrecks. McPherson's had taken the worst of it. Down to less than fifty percent after the first day, more than half of those surviving becoming casualties in repulsing Lee's final charge.

Yet, was it not at least as bad or even worse on the other side of Monocacy Creek this morning? Ord in his sacrifice had all but destroyed Early and part of another division. Phil's stand in what all now called the Hornets Nest had shattered Robertson, one of Lee's elite divisions, and savaged parts of two other divisions. Of the three divisions Lee had launched in the charge against Frederick, at least half of those men still littered the fields.

Grant had gone back into the town shortly before dawn. The grisly task of dragging out the Confederate dead was still going on. Fourth Street, for two blocks, was unlike anything he had ever seen, and he prayed he would never see the like again.

Every house in the town was a hospital or a morgue. Several hundred of his men, and all the available civilians, were already at work at the edge of town, digging mass graves.

In one frightful case, a woman had discovered her own out in the street, her husband and son, both with a Confederate regiment. She dragged them into her house and was found a half hour later in her bedroom, having hanged herself.

An argument had ensued when the men who discovered her and found her suicide note had gently removed her body, found the bodies of her husband and son in the parlor, and carried them out to be buried together. A town minister presiding over the burials refused to bury her in what he said was consecrated ground. One of the soldiers leveled a revolver on him, and the service continued.

It was the talk of the men this morning. Strange how one such tragedy became a metaphor for all the madness and tragedies. A delegation of citizens had sought Grant out, demanding that the soldier be found and arrested for having threatened a man of the cloth. He said he would. He watched them leave, and did nothing. The soldier who drew the revolver was right; she was a casualty of this war the same as her husband and son.

He had received word Ord was a prisoner; more than half of his division and brigade commanders were dead or wounded, but this army still had to fight. That had always been the mistake of the Army of the Potomac in the past. The Army of the Potomac had fought battles but had never been able to sustain a campaign. A battle can go on for a few very hard, bitter days, but then it dies out from sheer exhaustion. A campaign is not just one day, or two, or three . . . a campaign is a continuum until either one side or the other can no longer stand up . . . and he still had enough men standing to press the issue. Battles had proven they were indecisive and could not end the war. But a campaign pressed home with sufficient resolve just might get the job done and end the killing once and for all.

Phil finished his cup of coffee, and an enlisted man came up, offering him a plate with some fried salt pork. Phil paled and shook his head.

"I need you to keep the pressure on Lee," Grant said again.

"I realize that, sir," Phil finally replied. "I can still muster maybe three thousand out of the Ninth Corps."

"What's left of Ord's is in your hands as well," Grant said.

"Yes, sir."

Grant had essentially promoted him again at this moment, but Phil showed no reaction.

"Hunt is resupplying the guns he has left; they will resume their old position and bombard the line. If an opening develops, we push it. We also captured ten of their guns, Napoleons. Hunt is incorporating them into his command. Call on him if you need close-in support."

Phil said nothing, finally put his cup down, and saluted.

"I better get back to the men I have left," he said and walked off.

"Sir?"

It was Ely.

"Yes?"

"Sir, I have some returns," he said quietly.

He held up a sheaf of papers in his hand.

"Just tell me," Grant said.

"Sir, we might have upward of twenty-five thousand casualties for the last three days."

"What I figured," Grant replied, looking over at Ely.

The men of his staff were all silent. Nearly half their own men had fallen in the melee yesterday; all were in shock at the horrific losses. He wondered at this moment whether Ely, in presenting the returns, was offering a suggestion, that it was time to break off the fight.

Grant turned and looked at him.

"How many do you think Lee lost?" he asked.

"I'd judge as many or more. The Hornets Nest, we might have lost more than them, but it absolutely shattered Robertson's command. It was up here, though, that Lee was really pounded. The estimate is we lost somewhere around three thousand repulsing the attack; estimates are he might have lost eight to ten thousand."

Grant could not speak.

He did not want to say more. If he dwelled too long on just how much suffering had been created, and, yes, created by his own hand, he'd break. There was many a bottle to be found in town. It would be easy enough to say no fighting today, to find a bottle, get good and drunk, and try to get some sleep.

He sighed, pulling his hat brim low against the steady drizzle.

"Push him," he finally said. "I'm taking over Banks's Corps personally. After Sheridan feels better, I'll cut orders for him to consolidate his command with that of Ord while I incorporate McPherson in with Banks. That should give us two light corps for maneuver. No one is fit to move today, but I want Lee to know we are still here."

"Yes, sir," Ely replied quietly.

"Look, Major Parker," Grant said softly, so quietly only Ely could hear. "The question now is simply this: Who will decide to quit? I can turn this army around today and retire over the mountains, and every man in it will then believe that we were fought to a standstill and lost.

"But if I stand this ground, if we continue to stare Lee in the face, if tomorrow we advance, those same men will march believing they have achieved victory. Yes, a victory bought at a terrible cost, but victory never-theless, and they will march and fight as victors. If we stand and then move forward while Lee is forced to retreat, his men will reach the oppo-site conclusion, and they will withdraw from Frederick as a defeated force. That, in its simplicity, is often the essence of war. That will set the groundwork for the next step in this campaign."

Ely said nothing. Grant was slightly embarrassed that he had felt it necessary to explain himself.

"Go about your duties."

"Yes, sir."

"Ely, is the telegraph connection back up?"

"No, sir."

"Why not?"

"The telegraph wagon for headquarters was smashed in the fighting. The wire from town to halfway up the pass was cut in hundreds of places. Several hours ago, when I realized how long it would take to get service back up, I did send a courier back with news to Hagerstown."

"I wish you had done that sooner," Grant said, and there was a slight note of chastisement in his voice. "The president must be worried sick by now. Besides, our other commands must have clear news of what hap-pened here."

"Sorry, sir," Ely replied. "It's just that with all that had to be done, I let it slip. I'm sorry."

"Too late now. How long for another telegraph wagon to get up?"

"It should be here by late morning. Ten miles of wire are to be brought up."

"Thank you, Ely."

"Sir."

He stood silent, hands in pocket, and wondered what was being said in Washington now. Was Sykes continuing to advance, or had something gone wrong there? Were the fortifications at the fords strong enough to hold if Lee should turn that way? As he looked across the rain-soaked battlefield, he felt that never in his life had he been so lonely as now.

9:00 A.M.

General Lee rode across the field parallel to the road down to Hauling Ferry. It had been a hard choice, one he had agonized over ever since rising shortly after midnight.

Upon awaking, his first temptation was to reverse his decision and keep the army in place for the day, to see if Grant just might counterattack.

But the realization that his rear was now threatened had settled the question. Jeb had come to him shortly after one in the morning with a report that Yankee cavalry was astride the Baltimore and Ohio, nearly cutting Armistead off. Behind the cavalry it was believed additional Yankee infantry was moving, possibly only the militia that had fooled them a week ago into thinking Grant was coming due south, but fresh troops, nevertheless.

Lee could sense that a vise was beginning to close. *If I wait, Grant will indeed wait in response until I'm hit from the rear.*

His hand forced by events, he and his men, the veterans of Hood's and Beauregard's Corps, had set out before dawn. Hood had indeed lost his arm and was out of the fight. Beauregard was now complaining that he was sick and could not move.

Ahead, skirmishing began to flare, Jenkins's cavalry, probing down the road to Hauling Ferry.

The men marching on the road, as he gazed over at them, filled his his heart with anguish. They were what was left of Beauregard's two divisions in the attack. Their ranks were painfully thin, around more than one regimental flag barely fifty men now marched. They were numbed, shocked, shuffling through the mud, heads bent low. He thought of but two weeks before, the march north from Washington, toward Gunpowder River. Though the heat was terrible they were at a floodtide of youth, of enthusiasm, of belief in victory, heads held high as they marched forward.

And now this.

One more fight, that is all I need out of them this day. One more fight. Surely they will rally to that if I lead them. Secure the crossing, Longstreet comes down tonight slipping out of the trap, and we are across the river. From there all things again become possible. Though Grant was not driven from the field, Lee still believed he had beaten him. *If I have lost my offensive power, so has he.*

He came on arrogantly, but if allowed to stay in command, he will never do so again.

The Yankees will have to reorganize, recruit, and how can they recruit after three such stunning blows delivered against them in less than two months? Surely Lincoln will collapse now or at worst they will stop on the banks of the Potomac and wait till spring. Time enough for the wounded to heal, the ranks to be replenished, perhaps France still to come in and break the blockade.

We can still win this, he whispered to himself, even as he rode toward the distant rattle of gunfire coming from the Potomac crossing.

The Road to Hauling Ferry, near Buckeystown Ford

10:00 A.M.

When the column stopped again, Cruickshank rode wearily forward. The road was getting muddy and one of the huge wagons had skidded off to one side, a wheel sinking into a culvert. The dozen mules hooked to the wagon were clawing at the ground and braying as the driver, swearing furiously, lashed at them.

"Stop it," Cruickshank said, his voice barely above a whisper, having long since shouted himself hoarse.

"Goddamn stupid bastards," the driver shouted. "Hate goddamn mules."

"Lashing them won't change it," Cruickshank replied. He felt little pity for the beasts; years out west before the war had burned that sentiment out of him, but still, the poor animals in the traces now were straining, the wagon not moving. Behind them twenty more wagons with their load of pontoon bridging were backed up for almost a half mile.

It had taken nearly an entire day to round up the animals needed to haul the wagons, half the teams having been commandeered from an artillery battalion on direct orders from Longstreet. The gunners had been less than happy with thus being rendered immobile and had tried to pawn off the worst of their nags. It had taken several hours of screaming and threats to get the necessary teams, lead them back to the track, off-load the wagons, and hook them up.

A column of infantry, men bent double, hats pulled low against the rain, staggered by on either side of the road. In another time a mere request would have sent an entire regiment to his aid. He spotted an officer and rode up to him. The man at first actually averted his gaze at Cruickshank's approach.

"Colonel, I need your help," Cruickshank said.

"Sir?"

"Your help," and pointed back to the wagon, tilting over, pontoon boat atop it leaning precariously.

"My boys are just beat," the colonel said. "Besides, we've got orders to move as fast as possible to the ferry."

"If we don't get these boats down to that ferry to make the damn bridge, you ain't going nowhere," Cruickshank replied.

The colonel sighed, turned, and called for a sergeant.

"Robinson."

The sergeant major came up without comment. The colonel pointed to the wagon and Robinson sighed.

"Yes, sir."

It took several minutes for him to gather up thirty men. Some of them, once stopped, simply went to the side of the road and collapsed into a nearly instant, exhausted sleep. Cruickshank directed them around the wagon, and a couple of ropes were run out for the men to grab hold of.

Meanwhile, behind them the convoy of wagons was stalled; order of march was breaking up as troops stopped, men just going to the side of the road to lie down.

Finally, with a lot of whip cracking, cursing of men, and tragically one man having his foot broken when a wheel ran over him, the wagon was back on the road.

The infantry walked away without comment, the sergeant major shaking men awake, shaking hands with the injured soldier left behind, and the column starting back up again, rain coming down, mist rising from the creek, mules braying, an elderly captain sitting by the side of the road crying, head bowed, no one stopping to ask why.

"General Cruickshank, sir!"

He turned and looked back.

God damn! Another wagon had just stalled in the same place as the first one. He wearily turned and rode back.

Monocacy Creek

10:45 A.M.

The sharpshooting back and forth was constant, but Sergeant Hazner could sense it was a halfhearted effort by the other side, as much as it was halfhearted by his.

Here and there a few men, the type that took a perverse delight in such things, banged away as ordered. But most of his surviving men were sitting in the bottom of the mud-filled trench, soaking wet, miserable, exhausted.

"Think I got one," a sharpshooter announced. The men to either side of him said nothing, a few looking at him with disgust.

"Ain't you had enough killing?" Hazner asked.

The sharpshooter looked over at him and grinned while reloading.

The man stood up and a second later pitched over backwards, slumping down into the trench, dead, shot clean through the forehead. No one spoke for a moment. They just stared at his body.

"Someone wave a white handkerchief," Hazner said.

One of the men pulled out a dirty piece of cloth, held it up over the lip of the trench, and waved it back and forth for a minute.

"OK, push the dumb son of a bitch out," Hazner said.

Several men grabbed the body, hoisted it up, and rolled it over the rear of the trench. As they did so, Hazner risked a quick look.

The landscape below him and on the other side of the creek was blasted, like a painting of hell. The ruined bridges, the raw slashes of earth from trenches, and bodies everywhere, one of them hanging inverted from a tree that had been split in half by a shell.

The area around the Hornets Nest was a nightmare of bodies lying in the rain, heaped up around the sides of the railroad cuts. A party carrying a white flag, and followed by several ambulances, was at work, pulling wounded out of the tangle.

A minié ball zipped high overhead, and he sensed it was nothing more than a warning shot, that the Yankees on the other side of the creek had allowed the little truce for them to get rid of the dead sharpshooter but now it was back to business. He waved and slid down to the bottom of the trench, and squatting in the mud he fell asleep.

Three Miles East of Monocacy Creek on the Baltimore and Ohio Line

Noon

 I want the ammunition off of these trains now!" Pete Longstreet shouted.

He thought they had been off-loaded during the night. Three million rounds of rifle ammunition and ten thousand rounds of artillery, enough to sustain the army through another pitched battle if need be.

Organization was breaking down, that was becoming obvious. Some of the boxes of rifle ammunition were stacked up beside the track, out in the rain. Eventually the water would soak through the wood siding and ruin it. A few wagons and ambulances had been pressed into the service, men loading up, but there was no real effort here, no efficiency. Some batteries had sent their limber wagons back, others, especially the new batteries made up primarily of infantry volunteers, had yet to show up. They were short of horses as it was. They had organized for this battle to fight mainly in place, and now they just didn't have the transport to get their supplies up to the fighting men.

Lee should have stayed here, he thought. In one day the general of the army had gone from near victory to field commander of a battered, makeshift corps in retreat. *He should have stayed here to organize and he sent me instead.*

A courier came up the line from the east, riding fast, and Longstreet saw the man, who had just about ridden past without stopping. He stepped out into the middle of the track and waved him down.

The courier reined in.

"General Longstreet?"

"Yes, that's me."

"Sir, a report from General Armistead, sir."

"Go on."

"Sir, he reports he must abandon his movement along the railroad track. At least a brigade of Yankee cavalry has flanked him; in fact, sir, they almost got me right after I started out. They are linking up with General Sykes, whose men are advancing along the National Road. General Armistead reports, sir, that he will continue his withdrawal marching to the southwest toward Urbana and attempt to link back up with the army that way."

"Where is he now?"

"Sir, about ten miles back from here, at Marysville."

"Do the Yankees have trains?"

"Yes, sir, damnedest things. Big heavy guns mounted in front of the locomotives. We were breaking up the tracks and slowing them down good yesterday, but when their cavalry started coming in, that pushed us off the tracks."

They could be here in a couple of hours, Pete realized and looked over at the ammunition trains.

"Did you see any of Stuart's men?"

"A few patrols, sir, along the track. I warned them as I rode past."

"Fine. Get back to Armistead, tell him to push hard to link up with us."

He didn't say anything else about the army evacuating. The courier turned about and rode off, angling southeast, away from the rail line.

I have to get this ammunition off the train and up to the line, Pete realized. Behind him, back toward the front line, he had passed dozens of locomotives, hundreds of cars, all frozen in place, the boilers having gone out. The three ammunition trains were the last to get out, all the stalled trains now a barrier that wagons had to squeeze around to get through for a load.

There was the equivalent of a hundred and fifty wagonloads of ammunition on these trains, and so far he had moved less than fifty of them. That and a hundred double-caisson loads for the artillery.

At the rate it was going, he sensed they'd never get it all off in time.

He turned to his staff.

"One of you get back to headquarters. Tell Walter Taylor I need more wagons sent back here now, anything, ambulances, anything. Another of you track down Alexander. Tell him we have enough ammunition to resupply one hundred guns . . ."

He hesitated.

"And tell him to prepare to abandon any of his pieces that cannot get together full teams by nightfall."

The two couriers galloped off, and Pete stood alone in the rain, looking east, wondering if at any minute he might see an armored train coming down the track.

A major was supervising the off-loading, and he called him over.

"Major, post some sentries down the track a few miles. The Yankees are coming in on us from that way. The moment you see them, blow the rest of this up."

"Sir?"

"You heard me, blow these trains up. Then as you pull back, set fire to every train on these tracks."

"Hard to do sir, nearly all the locomotives are cold, their fires out."

"Be ingenious, son," Pete said, trying to smile. "I'm giving you the chance to put the damned B and O out of business for a long time; you can claim to be the biggest train wrecker in history."

The major smiled back.

"We'll find a way, sir."

Pete mounted and rode off, weaving his way around the long strings of boxcars, flatcars, hoppers, and locomotives. He passed the spot where Lee had almost been killed, wreckage still strewn across the track, and to the empty flatcars where Cruickshank had finally managed to get the damn pontoon bridges unloaded and moving.

Ahead there was a distant thumping, occasional muffled rattling of rifle fire, just when he had assumed there was nothing serious going on. Grant was just waiting them out now.

Headquarters, Army of the Susquehanna

12:15 P.M.

 The reassuring click of the telegraph sounded behind him, the replacement crew sending out the first test signal a half hour ago, and now forwarding a full report of the battle and a coded signal by Grant, indicating his belief that Lee was moving his forces toward Hauling Ferry.

Treasury Office
Washington, D.C.

12:40 P.M.

The cost, merciful God," Lincoln sighed as he sat down, holding the tear sheet just handed over by the telegrapher. "The cost."

Elihu was by his side, reading over his shoulder.

"Grant held, though," Elihu said. "He held."

There was a touch of exuberance in Elihu's voice, but for the moment Lincoln could not react.

"Estimate our losses at twenty-five thousand or more."

He kept rereading that one line.

The signal had been sent directly from Grant, to Hagerstown, from there to Harrisburg, then repeated down to Port Deposit. With the recapture of Baltimore, a victory heralded on the front pages of all newspapers across the country, the telegraph line had been restored directly back to Washington.

That number, twenty-five thousand, was now public knowledge. He could picture by this evening hundreds of thousands gathering at telegraphy stations across the nation, anxious parents, wives, children, all waiting for the first casualty reports to come through, names, more names, and yet more names, each one tearing a tragic hole into a family that would never heal.

"Sir?"

It was Elihu, lightly touching him on the shoulder.

Lincoln stirred from his thoughts and looked up.

"Sir, Grant held at Frederick. In fact he reports Lee is retreating, trying to flee Maryland and get across the Potomac to Virginia. That is the coded part which just came through. We have Lee on the run."

Lincoln could only shake his head and sigh.

"Yes, I know, Elihu. As we did last year after Antietam. He slipped the net then and the war continued."

Lost in gloom, Lincoln stood up and walked out of the room. A moment later Elihu heard a clamor out in the street as a cavalry detachment pushed the waiting crowd back, reporters shouting questions, as Lincoln slowly walked across Lafayette Park to return to the White House.

Elihu watched him disappear into the rain, his heart breaking at the sight of the man, who appeared, like Atlas, to be carrying an impossible burden upon his shoulders.

Elihu turned back to the telegrapher.

"A message to Hancock, coded. Inform him to expect a full attack by Lee before the day is out."

Hauling Ferry

2:45 P.M.

"Mr. Bartlett?"

Jim was asleep, heading resting on the table. He stirred. It was a white officer.

"Yes, sir?"

"General Hancock wishes to see you, Mr. Bartlett."

"Of course."

Jim stood up, rubbing the sleep from his eyes, taking a few seconds to wipe his spectacles with a dirty handkerchief. Like so many who fall asleep at midday he was surprised by the bustle of activity around him even as he had dozed. Men were setting up awnings to protect boxes of ammunition being off-loaded from a canal barge, a company of a hundred men, shovels and picks on their shoulders, were coming off the line to eat their noonday meal. They were all covered in mud, soaked to the skin, but their spirits were still high, a team of a hundred moving from the kitchen area back up to replace them, gibes about the food awaiting the returning crew being exchanged.

Jim followed the officer out from under the awning, glad when one of his assistants came up and offered him an army poncho and an army slouch cap to cover himself. The immaculate clothes he wore as a butler at the White House, black coat, trousers, boiled shirt, black cravat, were now filthy, most likely beyond any hope of repair.

He mounted his old swaybacked nag and fell in with the officer by his side.

"Your men, Mr. Bartlett. I never seen such workers," the officer said. "They just don't stop."

Jim smiled at the compliment.

"Thank you, sir. These boys have a reason to be here. Mr. Lincoln gave them that, Mr. Lincoln and you soldiers. We'll dig till we hit China if that is what you need."

The officer chuckled and shook his head.

"Maybe get a few million of them to help us, is that it?"

"I heard say those working out in California on the railroad are mighty fine workers."

"How the country is changing," the officer said.

"How is that, sir?"

He reddened slightly and shook his head. "Oh, nothing."

"You mean us colored, the Chinese, and such?"

"No offense, Mr. Bartlett."

"None taken, young sir. Yes, the country is changing."

They crested the top of the slope and Jim smiled with satisfaction. Little more than a day ago this had been open fields, woodlots, and just the beginnings of a trench. The entire landscape had been transformed by the terrible needs of war and he smiled because he had had a hand in achieving what needed to be done.

A rectangular bastion was before him, a hundred feet long and about fifty feet broad. The earthen ramparts were eight to ten feet high, all sides around it dug out into a moat. On a raised platform in the center was one of the huge cannons, what the officers were calling a Parrott gun. Four other smaller guns were inside the bastion as well. The entryway was a rough-hewn bridge made of logs split in half.

"Be careful," the officer said, "it's a bit slippery."

Not too sure of himself on horseback Jim decided to dismount and walk in.

Sentries were posted at the entryway. Just behind them, inside the fort, was a stack of logs that he realized could be thrown across the entrance to block it if the fort was surrounded. Within, hundreds of men, all of them soldiers, were forming up, some already positioned at the guns. The officer led the way for Jim as they walked across the muddy ground and up a sloping ramp, paved with logs, to where the great gun rested. Hancock, leaning heavily on his cane, was standing by the muzzle of the gun, field glasses raised, looking toward the road that headed north.

The ground before them was completely transformed. Everything had been cut back for several hundred yards. Trees dropped, brush cleared, sharpened stakes driven into the ground, entrapments dug. Looking north and south Jim saw where long zigzagging entrenchments had been dug in each direction. The one to the left sloped down to the Monocacy. The stream itself was now blocked by a half dozen barges, each mounting a light artillery piece; a rough-hewn bridge, now spanning the creek, was wobbly, and looked as if it would collapse if more than a few men were on it at any time, but it gave them a means of moving men across the creek without relying on the barges and canal.

On the far side there was another bastion, another of the great guns within, more entrenchments, connecting to yet another bastion. Men were still out in the fields forward, working, cutting down trees, even trampling down the corn to deny concealment.

To the south the line continued for over a mile before finally sloping back down to the canal and the Potomac behind it. The position was firmly anchored by two more bastions on this side of the river.

Hancock turned, looked at Jim, and, releasing his cane, eagerly extended his hand. Jim shook it.

"Mr. Bartlett, I felt you should see what your men have done while you slept."

Hancock smiled.

"Sorry, sir. Guess exhaustion caught up with me."

"I told everyone not to disturb you. I know you were up most of the night."

"Sorry, sir."

"Mr. Bartlett, how old are you?"

"Not rightly sure. Maybe sixty."

"Men half your age have dropped doing less work. I must say, this would have been impossible without you."

Hancock extended his hand, pointing to the defensive line, swayed a bit, and clutched his cane again, using his other hand to brace himself against the iron carriage of the Parrott gun.

"And now we shall need it!"

"Sir?"

"I guess you didn't hear," Hancock said excitedly. "The telegram just came in from Washington. Lee has been defeated at Frederick and is believed to be retreating this way."

"My God," was all Jim could say. His feelings were now so mixed. His son and grandson were up in Frederick, what of them? Yet if Lee was defeated, perhaps that might mean all this was coming to an end. It would also mean he was coming this way.

As if reading his mind, Hancock nodded.

"Lee is undoubtedly coming straight here. Skirmishing just a couple miles up that road is getting heavy. Infantry has been reported. I think he will try to force this position by the end of today."

"Then we keep working till he does show up."

"No, Mr. Bartlett. I think it's time I sent your people out. You've done a magnificent job. I'm convinced we can hold this place now. I wasn't so sure yesterday, but I am today. But still, you are civilians, and I guess I must add, colored civilians. I don't want you and your men here if things turn bad."

"We are staying, sir. No disrespect intended, but we are staying."

Hancock looked at him, not responding.

"Sir, how many cooks in your army? How many stretcher bearers, how many wagon drivers, how many men hauling boxes of ammunition once the fight starts?"

Hancock smiled.

"Quite a few."

"Put rifles in their hands, put them on the line, my men will do whatever is needed. We can fight that way, and we will keep digging right up until the bullets begin to fly."

Hancock hesitated, and then nodded.

"It's against my better judgment sir," he said, and Jim was startled by that one word—"sir." Few whites had ever called him that before.

"Keep your men well organized. Detail off reliable ones to do the tasks you've suggested. The rest of you I want back behind the canal when the shooting really starts."

"Yes, sir," Jim replied with a smile.

"It won't be long now," Hancock said, and he motioned to the north.

In the distance there was a muffled thump, followed seconds later by a crackling sound.

"They're coming up," Hancock said.

He turned away and Jim walked back out of the fort, mounted his old swaybacked horse, and rode back to his own "headquarters." His assistants were gathered round, waiting anxiously.

"We staying?" one of them asked.

Jim nodded.

There were exuberant shouts and Jim held up his hands for silence.

"This will be no picnic," he shouted, and all fell silent.

"A lot of men are going to be dying soon. A lot of men are dying for us. Some of us are going to join them in the dying."

He thought of his own son, his grandson, but forced that thought aside. *I can't dwell on that now,* he realized.

"We have to get organized to do our part. Here are your assignments."

He detailed men to find and assign drivers, hospital workers, cooks to bring up hot food to the troops. He then fell silent for a moment.

"And the rest of the men?" someone asked.

"Behind the canal embankment. Every man with a shovel, axe, or pick. They'll know what to do if the rebels break through."

In Front of Hauling Ferry

4:30 P.M.

Robert E. Lee pushed forward, watching as his men to either flank deployed out into line of battle.

Phil Duvall, former captain, now colonel, rode up to his side.

"Sir, the news I've got isn't good," he announced as he came up to Lee's side.

"Go on, Colonel."

"They extended their fortifications during the night. Nearly a mile now farther south than what they had yesterday."

"It was to be expected, Colonel."

"Sir, I must warn you, the fortifications ahead, it's like a week or more of work done in just a day. I don't see how they did it."

"Their numbers?"

"I counted six regimental flags, sir, maybe three or four thousand, and a lot of colored."

"What?"

"Workers, they're still digging."

"That explains the fortifications."

"What I thought, too, sir."

Phil hesitated. Two weeks ago he was just a lowly captain on outpost picket at Carlisle, now he was leading the forward edge of a desperate attempt to seize this river crossing. But he had to speak out.

"Sir, assaulting this position looks like desperate work to me. Give me to tonight, sir, and I'll find some flanking lanes that can put us down between here and Edwards Ferry."

Lee shook his head but smiled at the offer of this young officer.

"In other times and places, perhaps, Colonel. But would those roads be wide enough for our pontoon bridges? I doubt it. We crossed this ground last year, and I know it well. We'd have to march ten miles south to Poolesville then back west again to the next crossing down. In the meantime they have the canal to move their troops and laborers.

"No, Colonel, we must strike them right here. We go forward, seize the ferry. The river will act as a shield to our right flank and then we put our bridge across. We must do this now, tonight."

Phil sighed and nodded.

"Sir, let me show you a good vantage point."

Lee followed the colonel as he trotted down the muddy road. Troops ahead were falling out, forming up into lines of battle. Three batteries of guns, still limbered, waited in the middle of the road under a canopy of trees dripping moisture.

He turned and rode off, following Duvall up the slope to where he reined in.

The battlements were before him, half a mile away, skirmishers out, already firing from long distance, a scattering of shots from the fortress line coming back.

If this was an open-field fight, he thought, *I'd have the crossing in half an hour. I have more than ten thousand of my best with me; they can't have more than three to four thousand here. One solid charge would have swept them aside.*

Now, at best, with all those entrenchments and heavy artillery, it's an even chance.

He took a deep breath.

"Order the artillery forward," he said.

The order was passed and a few minutes later a cheer went up from the road, the batteries racing forward, reaching the crest. They did so with their usual élan and precision, turning at right angles at the full gallop, mud and dirt spraying up, two batteries to the south of the road, one to the north. Even before the last gun had appeared three shots ranged out from the bastion line, thirty-pound shells winging in, well aimed, most likely already practiced, one of the shells blowing directly over a double limber wagon, the two caissons of ammunition exploding in a fireball.

The guns swung about, dismounted, and in less than a minute opened up, pounding the bastion with solid shot and case shot.

And then the heavy hundred-pounder erupted. There was a brilliant flash, four seconds later a thunderclap roar as the shell hit the ground just forward of the slope, sending a geyser of dirt and mud a hundred feet into the air, dropping several gunners.

In the fields behind the slope the first wave of infantry was beginning to advance. There was no cheering, just grim determination.

He could no longer contain himself. Turning about, he raced down the slope and reached the left flank of his advancing line, the few battered men of Hood. Standing in his stirrups, he drew his saber.

"Come on, boys, come on!" he roared. "Win this one and we are back in Old Virginia. Virginia, boys, covered with glory for all that we have done. Do this and victory is still ours!"

There was a desperate tone to his voice, conveyed to the men.

"I am with you, boys."

He turned about, taking the lead, as the battered battalions, fifty to a hundred men behind each flag, swept forward, and for some the dream was still alive. Win this one and we are across the water, safe, to live another day, perhaps to still win this war.

4:45 P.M.

Sergeant Major Robinson was at the fore of his regiment. Seventy-two men left, according to roll call just before going in. Seventy-two men gathered round one tattered flag. But at the sight of Lee their hearts were full. If Lee was before them, then victory was still before them. They marched up the slope, guns silhouetted at the top of the crest, wreathed in smoke, pounding away, every few minutes a terrible explosion erupting along the line. Robinson looked to his right. Other regiments were coming forward: He saw the men of the Fourth Texas, not more than a hundred, a few score with the Second Texas. Next to them men of a brigade he didn't know, most likely some of Beauregard's men.

Gone were the days when Hood's Texans went forward in their glory, thousands of them, their wild cheer, the knowledge that when they went forward all would flee before them.

But Lee was in the front. What waited ahead, after the nightmare of yesterday, could not be anywhere near so bad.

"Come on, boys!" Robinson roared. "Do you want to live forever?"

5:00 P.M.

The first wave of the charge crested the slope and Winfield Scott Hancock stood silent, field glasses raised. If what was coming forward was a beaten army, it most certainly did not look so at this instant.

Though ragged, their lines were coming forward. He looked about the bastion. Gunners were in place, orders shouted to shift fire from the enemy guns to the infantry, fuses cut to two seconds. The bastion on the far side of the Monocacy was opening with enfilade, thirty-pound shells bursting in air.

"Stand clear!"

Hancock stepped back and covered his ears. The hundred-pounder lit off, its heavy shell screaming downrange, bursting in the air two seconds later, dropping several dozen of the advancing infantry.

"Reload with canister!"

He was about to shout a countermand, but then realized these men knew their business. The heavy monster took minutes to reload, and by that time the waves of infantry would be in range. Four twenty-five-pound bags of canister and grape were loaded into the barrel, over a thousand iron balls, propelled by thirty pounds of powder. One gun with the firepower of two batteries of Napoleons.

The charge was coming closer, still out of rifle range. He caught a glimpse of an officer mounted on a gray horse, turned his field glasses on him. My God, it was Lee himself. He was surrounded by a half dozen cavalryman, who were forcibly pushing before him, holding him back.

That revealed much. Lee was here, and he was desperate, wanting to lead this mad charge.

All the guns were loaded with canister, and they waited.

The charge was down to three hundred yards and then started to hit the edge of the entrapments, men tripping into spider holes, falling, lines breaking apart as they pushed through rows of sharpened stakes and tangled piles of brush.

Three hundred yards.

"Stand clear!"

He stepped back again and the hundred-pound Parrott recoiled with a thunderclap.

The hurricane of iron swept through the ranks of the Texans. Dozens dropped from the blast of the great Parrott gun. It looked as if the entire Fourth Texas went down from just that single blast.

Lee was no longer in front of them. A cavalry colonel and his men were forcing him back in spite of his protests.

They were down to two hundred yards and something spontaneous now happened up and down this line of hard, bitter veterans. They knew that the next two minutes would decide their fate forever.

They had been in enough charges to know that moment when, if but one man wavered, if a foolish officer shouted for them to stop, to return fire, they would be slaughtered. Their only hope was to charge! To charge with mad abandon, the way they had at Gaines Mill, Groveton, Sharpsburg, Chancellorsville, Taneytown, Gunpowder River. To stand out here even for a few minutes longer was death.

"Charge!"

The cry was picked up. It wasn't the officers, it was the men, the veterans, the final chosen few, who knew that if there was any hope of personal survival, any hope of getting back across the river, any hope of their cause surviving, it had to be now.

Robinson was in the fore, looking back, screaming for his men to charge, to run straight at them, to get over the wall and into the fort.

The wavering line took strength and set off in a wild run. Spontaneously, driven by no one mind, but imbued with the spirit of the general who watched them, whose face was streaming tears, they sprinted across the open field, dozens dropping, falling into the spider traps, knocked over by volleys fired from the battlement walls.

And then he saw the heavy guns rolling forward in their embrasures, barrels cranked down.

"Texas!"

The four thirty-pounders and the hundred-pounder recoiled—and hundreds dropped.

Robinson was jerked off his feet, thrown backward, his left side numb. He looked to his shoulder, his arm shredded, nearly gone. Beside him was the flag bearer of the First Texas, colors on the ground beside him, the man dead.

His flag, his beloved flag. The one he had carried for a few minutes at Fort Stevens, the one in his hand when he had stopped Robert E. Lee at Taneytown. His flag . . . his beloved flag.

As if in a dream he stood up, picked up the flag from the mud.

"Texas!"

He wasn't sure if any were behind him now. The crest of the bastion was ablaze with fire.

"Texas!"

He went down into the muddy moat and crawled up the slope of the fort, using the flag as a staff to keep himself upright.

My God, give me the strength to do this today. All other thoughts were disappearing, of his wife, of his young son Seth, at fifteen wanting to join the army, of his three-year-old baby girl, of his home. It was now just the flag he carried, praying that someone, anyone, was still behind him.

He reached the top of the slope, planting the flag atop the crest.

There was a brief, an all-so-brief moment when he looked down the length of the battle, dreaming that dozens of flags like his, from Arkansas, Georgia, Virginia, and the Carolinas crowned the heights, the way they had so many times before.

His was the only one.

"Sergeant!"

He looked down. A Yankee officer, a general leaning on a cane, had pistol raised, pointed straight at him.

"It's over, Sergeant."

He collapsed inside the wall of the fort, colors falling over with him as he clutched the staff.

Several men rushed to pull the flag from Robinson's hand, but the general holstered his pistol and knelt down by his side.

"You can keep your flag, Sergeant. You're one of the bravest men I've ever seen. You got farther than any other man in your army, but for you the war is over."

Sergeant Major Robinson looked up at him, unable to speak. All he could do was nod.

"My surgeon will tend to you, and I'll make sure you get home."

General Hancock patted him on his good shoulder, then stood up and limped off.

5:15 P.M.

Lee stood silently, head bowed. The charge was over before it had barely begun. He knew in his heart he had asked far too much of these men. Rest, ranks replenished, officers replaced, the men well fed, perhaps it might have been different.

The beaten survivors were falling back, not many of them. Out in the field, to his horror he saw many with their hands up in the air, casting aside rifles. The heavy artillery which had so frightfully decimated the charge, perhaps dropping a thousand or more in a matter of seconds, now resumed fire on the light batteries brought up in support.

A gun was dismounted, fragments flying in a deadly spray,

Around to the south, come dawn, he now wondered, still not ready to give in. He could catch a glimpse of the canal, which was filled with barges coming up, many of them loaded with additional troops.

The door this way was closed. He would have to find another way out. That realization, he knew, had just cost him several thousand more men as he surveyed the stricken field.

I am bleeding out by the minute.

He looked over at Colonel Duvall, who was silent, a bit red-faced, for only minutes before Lee had threatened him with a court-martial if the colonel did not release Traveler's reins and let him go forward.

"My apologies, Colonel," Lee sighed. "You were doing your duty."

"Thank you, sir. It was your safety, sir. The army needs you."

"Yes, son, I guess it still does," Lee said.

"Scout that road down to Poolesville," he said softly. "See if we can move that way. Send a courier up to General Longstreet as well. Inform him of our failure to breach the line here. He is to abandon his position tonight and move down here. We must find a way across this river tomorrow. I will need him with me."

7:00 *P.M.*

Grant read the telegram and sighed with relief. Hancock had held. The fight, according to the report, was over in a matter of minutes and Lee was already withdrawing.

Grant looked over at the map Ely had spread on the table.

It had to be Poolesville. That was the only other way out now. Strike for Edwards Ferry or a crossing in between. But moving the bridges over that road would be a nightmare.

"Ely."

"Here, sir."

"Orders to General Sheridan. General advance along the line the hour before the dawn. I suspect General Longstreet will abandon the line here during the night. Orders to Hancock to move the Edwards Ferry garrison up to Poolesville to block that road. Also to bring down the garrisons at Point of Rocks, they are no longer needed there. Sykes to now turn due south."

"Yes, sir."

Grant sat back down in the chair he had occupied most of the day, looking out across the Frederick plains. The air was heavy with the cloying stench of bodies rotting. It would be good to leave this terrible place.

Behind him, an endless train of supplies was coming down the mountain pass, priority now given to medical supplies. The first of the wounded who could be moved were being sent back to Hagerstown and from there to hospitals in Harrisburg.

To the east the sky was beginning to glow and he knew what that

meant. He lit a cigar and watched the glow begin to rise, punctuated by distant explosions.

On the Baltimore and Ohio

All over, goodbye, now blow it to hell!" Pete shouted.

Men were running down the tracks, throwing torches into boxcars, tossing in cans of coal oil, loose straw, anything to get them burning. Fires had been lit in several train boilers, steam was up, and the locomotives were now rolling down the tracks, crashing into burning cars, or tumbling off where rails had been severed.

One full ammunition train, a half mile away, went up with a tremendous roar, fireball rising hundreds of feet into the air. He watched it with grim satisfaction. Enough ammunition to keep an entire corps in action for a day, but he would be damned if the Yankees would have it now. And as far as the wreckage to the Baltimore and Ohio—the hell with them. *If we have lost this war, it was their blame as much as anyone's.* He was in no mood to be forgiving now.

He caught the eye of a colonel, leading a detail of men and an ambulance.

"Ammunition's gone," Pete said.

The colonel shook his head.

"Damn sir, I'm down to maybe twenty rounds a man."

"Just get your men formed up. We're marching at midnight."

"To where, sir?"

Pete smiled sadly.

"To Virginia if we can, but to hell if we must."

Chapter Twenty

The White House

August 30, 1863
1:00 A.M.

"How are you, Mr. President," Elihu asked as he came into the office.

Lincoln, sitting behind his desk, looked up, offered a weak smile, and set down his pen.

"Just a minute more, Elihu. Why don't you sit down and relax."

Elihu went over to the sofa and collapsed. He had not slept in a day and a half. He felt as if he had been trapped in a small boat, tossed back and forth by waves coming from opposite directions. There would be moments of exultation, followed minutes later by contrary news that plunged all into gloom.

Renewed rioting had broken out in New York when it was reported in the *Times* that Grant had sustained over thirty thousand casualties and was retreating.

The *Tribune*, in contrast, was reporting victory, but its headlines were ignored and the rioting had swept into city hall, the building torched by the mob.

Sickles was up to his usual destructive behavior, denouncing the removal of Stanton, calling for Lincoln's impeachment, and demanding that both he and Stanton be returned to positions of authority, in order to "save our Republic from a dictator who has led us to the brink of disaster."

The news had fueled protests in Philadelphia and Cleveland and many other cities of the Midwest, particularly those that had provided so many regiments to Grant's army.

Yet the waves would then rush in from the other direction. Sherman had just reported a sharp victory against Bragg about thirty miles north of Atlanta; if he could now beat Bragg in a race to secure Kennesaw Mountain, he'd be in a position to take Atlanta under siege within a matter of days.

Elihu closed his eyes, glad for the momentary respite. He heard Lincoln scratching away with his pen, a sigh, the sound of paper being folded.

"Elihu?"

"Yes, sir?"

"Asleep?"

"Wish I could, sir."

Lincoln was looking over at him. He seemed to have aged another decade within the last few weeks. He had lost weight, his eyes were deepset, dark circles beneath them, hair unkempt, bony features standing out starkly in the flickering light of the lamp on his desk.

Lincoln stood up, walked over, and sat down in a chair next to Elihu, handing him a sealed envelope.

"I need you to do this for me now."

"What is it, sir?"

"I want you to personally deliver this memo to General Grant."

Elihu took the envelope.

"Now, sir?"

"Yes. The railroad line has been restored to Baltimore. I've already sent a message down to the rail yard, and a car is waiting for you. You should be able to get a little sleep on the way up. From there proceed as far as possible west on the B and O, then find Grant and deliver this message. It is absolutely crucial that you do so."

"Yes, sir," Elihu replied wearily.

"Elihu, this is important. Once aboard the train, feel free to open the envelope and read it. You will then see why. Once you have linked up with General Grant, you are to stay with him." Lincoln spoke with a deep sense of urgency and almost foreboding.

"Sir?"

"Stay with him until it is decided one way or the other."

Elihu nodded.

"It's still not certain, sir," Elihu said. "Hancock repulsed Lee, but he has escaped us before. He still might slip back across the Potomac, and if so, the war will drag on for another year or more."

Lincoln nodded.

"I know that. The country knows that. And I am not sure the country can take another year of this kind of bloodletting without achievement."

He sighed, stood up, and walked over to the window, as Elihu noticed was his habit when thinking. He gazed out over Lafayette Park, the crowd gathered there, the ring of sentries.

"Another year. I don't think I can bear it. Nearly four hundred thousand Americans have died on both sides already. Another year, my God, six hundred thousand, seven hundred thousand?"

He turned away from the window.

"Are our sins so great that we must be punished so? I first asked myself that question after we failed so miserably at Second Bull Run a year ago. Now I feel a redoubled sense of trying to understand what God intends by this terrible agony for our nation."

Elihu could not reply.

"Just do as I've requested," Lincoln finally said. "And let us pray that when we meet again, all shall be well."

5:15 A.M.

The army had started moving fifteen minutes ago, the first light of a hazy, fog-shrouded dawn concealing their movement. Grant, staff following, was mounted, heading down toward McCausland's Ford, horses nervous as they gingerly moved around the carpet of dead covering the field. More than one of his men had already vomited from the stench.

He clutched his cigar firmly in his mouth, puffing furiously to block out the smell. The migraine still bedeviled him, and he feared that if he took too deep a breath of the fetid air, he would humiliate himself by vomiting as well.

He kept his eyes fixed straight ahead, unable to bear looking down at the ground. The few glances were out of a nightmare, made worse by the half light, the wisps of fog drifting off the ground . . . men tangled together, his and Lee's, black and white, corpses swollen, both sides mingled together. To his right a circle of lanterns lit up a Confederate hospital area. He did not dare to ride near it, for he knew the sights within, and his courage faltered at the thought of approaching it. Some generals did so after a fight, calmly walking in to visit their men, but that was something beyond him, something that he knew would break his will. As a result, some said he was heartless; few realized just how heartfelt his decision truly was.

To the east, fires continued to glow, a clear sign to him that the rebel army was pulling out, burning the trains and their abandoned supplies.

He reached the ford, and from the far side there was a loud splashing, the escort around Grant nervously raising revolvers.

"Who goes there?" someone shouted.

"Union!"

"Come forward. Union here."

Riders approached, fog swirling around them, and Grant smiled. It was Ben Grierson.

"General, good to see you looking so well," Grant said happily.

"And you, too, sir. Been wandering around out here since midnight trying to find you."

The two saluted, and then Grant leaned over and warmly shook his hand.

"A lot is happening, sir." Grierson said excitedly.

"First off, where are the rebels?" Grant asked.

The mere fact that Grierson had met him here, literally in the middle of the Monocacy, meant that Lee had abandoned his position on the line, a move he had anticipated. But the presence of Grierson confirmed it.

"Sir, we linked up late yesterday with Sykes and the Army of the Potomac just outside of Marysville. I have two brigades of cavalry with me. We moved along the railroad, and shortly after midnight we reached the trains."

Grierson pointed back to the glowing horizon.

"Lord, what a mess they made of it. Must be over a hundred wrecked and burning locomotives back there, everything blown to hell. We rounded up a few prisoners. They said they were with Longstreet's Corps, which pulled out during the night. Lee pulled out yesterday with two corps."

Grant nodded. It was what he had assumed. The report of Lee being seen down at Hauling Ferry was now confirmed by this report.

"Go on."

"Must confess I got a bit disoriented around here. Couple of hours ago we followed the tracks to the river, tried to cross, but some of your boys on the other side were a bit trigger-happy, and I felt it best to sort of wait things out till dawn.

"About an hour ago, we ran into your skirmishers crossing the river, and they directed me down to this ford. Glad I ran into you."

"As I am glad to see you," Grant replied.

"Longstreet's Corps is in full retreat. Apparently they started evacuating this position around midnight. I have my two brigades dogging them on the two roads leading down to Hauling Ferry."

"What about Sykes?"

"He is over toward Urbana. About six or seven miles southeast of here. Couch's militia is falling in behind him."

Grant smiled.

The net was indeed closing in.

"Sir, what happened here?" Grierson asked. "I tell you, coming up these last few miles, I've never seen anything like it before. Hospitals packed with Confederate wounded. Came across thirty or so field pieces, spiked, wheels smashed, abandoned. And good Lord, the smell. What happened?"

The mention of the smell finally got through to Grant.

"Excuse me, gentlemen," he said softly. "Must relieve myself."

He took his mount to the east side of the Monocacy, the ground held so tenaciously by Lee, then by Ord, and then again by Lee. He hurriedly rode up the embankment and dismounted. He walked over to a small tree, branches stripped clean by the gunfire, grabbed hold of it, leaned over, spitting out his cigar, and vomited.

He stood there for several minutes, gagging, vomiting again, each convulsive breath carrying with it the terrible cloying stench of the dead all around him, men lying in the mud, bodies half floating in the water, ghostlike faces looking up at him as if in reproach.

Tears streamed from his eyes as he struggled to breathe.

"Sir?"

Embarrassed, he looked up. It was Ely, holding a canteen.

He nodded his thanks, took the canteen, and swished a mouthful, then got sick again.

Ely stood by his side.

"It's alright, sir," Ely whispered. "It's hit all of us. Sir, nothing to be ashamed of. It's hit all of us."

Another mouthful spit out, and then a deep, long drink. For a second he wanted to ask if the water was clean, for if it had come from the river he knew he'd vomit again.

"That's it, sir," Ely said softly. "Take another. Believe me, sir, all of us understand."

He drank again and fought against the wish that it was pure whiskey, a quart of it. *No, don't think that.*

He took another sip, spit it out, and handed the canteen back.

"Thank you, Ely."

"Of course, sir."

Ely stood formally to attention, as if the exchange that had just taken place had never happened and would be forever forgotten, something that history would never record, how the victorious general had vomited like a sick child on the field of victory.

He let go of the tree, took his hat off, and, taking out a soiled handkerchief, wiped his face and brow. He nodded, indicating that he was all right. Ely turned and walked away.

Grant returned to his horse and mounted. Only then did the rest of the staff and Grierson cross the stream.

Not a word was said for a moment.

"We must push them," Grant said at last. "Grierson, ride with me for a while. Tell me everything that's happened over the last week. Ely, detail off some couriers, get word up to Sheridan. His men are already across. Push Longstreet and push him hard. Not one of them is to escape, not one of them. A courier over to Sykes as well."

He thought for a moment, the maps memorized.

"Tell Sykes I want him to swing wide. March toward Clarksburg, then due south to the Potomac at Darnestown. He will be our screen to the east, cutting off any attempt by Lee to move in that direction. A courier to Couch as well, that the militia is to follow Sykes and provide support. General Grierson, I suspect that is the route Lee might try to take. Once we are clear of this area, ride with all haste to Sykes with your men, push ahead of him to Clarksburg and down to Darnestown and from there to the canal.

"You know how to move fast, and I want that now. I'm behind Lee and will act as the barrier. You and Sykes are to be the pushers, bringing him back toward me. One of my staff will sketch out a map for you as we ride. Do not let Lee slip off to the east. His one chance is to slip past you and Sykes, perhaps make a lunge on Washington or to find a crossing place further down the river. I expect you will prevent that at all costs."

Grierson grinned and nodded.

"Better orders than when I rode through Mississippi," Grierson replied.

Grant nodded. This was the kind of officer he liked and trusted. Grierson would make sure, in what would be a forced march of twenty-five miles or more, that the back door was definitely slammed shut.

"Finally a telegram message to Hancock," Grant said, looking back at Ely, who was again all business, not an indicator at all of what had transpired but minutes ago. "Tell him to anticipate that Lee will now try to shift east and to ensure continued blockage of any potential crossing."

The group set off, riding at a slow trot, weaving around more bodies, past the ruins of the McCausland Farm, the hospital area around Dr. Field's house where McPherson had died, several thousand Confederates wounded around the house.

They rode on as dawn broke, the rain having stopped, coiling mist rising from the fields and woods.

"Push them," Grant repeated again, like a mantra. "Keep pushing them."

Headquarters, Army of Northern Virginia
Near Barnsville, Maryland

6:00 A.M.

General Longstreet rode into the encampment, mud splashing up from his mount as he trotted along the road. Troops were encamped to either side, a few had pitched tents, most had just collapsed in the open fields and were now sitting around smoky campfires, cooking their breakfasts.

Lee's headquarters area loomed up out of the mist, flag hanging limp, tents pitched in a half circle, awning canopying the middle, a knot of officers gathered round the fire. They looked up as Longstreet approached, coming to attention, saluting.

"The general?" Longstreet asked.

"Still asleep," one of them replied softly.

"He was up most of the night," another interjected, as if to apologize for the general sleeping so late.

Longstreet said nothing, taking a cup of coffee offered by one of the staff.

Walter came out of a tent and approached Longstreet.

"He's awake, sir, and begs your indulgence. He'll be with you in a few minutes."

"Thank you, Walter."

Longstreet sipped on his coffee, looking around at the staff. All were silent. Gone was the levity, the high spirits, the usual gibes back and forth, the sense of confidence. None of them had changed uniforms or had them cleaned in days.

"General Longstreet."

Lee was standing at the entry to his tent, beckoning him to come in. He did not have his uniform jacket on, nor vest, having obviously just been awakened.

Longstreet went into the tent and sat down in a camp chair Lee motioned him to while he sat back down on his cot.

"Your report, sir," Lee asked without greeting or the usual polite small talk before getting down to business.

"Sir, I started the withdrawal just after dark. The last troops pulled off the line at around midnight. The head of my column is within two or three miles of here. The tail of it most likely back near the Buckeystown ford. I regret to tell you, sir, there's bad news."

"And that is?"

"Sir, I abandoned over a hundred guns. The pieces we captured at Union Mills. All of them were spiked and wheels smashed."

"I expected that," Lee said. "They were of use at the moment but are a hindrance now."

"I thought so, too, sir. That frees up several thousand infantry who are back in the ranks. The ammunition, though, sir."

"You did not get all the ammunition off the trains?"

Longstreet shook his head.

"Why not, sir?" Lee asked sharply.

"Sir, we are short of horses, transport. I had to strip out an artillery battalion of its horses in order to move the pontoon train. At best we managed to retrieve about a million and a half rounds of small arms ammunition, maybe five thousand artillery rounds, before being forced to set the rest afire."

"Yes, I saw the fires," Lee said quietly. "But why?"

"That's the other bad news, sir. Grierson is at our rear. He came down onto the B and O line late yesterday afternoon with at least two brigades of cavalry. I fear Armistead might be cut off. I've not heard from him since nightfall. Sykes, with a corps strength, has pushed up and is in Urbana."

"That's less than ten miles from here," Lee replied.

"Yes, sir, I know."

Lee looked over at one of Jed Hotchkiss's maps on his field desk.

"Then the only ammunition we have is what our men are carrying, the small reserves at division level, and what you salvaged."

"Yes, sir."

"Enough, though, for one good fight if need be," Lee said, and he forced a smile.

"If required, sir. Yes, sir."

"The pontoon train. Everything rests on that now."

"Sir, it's proving difficult. Even on the best of roads they are difficult to move. The going has been slow. I estimate they are five miles back on our line of march."

Lee sighed, his gaze returning to the map. "We can still retrieve this situation, General," he said.

Longstreet did not reply.

"Do you believe me, General Longstreet?"

Pete looked into Lee's eyes. The gaze was intense, filled with determination, and yet again he found he could indeed believe in this man.

"Yes, sir. If we move swiftly and with daring. Yes, I think we can get back across the Potomac."

"Not just back across the Potomac, General. In the last two months we have dealt repeated blows to the North from which they can ill recover. This one reversal shall not stop us. We hold the line of the Potomac through the winter and into next spring, and surely their political coalition shall collapse."

Pete did not reply for a moment.

"Do you believe that, sir?" Lee asked, and Pete detected that there was a questioning in Lee's voice, a wish to be reaffirmed in his confidence.

"Sir, the first concern, at the moment, is to get this army safely out of Maryland. Then I will think of other things."

Lee finally smiled.

"Fair enough."

Lee pulled Hotchkiss's map over.

"We must move swiftly this day. You take your column, head down toward Poolesville. Then see if there is any chance we can secure Edwards Ferry. I know they are dug in there, but if in your estimate it can be stormed, do so. If not, move parallel to the river and find an appropriate place to cross. I will take the rest of the army and advance toward Darnestown and secure our flank in that direction. Grant's forces are worn, but the men coming down on our rear under Sykes must be turned, if possible defeated, and driven back. Succeed in that and we have bought some time."

Longstreet, looking at the map, nodded in agreement.

"We must move swiftly, sir, and the pontoon train must be pushed forward with all possible haste."

"Yes, sir."

Longstreet left the tent and mounted up. He started to ride back in the direction he had come from. Out in the fields the men were breaking camp, some loading up with backpacks or blanket rolls, but many just leaving them behind. They were stripping down for hard marching.

To the east the sun was clear of the horizon, promising a warm and humid day.

Headquarters, Army of the Potomac
Near Clarksburg

8:00 A.M.

 Sir, who is that man?" one of Sykes's aides asked, pointing up the road behind them.

Sykes turned in his saddle. An officer, riding a splendid white mount, was moving along the side of the road at a canter. He was pale-faced, gaunt, and almost seemed drunk the way he was riding, barely able to hang on.

Sykes smiled.

"I know him."

He turned about, moved to the side of the road, and grinned as the officer approached.

"Colonel Chamberlain, isn't it?" Sykes asked.

Joshua Lawrence Chamberlain saluted and forced a weak smile.

"Yes, sir, it is."

"My God, sir," Sykes exclaimed. "Last I heard you were dead."

"A premature report," Chamberlain replied.

"But you were captured?"

"Yes, sir. A friend of mine on the other side arranged my unconditional parole. I was officially exchanged last week and immediately came down to report for duty."

Sykes looked at him appraisingly. The man was barely able to keep to his saddle.

"I think, sir, you are not yet recovered from your wounds."

"Sir, may I be the judge of that," Chamberlain replied. "I have been following the news. I was with you and the boys of our glorious Fifth Corps at Taneytown, I wish to be with you now. I took a train down to Baltimore yesterday, paid a rather handsome amount for this magnificent horse, and have been trailing you ever since."

Sykes chuckled and shook his head.

"Such determination cannot be denied, Colonel. I have no posting for you, but you are welcome to join my staff."

"Thank you, sir, an honor."

"Fall in with my staff then. We have Bobbie Lee on the run. We are flanking to the east of him, boxing him in. I just received orders from Grant to push toward Clarksburg and then Darnestown. By God, sir, the Army of the Potomac must be in on this one. We will not lag, we will not slow, I will not let some damn Westerner claim he's won this war against Lee after all we've been through."

Chamberlain smiled.

"An honor to be here, sir."

He fell in behind Sykes, breathing deeply, glorying in the fact that he was back, he was with his "Old Fifth," the core of survivors of his beloved Army of the Potomac. The agony of his wound was forgotten for the moment, though each jostle of the horse beneath him sent shock waves through his barely healed hips and up his spine. Nor did he think of home, of his wife's threats to leave him if he followed through on such foolishness. No, this was the center, the core of his life, the reason for his existence, to be here, now, to help shape history, to ensure that the cause of freedom won.

Hauling Ferry

10:00 A.M.

Winfield Scott Hancock, barely able to stand, leaned against his cane, watching as the canal boats loaded up with "Mr. Bartlett's army," as it was now called. By the hundreds the men were scrambling aboard, as fast as a barge was loaded up, the mules or horses towing the boat dug in and set off, the men aboard cheering.

From up the river more barges were coming around the bend, carrying the last of the troops who had garrisoned Point of Rocks. They were heading back east and south, back down to Edwards Ferry and the crossing at Seneca Crossing.

Lee's men could march at two to three miles to the hour, but aboard the barges they could move four miles to the hour while the men relaxed, sang, ate, or slept.

It was a complex maneuver to keep boxing Lee in. The garrisons at Nolands Ferry and Hauling would hold in place, as would the garrison at Edwards Ferry. Hancock felt supremely confident. Though he had yet to meet him, he also felt supreme confidence in Grant. Here was a man who, at last, was thinking on a broad scale, maneuvering what were three armies at the same time, each one stepping into place and closing the ring around Lee. Gone was the indecision of the past.

An empty barge pulled up, and Hancock slowly shuffled aboard, Mr. Bartlett behind him, their staffs following.

Within minutes the horses were run over the low bridge arching the canal, cables attached to the harnesses, rudder pulled out from what had been the stern and carried to the rear of the boat and set in place.

"Heave away!"

The horses leaned into the traces, and the barge was moving, picking up speed.

Hancock gladly sat down on a camp chair set up near the bow, Mr. Bartlett coming up by his side.

Hancock looked up at the man and smiled.

"Boxing him in, Mr. Bartlett. That's the game now. Lee's a wily fox, he is. He still might slip past us, he surely will try, but you and I, we have other plans for him."

Near Edwards Ferry

12:00 P.M.

The marching was hard. The sun had broken through the overcast, at first a welcome relief after the rain of the past two days. Within a few hours it started to dry the roads, making passage easier, but the heat and humidity were climbing, thick clouds building overhead, a clear sign that by late afternoon thunderstorms would lash down.

The head of his column was already through Poolesville, where they had waited for a half hour while he and Colonel Duvall had ridden forward to Edwards Ferry. He had hoped against hope that perhaps here might be the crossing. A few minutes of surveying their lines had turned his opinion against it.

The Yankees were well dug in, same as at Hauling Ferry. Entrenchments encircled the crossing he had so easily taken a year earlier during the Sharpsburg campaign. Four of the dreaded, hundred-pound Parrott guns guarded the crossing, backed up by at least two batteries of thirty-pounders and at least five thousand infantry.

If I had a fresh corps up, two or three battalions of artillery in support, I might venture it, Longstreet thought. *It would cost, but we could do it.* But that would take the rest of the day, his column staggering along behind him, ten miles to the rear. *Gather here, and it will be dusk before we can even hope to force the position, and that will give Grant time to close in from the rear.*

Even as he surveyed the position, canal boats were passing by, ladened down with infantry and hundreds of colored civilians, all of them carrying shovels, picks, saws.

Has Lincoln drafted the colored of Washington? he wondered. If so, that would explain the massive fortifications confronting him.

He saw a banner draped on the side of one of the barges: WASHINGTON COLORED VOLUNTEERS.

He rode back to the head of the column, men standing back up after their noonday break, ready to resume the forced march.

"Duvall, scout ahead. We parallel the canal but out of sight of the Yankees along it. Find a spot where we can force a way across. The river can't be too wide where we cross, ideally with an island in the middle. Now ride!"

And the column had set off, afternoon sun blazing down.

Headquarters, Army of the Susquehanna
Near Barnesville, Maryland

1:00 P.M.

The distant rattle of skirmishing echoed from farther down the road. The men in the column, which had stopped, leaned wearily on their rifles, ordered to stand in place, to not break ranks.

Since late morning, any break had resulted in scores and hundreds of exhausted men refusing to get up again, regardless of the threats of their officers or provost guards.

Grant could not blame them. They were numb from exhaustion. These were men pushed to the limit and beyond, survivors of the Hornets Nest. Many of the regiments were reduced to little more than company size—a mere fifty men gathered around a flag where there would once have been five hundred.

Phil Sheridan came trotting up the road toward him, grinning.

"We're hitting the back end of Longstreet's column just ahead," he announced. "We're right behind him."

"Then keep pushing," Grant replied sharply. "Keep pushing."

Five Miles West of Seneca Crossing on the Potomac

2:15 P.M.

Col. Phil Duvall slowly stood up, General Longstreet by his side. The crossing below was swarming with Yankee troops getting off canal boats and starting to form up. They both scanned the line with their field glasses.

Duvall lowered his glasses and looked over at Longstreet.

"We have to try it," Longstreet said.

Duvall nodded, not replying.

Longstreet looked over at the young colonel. General Lee had pushed ahead to try to secure their flank at Darnestown while Pete had been ordered to take a narrow lane down to this crossing with his troops to see if they could somehow seize the position.

He had most of Scales's men up, two thousand men, concealed in the woods, nearly a brigade of cavalry with him.

"All at once," Pete said, turning to look back at Scales. "No artillery, complete surprise. Sweep down and into them. You must take that position."

Scales nodded.

"I can do it," he said quietly.

"Then go."

 Sergeant Hazner was at the fore of the charge, Colonel Brown by his side.

Both were panting for breath. The day had turned scorching hot, and they had not had a drop of water in hours, but both knew that this charge, out of so many charges, was different. This was a race for the survival of themselves and their army.

They had indeed caught the Yankees by surprise. They could see them forming up, struggling to create a volley line.

They were down to less than a hundred yards, running full out.

No volleys, just a scattering of fire to start, and then the volume increasing. Men began to drop.

"Come on!" Brown screamed. "One more time, boys, just one more time!"

Hancock stood up. Leaning against the bow of his canal barge, he saw the smoke roiling up from a field just around the bend in the river.

Damn!

"Get us ashore here," he shouted.

The steersman angled the boat over and slammed it against the embankment, Hancock nearly losing his footing. A couple of enlisted men, already on the embankment, reached over and half-lifted him out of the boat.

Bartlett started to jump off, but Hancock turned and looked back at him.

"No! Your people stay here!"

"We're needed, too," Jim tried to argue.

"No. You stay here. They've caught us by surprise. Chances are we'll get pushed back, at least for now. Get your men out. Move them back up that way."

He pointed farther along the canal, to a gently rising slope.

"Start digging in there. Build a redoubt. That's what we need now!"

Jim pointed the way, and his men, following in a half dozen barges, leapt for the shore and ran up the slope. Within minutes he had them at work, furiously digging, dragging fallen timber out of a nearby woodlot, tearing down split-rail fences and piling them up, forming a fortification for the Union troops to shelter behind.

C.S.A. The charge began to slow out of sheer exhaustion. They were but fifty yards off, but had run nearly a quarter of mile to gain this ground. One man stopped, and then another, and raised his rifle and fired.

"Come on!" Brown shouted, but the men of the Fourteenth came to a stop, raised rifles, and fired.

"Keep moving!"

The thin Union line before them offered another ragged volley. Several more men around Brown and Hazner dropped, but they continued to push forward and the Yankees broke, falling back, most turning to run along the towpath to the west.

The last few yards were covered, and Hazner, bent double with exhaustion, stood at the edge of the canal.

They had made it!

C.S.A. Pete Longstreet rode up, General Scales by his side, and quickly surveyed the ground. A half dozen abandoned barges were floating in the canal, a hundred or so Union casualties along the embankment.

Just below the canal was a short, open flood plain, and beyond the Potomac, on the other side, Virginia! Duvall had picked the spot well. A wooded island lay in the middle of the river, significantly shortening the distance they needed to traverse. On the far shore he spotted a couple of mounted troops, the men standing in their stirrups and waving. Mosby's men. He waved back.

Virginia!

He turned to Scales.

"Keep pushing them back. I need an opening here at least two miles wide or more. Keep pushing them back. I will send you everyone I can, and you keep pushing out to form a bridgehead that we can move the pontoon bridge through."

Scales saluted and rode off. Longstreet looked around at his staff.

"Venable, a courier to General Lee. Tell him we've seized a crossing point five miles west of Seneca. Second, a courier up our column to Cruickshank, and tell him to get those damn pontoons forward with all possible speed. The rest of you, as additional men come up, get them to work."

He pointed to a nearby farm, a gristmill, some sheds, and outbuildings.

"Tear them apart. Get any lumber out that we can use for bridging material. Use the barges here to build a bridge across the canal. We need more than what is here and then a corduroy road down to the river. Now move it!"

Longstreet watched as the men set to work.

Maybe, just maybe, we've pulled it off. By tomorrow morning we will be across the river and be out of this damn state.

Near Poolesville

3:00 P.M.

Cruickshank returned the salute of the officer who had come up.

"General Longstreet has seized a crossing point, sir."

"Where?"

"About three miles from here, west of Seneca Crossing."

"Damn all to hell," Cruickshank said, shaking his head.

The courier looked at him confused.

"The general insists you come up with all possible speed to bring up the pontoons. I'm to guide you in."

"All possible speed? Just what the hell do you think I've been doing all day?" Cruickshank asked.

"Sir, I'm just carrying orders."

"Yes, I know."

Ahead of him an artillery limber wagon had just lost a wheel, the load collapsing, again stalling traffic on the narrow, rutted road. The crew was struggling to jack the wagon up and replace the wheel, everything behind them stopped.

Cruickshank looked over at the courier.

"Got a drink on you."

"Sir?"

"A drink. Bourbon, gin, anything?"

"I'm a temperance man," the courier replied a bit stiffly.

"I bet you are, damn it."

It took five minutes for the artillery crew to maneuver the wheel into place, secure the lug nut, and the piece lurched forward.

Behind him, with much cursing and swearing, his crew lashed their horses and mules, the twenty-four wagons again rolling forward, wheels sinking deep into the mud that still clung to the road down in hollows and stream crossings.

They edged up to an open field where the artillery crew had pulled over and unhitched their horses to let them graze while men hauled up buckets of water from a stream. An infantry regiment was resting by the side of the road, men sprawled in the damp grass, some taking down fence rails to make fires.

There was a distant rattling behind them and the less weary looked up, turning toward the north. Stuart, in spite of his injuries, was in the saddle, guarding the rear, trying to slow down the relentless advance of Grant. From the sound of gunfire the Yankees were only a couple of miles back.

"Keep it moving," Cruickshank shouted, urging his exhausted teams on. "Keep it moving."

Darnestown, Maryland

3:15 P.M.

His men had covered nearly twenty-five miles since dawn. The militia had long since been left behind, but that did not worry him. The crossroads of this small village was just ahead. General Sykes reined in, shouting orders, the head of the column shaking out into line of battle.

To his right, a mile away, across open fields he could see them coming, red flags held high, shifting from column to line as well. It was a race to secure the village crossroads.

He rode across the front of the line, sword held high, trailed by his staff.

"Men of the Army of the Potomac!" he shouted. "This is your time. This is your time to regain our honor!"

A resounding cheer rose up, grim, determined.

The battle line swept down toward the advancing foe.

L ee watched with field glasses raised, heart pounding. *But an hour more and we could have been into this village, secured it, then turned south toward the Potomac, where surely Longstreet even now is securing a crossing place. And now this.*

At the front of his column men were deploying out, the same men battered before Hauling Ferry the day before. There was no cheering now, no defiance. Only a grim silence as lines were formed, ramrods drawn, rifles loaded. One battery was up, unlimbered, opening with a salvo as the advancing blue wave closed to eight hundred yards.

The enemy charge came on, relentless, their cheers filled with a terrible anger.

More of his men were coming up, moving to either flank to broaden out their front, but the men moved slowly, without the élan of but three days past.

The enemy were six hundred yards off. Another volley from the guns, several striking the line, but the charge continued forward.

He drew back to a wooden knoll, staff gathered around him. No one spoke.

Four hundred yards, then three hundred. A regiment in the center raised rifles and fired, too soon he thought, others began to fire as well. Clouds of smoke billowed across the field, and still the charge came forward.

They were relentless, bayonets glistening, cheering madly, not as Union troops cheered in the past, the disciplined three hurrahs, but an almost guttural roar, a scream of rage. An officer on a white horse was in their middle, sword raised, pushing forward, other officers, mounted, joining in as well.

Two hundred yards, and then a hundred yards. They did not slow or waver. The massive blue wave broke into a run.

Several of his regiments presented and fired disciplined volleys. Scores of Yankees dropped, but the charge pressed in.

And then his men broke.

One or two turned at first, then dozens, and finally the entire line shattered apart, men streaming to the rear.

Horrified, Lee said nothing, watching as his valiant army disintegrated under the hammer blow rolling toward them. Above the smoke he saw the Maltese cross of the Fifth Corps. This was not Grant; this was a ghost resurrected—this was the Army of the Potomac, and in that instant he understood the rage, the élan that drove them forward. On this field they were bent on restoring their honor and inflicting their revenge.

He turned Traveler and rode back to the west, joining in with his retreating men.

Headquarters, Army of the Susquehanna

3:45 P.M.

Elihu Washburne?" Grant exclaimed in surprise as the secretary of war came riding up, escorted by several dozen cavalry troopers.

"General, how are you?" Elihu exclaimed, leaning over from his horse to shake Grant's hand.

Grant could not reply at first. He had felt deathly ill all day, barely able to remain in the saddle.

The march had been tedious and frustratingly slow. His own men, to be sure, were exhausted, but then again, so were the rebels they were pursuing. The rebel cavalry, though, was still doing a masterful job of contesting every ford, every place where defendable ground could buy the retreating columns ten or fifteen minutes' respite.

Sheridan was at the fore, driving relentlessly, but for the men in column behind the advance, it was the most exhausting kind of march. Advance a few hundred yards, wait in place maybe for a minute, maybe for a half hour, then sprint forward a quarter mile, then slow down, stop, then lurch forward again.

The sides of the road for miles was littered with the castoffs of an army in retreat. Broken-down limber wagons, overturned and destroyed supply wagons, and prisoners by the hundreds, men who had given up and collapsed.

But it was littered as well with the debris of an exhausted army in pursuit, yet more cast-off equipment, gray-faced soldiers lying by the side of the road, unable to advance another step after so many hard days of marching and three days of pitched fighting.

He could so easily sense the inertia that built at such times, understand why so many generals would, at this moment, call a halt to allow their men to "rest, reorganize, and refit." Regiments were jumbled together, not just men from one regiment slowing and bleeding back into the unit behind them, but entire brigades and divisions were mixed together. All that kept them moving forward now was their own will, the will

of each man who, sensing victory, would not give out, and his will as well, driving them forward even if but one man was left standing at the end.

"I have a dispatch from the president. I think it is important that you read it, sir," Elihu said.

Elihu handed the envelope over.

"Yes, sir. Is it urgent?"

"Well, sir, I think you should read it soon, but for the moment it can wait."

"I want to keep pushing," Grant said. "Ride along with me. I'll tell you what is happening and we can discuss the president's wishes when we stop for a few hours."

"Fine with me," Elihu said, and he fell in by Grant's side.

4:00 P.M.

CSA Men were swarming about Longstreet. Some planking had already been laid across the tops of the canal barges to form a rough walkway, not yet secure enough to move wagons on, but in another hour that should be accomplished. Hundreds more were on the narrow ground between the canal and the river, dropping logs down to form a corduroy road. Down at the river's edge men with axes were dropping trees to clear an access way. A dozen men had volunteered to swim out to the island in the middle of the river and even now were hacking a path across it.

Where are the damn bridges?

And, as if in answer to a prayer, he saw the first of them coming down the road, Cruickshank in the lead.

"My God," Longstreet sighed, "we just might pull this off after all."

US Jim Bartlett paced back and forth along the line, his men digging furiously. Down by the canal more boats were coming up, off-loading infantry, and more of his own men. Along the towpath an artillery battery was coming up fast, an officer directing them to swing off the path and up the slope to where positions were being dug.

Ahead there was a constant rattle of musketry, drawing closer. Walking up the slope Jim saw Hancock atop the rise, astride a horse, field glasses raised. Jim went to his side.

"You can presently see them down there," Hancock said, and pointed.

Jim looked in the direction Hancock was pointing and just under a mile, perhaps three quarters of a mile away he could see a swarm of men at work, tearing the siding off a mill. Closer, far closer, a line of infantry was advancing in open order, some mounted troopers joined in. A harassing fire buzzed across the field, cutting down stalks of grass around them.

The rough entrenchment, after barely an hour's work, was not much more than knee to thigh deep, but it offered protection enough with the sod and dirt piled up in front, fence railing and logs atop that.

Hancock turned and rode back, shouting for his men to drop their tools, pick up rifles, and get to work.

All up and down the line men fell into place, and within a few minutes fire rippled along the line. Jim stood and watched.

Several men around Jim dropped, some screaming, some just collapsing silently.

"Get down, you damn fool!" someone shouted.

He knelt down inside the trench but continued to watch. He was strangely fascinated by what was happening. His vague memories of 1814, the years in the White House, the memory of watching Lincoln reading the latest casualty reports and walking the corridors alone in the middle of the night. *So this is what it is like,* he thought. *This is battle in all its horror.*

He could see the men who were supposed to be his enemy not a hundred fifty yards away, lined up, all of them moving as if in some nightmare, men aiming rifles, apparently straight at him, disappearing from view behind a flash of fire and then smoke, others reloading, others falling. The Union soldiers around him, secure behind the low entrenchment, stood firm. Men tore open cartridges, pouring powder down barrels, one was shot even as he poured, the cartridge flying into the air as he tumbled over a man turning to grab his fallen comrade. The battle continued to rage on, while overhead the skies darkened.

Five Miles West of Seneca Crossing

4:05 P.M.

The thunder of battle was close, damn close to his right as he led the column down a farm lane, the wagons behind him barely squeezing through between the trees, and then he saw it, the Potomac.

"I'll be damned." He spurred forward, heading across an open field, riding past a small mill which troops were struggling to tear apart, some with their bare hands. Down at the canal he saw Pete and rode up, saluting.

"General Longstreet."

"Cruickshank, it's about time you showed up."

Pete glared at him for a second, and Cruickshank began to bristle. After all that he had been through, if this was the reception, then the hell with him.

Pete smiled and leaned over to shake his hand.

"Get the damn bridges down there and start laying them."

"What?"

"You heard me."

"Sir, I thought my job was just to get them here. Where are the engineering troops? That's their job."

"Scattered to hell and gone."

"Oh, God damn," Cruickshank sighed, and knew there was no sense in arguing.

"Venable will stay with you. Tell him what you need and he'll see that you get it."

"Yes, sir," Cruickshank said as he turned about. The first of the wagons was coming out of the woods, cutting across the open field, driver hunched low since shot was dropping into the field from the fighting going on to the west.

Venable came up and saluted.

"He said you can get me what I need."

"Yes."

"There must be some engineering troops mixed into this mess. Have someone ask around for anybody who's built one of these damn bridges before and get them down to me."

"I've already done that. We have fifty or so who claimed to have worked on the bridge across the Potomac when the campaign started."

"Fine, then. Also a bottle of whiskey."

Venable reached into his haversack and pulled one out.

"The general said you can have one good slug now, the rest when the bridge is done."

Cruickshank made sure it was a damn big slug before he handed the bottle back.

The first wagon passed, crossing over the roughly made pontoon bridge across the canal, the boats underneath bobbing and swaying. The hard part now was getting down the side of the canal embankment, the driver lashing hard, the wagon skidding sideways and nearly lurching over. Then across the muddy flats and finally to the edge of the river.

Cruickshank rode alongside the wagon till it reached the river, and he dismounted, looking around.

Now what in hell do I do? Men were standing about. He eyeballed the crossing point. Maybe a couple hundred yards to the island where he could see men already at work, cutting a path. Hard to tell how far from the other side to the Virginia shore, maybe a hundred yards. *We should have enough.*

"Get the wagon into the river, back it in, and float the boat off. The stringers and cross ties, off-load here on shore first."

Men set to work pulling off the heavy lumber and stacking it up, the driver then urging the team to turn in a half circle, the wagon sinking deep into the mud as soon as it ran off the corduroy approach. There it stalled, sinking halfway to its axles.

"God damn it," Cruickshank cried. "Alright, get men to push the damn thing off, gently now, and into the water. I want fifty of you to start building a corduroy turnaround here so we can swing the wagons around."

The second wagon was coming down the canal embankment, barely making it, and Cruickshank ran back to it, yelling for them to stop and wait. The work crew around the first wagon, with much pushing and cursing, finally slid the pontoon boat off the back of the wagon. Cruickshank winced as they pushed it across the rough corduroy of logs, half expecting the bottom would be torn out. At last, the forward end was in the water, the load lightened, and the boat floated.

"Anchor lines should be in the boat," a sergeant announced and he waded out to the boat and jumped in.

The sergeant seemed to know what he was doing, so Cruickshank left him to his work as the sergeant tossed out two cables, anchors on the end of them, and directed men to wade upstream and set them in place. The boat was jockeyed parallel to the shore about twenty feet out, and two more anchor lines were run out downstream and dropped into place.

The sergeant jumped out of the boat and waded back to shore, shaking his head, coming up to Cruickshank.

"Assume you're in charge here, sir?" the sergeant asked.

"That's what they tell me."

"Ever lay a bridge before."

"No."

"Well, sir, the setup here is all wrong. You have just this one approach down to the river. You need a second one alongside it and upstream. That's where the boats should be hauled up to, backed around, and then pushed in. Once we get three or four boats out, it's gonna get tricky with this current maneuvering the following boats in place. You just can't run the following boats onto the bridge and dump them off the end."

Cruickshank nodded. This man knew the job; he didn't, and he realized he had better listen.

"Sir, let me go back and get my regiment. Some of us helped with the pontoon crossing back in the spring. We'll need at least two hundred men to cut the second approach."

"Go get them."

Venable, who was still by Cruickshank's side, rode off, the sergeant jogging alongside him.

The first stringers were laid in place and run out to the anchored boat. Within a couple of minutes he saw another problem. The stringers had been set into the mud on the bank, and, as the crosspieces were laid atop them, the whole thing started to sink.

"God damn it, take it apart," Cruickshank shouted. "We need supports, gravel, logs, something under here. Take it apart!"

He heard shouting and cursing behind him and then a rendering crash. Turning, he looked back. The third wagon had tried to negotiate the steep drop-off from the canal and rolled over on its side, mules tangled up in the mess, kicking and thrashing.

He struggled through the mud, men running toward the wreck. The driver, damn him, was dead, tangled up with his mules and kicked to death. The pontoon was completely staved in on one side.

"Get this wreck cleared," Cruickshank shouted, and then looked at the embankment.

They couldn't cut it down to level it, that would breech the canal. Men would have to be set to work. There wasn't enough time to extend the grade out, that would take hours and hundreds of men with shovels. He'd have to post a hundred here, rig up some cables with men hanging onto them to ease the load as it slid down the embankment.

Venable was coming back, Longstreet by his side. He could see that a regiment was moving behind them, the men obviously not too happy with their sergeant volunteering them for heavy labor.

Longstreet crossed the short bridge over the canal and nearly lost his mount sliding down the embankment slope.

"You've got to straighten this out," Longstreet snapped angrily.

"I'm trying, sir."

"The entire army will start passing through here tonight. This embankment, the grade has to be extended out, paved over with logs, better yet, gravel. We'll lose every artillery piece trying to negotiate it. We need a good approach to the bridge, well paved as well, otherwise the entire army will just flounder into this mud. Now get to it. I don't know how long we can hold this position, so get to it, Cruickshank."

Cruickshank just lowered his head.

"God damn it, sir, I'd like you to accept my resignation," he said wearily.

"What?"

"I'm resigning from this goddamn army. I'm a mule skinner, sir. First you gave me these damn bridges, which I don't know a damn thing about. Then you give me the goddamn railroad, which I definitely knew nothing about, and then you give me these sons of bitches again. Now you're screaming at me to build a goddamn road and a goddamn bridge, which I definitely know goddamn nothing about, goddamnit. I quit."

Longstreet looked down at him and actually smiled.

"You know, Cruickshank, if I wasn't so desperate, I think I'd shoot you."

There was no malice in his voice, just a sad weariness.

"I'd consider it a favor, General."

He dismounted and motioned for Cruickshank to follow him. The two walked off, Longstreet pulling out two cigars, lighting his own and handing the other to Cruickshank.

"We're trapped," Longstreet said softly. "The army is a shambles. I got men from two other corps mixed in with mine right now. My supply train is abandoned. Except for Scales, every one of my division commanders and over half my brigade commanders are down.

"If you don't get that bridge across and damn quick, we are lost, and with us gone, the cause is lost. Do you understand that?"

Cruickshank could not reply. Strange his feelings for this man. There had been times in the past, if given the chance, he'd have kicked his brains out, not even giving him a chance to duel, and then other times, like now, when he couldn't help but like him.

"I'll see what I can do," Cruickshank replied.

"Good, then, damn you. Part of it is my fault. I was too focused on the fight to take this place. I already should have had more men clearing the approach. You'll have a brigade of men working on this shortly."

"A brigade? Three thousand men."

"In this army," Longstreet replied sadly, "a brigade now means five hundred men. Get to work."

Headquarters, Army of Northern Virginia
Five Miles Southeast of Poolesville

4:45 P.M.

CSA All around was chaos. Men were staggering back up the road they had forced-marched down but four hours earlier in their drive toward Darnestown, "Damns-town" as they were now calling it.

Supply wagons had been abandoned, pushed to the side of the road to clear the way. Men were told to pull out what they could, especially ammunition. Wounded and exhausted men were mounting horses and mules being cut loose from the traces.

How many times in the past have I seen this? Lee thought. *But always it was the other side. Always it was their wagons abandoned, their exhausted men lying by the side of the road, their men collapsing into disorder and disintegration.*

"General Lee!"

A courier came up, one of Stuart's men, a newly promoted regimental commander, Colonel Duvall, followed by several dozen troopers.

"Sir, we got a crossing. The bridge is being built even now," Duvall cried excitedly.

"Where?"

"Sir, it's a rough track down to it. A lot of your men have already marched past the turnoff. General Longstreet, as ordered, tried for Edwards Ferry but it was too heavily fortified. He finally pushed down, about halfway between Edwards Ferry and Seneca. It's a good spot, sir, island halfway across."

Lee looked over at Walter and smiled. "Pete came through for us," he said.

Walter, expressionless, could only nod in agreement.

"I want a solid rear guard to be maintained. Slow down the Army of the Potomac behind us. If need be, sacrifice some of the artillery to do so. We need breathing space. I'm going up to see what we can do with this."

Lee set off with Duvall. In the column he spotted Judah Benjamin and reined in beside him.

"Good news, Mr. Secretary," Lee announced. "We have a crossing."

Judah nodded wearily but said nothing, silently falling in by Lee's side as the general continued to push his way up the road.

The Crossing

5:45 P.M.

C.S.A. Some semblance of organization was taking hold. Hundreds of men were dragging logs, brush, anything to lay down to create a roadway from the canal to the crossing. The sixth pontoon was in the water, the bridge now extending out over sixty yards. The sergeant in charge of construction was hurrying back and forth, urging men on. The crews were starting to learn the routine of maneuvering a boat into place, anchor it, span the gap with the heavy thirty-foot-long stringers, bolt them down on to the gunwale of the boat, then start laying the cross ties of heavy planking.

Cruickshank stood at the edge of the bridge watching as the sixth boat was steered down from where it had been pushed in forty yards upstream, men along the gunwale using bits of board and planking as oars and poles.

The current was stronger as they approached the middle of the river, the maneuvering more difficult, men shouting at each other, contradicting each other. The anchor lines went out and the boat stopped, but it was not lined up correctly, having drifted a dozen feet below the axis of the bridge. There was more swearing and yelling. A couple of men jumped over the side, but the river was too deep and they were swept away, one disappearing, the other floundering back to shore.

Men up at the bow pulled on the anchor lines, gradually hauling the boat into a near alignment, a couple of feet off center but about as close as they could get.

"Stringers!"

Cruickshank stepped off the bridge and down into the pontoon bridge, feeling it rock and sway as men ran up, pushing and struggling. Men aboard the anchored boat threw lines over, the lines were lashed to the ends of the stringers, and between the crew on the next boat out pulling and men on the edge of the bridge pushing, the stringer went across and was locked into place.

More men came up, two to each plank, dropping the cross ties into place, and another thirty feet was spanned.

The next boat was now easing into the river and Cruickshank actually felt that for once he was pulling something off correctly. Every man about him knew what was at stake, and though more than one man finally had to stagger off to one side to collapse from total exhaustion, others filled in. The survival of the Army of Northern Virginia was as dependent on them now as it had ever been on any volley line.

To one flank the rattle of musketry continued, Scales holding back the Yankees to the west.

Hancock grinned as the team of black laborers, a hundred of them to each piece, urged on by Jim Bartlett, dragged two of the thirty-pound Parrotts up the slope. The horses had been left behind, but the men were here to help maneuver the weapons into place. Others were hauling up the shells and wooden tubes containing the ten pounds of powder needed for each shot. Two more guns were on the next barge, teams of men struggling to off-load them.

The first two guns were rolled into place. The range was just about a mile, long shooting for a three-inch ordnance rifle, but well within the capability of the heavier pieces.

A captain of artillery came up to Hancock's side and saluted. Hancock merely pointed down to the river.

"Lovely," the captain exclaimed, "just lovely."

"Let's try some case shot for openers, nine-second fuses!"

The crews set to work, the captain standing behind each piece, carefully setting the rear sight in place, gunnery sergeants following his directions as they dropped elevation screws.

Powder was rammed in, followed by the shells.

The captain stood back and looked over at Hancock.

"Care for a shot, General?"

Hancock grinned and limped over, picking up the lanyard. He caught Jim's eye.

"Mr. Bartlett, after all you've done, why don't you take the other one."

Jim nervously walked up to the breech of the gun, the sergeant looking at him over with a jaundiced eye, but then under the gaze of the general he relented and handed it over.

"Just step back till it's taut," the sergeant said. "When the captain gives the command, step back hard, jerk, and turn away."

Jim did as directed, the line taut in his hand.

"Fire in sequence so we can judge the shot," the captain announced.

"Number one!" He pointed toward Hancock.

"Fire!"

The thirty-pounder leapt back with a sharp recoil, a tongue of flame bursting from the muzzle. The noise was stunning.

"Number two!"

Jim gripped the lanyard and thought of his son and grandson, wondering what they would say of this moment. Though he and his men had not been in the fight directly, still here, at least, was one shot that might count.

"Fire!"

He stepped back, pulled, but nothing happened and several men laughed good-naturedly.

"Harder!" the sergeant yelled.

This time he threw what little weight he had into it, and nearly stumbled backward. The gun leapt back with a roar.

Grinning, he looked over at Hancock, who gave him a friendly salute.

"Something to tell your grandkids about," Hancock shouted.

Cruickshank looked up, heard the shell screaming in, a geyser of water erupting about fifty yards upstream. Men working along the bridge flattened themselves. Seconds later a second shot, this one overhead, a sudden flash, water around the bridge spraying up from the cascade of case shot, several men dropping. A heavy shell fragment slashed into one of the boats, seconds later someone was crying they had a leak.

Cruickshank stood up, looking to the west, and saw the two puffs of smoke from a distant rise.

Must be thirty-pounders, he thought, and then a bit forward there were more puffs. Seconds later half a dozen lighter shells rained in, five of the six scattering wide, dropping into the muddy embankment, one kicking up a geyser in midstream, but one striking and exploding on the embankment of the canal.

"Watch it!"

He turned to look back. The crew of the seventh boat had ducked down when the first two shells came in and now the boat was broaching, turning sideways. Carried on the current it slammed into the sixth boat, which had just been anchored.

The anchor lines of the sixth boat let go from the impact, and now the entire front of the bridge started to buckle, bending, groaning. Men ran about shouting. He could feel the entire bridge swaying beneath him.

"Drop the front end!" someone screamed; it was the sergeant in command.

The men in the sixth boat worked frantically, trying to pull the bolts from the stringers that locked them to the gunnel, and then the gunnel itself just ripped away, stringers dropping into the water, half sinking, the sixth and seventh boats now wrapped around each other and drifting downstream.

The pressure on the bridge eased off, and it straightened, planking that had connected the fifth boat to the sixth dropping into the water until only the two stringers were left, bobbing in the water.

"Damn all to hell." Cruickshank sighed as he sat down and buried his head in his hands.

C ruickshank!"
It was Pete, coming toward him.
He didn't even bother to look up.

5:45 P.M.

 T his is it?" Lee asked as Duvall reined in and pointed down a narrow farm lane.
"Yes, sir."
Lee looked at the road. It was barely a dirt track, a pathway used occasionally by some farmer gathering wood for the winter, perhaps cut through years ago when the forests here were first harvested and now barely used. It was apparent, though, that it had seen recent heavy use, the track muddy, torn up by the passage of troops.

"The road General Longstreet used was a bit farther over, but this is the quickest way down to where the bridge is going in."

The men filing along the road back toward Poolesville had been passing this point for at least an hour or two. He would have to send someone forward to stop and reverse them and it would be a mad tangle, for the rest of his column five miles back would have to turn off here as well.

Lee looked around, watching as men continued to file past.

He turned to a cavalry sergeant who along with several other troopers stood by the side of the road.

"Halt the column, Sergeant," Lee said. "Have them stop right here, and pass the word back up the line for the men to fall out for rest and to eat. I should be back within the hour."

He turned down the track, Duvall in the lead, his men drawing pistols as they rode into the woods. From nearly all directions could be heard distant fire, the thumping of artillery, joined now by a deep rumble ahead.

6:15 P.M.

T he light was rapidly failing, the combination of the sun setting and the storm clouds continuing to build up to the west.
Two more boats were out in the river, being jockeyed into place. Yet another boat was almost across to the island, Longstreet suggesting that

they start building the bridge from both sides, something that Cruickshank knew he should have thought of, but exhaustion was completely overwhelming him.

After the shock of the first two shells coming in, the men had set to work as if the enemy fire was a goad. Watchers kept an eye on the distant ridge, and the moment they saw the flash of what were now four of the thirty-pounders, a warning went up.

Another boat had been destroyed, as it was being rolled up to be offloaded into the river, taking a nearly direct hit and just shattering. The two boats that had washed downstream were slowly being kedged up, and were now waiting to be shifted into place.

Another shell came in, this one nearly striking the bridge at midsection, the pontoons rocking and swaying from the impact, another boat springing a leak, a man tearing his jacket off to use as a plug.

Nearly all of the pontoon train was now parked in the flat land below the canal, crews manhandling the boats off rather than waiting for each to be backed into the water, and simply dragged along and pushed in. More leaks were being sprung but the time saved was worth it, bailers would be set to work in each once they were in place.

The bridge was pushing forward. They were out to their tenth boat now, well past midstream, the crews on the other side within hailing distance, one of them shouting that they only had to span seventy-five yards or so once across the island. The good news was that infantry could wade the last few yards through chest-deep water to Virginia soil once they were across the island.

Additional boatloads of men were already being sent across, armed with axes and shovels, to clear a road across the island and start work on the approach on the far side.

The eleventh boat was anchored into place, two more shells detonating over the river, more men dropping, but the work continued. Stringers were run across, planking laid. A man leapt off the boat on the far side and stood in the water, bracing against the current.

"Its getting shallower!" he shouted, a ragged cheer rising up from the makeshift engineers.

6:15 P.M.

General Longstreet!"
 Pete looked up and to his amazement saw Lee approaching, guided by Duvall.

"Sir!"

Pete rode the last few feet to Lee's side.

Lee said nothing for a moment, looking down at the bridge spanning the Potomac and a shell exploding among the wagons where the pontoons were being unloaded.

"I can have it finished in another two or three hours," Pete said.

"Those guns, though," and Lee pointed to the west, the distant puffs of smoke.

The two batteries Pete had brought up were trying to suppress the enemy fire, but only one of them was comprised of rifled pieces, the others were smoothbores, and so far they had had no effect either on the thirty-pounders or the lighter ten-pounders.

"Can you not push those guns back?" Lee asked.

"I have Scales covering that flank. He's trying as hard as he can, sir. But the numbers are about even and their forward line of infantry is dug in."

Lee took it all in. It was a marvel that Pete had indeed accomplished this, but the approach would be difficult. It might very well mean abandoning nearly all their remaining artillery and wagons.

"Did you receive my dispatch about what happened at Darnestown?"

"Sir?"

Lee shook his head.

"We are flanked to the east, Pete. Our old adversaries, the Army of the Potomac. They closed off that approach. Even now they are pressing the rear of my column."

"I didn't know, sir. I thought we had destroyed the Army of the Potomac twice now. Their resilience is amazing."

"You must watch your own flank carefully," Lee said, pointing east.

"I barely have the men left," Pete replied. "What's left of Rhodes and Anderson?"

He pointed across the open field where scattered commands were resting, waiting for the bridge to be finished.

"Form them up now," Lee said. "I fear that part of the Army of the Potomac might advance along the canal and try and strike you here."

"I have patrols out, sir. I need to rest these men in case they are needed as a reserve. They fought all day yesterday and have been on the road since midnight. Rations are short as well. Some haven't had a bite to eat all day."

"Please see to it anyway. Form them up now."

"Yes, sir."

"I will shift my column down this way. Expect the head of it to arrive within two to three hours."

"Yes, sir."

Lee turned and Duvall fell in by his side to provide escort.

Lee rode slowly, looking back occasionally toward the river. So tantalizingly close. *We could have the bulk of our men across by tomorrow morning.* Something in his heart told him not to exult just yet.

As they reached the edge of the woods there was a tattoo of rifle fire from the east, and within seconds it rose to a shattering explosion of volley fire.

CSA Pete Longstreet turned away as Lee rode north. He could see that another boat was being maneuvered into place, men standing in the water. Now that it was shallower, the work would go quicker.

And then the first pistol shots echoed.

Looking toward the east he saw several mounted men, riding hard, one firing his pistol in the air as he galloped. Behind them, a hundred yards back, a darker mass was approaching . . . Union cavalry!

Across the field where the rest of his corps had been keeping low, waiting for the bridge to be finished, men were stirring, standing up, grabbing stacked rifles, starting to form.

The column of Yankee cavalry came on at a gallop, reaching the edge of the field, spreading out as they did so. Behind them a column of infantry was visible, coming at the double.

He raised his field glasses, focused on the lead flag . . . a fluttering triangle, a red Maltese cross in the middle.

"Damn, the Army of the Potomac."

US Winfield Scott Hancock stirred, looked up as his staff began to shout, pointing down toward the crossing.

Behind him an assault column was forming up, men brought down from Point of Rocks and Nolands Ferry. He had kept the garrison at Edwards Ferry in place, except for the removal of the four thirty-pounders. There was always the chance that if he stripped out there, Lee could swing on the position and still try to take it. His reinforcements were coming, but it was taking so damn long, and now they were arriving at last. In another half hour, just before full dark, he planned to go in with everything he had and try to dislodge them before they finished the bridge.

"It's our boys!" someone shouted. "Look over there, our boys!"

Winfield raised his field glasses and looked to where they were pointing, the view momentarily obscured from the smoke of one of the thirty-pounders going off.

And then he saw it, cavalry, a regiment at least, maybe two, but behind them, infantry, a dark blue mass, national colors at the fore, and alongside them, fluttering out for a second, a large triangle, red Maltese cross in the middle.

He wept unashamedly at the sight of it. It was the old Fifth Corps, men of his army, men of the Army of the Potomac, trusted comrades in so many fights.

"Up, boys, up!" Hancock shouted.

The troops lying in the field on the opposite slope were already on their feet, sensing from the excitement of the officers around the guns that something was about to happen.

Hancock turned back to face them.

"It's the Army of the Potomac!" he shouted. "They're closing in from the other side. Let's join them and finish this!"

A resounding cheer arose. The men who but a minute before were nervously awaiting the orders to charge could not now be held back. They started up the slope, passing through the guns, which fell silent.

Several of Hancock's staff helped him to mount. He fell in alongside the advancing lines, struggling to draw his sword, pointing it forward. A rider came up beside him, wearing an army slouch cap that looked rather absurd when contrasted with his mud-covered butler's jacket.

"I'm not missing this, sir!" Bartlett shouted.

"Come on then, old man!" Hancock roared.

The charge swept down the slope.

Bartlett looked back. Mingled in with the infantry were many of "his" men, carrying axes and shovels, racing forward as well.

6:40 P.M.

Pete Longstreet was silent, turning back and forth, watching as the vise closed. *If they had planned this, it could not have been done more masterfully,* he realized. *We could have been to the island in another thirty minutes; if need be, men could have started crossing and waded the last few yards to the other side, to Virginia.*

Panic was breaking out. Scales's men were on the run, falling back toward the center, a wall of Union infantry in pursuit. From the other side of the clearing Anderson and Rhodes's men were holding for the moment, but more and more infantry were coming up the towpath on the double, pushing into the fight.

"General, we have to get out!"

It was Scales, wide-eyed, hat gone, his voice edged with hysteria.

"Can't you hold?" Longstreet cried.

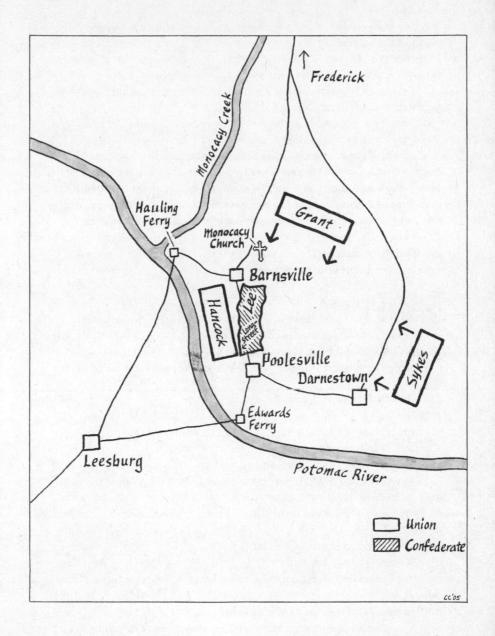

Frederick

Monocacy Creek

Hauling
Ferry

Monocacy
Church

Grant

Barnsville

Hancock

Lee

Longstreet

Poolesville

Darnestown

Sykes

Edwards
Ferry

Leesburg

Potomac River

Union

Confederate

cc'05

"With what, sir? If I had the men I had at Fort Stevens, if I had the men I had but three days ago, yes, but not now. Not now, damn it!"

The work crews at the bridge had stopped, were looking in one direction and then the other.

From the far side of the field men were beginning to break as more men of the Army of the Potomac surged into the fight.

More officers were coming up to Pete, shouting, asking for orders, yelling they had to get out.

Pete was silent, gazing at the bridge . . . the damn bridge. *If we had had it in but one day ago, we'd all be across. We'd still have an army.*

A shell detonated down where the remaining bridging material had been unloaded, striking a wagon with a pontoon still on it, the entire affair blowing apart, mules collapsing, screaming, and that set the panic off. Men turned away and started to run toward the canal embankment to get out. Others stormed onto the bridge itself as if instinct was telling them safety lay to the south.

"Order the men out," Pete said. "Full retreat."

He turned his horse, and started north, staff falling in with him.

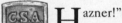 H azner!"

He turned and saw Brown, down on the ground.

Hazner turned and ran back to the colonel's side. Horrified, he saw that the colonel had been shot in the back.

Hazner tried to pick him up, but the man screamed and he gently set him back down.

"Hazner. Guess this is it," Brown said.

"No, sir. I'll get you out."

Brown feebly motioned back. The Yankees, advancing in the twilight, were less than fifty yards off.

"Not this time, my friend," Brown said.

Brown fumbled in his breast pocket and pulled out a small notebook and a pocket Bible.

"My diary, a few notes inside the Bible for my wife. See that she gets them."

Hazner gulped hard and nodded.

"Now go!"

Hazner stood up and stuck them in his haversack, to rest alongside another diary, that of his old friend killed at Union Mills. He felt as if the burden he carried was more than he could bear.

He saw young lieutenant Hurt limping along, blood dripping from a flesh wound to the leg.

"Come on, Lieutenant," Hazner shouted, gulping back his tears. "Let's get the hell out of here."

He grabbed the lieutenant, half lifted him, and together they ran.

They were running. Never had Chamberlain seen the rebels run like this before. Not at Fredericksburg, definitely not at Taneytown. He rode at the front of the advance as it swept along the canal path. Men were no longer shooting, just charging past the rebels as they dropped rifles, some putting their hands up, some collapsing, others still running. A mob of them were pouring over a makeshift bridge spanning the canal, and he pointed toward it. Though this was not his command, the men seemed to follow his orders, and they raced toward the canal crossing, shouting and cheering.

He fell in with them, crossing the canal, then nearly losing his seat as his horse slid down the far side of the embankment. He grimaced, the agony in his hips feeling as if someone had stuck a hot poker through his side.

The infantry with him spread out across the flood plain, driving hundreds of rebels before them, the enemy running, nearly all of them without weapons. They funneled onto the bridge, and he pushed forward. He had his sword out, could barely wield it, but when he did, he struck out with only the flat side of it.

They reached the approach to the bridge, the rebel mob running before them. An officer on horseback came riding up, infantry following

"Form a volley line!"

He turned and saw the men spreading out, raising their rifles.

"Volley fire on my command!"

"For God's sake, no!" Chamberlain cried, and rode directly in front of the men.

"Who in goddamn hell are you?" the officer roared.

"Colonel Chamberlain."

"Well, Colonel, this is not your command, and I outrank you."

Chamberlain saw the glint of a single star on the man's shoulders.

"You will not fire!" Chamberlain shouted, looking past the general to the infantry forming up.

"They're beaten. It would be murder." He paused. "They are no longer our foes."

The infantry lining up, as if guided by a single hand, grounded their rifles, some nodding. "Bully for you, sir," one of them shouted.

"I'll have you for this, Chamberlain," the general shouted.

"Yes, sir, report me to General Sykes. We are soldiers, not murderers, and if you plan to shoot, I will be in front of you when you do."

There was a long pause, and with a curse the general jerked his reins and rode off.

Alone, Chamberlain turned and rode onto the bridge. The back of the mob was barely visible in the twilight and then they just seemed to disappear, men leaping off the sides of the bridge, off the front of it. Some were down in the boats hiding. He rode on, saber drawn but down by his side, and he heard some infantry behind him, the men it seemed whom he had unintentionally taken command of.

Hundreds of rebels were in the river, heads bobbing, those who could not swim being swept away, their cries horrifying. Others were already crawling up onto the island, standing silent, looking back.

He rode to the end of the bridge. A lone man was standing there, arms folded, hat brim pulled low, a general, with a roughly made star stitched to his collar.

"I think, sir, you are my prisoner," Chamberlain said.

"Goddamn," the man sighed.

"Sir?"

"Just that, goddamn," the rebel said.

Chamberlain smiled.

"Profanity won't change it."

"Frankly, I don't want it changed. I'm goddamn glad it's over."

"I see."

The man looked up at him.

"Would you happen to have a bottle on you, some good bourbon perhaps?"

"I'm a temperance man," Chamberlain replied.

"Typical of my luck," Cruickshank replied. "Get taken prisoner by a temperance man."

C.S.A. "My men, my men," Lee sighed, watching as what was left of Longstreet's once valiant corps came staggering across the fields and into the woods.

And then he saw Pete riding up to him and let out a cry of relief.

"I'm sorry, sir," Pete said woodenly. "Sorry, I just wish . . ."

"Come along, General," Lee said softly. "If there is fault, it is mine. Come along now. We must plan for tomorrow. It is not over yet."

Chapter Twenty-one

The rain unleashed like a shattering deluge shortly after nightfall, striking with such intensity that he had called a halt to the march. As he looked out the window of the small farmhouse requisitioned as headquarters, he had to confess to a sense of guilt. In the past he had usually tried to set the example. If his men were forced to sleep in the rain, then so would he. But tonight, the migraine, the exhaustion, and also the fact that the secretary of war was by his side argued against that example, and he had Ely approach the darkened house.

It was, in fact, abandoned, the family most likely having fled because of the armies marching back and forth. It was a ramshackle affair, not much more than a rude cabin concealed beneath the trappings of clapboard nailed over the logs and a rough coating of plaster and whitewash on the inside.

The barn was empty as well, his staff piling into it, bedding down with their horses.

A flash of lightning revealed his troops hunkered down in the open fields, crouched under ponchos or shelter halves. In the woodlot nearby some intrepid souls had actually managed to get a fire going and were piling on logs, a circle of drenched men standing around the smoldering flames.

Grant turned back to Elihu and sat down, the room illuminated by a coal oil lamp hanging from the ceiling.

Their meal, what little he could stomach, was the same as the men outside ate, cold salt pork, hardtack, but he did have the luxury of coffee that one of his staff brewed in the open fireplace. Water was pouring down the chimney, and the fire was starting to hiss, smoke backfilling into the room.

Ely came in, stamping his boots, poncho dripping water on the rough-hewn floor.

"Sir, thought you should know a courier managed to come in from Hancock a few minutes ago."

Grant reached up to take the note.

"Sorry, sir, the paper, well, it just got soaked and disintegrated."

"Go on then."

"Hancock reports they've sealed off the Potomac and have linked up with the Army of the Potomac about five miles below Edwards Ferry."

Ely grinned.

"He also begs to report, sir, they bagged most of Longstreet's Corps and an entire pontoon train. The rebs had the bridge halfway across the river when they attacked and cut them off. He estimates between his command and that of Sykes and Grierson they've taken nearly five thousand prisoners."

"They did it," Elihu exclaimed, slapping the table with his hand, the sound of it causing Grant to wince.

Elihu jumped to his feet, came over to Grant's side, and grabbed his hand, shaking it.

"You did it, Grant. By God, you did it!"

"That they did, sir," Ely grinned. "Hancock suggests, sir, that what is left of Lee's army will be coming back toward us in the morning. He has linked up with Sykes, and they will begin pushing toward us and closing the trap, come dawn."

Grant nodded and offered a weak smile.

"Thank you, Ely."

There was a note of dismissal in his voice, and Ely, a bit confused, withdrew, closing the door.

"My God, Grant, this could be it."

Grant looked out the window.

"Perhaps."

"What's wrong."

Grant rubbed his forehead.

"Maybe I'm just tired."

"The letter from the president," Elihu said.

Grant nodded, and Elihu reached into his breast pocket and took it out, pushing it over to Grant. Grant saw that the envelope was open.

"Yes, I read it," Elihu said. "The president told me to, even though it is addressed to you. I think you need to look at it now."

Grant nodded, sat back, unfolded the sheets of paper, and began to read.

The room was silent as Grant read the memo carefully. Finished, he put it down, then picked it back up, and read it one more time.

Finished, he looked over at Elihu.

"And this was written after the casualty reports from Frederick?" he asked.

"Yes, General, it was."

Grant sighed and folded the document up.

"I half expected when you arrived that it was with orders to relieve me."

"That's absurd, Grant."

"Frederick was a near-run thing, very near run."

"You warned us of that cost a month ago. You warned the president again just last week. He was prepared for it, though I know the news did come as a shock. But Grant, even if you had lost the field at Frederick, you accomplished the goal you set before us a month ago, the one mandated to you by the president. You destroyed Lee's army in the process. Even if you had abandoned the field, the combined commands of Hancock and Sykes would have cornered him."

"Perhaps," Grant said quietly.

He looked out the window.

"The cost. I never quite realized the cost. I think history will remember me now as 'the Butcher.'"

"Grant, what is war but butchery?" Elihu replied sharply. "Isn't that why you hated the army even as you served in Mexico? Isn't that why you quit? Any man who loves what he does too much, I would not give two cents for, nor would the president. The president just said to me a few days ago that a good general is like a good doctor facing a cancer or an amputation. He cuts because he has to, not because he loves it. You need men under you like that young Sheridan, who get caught up in it, but the man who runs it all must balance things. You did so, and the survival of the Republic was in the balance."

"I wish it could have been done with less cost," he paused, "to both sides."

"If this war dragged on another year, how many more deaths? A hundred thousand, two hundred thousand? That's the other side of the equation the president asked me to convey to you. He anticipated what you might have to do to win. 'The cost up front might be high,' he said, 'but if the cost is high up front, let us pray it saves more lives in the long run.' I think, Grant, that is what you are accomplishing now."

"If we still bag Lee."

"What do you mean? He's lost his one pontoon bridge. This deluge will bring the creeks and rivers up. You have him cornered."

"Too many generals claim they have their opponent cornered and wake up in the morning to find him gone."

He looked out the window as another flash of lightning ripped the heavens.

"He can still run. He can still drag it out under cover of this storm, break up his army, and slip part of it across the river. If he does, this will still drag on."

Elihu did not reply.

"I think I need to try and sleep, sir. You can have the bunk here, I'll take the one in the loft."

Elihu did not argue with him. He could sense the melancholy, the burden Grant was carrying as he slowly climbed up the ladder and collapsed on the bed in the loft.

Elihu turned, and picking up a stick, he poked at the fire, unable to sleep.

Headquarters, Army of Northern Virginia
One Mile South of Monocacy Church

10:00 P.M.

The small village of Beallsville was nothing more than a hamlet of a half dozen homes, a general store, and a small Episcopal church. Lee sat within the church alone, head bowed in prayer.

For once, given the violence of the storm, he had broken his rule and allowed his men to move into the houses, the sick and wounded to be brought into the church. The men were silent as he sat in the front pew.

He finished praying and stood up, then walked to the back of the church where a surgeon was at work. A Union soldier was on the table, leg shredded just below the knee, the boy looking up with pleading eyes at the doctor.

"It will be just fine, son," the doctor whispered. "Son, I have to take your leg off, but you still have your life. Think about your mother. Will it matter any less to her if you come home to her injured?"

"No, sir, I guess not."

"Of course not. She'll greet you with open arms. Now go to sleep, son. You'll be just fine."

The doctor nodded to his assistant, who placed a paper cone over the boy's face.

"Breathe deeply."

"Hail Mary, full of grace . . ." the boy began to whisper, and then his voice drifted off. The doctor nodded to his other assistant who handed over a bloodied scalpel, and the doctor set to work. Lee turned away.

He heard a polite cough behind him and turned to see Walter in the doorway, illuminated by the flashes of lightning outside. Behind Walter was a gathering of officers, Longstreet, Stuart with head and arm bandaged, Jed Hotchkiss, several brigadiers, and Judah Benjamin.

"Sir," Walter whispered, coming to Lee's side. "These gentlemen wish to speak with you."

"I assumed that," Lee said.

Walter opened the door into the vestry and the men followed him in. Walter struck a match to light a lamp, then closed the door.

Lee sat down in the only chair, the others standing formally before him.

"Go on, gentlemen. I thought our plan of march had already been laid out for tomorrow, but if you have a concern, please share it."

They looked one to the other, and finally it was Jeb who stirred and stepped forward slowly.

"Sir, we have a request to lay before you."

"I am always open to suggestions from my trusted officers," Lee said. "Please go ahead, General Stuart."

"Sir, perhaps this storm is heaven-sent."

"How so, General Stuart?"

"Sir, we are requesting that you break the army up tonight. Every man to head for the river by his own means. Under cover of this storm thousands might get across to the other side. Come tomorrow, we turn west and head into the mountains. From there, sir, we can dig in and play havoc with them for years."

Lee said nothing, just stared at Jeb.

Longstreet stepped forward.

"I concur, sir. We might be able to get five to ten thousand across the river under cover of this storm."

The others, all except Walter, nodded in agreement.

Lee lowered his head, and all were silent.

God, give me wisdom now, he silently prayed. *Guide me in what I am about to do.*

He continued to pray and at last the words came to him and he looked back up.

"The One Hundred Forty-third Psalm, gentlemen."

"Sir?" Jeb asked.

"'Teach me to do thy will, for thou art my God.'"

No one responded.

"I was just meditating on that psalm before you gentlemen came to visit. When I first started to pray in this church my heart was drawn to the last stanza of that psalm, 'And of thy mercy cut off mine enemies, and destroy all them that afflict my soul for I am thy servant.'"

Jeb nodded as Lee spoke.

"Did you see that Union boy being operated on when you came in?"

No one spoke.

"Is that my enemy?" he asked.

"He fights for our enemies," Jeb replied.

"No, sir," Lee said and now his voice was forceful. "That boy is not my enemy anymore. If we have an enemy now, it is this war itself. It has swept us up into its dark soul. It has killed and crippled thousands like that boy out in the chapel who is being cut apart even as we speak. We have spent more than two years at this, tearing each other's hearts and souls out."

He lowered his head for a moment and then raised it again.

"We're all sorry about that, sir," Longstreet replied.

"Of course we are. We always say we are sorry. Generals have been saying 'I'm sorry' since war began.

"All right, General Stuart. Let us say I do follow the suggestion you gentlemen have put before me. We shall break camp tonight, pass the word to our officers to tell our men to disband and head for the river. We shall destroy the artillery we have left and abandon our medical supplies and every man will make a run for it."

Jeb looked at him hopefully, as if he were about to change his mind.

"Then what?" Lee continued.

"Sir, like I said," Jeb pressed. "We tell the men to head west once they're across the Potomac, up into the Blue Ridge, set some rally points, and there carry on the fight."

"With what and how? All organization will be gone. Individual men will be hunted down, cornered, or killed. No officers in control, our men reduced to brigands and thieves in order to survive as they head cross-country. Those that make it. What then? They will be outlaws, not an army. It will be bushwhacking, murder, and reprisals on both sides for months, maybe for years to come."

He paused.

"Maybe forever."

He stood up and went to the window, the men parting before him.

"If I were Grant and presented with such a situation I would hunt us down without mercy. I would be forced to. There would be no honor in it, no rules of war, just a merciless hunt. Those of you who served out west saw it at times, the brutality of raids and reprisals against the natives, the executions, the torture."

He turned and looked at his men.

"You have been with me for over a year and a half, my friends." Now his voice was softer. "We have served our country with honor, and we have one more service to render to her."

He lowered his head.

"We must serve her with honor to the end." He smiled sadly. "Is not the will of God evident to us this night? We have placed our trust in him. We have sought his guidance and strength. We have prayed and always our prayers ended with "'Thy will be done.'"

He stared intently at the gathering.

"Do we not now see his will in this?

"Things have turned against us and in that I see his will. I have sought God's guidance every day of my life and I sought it again tonight. Yes, I contemplated the same thing you gentlemen suggested, but then the psalm was my answer. I must do his will, and it is clear to me now, gentlemen, that his will is that we shall continue with honor, and then, if need be, submit with honor.

"If we do not break through Grant's lines tomorrow, if we do not win and are forced to surrender, then I expect each and every one of us will do so with honor, and then together we shall rebuild this shattered land. I think in doing that we will answer my prayer and fulfill God's wishes for us. To do anything else, gentlemen . . ."

He raised his head and looked each of them in the eyes.

"To do anything else would be a sin and turn God against us, and our country forever. The South will be reduced to an occupied land, marauding bands fighting like thieves in the night, our families displaced, farmlands destroyed, everything turned to wreckage and ruin and a hatred burned into all hearts that will never die, a curse passed on to our children's children."

No one dared to speak, heads were lowered. Finally, it was Judah who stepped forward.

"Sir, may I shake your hand," Judah whispered.

Lee looked at him with surprise and took it.

Judah turned and left the room without comment. One by one the others followed. Walter hesitated to leave, but Lee looked up at him and smiled, nodding for him to go as well.

Walter gently closed the door, and Lee sat back down and looked out the window, watching as the rain came down.

Headquarters, Army of the Susquehanna

August 31, 1863
Dawn

The storm had finally passed an hour before dawn, leaving a cooling breeze out of the west. Grant stood on the front porch of the small cabin which was now his headquarters and handed up the dispatch to a trooper who saluted and rode off, mud splashing up around him.

Phil watched the trooper ride off.

"Should you signal your presence thus?" Phil asked.

"Yes, I think I should," Grant replied.

"How's the headache?" Phil asked.

Grant looked over at him coldly and felt it had to be discussed.

"General Sheridan, if you wish to serve with me, there are a couple of rules."

"Sir?"

"No drinking in my presence, and never a mention of my headaches, do we understand each other?"

"Yes, sir."

Headquarters, Army of Northern Virginia

Troops were forming up, skirmishers deploying out, heading north on the road to Frederick. This would be his final gamble. If he could catch Grant in column on the road and push him aside, there would be nothing behind him. It would then be a renewed race. Gain Frederick, take the Catoctin Pass, which was most likely unguarded, hold there while the rest of the army crossed over the South Mountain range, and then seek passage over the ford at Sharpsburg.

It was a desperate move, but if done with enough push, it could still work. His only wish now was that his men had found at least some sleep during the night, for today they would be expected to fight and march nearly thirty miles.

"White flag!" someone shouted.

Lee saw coming toward him a Union officer, about a quarter mile off, holding a white flag aloft, waving it back and forth.

"Maybe they wish to surrender," someone quipped, but there was no laughter.

Lee mounted and rode toward him, Longstreet and Walter at his side.

Skirmishers surrounded the trooper. One of Jeb's men went up to the Yankee, there was a quick exchange of words, and the trooper escorted the Yankee up to Lee. As he approached, the Union captain stiffened and saluted.

"Sir, I am Capt. Daniel Struble, on the staff of General Grant. He asked that I personally present this letter to you and await your reply."

"Captain Struble," Walter said, "you understand that under the rules of war you cannot report back on anything you see while within our lines."

"Of course, sir."

Walter nodded his thanks and returned Struble's salute.

Lee opened the letter even as his skirmishers pressed forward, in line of battle, some of them Armistead's men, who had shown up miraculously during the night.

To Gen. Robert E. Lee

Commander, Army of Northern Virginia

Sir,

> *I believe that the situation now warrants that we meet to discuss terms for the surrender of your forces. You are surrounded on all sides and your line of retreat across the Potomac has been severed. Further resistance can only result in the tragic loss of more lives.*
>
> *I await your reply.*

(Signed)

U. S. Grant

Lee folded the letter and stuck it into his breast pocket.

"My compliments to General Grant for his thoughtfulness, Captain Struble, but please tell him that I disagree with his assessment of the situation. That will be all."

Struble hesitated, saluted, and then started to turn away, then looked back.

"Sir, I doubt that you remember me. I was at the Point while you were superintendent. You left the end of my plebe year."

"I am sorry, Captain," Lee said politely, "but I do not recall you."

"Sir, a personal appeal. You taught us at the Point to always deal with our fellow officers as comrades and with honor."

He hesitated.

"Go on, Captain."

"Sir, on my word of honor to a fellow officer, you cannot win this day. I have seen both sides now. Honor binds me from saying or revealing more to you, but I do appeal to you to reconsider."

"Thank you, Captain Struble, but my decision is final."

"I am sorry, sir."

Struble turned and, with his Confederate escort, raced back down the road, mud flying up as he passed, a few of the skirmishers offering catcalls once Struble was clear of their lines.

Lee looked over at Pete.

"I think we should press forward and see what Grant has prepared," Lee said.

Struble appeared out of the distant woods, riding hard. Grant raised his field glasses and could tell the answer already.

Struble drew up and saluted.

"He didn't accept it."

"No, sir. He refused."

"I'd have done the same," Grant said softly.

"How many are coming?" Sheridan asked.

Struble looked stiffly down at Sheridan.

"Sir, I cannot tell you."

"Nor should you," Grant interjected. "Captain, please stand by."

The crackle of skirmish fire erupted ahead, and some mounted skirmishers came out of the woods, pulling back. Tragically, two men down the road dropped from their saddles.

The field was nearly six hundred yards wide, open pasture land, grass waist high. At the center of the field was a crossroads, a lane coming down from the right leading back up toward Hauling Ferry. Troops from that position had been coming down it during the night and were concealed in the woods to his flank, led by Hancock, who had turned over command of the rear guard to Sykes and was now commanding troops covering the western flank of the net. At the crossroads was a small chapel, apparently abandoned.

Grant looked behind him. It was not the best of tactical arrangements, but he prayed that what he had deployed would have the desired effect.

CSA His skirmishers reached the edge of the woods, this morning seeming to advance with a bit of their old spirit, or was their élan just a final, mad desperation? During the night scouts had reported some campfires just on the other side of the woods. Grant had to be there, the courier had proven that. The question to be answered in the next few minutes was simple enough. Was Grant's army beaten down and worn? Had the pursuit been one of troops exhausted and strung out on the roads, or had he managed to bring up sufficient strength?

If he is off balance, then we push through and roll him up.

Every man had been spoken to by their officers just before daybreak, told of the task ahead. Dry ammunition from the few remaining wagons had been distributed to the advancing lines of Armistead.

As they advanced, Lee rode just behind the main battle line, his staff around him. He would not let them hold him back this morning, he had already made that clear. Somehow Walter had managed, during the night, to clean his other uniform and presented it to him when he arose. Stains had been sponged out, the brass polished. He felt strange dressed thus, for all his men were ragged, filthy, hollow-eyed from lack of sleep.

Moving cautiously, the skirmishers advanced a hundred yards out of the woods and into the field. There they halted, officers calling for the men to dress ranks.

Then he could see them. A heavy line of cavalry on the far side of the field, men mounted, perhaps two or three regiments.

For a moment his heart swelled. *Cavalry, we can push them back.*

"Bring up the guns," Lee said.

Walter looked back and raised a fist, then pointed forward. A battalion of guns that had been waiting on the far side of the woods turned into the road and started to struggle forward, mud splattering, the first of them reaching the edge of the woods then turning left and right to deploy out.

In another few minutes it would begin.

And then the Yankee cavalry men turned about, some riding off to either flank, into the adjoining woods, others heading toward the rear.

Behind them was a solid line of guns arrayed hub to hub, more than fifty, covering the width of the field. Directly behind the guns battle flags were suddenly raised up, dozens of flags, national colors, state flags, a solid wall of infantry, thousands strong.

The first gun recoiled, then down the line the others fired nearly in unison. Walter moved in protectively to Lee's side. Several seconds later they heard the shells . . . all of them aimed high, arcing up over the trees, all of them solid shot, no explosions, only the sound of their passage as they disappeared to the rear.

Lee raised his field glasses and scanned the line. The gun crews were at work, this time turning up the elevation screws, lowering the muzzles.

Grant had just given him a warning. The next salvo would plow straight into the Confederate lines.

Gunners to either side of him were unlimbering, looking nervously across the field, officers already shouting for case shot with three-second fuses.

Time seemed to drag out. The last of the Yankee gunners loaded, rammers stepping back, sergeants hooking in lanyards, rolling them out and waiting, facing their commanders, waiting for the order to unleash hell.

Lee looked over at his men at the edge of the woods. Bayonets had been fixed, men were arrayed, breathing hard, eyes focused across the field. Armistead was nearby, arm in sling, sword drawn, his hat on its tip.

Some of the men were kneeling, praying, many reciting the Twenty-third Psalm.

Still the Yankees were waiting. They should have opened the bombardment, fifty guns slashing across the field, trees shattering, guns dismounting, men screaming, his batteries smothered under, Armistead then going forward into the maelstrom.

Grant waited, not firing.

"Thy will be done, Lord," Lee said out loud.

US "You are not to fire until ordered to do so by me!" Grant kept shouting, as he rode back and forth just behind the gunners, Henry Hunt riding by his side.

"Relax, boys, relax," Hunt interjected. "If they come, it'll be Malvern Hill all over again. Just relax, boys, relax."

Men stood tense, wide-eyed, staring across the field. The rebel skirmish line had stopped a third of the way into the field. Most were kneeling in the high grass.

"A flag!" someone shouted. "A white flag!"

A staff officer was pointing to a Confederate officer riding forward at a gallop, his saber raised, a dirty white towel or strip of cloth tied to the point.

"Struble and Ely!"

The two left his side, Struble still with his white flag, Ely by his side.

The two galloped out and met the officer halfway. They talked but for a moment, then the three turned about, Ely and Struble now galloping back, Ely standing tall in his stirrups, hat off, waving it.

"It's over!" he screamed, *"Lee's surrendering! It's over!"*

Men stood silent for a moment, comrades turning to each other in amazement, and then the cheering began. A wild, triumphal roar.

"Silence!" Grant screamed, and he rode out in front of the guns, turning to face his men.

"Silence!"

The cheering died away.

"There will be no demonstrations, no cheering," he cried, his voice carrying across the field. "Gunners, stand down, remove primers carefully. Infantry to stack arms and remain at ease!"

All fell silent and more than one man removed his hat. In an instant the mood was transformed. Some shook hands, as comrades of so many hard-fought campaigns looked at each other. "Looks like we'll live out this day," "My God, we're going home," "It's over, it's really over," rippled up and down the line. Some went to their knees in prayer, some wept, some laughed and began to slap each other on the back, others stood silent, heads bowed.

Ely and Struble came up to Grant.

"Sir, General Lee wishes to discuss terms."

Grant said nothing.

"Sir, I suggested the abandoned chapel in one hour," Struble interjected, pointing to the dilapidated church at the crossroads.

"That's fine."

Grant turned about and rode back through his line to his headquarters, where Elihu stood on the front porch.

"It's over," Grant said.

Elihu smiled, then lowered his head and wept.

Monocacy Church, Maryland

8:00 A.M.

All were silent as Gen. Robert E. Lee rode through his lines, flanked by Walter, Longstreet, and Judah Benjamin. Men lined the road to either flank, battle flags held aloft, and he read the golden lettering on many of them . . . FAIR OAKS, GAINES MILL, MALVERN HILL, CEDAR MOUNTAIN, SECOND MANASSAS, SHARPSBURG, FREDERICKSBURG . . .

so many of them fields of triumph. Some of Beauregard's men were deployed as well, SHILOH, CORINTH, CHARLESTON . . .

Beauregard was nowhere to be found. Lee had not seen him since the beginning of the retreat.

The men stood at present arms, but as he passed them, a shudder ran through the lines, men taking their hats off, some holding them silently aloft.

"God bless you, General," "We're with you, Marse Robert," "Tell us to go back in and we will," an officer cried out.

Lee paused and looked over at the man.

"That time has passed," Lee said quietly, and the man lowered his head and stepped back into the ranks.

They passed Armistead's Brigade, the general standing at the center front, saluting as Lee rode by. From the corner of his eye, he saw Pickett standing behind the men.

"I thought that man was no longer with this army," Lee whispered, vexed.

He pushed the anger in his heart aside and continued through the cool damp woods, where yet more men were drawn up, and then back out into the sunlight. The batteries on his side were still deployed, but guns had been unprimed, crews leaning against their pieces, one crew gathered around a smoking fire, trying to cook a meal. All looked up as he passed; all were silent.

Walter pushed out ahead, again holding aloft the dirty white towel tied to the tip of his sword. He waved it, and from the other side of the field a flag was waved in response, a cavalcade of a half dozen riders setting forth.

To his surprise, a troop of Union cavalry, joined by several Confederate troopers, was already at the chapel with brooms and shovels, cleaning out the inside even as they approached. The skirmish lines from both sides had slowly drawn closer, at last came together, and men were leaning on their rifles, sharing tobacco, smoking, chatting freely, watching as the generals from both sides approached.

As Lee rode up, a minute or so ahead of Grant, Phil Duvall came out and saluted.

"Sir, the inside was a bit of a mess. Chapel was abandoned. Unfortunately some Yankee troopers used it as a stable last year. I think we've got it fixed up, though."

Lee dismounted and walked to the entryway. It was a small Episcopal church and he took comfort in that. A cornerstone indicated it had been dedicated more than a hundred years before, in 1747. Several windows were broken. Within, there were clouds of dust as troopers, Union and

Confederate, side by side, hurriedly swept the floors and took some pews, arranging them to face each other, a table in the middle, with two chairs, an inkwell and paper on the table.

He took a deep breath and waited.

Grant came riding up. He was mud-splattered, wearing the shell jacket of an ordinary infantryman, the only mark of rank the three stars on his shoulder. He was joined by a half dozen officers, most of whom Lee did not recognize, except for Winfield Scott Hancock, gave a who salute, which Lee returned.

The Union officers dismounted.

There was an awkward pause, then Walter and Ely Parker took over, offering introductions, the men shaking hands.

"Gentlemen," Ely finally said, motioning them into the chapel. They walked in, the dust having cleared with all the windows open, a cool breeze wafting in.

Grant walked over to the table in the center of the chapel and motioned for Lee to join him on the other side.

Grant cleared his throat nervously.

"General Lee, I am not sure if you recall. Back in Mexico, with General Scott, we met on several occasions."

Lee, taking off his hat, sat down, smiled, and shook his head.

"My apologies, General Grant, I am sorry but I do not recall you. I hope you do not take offense."

"No, sir, of course not.

"Sir, I feel I should inform you that the president has personally looked into the case of your son, Rooney. He has already been paroled and should be home by now with your wife. The president apologizes for any distress this might have caused you by his capture and confinement. He wished for me to express to you that the moment he heard of the situation he ordered his parole and release."

"Convey my thanks, sir."

Grant nervously cleared his throat again.

"Sir, I hope you accept my compliments that you and your men fought masterfully these last few months."

Lee did not reply for a moment and sighed.

"General Grant, perhaps we should get down to the business at hand."

"Yes, sir, of course."

Grant motioned to Ely, who opened his haversack and drew out two sheets of paper.

"Sir, I've drawn up a draft of terms." He slipped the paper across the desk.

Grant looked at him carefully as Lee drew out his spectacles and adjusted them.

"Sir, I do not see this as an unconditional surrender as I have done so in the past. The situation here is different. I have been in communication with the president these last few days."

He nodded over to Elihu, who stood in the corner of the room.

"These terms are a reflection of communications with President Lincoln, but also my own heartfelt convictions as well.

"Upon the signing of this document, you, sir, all your staff, all officers and men, are to be paroled until exchanged."

Surprised, Lee looked up at him.

"Paroled?"

"Yes, sir. We are bringing down a printing press from Frederick. It should be here later today, and the forms can be turned out. Each man is to sign his parole, once done he is free to go home."

Lee looked at him in surprise. He expected that by this evening his men would be marched north to prison or, worse yet, paraded in triumph through the streets of Washington.

"But there is one clause in here I feel I should tell you about now before you sign."

"And that is?"

"The president, as of two days ago, has placed a ban on any further exchange of prisoners. You are paroled, sir. You and your men may go home, but you will not be exchanged for an equal number of our prisoners that you now hold or have paroled as well. In short, sir, you and your men are permanently out of this war. I want you to understand that. Go home, but it is over for all of you."

Lee sat back in his chair and hesitated. Traditionally, for the last two years, prisoners had indeed been held, but always there was the promise of exchange, an equal number of privates for privates, generals for generals. Once officially exchanged, the men were released, whether in a holding camp behind enemy lines, or back home . . . and allowed to return to the fight.

"I must think on this a moment, sir," Lee said.

"Take your time, sir," Grant replied. "But, sir, if you refuse, we will be forced to fight this day, and tomorrow the surrender will be unconditional."

He hesitated, not wishing to push too far, but feeling he had to.

"Sir, I shall lay my cards on the table to you. To your left flank General

Hancock has massed more than fifteen thousand men. General Sykes is behind you with fifteen thousand more. Grierson is on your right flank, and I have thirty thousand blocking your way in this direction. I force-marched my men throughout yesterday and deployed them out here. Many are already dug in. Sir, you are trapped. I promise you, that is not a threat or a bluff. I would not stoop to that. It is the reality of this moment."

Lee looked at the other Union officers, Hancock, leaning heavily on his cane, nodding in agreement, Elihu Washburne, standing the corner, nodding as well.

"I am here as a representative of the president," Elihu said, "as secretary of war. I will take an oath affirming the truth of what General Grant has just told you, and the promise, as well, that if we are forced to fight again, unconditional surrender will be the tragic result. Please, sir, that is not the wish of President Lincoln now."

Lee glanced at Judah, who looked over at Elihu and then back to Lee and nodded an assertion.

"Then I believe it is my duty to sign," Lee replied softly.

Grant smiled.

"Thank you, sir. I think you are as weary of the fighting as I am. Let us end it this day."

"Several favors, please," Lee asked.

"Certainly."

"Many of the mounts belong to the men themselves. May they please take them home with them. Fall harvest is about to come in, and it would be a tremendous help if they could return with their horses and mules."

"Of course."

"Officers to retain side arms. That is a traditional mark of rank and will help to maintain order as well if any men might rebel against this surrender."

"I understand."

"Finally, it humbles me to ask this. Some of my men have not eaten in two days."

Grant smiled.

"Our own supply wagons are stuck in the mud, but I promise I shall see what I can do."

"I have enough rations on the canal boats," Hancock interjected. "I will have them brought up with all possible speed."

Grant motioned to Ely, who quickly added in the extra provisions on the two copies of the document.

A minute later Ely carefully slid the document over to Lee, who scanned it one last time, took up a pen from the inkwell, and without hesitation signed it. He passed it back to Grant. The second copy was signed, both of which Grant now countersigned, and then there was a long silence.

"Once the printing press is up and paroles printed out and signed, your men will stack arms. That done, you and your army are free to march out of here and back into Virginia. I think we can make those arrangements by late tomorrow."

"General, I think I shall return to my men," Lee said. "I must break the news now and see to their welfare."

Grant stood up, hesitated, then extended his hand, which Lee took.

Lee walked out, staff and officers following, mounted, and rode off.

"He didn't offer you his sword," Elihu said as the room emptied out.

"Nor should he, nor would I have taken it," Grant said softly. "He is an honorable man and I would have been ashamed to take it. Elihu, we fought him for two years, perhaps this final action by him has saved this country after all. He may keep his sword."

Elihu looked over at Grant and smiled.

"I know I shouldn't ask, but how's the headache?"

"What headache?" Grant said with a grin. "It disappeared the moment I saw that white flag."

Grant stepped out of the chapel, all order having broken down around it. Hundreds of men, Union and Confederate gathered around the outside.

As Lee mounted, he looked around and offered a salute, every man returned it. He set off at a slow trot, riding back to the South.

8:00 P.M.

CSA "General Lee?"

It was Walter Taylor standing in the doorway of the vestry that Lee now used as his headquarters. Walter knew he had been asleep for several hours, and Lee, a bit embarrassed, stirred and sat up.

"Yes, Walter."

"Sir, a messenger just came from General Grant. He requests that you meet him back at the chapel, you and Secretary Benjamin."

"I'm coming."

Lee stood up, brushed himself off, and almost picked up his saber and side arm to snap on, then left them in place. Outside the church Traveler was waiting, Benjamin already mounted.

The two rode off together, Walter and a dozen cavalry troopers providing escort.

The encampment area was quiet, as it had been throughout the day. The men were so exhausted that the shock of what had transpired this day had caused a complete collapse. Men had simply lain down in the fields and gone to sleep. With the coming of evening a few managed to get fires going, but there was little to cook until something absolutely remarkable happened.

At first it was just one or two, then a few dozen, and then by the hundreds; Yankees had crossed the field, drifting into the camps, shyly pulling out a few pieces of hardtack, a tattered bag filled with coffee, a little bit of salt pork or a chicken snatched from some farmyard. They sat peacefully together, chatting away, comparing notes of who had fought where. Officers were doing it, too, especially the West Pointers, seeking out classmates and comrades from so long ago.

As Lee's party approached the chapel, Grant was leaning against the doorway, smoking a cigar, and he stood up formally as Lee dismounted. The two stood silently for a moment, neither quite sure of protocol, and finally Lee offered a salute, which Grant returned.

"Sir, I felt we should talk," Grant said and he motioned Lee to the door, then looked back at Judah Benjamin. "Just the four of us. The secretary of war waits inside."

The table in the room was set about with four chairs, a coal oil lamp in the middle and a few candles by the altar shedding the only light. Souvenir hunters had been busy throughout the day in the abandoned chapel. It was reported Phil Sheridan had snatched the table the surrender had been signed on, while others had hauled out pews, even a couple of the stained-glass windows. The table between them now was a rough-hewn affair, carried over from Grant's headquarters, as was the lantern and candles.

A pot of coffee, still warm, was on the floor, and Elihu produced four tin cups and poured the drinks as the small group sat down.

"I think we need to talk," Grant said, opening now without any nervous preamble.

"I agree, sir. And again my thanks for the generosity shown to my men this day."

Grant unconsciously let his hand drift to his breast pocket, which contained the missive from Lincoln: "Let them down easy," had been written not once, but twice, in his directives not only to negotiate the surrender of Lee but to discuss broader issues as well.

"General Lee," Grant continued, "I realize there is a difference in our ranks. I command all of the armed forces of the United States of

America now in the field, while you but command the Army of Northern Virginia."

"Yes, that is true."

"But I would like to enter into negotiations to end all fighting, to end this war. The president in a memo sent to me yesterday reaffirmed my authority to do so in a military sense, and he asks if you would consider such a proposition."

Lee sat back and shook his head.

"General Grant, I have no authority to do so. You are right, I command the Army of Northern Virginia, which has laid down its arms this day. As for the other armies in the field, I have absolutely no authority to speak for them."

"As I knew you would reply," Grant said.

"Then why ask?"

"Sir, I think I should explain a few things that now confront us both."

"Go on."

"As I told you this morning, you and all your men will be paroled home. I offer as well to you my personal pledge that, once home, no one will bother or molest you or your men. The president made that clear in his memo to me. As far as he is concerned, your war is over, or should I say, our war against you. Obey the laws of the United States of America, and nothing more will be done to any of you."

"And as I said before, that is most generous."

"And yet the war continues."

"I have no control over that."

"I think you do, sir."

Lee shook his head and remained silent.

"I shall share with you the rest of the memo sent by the president."

He looked over at Elihu, who nodded in agreement.

"We are to help you and your men return to Virginia. Even now my engineers are completing a bridge at Edwards Ferry. You can march out, once disarmed, and stack your colors before crossing the river. I suggest you then take your troops to Richmond and there disband them."

He took a deep breath.

"The day after you return to Virginia, I will move my army across the Potomac as well, but advance no farther than the Rappahannock River, occupying the positions held by our armies prior to the Chancellorsville campaign. This I do as a military necessity to shield Washington, but also to position myself for an advance on Richmond."

Lee nodded, looking straight at Grant.

"And then?"

"Sir, if the Confederate government does not seek a general armistice leading to their disbandment at the end of thirty days, I am ordered to drive straight on Richmond. I will also detach one corps to occupy Shenandoah Valley and, if need be, destroy any material of military worth."

"Please, sir, define military worth?" Lee asked.

"The fall harvest, all barns, railroads, everything clear down the valley to Tennessee. I will do the same as I advance toward Richmond."

"I see," Lee replied, shaking his head. "A new kind of war, isn't it, General Grant?"

"A kind of war that will become necessary if your government does not see reality and disband. I will regret it, sir, but I will order it without hesitation.

"We do not need to play any bluff games with each other, General Lee. You have absolutely no forces left in Virginia, other than some militia. Once I start this next campaign I shall be in Richmond within the week.

"I regret to say this, but I am ordered to carry my campaign forward with full and absolute vigor. That means my army will live off the land as we advance. We will cut a swath fifty miles wide and destroy everything in our path."

Lee sighed.

"General Grant, so far, this war has been fought with a certain degree of civility, with respect to the property rights of civilians."

"That is war, this new kind of war," Grant replied, and there was a sharpness to his voice. "I do not like it any more than you do. It is the prayerful wish of our president that the terms of surrender granted here today will send a positive message across the South. We want peace, we wish it as much as you, and we can have it with honor. But if there are some who wish to continue the fight, then utter devastation will be the result.

"I am not sure that you heard the news from Atlanta today," Grant said.

"No, sir."

"Sherman has soundly defeated Bragg again, near Kennesaw Mountain. We received word that your president is finally relieving Bragg and replacing him with Joe Johnston, but it is too little too late. Sherman declares that his armies will start the bombardment of Atlanta within days; in fact, he is holding back until I authorize him to do so. He believes he can take the city in a matter of days.

"If your resistance continues, he has already suggested the plan to burn Atlanta to the ground, tear up the railroads, and then march from there straight to Savannah, again living off the land, destroying most of Georgia in the process."

Lee glared at Grant.

"Sir, I saw a certain compassion in you this morning. Your words now challenge that first assumption."

Grant leaned forward and stared at Lee intently.

"Sir, we are soldiers. We have seen nothing but hell the last two years. You know and I know your cause is lost. To me, the wasting of but one more life would be a sin. Yes, there has been a threat offered, but also a hope, a hope that you and I can work together to end this terrible slaughter and return peace to our land. Sir, I must repeat, any more deaths will be a sin, and they will rest upon your soul and mine."

Lee, a bit flustered, took up the cup of coffee Elihu had offered and looked down as he took a sip. Then he looked up.

"I believe you," Lee said.

Grant sighed, sat back in his chair, and nodded his thanks.

"But I repeat, I have no authority beyond that of the Army of Northern Virginia," Lee replied.

"Gentlemen, may I interrupt?" Elihu said and he leaned forward, placing his hands on the table.

Grant nodded his assent, and Elihu looked over at Judah.

"I hope you don't mind that I call you Judah," Elihu said. "The rules of diplomatic protocol forbid me from addressing you by your title since we have never recognized the legitimacy of your government."

Judah smiled.

"Of course, Elihu."

"The generals have had their words. I think you and I should now share a few thoughts."

"And your thoughts are?" Judah asked.

"Your government declares that you are secretary of state. All know that you are the one who is always at the right side of your president Davis. You, more than any other, have the power to persuade him."

"You confer upon me more power than I think I have," Judah replied with a smile.

"Let me tell you the terms President Lincoln now offers."

"Go on."

"I carry with me an additional letter, which I shall turn over to you at the end of this meeting, outlining the terms, which are as follows.

"Your Confederate government is to vote to surrender to the government of the United States of America. It is then to vote full allegiance to that government and its Constitution. Then it must disband itself and go home.

"Upon doing that, a military armistice shall be declared and all armies of the federal forces will stop in place, except for two forces. General Grant's will occupy Richmond and Sherman's will occupy Atlanta.

"All troops are to surrender their arms to the nearest federal forces, sign paroles, and return home. State militias behind the lines are to report to their respective capitals, disarm, sign paroles, and return home as well.

"In return, and you will have it in writing from President Lincoln, there will be no arrests, no incarcerations, no trials, no retributions, no confiscations of property"—he paused—"other than slaves."

"Sir?"

"The Emancipation Proclamation shall become law across all twelve of the states in rebellion; all slaves at the moment of the surrender of your government are forever free."

"A bit hypocritical," Judah offered back. "What about those states which remained in the Union, where slavery still exists?"

"I agree, and given some things I've heard about you, I think this is a moral issue for you as well," Elihu replied. "In his message to Congress, come December, the president will set forth several measures. The first is a constitutional amendment forever banning slavery and granting full rights of citizenship. Second, when your various state legislatures reconvene, those men, who have signed an oath of loyalty to the Union and agree to support the constitutional amendment ending slavery, will hold their seats and will then vote for senators and, for the present, congressmen to be sent to Washington. The one stipulation for those elected to federal office is that they must sign oaths of allegiance as well and an oath in support of the constitutional amendment banning slavery. That is their only requirement.

"The government will resume in January with full representation from the South."

The room was silent for a moment, Judah taking the information in.

"No reprisals?"

"No, sir. The president is emphatic on that. He said the other day that we are like a family that has been divided too long, until a beloved child within the family dies. That child is the four hundred thousand sons so far lost. In spite of our differences we must now gather to mourn him and to repair all that we have done to each other.

"This is unofficial, but the president has authorized me to state this to you two gentlemen in private. If the South returns thus, come next summer, he will place before the Republican Party a nomination of a Southerner as his running mate and will promise one or two cabinet-level offices as well. The party will run on a unity and reconciliation platform."

"The terms are generous," Judah conceded. "but the issue of the blacks. Where are they to go? How will they live?"

"I saw the field carpeted with dead black soldiers at Frederick," Grant said coldly. "If any have earned the right of full citizenship, it is they."

He looked over at Lee, who lowered his eyes and then nodded in agreement.

"It will be hard. But I believe, as Lincoln said to me a few days back, 'Every drop of blood drawn by the bondsman has now been repaid.' We must learn to live together. And I pray that we can. Lincoln will propose a program in December opening up land in the west as part of the Homestead Act for any who wish to go there to start life anew. He is proposing as well federal moneys for schools and colleges, and, if need be, the direct loans for the purchase of land in the South, at fair market value, for any who wish to sell part of their farms and plantations to those who once worked them."

"That will be expensive."

"The war cost nearly two million dollars a day. The price will be cheap in comparison to another year of war. If your congressmen and senators vote for the appropriations, well, to be cynical, they will profit, because they are some of the biggest landholders, but in so doing will set the example as well. Sir, I must warn you, the president and I have talked about this at length. If maneuvers are played by former owners, to try to rebond their former slaves to the land, through sharecropping, or contracts of service that are impossible to fulfill, the offer of direct purchase will be withdrawn, and confiscation might then be considered.

"It is the clear and stated policy of this administration that the black man is now an equal citizen, in a nation of equals. Many of them paid that price in blood, as both Generals Grant and Lee can affirm. If this nation is to heal, that must be one of the cornerstones. We do not wish this issue to haunt us for the next hundred years. We can end it here."

Elihu leaned forward and stared straight at Judah.

"Sir, if we do not agree to this point, I fear that what helped to cause this war, the issue of slavery and race, will continue to fester within us for the next hundred years. I do not wish to sound overly sentimental or patriotic, but the Declaration did declare that all men are created equal. I want to believe that the four of us, sitting here, can help that to come true."

Judah sighed.

"And yet human nature being what it is, I hope your dream is true, Elihu. I have a friend in Baltimore, a rabbi, who shared basically the same thoughts with me just a few weeks past. Yes, he is right, and so are you. As a Jew I should be more sensitive to that than most. The history of my people is replete with persecutions, and I fear in times to come it will happen again, perhaps even worse than what was endured before. But we here now rail against the deep-seated fears of so many."

"Then we set the example," Grant interjected. "The example the president will set as well. The example I know you, General Lee, have always set. I received a report yesterday how you personally intervened and protected some of our black prisoners of war. I thank you for that, and I can assure you word of that will spread."

"They were honorable soldiers, I could do no less."

"I think, gentlemen, we are all in agreement on this," Elihu interjected.

Elihu looked over at Grant and sat back.

"Gentlemen, I think it has nearly all been said."

Lee nodded.

"I promise you, General Lee, rations shall be up by dawn for your men. The signing of paroles will start tomorrow as well. Might I suggest a formal stacking of arms and colors on the morning of September 3. At which time I will try to issue out five days' rations to each of your men to help them on their way home."

"Thank you, sir."

The group stood up and was silent, not sure how it was to end.

"It is our duty now," Grant said, "to heal this nation."

The White House

August 31, 1863
10:30 P.M.

 The serenaders had gathered around the White House at dusk, when the first newspaper extras had been rushed out into the streets, newsboys crying, "Lee surrenders at Frederick!" "Grant saves the Union!"

The crowd, which only days before had been on the verge of rioting, was now exuberant, cheer after cheer rising up as two batteries in Lafayette Park fired off a hundred-gun salute.

He had finally relented and stepped out onto the balcony, unable to speak for several minutes as hysterical cries greeted him.

Finally he lowered his head. Then all fell silent, and he looked up at them.

"Now is a time of celebration," he said, "and I join with you."

Again long minutes of cheering. "Hurrah for Old Abe." "Hurrah for Grant." "The Union."

"And yet, our task is not finished," he began, the crowd falling silent with his words. "There is much to do. Let us all join in prayer that our former brothers and sisters of the South shall see the will of God in this decision and that soon the guns will fall silent forever. That the chorus of the Union shall again swell as one voice and that the better angels of our nature shall again prevail.

"Now is a time of celebration but it must be, as well, a time of forgiveness. Forgiveness of our former foes, and yes, of ourselves as well, for all that we have done to each other. God has placed this test before us and let us rise to the occasion, not just now but in years to come. Let us set aside our hatreds, our fears, and join hands once more. Let us show compassion for the wounded and the widow"—he paused—"of both sides.

"And let us honor, as well, the pledge made by our forefathers in the Declaration, in which it is written, that all men are created equal. Let us now honor that pledge as well."

There were no cheers now, only a somber silence, some in tears.

He forced a smile and looked down at the band on the front lawn of the White House.

"Bandmaster, I think we can claim right of conquest to a song I have loved dearly for years, but have seldom heard in this city of late."

"Whatever you desire, Mr. President," the bandmaster shouted back, and a certain levity returned to the crowd.

"'Dixie.' I would dearly love to hear 'Dixie' once more."

Chapter Twenty-two

Edwards Ferry
The Banks of the Potomac

September 3, 1863

The roll of drums echoed from the woods, sending a shiver down his spine. It was not the long roll signaling the charge, just a steady thumping beat, growing louder and louder.

A cool breeze swept across the Potomac, ruffling the water, flags whipping out around him, the national colors, corps standards, regimental flags, his own headquarters flag.

The morning was cool, rain having passed during the night, the dawn breaking fresh and clear with a hint of autumn to come.

The drumroll grew in intensity and then he saw them, the head of their column coming out of the forest.

The head of the column was a sea of red battle standards of the Army of Northern Virginia and inwardly Gen. Ulysses S. Grant felt a chill.

How often I have seen those flags through the smoke of battle, coming on relentlessly, gray-clad warriors charging forward beneath them, their wild shouts echoing to the heavens.

But now they marched in silence.

There must have been a hundred or more flags at the head of the column, the colors standing out bright and clear in the early morning light. Ahead of them rode a single man on a gray horse, followed by several others.

The flags cleared the forest, and behind them came the column of infantry, ranked in column of fours, officers to their front, drawn sabers resting on shoulders, but the men behind them no longer carrying rifles. Their weapons had been stacked at dawn, when they had fallen into ranks, cartridge boxes slung over weapons and left behind.

They were now less than three hundred yards away, entering the open fields cut back but days before in preparation for battle to defend this crossing, roughly dug graves from that battle covering the ground in front of one of the forts. They approached the wide temporary bridge laid across the canal. As they reached the embankment they would be able to see what awaited them on the open ground leading down to the Potomac where he waited at the edge of the pontoon bridge across the river.

Grant turned and, saying nothing, nodded to Ely Parker.

Ely rode forward a few feet out into the middle of the road, drew his saber, and rested it on his shoulder.

"Battalions!"

The cry echoed down the length of the road, picked up by the thousands of Union troops deployed.

"Atten-shun!"

The troops flanking to either side of the road came to attention.

"Present arms!"

The echo of the command startled Gen. Robert E. Lee, who had been lost in melancholic thought. He raised his head, looking straight ahead. The road was flanked to either side by several divisions of Union troops, standing a half dozen ranks deep. As one, all raised their rifles up to present arms, the traditional military salute.

Lee stiffened in the saddle and slowed. He looked over his shoulder. Walter Taylor was carrying his headquarters flag, Pete Longstreet by his side. Judah Benjamin was with him, as was John Bell Hood, gray-faced, with a bandaged stump of an arm, but insisting over all protests that today he would ride out and look "those Yankees" straight in the eye.

He had not expected this. Never across the last several days had there been mention of it by Grant. The agreement reached was simply that the men were to stack arms on the morning of the third, break camp, march to the river, and there surrender their colors before crossing the river.

He had half-feared that the surrender of colors might be a difficult moment and even wondered if the earlier surrender of arms was a subtle way of preventing trouble. For surely, when the cherished banners behind him were turned over, emotions might overflow for those who had followed them for so long, had given so much for so long. He had agreed with Grant's suggestion that all flags to be surrendered were to be massed

at the front of the column rather than to be directly turned over by their own men.

Never had he expected this.

He looked to his comrades.

"Tell the men to march with pride," Lee said solemnly. "Honors are being rendered to us."

The column had come to a halt behind him, drums stilled.

Lee looked over at Pete, John, Walter, and Judah.

"Forward, gentlemen."

The drums picked up again, a steady marching cadence, orders shouted back down the line, and though there was no longer that reassuring sound of men slapping the barrels of their rifles as they shifted them to present, he could sense that all had braced up, heads raised, eyes level.

The first of the Union troops were directly ahead, their colors held high, tough, lean men, Westerners by the looks of their battered hats, threadbare jackets, and patched trousers. Their officers, mounted, came to attention and saluted with drawn sabers, and Lee returned the salute.

The Union troops were silent, most with eyes straight ahead, but some looking up at him wide-eyed, some offering subtle nods as he rode between the flanking lines. Before each regimental standard, were more officers, all saluting.

He felt overwhelmed, recognizing more than one face as he rode between the columns, friends from long ago in Mexico, younger faces now prematurely aged, cadets of his from West Point, a few of them, when saluting, whispering, "Good day, sir," or simply, "General Lee."

He gave a glance back. The flags of what was once his army were still held high; behind them the men were marching, not a word said by either side.

And then ahead, he saw him, waiting by the bridge over the Potomac, General Grant.

Grant took a deep breath. *If ever there is a moment when I can truly serve our country*, he thought; *it is here, it is now. God give me guidance.*

He nudged his mount and came to the center of the road, Ely drawing back. He was unarmed, his dress uniform having been lost somewhere in Frederick, so he was turned out instead in his traditional field dress of a simple private's sack coat with three stars on each shoulder.

Lee was closer, just a few dozen feet away, the flags behind him. Grant stiffened to attention.

Lee held up a hand, signaling a halt, the command racing back down the length of the column. Lee came to attention, saber in hand, and saluted.

"General Grant, sir."

"General Lee."

Lee looked about and then focused on Grant.

"Sir, why are you doing this?" Lee asked.

Grant took a deep breath.

"I am not saluting a defeated foe," Grant said, and this time he raised his voice so it would carry. "The war between us is over. Today we are saluting brave fellow Americans, men of honor and courage."

Lee found he could not reply. He advanced a few more feet, taking the sword from his shoulder, holding it lovingly for a few seconds. It was the sword his father, Light Horse Harry Lee, had carried in the Revolution. He inverted it, and offered it to Grant hilt first.

Grant held up a hand and shook his head.

"No, sir. That sword helped to win our independence. It is a cherished heirloom of your family. Keep it today in remembrance of our friendship."

Again, Lee found he could not reply. He then looked back to the column behind him.

"Surrender the colors," Lee announced.

Since none of this had been planned or discussed, there was a moment's hesitation, the flag bearers not sure what to do next. Some clutched their treasured standards tightly, tears streaming down their faces.

Across from Grant stood several hundred men who were unarmed, drawn up in ranks. They began to step forward, going up to the Confederate flag bearers and saluting.

"Your colors, sir," one of them said.

The first approached, looked up at Lee, eyes pleading. Lee forced a smile and nodded.

The soldier, with head lowered, reluctantly handed the flag over. More and more came up, each saying the same, "Your colors, sir," and without protest the flags were handed over.

One of the Union soldiers took a flag and looked up at it, breaking discipline.

"Fourteenth South Carolina?"

The rebel looked at him defiantly, and Grant was just about to raise his hand, to signal Ely to have officers prepared for this moment to intervene.

"You took our flag at Gettysburg," the Union soldier said. "I will treat yours with honor."

He saluted and stepped back, the Confederate looking at him wide-eyed and then saluting in turn.

The Union soldiers taking the flags then stepped back to the side of the road. Lee watched them carefully. The flags were not laid on the ground, or tossed down. Staves were simply rested, the men returning to attention. The colors of the Army of Northern Virginia were turned over, all except one, the personal flag of Lee, carried by Walter. No one approached him and Walter looked around in confusion.

"General Lee, your flag is your keepsake as well," Grant said.

"I thank you, sir."

There was a long silence, no cheering, no shouts of triumph, no patriotic airs, only the sound of the wind, the fluttering of the flags, of which only one was now held high, the colors of Grant's headquarters.

"God be with you, General Lee," Grant said, and he drew to the side of the road, clearing the way.

Lee rode a few feet forward, leaned over, and extended his hand, and there was a muttering from all gathered at the sight of this.

"Today you are a friend of the South," Lee said loudly. "God be with you, General Grant, and with all of your honorable men. We shall never forget the respect you have rendered us this day."

Grant took his hand firmly, and then he leaned over and whispered, "For heaven's sake, sir, please try and end all the fighting. Please, sir, help me with that."

"I shall."

Their grasp tightened for a second, and then Lee let go.

He looked over his shoulder, men staring at him, the column stretching deep into the woods.

"Pass the word down the column," Lee said, not too loudly, but clear enough for those in the front ranks to hear. "Pass the word that we have been today treated with honor, and we shall return that honor."

He turned to face forward, nudged Traveler, and as he passed the national colors he slowed and raised his sword in salute.

He rode on and made it a point to turn and look back. His officers behind him hesitated for a second, not sure of what to do, but his gaze made it clear to them. Longstreet did it first, slowing and saluting the flag. Hood, once the fire-eater, right arm gone, but with tears streaming down his face, raised his left hand to render honors.

He could hear word of this racing back down the column, the discipline of silence broken for a few seconds.

"The general's saluted the flag. Salute the flag as you pass, men. They saluted ours."

Drummers picked up the beat of the march, and the column went forward, Lee at the front. As they stepped onto the pontoon bridge across the river, command was given to break to route step.

The column flowed past, an endless sea, it seemed, of battered, worn men in gray and butternut, blanket rolls over shoulders, some limping along with a bandaged leg or arm in a sling, some being helped by comrades.

Grant gazed into their eyes, accepting the salutes of their officers.

He looked carefully at his own men. Their features had softened in the last few minutes. Some would nod or whisper a few words as the Confederates continued to march by. He had worried about that, the slightest breach of discipline, a taunt, a comment, that would be repeated and remembered. But he realized now there had been nothing to worry about at all.

If any were bonded together by a war, it was these men, these men of both armies. The politicians of both sides who had started this nightmare might now scream for vengeance—never to give up, never to forget, always to hate and be hated in turn—but not these men. They had, together, faced the fury of battle, and so many of their comrades had disappeared into those gray smoke-enshrouded fields, where they would remain forever.

Those here, at this moment, understood far better than any what it had cost, what it now meant. They had shared the crucible of war and drank from its scalding contents and the taste of it had burned the final hatreds away.

After long minutes became a half hour and then an hour, the command was given for the front rank to step back and go to at ease, the rank behind them stepping forward to replace them and coming to attention. And yet still he remained motionless, watching the column as it continued to pass.

Discipline did ease slightly when a reb marching by looked over and recognized a few, a tragic few in their tall black hats. The reb saluted. "Iron Brigade, fit you at Antietam. You boys have grit."

The men of the Iron Brigade nodded. "Texas, ain't you? You're good men."

The reb nodded and moved on.

And so the column crossed over the bridge, dust rising up as the hours passed, a rider astride a gray horse at the fore, followed by a single flag disappearing from view, marching into the realm of legend.

Chapter Twenty-three

Richmond, Virginia
The Confederate Capitol

September 10, 1863

Gen. Robert E. Lee dismounted from Traveler, returning the salute of the men lined up in division strength to either side of the road. He was dressed in his formal uniform, sword at his side. The men saluting him were a mixture of troops from several of his old divisions, mostly Virginian boys.

Out on the front lawn before the old state legislature building of Virginia, now the capitol building of the Confederacy, thousands of civilians had gathered, and an ovation went up at the sight of him walking up the steps.

Many of his old comrades were already waiting for him, Pete Longstreet, A. P. Hill, who seemed, at the moment, to be recovering from the illness that had taken him out of the last campaign, and Judah Benjamin.

Judah stepped forward to shake his hand.

"Did he do it?" Judah asked.

"You mean the president?"

"Yes, of course I mean the president."

"Yes, he did. And I think you know what I shall say now."

Lee walked into the legislative hall, which was packed to overflowing with members of the Confederate Congress and the Senate. A ripple of applause broke out at the sight of him and turned into a standing ovation. He said nothing, merely nodding and stepping to one side of the door.

There was one person still missing.

Several minutes passed in silence until again there was cheering outside.

The sergeant at arms came to attention and banged his staff on the floor.

"Honorable members of Congress. The president of the Confederate States of America."

Jefferson Davis walked in, and after a brief applause the room fell silent. The tension was electric as the members of Congress looked from Davis to Lee and back to Davis, wondering what had transpired in their meeting of an hour ago. Not just Richmond, but the entire South was waiting, citizens as far off as Savannah, Mobile, beleaguered Atlanta, standing before telegraph stations.

The Speaker of the House took the podium and called for order and then without flourish or ceremony simply announced, "Gen. Robert E. Lee."

Lee took a deep breath, looked over at Judah, who nodded, and walked up to the podium, turned, and faced his audience.

"President Davis," General Lee began, nodding toward President Jefferson Davis, sitting in the back of the room, "members of the Congress of the Confederacy and members of the president's cabinet, fellow citizens.

"I have come here to report on the military situation of our Confederacy. I speak not as a politician but as a military man. My facts are the facts of war, not the hopes of politics and civilian speeches."

The crowd began to straighten up and watch carefully at these unexpected words and the sober, indeed somber, tone of Lee's words.

He paused for a moment.

"This morning I met with President Davis to discuss those facts. As a serving military officer I am honor bound to obey the orders of the commander in chief."

Again a pause and he lowered his head, then, realizing that what he had to say required him to look Davis straight in the eye, he stiffened, features grave.

"But this morning I have refused the orders of President Davis and have no recourse but to resign from the service of the Confederacy."

Davis, red-faced, glared at him.

Lee knew the gesture was melodramatic, but Judah and Pete Longstreet had both told him he had to do this symbolic move to rein-

force his point. He stepped back a foot from the podium, drew out his sword, and laid it upon the podium.

"I resign from service and shall return to private life."

There was a moment of stunned silence, and then the audience erupted. Some cheered, but there was also cries of "No, never!" and even a few who cried, "Traitor!"

He waited for the audience to fall silent, obviously not yet done speaking.

"I shall speak to you now, not as a general, but as a private citizen and shall say what I could not say before when I still carried a sword by my side pledged to this government."

The room fell into a tomblike silence.

"This morning I met with President Davis and offered my formal report on the surrender of the Army of Northern Virginia and the signed agreement between myself and General Grant.

"President Davis ordered me to violate the terms of that surrender."

There was a low murmuring in the room. All knew what the issue was, and now they would hear of it directly from Lee.

"The president ordered me to violate the terms of parole and return myself and all my troops to active service. He stated that President Lincoln had violated the rules of war by the ending of the exchange of prisoners and therefore I could break the oath I gave to General Grant.

"I cannot, I will not, accept that. I signed a fair and generous agreement with General Grant with full knowledge of the terms. To order me to go back on my word is a violation of a code of honor that has guided my entire life.

"I have resigned. I suggest to all my fellow officers who were with me at the surrender to do the same. I shall inform my gallant and honorable men in the ranks, who stand arrayed outside this building, to refuse any order to return to the ranks as well."

"Traitor!"

It was a lone voice, a congressman from South Carolina, and several joined in, but those around the protesters shouted for silence.

"With my refusal and that of my officers and men to violate a sacred oath, given to an honorable foe, the simple fact now confronts you, the civilian government, that we no longer have the military capacity to stop the Union army."

The crowd gasped and men began to fidget in their seats. Some of the hotheads began to say something but realized this was General Lee speaking, and their respect for him stilled their voices.

"General Grant and President Lincoln"—at the very sound of his name the room turned frigid—"have both treated the Army of Northern Virginia with honor and with dignity."

To the restive members of the audience he interjected, "I was there, gentlemen. I am reporting on facts not wishes, events not fantasies."

He went on. "As I just stated, this morning President Davis ordered me to take the field once again to save our capital. I cannot.

"As a matter of honor I have given my word before God that I would accept parole and understood when I accepted it that I would not be exchanged and therefore am out of the war.

"I gave my word for the entire Army of Northern Virginia serving with me.

"Now let me address the second issue, which is simply that of practicality and reality. I surrendered, and now urge this entire government to surrender, because to not do so will guarantee the needless killing of thousands of our young men in a situation in which we have no hope of winning against overwhelming Union forces."

"Hell, no!" someone shouted. "We'll fight the damn Yankees to the death."

Lee's features reddened and he stared at the senator who had challenged him.

"Whose death? I have seen tens of thousands die. In war, always it is the old men such as we who create it, but it is the young who must do the dying."

"How dare you, sir," came the reply.

"I dare because I must," Lee retorted. "There is no Confederate army capable of defending Richmond. We lost our artillery and our ammunition trains north of the Potomac. There is no possibility of stopping General Grant and his forces. President Lincoln offered us an armistice of thirty days. Seven of those days have now passed, and I tell you this without embellishment. On October 3, if we do not surrender, Grant will cross the Rappahannock in force, and Sherman will resume his attack on Atlanta . . . and devastation will follow.

"Grant will lay waste the state of Virginia and then move across the Carolinas until he meets with General Sherman. Between them they will burn every barn, lay waste every field, and tear up every town, destroy every mill, every mile of railroad track, and they will leave utter ruin in their wake. Those who wish to wage war in these circumstances will find themselves fleeing across a wilderness of destruction.

"So far this war has been fought with a certain degree of civility. The patience of our opponents is at an end. If we defy the truth that is before

us now, we shall reap a terrible whirlwind that will scar our nation for generations to come.

"And hundreds of thousands more will die."

As he described the apocalyptic scene there was silence.

"As a man of honor and a man of military training I cannot support or condone such a future for my state.

"You gentlemen are politicians. You have every right to reach a different conclusion than a military man. However, neither I nor any member of the Army of Northern Virginia who is loyal to our good name, to our honor, and to my given word will break that word.

"Gentlemen, I beg of you, as a simple citizen, setting aside my former military position, the war is over, the cause is ended. Let us save our families, our young men, and our land from inevitable devastation. Let us end with honor that which we began with honor. I can do no less."

He paused and lowered his head.

"I urge you this day to accept and honor the terms offered by President Abraham Lincoln, terms carried back from Maryland by Secretary Judah Benjamin. At this very moment copies of those terms are being printed up and distributed not just here in Richmond but across the South."

He looked at Judah who nodded and motioned to several boys who had come in carrying bundles of paper, word for word reprints of the letter from Lincoln, given to Judah by Elihu Washburne.

Lee waited for several minutes as the papers were distributed.

"This is a violation of confidentiality between myself and the secretary of state."

It was President Davis, who throughout Lee's speech had remained silent.

Lee looked over at the Speaker of the House, who came to his feet.

"The chair still recognizes the general," he paused. "Mr. Robert E. Lee, Mr. President. He still has the floor."

Davis, fuming, turned and walked out of the room.

Senators and congressmen snatched up copies of the letter, some sat down, reading in silence, a few crumpled the papers up and threw them to the floor, several stormed out of the room after President Davis, one of them turning and shouting that all who remained and listened were cowards.

But the vast majority stayed, read, and looked up at Lee.

"The terms are just, fair, and liberal," Lee said as he resumed. "Rarely in the annals of history has such an offer been made to end an internal re-

bellion, with the victor extending his hand in a gesture of peace and reconciliation. It is an offer imbued with Christian charity, and I pray that
you accept it."

He paused, again scanning the room, looking at each of the men gazing up at him. The features of many had softened, more than a few were
in tears, some sat woodenly, in shock, as the reality of what they confronted was put before them.

"I believe I have said enough," Lee said. "I suggest, gentlemen, that
when I yield the floor, you recognize Mr. Judah Benjamin, who sat by my
side during the surrender negotiations and will discuss the details. I know
what he will say, and I urge you to listen to him.

"But before I leave, I ask but this. Look out the windows of this
building. Gathered outside are the men who were once the proud Army
of Northern Virginia. They have fought with honor across two years and
won great victories and have now suffered a final defeat. But for each one
who stands there, how many are vacant from the ranks? How many of
our sons, our comrades, our friends are perhaps gathered here only in
spirit."

He felt as if his voice was about to break. He took a deep breath and
went on.

"Jackson, who fell at Chancellorsville, so many who rest in unmarked
graves, so many who will never return home. Some might now say that
we must shed more blood, otherwise their sacrifice would be in vain."

Lee shook his head.

"Thus it is always said across history, and yet never have we heard the
dead themselves speak, telling us what they would want. Would they
want more blood poured upon their graves as atonement? I think not. I
believe, instead, it would be their voices that would be the loudest, urging us not to waste the blood of one more young man for a cause that is
now lost. Let the dead who fought for this cause rest in honored peace.
Let the living who survived . . ."

And now his voice did come close to breaking.

"Let the living go home to the waiting embraces of their loved ones.
Let them go home with heads high, knowing they are men of honor,
whose former foes wish now to extend the hand of friendship and
peace.

"My friends, across two years we have prayed to God for guidance and
victory. Our opponents have done the same. There is a terrible irony in
that, for both sides to pray to the same Prince of Peace for the destruction
of the other. The prayers of neither side have been answered fully. Yet, is

it not evident that the will of God is revealed? For whatever reason, he has judged against us. We have prayed to him with humility, as men of honor, and that honor is intact.

"I believe firmly, that to continue the struggle now is to turn against God's will, and in so doing, we shall face a terrible judgment."

He lowered his head in the silent room.

"Gentlemen, may the blessing of the Almighty be upon you and guide you this day. I shall now return to private life. Good day."

He stepped down from the podium and with head high walked out of the room. As he started to leave, Pete Longstreet came forward, followed by other officers, and without comment or fanfare, they drew their swords, laid them at the foot of the lectern, and followed their general out of the room.

As he stepped out onto the steps of the capitol his men, his gallant men, were drawn up in ranks, coming to attention, saluting.

"We're with you, General!" someone shouted, and a wild cheer, the rebel yell went up, sending a chill down his spine.

How many times, dear God, how many times did I hear that yell, their going forward, colors at the fore, that wild cheer that signaled victory.

He waited, the cheer dying down, something in his demeanor commanding silence.

Behind him the doors to the capitol were open and he could hear the speaker pounding his gavel. "The chair recognizes the Honorable Judah Benjamin."

Before him was a sea of upturned faces.

"My comrades," he began, then paused, "my friends . . ."

No one spoke. All were silent.

"After two years of arduous service, marked by unsurpassed courage and fortitude, the armies of the Confederacy must now yield to overwhelming numbers and material. We must humbly, and yet honorably, yield as well to the will of God. The war is over. Disband and go home. May you be as good citizens of the United States of America as you have been soldiers of the Confederacy. That is my last order to you. Farewell."

Mounting Traveler, he rode past their silent ranks. One by one men reached out to touch him as he passed, some saluted, some stood silent, hats clenched in hands. As he looked into their eyes he was filled not with sadness, but with hope. He could see in the eyes of so many, not anguish, but a dreamlike realization . . . they were alive . . . they had outlived the nightmare . . . they were going home, home to families, home to farms not ravaged by war, home to waiting children, parents, and wives. They were going home.

The war was over.

Frederick, Maryland

November 19, 1863

After the long two-hour speech by Edward Everett, formally dedicating the cemetery at Frederick, a band was now playing a patriotic air.

For Ulysses S. Grant all music was an annoyance. He had a tin ear, and music, especially loud military marches, could often trigger a headache.

Sitting on the raised dais, he looked out across the field, and there was the nightmare memory of this same field, little more than two months back, the same field across which Lee had launched his final charge on Frederick.

The town behind him was quickly rebuilding, but the land around Frederick still bore mute evidence of the shock of war. Destroyed fields, gutted farmhouses and barns, and, directly before him, earth still freshly mounded over, row upon row upon row, nearly six thousand graves so far.

The crowd that had gathered for the ceremony stood in a vast semicircle around the new cemetery, but a scattering of men and women stood within, an informal understanding that those who had a comrade or loved one resting on this sacred ground could stand by the remains of their fallen.

Near the front he saw Emily McPherson, dressed in black. He caught her eye for a moment and was filled yet again with the memory of his old comrade. Near her was a soldier in Confederate uniform, a young colonel, standing next to the grave of Custer.

A fair number of former Confederates were actually present, though he did not know their names. Sergeant Hazner and one-armed Sergeant Robinson were present, standing by the mass graves for the unidentified Confederate dead, who, at the insistence of President Lincoln, were to be interned in the same cemetery, though in a different section, a compromise Lincoln made when some hard-liners protested that decision.

Another decision that Lincoln had made—and stoutly shut down any protest over—was that black soldiers' graves were to be mingled with white. Grant recognized Major Bartlett, a Medal of Honor around his neck, and by his side an elderly black gentleman whom he recognized as well,

Mr. James Bartlett, now special adviser to the president for the Freedmen's Bureau. They stood together by a grave, hands resting on the temporary wooden cross. He caught their gaze for a second, and Major Bartlett came to attention and saluted. Grant nodded in return, knowing that they were standing by the grave of their son and grandson.

The music continued, and Grant waited patiently for it to finish.

"Well, General, it is over, and you did it," Elihu Washburne said, leaning over to whisper to him. "Looking back, did you always think it was going to end this way?"

Grant shook his head, glad for the momentary diversion of conversation.

"No, sir, I did not think victory was inevitable."

Elihu looked at him with surprise.

"From the moment you were assigned command and first met President Lincoln, you said we would win."

Grant smiled.

"All generals must say that if they are indeed to win. What kind of confidence could I give to my men, to you or the president if I said, 'Maybe'? Men must go into battle with confidence, and that was my job, sir, to instill that confidence, and frankly to believe in it as well. To do otherwise would mean defeat.

"But now that it is over, I can confess, there were times that I did doubt we could do it."

"How so?"

"The South was trying to leave, and we were trying to force them to stay. Conquering a region is vastly harder than defending it. We had no real army when this war began. Many of our best officers left to defend their home states.

"Only one man stood between ending the Union and preserving the Union, and that man is sitting over there."

Grant pointed toward Lincoln, who was sitting next to the speaker's podium.

"It ultimately rested with him. Without his will and his ability to survive defeat after defeat and discouragement after discouragement the South would now be a separate country and the Confederacy would be our rival on the North American continent. General Lee had the South at the edge of victory after Second Bull Run, after Fredericksburg, after Chancellorsville, and after the great victories of this summer. A weaker man than President Lincoln would have broken, and an armistice would have been signed. Once a truce was signed, there would never have been the will to start fighting again. No, sir, this victory was a long way from inevitable, and every young American ought to learn just how important one man can be. How one man can shape history and, in that moment, save a nation.

"And General Lee as well. He stood up for the honor of the South at the end. His actions in Richmond spared us a year or more of terrible conflict, and he is now helping to heal the wounds. I thank God for him as well."

The band finished playing, and ever so slowly Abraham Lincoln, sixteenth president of the United States, came to his feet and stepped up to the lectern. Reaching into his breast pocket, he pulled out several sheets of paper, laid them out, and then raised his head and began to speak, his high tenor voice carrying far across the cemetery and the fields beyond . . .

"Four score and seven years ago . . ."